Methodist Episcopal Church Conferences

The New Jersey Conference Memorial

SALZWASSER
VERLAG

Methodist Episcopal Church Conferences

The New Jersey Conference Memorial

Reprint of the original, first published in 1865.

1st Edition 2022 | ISBN: 978-3-75259-041-8

Verlag (Publisher): Salzwasser Verlag GmbH, Zeilweg 44, 60439 Frankfurt, Deutschland
Vertretungsberechtigt (Authorized to represent): E. Roepke, Zeilweg 44, 60439 Frankfurt, Deutschland
Druck (Print): Books on Demand GmbH, In de Tarpen 42, 22848 Norderstedt, Deutschland

THE

NEW JERSEY

CONFERENCE MEMORIAL.

CONTAINING

BIOGRAPHICAL SKETCHES

OF ALL ITS

DECEASED MEMBERS,

INCLUDING THOSE WHO HAVE DIED IN THE

NEWARK CONFERENCE

"THE RIGHTEOUS SHALL BE IN EVERLASTING REMEMBRANCE."

PUBLISHED BY ORDER OF THE CONFERENCES.

PHILADELPHIA

1865.

CONTENTS.

TO THE READER.

A FEW words of explanation are appropriate in connection with this volume.

At the session of the New Jersey Annual Conference of the Methodist Episcopal Church, held at Salem, March, 1860 ; in view of the large number of honored members of this body who had died in the triumphs of the Christian faith, since its organization, Rev. George Hughes offered resolutions, which were unanimously adopted, that the deeds of these fathers and brethren demand at our hands a fuller recognition, and more enduring memorial than is found in the Annual Minutes.

A committee of five was immediately appointed to prepare and publish a volume which would give to these men a proper and permanent record.

Similar resolutions were passed the same year, by the Newark Conference, with the view of incorporating in the work biographies of those ministers who had died within their bounds.

The hope of a speedy and successful issue in this interesting enterprise was entertained, but difficulties of various kinds arising, little progress was made.

The present year, however, seemed auspicious, and the work is now accomplished.

The labor of collecting materials has been arduous, and often embarrassing. Still, many of the memoirs are full, and there was matter for making them larger, but its further use was prevented for want of space.

In other cases, however, we have but meagre sketches. This is regretted, but the fault is not ours. Information was sought, at different times, through the Christian Advocate and Journal; large numbers of private letters were written, some of them in the most beseeching tones, and numerous personal inquiries were made, without success, and the conclusion reached was, that facts and incidents, such as were sought, did not exist, or, if they did, the length of time since their occurrence, the vagueness of memory, and, possibly, in some instances, inattention to these calls, left such facts beyond our reach.

In these instances, the materials furnished by the printed Minutes have been used, and the best possible record for these brethren made.

Still, we shall be greatly disappointed if the reader does not find an *intensely interesting book.*

It records the toils and triumphs of *fifty-three* devout and earnest men, all familiar to New Jersey Methodism, the aggregate of whose ministerial labors is *over one thousand years.*

What they suffered and what they accomplished, as far as known to us, is here set down in unvarnished narratives, and had they all kept records of their lives, the volume would have been still more interesting and complete.

The committee is under lasting obligations to several families of these honored fathers and brethren, for the use of valuable papers. To them, and all others, who have kindly assisted in this work, sincerest thanks are tendered. It would afford pleasure, could the names of all such be given, but as the number is large, this general acknowledgment must be sufficient.

The volume is published with the approval of the New Jersey and Newark Annual Conference, but as all the members of these bodies could not possibly examine the manuscript, the committee alone must be responsible for the sentiments which the book contains.

The arrangement of the subjects, as they stand in the volume, is according to the chronological order in which the deaths occurred.

The work, as here presented, while it has involved a vast amount of anxiety and toil, has also given rise to many pleasant memories; and it is earnestly hoped, it will prove, not only a source of spiritual profit to the reader, but will also be what the Conferences desired, "*a fuller recognition, and more enduring memorial* of the noble achievements of our honored fathers and brethren who have finished their course on earth."

Our labors, which have been gratuitously, yet cheerfully rendered, are closed.

May the benedictions of the blessed rest upon the readers of this book, until readers and writers shall greet the sainted men whose lives are here recorded, in our Father's house above.

Yours in Christian fellowship,

S. Y. MONROE,
E. H. STOKES,
A. E. BALLARD,
G. R. SNYDER,
J. B. DOBBINS,
Conference Committee.

THE

NEW JERSEY CONFERENCE MEMORIAL.

REV. THOMAS MORRELL.

AMONG the honored names that adorn the ministerial list of the M. E. Church only a few are entitled to greater prominence than that of Thomas Morrell. Very few can more safely be set forth as examples for imitation, or reproduced in the hearts and lives of succeeding generations. His fallen mantle may well be coveted by his sons in the ministry. And if "biography teaches history by example," that of such a man clothes its lessons with a halo of light, and invests them with an evil restraining and good stimulating impulse.

He was born in the city of New York, Nov. 22, 1747, his parents having formerly resided at Newtown, Long Island. In 1772 the family settled in Elizabethtown, N. J. Jonathan Morrell, the father of Thomas, was a man of sterling character and worth. His earthly pilgrimage covered eighty years, one half of which long life was adorned by a Christian profession. This places his conversion about 1765, seven years prior to his removal to N. J. But when he joined the church or what positions in it he occupied, are not now known. But evidently he was a leader in Israel, for "when the circuit preachers were not present, he would exhort the people, sometimes taking a text, and pray with them." He died in Sept. 1805, in full hope of a blissful immortality.

Mrs. Morrell, the mother of Thomas, held a prominent connection with early Methodism in America. She was converted under the ministry of Philip Embury, the pioneer American Methodist preacher, was a member of the first class in old John St. N. Y., and to the end of life was an eminent Christian and a fast friend of the Church. When she went to Elizabethtown there were no Methodists in the place, and she joined the Presbyterian Church. In 1785, when the first class was formed in the place, she rejoined the people of her choice. These facts help us to estimate the qualities of her piety and integrity. She had the moral courage to attend the meetings of the "sect everywhere spoken against," and when converted through their instrumentality, to cast in her lot among them. Then when placed beyond the reach of this people, she was too devout and liberal to remain without Christian communion. Nor was this change prompted by a mere desire to go with the multitude, regardless of duty or principle. From this reproach she stands nobly vindicated, by a return to her chosen people at the earliest opportunity. In doing this she left the popular and associated with the despised, and that too when pecuniary interests were thereby jeoparded, for her husband was a merchant. Thus to obey conscience against both popular favor and interest, is to display true moral heroism. Dr. Murray says:—"She lived a pious and exemplary life, and died on the 30th of July, 1796, in the sixty-eighth year of her age."

Thomas was a military, before he was a Christian soldier. Of his early life, we have no specific information. From all that appears he was an exemplary youth. He was employed in his father's store, till the stirring events of the Revolution called him out. The following account of his military career is condensed from Rev. Dr. Murray's interesting narrative in "Sprague's Annals." The battle of Lexington led to the formation of a company of Militia in Elizabethtown, of which he was elected Captain. His first adventure was important and successful. A British transport was said to be on the coast, and four armed boats were sent to capture her. She was overhauled about forty miles from Sandy Hook. The men being concealed, the boats were mistaken for pilot or fishing boats. Two of them outsailing the others and reaching the ship, the men suddenly emerged, rushed on deck and effected her capture without the loss of a man or scarcely any show of resistance. She proved to be the "Green Mountain Valley," with twelve guns manned by forty men, and laden with provisions for the British army. Capt. Morrell had charge of one of the successful boats. This was in the Summer of 1775.

A squad of two hundred men, of which he was second in command, were stationed for a time, on Staten Island, in order to make observations and awe the tories. And the next Spring, he superintended the building of "Stockade Fort" at Elizabethtown Point, a breastwork of a mile in length, intended to keep the enemy from landing. About this time, some powder, passing from Maryland and Pennsylvania to Gen. Washington at Boston, had to pass through a hostile population before reaching a vessel on the North River. Maj. Barber and Capts. Morrell and Lyon, placed it in rum hogsheads, and succeeded in delivering it. This was regarded an expedition of great intrepidity.

In June 1776 he received a Captain's commission from the Continental Congress, then in session at Trenton, with directions to enlist a company of seventy-five five months' men, and report to Gen. Washington in New York. He convened two companies of Militia, and addressed them in a speech of such patriotism and power that in five minutes, more than the required number offered their names. "With great difficulty and at great private expense, this company was equipped and reported in New York by the 10th of July." It was soon ordered to Long Island, as part of the New Jersey Brigade, commanded by Gen. Heard of Woodbridge. On the fatal 27th of August, they were in advance of the main army on the heights of Flatbush, and received the first fire of the British. They were badly cut to pieces, and he fell pierced by two balls. One passed through his body above the lungs, fracturing his shoulder blade, and the other through his hand. Hailing the advancing commander of the enemy, he asked to be removed, as he was badly wounded. *The response came in a volley of bullets*, which God seems to have turned aside. He feigned death, and was left, but was soon found and cared for by a young volunteer. He was carefully conveyed to New York, thence *carried by six soldiers* to his father's, and afterward, as a matter of safety, taken to Rev. Jonathan Elmer's at New Providence. By God's blessing upon medical skill and kind attentions, he finally recovered.

So highly were his soldierly qualities appreciated, that he was appointed a Major in the 4th New Jersey Brigade, before his wounds were healed. He was in the battle of Brandywine, Sept. 11, 1777, said to have been one of the hottest engagements of the war. "He belonged to the division which guarded the passage of Chadd's Ford with great gallantry, but which eventually gave way under the furious assault of Knyphausen. In this engagement the Regiment of Maj. Morrell suffered most severely."

His health was now rapidly declining, but his ardor in the cause kept him in the field. He marched with the army to the attack of Germantown. The battle began with the dawn of Nov. 4th, and raged with great fury nearly all day. He was in the heat of the contest, which, though not entirely successful, gained unfading laurels for Washington's army. With it dates the close of the Major's military career, his failing health compelling him to retire. To this, Washington, after a long interview, reluctantly consented, regretting the loss of so skillful and brave an officer. Over two and a half years had elapsed since the first battle for American freedom, during most of which time he had either been in active service or laid aside by wounds received in battle. Nor did he now leave the service from choice, but necessity.

He was now thirty years old, and though a true patriot, a brave soldier, and a skillful officer, he was not a Christian. He returned from the army to the home and business of his father, but did not seek religion till eight years later. He was awakened, October, 1775, under a sermon by Rev. John Hagerty, but was not converted till the following March, when, he says, "I received the witness of God's Spirit to my acceptance." This was about the time the Society was first formed in Elizabethtown, of which, probably, he was one of the original members. And our Church in that city is largely indebted to his long-continued and eminent services for its present prominent position.

He had been prompt to respond to the call of his country at an earlier day, and honorable scars testified to his patriotism and bravery. Nor was he less prompt now that the Master and the Church called. He was licensed as a local preacher, in about three months after his conversion. He says, "In June, 1786, I began to preach as a local preacher in Elizabethtown, and several parts of that circuit. In March, 1787, I began to ride as a traveling preacher, and rode on Elizabethtown circuit with Robert Cloud. At the Conference in New York, in October, 1788, I was ordained deacon, and appointed to Trenton circuit with John Merrick and Jethro Johnson. At the June Conference in New York, 1789, was ordained an elder, and appointed to that city with brother Cloud, who was with me twelve months, and brother Merrick four." The present rule, requiring a course of study, two years' probation before receiving orders, and two years afterward, before graduating to the full ministry, was not then in force. And the brief period between his conversion, admission to orders, and appointment to New York city, shows how highly his abilities were appreciated at the beginning of his career.

We are not informed what success attended his labors on Elizabethtown and Trenton circuits, but not so as it regards New York. When he began his labors there, some twenty years had elapsed since the erection of the Church on John St. There had been time enough since peace was restored to bring a return of prosperity. The need of a second Church had been felt for some time. After much deliberation by the laity and the Conference, he received the following remarkable paper, signed by Bishops Coke and Asbury. "Thomas Morrell is appointed and ordered by the bishops and Conference to raise a subscription in the City of New York, in order to erect a new Church, on a convenient spot in the North, or North-east part of the city; and shall call to his assistance any person or persons recommended by the bishops or Conference, or in their absence, any person he shall judge proper. The bishops and Conference do also order that all the subscriptions and collections that shall be raised from time to time in the new Church, when erected, shall be applied for the benefit, support, and interests of the new Church. And they do also give Thomas Morrell authority to appoint trustees for the said new Church."

This significant document shows to what extent *authority* was then exercised, the contrast between then and now, in the *manner* of doing such things, and also the great confidence reposed in the capacity, integrity and energy of Mr. Morrell. He was not only appointed, but *ordered* to secure the erection of a new church. No possibility of failure is recognized, and no door left open for convenient retreat. The whole responsibility was thrust upon him, with the sole exception of a reserved *right* to interfere, which seems never to have been exercised. He was to appoint trustees and call in such aid as he deemed necessary. Then, with the council of such advisers as he chose to gather around him, was to determine the site, size, materials, architecture, cost, everything in regard to it, and, also, procure the funds. He had been in the itinerancy but two years and three months, and in the church but a little over three years. Does our history as a church furnish a similar instance? But the extent of the case is not yet reached. Serious division of feeling and consequent opposition and difficulty had to be encountered. In view of this, he applied to Bishop Asbury, and received the following reply:

"MY VERY DEAR BROTHER.—It is impossible for me to give you any decided advice in the critical circumstances of your case, and the fickle tempers, you have to deal with, which may tack and change more frequently than the wind. In brief I advise you to do the best you can, *but build the house.* I will cancel your obligation to the Conference and myself. I wish you to be under no shackles on our side. I would not have you outdone." In another letter he says, "O brother, piety, patience, courage, zeal and industry will carry you through!" The following is from Dr. Coke, and speaks for itself.

"ON BOARD THE UNION, NEAR IRELAND, *June* 6, 1789.

"MY VERY DEAR BROTHER:—I beg your pardon for my great forgetfulness in not leaving behind an address in behalf of the new church we are going to build in New York. I hope you will be able to accomplish that important undertaking. Fear not, thou worm Jacob; for thy Redeemer is the Lord of hosts, etc."

The nature of these troubles is only hinted at, nor need they be exhumed from the burial time has afforded. But evidently there was much friction to retard the movement, and much motive power required to overcome it. This the bishop fully recognized, and yet the only advice he ventured to give, was, "Build the house." This was speedily accomplished. Rev. J. B. Wakeley says, "On the 11th of August, 1789, just two months and eleven days after the Conference ordered Mr. Morrell to build the church, the first stone of the foundation was laid, and it proceeded with such rapidity that it was completely enclosed, floors laid and ceiled, by the 8th of November, when it was dedicated." Referring to its completion, the Bishop drops other significant hints:

"My Dear Brother, I am pleased you have made out so wonderfully. I can figure to my own mind the difficulties you have had to struggle with. The hints you gave me as to the management of temporalities are very just. The members are welcome to act, but who are to appoint them, is the question. I find it hard if a preacher cannot draw a collection for a Mission or Conference or Station without complaint. I have nothing at all to complain of, and it would have been impossible to have carried your great design into execution without your method."

It was located on the site of the present Forsyth St. Church, then called Second St. God approbated the enterprize, not only by crowning the efforts of its friends with success, but also by a speedy outpouring of the Holy Spirit. Mr. Morrell says, "On the 4th of this month (January, 1790) a revival began in the prayer-meeting, and on the 12th it broke out in the Church, and continued, with some small intermissions, till the latter end of February. In this time about two hundred joined the society: perhaps about four hundred were converted in about eight weeks. Many of these joined afterward, *and from this revival we may date the prosperity of our Church in New York.* Very few of them fell away."

This edifice stood till 1833, when it gave place to the spacious building that now occupies the same site. As Mr. Morrell had dedicated the former, he was invited to perform the same service at the opening of the latter. But, being in his eighty-seventh year, his infirmities led him to decline.

He continued in the city two years and five months, and then returned to it after a brief absence. During this time the membership increased from three hundred to upwards of six hundred in the two Churches. But his toils were arduous and wearing as well as successful.

In the Fall of 1791, he took a tour for health, with Bishop Asbury. After a brief halt at his father's, they proceeded by land to Charleston, S. C., where he was stationed till the following June. "Secession" is no modern invention in that famed city. A Mr. Hammett, who had been stationed there, became a "disturber of Israel." He had bitterly attacked the bishop, seceded from the Church, and so drawn the members with him, that only the blacks and a few whites, were left as sheep without a shepherd. Mr. Morrell so answered his attack on the bishop, and vindicated the Church, that a large portion of the seceders saw their mistake and returned to the forsaken fold. The defence was published, and is said to have been masterly and triumphant. Having gained much invigoration, and to a great extent quieted the disturbed elements in that city, he returned to New York by sea.

He resumed his labors in June, 1792, and remained till March, 1794. The following entry refers to the yellow fever, which raged in Philadelphia from August to October, 1793, with such fury that four thousand persons fell victims to its ravages. "Sept. 26th there was a day of fasting and prayer, held in New York, in every Church. Such a solemn time was never seen in the city. The churches were all crowded. Ours (the new Church) was not only full, and the house adjacent, but also the burying yard. I preached from Jonah iii. 5, 'So the people of Nineveh believed God and proclaimed a fast,' &c. It was a most solemn season indeed. The occasion of the fast was to entreat the Lord to put a stop to the malignant fever in Philadelphia. We had prayers at six and preaching at ten A. M., and preaching at three and six P. M." At this time, Rev. Freeborn Garrettson was stationed in Philadelphia, and in March, 1794, they exchanged places. He says,—"On Friday, 28th, I left the city and came to Elizabethtown, having been stationed in York from June, 1789, to March, 1794, near five years:" (this included the trip south.) "Blessed be God for the gracious assistance he gave me in preaching to that kind and loving people, and I desire to be humbled under a sense of God's goodness to me in owning and blessing my labors to them. When I entered upon my station there, I found about three hundred members, and when I left them about eight hundred and fifty. This great work has God wrought, and the glory be ascribed to him." So the increase, after he returned from the South, was about two hundred and fifty.

He was prostrated, Dec. 1, 1794, by a severe attack of inflammatory fever. After this he only preached five times in Philadelphia. His recovery was considered doubtful for a long time. This near approach to eternity led to close heart-searching, and the recording of the following solemn vows in case of recovery:

"1. Not to abandon the ministry.

"2. To be more watchful than formerly.

"3. To be more charitable according to ability.

"4. Never to omit private prayer three times a day."

Truly, as Deity is unveiled, the world and self sink in our estimation! April 21, slightly over a year after going to the city, and nearly five months after he was prostrated, he went to his father's, where he remained in feeble health till May, 1799. At this date he began a two years' term in Baltimore. The labors of himself and colleagues there were largely owned of God. At the beginning of the second year, the General Conference sat in the city, during which a gracious revival occurred. Over one hundred were converted before its close, and the work spread till four hundred were added to the church.

Mr. Wakeley says, "In consequence of ill health he located in 1801, but consented, at the earnest request of Bishop Asbury, to be stationed in New York in 1802, where he remained till 1804." But his name in the minutes is connected with New York for 1801–1803. Which is in error I have not the means of determining, not having his private papers. Of the immediate fruits of this last term, we are not advised. But Methodism in that city is largely indebted, under God, to Thomas Morrell.

It had become partially fossilized in old John St. The more sagacious and liberal among the membership felt the need of a second church, and were anxious to build it. But the other sort resisted with such pertinacity that they came near defeating the attempted forward movement. The exigency was important, and something must be done to meet it. The skillful, courageous Major was promoted to a Generalship, and placed in command of the advancing forces. The battle was severe, but with great prudence and energy he led them to victory. The fossil shell was broken, and an expansion begun which has continued till the Church has reached its present enlarged and influential position.

Near seventeen years had now elapsed since he began "to ride as a traveling preacher." But he was laid aside over four years, and if he spent one in his father's store, less than twelve are left to the effective ministry. But these were years of incessant toil, great responsibility and signal success. Most of this time was spent in four of our principal cities, and more than half of it in New York. He corresponded with Wesley, Coke, Asbury and other leading men in the Church, while his whole ministerial career shows that he occupied a prominent position and exerted a decided influence in her early councils. Nor did his labors abate only with his strength. Referring to his last term in the city, he says, "This was my last station out of Elizabethtown, but for sixteen years I continued to preach as often as when I traveled." Dr. Murray adds, "After that he generally preached once every Sabbath in Elizabethtown, unless prevented by ill health, until he reached his eighty-seventh year." He was eighty-eight years and nine months old when he preached his last sermon.

He was married, May 24, 1802, to Lydia, daughter of George Frazer, of Westfield, N. J., then in his fifty-fifth year. His wife joined the M. E. Church soon after, probably leaving another communion for this purpose. She was a woman of deep and uniform piety, and reached a peaceful end, Oct. 11, 1808, leaving three children, one of whom, Rev. Francis A. Morrell, is still (1864) living. He afterward married the widow of Theodorus Hamilton, who survived him some twelve years, and left a daughter, the wife of Judge Elmer, of Elizabeth City, N. J.

In 1804 the minutes assign him to Elizabethtown. The next year his name only appears in the list of elders, and in 1806 it is marked "located." And though his labors were incessant, his name does not appear again till 1825, when it is marked "supernumerary," which relation he held to the end of life.

Dr. Murray gives this striking and instructive portrayal of his personal appearance and social habits. "When I first knew Mr. Morrell, he was in his eighty-ninth year. His appearance was unique and striking. He was rather short, his head not large, his eye bright and blue, his lips thin, and his whole appearance indicative of much more than ordinary firmness. He always wore a covering on his head like a smoking-cap, from beneath which his hair fell gracefully on his neck. For his age his step was quick and his conversation vivacious. He was neat in person, and always appeared as if dressed for company. He wore a long frock-coat, buttoned to the chin, and, without the least ostentation, was a man of the old school. His personal and social habits were worthy of all praise. Through the whole course of his life, he rose early. He was frugal and temperate in all things. He was remarkably punctual in all his engagements. He never put off the work of one day to another, or of one hour to another. Hence everything around him and belonging to him was in order. It was also one of his standing rules to owe no man anything but love; and at the hour of his departure, there was not probably a man living to whom he owed a penny. He possessed great energy and activity. He was always occupied with something. And hence to the last he was cheerful, contented, and happy."

The fires of patriotism, which burned so brightly in his early manhood, only went out with his life. Dr. Murray bears this testimony: "He was always an earnest patriot. His love of country increased with his years, and was second in intensity, only to his love to God and his zeal for the salvation of men. On the 4th of July, 1828, when he was eighty-three years of age, he delivered an address in the Presbyterian Church in this town, worthy of one whose blood had actually formed part of the price of his country's liberties."

He did not receive a thorough literary training, and made no "pretensions to extensive learning, philosophical acumen or critical research." His mind was not massive or brilliant, but quick, penetrating and energetic, and at the same time elastic and tenacious. His perceptive faculties were of a high order, and combined with quick intuition, accurate observation and careful reflection, enabled him to acquire a good degree of mental discipline, and also, accurate and extensive knowledge of men and things. Nor was he deficient in a knowledge of his mother tongue or of theological and general literature.

As a preacher he ranked among the first of his day. Rev. John Lee, who knew him well, says: "His appearance and manner in the pulpit were grave and dignified, befitting the ambassador of God. His sermons were characterized by strong sense and sound theology; his deductions were logical, his analyses clear, and his application forcible, discriminating and faithful. Not unfrequently his preaching was attended with an unction that affected his own heart, causing the tears to trickle down his cheeks, and being communicated to his hearers, a large part of his audience would be melted down into tenderness, humility and love." Dr. Murray says, "Possessing a rich Christian experience, he was peculiarly felicitous in exposing the deceitfulness of the human heart, and in edifying believers. And when, at times, he denounced the wrath of God against the impenitent, he did it with an authority and power which spread awe and solemnity over the whole assembly." Rev. Dr. Sprague, having examined one of his sketches, says, "It is written with marked ability, and would be highly creditable to any of our most highly educated ministers, indicating a high degree of intellectual culture." These testimonies are corroborated by the notice he attracted, the positions he occupied and the success that attended his labors.

Though not converted in early life, he became a deeply experienced Christian. January 1, 1838, he entered the following remarkable item in his journal :—

"Through the tender mercy of God I have lived to see the beginning of another year, being now ninety years, one month and nine days old, a longer period than any of our family have lived. I have many things to be thankful for, my life being prolonged to so advanced an age, having the faculties of my mind in perfect exercise, my health tolerably good, sleep sound, appetite good, my wife in health, my children all religious and in health, my son successful as a preacher, my soul devoted to God, and everything in plenty of temporal things. Would to God I was more thankful, more holy, more heavenly-minded. This morning I have devoted my soul and body to God; and though I am unable to preach as formerly, yet I am endeavoring by grace to walk with God. The church here is in a low state. Lord, revive thy work in my soul, and in our and other churches for Christ's sake. Amen, and amen." Was any other man ever able to indite such a record? or was any mortal ever more highly favored or richly blessed of Heaven?

His son says, "His favorite themes in preaching were the universality of the atonement, justification by faith, and especially the doctrine of entire sanctification, of which, for some time before his death, he had the clear witness. I seldom heard him preach, but the tears flowed from his eyes, evincing the deep earnestness of his soul. His absorbing aim was to lead the soul to Christ and heaven." Observe, too, his recorded vow, "never to omit private prayer three times a day," showing him to have been familiar with spiritual exercises, and to have walked and talked with God. Dr. Murray says, "He possessed a rich Christian experience," and that, "he was a good man full of the Holy Ghost and of faith." And especially significant is the above statement that "for some time before his death he had the clear witness" of entire sanctification.

It was fitting and to be expected that such a life should be crowned by a triumphant death. His son shall relate the manner of its occurrence. "In his last illness, which was protracted, he suffered much from soreness of throat, accompanied with an asthmatic affection. Yet he uttered no complaint—not a murmur was heard; and though he desired the hour of deliverance to arrive, yet was perfectly resigned to the will of God. He repeated audibly three times,—'Though I walk through the valley of the shadow of death, I will fear no evil, for the Lord is with me.' To our deeply affected mother, he said, 'Why do you weep? I am going to glory.' At his request the 23d Psalm was read. We sang the 'Christian's Home,' in which he made an effort to join. He said, 'I shall soon be there,' and often prayed, 'Come, Lord Jesus, come quickly.' When asked if death was a terror to him, he replied in the negative, and added, 'I have gotten the victory.' He exclaimed,—'How good to feel a Saviour's love amid so much suffering.' He remained conscious to the last, and uttered as his last audible words, 'All is well,' and then without a struggle or a sigh, sweetly fell asleep in Jesus. Of those who thus die it may be truly said,—

'They sleep in Jesus and are blessed;
How sweet their slumbers are!
From suffering and from sin released,
And freed from every care.'"

Thus triumphantly ended an eventful and noble career, that had been extended to the rare length of ninety years, eight months and seventeen days, on the 9th of August, 1838. And how full of instruction and comfort is the fact, that aftr a manly and high-toned devotion to God and his work had characterized his Christian and ministerial life, no cloud was permitted to shade the closing scene. But the light and warmth from the Sun of Righteousness, which had so richly cheered and invigorated him amid the toils and trials of life's long day, beamed upon him with increasing fullness as he neared the final hour. How touchingly is the saying of the wise man thus verified,—"The path of the just is as the shining light, that shineth more and more unto the perfect day."—Prov. iv. 18.

N. B. The materials for the above memoir were gathered from Rev. Dr. Murray's contribution to Sprague's "Annals of the American Methodist Pulpit," to the use of which Dr. S. kindly consented,—from Wakeley's "Lost Chapters," and from Lee's sketch of "Methodism in New Jersey," together with some direct information from Rev. F. A. Morrell.

REV. JAMES BUCKLEY.

THE Methodists of America are indebted to England not only for their denominational origin—but also for very many in their communion who have proved themselves able ministers of the New Testament. Of this class are the two brothers Buckley. They were born in Lancashire, but in the providence of God were transferred to these shores, where they became the subjects of redeeming grace, through the agency of that Church, whose ministry they subsequently adorned.

James Buckley, the subject of this sketch, was born in 1810. He came to this country at the age of seventeen, and three years after his arrival embraced religion. It soon became evident to the Church that he possessed the necessary qualifications, both of gifts and grace, for an effective minister of the cross. Being satisfied himself of a Divine call to this sublime work, and finding his way open to the regular ministry in the latter part of the year 1833, he entered upon it, under the direction of Rev. J. J. Matthias, Presiding Elder of the East Jersey District.

The following spring he was received on trial in the Philadelphia Conference, and appointed to Mount Horeb, N. J. In 1835 and 1836 he was stationed at Elizabethtown, and in 1837 at Morristown, in the same state. He went to this last charge in a feeble state of health, and continued gradually to decline, until in the following winter it was found there was but little hope of his recovery, when he was removed to the house of a relative in Bloomfield, where he lingered through several months. He was not confined to his bed until the last two or three days of his life, though his disease, which was a clearly marked case of pulmonary consumption, left him no hope, during these months of suffering, of a favorable issue. He walked, however, even cheerfully into the evening twilight; and witnessed the deepening shades of the approaching night of death, not only without dismay, but with continually brightening hopes of immortality and eternal life. He possessed an unshaken faith in God his Saviour, and, in the spirit of abiding trust, declared, "My hopes of heaven are firmly based on the atonement of Christ."

The evening before his death, he seemed better than usual; was cheerful, and conversed freely with his friends, but on the following morning a change for the worse had evidently taken place. His speech had partially failed. He was sinking into the arms of death. A friend inquired, "Is the great sacrifice which has been offered sufficient?" to which he responded with emphasis, "Oh yes, yes." After his speech had entirely failed, he was requested, if all was well, to raise his hand, which he did at once; and, as if to emphasize the response, he repeated immediately this token of the victory which he realized through the blood of the Lamb. His friends kneeled around his bed, and in prayer commended his spirit to God. Soon after which, on the morning of the 15th of March, 1838, he sweetly fell asleep in Jesus.

The piety of James Buckley was not of a vacillating or doubtful character; but deep, uniform, constant, practical. The graces of the Christian shone in him with distinguished lustre. Grave and serious in his manners, he was at the same time amiable and cheerful.

His talents were of a superior order. Gifted by nature with a mind strong and discriminating, his habits were studious, his application close, and his improvement consequently rapid. In the pulpit he was eminently popular and successful. The zeal, pathos and energy with which his sermons were delivered, rendered them deeply impressive. He was a most faithful and devoted pastor, always awakening a healthful religious influence in his pastoral visitations. He was, in a word, in every department of his calling "a workman that needeth not to be ashamed."

Though called at the early age of twenty-eight, to lay down with his life the work for which he was so peculiarly qualified, he still lives in the fruits of his labors, and his crown of rejoicing will be decorated with many stars.

REV. JAMES CAMPBELL.

He was born in Ireland, in the year 1762. It is not now known, when he came to this country, but it must have been at an early age, as we find him living in the State of Maryland, where he was converted in his eighteenth year. At the age of twenty-seven, he entered the itinerant ministry—his name first appearing in the Conference minutes for the year 1789. He continued in the effective work for a period of sixteen years, and in 1805 permanently located in the Borough of Pemberton, New Jersey.

We find his name connected, at different periods, with the Virginia, New York, Philadelphia, and New Jersey annual Conferences, in connection with which he traveled and preached in most of the States then in the Union.

His location was occasioned by a charge seriously affecting his moral character, under which he suffered for a time, when God in an impressive manner vindicated his innocence. His accuser, who was a woman, was brought upon her death-bed, and with the fearful guilt of this crime upon her conscience dared not pray nor hope for the Divine forgiveness until she should relieve the victim of her malignant slander from its bitter consequences.

She accordingly sent for Mr. Campbell and several prominent and influential members of the church, and in their presence made a full confession of her falsehood and perjury, which was taken down at her request, and duly attested. At the next Conference, he was promptly and honorably restored to the Church and ministry. He however never re-entered the regular work, but continued in business, by which he acquired a considerable fortune, a large part of which at his death was left to the church.

As a preacher he was plain, practical, and energetic, and during his long residence in Pemberton was greatly respected for his earnest consistent life. His regard for the sanctity of the Sabbath was quite remarkable. No one was ever more careful to "remember the Sabbath-day and keep it holy." The precept did not devolve upon him an irksome task to be performed reluctantly, but it seemed rather the charter of an unspeakably precious privilege. The dawn of the Sabbath's heavenly light always stimulated his devotions and gladdened his heart, and its recurrence was hailed as among his most coveted enjoyments.

He cherished also a very ardent love for the inspired word. He read it habitually and with great interest, and treasured every favorable expression of the sacred volume which he met in his reading as we might suppose he would have done if it had been a personal compliment.

The Jews, we are told, regarded the name of Jehovah as too sacred for utterance, and Mr. Campbell's veneration for it was scarcely less marked, for it is said he never uttered it nor heard it uttered but with uncovered head.

He lived to a ripe old age, having reached nearly the divinely-prescribed limit of probationary life. His evening was without clouds, and his sun went down amidst bright skies on the 31st of December, 1840, in his eightieth year.

REV. THOMAS WARE.

THERE seems to be no authentic record of the date of his birth. The part of the family register containing it having been, by accident, so effaced as to render it illegible. He says: "For the only knowledge I have of it, therefore, I am indebted to the memory of my excellent mother, from whom I learned that it was on the 19th of December, 1758." He was born in Greenwich, Cumberland Co., N. J.

His paternal grandfather was an Englishman by birth, and was a captain in the British service under Queen Anne. He says, "I remember him well, as he lived until I was sixteen years old. His personal appearance was fine, and his mind cheerful. The caresses, anecdotes and lessons of instruction received from him are among my earliest recollections. He had high notions of liberty, and was the first man I ever heard eulogize the Indian character. Most people seemed to think the Indians ought to be exterminated."

"When this venerable man came to spend a few days with us," says Thomas, "we were always delighted, and vied with each other in our efforts to please him. His company was interesting on account of his cheerfulness and the stories with which he was always ready to entertain us. He was in the habit, too, of advising my father with respect to the education of his children. On this subject he used to say the mind must be made strong, as well as the body . . . . and in view of this a beginning could not too soon be made to guard children against the fears which vulgar stories about ghosts, &c., were calculated to produce, and to store their minds with correct ideas. My grandfather lived to the great age of more than five score years."

His maternal grandfather was a native of Scotland, named Reed, who was wrecked off the Capes of the Delaware, on his way to this country. He reached the shore by clinging to some fragments of the broken ship, and was found nearly exhausted on the beach by a farmer named Garrison, whose daughter he afterward married.

The father and mother of Thomas were pious persons, and lived together in the fear of the Lord. His father died when about thirty-eight years of age. He was remarkable for his kind and gentle disposition, and was the only one of the family who professed to know that God, for Christ's sake, could forgive sins. "The whole deportment of my father," (said Thomas) "tended to fix in me a habit of serious reflection on the subject of religion, and his triumphant death made an impression on my mind that time could not obliterate."

He seemed to have been a man of considerable reading and intelligence. Milton was his favourite poet, and it is said that persons of taste and cultivation were always delighted to hear him read Paradise Lost. It seems that while his parents were both pious, they differed very decidedly in their views of doctrine. The mother was a firm believer in the Presbyterian faith, while the father was not, and refused to join that church unless he could be permitted to think for himself on the subject of Divine decrees. He believed in the doctrine of the universality of the atonement: but in compliance with his wife's wishes suffered Thomas to learn the Larger and Shorter Catechisms. In view of the long dark night of sorrow occasioned by these Calvinistic prepossessions he afterward said, "Alas! how many children are injured, and go halting all their days, for want of skillful nursing."

His account of the mother's first effort to conduct family prayers after his father's death is quite affecting:—"It had been usual for my mother in my father's absence to pray with her children, morning and evening . . . . After his death she collected her children as usual around her. While thus seated, eight in number, and the eldest only in her seventeenth year, she attempted to read, but could not. She sat and wept. My eldest sister at last said, 'My dear mother, why do you weep?' 'Alas!' she replied, 'death has made you all orphans, and your mother a disconsolate widow. I am not worthy to fill the place of your excellent father; had I been so, and you been dutiful children, we should not have been left in this forlorn condition. Go, my children, and pray for yourselves: these little ones,' (meaning the younger four of the number) 'I will take with me into the closet.' On hearing these words from my bereaved and much afflicted mother I arose quickly, went out into the field, and wept bitterly."

The gloom which hung over the mind of this good woman, at the loss of so kind and affectionate a husband, devolving upon her as it did the whole responsibility of a large and dependent family, was heightened by the doubts she often indulged about her own election, or gracious state, as she expressed it. She was harassed with fears, that what she had fondly taken for saving grace was nothing more than common grace.

A deep gloom was cast over the morning of young Ware's days by his early instruction in the doctrines of the Calvinistic faith: he says, "A spirit of melancholy seized me, and I became subject to desponding fears; in this state I wandered in lonely places, and having heard that departed spirits did sometimes return as messengers of good to those they loved on earth, I often invoked my father's appearance, hoping that for the love he bore us while he was with us, he would return and tell me if my mother's name and my own were written in the book of life."

Soon after this he says, "The younger two of our family were taken away by death. As they died in infancy, there is no just ground to doubt of their being happy. But to a mind exercised as mine then was, there was no satisfactory assurance of it: for according to our creed the condition of infancy could not be considered as a security against being finally lost." He inferred from his creed, as he tells us, that, "Our dear little Lydia and Enoch were more likely to be in hell than in heaven," as he supposed the non-elect to be much more numerous than the elect, and thus the moral gloom through which he walked was deepened almost to the blackness of despair.

He was now some twelve years old, and from this time until he reached his twenty-first year, when under the preaching of the sainted Pedicord, the light of gospel truth chased from his mind the dark clouds of this "horrible" system of decrees, he seems to have walked in darkness and the shadow of death, sometimes meditating suicide as a remedy for his mental anguish, but deterred from cherishing the fell purpose more by the love he had for his mother, and the effect "the tale of horror" would have upon her, than by any fear he had of the sleep of death, which, as he tells us, he "sometimes much coveted." At other times he would try to dismiss all serious thoughts from his mind, and give himself up to levity and indifference—to singing songs and reading novels and indulging in wicked jests, but his conscience, still awake and alarmed, gave him no quiet.

Speaking of his condition, on one occasion he says, "I was now for several months little better than a maniac. I delighted in nothing so much as being alone: to wander in retired places, and indulge the reveries of my own mind: sometimes I cherished the delightful thought that I had an interest in the Parent of all, and was an object of his pity. At other times I was led to adopt the language of the poet,—

> 'Ten thousand midnights rolled their midnight gloom,
> In solemn pomp along a starless sky.'

"At times I devoted myself to much reading. Interesting histories I preferred to any other solid works: but novels took the lead, and I devoured all I could procure. With my jaundiced eyes I could find nothing in the Bible whereon to build but a doubtful peradventure—a mere shadow—and with this I dare no more converse than with a spectre from the dismal shades. In such a state, where or to whom could I go for instruction and relief?"

At about this time a preacher, who was one of the most rigid predestinarians of that age, came into the place, and revived the clamor against the Methodists. The story which was put in circulation was that the Rev. Messrs. Richard and Rowland Hill had written them down in England, and that they were flocking to America: and a clergyman of an adjoining parish apprehending that no time was to be lost, commenced a course of sermons on the decrees of God, in which he extended their application to the falling of every leaf as well as to all the minutia of human actions. He was very severe on the Methodist tenets, denouncing them as Arminian, Pelagian and Popish heresies, &c. During this agitation a son of Col. S., one of the minister's chief parishioners, returned from college with two of his fellow-students to spend a short time at home. These young men were studying for the law. They attended church for two successive Sabbaths, and listened to the discourses on the divine decrees. On the following Sabbath, however, while the parson was pursuing his subject in the church, they were playing at cards in a pleasant shade near it, without any apparent concern about being concealed from the public view. Of this daring impiety the pastor was soon informed, and on the following day in company with two of his elders he waited on Col. S., whose son had evidently taken the lead in this open contempt of the day, the ordinances, and the minister of God. The clergyman opened the subject to the father, and the son was called to answer for himself. The youth frankly confessed what he had done: and on being sharply rebuked for an offence so enormous, and shocking to the moral sense of all good people, he boldly took refuge under the doctrine taught him from the pulpit. "If your reverence please," said he, "the Lord made me to do this bad deed, and I hope you will excuse or at least pity me, seeing it was from all eternity decreed," and then drew from his pocket and handed to the preacher an abstract which he had taken of one of his sermons, in which it was affirmed that the decrees of God extended to all the actions of men. With this repartee the Colonel saw the parson was greatly embarrassed; nor could he relieve him other than by an exercise of parental authority in reproving his son for being guilty of so wicked an act, and obtaining from him a promise that he would not be guilty of the like again. But the son gave point to the whole by begging his father in the most respectful manner not to urge his demand with too much decision, lest he should be guilty of greater impiety, not knowing how the decrees of God might run.

In his sixteenth year the subject of our sketch left his native place and went to Salem, N. J., about twenty miles distant, to reside with his uncle. This uncle was an ingenious mechanic, intelligent, witty, and sarcastic, but lax in his moral and religious principles. His associates were like himself, skeptical and profane. Under the corrupting influences of these vicious examples young Ware for a time lost his seriousness; he imbibed their spirit, joined in their merriment, and having a good voice he was soon caressed by them as being able to sing a good song and say some smart things.

While residing with his uncle the quarrel between us and the mother country raged with great violence. Thomas, young and ardent, had all his feelings enlisted on the side of America, and seemed justly to appreciate the issues involved, as will appear from the following: When one asked him for an explanation of the principles which controlled the colonists, he replied, "They consist in never invading the rights of others, nor in allowing others to invade ours, at the risk of life. But understand me, sir," he continued, "I do not mean as a duelist, for no man in his individual capacity has the right of life or death;" and he proceeded to explain an invasion of rights as consisting in attempts to compel us to believe and act contrary to the dictates of our own rational convictions.

When the struggle commenced his uncle was on the side of America, but on the adoption of the Declaration of Independence he changed sides, and Thomas left him and volunteered in the Colonial service, and was one of the nine thousand troops quartered at Perth Amboy in 1776.

The responsibility and dangers of his new position led him again to serious thoughts of God and eternity, and he prayed until a confidence sprang up within him that he should be returned to his home and friends in safety; and "so it was," he concludes, "that as a soldier in the army I was more devout than when at home."

While they were lying at Perth Amboy their general reviewed them in full view of the enemy, and with only a narrow river between them and the enemy's guns. As might have been expected the British opened their artillery upon them, and if they had directed their fire with skill many would have been slain: but they shot over them, and though none were injured many were dreadfully frightened, and indignant at the officers for unnecessarily exposing their lives to such imminent hazard.

The incompetency of the officers was but too obvious. For instance, instead of drilling and exercising their men in the arts of war they permitted them to spend their time in foot-races, wrestling, jumping, &c. By an inadvertent remark on this subject, Thomas came near getting into serious difficulty. He said, "Our officers undoubtedly depend more upon our heels than our arms," alluding to the exercises of the men in running and jumping. For this he was reprimanded and threatened with an arrest.

He afterward volunteered to reinforce Washington on Long Island. They marched with all possible haste to Paulis' Hook; but before they arrived the British got command of the Hudson River, and they were prevented crossing to Long Island. After this forced march, the day being very sultry, and having no tent or quarters for the night except a damp filthy hovel, he was seized with what was called the camp fever. The physicians pronounced it a hectic. Whatever it was, it cost him several years of the prime of his life.

He returned home, sick, but from the cruelty of the tories who infested the lower part of this State, and treated him with all sorts of indignities, came near losing his life on the way. He afterward enlisted again, but found himself incapacitated by sickness; and among strangers and nigh unto death, with a conscience ill at rest and a religious creed which obscured the way of life and shrouded his mind in a worse than Egyptian darkness, his case was pitiable indeed. He says of himself at this period: "My physical powers were prostrated by disease, and my mind bewildered by the religious opinions I had been taught in my childhood, without being able to understand them. It is true I sometimes read, but superstitiously believing that God's effective will was hidden from man, I doubted much if what I read was true."

About this time, while residing in Mount Holly, he contracted an acquaintance with a young man of insinuating manners, who was completing the study of navigation. He was expecting to go to sea with his brother in-law, as his mate, in a brig which was nearly fitted for the voyage. This young man induced young Ware to engage in the same study with him, promising to give him all the aid he could until the brig was ready, and that he should have the steward's birth on board, when he would assist him in his studies until he had acquired a knowledge of the art. He said he had no doubt they would both make their fortunes, as the brig was to have a picked crew and outsail everything on the seas. Thomas entered heartily into the enterprise, without, however, knowing its true character. This brig, as facts subsequently proved, was designed to carry on a contraband trade with the British. Between the owners and the enemy there was an understanding: the vessel laden with provisions was to be thrown in their way and captured; and then a liberal price was to be paid for the cargo, and she permitted to escape.

Ignorant of his wicked design and treachery, he was drawn to the very verge of the abyss, without suspecting it. Impatient for the time to arrive when he was to sail, and when the preparations were nearly complete, he wandered into a neighboring grove to think over the subject of the adventure. While musing there alone, a stranger passed him, though without seeing him. As he was going by he began to sing,

"Still out of the deepest abyss
Of trouble, I mournfully cry,
I pine to recover my bliss,
And see my Redeemer and die.

"I cannot, I cannot forbear,
These passionate longings for home.
Oh! when shall my spirit be there,
Oh! when will the messenger come?"

Thomas was greatly touched by this singing, especially the couplet:—

"I cannot, I cannot forbear,
These passionate longings for home."

He followed the singer, hoping to hear more of it, until he saw him stop at the house of a Methodist and dismount. He concluded the stranger must be a Methodist preacher, and had probably come there to preach that evening.

A Methodist man in the town, suspecting Thomas to be under religious impressions, went to him and informed him that Mr. Pedicord, a most excellent preacher, had come into the place and was to preach that evening, and expressed a very earnest wish that he should hear him. Thomas knew very little of the Methodists at this time. He had been led to believe they were disloyal; and had been charged by his mother, who was strongly prejudiced against them, to refrain from going after them. Through the influence of his Methodist friend, however, he was induced to go, and for the first time, heard the doctrine of a free and present salvation. The text was Luke xxiv. 45–47. He says: "I was soon convinced that all men were redeemed, and might be saved—and saved *now* from the guilt, practice, and love of sin. With this I was greatly affected, and could hardly refrain from exclaiming aloud, 'This is the best intelligence I ever heard.' When the meeting closed, I hastened to my room, fell upon my knees before God, and spent much of the night in penitential tears. I did not once think of my engagement with my sea-bound companions, until the next day, when I informed the young man who had induced me to enlist in the project, that I had abandoned all thoughts of going to sea. They, however, proceeded in their perilous undertaking, were betrayed, their officers thrown into prison, and the brig and cargo confiscated. When I heard this, I praised the Lord for my deliverance from this danger and infamy, which I considered worse than death."

He now gave up the study of navigation, and abandoned all company but that of the pious. He read the New Testament over and over, and was charmed with the character of God his Saviour, as revealed in it, and esteemed reproach for his sake more desirable than all earthly treasure.

"Mr. Pedicord," he says, "returned again to our village. I hastened to see him, and tell him all that was in my heart. He shed tears over me and prayed: I was dissolved in tears: he prayed again. My soul was filled with unutterable delight. He now rejoiced over me as a son—an heir of God and a joint heir with Christ. I felt and knew that I was made free."

He was now twenty-one years of age, and his regenerated

nature was wholly consecrated to God and his service. Among the stirring incidents in his new experience and associations is an interesting account of a quarterly meeting held in Mt. Holly by Rev. George Mair, when that was missionary ground, in the year 1780. His picture of the Love-feast, on that occasion, held in a barn, contains several touching experiences, one of which I know the reader will enjoy: it is as follows:—

"A German spoke next, and if I could tell what he said, as told by him, it would be worth a place in any one's memory. But this I cannot do. He spoke, however, in substance thus:—When de preacher did come to mine house, and did say, 'Peace be in dis habitation: I am come fader to see if in dese troublesome times, I can find any in your parts dat does know de way to dat country, where war, sorrow and crying is no more; and of whom could I inquire so properly, as of one to whom God has given many days?' When he did say dis, I was angry, and did try to say to him, 'Go out of mine house;' but I could not speak, but did tremble, and when mine anger was gone, I did say, I does fear I does not know de way to dat goodist place, but mine wife does know; sit down and I will call her. Just den mine wife did come in, and de stranger did say, Dis, fader, is I presume yourn wife, of whom you say she does know de way to a better country, de way to heaven! Dear woman, will you tell it me? After mine wife did look at de stranger one minute, she did say, *I do know Jesus*, and is not he de way? De stranger did den fall on his knees and tank God for bringing him to mine house, where dere was one dat did know de way to heaven; he did den pray for me and mine children, dat we might be like mine wife, and all go to heaven togeder. Mine wife did den pray in Dutch, and some of mine children did fall on deir knees, and I did fall on mine, and when she did pray no more de preacher did pray again, and mine oldest daughter did cry so loud.

"From dat time I did seek de Lord, and did fear he would not hear me, for I had made de heart of mine wife so sorry when I did tell her she was mad. But de preacher did show me so many promises, dat I did tell mine wife, if she would forgive me, and fast and pray wid me all day and all night, I did hope de

Lord would forgive me. Dis did please mine wife, but she did say, We must do all in de name of de Lord Jesus. About de middle of de night, I did tell mine wife I should not live till morning, mine distress was too great. But she did say, Mine husband, God will not let you die; and just as de day did break, mine heart did break, and tears did run so fast, and I did say, Mine wife, I does now believe mine God will bless me, and she did say, Amen, amen, Come, Lord Jesus. Just den mine oldest daughter, who had been praying all night, did come in, and did fall on mine neck, and said, O mine fader, Jesus has blessed me. And den joy did come into mine heart, and we have gone on rejoicing in de Lord ever since. Great fear did fall on mine neighbors, and mine barn would not hold all de people dat does come to learn de way to heaven." His looks, his tears, and his broken English kept the people in tears, mingled with smiles, and even laughter, not with lightness, but joy, for they believed every word he said.

In those days when conversion implied devotion to God's work, it could hardly have been otherwise than that our subject, ardent and gifted as he was, should be in labors more abundant. He was soon appointed leader of a class, and also licensed to exhort, and though he did not deem himself called to the work of the ministry, yet his zeal often led him to extraordinary efforts for the salvation of souls. Some of these he relates in his account of his first meeting with Bishop Asbury.

"Bishop Asbury came to New Mills, about seven miles from Mount Holly, and sent for me to come and see him. We had not previously met. On entering his room, he fixed his discriminating eye upon me, and seemed to examine me from head to foot. As I approached him, he reached me his hand, and said, 'This I suppose is Brother Ware, or shall I say Pedicord the younger?' I replied, my name is Ware, sir, and I claim some affinity to the Wesleyan family, and Mr. Pedicord as my spiritual father."

After an informal though thorough examination of the young man on his doctrinal views, "The Bishop (he continues) looked at me very sternly, and said, 'What is this I hear of you? It is said that you have disturbed the peaceful inhabitants of

Holly by rudely entering into a house where a large number of young people were assembled for innocent amusement, and when welcomed by the company and politely invited to be seated, you refused, and proceeded to address them in such a way that some became alarmed and withdrew, and the rest soon followed.' To this I answered. 'My zeal in this affair may have carried me too far. But I knew them to be generally my friends and well-wishers, and felt to do as the man out of whom Christ cast the devils was directed, namely, to go and show my friends how great things God had done for me. It it true, when I entered the room some appeared delighted to see me; but those who knew me best appeared sad. And when invited to take a glass and be seated I told them I must be excused, for I had not come to spend the evening with them, but to invite them to spend it with me. 'You know me,' I said, 'and how delighted I have often been in your company and with the amusements in which you have met to indulge; but I cannot go with you now. My conscience will not permit me to do so. But as none of your consciences forbid your going with me I have come to invite you to go and hear the excellent Mr. Pedicord preach his farewell sermon. Pardon me, my friends, I am constrained to tell you the Lord has done great things for me through the instrumentality of this good man.' Not a word of reply was made to what I said. Some were affected, and left soon after I withdrew. It is true, some of the citizens were offended, and said it was too much that the Methodists should give tone to the town. 'Must the youth of Mount Holly,' said they, 'ask leave of the Methodists, if they would spend an evening together?' Others said, 'The young man must have acted from a Divine impulse, or he could not have done it, as he is naturally diffident and unassuming.' But I never knew that any of the party was offended."

"The Bishop listened attentively, but without relaxing the sternness of his look or making any reply. He then branched off to another subject. 'Was it not bold and adventurous,' said he, 'for so young a Methodist to fill for a whole week without license or consultation the appointments of such a preacher as George Mair?' I replied that 'Mr. Mair was suddenly called from the circuit by sickness in his family, and I saw he was deeply affected because of the disappointments it must occasion on a part of the circuit where a good work was going on; that some of these appointments were new, and there was no one to hold any meeting whatever with the people; and that I was therefore induced soon after he was gone to resolve on going to some of these places and telling those who might come out, the cause of the preacher's absence; and if I was sometimes constrained to exhort, it was with fear and trembling, and very short, unless when the tears of the people caused me to forget that I was on unauthorized ground.' "

The Bishop made no reply; and the young man being under the impression that his remarks were designed to mortify him for his course at the Ball and on the Circuit, said, "Mr. Asbury, if the person who informed you against me had told me of my errors I would have acknowledged them." Here he stopped him by clasping him in his arms, and saying in an affectionate tone, "You are altogether mistaken, my son; it was your friend Pedicord who told me of your pious deeds, and advised that you should be sent to Dover Circuit, saying that he would be responsible that no harm, but good, would result from it." Though not yet a preacher, he consented to go, quite reluctantly, however, to assist in keeping up the appointments until another should be sent.

Having made the necessary preparation, he set out from Mount Holly in September, 1783, for his new work on the Peninsula. He was received kindly by the people, and soon saw, as he expressed it, that Dover Circuit was the place for him. He found some of the members wealthy and in the higher circles of life, not ashamed to bear the cross. Among these were some females distinguished for piety and zeal such as he had never before witnessed. A number of these possessed the true missionary spirit in an uncommon degree, and greatly aided the young preachers, by whom principally the work was carried on on that favored shore.

At almost every meeting some were converted, and "frequently his rejoicing in the Lord was great." In the meantime, he tells us, he "*prayed* and *read* and *wrote* much." The

Bible was his chief book, which he constantly studied with such helps as were within his reach.

In the Spring of 1784 the Conference sat at Baltimore. He went to this Conference under the impression that he ought to go home and give himself to study for a year before entering fully upon the work of the ministry. But when he saw so many of the preachers overworked and broken down in their efforts to meet the calls everywhere made for laborers in this spiritual vineyard, he yielded to the advice of his friend Pedicord, and consented to continue in the work, and was appointed with James O. Cromwell and Wm. Lynch to the Kent Circuit, Eastern Shore of Maryland.

There he was also very successful, especially among the young, of whom he gathered great numbers into the church, and many of them from the first families on the Eastern Shore.

At this time the whole number of itinerant ministers in America was eighty-two, and the number of members, 14,983.

During this year Dr. Coke, having been ordained by Mr. Wesley to the office of Superintendent or Bishop of the societies in this country, arrived in New York with authority to ordain Mr. Asbury to the same office. These eminent men first met at Judge Barrett's, in the State of Delaware, and after some consultation agreed to call what has since been known in our history as the celebrated "Christmas Conference." where the societies were organized under the name of the "Methodist Episcopal Church." It had been fifteen years since Boardman and Pillmore had introduced Methodism into this country, and during all these years the ministers had been without ordination, and societies without the Sacraments, except as they received them at the hands of a ministry by whom they were held in utter contempt, and for whom as Christian ministers they could have no respect. These long-suffering preachers and their societies were greatly rejoiced at the prospect of an organization by which they could consolidate and build up a symmetrical and effective church. After the organization at this Conference, the first thing was the election and ordination of a sufficient number of elders to visit all the Quarterly Meetings and administer the ordinances, and thus originated in our church the office of Presiding Elder.

Mr. Ware had many opportunities of seeing and conversing with Dr. Coke, and though not favourably impressed with him at first, became greatly interested in him after further acquaintance. He thinks he was the best speaker in a private circle and on the Conference floor he ever heard.

From this Conference he was returned to the Peninsula. After a season of great prosperity he had a sudden and severe attack of illness, accompanied with great gloom and mental depression, and also by serious doubts of his call to the ministry; and after recovering his health made up his mind to leave the work. At what he intended for his last appointment in the circuit, he received such a Divine anointing, and the people were so moved under his word, that his doubts all left him, and he went on his way with great rejoicing and success. Before the next Conference, however, his despondency returned, and he wrote Bishop Asbury, declining to take an appointment, and returned to his home in Salem, N. J. This Conference, notwithstanding his request, appointed him to Salem Circuit with Wm. Phœbus and Robert Sparks, and the year was to him, upon the whole, a very pleasant and successful one.

In 1786 he was appointed to Long Island, in the State of New York, and with the aid of local preachers extended his labors accross the Sound, and preached at New Rochelle, Peekskill, Bedford, Croton, &c. At the last named place he was invited to the house of Lieutenant Governor Van Courtland, where he was charmed with their Christian courtesy and hospitality.

After preaching at Bedford, a Presbyterian minister arose in the congregation, and accused him of preaching false doctrine, but the people were all with him, and the Presbyterian got decidedly the worst of it. A Mr. Eames then arose in the audience, and invited him to go home with him and remain and preach at his house. He accepted the invitation; and when Mr. E. introduced him to his wife, he said, "You know I told you God would send the Methodist preachers among us, when I dreamed that I saw Mr. Wesley riding through the country with his Bible open in his hand." Here he preached repeatedly, and formed a class. On his return to Long Island, he was overtaken by a terrible snow-storm, and "driven to the necessity of putting up at an inn," where he was detained for a week. "Thirty years after this," says Mr. Ware, "I was again appointed to Long Island, where my host visited me. On meeting me he said, 'Father Ware, I am happy to see you once more. Have you forgotten the snow-storm which brought you and salvation to my house?' "

EAST TENNESSEE.

At the Conference of 1787 Mr. Ware volunteered with two other young men, who esteemed the reproach of Christ greater riches than earthly treasure, to accompany Mr. Tunnell to the Holston Country, now called East Tennessee. Here they found a population spread over a territory equal in extent to East Jersey, almost wholly destitute of the gospel. They found the community greatly demoralized. The leaders were many of them the worst of men: such as had been guilty of some heinous or scandalous crime, and had fled from justice. Some who had borrowed money or were otherwise indebted, and left their creditors and securities to suffer by their dishonesty. Among these were several apostate preachers of different sects, whose profligate lives had greatly prejudiced the community against ministers as a class, and which caused most of the persecutions which this little pioneer band of Methodist itinerants were called to endure. Societies, however, were formed, and a number of log chapels erected, and on the circuit three hundred members were received the first year.

In the fall of this year he extended his labors by direction of the Presiding Elder lower down on the Holston, to a section through which Indian savages were constantly prowling, with the object of destroying or capturing the white inhabitants. On one occasion, as his course led him through a "fine bottom covered chiefly with the crab apple-tree," and as he approached a lofty grove, his horse suddenly stopped, snorted, and wheeled about. As he turned he caught a glimpse of an Indian with a rifle; he gave his horse the reins, hasted to the nearest settlement and gave the alarm. On another occasion a woman was killed within a quarter of a mile of where he was preaching, by an Indian, who came stealthily to where she was spinning, and "drove the tomahawk into her head before she knew they were near, and her two children came screaming into the place of meeting, 'The Indians have killed mother.'"

During this winter he narrowly escaped death on several occasions, from long exposure to cold and rain in his journeyings through the trackless wilderness.

The first Conference in Holston was held in 1788. As the road by which Bishop Asbury was to come, was infested by hostile savages, so that it could not be traveled, except by considerable companies together, he did not arrive until a week after the time appointed to commence it. Meantime the preachers were earnestly engaged in holding public religious services, which resulted during the week in a large number of conversions. Among the first converts were General Russell and lady, the latter a sister of the illustrious Patrick Henry. His account of the conversion of this interesting couple is as follows: "When the meeting closed on Sabbath morning Mrs. Russell said to me, 'I thought I was a Christian: but, sir, I am not a Christian—I am the veriest sinner on earth. I want you and Mr. Marten to come with Mr. Tunnell to our house and pray for us, and tell us what we must do to be saved.' So we went, and spent much of the afternoon in prayer, especially for Mrs. Russell. Being much exhausted, the preachers retired to a pleasant grove near at hand to rest. After we had left the General, seeing the agony of soul under which his poor wife was laboring, by the advice of his pious daughter, read to her Mr. Fletcher's charming address to mourners. At length we heard the word 'Glory!' often repeated, accompanied with the clapping of hands. We hastened to the house, and found Mrs. Russell, praising the Lord, and the General walking the floor and weeping bitterly, uttering at the same time this plaintive appeal to the Saviour of sinners: 'O Lord, thou didst bless my dear wife, while thy poor servant was reading to her—hast thou not a blessing also for me?' At length he sat down quite exhausted. This scene was in a high degree interesting: to see the old soldier and statesman—the proud opposer of godliness—trembling and earnestly inquiring what he must do to be saved, was an affecting sight. He rested not until he knew his adoption: he joined the church, was faithful, serving the church in various offices until the end of his life.

From this Conference, he was appointed to East New River, with a colleague younger than himself, where, during the year, they received eighty persons into the church. There was not within the bounds of this circuit a religious meeting, except those held by these young itinerants. Here they were called to endure great hardships, from the effects of which he suffered until the close of his life. Through all this country, the people brought their children to him to have them baptized. He says, on this subject, "I cannot but regret that I did not keep a record of the number of these lambs of Christ's flock, which I have held in my arms and dedicated to him. For a time I attempted it: but in Holston and the other circuits so many were presented for baptism that I gave it up."

During his stay in New River Circuit, a young licentiate of the Baptist order came into a part of the charge, where were a few members of his church. He seemed to possess much of the spirit of love, says Mr. Ware, and was with me several days. He frequently exhorted and closed our meetings by prayer. He was present at a meeting where several children were brought forward to be baptized. On this occasion I stated some of our reasons for baptizing infants, and then called on my young friend to close as usual. He rose up, and to our surprise, whether by a previous understanding or not, I cannot say, a Baptist woman in the congregation presented him her child. He took it into his arms and pronounced a blessing upon it, and returned it; and then proceeded to say, "Jesus took little children into his arms, not to baptize, but to bless them. No, my friends, neither Jesus nor his disciples ever spent their time in baby-sprinkling." Here he paused, holding his hand to his eye, as if in great pain; and the people were at a loss to know what was the matter. He finally told them that a hornet had stung him in the eye; and the woman upon whose child he had pronounced a blessing stated that she knew a remedy for it, at which he immediately left and went with her, and I never saw him after."

In the Spring of 1789, he accompanied Bishop Asbury into North Carolina, and was appointed to Caswell Circuit from the

Conference held at McKnight's Church on the 11th of April. He set out for his field of labors poorly clad, and nearly penniless. He says, "My coat was nearly through at the elbows, and I had not a whole garment left, and as for boots, I had none." He had a very fine and valuable horse, his sole worldly property at that time. But he had borne him through so many dangers, and once at least, by his instinctive sagacity had saved his life, and he could not therefore consent to part with him. By a mysterious providence, in a few days this noble animal sickened and died. God however raised him up friends who supplied all his wants; and this year was among the most pleasant and successful of his life. He visited a settlement of Episcopalians; at their request he preached for them, and they brought scores of children to be dedicated to God in baptism. And such was the Divine influence that accompanied the services of that afternoon, that the people could not be induced to leave; and he continued to pray and exhort till midnight. In six weeks he gathered a society in that place of eighty members, mostly heads of families. "This event," he says, "I have always deemed a Divine sanction of infant baptism; for this work, evidently, commenced with the baptism of infant children."

In 1790 he was appointed Presiding Elder in this district. At one of the Quarterly Meetings in New River, a religious concern was awakened, which pervaded a large district of country, and suspended for many weeks almost all worldly concerns. In the family of General Bryan, who was a barrister at law, thirty persons professed conversion; twelve of whom, including the general himself, were whites. In this family Mr. Ware spent many happy days. In this district he was permitted to see some of the most wonderful displays of Divine power.

A short time before he left North Carolina, he was confined by indisposition for several days, at the house of a very aged couple, who had been brought from a merely formal religion to the enjoyment of its life and power through his instrumentality. While there they wanted him to write their will. He objected on the ground of not understanding the form which might be requisite. They said it was very simple, and might easily be drawn; it was that on condition of his remaining with them through their short stay in this world, (as they had no children,) all the property they had should be his. They were the owners of a large farm, and mill, and other property. "This," he writes, "was a strong inducement to exchange a life of poverty and toil for one of affluence and ease. Had I accepted the offer, my history would doubtless have been very different from what it is, but I could not do it with a good conscience; so I bid them and North Carolina adieu for ever, and returned to see my friends in New Jersey."

He arrived in time to attend the Philadelphia Conference for 1791, and was appointed to Wilmington, Delaware. This was his first station; but it was not congenial; and he sighed, as he tells us, for the back woods, which were a paradise to him compared with this suffocating borough. Religion was low, and rowdyism so rife, that they could not hold meetings at night without insult and abuse from street ruffians.

In 1792 he labored for a short time on Staten Island with success, but was soon taken up and appointed to the charge of the Susquehanna District. From this time he continued to fill this very laborious office, till 1808, a period of sixteen years, in succession. During his years on the Susquehanna and Albany Districts, he had many long, dreary and dangerous rides. He met with much opposition and many bitter revilings from the godless ministers of a hardly formal religion. They were, however, years also of great success.

He was appointed, in 1796, to the Philadelphia District, and resided at Strasburg. There he formed the acquaintance of Miss Barbary Miller. "A person," he says, "whom I selected above all others as a suitable companion for me; and on the fifteenth of October, 1797, we were joined in holy matrimony, she being thirty-five years of age and I thirty-eight." This year was remarkable in his district for some very powerful and extensive revivals.

In 1800 he was changed to a District on the Peninsula. His first year on this district was one of the happiest of his whole life. "My health," he writes, "was good, as was also that of my wife and child. The vine we were exerting our utmost skill to dress, grew until it shaded all the land, and regaled us with odoriferous flowers, and delicious fruit. Every thing went on pleasantly . . . . The candle of the Lord shone brilliantly about my path: and my cup was sometimes full to overflowing."

Camp meetings had not yet been introduced, and they knew not what to do with the thousands of people who attended their quarterly meetings. They were sometimes forced to resort to the woods, and even to hold their Love-feasts in the grove. "Some of these revivals," he says, "exceeded anything he had ever witnessed." The revival which commenced in the Strasburg circuit extended through the peninsula, and embraced all classes, governor, judges, lawyers and statesmen, old and young, rich and poor.

At the Smyrna Conference, the work of revival went on with great power, so that at the close of the Conference five hundred persons were received on trial, in the church.

His cup of felicity, however, was not unmixed; for about this time he was called to bury his infant son. He suffered also by some opposition growing out of political excitement, while in this district. His position in his Conference on the question of an address to President Adams, approving his administration and promising him support, when it came to be known in the district, rendered him exceedingly popular with the one party, but lost him entirely the influence of the other. These latter, though they treated him with great kindness, had the address to effect his removal from the district.

In 1801, he again returned to the Philadelphia District. The next year he took charge of the New Jersey District, and continued there four years. After this he was stationed two years in the St. George's charge, Philadelphia. Toward the close of his term in this charge, he was attacked with a violent fever, and he says, "my physician deemed it proper for me to be bled. Until this time I had not been sensible of any material decline in strength, agility or sight: but now I could distinctly perceive failures in each of these." At the following Conference, his debility was such as to render it necessary for him to take a supernumerary relation.

At the Conference of 1810, on account of continued ill health, he became superannuated. During this year, however, his health improved so as to enable him to take an appointment; and he was sent to Lancaster, Pa.

At the General Conference, which met in New York, in 1812, he was appointed one of the book agents. He continued to serve the church in this office four years.

At the expiration of his term in the book room he was appointed to Long Island, for the second time, where he found some of the fruits of his former labors still faithful. Mr. W. continued in the effective work till 1825, and thus rendered full service as an itinerant for the long period of forty years. He was the last of the effective men that composed the Christmas Conference in 1784. All had been shrouded in the grave, or retired from the active work, before his name was transferred to the superannuated list.

Mr. W. had been in every General Conference from the organization of the church in 1784, to that which met in Philadelphia in 1832, where he was the sole survivor and representative of that noble band of faithful men who originally constituted the Methodist Episcopal Church. A body of men, who, for earnest self-devotion, real Christian heroism and wonderful ministerial efficiency have never been surpassed in the history of the church.

After he became supernumerary, Mr. Ware removed to Salem, N. J. where the closing years of his life were spent; and where he enjoyed in a high degree the respect and confidence of the entire community. He engaged occasionally, in active service as long as his strength would permit, and when his ability to labor ceased he still continued to bear an effective testimony for his Master, by a spirit of serene submission and joyful confidence in God. He died at his residence, in Salem, N. J., on the 11th of March, 1842.

Rev. Dr. Bangs, who knew him well, during his connection as book agent with our publishing house in New York, says of him: "Mr. Ware had a fine commanding person, and an expression of countenance at once pleasant and dignified. There was nothing in his manners that savored of moroseness on the one hand, or of levity on the other. He was a man of excellent common sense, and his judgment in difficult cases could generally be relied on with confidence and safety. He lived through an eventful period in the history of Methodism, and indeed in the history of the country and of the world; and his influence for good has gone out through innumerable channels."

REV. DANIEL FIDLER

WAS a native of Hunterdon Co., N. J., and was born August 26, 1771. Of his parents, Timothy Fidler and Ann Wilson, but little is now known. They were in moderate circumstances, industrious and respectable, and were humble followers of Christ, and worthy members of the Methodist Society. When Daniel was quite young, they settled upon a farm near Hancock, Pa., where the father spent the balance of his days. All their sons, except Daniel, emigrated to Ohio, in which state, together with that of Indiana, many of their descendants are now living. The widow survived her husband several years, and closed her life in the West. But neither the extent to which either pilgrimage reached, nor the date, nor manner of its close, can now be given. Daniel assumed a profession of religion in his sixteenth year. Of the circumstances of his awakening and conversion he has left no account. But his subsequent stability, and rapid growth in piety and zeal, prove the work to have been genuine. The Conference Obituary says, "According to his own account, from that time till the day of his death, he never lost the evidence of his acceptance with God."

At this period there were no conference boundaries, the bishops convening the preachers, at times and places, to suit the demands of the work. Then the minutes for the year were arranged as if there had been but one Conference, and thus headed, "Minutes taken at the several Annual Conferences * * * for the year 1789." No date, place of meeting, or names of those admitted at each separate session, are recorded. Hence the exact date, and place of his admission, are unknown. If earlier than August 26th, he was under eighteen years old. His name is strangely omitted from the list of appointments for this year.

In 1790 he was continued on trial and sent to "Ohio." In

1787, and the next two years, two preachers had been sent to Ohio. Now the name of the stripling stands alone. How gladly would we of this day, trace the footsteps of our venerated fathers in the ministry, in their heroic journeyings through the desert wilds of what were then frontier settlements. But this, unfortunately, they have not left us the means of doing. One of his sons says, "Ohio at this time was very sparsely settled, and I have heard it stated, that in his long journeys from one appointment to another, through paths seldom traveled, and often guided only by marks on the trees, he was frequently exposed to danger from the unfriendly Indians." Still, how little do we know of these dangers, of the harrowing fears they awakened, or of those occasioned by the less unfriendly and scarcely more savage beasts of prey, prowling through the same inhospitable regions, or, of the fatigues and exposures of those long journeys, their cold receptions or cruel repulses by the unfriendly; the coarse food, uncomfortable houses, scanty beds, in a word, the toils, privations and hardships of this missionary life! "But the back was fitted for the burden." And then this dark background was not unrelieved by bright contrasts. The constraining love of Christ, the comforting presence of the Holy Spirit, giving support under trials, and the Divine sanction by which labor was crowned with success, these, together with the warm congratulations of friends, the holy revivings of Christian fellowship, and the joyous anticipations of rest in heaven, were among the offsets to their hard lot. And richly, blessedly did they perform their kindly offices.

In 1791 he was received in full connection, ordained Deacon, and placed in charge of Redstone Circuit, with James Coleman for a colleague.

In 1792 the minutes read, "Rockingham, Daniel Fidler, Elijah Sparks." The exact scene of his labors up to this time cannot be determined. Dr. Stevens, after referring to the absence of his name from the list in 1789, says, "During the next four years he traveled circuits, which extended through the western sections of Virginia and Pennsylvania into Ohio, a region which then lay on the western frontier of the nation." This, though indefinite, is probably correct, as to the scene of his labors, but not as to the extent of time. He spent about three and a half years, including the first, in the region named, and was then sent by Dr. Coke, to Nova Scotia, to aid in carrying out his self-sacrificing and zeal-taxing missionary enterprizes. Stevens' "Memorials, and the Conference Obituary, which he probably followed, fix the time of his going East, in 1794. But Dr. Coke says, he was in that service six years, which he left in the fall of 1798. And he himself says, "May 30, 1794. After spending near eighteen months in Liverpool, I embarked for Halifax, &c." This fixes his arrival in the Province at about December, 1792.

In 1793 the minutes contain his name as a Deacon, but not in the list of appointments. Nor is Nova Scotia mentioned. But in 1794 this entry occurs. "Nova Scotia, Wm. Jessop, Isaac Lunsford, *Daniel Fidler*, Benj. Wilson, James Boyd, James Mann, John Mann, Richard Sockett." After this, Nova Scotia is again omitted.

His first circuit in the Province lay on the South-eastern coast. At the end of one year he began to keep a private diary, or, as seems likely, from its abrupt beginning, the parts dating earlier have not been preserved. It contains various interesting incidents of travel, observation and experience. Want of space will compel us to be sparing of extracts. We insert the first entry on account of its singularity. "January 1, 1794. Yesterday I was at the burial of Mrs. Cheevers, who by all appearance has been possessed of the devil for eighteen months. She used the most profane language and horid imprecations I ever heard from any mortal being." Here is another, showing the prevailing religious destitution. "It is very lamentable that there are about one hundred persons now out of this place (Liverpool) gone to the West Indies, and not more than three or four professors of religion among them. It appears Jacob is very small, by whom shall he rise?" Still God was with the few. He says, "Last Thursday evening at class, we had a signal display of sovereign grace." He also gives account of numerous other gracious seasons, and of personal religious comfort and growth. Accessions to the society were gradual, with increase toward the close of his term. Of a visit to an out appointment, he says, "Sailed in a shallop to

Port Moulton, preached three times, and baptized an adult and eight children. Bless God, I had a comfortable time, liberty in speaking, power in prayer, and satisfaction in conversation. The Lord has begun a good work here in the hearts of several persons."

After eighteen months they met in Conference at Horton, in the central part of the Province. His next field was Annapolis, on its Western shore. He found the society in a good condition. Referring to his second sermon, he says, "I have hardly seen such a time of power, since, in Nova Scotia. I added two to the class." Again he says, "July 16th, I preached at a Mr. Shaw's, ten miles below Annapolis. The Lord was present. Several were much affected. Glory to God, I trust my labors are not in vain on the circuit. I see a good prospect, and feel my soul more and more given up to God and his work."

An episode now occurs. After spending ten weeks on this circuit he crossed the Bay to St. John's, New Brunswick, and, September 1, 1794, sailed for New York. The vessel halting off Martha's Vineyard, he went on shore, and preached to a numerous audience, principally from theirs and other vessels. He had much liberty, and received the warm congratulations of several hearers. The passage was so tedious that they were twenty days in reaching New York, but all arrived safely and well. He was barely in time to meet the Conference, and enjoy, for a few days, the society of his brethren. He was elected to Elder's Orders, and was ordained, September 26, by Bishop Asbury.

He made a hurried visit to an uncle's in Princeton, N. J., where he preached; thence to Trenton, Philadelphia, and Baltimore, all by stage. Here he spent a precious Sunday. He assisted Rev. J. McClasky at the communion in the morning, and preached afternoon and evening. He arrived at his father's, Oct. 11th, after an absence of about two years. He remained till the 22d, and preached with much comfort to his old acquaintances. He then took affectionate leave of relatives and friends, and set out to retrace his tedious journey. He spent another Sunday in Baltimore. Bishop Asbury preached, and ordained five elders and seven deacons. He tarried three days in Philadelphia, and on his arrival in New York had an affecting interview with a convict, who expected to be executed in a few days. He believed he was converted, and went to attend his last moments. But a respite for three months came to hand just previous to the fatal hour. November 16th he preached in Brooklyn, and for the first time administered the communion. He sailed, December 5th, for St. John's, and arrived on the 11th, thankful for a brief, pleasant passage.

While absent, he had been assigned to St. Ann's Circuit. This threw him in the Province of New Brunswick. After a pleasant Sunday in St. John's, he says, "Monday I set off for Sheffield, and arrived there on Saturday. I suffered more in traveling than ever in my life before. But, bless the Lord, I found his presence, and am still resolved to press on to declare the council of God, though my trials are heavy. January 1st, 1795, set off for St. Ann's. The next day I arrived there, and waited upon his Excellency, the Governor. He gave me his approbation to preach. Blessed be God, now I have full liberty." After nearly five months, for some unexplained reason, he was sent to another field. He says, "I left the circuit with great reluctance. I find my heart much united to this people."

The Conference met at Windsor, N. S., but he could not get across the Bay in time. While waiting in St. John's, he preached, and a notorious sinner was awakened, whom he baptized, together with his wife and six children. He finally got across the Bay only to learn that his field was St. John's, and then had to wait two weeks before he could get back. He soon learned of some disorder in the society, which greatly oppressed him. But he cast his burden on the Lord, and was sustained. Aug. 26, 1795, he writes, "My birthday—twenty-four years old. I see the goodness of God in preserving me. I bless his holy name, more than eight years I trust I have enjoyed the love of God, and about six have been in the line of a traveling preacher. And I can say, I am not weary of his service." Much of his time was spent on the outposts of the circuit, and the latter part of the year on that of Frederickton. This year closed his labors in New Brunswick. They had been attended with considerable success, with many profitable seasons and much personal religious enjoyment. But he also passed through seasons of severe trial and discouragement.

The Conference met in Windsor again in May, 1796. Only six preachers were present. He says, "We conversed freely, and transacted our business in much love. Religion is prospering in Windsor. More than twenty have been added to the society, and many of them truly converted to God." From this and other remarks, it appears that nearly all who then joined on probation, did so as seekers. He was now sent to Shelburne, far down on the south-eastern coast, and a long journey from Frederickton. But he was a lone wanderer, with but few effects to impede his travel. He gives several interesting incidents of the journey. Two young evangelists by the name of Newton had been instrumental in promoting a great revival in Liverpool and vicinity. He preached to his old friends with unwonted power. The occasion was affecting and profitable in a high degree. The flame had also spread to Port Moulton, and began to extend over his new circuit. Many were converted at "Sable River." Up to Dec. 1 he baptized one hundred adults and children. And though he made many long journeys on foot, and passed through severe trials and hardships, yet these rounds on his extensive circuit were like the triumphal marches of a conqueror. He preached with great freedom, and the word was often "in demonstration of the Spirit and of power." He exulted much in the triumphs of the cross and in the rich indwelling of the love of Christ.

He remained on this circuit till June 1, 1798, and then went to Halifax to take the place of Rev. Wm. Black, the Superintendent, while he made a tour of supervision. Preserved letters show that a confidential and cordial intimacy existed between these co-laborers. In reference to Halifax, he says, "I found great liberty and satisfaction in preaching here. The congregations are very large." The Conference met in the old place, June 13. He was returned to Halifax. The trip to and from Conference was a tour of successful evangelical labor. Referring to his term in Halifax, he says, "Spent my time agreeably and profitably till October 11th. Then left my dear Halifax friends, and sailed for Shelburne; called at Liverpool, and spent a few hours very agreeably with my dear old friends: arrived safely at Shelburne on the 13th. . . . I still find various trials and powerful conflicts, but the Lord is my helper; in Him I find comfort.

He is my portion; may I glorify Him in my body and spirit, which are his." He was detained in Shelburne one month with that loathsome disease, the small-pox, but did not have it badly. Thus singularly closed his eventful and successful career in this distant, and then dreary, region. He sailed for New York Nov. 13, 1798, and landed on the 21st.

His diary, which covers not quite five years, shows that he traversed most of the Province of Nova Scotia and a large portion of New Brunswick, preached to crowded houses in the two capitals and other large towns, and was favored with considerable success in these centres of population. But his labors were not confined to them. He took long journeys into sparsely-settled districts, preached wherever openings offered, went from house to house, visiting the sick, burying the dead, warning sinners, instructing penitents, and freely mingling with and encouraging the humble poor in a most unostentatious and laborious manner.

His after fields were: 1799, Wilmington; 1800, Sandwich; 1801, Greenwich and Rhode Island; 1802, Harford; 1803, Caroline; 1804, Prince George's; 1805, Allegheny; 1806, Baltimore Circuit; 1807, Fell's Point; 1808, located. In 1811, New Mills; 1812, Bergen; 1813 and 1814, Cumberland: 1815, Gloucester; 1816, Dover; 1817, located. In 1818, New Mills; 1819, Freehold; 1820, Cumberland; 1821, Cecil; 1822 and 1823, Bristol; 1824, superannuated. In 1825, Juliastown and Wrightstown, as supernumerary; 1826, New Mills; 1827, Caroline: 1828, Dover; 1829, Chester; 1830, Waynesburg; 1831, supernumerary. He retained this relation till 1842, when it was changed to superannuated.

The above transcript from the minutes is an interesting record. Together with what precedes it covers fifty-three years, during four of which he was located, superannuated, one; and supernumerary, twelve, leaving thirty-six to the effective ministry. And then how wide the range and how checkered the pathways of his itinerant meanderings! After nearly three years and a half on four extended fields in the far West, he passed to the distant Provinces of Nova Scotia and New Brunswick, large portions of whose territory he traversed during six years on as many circuits. Then one year in Wilmington, Del., one in

Massachusetts, one partly in that State and partly in Rhode Island. Then one in Harford, Md., one in Carlisle, Pa., next Prince George's in the southern part of Md., then Allegheny, in its western extremity, and then Baltimore and Fell's Point. His name next stands at New Mills, now Pemberton, N. J., then Bergen, near New York, and then back to South Jersey, at Cumberland and Gloucester. Thence across to Dover, Del., and then back to New Mills. Then in turn at Freehold and Cumberland. Thence Cecil, Md., next Bristol, Pa., and then a third time at New Mills. Next to Caroline, Md., then Dover, somewhere in West Jersey, and finally Chester, and then Waynesburg, Pa. As supernumerary his name stands in connection with Juliustown, Pemberton, Medford and New Egypt. By noticing how frequent and long these removals were, we see how thoroughly the itinerancy of our fathers stands in contrast with that of the present day.

He is twice marked located. That in 1808, is readily accounted for. He was married, June 6, 1806, to Sarah, daughter of Abraham Larsh, of Baltimore. At this period, the lack of support drove nearly all married men out of the itinerancy. For two years his fields of labor were convenient to the home of his wife. Then he entered the mercantile business in Baltimore. But his wife died Feb. 14, 1811, leaving one child, who is now (1864) a local preacher in Cape May County, N. J. This sad bereavement furnished both an opening and a call to resume his life-work, which he at once did. The other location was the result of a difficulty in the administration of discipline. He retired as a peace measure, but at the close of one year resumed his work, the matter having been amicably settled.

January 12, 1812, he was married to Margaret, daughter of Levi Budd, of New Mills, and sister of Rev. T. L. Budd, late of the Philadelphia Conference. Six sons were the issue of this marriage. Isaac Hilliard, Esq., of Pemberton, a brother-in-law, says of Mrs. Fidler, "I had full opportunity of witnessing her manner of life. I never in all our intercourse, heard her utter an improper word or saw her do an improper act. She was truly an 'Israelite indeed.' She was a remarkable woman. 'Take her for all and all, I never expect to look upon her like again.'" He also says, "I must reiterate in substance what I have above written, that in my earthly pilgrimage, now somewhat lengthened out, I have never met her equal."

She was a woman of superior natural parts, more than usual literary tastes, considerable culture, and of such industry, frugality and good management, as to make a slender income minister to the comfort of her family. After 1817 she did not move with her husband, and the care and training of the children devolved mainly upon her, which she managed with skill and success. She survived her husband over fifteen years, the last three of which were spent in Lambertville with her son Thomas. Her last illness was protracted and severe, but did not find her unprepared.

"Life's fitful fever over, she sleeps well."

She joined her companion in Paradise, October 27, 1857, being in her seventy-first year. The hard necessities of our itinerent fathers are shown by an incident connected with her funeral. The friends were invited to the house of Mr. Hilliard. This was the only time all the children were ever together at once. The eldest had left home before the youngest was born, and they were never all at home at one time; nor will they all meet again on earth, for one has since crossed the cold river. May the parents, who never yet saw all their children together, greet them all in their heavenly home!

Our materials and space are both limited, so that we cannot farther trace the toils and successes of our subject. His early literary advantages were evidently quite limited; and if he failed to push his after researches to the extent of some of his compeers, still he possessed qualifications which rendered him an able and successful herald of the gospel. Sterling sense presided over all his movements. He reared the standard of the cross, and kept its banner to the breeze with a steady arm and an unfaltering step. But he sought to conceal himself behind that waving banner. Indeed, no man whose name adorns our history, presents a more striking instance of self-abnegation. His diary shows that he passed through many hardships. *Yet he does not utter a single complaint, nor once refer to his fare or compensation.* But it is full of allusions to kind friends and to the supports and comforts of religion. The figures that represent his salary would afford an interesting item, but owing to his great modesty and unselfishness, he did not preserve them. Stevens' "Memorials" give them for one of the years he was in New England. "Timothy Merritt had received during the year $63.50; Epaphras Kibby, $35.50; Joshua Soule, $45.36; *Daniel Fidler*, $32.25, the smallest amount recorded. He had suffered well, as a volunteer, the privations of the New England itinerancy for two years, and was allowed now to retreat southward, to his original and more favorable fields of labor in the middle states." His pay is understood to have been unusually small even for those times. One of his sons says, "I do not know what father received from the church while he was in active service. He was never known to complain. His own and his wife's patrimony, with their economy and frugality, made up for all deficiencies." His cheerful, hopeful, happy piety, stands in most striking and instructive contrast with his meagre support, his toils and hardships.

He was held in high esteem by Dr. Coke. In the year 1800 the Doctor selected him for a missionary to the "Providence Islands," but for some unknown reason he did not go. Drafts on the missionary funds, and letters of introduction to different parties, were prepared. To the Governor General of the Bahama Islands the Doctor says, "The bearer, Rev. Mr. Fidler, is a minister of the gospel and my friend. He labored in the ministry for six years, under my direction in Nova Scotia. I have a very high opinion of his honor, integrity and loyalty. His primary design is to be beneficial to the blacks and colored people, but he is a man of ability sufficient to be beneficial to any." To a brother minister the Doctor writes, "He has traveled eleven years, and is therefore your senior, and consequently will rank as the chief superintendent of the work." Of his term in Nova Scotia, the Doctor says, "I have reason to believe he gave very complete satisfaction to the government, to our societies, and to all who knew him." A long letter addressed to him, shows that the Doctor felt it no disparagement to hold with him relations of cordial intimacy.

His social qualities were of a high order. Mr. Hilliard says, "He was courteous and conciliatory in his manners, very agreeable in social intercourse, and punctual to all the duties pertaining to his ministerial office. As a husband he was always kind, attentive and affectionate. Similar terms will also apply to his care and treatment of his children." And when he asked his wife what he should say of her brother-in-law, she replied, "Say he was a good man, punctual to all his appointments, kind and courteous to all." Rev. T. M'Carrol is said to have enlarged, at his funeral, upon his amiability of disposition, his uncomplaining manner in receiving and prosecuting his various fields of labor, and his faithfulness in striving to cultivate them all with credit and success.

We have not the means of giving a distinct estimate of his talents as a minister. His preserved written preparations are mere skeletons. A majority of the texts are taken from the Old Testament, but the themes are full of the marrow of the gospel. They are treated in a plain, unpretentious way, but with a directness and earnestness of appeal that aimed at both immediate and lasting fruits. He is not understood to have ranked high as a pulpit orator, but his strong sense, his familiarity with the Bible, and his ready gifts in expounding and enforcing its teachings, aided by a deep Christian experience, an impressive manner, and an earnest desire for success, rendered him an efficient minister of the gospel.

His diary, pulpit themes, and the genial, mellow temper with which he came out of the severe trials of his long and eventful career, combine to show that he had attained large measures of saving grace. It is not possible to human nature, for one to pass through what he did, and not thereby be rendered morose, imperious and inflexible, without a deep imbuement of the spirit of holiness. Nor is this a mere inference in his case, as his written sketches and recorded struggles and conquests clearly show. Dr. Coke, also, says to him, "I am glad to find by brother Asbury, that you universally press upon your believing hearers, the necessity of sanctification and entire devotedness to God; and that you guard them from seeking this, as it were, by deeds of the law, and that you urge them to believe now on a present Saviour, for a present salvation." This none do, who are not themselves familiar with this great salvation. "Mark the perfect man and behold the upright, for the end of that man is peace."

The Conference Obituary says, "In the year 1831, he was induced from the infirmities of age, and other considerations, to take a supernumerary relation. He continued, however, as his health would permit, to preach and labor with increasing zeal and acceptance, till within a few months of his death. After having served the church, as a faithful and accredited minister, for more than half a century, he preached his last sermon, Sabbath evening, June 30, 1842, from Ex. xxxii. 18: "And he said, I beseech thee show me thy glory." While the venerable man of God, was elucidating this impressive text, and especially, while he contemplated the manifested and unvailed glory of God, which the faithful finally shall enjoy,

> "When the voyage of life's at an end,
> The mortal affliction is past,"

his soul seemed to kindle into rapture, as he realized the time of his departure at hand. About this time his health began more rapidly to decline, and his mind, sympathizing considerably with his failing tenement of clay, was bewildered, which made it difficult for him sometimes, to fix his thoughts for any length of time on temporal subjects; but on the subject of religion, he was clear, calm, and dispassionate, up to the latest hour of life.

The last time he met with the people of God on earth, for public worship, was about four weeks previous to his death, on a quarterly occasion. It was peculiarly affecting to see him as he knelt with solemn reverence at the table of the Lord, and received in his trembling hand the affecting emblems of the broken body and shed blood of his Divine Redeemer. Indeed he appeared to engage in all the religious exercises of that blessed Sabbath morning, with more than ordinary interest and spiritual fervor. Many of the members of the church in Pemberton will long remember the deep-toned feelings with which he spoke in the Love-feast, of mercies past and present, and of his brightening prospects of a certain and glorious immortality. From this time he gradually failed, until the morning of the 27th of August, when he fell asleep in Jesus.

REV. JAMES MOORE.

"He was a good man, and full of the Holy Ghost, and of faith: and much people were added unto the Lord."

THERE are many beautifully-winding streams around us, rolling their broad, deep, silvery tides to the ocean, of whose sources in the distant mountains we know but little. The same is true of some men. They come upon the stage of action, perform their life-parts well, and then sink down into death, and are buried amongst us, of whose early history we have little knowledge.

These remarks apply to James Moore, the subject of this sketch. After his death the following little memorandum was found amongst his papers, which contains nearly all the reliable information we have of his early life.

"I was born in Ireland, in the county of Tyrone, 1760; joined the Methodist Society in 1786: came to America 1792; joined the Philadelphia Conference in 1794; now in the fortieth year of my age; still bound for heaven; happy in my soul this morning. All glory to God. JAMES MOORE."

SALEM CIRCUIT, *June* 3, 1809.

Before coming to this country, however, he received license to preach, and subsequently married, and two or three children were born to him; but, while on his way to America, his wife died, and was buried in the sea; so that when he arrived here, he was a widower, with these little helpless children, a stranger in a strange land. But his trust was in God, who did not forsake him.

Our narrative commences more particularly with 1794, the year he joined the Philadelphia Conference. In those days the Methodist itinerancy was more than a name; it was a great system for evangelizing the world, involving labor, sacrifice, and suffering. Yet these old Gospel heroes endured all with such uniform cheerfulness, that the contemplation of it is refreshing and inspiring to the soul.

James Moore's first appointment was to the rough regions of Tioga county, Pa. There were then but one hundred and thirteen members of the Methodist Church, within the bounds of his widely-extended circuit, and we may well suppose his fare was rough, and his remuneration, apart from an assurance of the Divine approval, almost nothing. Persons sometimes objected to admit him to their houses; he had to go without regular meals, swim rivers, face the mountain tempests, and, on one occasion, refused lodgings in the house, he slept all night beside a hay-stack.

From this rough country, he was sent in 1795, to the more congenial scenes of Cecil Circuit, Md., and in 1796 to Frederick Circuit. While these were years of much sacrifice and suffering, they were also years of great spiritual power, so much so, that the Conference ordered the last Thursday of October, 1796, to be observed as a day of general thanksgiving, "for such signal displays of Divine power in the Methodist Society within the space of twenty-six years, through the continent of America; for the late powerful and glorious work we have had in Virginia and Maryland, and which still continues in an eminent and special manner in some parts of our American connection," &c., &c.

In 1797, he was stationed with Wilson Lee, in the city of Philadelphia. The district with which Philadelphia was then connected, stands on the minutes of that early day, as follows. Thos. Ware, Presiding Elder; Wilmington, Ezekiel Cooper; Chester, Wm. Colbert; Strasburg, Wm. P. Chandler; Bristol, Chas. Cavender, Rich. Lyon; Northumberland, John Lacky, D. Higly; Wyoming, R. Benton; Tioga, James Stokes; Seneca, Anning Owen, J. Dunham; Philadelphia, Wilson Lee, Jas. Moore.

It was a vast district, covering territory now occupied by parts of several of our leading and most influential conferences.

But large as was the field, the entire membership on all that ground, including the city of Philadelphia, which now contains about forty Methodist Churches, was less than two thousand, of which number, between two and three hundred were colored. But the men who fought the Lord's battles in those days, were mighty through God, to the pulling down of the strong-holds of sin. Anning Owen was on this district. Seeing his name, reminds the writer of a conversation, serving to illustrate the character of the men who preached the gospel in our church at that early day.

I was riding in 1858, through the far-famed, and romantic Wyoming Valley, in company with Rev. A. H. Schoonmaker, of the Wyoming Conference. Approaching Kingston, Brother Schoonmaker pointed out an old frame building, by the road-side. "There," said he, "is the dwelling of the first Methodist, who also became the first Methodist Minister in Wyoming Valley, Anning Owen." It was truly an humble dwelling, but I looked at it with a kind of reverence, when I learned it had been the home of one of God's nobility. "Yonder," continued Brother Schoonmaker, pointing towards the west, "is Ross hill, on the farther side of which, Brother Owen formed the first class that existed in this part of the country, from which sprang the Oneida, Genesee, Black River, Michigan, and part of the Ohio Conferences." Brother Owen was a man for his times. Walking with an infidel one day, they came to where the road divided. As they separated, Brother Owen said to his companion, solemnly, "Eternity is long, and hell is hot; good-bye." The next time they met, the infidel was a Christian.

In 1798, Brother Moore was appointed to Bristol Circuit, Pa., and in 1799, with Benjamin Bidlack, to the classic Wyoming and Northumberland vallies, through which the peaceful Susquehanna pours her silvery waters to the sea. Benjamin Bidlack is an historic character; Wyoming was not only the home of his childhood, but here he resided a number of years in after life, and finally died, and was buried in the midst of its unequaled beauties. In order to give a clear view of the men of those times, the reader will be pleased with a few facts, concerning Benjamin Bidlack, the colleague of James Moore, in 1799. Dr. Peck, in his work on Wyoming, says:—

"Benjamin Bidlack served his country under General Washington, through the entire period of the Revolutionary war. He was at Boston, when Washington took charge of the army to oppose General Gage. He was at Trenton on the taking of the Hessians. He was at Yorktown, on the occasion of the surrender of Cornwallis; and was in Washington's camp at Newburg, when the army was disbanded. He was a tall, large-boned, powerful man, and a good soldier."

"Some time before the close of the last Pennamite and Yankee war, young Bidlack undertook some sort of a commercial expedition down the Susquehanna river. At Sunbury he was made a prisoner by the Pennsylvanians, and confined in a place which they called a jail. He was a splendid singer, and a merry fellow. Like many of the old soldiers, he was addicted to strong drink, and on evenings, when jolly circles love to assemble to while away an hour, to shake off the burdens of business, or to stimulate their exhausted nerves, by the exhilarating draught, a company were accustomed to gather upon the stoop, and hear Bidlack sing songs, of course offering him a sufficiency of the desired stimulant. The number of those gatherings increased from evening to evening, and the songs, the romantic stories, and the jokes of the soldier, became increasingly interesting, until he had become an object of more absorbing interest in the little town of Sunbury, than a company of minstrels is now in one of our large cities."

"The company were finally not quite satisfied with seeing the face of their interesting prisoner through the grates of the prison, but wished to view him at full length, as he poured out his harmonious and powerful numbers. The door was accordingly opened, and he stood upon the threshold; but here he was too much cramped, and his gestures were evidently impeded by his position. 'What's the use,' said one, 'let him have room.' And he was then allowed to come out and give himself free scope in gesticulation. He was a tall, straight, majestic figure. The more room he had, the more fully did his sallies, cuts, and thrusts, illustrate and enforce the sentiment, either sense or nonsense, of the poetry, and the higher was the excitement, and the louder the bursts of laughter amongst the merry companions of the gathering."

"Evening after evening passed away in these exercises without the least abatement of interest, when, at a late hour, the gallant hero of the farce would throw himself upon his pallet of straw, and sleep away the excitement of the maddening bowl."

"Understanding perfectly his position, and noticing that the sympathies of his nightly visitors, and the confidence he had inspired in their minds, had completely put them off their guard, he began to meditate turning the advantages of these circumstances to his account. He studied the matter thoroughly, and arranged his plans."

"He finally came out with a new song, entitled, 'The old swaggering man.' 'That's the song for me,' said one. 'The best one yet,' said another. 'Let's have that over again,' roared a third. 'Well,' said the performer, 'let me rest a little, and take a good drink.' 'Yes, yes,' all responded. After a few minutes intermission, and the drink of course, 'Now,' says the actor, 'if you want a rouser, I must have a cane, and room to act it out. I want the whole length of the stoop.' 'Bring on the cane! clear the way, clear the way!' bawled a dozen. He sang one stanza, and then came on the chorus, 'Here goes the old swaggering man.' He brandished his cane, and staggered and plunged from end to end of the stoop. A roar of merriment, and shouts of applause resounded through the whole neighborhood. He now faced about, breathed hard, took another drink, but this time his movement was in the direction of Wyoming. He sang another verse, and then roared out the chorus, 'Here goes the old swaggering man,' and in a trice sprang from the stoop, leaped the six foot rail-fence, which surrounded the premises, and was out of sight."

"Some were petrified with astonishment, others cursed, while others laughed immoderately. 'After him! after him,' cried the jailer. Half a dozen ran a few rods in the dark, and then pausing to listen, heard his heavy tread dying away in the distance. 'There's no use,' said they, 'he can out-run a deer.'' They returned to have a hearty laugh over the romantic adventure of the jolly Yankee prisoner."

"The next day our hero arrived safely at his father's house in Plymouth, a distance of fifty miles, performed on foot, *having sung himself out of prison.*"

"Young Bidlack married an Alden, a descendant of a family of that name, who came to this country in the *May Flower.* He struggled hard with poverty, and still harder with his old army habits, but made no progress, and there seemed no human probability of his improving either his character or his fortune. At length he became awakened through the instrumentality of the pioneers of Methodism, and finally became a Methodist preacher. He had great pulpit power, and was as great a singer of the songs of Zion as he had been of the old patriotic ballads."

Such was the mettle of some of the men with whom James Moore was associated. And such men, changed by the gospel, and nerved for their work by the Divine Spirit, were overwhelmingly powerful in their efforts for good. Brother Moore's subsequent appointments were numerous and widely separated. Leaving Wyoming, we find him in 1800 up in New York on Oneida and Cayuga Circuit. In 1801–2 he is down in Maryland on Talbot Circuit. His years on this charge were perhaps the most extensively successful of any of his protracted ministry. *Eighteen hundred souls were converted* during his term of service there, so that at the close of his labors he reported a nett increase of *sixteen hundred and eighty-three members.* In 1803 he was appointed to Queen Ann's, and there was an addition of *five hundred and twenty-two souls.* 1804 was spent on Lewistown, and 1805 on Chester Circuit. In 1806 he crossed into New Jersey, and labored on Freehold Circuit. and then in 1807–8 on Elizabethtown.

In that day all the circuits were large. Elizabethtown extended from the Raritan on the south to Haverstraw on the north, taking in Staten Island and all the ground from the Hudson back to Morris County, including Newark, Belleville, &c. Jacob Hevener was Brother Moore's colleague the first year. and Thos. Stratton the second. Joseph Totten was Presiding Elder. There were accessions to the Church all over the circuit, and all hearts were joyful. At that time there was a quarterly meeting held at Belleville. The preacher in charge had been all round the circuit, calling on the people to come up to this great feast of the Lord. The attendance was likely to be large. John

Williams, but recently deceased, was then a young man, and just converted. Knowing that very few of the members of the church in that place had *barns*, he wonders what they will do with the horses at quarterly meeting. Fortunately there was in the immediate vicinity of the church a six acre pasture lot. This occurred to his mind, and, going to its owner, hired its use. When quarterly meeting came, they turned their horses in. It was an exciting scene. The boys of the village, to whom all these things were new, looked and wondered; and as they sat on the fence surrounding the lot, counted forty horses, grays and bays, black and white, well fed and lean, all feeding harmoniously together, while their pious owners were shouting the high praises of God in the church a few hundred yards distant. At night, the good sisters would divide and subdivide their beds, spread out their quilts and comforters upon the floor, so that long lines of happy and welcome visitors might rest their weary limbs. These quarterly meeting occasions were great events, and looked forward to with high anticipations. So numerously were they sometimes attended, that at one of these gatherings in Belleville the table of Rev. John Dow, a celebrated local preacher there, supplied the wants of one hundred and eighteen persons.

While James Moore was on Elizabethtown Circuit, the brethren in Belleville conceived the idea that measures should be taken to build a church in Newark. A meeting was accordingly called, and three men, Richard Lecraft, John Dow, and Charles Marsh, all that were present, resolved to build a church in that town. The result was, that in a little over one year the Halsey St. Church was completed, at a cost of nearly three thousand dollars.

From 1809 to 1816, his appointments were as follows: Salem and Asbury, N. J., Union and St. George's, Philadelphia, Cecil, Talbot and Caroline, Md., and Dover, Del.

In 1817 he labored on Burlington Circuit with the saintly Joseph Lybrand for his colleague. An amusing incident occurred at a quarterly meeting on this circuit. Brother B. W., who had license to *exhort*, would sometimes take a text and try to *preach* from it. Brother Moore thought this course highly improper, and brought the matter before the Quarterly Conference, asking the Presiding Elder "what was to be done with an *exhorter* who took a text and *preached* from it." Before the Presiding Elder had time to speak, Brother Stiles, one of the stewards, sprang to his feet, and asked in reply, "what was to be done with a *preacher* who took a text and *exhorted* from it." As the latter was Brother Moore's frequent practice, a hearty laugh was had at his expense, and Brother B. W. was allowed to take his own course.

From 1818 to 1821, he is again on the lower section of the work, laboring on Smyrna, Kent, Caroline, and Somerset Circuits. In 1822 he is up amongst the hills of Warren County again, preaching to his old friends on Asbury Circuit. In 1823, he is on Gloucester Circuit. 1824, Lancaster, Pa. In 1825 he returns to Freehold: in 1826, Trenton; in 1827, after an absence of eighteen years, he returns the second time to Salem, N. J. In 1828–9 he is along the sea-shore, on Bargaintown Circuit. Here, after an uninterrupted course of ministerial labor extending over this wide and varied territory for a period of thirty-five years, his physical energies gave way, and in 1830 he was obliged to ask for a supernumerary relation, and the years of his effective ministry closed. Is it not remarkable, in view of the hardships and exposures of those early days, that it did not close before? But these men were not only divinely fitted for their work, they were also divinely sustained while engaged in its performance.

During all these years of exhausting labor, he was without the enjoyments of a settled home, having, as already stated, lost his wife at sea, and never re-married.

James Moore was not a man of learning; his opportunities for mental culture were few, and yet he was a man of marked power. That power was largely attributable to his wonderful simplicity. His public exercises were conversations with his congregation rather than formal sermons. But there was a power in his words that few could resist. Christian experience was his great theme; and so confident was he of the truthfulness of his statements, that he would often exclaim in the midst of his discourses, with a great deal of genuine Christian and Irish fervency, "*It's as true as ould Jeemes Moore stands here this day,*" and then appealing to any one in the congregation whose eye chanced to meet his, would continue, "Ain't it so, Brother A.?" and then Brother A., and perhaps a score of others, would respond with an emphatic "Yes," a volley of hearty amens, or floods of tears. He was a great singer, too, and would almost invariably come down the pulpit steps, after sermon, singing his favorite air,

> "Is there anybody here like a weeping Mary?
> Call on my Saviour and he'll draw nigh."

Advancing in his song, he would insert in the succeeding couplets in the place of "weeping Mary," "a doubting Thomas," or "a sinking Peter." Then, having gained the sympathy of his audience, with tears streaming from his own eyes, his whole soul would break forth:

> "Is there anybody here that wants their souls converted?
> Call on my Saviour and he'll draw nigh,
> O glory, glory, glory be to my God on high."

It was a rare thing that some did not respond to these calls; and thousands newly born to God have united with him in singing:

> "O glory, glory, glory be to my God on high."

He excelled in prayer. His petitions took hold of the strength of God, and his unyielding faith and fervent supplications were uniformly successful. The following instance will illustrate this point. James Moore was a frequent visitor at a relative's of the writer, where he was highly esteemed. He happened there one day in midsummer, while they were engaged in gathering hay. Several acres of grass had been cut and cured, and were now ready to be stored away for winter use. The farmer, his sons, and all the help he could procure, were taxing their energies to secure the crop before it should be injured by a heavy thunder shower which was rapidly approaching. The heavens grew darker and darker—the loud thunder roared and the lightnings flashed. They were now ready to commence on their last load, but the rain was pouring in torrents only a few hundred yards off, and seeing they could not finish, orders were given for a hasty retreat to the barn. The field was near the house, and just at that moment, Father Moore came to the door, and seeing how matters were, called aloud to the men, saying, "Continue your labors, and while you work, I will stay here and pray for the rain to be stayed." The venerable man then took his stand in the doorway, and lifting up his hands and eyes and voice to heaven, prayed most fervently for God to stay the rain till Brother Shinn should secure his last load of hay." The prayer was heard, and my uncle used often to affirm with tears in his eyes, as he recalled the scene, that the rain came up even with the fence that bounded the field where they were at work, where it poured in torrents, but over which it did not cross until they had finished gathering the hay, and then, as soon as they were all sheltered in the house or barn, it came down over all the farm with tempestuous fury.

He was a man of great fervency of spirit too, which he retained with little or no abatement up to the close of life. The following incident from the pen of Rev. Anthony Atwood, of the Philadelphia Conference, occurring but two years before his death, will strikingly illustrate this statement. The scene took place at the Session of the New Jersey Conference, held in Trenton, April, 1839.

Brother Atwood says, "Bishop Hedding was in the chair, and we were receiving the young men. A case came up of a young man who was said to have a good mind, and some preaching talents, but was reported as slow, and very sluggish in his manner, and very much lacking in fire and zeal. This, I consider a sad defect in a man so young, and remarked, 'if he was so deficient in natural fire now in youth, he would in a few years be unbearable, as it was common for men to lose much of their zeal, when age had dried up their youthful activities.' Bishop Hedding turned to Father Moore, who sat in the corner at his left, and said, 'Brother Moore, how do you like the doctrine of Brother Atwood? Do you think a minister is apt to lose his fire as he grows old? I want to hear your opinion.' I saw I was totally annihilated. The church was full in every part, listening to what was said, and as the man who fell under the wheel, and saw that to be run over was inevitable, made himself as *hard* as possible, I prepared myself for the storm I knew was coming. Brother Moore rose up slowly, and began to speak of his interest in the work of God formerly and now. As he proceeded he rose to a state of feeling the most sublime and inspiring that I ever witnessed. He shook with deep emotion. He usually had a rapid utterance, but now faster than ever, until the whole house was perfectly convulsed with intense excitement. As usual the shout began amongst the preachers, then the galleries caught the spirit and followed, until the noise of shout and praise went up like the sound of many waters. For a length of time no business could be done. The good Bishop shook, wept, and praised God with all the others. It was a wonderful scene, worth traveling many miles, to witness and enjoy. A feeling that no man could wake up but James Moore, and he could, and did do it often. The Bishop was aware of this, and seeing a good opportunity to wake up an unusual shout, could not afford to let it pass unimproved. I, of course, could only say, I thought my position a sound one in general, but Bishop Hedding and James Moore were exceptions to the rule, and business resumed its usual course."

He was attractive in his manner. Mrs. Mary James, who, knew him when she was a little girl, says, "His life was so holy that I felt an awe in his presence, and yet so winning, loving, and beautiful was his conduct, that he drew all, even the hearts of little children to him."

He was a successful minister. Large revivals as have been seen crowned his labors in many places, and perhaps in none of his fields was he entirely without fruit.

The following reminiscences of James Moore are from the gifted pen of Mrs. Anna R. Harlow, wife of Dr. Lewis Harlow, surgeon in the United States Army, and daughter of James Rogers, Esq., at whose house in Medford, Burlington County, N. J., Father Moore died.

"My earliest recollections are connected with Father Moore. My father's house he always used to call one of his homes. The children of our household were taught to venerate him. He ever seemed to us as a dear friend, and a member of our family.

Whenever he was expected at our house, it was a jubilant time with us, and the entire family, servants and all, assembled to greet him. I have sat upon his knee, and listened to the story of the birth of the Saviour, the tidings of the angel to the shepherds, and the song of the heavenly host, and felt that no one could tell it so sweetly as he. He used to talk to us of young Timothy and Samuel, and urge us to be early good, as they were. Almost the first question he would ask when he came to see us was, if we had given our hearts to the Saviour. I remember well the last time before I could answer this question affirmatively I felt such regret that I must meet him, and say, not yet. He loved children, and conversed freely with them. In family devotion it was his custom to mention every member by name, and pray earnestly for them. His faculty for remembering names was remarkable. He was never told a name but once, and recollected it for years afterward.

"In asking a blessing he always stood with out-spread hands and open eyes, observing all before him, and would thank God with reference to the food prepared—the fish from the sea—the fowl of the air—the beasts of the field, and the grain from the storehouse.

"In conversation he was animated and interesting—possessed a rich fund of amusing anecdotes, which made him the life of the circle. He was never unemployed. He could not endure sloth in any form. He used to tell us children never to be indolent; that such habits would ruin 'soul and body;' that the *wicked one* would take possession of us, if he found us unemployed and lazy.

'For Satan finds some mischief still
For idle hands to do.'

"He was a model of neatness. He could not endure the least spot or speck of lint on his clothing. He never knelt on the most delicate carpet, without first spreading down his pocket handkerchief.

"He was very punctual, and carried the habit out in everything. When the bell rang for meals, he started immediately for the table; no matter how interesting the conversation, he would say we can finish another time. It won't do to keep the family waiting, it will tire their patience. If he made an appointment to preach, or attend a quarterly meeting, no storm, or anything ever seemed to alter 'his plan.' This course he pursued to the close of his life.

"He seldom spoke of his private religious exercises, unless particularly interrogated. The visit he made us before the last he was in feeble health, and could not attend church at night. I sat at home with him, and then drew him out in this respect. As he was inclined to be communicative, I was greatly profited, and shall never forget these interviews. He was rich in faith, and the recital of God's dealing with him and gracious deliverance in the dark hours of trial and sorrow, were so remarkable that I was led to stronger trust.

"Father Moore excelled in prayer. I have often thought he could appropriately embody in his prayers more subjects than any one I ever heard pray. There was a fervency in his supplications that every one felt. He was truly a man full of faith, and of the Holy Ghost. It was his custom on arriving at a place, after the usual ceremony of meeting the family, to ask if he could retire to his room, and if any one was near, the occasional out-breathings of his soul might be heard. At these seasons he prayed for the family, and so fully was this understood by us children, that we would say Father Moore is up stairs praying for us. He used to tell us that 'daily he remembered every one of us on his old knees before God,' and when he died, I mourned because I had lost an efficient praying friend—and such prayers as but few uttered for me. His attention to secret prayer was stated and never failing. Always after meals he retired for private devotion. If he could remain but a minute, the habit must be observed. He was an early riser; generally arose at four o'clock in the morning. When with us, Father Moore could be heard in his room at an early hour, breaking forth in Scripture expressions, such as 'Bless the Lord, O my soul, and all that is within me bless his holy name.' 'This poor man cried, and the Lord heard him, and saved him out of all his troubles.' And occasionally we would hear his voice ascending in hymns of praise. He ever was found in the spirit of devotion. It was his meat and drink to do the will of God. His was a beautifully green old age, and his loving presence refreshed the hearts of all his friends."

The following letter from Father Moore, to his friend James Rogers, is interesting and valuable, as it shows the current of his thoughts at a very late period of his life.

NEAR LONG BRANCH. *June* 30*th*, 1839.

MY VERY DEAR BROTHER:—I hope you are all well now, and still bound for the kingdom. Yesterday I received your long-looked for favour, dated 13th inst. For the information you give I thank you, kindly, and pray the great Head of all will bless you a hundred-fold in this life, and in the world to come give you everlasting life. You mention the good times you have in Medford. I pray that they may abound yet more and more. Amen, God grant it. We have here excellent preaching, but not much life or power. I daily pray and hope there will be a move amongst them, before long. You wish me to come up to your last quarterly meeting. I should like to be there, but it will not be convenient. Our quarterly meeting comes on the 9th and 10th of March, and other things are in the way.

I was really glad and thankful to hear that mother's health was better. Please give my best respects to her; I hope she is on the mountain top every day, viewing the promised land with delight and pleasure. I was also much pleased to hear that William was getting ahead, and I pray that he may be a pattern to the young men in the Conference; remember me to him if you write to or see him before I do. Please give my respects to grandmother. I wonder if her old soul is on the wing. My love to sister Anna, and thank her for taking notice of poor old Father Moore. My respects to Benjamin; tell him for me, he must be a good boy; he has got a good name. Susan and Rebecca I hope are good children. My respect to Sister Burdsall. Reading, I hope he is like one of those young men that old John mentions, strong in the Lord. Brother J. Goslin, I wonder if he sees, as his old namesake did, the dead, small and great, stand before God. Brother G. Idell, I hope he is not an *idle* and *slothful* servant. God bless their families, and all the members in Medford. The preachers, I pray God they may be like fire-brands in a dry stubble. Brother Cramer, I trust he is steadfast in the Lord. Do please give my respects to everybody you think would be glad to hear I am yet a Methodist: and I think if I know myself in heart and life I am. Hallelujah! Jesus reigns.

I have now entered on my seventy-ninth year; praise God, O my soul, &c. You talk of making me a *new hat*. This is unexpected, but I pray God to give you a *new commission* from heaven, so that all the powers of darkness cannot stand before you. You know Brother Rogers, God says, "One shall chase a thousand, and two put ten thousand to flight."

And now may all the blessings of heaven be with you, and remain with you all forever and ever, Amen, &c.

So prays your old friend,

JAMES MOORE.

Such were the warm outgushings of his heart, even down to the close of life. Residing most of the time while a supernumerary, upon the shore, he was on his way to Conference from that place when he died. The following interesting account of his death is likewise from the pen of Mrs. Harlow.

"He arrived at his 'old home,' (as he used to denominate it,) the residence of his friend, James Rogers, on Tuesday, 19th of April, 1842, on his way to the New Jersey Conference, which convened at Camden the ensuing week. With much difficulty he reached our house, and was supported to his chamber. Medical aid was procured almost immediately, as we feared he was dangerously ill. The doctor did not speak despondingly of his case, but at once expressed the fear he could not recover sufficiently to attend the Conference, as his disease was bilious pleurisy, and had already progressed too far to adopt the remedies used in the first stage of the disease. Father Moore received the intelligence with gratitude and composure, but did not abandon the hope of attending Conference until Thursday, the 28th, when he said, 'I fear I must relinquish this hope, and it will be the first Conference I have missed since I joined, which was forty-eight years ago.' His strength by this time had so far declined as to compel him to take his room. We often entreated him to lie down through the day, but he steadfastly refused while he had strength to sit or walk, saying, 'I have not lain down during the day for fifty years, and cannot think of indulging so indolent a habit until compelled.' We felt it a duty to have every thing arranged to make him as comfortable as possible. He would retire frequently into the adjoining room to pray. I observed him one day to retire nine times, and engage with so much fervency as to be overheard. Fearing it would be a disappointment to him not to be able to rise in the morning as usual, I said, on entering his room, 'Although you are unable to unite with us in the next room to-day, we will do all we can for you, Father Moore, and hope in a few days you will be better.' He replied, 'My Jesus hath done all things well: this affliction is for my good.' During the morning the doctor called, and after due deliberation, told him his case was hopeless, but presumed he was prepared for the solemn event; and if he had any arrangements to make relative to his business, &c., he had better attend to it without delay. He looked very composedly, and only said, 'I'm much obliged to you, doctor.' He afterward made his arrangements, and spoke of his departure with all the composure of one about to take a pleasant journey. In the course of a few hours his symptoms assumed a more favorable aspect; he seemed better; on Sunday more comfortable, and quite happy. When my father entered his room, he repeated the hymn commencing,

'Happy soul, thy days are ended,' &c.,

with a heavenly smile playing about his features. Whenever we would sympathize with him, or regret his suffering, he would immediately say, 'Patience must have its perfect work. Many are the afflictions of the righteous, but the Lord delivereth him out of them all. Our light affliction, which is but for a moment, worketh for us a far more exceeding and eternal weight of glory,' &c. Often would he call me to him, and repeat the hymn beginning,

'O what are all my sufferings here.'

And once I heard him praying thus: 'If consistent with thy

will, O Lord, take me to thyself; nevertheless, not my will, but thine be done.' Frequently he exclaimed, 'O blessed Saviour, give me grace and patience; not only me, but all who attend me.' He was averse to giving the least trouble, and manifested on all occasions perfect resignation: every thing we did for him, to use his own expression, 'was just right; I could not desire it better.' We frequently conversed with him about death and heaven, and his confidence never appeared in the least to waver. My father asked him, a few days prior to his death, if he could say with Mr. Wesley, 'The best of all is, God is with us.' He replied, 'O yes,' and repeated it. To almost every one that visited him, on parting he would say, 'Be thou faithful until death, and I will give thee a crown of life.'

"During the conference the doctor considered him better; the disease was subdued, and weakness appeared to be the only obstacle to his recovery. We were cheered for a while, and fondly hoped and prayed, if in accordance with the divine will, his life might be protracted. But at the close of the week our bright anticipations were blasted. Stupor, with an unpleasant train of symptoms peculiar to the last stage of the disease, too plainly convinced us he must die. On the Monday previous to his departure, I said, 'Father Moore, you have had a tedious night, and have suffered much; but I expect you have found the Saviour precious.' He replied, 'Yes, very.' I added, 'Soon we think he will transport you to a brighter and better clime than this.' He looked upward, and ejaculated, 'O blessed, blessed Saviour!' 'But you feel perfectly resigned, do you not? 'O yes,' he exclaimed, with much emphasis, 'His promises are sure.' This was a day of heart-rending suffering; he had but a half hour's intermission from a racking cough, which seemed almost to deprive him of life. Late in the evening it subsided, and all the next day he was on the verge of eternity. When aroused he would say, 'Jesus is with me all the time, nigh at hand to help whenever I call on him.' On Wednesday he seldom spoke, or observed anything passing around him, unless his attention was particularly directed to it. When asked a question he would simply reply, yes or no; and as the closing scene drew near he was deprived of speech. About fifteen minutes before the spirit took its flight, my father said, 'The conflict is almost over; you are going to receive your reward; you will soon obtain the crown.' His countenance brightened, and he tried to say yes. 'My father, we know you cannot speak to us; but if you feel that you are passing over Jordan, and the Saviour is with you, and your way perfectly clear, raise your hand in token of victory.' He raised it quickly, and soon after threw up both hands, and looked upward pleasantly, then closed his eyes for the last time on earthly scenes just twenty-two minutes after six o'clock, P. M. With a heavy groan this dear veteran of the cross yielded up his breath, and plumed his wings for glory, on the 11th of May, 1842, in the eighty-second year of his age."

Just as he breathed his last, Brother Rogers' who was near his bed, says, "I heard a sound, soft, sweet, and celestial, that seemed to fill the room, which after a little passed out of the window, and I thought it was the angels bearing his spirit to the skies." Soon after this, Rev. J. F. Crouch, who lived opposite, a few hundred yards off, came down to Brother Rogers, house, and said, "I hear Father Moore is dead." "Yes, he's gone," was the reply. "What time did he die?" asked Brother Crouch. "A little after six o'clock," was the answer. "It is very strange," continued Brother Crouch, "for the last three days I have been cast down to an extent beyond anything I have ever experienced, yet this evening, just at the time you mention, I was going from my house to the barn, and when half way down the garden, I heard a sound, like the rustling of wings, accompanied with soft, sweet music, and, at the same time, a Divine baptism came upon me, so great that I fell prostrate to the ground. As soon as I recovered I went to the house and said to my wife, I know Father Moore is gone, for I have just heard the angels bearing his spirit to the skies."

The coincidence was singular, and yet, singular as it may seem, it was only a verification of a verse of one of our beautiful hymns:—

"He's gone! the spotless soul has gone,
Triumphant, to his place above;
The prison walls are broken down;
The angels speed his swift remove,
And, shouting on their wings he flies,
And gains his rest in Paradise."

REV. BENJAMIN BENSON.

AMONG those whose lot fell in the New Jersey Conference when it was set off from the Philadelphia, was Benjamin Benson. His labors in the State of New Jersey covered only a very brief period, and beyond the record of his appointments and a brief biographical sketch in the General Minutes, it has been found impossible to collect any facts connected with his history.

He was born in 1807, and was consequently twenty-three years of age when he entered the itinerant connection in 1830. His conversion had taken place three years previously, and two years before he had been licensed to exhort. Entering the traveling ministry from the section of country known as the Peninsula, with the single exception of his last appointment, his labors were confined to that part of the Conference territory. Smyrna, Kent, Salisbury, and Accomac circuits and Elkton station were the charges to which he was sent. In the spring of 1835, being somewhat enfeebled, he took a supernumerary relation to the Conference. At its next session, with health slightly improved, he was appointed to Plainfield, New Jersey. The expectation that he would be able to perform effective work, however, proved delusive, and indications of a pulmonary disease soon became so marked, that he was compelled to leave his post and make a visit South. No good result following, he returned to die among his relatives in Cambridge, Maryland.

His afflictions were protracted and painful, but were endured with patience and resignation. His soul arose superior to his sufferings, and while death, with slow but unwavering step, carried on the dissolution of his earthly tenement, he rejoiced in the prospect of eternal life. His death, which occurred in October, 1840, was eminently peaceful.

"Such was the Christian's parting hour;
So peacefully he sank to rest;
While faith, endued from heaven with power,
Sustained and cheered his languid breast."

Mr. Benson is said to have been possessed of fair preaching abilities, a good voice, pleasant address and manners, and to have attained considerable mental culture and familiarity with books. But the insidious and enervating disease, of which he died, early marked him for its victim. He was thus prevented from developing his powers to the extent that would otherwise have been the case, or of reaching his full stature as a man or a minister. Still he was highly esteemed where known, accomplished some work for the Master, and then, after illustrating the power of religion, to give patience and fortitude through a wasting and painful illness, he passed to share the rewards of the redeemed in heaven.

REV. JOHN BUCKLEY.

JOHN BUCKLEY, the subject of the following memoir, was born in the village of Sholver, Lancashire, England, May 3d, 1805. At the age of seven or eight years his mother died, leaving him and a younger brother to a father, pressed with the cares of business, and struggling under embarrassments. About four years subsequently, the father, also, was taken from them, and they were left to the care of a step-mother. John was, however, soon, afterward received into the family of a maternal uncle, Mr. James Wilde, who, with his excellent wife, although having a large family of small children of their own to care for, faithfully acted the part of father and mother to the orphan boy. Here he was introduced into the Sabbath-school connected with the Wesleyan Methodists, which gave him an opportunity of listening to the gospel in its primitive simplicity and purity, and there is no doubt that here was laid the foundation of his religious character. He was ever remarkable for the earnestness with which he entered upon the accomplishment of any object, which may be illustrated by the fact, that while connected with the Sabbath-school, a small reward having been offered to the boy who would first learn and repeat correctly the Epistle of James, he applied himself to the task, and obtained the promised prize.

When nineteen or twenty years of age he broke through the restraints which had hitherto been placed upon him, so far as to become exceedingly fond of dancing, attending parties, and kindred amusements; although, to those who knew him only in after years, when Divine grace had changed his heart and life, it seemed difficult to realize that pursuits, so vain and frivolous, would have had any charms for him. Returning home, on one occasion, at a late hour of the night, from one of these scenes of festivity, he contracted a cold which resulted in a severe fit of sickness, and that brought him apparently near the grave. It pleased Providence, however, to restore him to health, but never again was he found in those places of folly and dissipation.

Soon after coming of age he accompanied his uncle's family to this country, and with them settled in Bloomfield, N. J. Before leaving England, and while on the voyage, he resolved that when he arrived in America he would devote himself to the service of the Lord, but not until about a year after he landed did he put his good resolution into practice. Then, which was in the spring of 1828, he connected himself as a seeker of religion, with the M. E. Church, of which the Rev. Isaac Winner was at that time pastor. It soon became evident that in this, as in other matters, he carried his peculiar earnestness with him. He was faithful and punctual in the discharge of his private duties, sometimes becoming so much engaged in his devotions as to cry aloud, and was frequently listened to by those in an adjoining room. He possessed an extremely tender conscience, and if in any case it could be appropriately said, it might of him, that he was "righteous over much," even before his conversion. Soon after his convictions had ripened into a resolute determination to seek the Lord, and while earnestly engaged in the discharge of every religious duty, even to praying in public, he suddenly left his work, on one occasion, went to his uncle, and informed him that he wished to be absent that afternoon. His uncle said, "Where are you going, John?" He replied, "To Bellville, (a village about three miles distant,) to converse with the Rev. Mr. Lee about this soul of mine. I am not fully satisfied. I must save my soul."

He was not long left in doubt, but soon after received such a baptism of the Holy Spirit as enabled him to go on his way rejoicing. He immediately commenced exhorting his friends and relatives to turn to God, and rested not until most of his cousins and his only brother, were walking with him in the way to heaven.

It was soon evident that the Lord had a work for him to do, and in order to qualify himself more fully he made his arrangements to spend a year at the Wesleyan Academy, Wilbraham,

Mass., over which, that eminent man of God, Rev. Dr. Fisk, then presided. He entered upon his studies with that ardor and determination which characterized all his undertakings; but, probably neglecting to take the exercise that was necessary, more especially as he had been accustomed to an active life, he was soon attacked with dyspepsia, which increased to such a degree that at the end of five months he was obliged to relinquish his studies and return to his uncle's in Bloomfield, and from the effects of which he never entirely recovered. Soon after his return he was licensed to preach, and the following spring was received into the Philadelphia Conference, and sent with the Rev. R. W. Petherbridge to what was then called Trenton Circuit, although Trenton was not at that time included within its limits.

The following year he was appointed to Essex Circuit, in both of which places his labors were owned and blessed of the Lord.

In the spring of 1833 he was sent to Mount Holly, then, for the first time made a station, where he labored for two years with great acceptability and usefulness. In reference to his labors in that place the Rev. G. A. Raybold says, in his "Methodism in West Jersey," "The year 1833 was an era in the history of Methodism in Mount Holly. The Church resolved to become a station, and the Rev. John Buckley was appointed pastor. The eminent abilities of that brother as a preacher, his solid piety, and strict practical Methodism, had the blessed effect of giving a powerful impulse to Methodism, and it then obtained a character, extension, and influence, hitherto unknown in Mount Holly."

In the spring of 1835 he married a daughter of Clayton Monroe, Esq., of Mount Holly, and was sent to Dover, Del., also, at that time first made a station. Here, likewise, he was made eminently useful in building up the Church. At the end of that year the Philadelphia Conference was divided and the New Jersey Conference formed. Preferring to be in the latter, he was removed from Dover and was stationed in Rahway, N. J., where his labors were blessed to the conversion of souls.

From Rahway he was sent to Burlington, N. J., and here, at the close of his first year, ended his active labors in the itinerancy. He had suffered more or less with dyspepsia, during all the period of his ministerial service; but this year his throat became very much affected, and, with the advice of his physician, he concluded to desist from preaching for a year, hoping by rest and relaxation, to be able, at the end of that time, to resume his labors. About this time, he met with a severe affliction, in the loss of his brother, to whom he was ardently attached, and who was also a member of the New Jersey Conference, and a young man of great promise. This mysterious dispensation of Providence, greatly depressed his spirits, and doubtless aggravated his disease. At the Conference of 1838, he obtained a supernumerary relation, and retired to Mount Holly, where he spent the year in such exercises, as were thought to be most conducive to his restoration to health. At the end of the year, however, he found himself still unable to render effective service, and as a further means of promoting his recovery, took a small farm in the vicinity of Mount Holly, the cultivation of which, afforded him abundance of out-door exercise, and proved to be very beneficial to his general health: so that, during the winter, he had strong hopes of being able, at the ensuing Conference, to enter again the regular work. But having preached a few times, toward the close of the winter, his throat was so seriously affected thereby, that he was obliged to relinquish the idea: and the painful conviction was forced upon his mind, that he was no more to be employed in that work in which his soul greatly delighted. Having previously made arrangements to leave the farm, he moved into the town, and soon after, an opportunity being afforded for engaging in business in Bridgeton, N. J., he availed himself of it, and removed to that place. While there he had the confidence and esteem of all who knew him. His pulpit labors, (in which he occasionally engaged,) and his private interviews were highly appreciated by the people.

His health continued with but little variation, for about a year and a half after his removal to Bridgeton, when his strength began visibly to decline. But so gradual was the decay, and attended by so few of the more distressing symptoms of the disease, that it was long before he realized that he was about to be removed from earth: indeed, until within two weeks of his death, he cherished hopes of recovery. But when he became fully convinced, that his sickness was unto death, perfect resignation possessed his soul, and the consolations of grace abounded. He conversed respecting his approaching dissolution, with the composure of one preparing for a journey. Death, to him, had no terror. He summoned one of the brethren, gave him explicit directions, respecting all his affairs, and then calmly awaited his change.

He was but three days confined to his bed, when the messenger came, and gently removed him to his home above, on the 28th of June, 1842, aged thirty-seven years.

As a Christian, his piety was deep and uniform. He always carried with him an atmosphere of purity and holiness. He was grave and serious in his manners, yet never gloomy or morose: indeed, in the entire consistency of his Christian and ministerial character, he had few equals. His talents as a preacher were of a superior order. His sermons were well studied, methodically arranged, and practical, searching expositions of gospel truth, which found their way to many hearts. It could be truly said of him, he studied to "Show himself approved unto God, a workman that needed not to be ashamed, rightly dividing the word of truth."

In regard to pastoral duties, he was a model, well worthy the imitation of his successors in the ministry. As a result of his faithfulness in this respect, many were led to embrace the truth, who will be stars in his crown of rejoicing.

REV. WILLIAM BAKER

WAS born in Washington, Litchfield Co., Conn., October 9, 1801. Of his early life but little is known. He says, "I had frequent operations of the Spirit, from my childhood. Yet I became more and more wicked, till the age of eleven, when it pleased the Lord to bring me to a bed of affliction." Believing he was about to die, and feeling unprepared, he solemnly vowed to seek religion, if God would spare his life. But, like nearly all who make such promises, he failed to keep it. He says, "My seriousness wore off, and I became more wicked and profane than ever, till I had scarcely any of the fear of God before my eyes." At the age of sixteen he went to Northampton, to learn the "Clothiers' Trade." About a year after this, he was again brought near to death, and was terribly alarmed. His broken vow haunted him like a spectre, till he feared to go to sleep, lest his waking should be in eternity. He exclaims, "Oh, the awful consequence of putting off repentance till a death-bed!" But alas, with the *sight* of danger, concern disappeared, and he became as careless as ever.

After recovering, he entered the Fulling Mill of his brother, near Englishtown, Monmouth Co., N. J. Here he attended the "Old Tennent Church," and soon became concerned for his soul. He says, "I felt I must lead a new life or be lost." He often thought he would open his mind to the minister and others, but was prevented by diffidence. The flame thus shut up in his heart, soon became a consuming fire. "Pilgrims' Progress" afforded him some help, but did not lead him to the Saviour. He often waited at the church door, hoping that the minister would inquire about his soul, but was disappointed. At length the preacher "told me all my experience," he says, in a sermon from, "Come unto me, &c." He began secret prayer and to seek light from good books, still, he says, "I became darker and harder, till it seemed I would die. I groaned in spirit and cried to the Lord, till one night the burden was removed, and I felt a change wrought in my soul." Yet this proved to be only a partial deliverance. He says, "Evil habits had become a second nature, so that to do evil was as natural as to breathe. I had hard fighting; however, I continued to struggle on." He did not join the church, but gratefully acknowledges his indebtedness to the Presbyterians. He spent the summer of 1823 in Connecticut, where he attended Methodist meetings for the first time.

He then entered the Fulling Mill of Andrew Winter, near High Point, Monmouth Co., N. J. This placed him out of reach of any Presbyterian meeting. For some time he did not attend any place of worship. He learned that meetings were held in a school-house near by, but felt reluctant to begin to attend. His mind was not at rest. At length he dreamed that he heard them singing and praying while he was breaking the Sabbath. His feelings became much agitated. Brother Samuel Bowne invited him to attend the meetings. He gladly went, and also stayed in class. He found that he did not enjoy religion, but soon sought it, joined the church, and took a decided stand for God and Methodism. Referring to this invitation, he says, "I went, and, glory to God, I cast in my lot among the Methodists, under Rev. John Walker. Memorable day! I shall never be sorry." For about one year fair winds and smooth waters attended him, then his bark was tossed and driven. He "reasoned with the devil," till driven to the verge of despair. He says, "None but the Lord and my own soul knew what I passed through for about eight months."

In the fall of 1825, he was married to Ann, the eldest daughter of his employer. She was a class-leader, which position she held for several years acceptably and usefully. She was his only leader till her death, which occurred some three and a half years after their marriage. She finished her course with great joy. One of their two children died in infancy, while the other, an industrious, upright man, is still living.

At first Mr. Winter insisted upon their business engagement

covering a term of years. But when Mr. Baker became a Methodist, Mr. Winter was as anxious to get rid of him as he had been to bind him fast. Finally Mr. Baker bought the stock and took the business upon himself. Not long after this his mind was drawn to the subject of preaching, which he soon felt to be his duty. He became greatly perplexed, but concluded to pursue his business in order to pay his debts, and at the same time preach in a local capacity. But God ordered otherwise. His wife died after an illness of only ten days. Business became so dull that he could not meet his liabilities. His father-in-law took the property back, and he gave up all to his creditors, including a dwelling-house on which he had paid $800. Thus in about one year he was left with only one child and a good conscience.

His way into the ministry was not a smooth one. He had attended school but little. His stores of information were very limited. His mind was not much disciplined. He did not possess ready gifts, and was extremely diffident. Hence the idea of his being called to preach seemed preposterous. For a long time he strove to reconcile his mind to another course of life. In this he failed. In spite of himself his reveries and his dreams were full of sermons. The struggle became so intense that he exclaimed, "I never in this world expect to be able to describe the anguish of my mind." But when he fully felt, "Woe is me if I preach not the gospel!" he gladly responded, "Here am I; send me." At the funeral of his wife he opened his mind to Rev. R. W. Petherbridge, who gave him license to exhort. This was in the spring of 1829. The next February he applied for license to preach. The Conference adjourned while his case was pending. This was a sore trial, but at the next session the vote was unanimous, and Rev. C. Pitman, Presiding Elder, at once sent him on a circuit.

In 1831 he was received on trial by the Philadelphia Conference, and sent to Haverstraw with Rev. J. H. Dandy. A friend lent him money with which to buy a horse, and he went on his way rejoicing. In the early part of this year he dreamed that as his feet were set on a large rock, it became innumerable pieces. He took this as an omen that God by his ministry would break hard and flinty hearts. There were several conversions, but no general revival this year. A singular incident occurred, March 12, 1832. He was preaching from the text, "If the righteous scarcely be saved," &c., at the house of Benjamin Geroe, near New Prospect. As he was opening the subject, the house was struck by lightning. He stood by the chimney down which the fluid passed. All seems to have been stunned, but none seriously injured. Mrs. Geroe and child were prostrated for a little while. Mr. Baker stood so close to the wall that the fluid did not produce a serious shock. *Yet it tore off the soles of his shoes.* The lights were put out, and he was so bewildered, that he rushed out of the house, sprang over a high fence, ran a quarter of a mile to the nearest neighbors, through a dashing rain, and gave notice that all were dead but himself. He returned, and, to his surprise and joy, found all alive. God having spoken, the sermon was omitted, and a prayer-meeting held. It was a solemn, searching time, in which some began to pray who had never prayed before. The house was much injured, but not set on fire. A singular phenomenon was found in the cellar. Under the fire-place was a ceiled arch, with stone floor and a tight plank door. Here were some eggs, and the underside of each was found to be perforated with innumerable holes, as if made with a fine cambric needle

He was returned to the same circuit the next year with Rev. J. V. Potts. The rock seems now to have fully gone to pieces. A revival began in the early part of the year, and many were converted under the ordinary means. They were also largely successful in their extra meetings. After the above-named occurrence we would expect to find him timid when he heard God's voice in the thunder. He describes a terrific storm that occurred August 7th, and which awed him into the deepest reverence and devotion. He also gives another instance. Having preached on the evening of September 9th, he had to go five miles to find lodging. Flashes of lightning afforded the only means of seeing a narrow road on the mountain-side, with a swollen stream at its base. He says, "I viewed myself as standing on the verge of eternity. Only the Lord and myself knew how I felt. O how good religion is at such a time!" As it began to rain he reached a house, but the inmates were so frightened that they did not admit him, and he took shelter in the cellar. Then, after waiting an hour and a half, and capturing his horse, which had broken loose, he proceeded, but did not reach his destination till after midnight. Oh! how his soul exulted in the mercy of God when he found himself safe and comfortable. A church was built during the year, at a place called "Thiets." The mis-called Reformers tried hard to defeat the effort, especially by the slang about the bishops being able to sell the property. The house was completed, however, and also one at Rockland. He usually preached two or three times on Sunday, and five times through the week, three weeks out of four. February 12, 1833, he says, "This is my rest week, and I feel the need of rest after so much labor. A good deal of the time I am as much fatigued as if I had been mowing." At times he was depressed and low-spirited. But light mingled with the shade. He saw the work prospering in his hands, and had seasons of rejoicing and holy triumph.

In 1833 he was admitted to orders, and sent to Milford, with Rev. V. Shepherd as a colleague. His wonder and admiration were excited by the rugged scenery of the country, and his warmest sympathies awakened for the lumbermen, on account of heavy losses sustained by a "freshet" in the Delaware. He took a deep interest in this plain, friendly people, and was the means of doing them much good. A quarterly meeting and a camp-meeting are described as scenes of unusual displays of Divine mercy. On Sunday, after the close of the encampment, seekers crowded the altar, while the most hardened sat in mute silence. Sixteen professed conversion during the service, and other good fruit was gathered afterward.

In the spring of 1834, he was greatly cheered and refreshed by a visit to Monmouth County. Since he left, the society at High Point had increased from thirty-five to one hundred and twenty-five. Business calling him to Connecticut, he spent a Sunday in New York, and on his return, one in Haverstraw. This was the day their new church was dedicated, on which occasion he preached twice. Both these Sundays were times of unusual "refreshing from the presence of the Lord." He spent another year at Milford, but gives no account of special success, except at a camp-meeting, of which he speaks in glowing terms.

For several years he had been a widower, and as an itinerant, a lone wanderer. Yet he was so timid, retiring, and desponding, that few could be found who so much needed a suitable companion. This he found in the person of Elizabeth Carhart of Bethany, near Keyport, N. J., to whom he was married September 20, 1834. She was a deeply-experienced Christian, and possessed gifts of a superior order. She often closed the public services, sometimes delivering powerful exhortations. She had few equals in prayer, either as to solemnity of manner, propriety of language, or attending divine unction. Both her public and prive labors were much blessed in the promotion of the work of the Lord. Then, after sustaining his active toils, she soothed his dying hours, and for a number of years acted the part of a faithful mother to his son, till she rejoined him in heaven.

The private memoranda from which we have drawn was not continued after his second marriage. Still our materials are fully equal to the allotted space. He received elders' orders in 1835. In 1835 and 1836, he was at New Prospect; 1837 and 1838, at Rome; 1839, at Sandyston and Port Jervis; 1840, at Sandyston; 1841, at Hope. These were years of unceasing toil, severe trials and varying successes. His health was precarious, and had to be watched with great care. He got wet by fording a stream while on his way to Hope, and took a severe cold, from which he never recovered. His debility so increased that he was forced to quit the field in August. After resting till the last Sunday in September, he consented to preach and administer the communion at a distant appointment. He did not return till Tuesday, and that night was prostrated by hemorrhage from the lungs. The bleeding was stopped, but the next night it returned, and in less than an hour had done its fatal work. He could say but little, yet "the few words he was able to utter, were expressive of the high confidence he reposed in the merits of Christ his Redeemer." He closed the career of his toils and sufferings at his home in Hope, Warren County, N. J., Sept.

30, 1841, in the fortieth year of his age and the eleventh of his ministry.

Wm. Baker was a man of great simplicity and integrity of character. He traveled the roughest portions of the State, endured many exposures and hardships, and received an unusually small support. Yet he left no recorded complaint. The nearest approach to one refers to Sandyston. "This was a trying year. The circuit was laborious, religion low, Methodism weak, my support insufficient, receiving but little more than half my allowance. But I would not complain, though I was very glad to leave, for we lived among a heathenish people." An amusing incident will illustrate his ingenuousness. In his early Christian life he imbibed the notion that certain frames of feeling were the standard of religious excellence. In order to secure the desired revery he would become so absorbed as to forget the proprieties of time and place. On one occasion the presiding elder publicly desired him not to draw his face so horribly. At the close of the service, he extended his hand to the elder, saying, "If I am wrong I want to be set right." Complaint was once made to his elder that he was unsociable. When spoken to on the subject, he frankly regretted his diffidence and lack of conversational gifts. But said that he disliked to converse on trivial subjects, and that he thought it best to talk only when he had something to say, hinting that this rule did not fully apply to those who had made the complaint.

He took a serious view of life, and was deeply grieved by the misdoings of others, and especially of professing Christians. But his complaints were uttered only to God in his secret prayers. Sometimes he gave way to despondent feelings till he walked near the verge of despair. Then he would gain the mountain heights and exult in holy triumph. He also learned the art of trusting where he could not trace, and of so clinging to Christ as to prove a conqueror in every struggle. Thus he became an eminently holy man. "His piety," says the Conference Obituary, "was of the highest order. For many years he lived in the enjoyment of perfect love, and his daily walk testified that his profession of such enjoyment was not vain. No one ever saw him light or trifling, or indulging in any dispositions or tempers inconsistent with the Christian character."

The same authority says, "He was a minister of good preaching abilities, possessing the power of exhibiting with great force and perspicuity, the essential doctrines of the gospel." He generally selected plain texts that directly embodied the vital truths of his mission. His usual habit was to ask and answer questions, which answers were mainly drawn from the Bible, and his own observation and experience. He was plain, pointed and searching, so that all saw that a devout, earnest man stood before them, who felt it to be a privilege as well as a duty, to preach Christ and seek the salvation of souls. He thus faithfully executed the trust committed to him, and then passed away to enjoy in its fullness that salvation which he so earnestly commended to others.

REV. JOSEPH BURN M'KEEVER.

TWENTY-ONE years the subject of this sketch has been in glory. A brief, earnest ministry of but five years wore out the frail tabernacle, and introduced the spirit to higher and holier scenes. It is well to preserve some memorial of departed saints for the good of the living, and as a record of what the grace of God can do for sinful man.

Joseph B. M'Keever was the youngest son of Captain John M'Keever of Philadelphia, and was born December 1st, 1811. He was a boy of bright talents and warm affections, peculiarly generous and unsuspicious in his nature. Having lost his mother at an early age he was educated in the family of his maternal grandparents.

His grandfather was a man of one set of ideas, and thought nothing so desirable as mercantile pursuits; therefore, without regarding the peculiar character of the boy's mind, he was placed at an early age in a counting-house.

While quite a youth he manifested a desire to study for some profession, and the business of a counting-house became utterly distasteful. But these aspirations were treated as romantic folly, and he was obliged to drudge on. When about eighteen years of age he became a member of a club, the chief aim of which was improvement in elocution. Here, under the influence of a company of thoughtless young men, he was led to believe he possessed peculiar talents for the stage. His family were not at all aware how far he had progressed in preparation for the final step, when, suddenly, it burst upon them. He was at that time a handsome youth, with a graceful form, fine voice, and considerable talent for public speaking. Discouraged by relatives in preparing for a useful and respectable profession, he had chosen his own, and imagined a field of glory opening before him. I can never forget the day when, filled with grief, I tried to dissuade him from the step which he was about to take. I can see him now, as he stood before me, with glowing cheek, trembling lip, and flashing eye, with an extended arm, expressing determination in every gesture, as he said, "Sister, I seek for fame." I remonstrated, but in vain.

Though he was tenderly attached to his only sister she had not power then to change his determination. He had made an engagement with the proprietor of one of the Philadelphia theatres, to appear on a certain night in the character of Sir Edward Mortimer, in the "Iron Chest." Placards were placed at the corners of the streets, announcing the appearance of a new debutante. His father in anger tore down the notices, and as he was still a minor, threatened the proprietor with prosecution.

His appearance upon the Philadelphia boards was, therefore, at that time prevented; but in the heat and impetuosity of youth, he packed up his clothes in a silk handkerchief, and started on foot for Lancaster, where he joined a company of strolling actors. His family had all discarded him, excepting his grandparents and sister. On parting with the latter, she bade him remember that she should never forsake him, and should still pray and hope for his return from folly. Fortunately, he fell in with a set of dishonorable men, who cheated him out of his earnings. He had dreamed of a company of high-minded, generous adventurers, and this experience was valuable to him.

During all the time of his estrangement, he regularly corresponded with his sister, and still clung to her with all the warmth of his nature.

When he returned to Philadelphia, he again made application to the city managers, and meeting with no more opposition from his father, who had given up all interference in his affairs, he made his appearance in his native city. He was warmly applauded, and the press predicted success for the young aspirant.

But before the evening of his first appearance, he sought his sister. This interview was affectionate, but brief. He seemed sad and tearful. Her last charge was, "Brother, you will appear on Friday night, remember, I shall then be at the lecture, thinking of, and praying for, you." Tears filled his eyes at this appeal, and in after-years, he said that the words rang in his ears all the evening. But he was not destined for an actor. A number of friends who deplored the perversion of his talents, and who saw the path of ruin before him, went in company on another appearance, and hissed him from the stage. This mortified his pride—it was his last appearance. Soon after this disappointment he brought all his play books to his grandfather, requesting him to burn them.

The situation of the young man was still very critical; without employment, despondent, and surrounded by bad advisers and worldly companions, he could not recover lost respectability in his own home, and felt that he must leave it for a while.

Then an Episcopal gentleman who was interested in him, offered him a clerkship in his factory, near Rockdale; and thither he went. An important step was now taken—cut loose from all his former associates, in the retirement of the country, he had leisure for thought.

At this time he was in constant correspondence with his sister, and it was manifest that deep and serious convictions were pressing upon his spirit. The same kind Christian friend invited him to his family-circle, which was one of refinement and piety; and, at last, he took a class in the Sunday-school, and became interested in the work. A good Providence was now leading him, day by day, by a way which he knew not.

Many months passed by, and returning to Philadelphia, he obtained a situation in the Southwark Bank.

For some months, in company with his sister, he attended upon the ministry of the Rev. Dr. Bedell of St. Andrew's Church. It was his desire, at that time, to connect himself with that communion; but Dr. Bedell, who knew of his former life, advised him to test his conversion thoroughly ere he came out openly as a follower of the Redeemer. About this time the Rev. Mr. Maffit visited Philadelphia, and became deeply interested in the young man. Under his influence his religious convictions were deepened, his hope made sure, and his course for time and eternity decided. He became a member of the

Methodist Episcopal Church, and from that time adorned his Christian profession. Soon after this event, he was united in marriage with Miss Pauline Morgan, of Philadelphia, who proved to be a most faithful and devoted wife.

The desire now to devote his talents to the cause of his Master became very ardent; and, after due deliberation and prayer, he came to the conclusion of resigning a lucrative situation, for the purpose of preaching the everlasting gospel. His first appointment was to Haddonfield Circuit, in 1838, with Rev. J. Long, where he preached and labored successfully for one year. His second, in 1839, was on Salem Circuit, where also he was a faithful laborer for his Master, and the Churches grew under his ministry.

In both of these places he bore his cross meekly, and, though sometimes sorely tried, he submitted with a sweet spirit of Christian forbearance to all that befel him in the way of privation, misconception, and hard labor in the vineyard of the Lord. From Salem Circuit he was removed to Bloomfield, where his lot was cast in more pleasant places, and he was universally respected and beloved by all classes and denominations.

His last charge was at Halsey St., Newark, where he made rapid growth both as a Christian and a minister: he had there a large congregation and useful membership, where he enjoyed the confidence and love of his own people, and the community in general. His labors here were much blessed, and his friends looked forward to a constantly increasing usefulness in the service of his beloved Master.

Here he was abundant in labors, not sparing himself on any occasion, but was always ready to do the work of a minister; preaching, exhorting, laboring, visiting, in season, and out of season, so that he might win souls to Christ, and finish the work given him to do.

In all these labors, he was encouraged and sustained by the partner whom God had given him, and who, as the wife of a Methodist minister, cheerfully bore her part in the labors and privations of the itinerancy.

He was distinguished for clearness, earnestness, and unction in proclaiming the message of his Lord. The graceful elocution and eloquent oratory once employed in the service of the evil one, was in his case most beautifully transferred to the ministry of the blessed Christ. As he preached, love beamed from his expressive eye, glowed upon his cheek, and breathed in every gesture of his impressive manner.

The following sketch of his labors at Halsey St., Newark, is from Rev. A. E. Ballard.

"The accomplished and talented William Roberts had been removed from Halsey St. in the plenitude of a popularity, probably never surpassed by any pastor of that time-honored sanctuary, and it became a matter of serious inquiry by the authorities of the church, who should succeed him. Brother M'Keever had been but one year at Bloomfield, which charge was growing rapidly under his ministry, but to their great dissatisfaction he was taken from them to meet the peculiar eircumstances of Halsey St. At first it was supposed no one could supply the place of Roberts, but a very slight acquaintance with the public exercises and personal character of M'Keever soon dispelled that idea. His popularity was of a solid and influential character, holding the congregation and impressing them for good. His health was feeble when he came, which was, while the church was rent with Millerism, and the anxieties attendant upon the distraction occasioned in the church, by its dissemination, contributed, as he himself assured me, to break down his strength and speed him to his grave. He preached up to the last of his physical strength, never intermitting it until he had become too feeble to go out for the performance of even a marriage ceremony. My last interview with him was at the time when he found himself unable to attend to this service. He was seriously alarmed for his health, but still thought *rest* would recuperate him, and he would soon be well. Probably had he rested earlier, he might have been spared, but Halsey St. is not an easy plaee to rest in.

In person, he was slight, but beautifully symmetrical. His voice was harsh, but with a sweet and tender undertone, which made it charming. His sermons were always short, clear, and to the point —delivered with great deliberation, and yet with impassioned energy. He was, perhaps, the only man I ever knew, who could combine the two. The great theme of his preaching was, faith in our Lord Jesus Christ. I heard him once in his startling, guttural tones, say to a lady, who had been long a seeker of religion, "Woman, I command you to believe *now* in the Lord Jesus Christ for salvation." The desponding penitent made the attempt, and immediately was saved.

In deportment he was always a gentleman, dignified and serene—never participating in the jests which might be passing round him, but always seemed to feel that *he* must be serious and solemn."

Mrs. Isabella Avison says, "He was a man possessed of every virtue which adorns human nature. As a minister, he had superior talents, and was deeply pious.

"The last time he met us, was in the lecture room of the old church, and I shall never forget it. The night was stormy, and but few were present. But as he addressed us for a few moments, his countenance was illuminated with a holy joy. It was a precious season." But this glowing ministry was short. In the fifth year, these constant and wearying labors began to tell upon his frame. He took a severe cold; continued preaching at a protracted meeting, while suffering severely; went to Philadelphia, on business in winter, increased his cold, and returned home very sick. His decline was rapid. A pulmonary disease settled upon his lungs, and it was very soon manifest that he could not continue long on earth. I was sent for, and was shocked to see the inroads which consumption had made. I knew that the sentence had gone forth, and, painful as was the task, it was mine to inform him of his approaching end. He received the intelligence calmly, but with much suppressed feeling. At first large tears stole over his pallid features, at the thought of a ministry so soon concluded, and a wife and young family to be left upon the cold world. Soon however his spirit rallied, and perfect submission to the will of his Lord henceforth marked the temper of his mind. Duty called me elsewhere, and I saw my brother no more.

Mrs. Avison says, "I spent four weeks with him in his sick room. It was a privilege to wait upon him. He was perfectly patient and happy, anxious if it was the Divine will, to live, but, said he, "I am in my Father's hands, as clay in the hands of the potter." He requested me to read a portion of God's word to him daily, and he enjoyed it very much. Once when I handed him a drink of water, he said, "I shall soon drink in my Father's kingdom, and I shall go out no more." His last words were, "*Jesus is precious.*" Soon after, on the 27th of April, 1843, in the thirty-second year of his age, he gently breathed his last."

The New Jersey Conference, of which he was a member, being at the time of his death in its annual session, appointed one of its number, Rev. Isaac Winner, to conduct the funeral services. These services were held in the church, where so often he had preached the word of life. Mr. Winner delivered a sermon of great feeling and power to a weeping congregation, from, "He was a good man, full of faith and the Holy Ghost." The remains were taken to Philadelphia for interment. When the cars arrived at New Brunswick, where the Conference was sitting, the members, in token of their high esteem, assembled at the depot, where they stood, with heads uncovered in solemn files on either side of the rail-road, while the train was passing. A funeral service was likewise held in Trinity M. E. Church, Philadelphia, where Rev. E. S. Janes delivered an appropriately solemn address, and several ministers assisted in the service.

The precious dust now sleeps at Laurel Hill, where he has since been followed by his wife and three daughters, called in the bloom of youth. But one son remains to represent the family.

Life is not to be measured by the years appointed, but by the work accomplished. If, therefore, in the short and glowing ministry of five years, our dear brother led many to Jesus, how long does that life appear, when compared to three-score years and ten, all spent in the service of the world? His life, short though it was on earth, stretches forward into eternity, where, in a state of bliss unspeakable, it is ever growing in love. Twenty one years in glory, who can tell what exalted service he has rendered there?

REV. WILLIAM LUMMIS

WAS born in Lower Penn's Neck, Salem County, N. J., May 4, 1776. He was early inured to the trials and hardships of orphanage, his mother having died when he was an infant, and his father, when he was eleven years old. He was then placed in charge of a man in Pittsgrove, who was to teach him the saddle and harness making business, when he should reach a suitable age. This, however, he never did, but scanted both his food and clothing, compelled him to work beyond his strength on the farm, and then, after seven years of cruel treatment, went West, and left him to shift for himself. He then apprenticed himself in Salem for two years in order to complete his trade. Matters went but little better here, and his hard experiences with these masters, both of whom professed religion, prejudiced his mind against Christianity, and led him to conclude that the whole subject could be resolved into superstition and priestcraft. He soon became a professed infidel, and began to eagerly pursue the pleasures of the world. He married and became a father, but did not, on that account, reform his wild and pleasure-seeking habits. And being fitted by temperament and talent to be a leader among his associates, he acquired the infelicitous sobriquet of the "Devil's Bell-sheep." Still the Holy Spirit did not leave him to the unrestrained pursuit of his own evil propensities. While in the shop, reflecting on his past life, he saw that it had not been such as he could approve. And as he called to mind how many around him had died, while he was spared, God's goodness so shone in contrast with his own vileness, that his heart was deeply affected, and he resolved to strive to conform his future life to the will of God.

Often while listening to Christians praying, he had criticised them severely, and thought if he could not do better, he would surely hold his tongue. But when he fell upon his knees beside his bench, in order to lift his heart to God, he was astonished to find that he could only say, "Lord, have mercy on me." He then sought a more private place, lest he should be seen and heard, but all his fine praying was reduced to the cry, "Lord, have mercy on me." Having fully determined to be on the Lord's side, he next offered himself as a probationer in the M. E. Church. But as his past life had been one of open profanity and profligacy, and as he had not yet been converted, some were afraid of him, but others were in favor of giving him a trial, and he was admitted as a seeker. His whole soul became so absorbed in seeking salvation, that he shunned no cross and shrank from no duty. He at once established a family altar and faithfully attended the means of grace. Still for nine months he walked in darkness, and blindly groped for the path. But he kept his face steadily toward Mount Zion, and proceeded carefully, feeling for the pitfalls and quagmires, in order to avoid them, and firmly planting his feet wherever he found solid footing. Thus unfalteringly did he press forward, till he found himself across the dismal, dangerous morass, in the delightful groves, the clear sunlight and the invigorating air of the "kingdom of heaven." This long struggle was ended while he sat in his room reading the New Testament. The Spirit shone upon the word, and so reflected the light upon his mind, that he was enabled to apprehend Jesus as a present Saviour. He sprang to his feet, exclaiming, "Glory to God, I can convince the world." And so certain did he feel of this, that he at once started on a mission among his neighbors and old associates, in order to lead them to the same light and love that now illumined and thrilled his own soul. But to his disappointment and sorrow, he soon found that it required more than human power to open their blind eyes and turn them from their idolatries to the true God. Still, though unsuccessful in this Christian effort, his concern for their soul's welfare did not abate. As he had opportunity he attended camp-meetings and all other places that afforded the hope of getting or doing good, prayed in public, used personal effort with sinners, and earnestly strove to promote the cause of Christ.

In the meantime his wife died, and he was again married. In 1809, some two years after his conversion, he received exhorter's license, and began to hold meetings at Quinton's Bridge, Logtown, and the house of a Mr. Gibbs, in each of which places he formed a society. There were some singular events connected with his ministry at Gibbs. This was a wealthy Quaker family, in which were several sons, one of whom had received an injury, which resulted in mental weakness. This was a source of trouble and mortification to his relatives. But God strangely used this afflicted youth as a door through which came saving truth, both to the immediate family and to other Quaker relatives and friends. He heard Methodist preaching, and embraced religion, and his changed life unmistakably attested the genuineness of his conversion and the reality of religion. Soon after this he was honored with a most triumphant death and an angel convoy to the heavenly world. He was in an ecstacy, and insisted that he saw the angels that had come to bear his spirit home. He left a request for Mr. Lummis to speak at his funeral. The attendance was large, and a special divine unction attended the services. In one week the mother died, and he was invited to preach on the occasion of her burial. This proved to be a time of great spiritual power, and the services had a wonderful effect upon her kindred and the neighborhood generally. A class was soon formed, and religious meetings regularly established at the house. The Quakers, whose narrow prejudices keep them from hearing other than their own preachers, made an exception in his favor. They knew he had but little learning, saw that a gracious influence attended him, and hence inferred that he was prompted and aided by the Holy Spirit. They would often say to him, "I know that thee has not learned thy preaching."

He was licensed to preach in 1813. We hardly know whether to approve or censure the delay of four years, after he began to hold public meetings, before giving him this license. Those who confer this authority, are charged with the solemn trust of guarding the sacred office from the intrusion of improper persons. In many cases this door has been thrown too widely open. And Mr. Lummis had been a neglected orphan, apprenticed to hard task-masters, whose glaring inconsistencies had destroyed his confidence in religion, and quickened his steps in the paths of vice and folly. Having been deprived of a proper literary and moral training, he must have come before the church with but little more than what nature and grace had done for him. And yet four years seem a long time for it to require observing men to discern that God was sanctioning his labors and thrusting him out into the work of saving sinners. But in view of the effective and constant employment of his gifts, all opposition finally subsided, and the voice of the Church concurred to the call of God.

In 1814 he was received on trial by the Philadelphia Conference, and sent to Dover, Del. As he entered the Church at the first appointment, he found a large congregation drawn together to hear the new preacher. Seating himself in the pulpit he began to sing,

"The fields are all white, and the harvest is near," &c.

The topic was so solemn, and his manner so impressive, that the whole assembly were melted to tears, many sobbing aloud. He gave a brief but powerful exhortation, urging to immediate action, and then invited seekers to the altar. Eleven came, of whom nine professed conversion before the service closed. This course accorded to his favorite maxim, viz., "The great end of preaching is to save souls." To reach this end he often laid aside the usual forms, and adopted the most direct method of attaining it. During this year four hundred were added to the church, chiefly through his instrumentality.

A prominent lawyer of Maryland related the following incident to the late Rev. T. McCarroll, as having occurred at a camp-meeting in Delaware. He said, "Several of my family were members of the Methodist Church. We had spent some days on the ground, and a number of popular men from the cities had preached. The meeting was to be held over the Sabbath, and I concluded to go home, as the circuit preachers were expected to conduct the services. But my family prevailed on me to remain. Mr. Lummis preached in the afternoon. In his introductory exercises I found but little to criticise. As he commenced his sermon, it was evident that he aimed directly at the heart and conscience. In a few minutes I was so absorbed in the subject as to forget that I ever had a thought of criticism. As he warmed in his theme, original and startling figures, burning words and overwhelming energy flowed like a torrent from his lips. When he closed I was completely overpowered, so that I trembled like an aspen. For some minutes I did not venture to move lest I should fall prostrate to the earth. Never before nor since did I feel so powerfully my guilt and danger as a sinner, or the necessity of salvation. I have always believed, that if some one had then taken me by the hand and led me to the altar, I should have embraced religion. Of all the men I ever heard preach none seemed more perfectly pervaded by his subject than Mr. Lummis."

In 1815 he traveled Cambridge Circuit, Md. In 1816 he and eleven others were elected to membership in the Conference and to deacons' orders, but for some unexplained reason were not ordained. This year he traveled Milford Circuit, Del. In 1817 he was ordained by Bishop Roberts, and sent to Annamessix. The next two years he was at Accomac, having been ordained elder by the same bishop in 1819. Lawrence Laurenson was his colleague for the three past consecutive years, a thing so unusual at that day as to be worthy of special note. The three next years he traveled Snow Hill, Somerset and Cecil Circuits.

What he learned during these nine years of labor on slave territory fully settled his convictions on the subject of slavery. The following incident made an ineffaceable impression on his mind. In 1819, while returning from an evening meeting, a peculiar sound attracted his attention. He halted, and by aid of the moon discovered a number of persons in double file. As they drew near, he saw two men on horse-back, one in front and the other toward the rear. They were driving a gang of about twenty slaves, who were hand-cuffed to a chain extending the length of the gang. He saw the rear driver use his long whip several times on the shoulders of a female, who seemed much jaded, and earnestly begged to be allowed to rest, declaring that she was unable to proceed. Having never seen a company of human beings driven in chains along the highway, his feelings became strongly excited; and as the brutal driver still plied his lash, he ventured to remonstrate, and urge that they be allowed to rest. The driver, with a bitter oath, replied that the woolly heads were his property, and that he did not need any instructions as to how he should manage them. "Well," said Mr. Lummis, "if I were in the place of those woolly heads, I would remember you if ever the time came when those hand-cuffs were loosed. None but a monster would drive even a brute under the lash when scarcely able to walk." They parted, but ever after that he regarded an institution which can turn a human being into a beast, and the owner into a brutal tyrant, as intrinsically wicked, and a curse to Southern society. His sympathies became warmly enlisted in behalf of the blacks, and his labors among those who attended his ministry were unremitting and largely fruitful in leading them to the Friend of the weary and heavy-laden. For years, besides averaging one sermon a day, he often led more than a hundred colored persons in the classes on the Sabbath.

His subsequent labors were chiefly in New Jersey, and were in the following fields:—1823, Freehold; 1824, Gloucester; 1825-6, Cumberland; 1827, Gloucester; 1828-9, Caroline, Md.; 1830, Staten Island, N. Y.; 1831-2, Tuckerton, N. J.; 1833, Bargaintown; 1834-5, Gloucester; 1836, Salem. In 1837, at the first session of the New Jersey Conference, he became supernumerary in connection with old Gloucester Circuit, and thus remained till the close of life.

Mr. Lummis was about five feet eight inches high, very broad-chested and firmly built, and was a man of great physical power and undaunted courage. His bold reproof of the armed ruffian slave-driver shows of what mettle he was made. At a camp-meeting where, as usual, he was one of the managers, a large, burly man, slightly intoxicated, came swaggering forward, bitterly swearing that he would take his wife out of that sheep-pen, as he termed the altar. Mr. Lummis was leading the meeting, and advanced to dissuade him from his purpose. But his utmost endeavors failed. When he saw that nothing short of force would avail, he seized the clothes covering the ruffian's chest with his right hand, and the right wrist with his left. In this way he backed him, locomotive-like, out of the circle.

When released the ruffian retreated to his associates, who rallied him for his defeat, and asked why he did not knock the old fellow down. "Why," said he, "when I attempted it he would gouge my breast with his knuckles as if he would mash it in, and my right arm might as well have been in an iron vise." And he was agile as well as strong. When fifty years old and weighing two hundred pounds, he would scale a five rail fence by placing one hand upon it, with the suppleness of a boy.

His natural endowments were superior, but his hard lot in early life prevented him from acquiring an education. Then several years were wasted in utter neglect of both mind and heart, nor did his after-reading take a wide range, while his studies were chiefly confined to the Bible, Hymn-book, Discipline, Clarke's Commentary, and Wesley's Sermons. With these, and especially with the Bible, he made himself familiar. His memory was tenacious, which enabled him to quote largely, and generally give chapter and verse. He also used freely and effectively the facts and incidents gathered from reading and observation. He had a voice of great compass, melody, and power, and was a remarkably gifted singer. Conscious of the power of this gift he diligently plied it. He often sang as a sort of prelude to the public services, and the compass and melody of his voice, together with the soul he threw into the sentiment, would so thrill and subdue the assembly as to prepare them to give a favorable hearing to the word. His language was unusually full, so that he was seldom at a loss for words by which to express his meaning. And in prayer, especially, there was a strength and fluency, a copiousness and conciseness, that would often remind the hearer of the Episcopal Liturgy. His gifts in exhortation, prayer, singing, and class-leading abundantly made up for any defects that might be found in his pulpit performances.

Had his culture and acquirements equaled his natural endowments he would, doubtless, have occupied a very prominent position as a preacher. But he took humble views of his abilities, made no attempt at the arts of oratory, and no pretensions to style. The love of Christ so constrained him that he became absorbed in his theme and seized with skill and energy the facts, truths, and imagery which most readily arose to his mind and promised to subserve his great aim most effectually. The Bible and nature, observation and experience, chiefly supplied him with matter which, being used in an artless, earnest, and impressive manner, and attended by the unction of the Holy Spirit, arrested attention, disarmed prejudice, defied criticism, and so threw the sinner off of his guard as to make him an easy, willing captive. His appeals were pre-eminently to the conscience, and were often so direct, searching, and powerful as to carry it by storm. The signal honor with which God crowned his labors is partly seen in the fact that he received not less than five thousand members into the Church.

We learn from the Conference Obituary that he labored with zeal and usefulness as a supernumerary till the autumn of 1843, when he had a severe attack of rheumatism, from which he suffered much, and which he bore with Christian fortitude. He had an excellent constitution, having scarcely ever been ill up to this date. It is said that he missed but a single appointment on account of sickness during the whole of his effective ministry. The disease of which he died was apoplexy, which terminated his life in ten days after the first attack. When taken ill he remarked with emphasis, "I shall die; and I am ready and willing at any time the Lord shall say the word and call me to himself." He was perfectly composed and resigned, while his chief desire was "to depart and be with Christ, which is far better" than to linger in pain and weakness. He had maintained an unshaken confidence in God thus far, which, as the last trying scene approached, became all conquering and triumphant. "To him death had entirely lost its sting, and he talked of dying with as much composure as one would of taking rest in sleep." His son Samuel, a local preacher, who has since followed him to heaven, came home, not knowing that his father was so ill, and approaching the bed, asked if he knew him. His speech had nearly failed, and his answer was indistinct. He looked up and began to weep, evidently because he could not utter his recognition and dying blessing. The son told him not to weep, that all would be well, for the kind hand of Providence had so ordered. He was composed in a moment, and continued in a peaceful frame of mind. At a later period, when asked if he could say, "All is well," he answered with a nod, and then gradually sank down through insensibility into the arms of death. Thus, like the setting sun, cloudless and beautiful, the sun of his life passed behind the western hill of death, Nov. 1st, 1843, in the sixty-eighth year of his age and thirtieth of his ministry.

Father Lummis was wont to say that he had learning enough to help him feel the need of more, and, if Providence favored, he would give his children a good education. The careful industry and economy of himself and wife led to the realization of this noble purpose, to a good extent. Two sons, Fletcher and Henry, and the son-in-law, Rev. H. L. Kelsey, are in the itinerant ranks. But God took care of most of their children, twelve of them having preceded him to the "happy land." The aged widow lingered on these mortal shores till the autumn of 1863, when she also joined the blood-washed throng with her partner and little ones.

NOTE. The above memorial is substantially from the pen of Rev. F. Lummis, but has been enlarged and re-arranged to adapt it to this work.

REV. WESLEY C. HUDSON.

"He was in duty prompt at every call,
He watched, and wept, he prayed and felt for all,
And as a bird, each fond endearment tries,
To tempt its new fledged offspring to the skies,
He tried each art, reproved each dull delay,
Allured to brighter worlds, and led the way."

THE sky is clear. Then a little cloud arises. With marked rapidity it spreads itself, pouring watery blessings upon the earth, then disappearing, all again is bright. Such is life. Man appears a little speck upon the world's horizon, then enlarging, pours upon humanity the benedictions of a holy life, retires from view, and, so far as the human vision is concerned, is as though he had not been.

But, though the cloud passes away, in after months, the watery treasures which it lavished upon us, crown the earth with beauty, and fill our barns with food. So with the good man. The human passes from our view, but his influence and example have blest the world for ages yet to come.

"Our mortal life, our influence is not gone,
When the material bonds around us break,
In other minds our spirit still lives on,
Though dead we speak."

May it be so in the brief record which we make of the brief but beautiful life of that young and ardent minister of Christ, Wesley C. Hudson.

He was born in the City of Philadelphia, October 18th, 1813. His mother was a godly woman, and, as soon as reason commenced its dawnings in her little son, she taught him the value of prayer; a lesson which can never be too early, or too deeply impressed upon the expanding mind of childhood.

From his earliest remembrance his confidence in God was very strong, and his belief in the Divine ability and willingness to answer prayer grew with his years.

With such views, he thought it was only necessary to pray, and, whatever he might ask, should be received. He soon had an opportunity to test the correctness of his theory. Returning from school one day, when between five and six years old, he was followed through the streets by two larger boys who ridiculed him on account of his red, curly hair. This greatly annoyed him. On reaching home he went directly to his bed-side, and with a heart sorely tried, because of the derision he had been exposed to, prayed most fervently that God would be pleased, for Jesus' sake, *to make his hair straight and black.* The prayer, not being a proper one for him to offer, of course was not answered, and his hair remained curly and red to the close of life. Similar mistakes are often made by older persons. They pray for objects which are not in the range of Scriptural propriety, and then, having asked, and failing to receive, rashly conclude God does not answer prayer.

His childhood and youth were marked with great activity of body and mind. Whatever he did was characterized by great earnestness. When he studied, all the powers of his intellect were employed, and he was generally at the head of his class. But, when the hours of relaxation came, whatever fantastic game or play might be performed, his physical energies were at once taxed to their utmost capacity, and he was a leader in all fun and frolic. Fond as he was of play, however, his love of study predominated, and often, when his young companions urged him to join them, he would decline, preferring to remain at home to improve his mind.

When about ten years old there was a fire, in which some property belonging to the father of one of his school-mates was destroyed. This gentleman engaged Wesley to assist his son in removing some bricks from the burnt building to the place where they were erecting a new one, agreeing to give the young workmen so much a wheelbarrow load.

Upon this new enterprise they entered with great zeal. The Fourth of July was near, and, in the hope of raising funds for that grand old holiday, they employed every hour that could be spared from school. When his money was paid him at the end of the week, greatly delighted with so large a sum, he hastened to show it to his mother.

"What will my little son do with so much money?" inquired his mother, with an approving smile.

Young Wesley's eyes flashed with well-earned joy, and wondering that such a question should be asked at such a time, exclaimed enthusiastically, "Buy fire-works for the Fourth of July."

His mother did not say much to this proposition, but after his first pleasure had somewhat subsided, asked him kindly if it would not be better to take his money and buy a good book, so that he could have something to look at in coming years. He thought it would. Cowper's Poems, in two volumes, were accordingly purchased. He had them carefully covered with parchment, and prized them highly all his life.

In referring to them, he often said they were purchased with the first money he ever earned, and with quotations from their classic pages, his sermons in after years were often adorned and enriched.

In his eleventh year he professed conversion. Soon after, he was admitted to the Church on probation, in which relation he continued up to his fifteenth year. At that time he became still more anxious for his soul's salvation, was received into full membership in the Church, and soon after began to exercise in public meetings.

Though only a probationer, for a period of four years, yet he felt the restraints of the Church, and, according to his own confession, from that fact alone, was often kept from doing things which were wrong. He often said, after he became a minister, that children who made a profession of religion were not sufficiently borne with. "Had I not been nursed and cared for," said he, "I might not have been so easily reclaimed."

When only a little past fifteen years of age his mother died, and he was left an orphan. Soon after, he entered an office in the City of Philadelphia, to learn the business of a printer. Here his talents rapidly developed, and after he had set type only a few months, was taken into a higher and more responsible position. Some time before the term of his apprenticeship expired, such was the confidence which his employers reposed in him, that nearly all the care of the office devolved upon him. One of his fellow apprentices, still living, and in the active work of the ministry, says, "His influence in the establishment was so great, that if apprentices, or, gray-haired journeymen, were standing and talking together, they would, at his approach, disperse as quickly as if it was one of their employers."

During these years, his opportunities for mental culture were unusually great, for a tradesman, while his gifts and graces, as a Christian, being constantly employed, were rapidly maturing.

When only twenty years of age, he was licensed to exhort, and shortly after, in 1833, to preach, as a local preacher. Three weeks after his apprenticeship expired, he was called to fill a vacancy on a distant circuit.

His employers offered him a thousand dollars a year, with the promise, that they would soon give him an interest in the business, if he would remain in their service. The firm was one of the oldest and best established in the city. The business was lucrative, and the inducements thus held out to a poor young man, were of the most flattering character, while the pay on a country circuit for a single man, was only a hundred dollars, the whole of which meagre sum in those days was rarely received.

Such considerations, with a mind less devout and resolute, might have had an influence. With him, however, much as he respected the persons who made the offer, the proposition had no weight. A voice was continually sounding in his ears,

"Go preach my gospel, saith the Lord,
Bid the whole world my grace receive,
He shall be saved that trusts my word,
And he condemned who won't believe."

And while this was the case, wealth or poverty were not subjects of debate, He therefore responded promptly to the Presiding Elder's call, and went to Milford Circuit, though, at the first quarterly meeting, he did not receive enough money to pay his traveling expenses to his new field of labor.

He remained on this charge until the spring of 1835, when he joined the Philadelphia Conference, and was appointed with Rev. I. Winner, to Belvidere Circuit. In 1836, he was sent to Whippany, but afterwards to Rockaway station. In this charge he preached three times each Sabbath, superintended two Sabbath-schools, and frequently led a large class immediately after the morning sermon, to which were added his extra meeting services, running almost entirely through the winter months. This labor, too arduous for the most robust, prostrated his physical energies, and his friends believe permanent injury was sustained.

In 1837 he was appointed to Jersey City, in the New Jersey Conference. His next field of labor in the spring of 1838, was Bloomfield, where, in the following November, he was married to Miss Margaret Wild, youngest daughter of James Wild, Sen., a lady worthy of the relation to which she was thus introduced into the church of God. On Christmas-day of that year, he was attacked with hemorrhage of the lungs, which, though he was under the care of skillful physicians, all winter, were several times repeated in a few months. These alarmed his friends, and he was induced at the next Conference to ask for a supernumerary relation. But how can an ardent nature, burning with the love of God, be silent? He preached the next Sabbath after Conference, and continued to do so up to August, when he took the charge of Orange station.

In 1840, he resumed his effective relation, and was appointed to Woodbury, where he labored for two years with great success.

In 1842, he was appointed to New Brunswick. Here he labored faithfully, though in much discouragement, for twenty-one months, in the fond hope of witnessing the fruits of his toils. He had already seen the tender blade shoot up, then the ear, and now the full corn in the ear was just appearing; but while uttering the first joyous shout, over the ingathering harvest, he was prostrated by disease, and obliged to leave the glorious work to others. It was a great affliction. He felt, sometimes, as if he could not give up to be sick. "I must go," said he, "and encourage the weeping penitents I have left at the altar." "I must go, and try to persuade others to flee from the wrath to come." His ardent nature, though prostrated by disease, longed to be in the heat of the conflict, and shout the victory.

"His sword was in his hand,
Still warm with recent fight,
Ready that moment at command
Through rock and steel to smite."

Rev. C. H. Whitecar, in speaking of his ministry, says, "He was in some respects like a comet, great, luminous, exciting admiration, and even wonder; more, he was a body of felt fire, warming, melting, purifying, enlightening, propelling and guiding others. He was studious, versatile, of good memory, fine taste, highly imaginative, apt to teach, beautifully descriptive, fervent in prayer, and of unconquerable energy. His soul was too great for his frail body: when his soul power was in exercise, the framework trembled. He loved his work, his brethren, and the church. His highest ambition was to see fruits of his labor."

He was systematic. His mornings were generally spent in his study. In the afternoon he went forth to visit as a pastor. He had the name, residence, and occupation of each member of his church in a little book, and, as far as practicable, called on them once a month, in order to inquire into their spiritual condition. As a consequence, the people loved him, and the church prospered.

His labors were generally successful, so that though his ministry lasted but ten years, many were added to the Lord through him.

The illness which seized him in the midst of his revival at New Brunswick, proved his last. It continued with great severity, for eleven weeks, from January to the second day of April, 1844. On that day, kissing his fond wife, and little cherub boy, he said, "I am stepping over Jordan," and in an instant his immortal feet stood upon the golden shore in endless bliss.

"They who die in Christ, are blest;
Ours, be then, no thought of grieving;
Sweetly with their God they rest,
All their toils and troubles leaving,
So be ours the faith that saveth,
Hope that every trial braveth,
Love that to the end endureth,
And, through Christ, the crown secureth."

REV. LEWIS T. MAPS.

THE following sketch has been condensed for this work from a valuable memoir, by Rev. T. Hanlon. The committee deeply regret that their limits do not allow its insertion entire.

Lewis T. Maps was born at Long Branch, Monmouth County, N. J., May 3, 1820. His ancestors, both on the father's and mother's side, were numbered among the most prominent and valuable citizens of the community in which they lived, and also held a distinguished place in the formation and perpetuation of the Methodist Episcopal Church. Long before the Revolutionary war the families were firmly planted in that county, and gave to the advent of Methodism that influential identification which, under the blessing of God, has resulted so largely in its establishment and steady growth.

These families were the first to welcome the itinerant preachers. In the days of Asbury and Coke their homes were preaching-places for the ministers of God, and from that time to the present their hospitable entertainment of the descendants of Wesley has been proverbial. The names of William Throckmorton and Michael Maps are known all through New Jersey Methodism as among its noblest and most honored sons, while their estimable wives are remembered by numerous ministers, both for the holiness of their lives, and the generous hospitality with which they ever greeted the servants of Jesus. Of the children of his maternal grandfather (Michael Throckmorton) four have been placed by Providence in connection with the work of the ministry. Samuel Throckmorton, his son, was an earnest and devoted preacher, so earnest, that his zeal consumed his life ere its early morning had passed away. One of the daughters is the wife of the Rev. William Barnes, of the Philadelphia Conference; another, of Rev. Samuel Jaquett; and still another, of Rev. Wm. Franklin, of the New Jersey Conference. His paternal ancestors were, as has been stated, equally devoted to the Church of their fellowship, and a union of these families, so alike in sentiment and feeling, could not otherwise than be attended with the happiest results; and Michael Maps and Hannah Throckmorton after their union in marriage, walked together for fifty-four years like Zachariah and Elizabeth of old, "in all the ordinances of the Lord blameless;" and of that marriage was born the subject of the present sketch.

"In his early boyhood it is said that he gave evidence of superior mental ability. His studies were mastered with ease, and he was soon prepared to assist his brother in his store, where he remained as clerk for several years. His affable and courteous manners, combined with his ready use of choicest language, made him almost invaluable as a salesman, while the facility with which he computed accounts gave promise of a mental strength which his after-life fully realized. At the early age of twelve, under the ministry of the sainted Stewart, he gave his heart to God and his life to the Church, maintaining an attendance upon religious duties, which kept alive the spiritual-mindedness which he had at that time received. A few years after, while Rev. J. L. Lenhart was stationed in that appointment, his religious life received an earnest impulse. Through his counsels he was induced to double his diligence; and, as he approached the years of manhood, the impression was powerfully made upon his mind that God designed him for the work of the holy ministry. He was deeply sensible of unfitness for the sacred calling, and earnestly sought the Divine direction.

He opened his mind freely to his pastor and other devoted Christians, and by their advice decided to yield to the heavenly calling and prepare for his great work. With this purpose in view he entered Wilbraham Academy. Here he applied himself closely to his studies, and made rapid advancement, so rapid, that his first public effort after his return surprised all who heard him. He had chosen the subject of universal freedom for his topic, and although the doctrine of the abolition of slavery was unpopular, yet he discussed the subject so ably that no one was found sufficiently bold to oppose him. In the spring of

1839, while but nineteen years of age, he joined the New Jersey Conference, and was appointed junior preacher on Toms River Circuit. The description of his leaving home for his first appointment is thus given by his brother. "Having been fitted out with a horse and saddle-bags—the usual equipments of a Methodist itinerant in those days,—he started for his work. He left home deeply impressed with the responsibility resting upon him, and seemed dejected and sorrowful. On his way through the pines and sands of South Jersey, in the vicinity of Kettle Creek, he was overtaken by a severe thunder-storm, which compelled him to take shelter in an old saw-mill near by the road. Here, sitting alone amid the vivid lightnings and pealing thunders, he wept as if his heart would break. But his spirit knew no retrogression, and after a tedious and lonely journey he reached his appointment, and was cordially welcomed by the people of the circuit.

He was marked as a rising man at the commencement of his ministry. His brilliancy of mind, close habits of study, and faithfulness in all departments of his work, impressed both the people of his charge and his brethren in the ministry, that a career of no ordinary promise lay before him. At the Conference of 1840 he was appointed to Bergen mission. Here also his ministry attracted large congregations, and his fervid eloquence charmed all listeners. During this year he was united in marriage with Miss Eunice H. Ferguson of Long Branch, a lady eminently adapted to the sphere in which she was called to move, and who was to him a most valuable helpmate in the work of the ministry. In the spring of 1841, at the earnest solicitation of the people of Toms River, he was re-appointed to that charge. Rev. N. Edwards, who was his colleague that year, speaks of him as a brilliant preacher, and also as one of the most affable colleagues with whom he had ever been permitted to travel. He says, "Though they both went to the circuit as married men, with a very poor prospect for competent support, yet, they had a pleasant and prosperous year. God poured out his Spirit upon the people, blessing them with far greater spiritual prosperity than had been usual for several years past." At the Conference of 1842 he was appointed to what is now known as Verona, in the northern part of Essex County. The appointment was one of unusual difficulties, but God blessed the labors of his youthful servant with marked sucеess. "At two appointments on this charge," writes his widow, "there were powerful awakenings and numerous conversions." His studies also were proseeuted with the same tireless energy that characterized every department of his labor. "Study to show thyself approved unto God, a workman that needeth not to be ashamed," was with him a motto of daily life, and in the midst of an extensive revival, his theological studies were pursued with undeviating regularity. He now began to attraet the attention of the church as a gifted and eloquent preaeher, and an appointment, usually intrusted only to men of both years and experience in the ministry, was given to him at Morristown. He followed Rev. D. W. Bartine, a man whose praise was in all the churehes, and many, while highly esteeming his abilities, were yet doubtful whether he would be able to fill the place of that eminent minister. But their fears proved groundless, for the youthful ambassador suceeeded in retaining his congregation, and also added largely to the material prosperity of his charge. His widow says, "Although he went to Morristown with fear and trembling, yet the Lord blessed his labors and prospered him abundantly. The eongregations had never been larger—there were numerous accessions to the ehureh, and in every respect the soeicty was greatly prospered." Here his kind manners and gentleness of spirit made him numerous friends, while his abilities commended him as an eminent minister of Christ, and after the lapse of twenty years he still lives in the memories of the older members as a man whose ministry cannot be forgotten. In a Morristown newspaper printed after his deeease, it is said, "Mr. Maps possessed brilliant talents, and during the two years he was among us made many and warm friends by his social manners, gentleness of spirit and untiring assiduity in the great cause of salvation."

At the session of the Conference of 1845 he was appointed to Prospeet Street, Patterson. Of this charge his widow says, "Here his duties were arduous, and he labored very hard. The society had just been organized with only about eighty members, yet the Lord blessed the little band with a glorious revival of religion, so that at the ensuing Conference he reported two hundred and ten members. To give some idea of how much his heart was in the glorious work I need only say that during the protracted meetings of this year, he himself preached seventy sermons in ten weeks. This was the most laborious and successful year of his whole life. In the three months intervening between the Conference and his fatal illness, he had made pastoral visits to all his members. But his life of labor and success was now ended.

On the 18th of June, 1846, he was prostrated with bilious fever. From the first he suffered deeply, and the care of his charge, which his sense of responsibility would not suffer him to dismiss, aggravated the disease. On the Sabbath, while only able to sit up for a few moments at a time, he desired to be conveyed to the church, that he might not lose an opportunity of preaching Christ to the people. But the disease ran its course with fearful rapidity, and it soon became evident to those who surrounded him that recovery was impossible. All that skillful medical attendance could perform, or that the Christian kindness of loving friends could offer, proved unavailing, until, on the 11th of July, before he had reached the midsummer of either his years or usefulness, he finished his course on earth, to develop in his heavenly home the powers which gave such glorious promise here.

> "His was the morning hour,
> And he hath passed in beauty from the day,
> A bud—not yet a flower;
> Torn in its sweetness from the parent spray.
> The death wind swept him to his soft repose,
> As frost in spring-time blights the early rose."

"During his protracted illness he suffered much, but realized the promised presence and support of his God. At one time he requested his mother to read for him the one hundred and seventh Psalm. And as she read he emphasized delightfully upon the amazing goodness and mercy of God toward the children of men. At intervals, during his sickness, he manifested a desire to recover, but grace enabled him to submit to the Divine will with becoming fortitude and patience. Never was he heard to murmur for even a single moment. On the Sabbath preceding his death, when he was thought to be dying, he took an affectionate leave of wife, mother, brother, and all friends who were present. When his two little children were brought to him he called them by name, embraced them, and then commended them to that God who had promised to be a 'father to the fatherless.' This was, indeed, a trying time, but it was a season in which the Divine presence and power were gloriously manifested, insomuch that those who were present were constrained to mingle their praises with his, as he shouted aloud, assuring them that his way was clear and his prospects bright for heaven. He requested his early friend, Rev. J. L. Lenhart, to give his love to the New Jersey Conference with the assurance that he was going to rest. He lived several days after this, but was seldom able to speak. When questioned as to his experience and prospects, he answered, generally by signs, that his way was open to the better land, and in his death he left ample ground for hope that he rests from his labors and awaits a blessed resurrection.

He died on Saturday, and on the Sabbath succeeding his remains were borne to their place of interment at Long Branch, followed by the broken-hearted widow and weeping orphans, whose light of life had so suddenly gone down in death. On that same afternoon, in the old church at Long Branch, where fourteen years before, in the tenderness of childhood, under the earnest ministrations of Thomas Stewart, he had found an interest in his Redeemer, lay, in the coldness of death, all that was mortal of the gifted and lamented Maps. The people gathered from all the country round about, and amid the most absorbing interest, his former friend and pastor, Rev. J. L. Lenhart, preached his funeral sermon, after which his body was interred in the beautiful cemetery adjoining the church, where the unceasing requiem of the ocean sighs over his memory, and the spray of the sea bedews the grass which covers his grave.

The Philadelphia Christian Repository said of him, "In his death, the New Jersey Conference has lost one of its brightest ornaments, and maturer years would have ranked him with its most eminent members."

A Trenton paper says, "Mr. Maps possessed a vigorous intellect, a pleasing address, and no inconsiderable share of the fire of genius, while the whole was chastened and adorned by an ardent and consistent piety."

His Presiding Elder, Rev. J. S. Porter, thus speaks of him. "I soon perceived that he possessed more than ordinary abilities for the work of the ministry, and when he had been but four years in the work, and had just graduated to elders' orders, I felt free to recommend his appointment to Morristown, then, as now, one of our most important stations. In that charge he remained two years with credit to himself and profit to the people. His social qualities were good, his preaching talents considerably above mediocrity, while his pastoral habits, and prudence in the administration of Discipline were such as commended him to the Church as one well qualified for the work in which he was engaged."

Rev. L. R. Dunn describes him, as possessing a brilliant imagination, which often made his sermons glow with the most beautiful and gorgeous imagery. Rev. W. P. Corbit says, "He was a burning and a shining light, and his sermons were in demonstration of the Spirit and of power. My whole soul has many times been filled with unutterable horror or unspeakable glory as he described the torments of hell or the transcendent bliss of heaven." Rev. C. H. Whitecar writes a most truthful and eloquent description of his character, which, it is to be regretted, cannot, from the short space allowed by the limits of this work, be inserted entire, and extracts from it would simply mar its beauty.

Brother Maps was a man of commanding appearance. He was tall, slender and erect in person, compact in structure, graceful in movement, and possessed a countenance from which his genial and intellectual nature was openly reflected. His eyes were black and expressive, soft and penetrating, and, when preaching, appeared to flash his meaning into the soul of the hearer. His abundant flow of animal spirits seemed to know no depression. His conversational powers were of a high order, and he was ever the centre of the social circle in which he might happen to be placed. He was said to have been "one of the most affectionate of sons, truest of brothers, kindest of husbands, proudest of fathers and warmest of friends."

As a speaker, it has already been said that he was brilliantly eloquent. The following anecdote of his preaching used frequently to be related by his venerable father. "One day while he was transacting some business in a Bank, the cashier mentioned his name. A few moments after, a stranger, who was standing by, approached and asked him if his name was Maps. On being answered in the affirmative he stated that he was from Philadelphia, and that a young man by that name from New Jersey, had preached, on the previous Sabbath, in that city, in the place of Dr. Durbin, for whom the appointment had been made, but who could not be present. At first the congregation were deeply disappointed in beholding so young a man in the place of the eloquent and revered Doctor, but the feeling soon gave way under the polished and glowing sermon of the youthful preacher, and emotions of admiration and delight were substituted until it was doubtful if the congregation were not pleased with their disappointment." "The written sermons which he has left behind illustrate the possession of a matured mind and extensive knowledge. He was familiar with the best authors, and would quote their language at pleasure. Indeed his memory was so astonishing that he could repeat almost verbatim any sermon that he heard."

In public prayer he had a remarkable gift. In leading the devotions of the people, he seemed to take them *within* the *veil*, and keep their spirits there until the sacred presence could be realized by every believer in the assembly. Language as sweet as his pulpit style was brilliant lent a tenderness to his petitions which it is impossible to describe, while the imbuement of his words with the most melting pathos, bound sentiment, and thoughts in closest unity, and when the Divine Spirit thrilled through these human instrumentalities, the effect was overpowering.

He has now, doubtless passed to that inner glory where his soul so delighted to expand, and tastes the fullness of that rapture whose foretastes were so often enjoyed by him below.

REV. DANIEL PARISH.

A MEEK-SPIRITED, intelligent child is an object of peculiar interest and loveliness. In this respect the case of our subject presents some unusually striking traits. Like Samuel and Timothy, he seems to have escaped the full wreck of the fall, especially the usual sordid feelings and groveling propensities, and from a child to have stood erect, with heaven-ascending aspirations. He had very few early helps. His childhood home was neither blessed with a family altar, nor with the restraining and enlightening presence of religious council and example. No father's voice taught him the sacred truths of religion, no mother's Christian influence distilled upon his young heart, religious sentiments and impressions. He was not even taught to say his prayers, nor did the Sunday-school come in to fill any part of this void. True, his aged grandfather often tried to lead his thoughts through nature up to nature's God, and to interest him with incidents of Bible history, and especially that of the Saviour. But it was with indirect cautiousness of a pious Friend. His mother also took him to church, but it was where every thing was so dead, that no convert was added for fourteen years. Yet from a child he had a nice sense of the pure and sacred, and shrank from contact with the coarse and vulgar. The elevated converse of his grandfather entertained and delighted him, but he had little relish for the childish sports of his playmates. Called of the Lord, as was Samuel, like him, he gave an attentive ear and a prompt response.

He was born at Oyster Bay, Queen's Co., Long Island, April 3, 1799. He says, "My parents, Ambrose and Deborah Parish, did not profess religion. They were persons of high standing in society, and remarkable for good morals. They instructed their children to support a good character, but nothing further."

When about seven years old, he found in his "Youth's Instructor," that immortal verse, "Now I lay me down to sleep," &c. It arrested his attention, and he thus mused: "That is a beautiful prayer; it is right to pray; I will pray that prayer." Thus early, and in this way did he take the first step in an eventful religious life. At first he repeated the prayer after laying his head upon the pillow. This he soon felt to be improper, and, so prayed at his bed-side. In a short time, feeling the need of giving fuller vent to his pent-up soul, he began to proceed "as the Spirit gave him utterance," after repeating the verse. Then he laid aside the form, and uttered to God the words that rose spontaneously from his anxious heart. His widow says, "He was wont to pour out his soul in strong cries and tears, that so disturbed the Quaker stillness of his home, that his kind father said to him gently, one evening, 'My son, can't you try to pray without making so much noise?' This remark gave him great pain, not because he wished to parade his praying, but he took that way to relieve his mind of the concern he felt for the spiritual welfare of the family."

He says, "As soon as I was able to read, I was very much pleased with reading the account of the Saviour's death. I would frequently cry, and express my wonder that the Jews could crucify him. Soon after this, I resolved to read the Bible through. I read five chapters a day. This course I have pursued ever since, with the exception of a little more than one year." This record was made in his 26th year, and his testimony to the advantage thus derived is very emphatic.

How safely the Spirit guides the humble, docile mind! His thoughts had not been made familiar with spiritual subjects. Neither by precept nor example, had he been taught to pray, to read the Bible in course, to kneel in time of prayer, or "pour out his soul in strong cries and tears." The Holy Spirit was his only guide in these several matters.

His early struggles afford some useful lessons. He says. "I had no evidence that I was converted, though I *felt* that I loved God. I would feel happy while reading certain passages of Scripture, which I would write down and put in my pocket." But to his surprise and perplexity, the re-reading of them did not produce the same emotions. Still the repeating of all the passages he could remember, after retiring, he found a useful exercise. Some of the expedients to which his perplexity led him, while they excite a smile, evince singular docility and earnestness. Fixing his gaze on a certain star, he would say, if that shoots, I will take it as an omen of God's favor. At length, while he gazed, his selected star did shoot, but to his great disappointment, there was no change in his feelings. This was but one of many tests tried with like success. In the garret of his father's house, he had a desk, a Bible, and a hymn book. This was his sanctuary, where he spent much time in reading and secret prayer. But his prayer before retiring was audible, and was so remarkable for depth of pathos and fluency of language, that the neighbors frequently collected to hear it. He also says, "I did not mix a great deal with the school-boys, and when I did, I always felt condemned. I would take two or three aside and talk with them on the subject of religion." He further says, "At the age of nine or ten I heard Methodist preaching for the first time, by Wm. Thatcher and Coles Carpenter. I was benefited by their preaching. They made the way so plain that I was encouraged." Not long after this he attended a camp-meeting. He had been told that if any one happened to fall the Methodists would convert him. He stepped cautiously, but did not escape the dire calamity. He says, "Oh how I was frightened. I jumped up, looked every way to see if they were coming, and then ran." But on recovering self-command, he returned and received good impressions.

Between the ages of seven and fourteen he pursued the even tenor of his way with great steadiness and fidelity. Then a crisis in his history was reached. He was placed with an uncle in New York City to learn the tailoring business. He was unwilling to go for fear the change would be unfavorable. Nor were his fears groundless. His surroundings were sadly averse to his feelings and religious interests. His uncle, who was a Universalist, had no sympathy with his religious views. The shop was full of wicked men and boys, who laughed at his seriousness, and taunted him with being a Methodist. Nor could he find any place for secret devotion. Poor boy, his courage failed him. Not only was his *loud* praying silenced, but he says, "I concluded to get into bed, pretend to be asleep and pray there. This course I pursued while I remained. But having lost the form I very soon lost the power. It was no longer a pleasure but a burden to pray. And then I soon indulged in idle conversation, though I never was tempted to swear since I was born." This was the year he neglected to read the Bible. Nor did he attend church, but "strayed about on the Sabbath." He frequently lamented his folly, but having let go his hold on God he was unable to change his course. After a lonely wretched year, while in the street one Sunday, pondering, the Spirit as by an audible voice, pressed these inquiries upon his conscience. "What are you doing? Where are you going?" He was powerfully aroused and greatly distressed. His health and his work were soon so interfered with as to enable him to get permission to visit home. He vowed to the Lord to resume his service if he would open the way for him to remain in the country. His parents saw the bent of his feelings, and acquiesced. Now he stood committed, and promptly began to redeem his vow. This he found no easy task. His relish for spiritual exercises was gone, and three tedious months passed before his suit was gained, and then, not with clear evidence at first.

At this period he dates his conversion, which was in his sixteenth year. Yet he says, "When I was converted I found it was the same that I had felt before going to New York." Doubtless it was the same, and if he was never converted before, it was because he had cherished his initial salvation till he backslid in the city. He now felt it to be his duty to make a public profession, and as his mother was of a Baptist family, his attention was naturally drawn to that church. But he soon found that he did not believe its doctrines, and as there was no Methodist church in reach, he deferred the matter. He says, "I strove in my feeble way to seek the power as well as to keep the form of godliness, and I think I made some little progress in religion." Still he sighed for Christian communion, but did not enjoy it till in his twenty-first year. The family now moved to Belleville, N. J., which event opened a new era in his life. He at once attended the public and social meetings, and entered the Sunday-school. He also examined the discipline, doctrines of the pulpit and usages of the church, with which he was satisfied. His serious demeanor and gifted praying soon attracted attention, and November 17, 1819, Rev. John Potts invited him to join the church. He consented, but wished his baptism to be deferred. This he did to give time for all to be satisfied of his piety.

Heretofore his helps in the Christian life had been very few. Now that they were enjoyed he advanced rapidly. In two months after joining the church, he took charge of a class, and also began to be exercised on the subject of preaching. His attention had been almost entirely confined to one book and one subject. Now he deeply felt the need of greater literary attainments. He was much perplexed, but when fully satisfied that "woe is me if I preach not the gospel," he felt assured that his way would be opened, and that he would be able to attain the necessary qualifications. When this conviction was fully reached, the storm of agitation through which he had passed, subsided, and he calmly awaited the openings of Providence and the call of the church.

On the 6th of August, 1820, an exhorter's license was thrust upon him, and on the 28th he was recommended for license to preach. But before this was conferred, he was sent, by Rev. L. McCombs, Presiding Elder, to New Mills Circuit, with Rev. John Finley, to take the place of Father Vannest, whose health had failed. He received license in December, and also a recommendation to the Philadelphia Conference, to which he was admitted in 1821. He spent one year with Rev. John Creamer on Asbury Circuit, and the next with Rev. R. W. Petherbridge on Hamburg. In 1823 he was ordained a deacon, and appointed to St. George's, Philadelphia, with Revs. Wm. Thatcher and Thomas Burch.

In March, 1823, he renewed his consecration to God, and expressed earnest longings for a higher Christian experience and a fuller unction upon his ministry. He also began to make note of his exercises and other items of interest, not for the public eye, but for his own profit. This unpretending diary is full of holy fervor, earnest self-crimination and deep concern for the glory of God and good of men. Rev. Messrs. Reese and Hannah, delegates from the British, to the coming General Conference, visited the Philadelphia Conference in 1824. Their ministrations were greatly blessed to him, and Bishop George also "preached as if he lived in heaven."

He was now transferred to Baltimore, and stationed at Fell's Point with Rev. Job Guest. Before removing he visited home, and writes, "I experience what I have long known, that the society of my friends cannot make me happy—nothing but religion can do this." On his return he spent a Sunday in Philadelphia. After preaching three times he exclaims, "Truly God was with me. I think he owned me as a minister of his. Oh, that I could always feel as I did yesterday!" At the close of the General Conference which sat in Baltimore, he says, "For several weeks I have preached but little. I find it no advantage to be idle." This was a year of severe trials, occasioned partly by a slight jar with his colleague and partly by small visible fruits. But even these were profitable, for they led to more earnest prayer and watchfulness.

He was ordained elder by Bishop Soule, April 10th, 1825, and sent to Great Falls, with Jacob Larkin. This was a year of much success. One hundred and seventy were added to the Church. He also dwelt much upon the subject of holiness both in the pulpit and the classes, and saw large fruit from this special tillage. He enjoyed more liberty in preaching than he had in the city, which, he says, "made up for the agreeable society I left there."

In 1826 he was placed in charge of Prince George's. This put his loyalty to a severe test. He shrank from taking the charge of a circuit. And then, why need he be torn from the lambs of the flock? And why must he be sent to the southern, sickly part of the state? Nor was the field desirable in other respects. The Church was in a cold state, and he was called to the painful duty of expelling several members. Reports, too, were circulated affecting his character. Referring to these, he says, "But under this I can trust God. I feel no hatred toward those who wish to injure me. I would do them a kindness as soon as others." He also writes, "Oh, the moral desolations of slavery! Oh, the dreadful influences of slavery! A view of it often sinks my spirits. I think slaveholders are the worst of sinners. They have their good things in this life, and their slaves evil. A righteous Judge will give to every man according as his work shall be. O, Lord, have mercy, have mercy!" At the close of the year he retrospects thus, "April 5th, 1827. Yesterday I closed on Prince George's Circuit. During the year I preached one hundred and seventy-five times. Most of the people treated me with great kindness, and I hope some little good has been done. The Lord has been better to me than my fears. I had not thought to see this day."

He was now re-transferred to his old Conference, and sent to Strasburg with Rev. Henry Boehm. When a few miles from Smyrna, the seat of the Conference, he was thrown from his gig and his right foot injured. He was carried back to the house of his hostess, Mrs. Gilmore, whose kind attentions he received from April 20th to May 8th. Then, by the aid of friends, he visited Baltimore and also Great Falls' Circuit. He started, June 13th, for his field of labor, which he found in gratifying contrast with the former. But his situation was most painful. He writes, July 26th, "Yesterday I was assisted to preach twice, and meet about fifty in class. My poor foot continues useless, but I make out to crawl in and out of my gig and to *stand upon my knees and preach.*" One week later he adds, "*During the last eight days I have preached eleven times.*" Do not these items exhibit an almost unequaled display of moral heroism? During the summer he visited Baltimore for medical advice, and was told that time and rest would bring all right. On his return his fractious horse nearly plunged him in a canal. His escape seemed marvelous, and deeply affected him. He ceased to travel during the winter, and Rev. John Nicholson took his place. "To be thus laid aside as useless," was very trying, but, he adds, "I dare not complain. No, I rather wonder that I was ever used at all." During the year he preached ninety-four times. He received every attention that kindness could bestow, and during the winter was furnished a home by a Brother Groff. Soon after leaving there he got word of Sister Groff's death, and hastened to condole with the family. Of her he leaves this memorial: "Such a light was scarcely ever blown out. I never knew one like her."

At the Conference of 1828, after great perplexity, he decided to resume his work, and was stationed in West Chester. During the summer he visited a camp-meeting, at which were unusual displays of Divine power. Concerning it he makes this strange record. "Several Quakers shouted and jumped more extravagantly than any of the Methodists. A preacher among them made the woods ring with her shouts, and leaped, I think, a rod at a time." At the close of the year he reviewed it with much satisfaction. His foot had been less painful than before, though it was still useless. The net increase of the membership was sixteen, and the tone of piety much improved.

While at his father's, in September of this year, the family having returned to Long Island, he and a niece narrowly escaped death by his unruly horse. After praising God for the deliverance, he thus moralizes: "My loss is considerable, (referring to his broken gig,) but I do not feel that as I do the strange unwillingness of my friends to bow down to Christ." Most of his relatives were yet unconverted. But from the rest he could turn to his venerated grandfather, who died February 7th, 1828. "Few live as he lived. I never saw such a man. When I was a child he often talked about religion. With tears in his eyes he would give the history of Daniel, the travels of the children of Israel in the wilderness, and dwell particularly upon the sufferings of Christ. He also gave me a Bible. Perhaps he was the principal instrument in my first convictions. His health, manners, and spirit were remarkable. He was never bled, never took a dose of medicine, and, I may say, was never sick. He lived on vegetables. He abstained from flesh, I believe, that animals might not suffer for him. He never injured any one, and all loved him. Let me live as he lived." This, truly is an enviable memorial.

In 1829 he was stationed in Elizabethtown, N. J. He did not wish to be removed, but bowed uncomplainingly. On first reaching the place his impressions were unfavorable. He says, "The Methodists are gay, and, I fear, deficient in love to God." Yet he speaks of a kind reception and good congregations. In

July he was terribly shaken by the ague, but in the fall his foot was cured in the following remarkable manner. He says, "I was induced to consult Dr. Sweet of Guilford, New England, who in a few minutes did all he wished to do. He said there was a bone out of place, and that he put it back. From the feeling since, I incline to think he did, though I felt hardly any pain. My foot was injured April 20th, 1827, and Dr. S. gave it a twist November 12th, 1829." The doctors told him no bone was displaced, yet he took no natural step for over two years and a half. But after Dr. Sweet *gave it a twist* it got well. Now he saw the hand of God, both in his removal from West Chester and in this strange cure. We also find another cheering entry. "December 22d, On Sunday I preached twice in Morristown. What a work has God wrought! Two years ago but five or six members in the place, now between two and three hundred, and a good meeting-house." The year was not specially prosperous, but his return was largely petitioned for.

In 1830 the Minutes read, "Burlington, Daniel Parish, Wm. A. Wilmer," and the next year, "Daniel Parish, Charles T. Ford." These were eventful years. On the 27th of April, 1830, he was married to Ann Maria Howard, of Long Green, Baltimore Co., Md. At this time his health was so poor that he did not preach for ten weeks, and then only for a short time. In July his wife had a severe attack of dysentery. Then, after a tour for health, some Church trials added much to his affliction. But he was able to resume preaching in September, and a gracious revival began in October, in which he received a large baptism, and his sister Eliza was converted. It continued through the second year, and reached all points on the circuit, except Mount Holly. During this year he was called to mourn the death of a sister, Mrs. Lyon, and to bear the loss of his wife's "dower" by intrigue. Referring to this, he meekly said, "Well, this may be for good also." His own and his wife's health continued feeble, and on the 25th of March he went to Mount Holly to preach his farewell sermon. He says, "Upon rising in the morning I began to raise blood, so I had to disappoint a large congregation."

In 1832 he became supernumerary, and removed to Long

Green, Md. But before going he visited his mother, expecting to witness her death, yet was compelled to leave just before it occurrred. She was happy in God, having been converted late in life. He preached once in May, and not again till December. The hemorrhage, which had ceased in September, returned on the 4th of February, and on the 23d his wife was attacked with it. This deeply oppressed him. He expected to die, but was anxious that she might live to care for their two babes. As this hope waned, despondency, for a time, threw its dark shadow over his spirit.

In 1833 the same relation was continued, but he took charge of the church in Morristown. After getting fairly at his work, he writes, "How is this? I find myself again in the field preaching twice on Sunday, and attending meeting nearly every night." But in November the hemorrhage returned, and his physician insisted upon his taking a sea voyage and a trip south. He yielded to a sense of duty, greatly against his inclination, and sailed for Charleston, S. C., December 2d, where he landed January 3, 1834, slightly improved in health. He was kindly treated, which he fully acknowledges. Yet he felt impelled to make this disparaging entry: "This is a miserably poor, sickly country. I should take the people to be lazy and ignorant. I find them kind, but taken up with politics to the great injury of religion." He sojourned in the city and at different points in the State till April 17th, and then came the entire journey home, on horse-back. He arrived, May 20th, after an absence of five months, partially restored to health.

He now settled in Spring Valley, a few miles from Morristown. He did not preach till August, and then only occasionally through the balance of the year. The next year he took charge of New Providence, with Rev. E. Sanders as a colleague. He met his appointments regularly, but was kept much at home by the failing health of his wife. As her body grew weak, her mind passed under a cloud. The struggle with the tempter was long and painful. But she got a glorious victory August 11th, and then gave up friends and relatives, and joyfully awaited her transfer to heaven, which occurred September 26. The husband was much cast down by this bereavement, but fled for and found refuge under the shadow of the cross. And the light of heaven not only shone in his own heart, but also on the charge in a gracious revival at Union Village.

In 1836 he resumed an effective relation, and was stationed in Paterson. He prosecuted his work steadily till January 30th, when the hemorrhage returned. Yet he so rallied as to be returned the next year. In retrospecting the former year, he says, "Last year we were favored with great prosperity, in both temporal and spiritual things. We have nearly finished a church, fifty by seventy feet, and received one hundred and sixty on trial." The church was dedicated Oct. 5, 1837, and the congregation nearly doubled as they entered the new house. But these were years of wearing toil as well as great success. Meanwhile he found in Miss Eliza G. Bonsal, of Spring Valley, what he much needed—a good companion and mother for his children.

He then spent a year at New Providence and two on Staten Island. The latter were years of great usefulness, especially in building up the church in faith and holiness. This, too, was amongst the pleasantest fields of his ministry. But even here darkening shadows crossed their pathway. A sweet babe was taken by him who said, "Suffer the little children," &c.

Many interesting particulars must be omitted for want of space. In 1841 he was returned to Paterson, but at the end of one month was transferred to the Trenton District, made vacant by Dr. Pitman's elevation to the Missionary Secretaryship. The out-door activities of this position were favorable to his health, which gradually improved. And though no man among us could fill Pitman's place,—and the attempt was no enviable task,—yet, on parts of the District, at least, he was scarcely less popular. His fervent piety, the unction that attended his ministry, his earnest solicitude for the church's welfare, and his agreeable social qualities, commended him to general favor, and rendered his quarterly visits occasions of no ordinary interest.

In 1845 he was placed in charge of Newark District, where he pursued the even tenor of his way for nearly three years. Then, during a quarterly visit to Little Falls, he found that his boot leaked, and fearing the effects of a wet foot, he borrowed one, which chafed his instep. Four days later, while on his way to one of the Newark churches to hold a love-feast, that foot was seized by an acute pain. It soon assumed the form of severe inflammatory rheumatism, but afterward of malignant erysipelas. He suffered extremely for seven weeks. Then mortification began, and amputation was thought to afford the last hope of saving life. The limb was removed, but his reduced strength was not equal to the shock. This occurred April 1, 1848, and in a few hours he was released from suffering, aged forty-nine years, and in the twenty-ninth of his ministry.

During life his varied and severe trials often weighed down his spirits. Now he could say,

> "Not a cloud doth arise to darken the skies,
> Or hide for a moment my Lord from mine eyes."

His widow says, "He possessed his soul in patience, not a murmur escaped his lips. He said, 'The Lord has not left me for a single moment.' He seemed waiting calmly for the heavenly messenger to convey him home. When told that amputation was necessary, he replied, 'I am prepared for the result, and hope my family are.' Nor did he flinch, but remained calm and peaceful under the painful operation. He would say, 'I can only whisper now, but how I will shout when I get up yonder!'" Thus a life of toil and suffering ended in peaceful, holy triumph.

Daniel Parish was respectably connected, but not favored with early advantages. He early learned to read, and soon became a diligent student of the Bible. But neither his school-studies nor after reading-habits took a wide range. His attention was chiefly confined to practical subjects, still he was not deficient in general intelligence, was unusually familiar with the theology of his own church, while his habits of reflection secured to him a good measure of mental discipline. Nature also dealt liberally with him. His mind was well-balanced. his address fluent, his style elevated and generally correct, and his sensibilities formed in the finest mould. His sympathies yearned for the common weal of all mankind, not excepting the down-trodden slave. He was never more in his element than when mingling with and ministering to the sick, distressed, or humble poor. His heart was in every good work. The benevolent enterprises of the Church found in him an earnest advocate, especially the cause of education. And his own lot in youth moved him to aid all young men as far as possible.

His early exercises evince true simplicity and transparency of character. These traits modified his whole life. He never had pet schemes, or personal projects on hand. He deferred marriage several years, for fear of burdening the church. His fields of labor were received with devout gratitude that God used and the people bore with him anywhere. He sought a place at the feet of the humblest, and thought of all hobblers he was the greatest, and that if any preferred him to others, they made a strange choice.

He prayed "without ceasing." Secret prayer, three times a day or oftener; frequently quite protracted, and from which little things could not divert him, was a life-long habit. He also breathed the spirit of prayer and gained the art of acting faith in God from moment to moment. In all this he *talked* with God solemnly, but with boldness and freedom of access.

He was a man of great conscientiousness. The calls of duty as he understood them, he obeyed, and left the result. In this there was neither bluster nor parade, but a firmness that seldom faltered, and a resignation that uttered no complaints. Nor did he fail in little things. He would neither shave, nor blacken his boots on Sunday, he deemed it a breach of faith, not to begin service at the *appointed* time, and especially did he refuse to travel on Sunday when, on his return from the South, Saturday night found him but three hours' ride from a sick wife and loved babes, whom he had not seen for five months. Thus a sense of duty was his guide, regardless of personal sacrifice.

His Christian experience was marked by striking contrasts. "A doubting Thomas," his conquests cost him severe contests. His growth was not rapid, but steady, for however buffeted by Satan, or discouraged with himself, he never let go of Christ. And if he had his gloomy seasons, they were alternated by those of rapturous ecstacy. As life advanced, he became increasingly imbued with the spirit of Christ, a bright example of the efficacy of the atonement to cleanse from all sin. He proclaimed a full salvation with great clearness and power, and though he seldom professed it by name, yet all felt that "he was a good man, full of the Holy Ghost and of faith."

His success was above the average. At several points large revivals attended his labors, while as a peace-maker, and in edifying the church generally, he was uniformly successful. In the pulpit he was easily embarrassed, and sometimes made humiliating failures. But when his thoughts flowed freely and he was favored with the desired unction, he preached with superior ability and "in demonstration of the Spirit and of power." "He being dead yet speaketh."

REV. THOMAS G. STEWART.

ALTHOUGH the subject of this sketch did not enter the itinerant ranks, until he had reached the period of middle life, and death summoned him from labor to reward, before he could have been called an old man, the impress which he left upon the charges to which he was appointed, was so remarkable, that we look for particulars of interest both in his character and history.

Thomas G. Stewart was born near the city of Burlington, N. J., October 30, 1790. On his father's side, his early religious associations were with the Church of England, but his mother, who exerted, perhaps, the greatest influence in his early training, was of the society of Friends. It was his sad loss to be deprived by her death, of the care and council of this devoted parent, while he was yet in his seventeenth year. The new matrimonial alliance which his father soon after contracted, does not seem to have contributed to the domestic comfort or religious culture, of young Thomas; and at the age of nineteen he left the parental roof, to work his own way in the world. After a brief apprenticeship to the woollen cloth manufactory, at the falls of the Schuylkill, heremoved to Cedarville, N. J., to occupy the position of manager in an extensive establishment then located in that place. Here he formed an acquaintance with the lady who subsequently became his wife, Miss Sarah B., daughter of Johnson Reeves, residing near Bridgeton. She was a young lady of more than ordinary intelligence, good sense, and force of character, who proved a helpmeet indeed, "doing him good and not evil all the days of his life." They were united in marriage, December 25, 1810.

In the providence of God, after brief residences, and varying fortunes, in other places, he was led, in the Spring of 1816, to take up his residence in Warren, Ohio. Three years afterward, the religious convictions which had followed him through all his earlier career, were brought to a crisis by an alarming providence and culminated in his conversion. Going into the street in Warren, to inquire concerning a fire that had broken out, he encountered an infidel, with whom he was acquainted. After conversing a few minutes, the man was suddenly seized with apoplexy, and fell dead at his feet. Startled by this unexpected and distressing event, he felt that it became him too, without delay, to prepare to meet his God. Earnestly seeking redemption in the blood of the Lamb, he soon found peace.

He was converted in a Young Men's Prayer-meeting, at which time, his wife, who had been a Christian for many years, entered the room while he was in the midst of his joy, and suggested that he should say something to the sinners who were present. Thus prompted, the first exhortation was delivered, by one from whose lips so many hundreds were afterwards to hear the gospel, as the power of God to their salvation, and like those which came after, it is said to have been distinguished by a warmth and feeling that moved the hearts of all who heard it. The impulses of an earnest nature, baptized by the Holy Ghost, forbade him to be inactive, and he was soon engaged, in the place of his residence and the region round about, endeavoring to move the people to the great subject of salvation. At the outset of his religious life, he united with the Presbyterian Church, of which his wife was a member. But they were both soon convinced that duty called upon them to change their church connection, in order to a fuller harmony of sentiment and greater facilities for usefulness.

The Methodists, whose circuits covered the county in every direction around, had, at this time, a small society at Warren, which they joined in 1821. He was soon appointed a class leader by Rev. Dennis Goddard, and in 1822, received license to exhort from Rev. Charles Elliott, in which position he continued active and useful until 1827.

He had made a visit to his father's house three years previously, during which his example and conversation had been blesed of God to their good. The occasion of his final return from the West, was a summons from his father, on the death of his step-mother, asking him to settle in Burlington. His deep piety, ardent zeal and effective gifts, soon attracted the notice of the authorities of the Church, and instead of being allowed to act in the more humble sphere of an exhorter, quietly in his own neighborhood, he was employed for two years, as a supply on Burlington and Tuckerton circuits. His call was so evidently of God, that in January, 1830, he was licensed to preach, and in the Spring of that year, received on trial by the Philadelphia Conference; New Jersey at that time being a part of its territory. The first appointment made by the Conference was to Pemberton Circuit, a charge consisting of eleven Societies, of which Pemberton was the most important. His residence was at Medford, where the effects of his life and labors were seen in a revival of religion, by which the numbers of that society were increased from seventeen to one hundred and fifty. His colleague was the now venerable Henry Boehm, noted as the traveling companion of Bishop Asbury, and the prudent, faithful and successful Methodist preacher, whose life and usefulness were continued through two entire generations. They labored pleasantly and prosperously together, and were permitted to see a healthful advance in the interests of religion on the charge generally. At a camp meeting held near Vincent-town, the displays of Divine power were very marked, and many look back to that feast of tabernacles, as the time and place of their conversion.

His next appointment was to a field of labor strikingly in contrast with the one which preceded it. Pemberton Circuit had long been the scene of the toils and successes of our ministry; part of it, indeed, was among the first ground occupied by the Methodists in New Jersey, and consequently the community was familiar with her doctrines and usages, while at the same time the societies had acquired strength and numbered in their membership many fathers and mothers in Israel. Here, of course, were sympathizing hearts, ready to enter into the spirit of his labors, and helping hands prepared to provide for his temporal wants. Bergen Neck Mission, to which he was removed, was new territory, in which at that time, it might almost be said, Methodism had scarcely an existence, "no, not so much as to set its foot on." Jersey City, Hoboken, and Fort Lee were the appointments, at all which he found only twenty members. Strong prejudices prevailed also in parts of the charge, so that it was found very difficult to secure a congregation at each place that would average more than from ten to fifteen. Large and influential churches, each sustaining its own minister, are now to be found within what were the limits of the Old Mission. But then it was indeed a "region beyond," where the "sect was everywhere spoken against," and its ministers found but few friends. Still the fervor of Mr. Stewart could not be chilled even in this cold region, and he went in and out among the people, "testifying of the gospel of the grace of God," in a way that was not without its good effects. Communipaw, at which place there was a class of living Christians, was added to the appointments on the charge, and other places also were taken up. A series of evening meetings in Jersey City was owned of the Lord in the conversion of a number of souls, and the year was closed with evidences that the servant of the Lord "had not run in vain, neither labored in vain."

At the succeeding Conference he was ordained a deacon, and sent to Freehold Circuit, which at this time was of almost primitive dimensions. Four hundred miles were to be traversed in going round it, which required three weeks of heavy toil, to be followed by a week of rest. But the soul of our evangelist was as large as his field of labor, through the length and breadth of which he traveled with a zeal and ardor that never flagged. His colleague the first year was Rev. David Bartine, a man of eminent ability as a close logical preacher, to whom, with his fiery nature in exhortation and appeal, Mr. Stewart was an invaluable adjunct. At the close of the year, the summing up of the result showed that some seven hundred had been converted. The great enlargement of the work compelled a re-arrangement of the plan of the charge, and Freehold was made a six weeks' circuit, with three preachers. The state of Mr. Bartine's health led to his taking a supernumerary relation, at the Conference in 1833, and Revs. James Long and Mulford Day became Mr. Stewart's colleagues. All of these holy men have since passed away from earth to the heavenly glory, where, doubtless, they together magnify the Redeemer's grace for what they were permitted to see and enjoy on old Freehold Circuit. Under the new arrangement good results were reached, though not equaling those of the glorious year preceding. Three hundred, however, were added to the communion, and all the societies were greatly strengthened. Long Branch, one of the principal appointments, had grown to such magnitude, that it was now constituted a station. Neither Freehold nor Red Bank had any Methodist organization or regular preaching by our denomination until they were taken on the plan of the circuit during the first of these years, and in each place a blessed revival resulted in the establishment of a permanent society.

Tuckerton Circuit, covering what are now several charges, was his field of labor for the succeeding two years. During the first, he was laid aside for a season by a hemorrhage, brought on by excessive exertion at a camp-meeting at Bargaintown. He preached on each of four successive days, and with an energy, too, that taxed all his powers. At the close of the meeting, quite hoarse, exhausted, and sick, he found that even his great capacity for physical endurance had its limits. As soon, however, as Providence permitted, he was at his work again, and even before his physician allowed him to preach a full sermon, he visited his appointments, telling the people in a few sentences of the power of the gospel. An incident in connection with this charge will show that beyond his own denomination he commended himself as a faithful servant of God. A Friends' meeting-house at Bass River, which was not occupied on Sunday evenings, was tendered to the Methodists till they could erect a church of their own. Here he preached again and again "in demonstration of the Spirit and of power." Thus the disciples of George Fox and the followers of John Wesley united together in upbuilding the Redeemer's kingdom. At other points, also, the work of the Lord prospered, and at the close of the disciplinary term, he found it trying to part with a people whose numbers and piety had steadily grown under his ministry.

On Crosswicks circuit he now spent a happy and prosperous year. The hand of God was evidently with him, and the churches under his care, "walking in the fear of the Lord, and in the comfort of the Holy Ghost, were multiplied."

The next Spring the first session of the New Jersey Conference was held at Newark. He was now appointed to New Egypt. As this charge had formed part of the Pemberton Circuit, when he traveled it six years before, he was returned to a people he had once served. But "a good man, full of the Holy Ghost and of faith," does not exhaust his usefulness in a short time, and this appointment proved to be of the Lord. Sinners were converted in considerable numbers, and especially from among the children of the established members of the Church. And believers were so stimulated by his preaching and example, that they earnestly pressed forward after holiness of heart. New Egypt, Wrightstown, Imlaystown, Cookstown, and other places, all felt the impulse of the blessing of the Lord, upon the efforts of this faithful herald of the cross.

For several successive years Mr. Stewart had been laboring on a belt of territory stretching well across the centre of the State, from the ocean to the Delaware river, on circuits lying almost contiguous to each other. And as he now reviewed this broad field, he could say of many, "The seal of mine Apostleship are ye in the Lord." He had gone in and out among the people, a man of one work, and in the face of the toils, trials and difficulties incident to the life of a faithful itinerant, had evinced the spirit of him who said, "None of these things move me, neither count I my life dear unto myself, so that I might finish my course with joy, and the ministry, which I have received of the Lord Jesus, to testify the gospel of the grace of God." No wonder that he lived in their hearts, and was followed on his departure, by their tears and prayers. To this day many speak of the time he spent among them, "as years of the right hand of the Most High."

He was now to spend another succession of years, on a number of adjacent appointments, in a different part of the State. The Spring of 1839 found him the preacher in charge of Cumberland Circuit, on the lower District in the Conference. With the exception of Bridgeton and portion west of the Cohansey, the circuit covered the whole of Cumberland County and a part of Cape May. On its North-west boundary lay Salem Circuit, to which he was sent after two years, and at the close of this term, took charge of Swedesboro, which lay next in order. Methodism had been early introduced, and long established through this region, and was then as it is now, the controlling form of religion, in most of its territory. Within it was the birth-place, both natural and spiritual, of Benjamin Abbott, and here had been put forth many of the most successful efforts of this wonderful man of God. In intense earnestness of soul, in that remarkable unction which attended his preaching and in the success that followed, Mr. Stewart largely resembled him. Taken together, perhaps, no six years of his ministry were more agreeable to himself than these. Though beginning to feel the advance of years, and the effects of toil, in the main his health was firm ; the charges were strong in numbers and well supplied with active and influential official boards ; his family was surrounded by kind friends and a pleasant community ; his colleagues were such men as Crouch among the dead, and Raybold among the living; and wherever he went "the hand of the Lord was with him, and a great number believed and turned unto the Lord." Indeed so greatly were many of the appointments strengthened by accessions, that charges were divided and sub-divided, at the time, or soon after his leaving them. Among the stations dating their origin about this period, are Millville, Cedarville, Penn's Neck and Pittsgrove. Bright, however, as was the state of things in the main, even here, he was reminded in a powerful manner, that this is not our rest. Jan. 2, 1843, while the family resided at Allowaystown, on Salem circuit, his son Joseph died, and in August of the following year, Martha, his third daughter, followed her brother. A pulmonary disease was the destroyer in both cases. Insidious was its approach, and rapidly did it do its work, leaving the stricken survivers to mourn over the desolation it had wrought. In both cases, however, religion displayed its power, enabling this good man to see in his own family how it can sustain in nature's great extremity.

Leaving Swedesboro in 1845, he was sent to Moorestown with Rev. Rodney Winans as a colleague, and was returned the next year with Rev. Wm. R. Rogers and John I. Morrow as assistants. This was his last appointment. Faithfully did he perform his work, and here, as elsewhere, many souls were given to his ministry. But another daughter followed her brother and sister to the grave, and at the close of the term he found himself compelled to ask for rest.

Eighteen years had now elapsed since he entered the traveling connection, during the whole of which time he had been in labors more abundant. Restricted to the State of New Jersey in the sphere of his movements, he traversed a large portion of its more southerly teritory, and that garden of Methodism was largely increased in productiveness by his zealous and divinely sanctioned labors in its tillage. In the revivals where he labored, about five thousand souls had been received into the Church, the piety of the membership greatly promoted, and every charge handed over to his successor in a better condition than when he entered upon it. These results were attributable, under God, to a faithful use of natural, combined with such acquired gifts, as his few early advantages and his limited opportunities for self-improvement, enabled him to secure. He studied, not in "the schools of the prophets," but the Bible and man, and preached the gospel, "not in the words which man's wisdom teacheth, but which the Holy Ghost teacheth." Perhaps never, than in him, was a more life-like illustration given of the lines of Charles Wesley.

> "The love of Christ doth me constrain,
> To seek the wandering sons of men;
> With cries, entreaties, tears, to save,—
> To snatch them from the gaping grave."

Carried away himself by his great theme, he often carried away his audience with him. Young and old, rich and poor, both sexes and all classes, felt, and confessed they felt, his power. Nor were the converts under his ministry altogether from the illiterate and obscure. Refinement, intelligence, and position, in many cases, marked the character and condition of those who gratefully acknowledged themselves among his spiritual children.

It was not possible for the active spirit of Mr. Stewart, even after he had retired from the effective ranks, to be content without employment, and, though a supernumerary after the

Conference of 1847, he continued to preach and travel considerably. In some cases the importunities of friends led him to overlook the dictates of prudence, but it was with him, as he said to a friend, when he had been prevailed upon to preach three times in one day, "Ask me," said he, "to do anything but preach, and I have the power to decline; but to refuse standing in a place where all my desires are centred, towards which an irresistible force moves me, and I can only be passive."

His last sermons were preached in Burlington, and the text of the final one, "The time is short," in view of the fact that he died in about two weeks after preaching from it, was very significant. On Friday, January 14th, 1848, he was attacked by Pleurisy, at the house of Rev. C. H. Whitecar, then stationed in that place. He repaired to his home in Bordentown, but the disease did not abate except at intervals. Before leaving Burlington he said to Mrs. Whitecar, "When I am sick I investigate my spiritual condition, to see whether, if God should call me, I am prepared to stand before him and give an account of the deeds done in the body. I am not fearful but that it is now well with me. I believe an abundant entrance will be ministered to me, into the everlasting kingdom of our Lord and Saviour Jesus Christ."

On Friday, the 21st, he suddenly became worse, his disease assuming a typhoid character. From this time his mind wandered. On Saturday and Sunday he was unconscious nearly all the time, and at two o'clock in the afternoon of the next day, his spirit took its flight. His last intelligible words were, "All is well." His funeral sermon was preached by Rev. John S. Porter, from Acts xi. 24: "He was a good man, full of the Holy Ghost and of faith, and much people was added to the Lord;" a most appropriate theme.

"Servant of God, well done!
Thy glorious warfare's past;
The battle's fought, the race is won,
And thou art crowned at last."

REV. VINCENT SHEPHERD.

As no responses to the requests of the committee, for information concerning him, have been received from his relatives, the writer is compelled to present the following meagre sketch, as *all* that can be given of a man eminently worthy of an extended memoir.

Rev. Vincent Shepherd was born in the town of Wantage, Sussex Co., New Jersey, in October, 1808.

His early days were spent amid the magnificent scenery of his native hills, which no doubt fostered a seriousness of mind that was ever afterward a marked characteristic of both the man and his ministry. In his youthful days, under the preaching of the venerable Benjamin Griffin, he was led to give his heart to God and connect himself with the church. Of this devoted minister Brother Shepherd always spoke in terms of endearing appreciation as his spiritual father.

The consistency of life manifested by Brother Shepherd, his warm interest in souls, together with marked abilities in public addresses, induced the church to license him in his twenty-fourth year as an exhorter. He was so abundant in labors, and his gifts improved so rapidly, that in six months more, they accorded him the honored and useful position of a local preacher among them. It was but a short time after this, that the indescribable urging, which the Holy Spirit presses upon those it calls to the ministry, came upon him, and the duty of an entire consecration to the work, became a certain conviction, and in a brief period after his license as a local preacher, he was received on trial in the Philadelphia Conference, and appointed to Milford Circuit. His year of labor here was successful, and the rapid developement of his abilities gave large promise of future usefulness. At the ensuing conference he was appointed to "Essex," then numbered among the prominent circuits. He labored here with zeal and assiduity, leaving behind him the impression of an earnest and devoted minister. In 1835 he was admitted into full connection in the Conference, ordained a Deacon by Bishop Emory, and appointed to Rockaway, where he endeavored to improve both his time and abilities in his Divine work. In 1836, he crossed the state lines, and spent a year toiling for the *Master* in the large and important town of Easton. In 1837 he again crossed the state lines into Delaware, and was stationed in Smyrna. In 1838 he was transferred to the New Jersey Conference, and appointed to Plainfield, where he remained two years preaching with great acceptability and usefulness to the people of that town. In 1840 he was sent to Belvidere. While here he was united in marriage to Miss Susan Dwight, of Dudley, Mass., a lady eminently qualified to assist him in the work to which he had pledged his life. Her companionship and tender sympathy during the rest of his career was invaluable to him, cheering the natural seriousness of his character, and brightening the despondency to which he was occasionally subject. His appreciation of her was commensurate with her worth, and the gentle deference of his manner to her gave ample proof of the regard in which she was held by him. This lady still survives him, and resides in Brooklyn.

In 1841 he occupied the important station of New Brunswick. In 1842-3 he labored in Jersey City. During his administration in this place he supervised the interests of the society at Bergen, Five Corners, and it was largely through his efforts that a church was built in that place and the influence of Methodism rendered permanent. Dr. Hornblower, a nephew of the late Chief Justice of that name, attended his preaching, and often spoke of the influence exercised upon the community by the gentlemanly demeanor and pulpit abilities of Brother Shepherd. In 1844-5 he was stationed in Rahway, where his health, naturally feeble, and rendered more so by his studious habits, gave way entirely, and he was compelled to take a supernumerary relation. He removed to Jersey City, where he lingered until July 1st, 1848, when, under the power of a sudden attack of apoplexy, he left the earth for heaven.

In person, he was slender but symmetrical. His countenance, grave and solemn, left upon all who came in contact with him, an impression of spirituality and holiness. His bearing was always that of a refined and cultivated man, and his conversation deeply and gravely religious. In pastoral habits and usefulness he had few superiors. In diligent study he might rank as a model. His preaching abilities were above the average, and secured him prominence of position. His spirit was progressive, and adopted the improvements of the age as necessities in the advancement of the Church, and, altogether, he ranked as a workman that needed not to be ashamed.

The following estimate of his character is from the pen of Rev. J. S. Porter, D. D.: "He was a good man and a good minister of the Lord Jesus. His talents were above mediocrity, his attainments respectable for his opportunities, and, had his health been sufficient to have borne close application, and his life been prolonged, he would have taken a high position in our Church and ministry. When we were associated in the work, I found him a true man and valuable fellow-laborer, in whose hands the work prospered."

This estimate of his character was that of all who knew him, and, while in his transition from earth, the heavenly mansions gained another occupant, the vineyard here lost a valuable laborer.

REV. JOHN WALKER.

On the walls of many of the dwellings in the southern part of New Jersey, is the likeness of a man whose thin and furrowed visage, show him to have been far advanced in years when it was taken. But the bright eye still beams with the fires of earlier days, and the lines about the mouth, and lower part of the face, indicate a character in which decision and energy have been strongly marked. This is the likeness of Rev. John Walker, one of the many venerable men who still lingered among the veterans of the itinerancy, and reflected honor on the New Jersey Conference, of which they were members and to which they were spared for some time after its organization. Of Faither Walker, the following sketch has been prepared by one who had every opportunity to know him well, and whose admiration and affection were strengthened and deepened by the intimacy and extent of that knowledge.

John Walker was born in Burlington County, N. J., Dec. 14, 1764. His parents both died when he was young, and left him, (an only son,) to the care of four elder sisters. At the age of fourteen he was apprenticed to the shoe-making business, in Mount Holly. In his nineteenth year, and during his residence in this place, he was converted to God, and joined the Methodist Episcopal Church. At the age of twenty-one he was licensed to preach, and sustained that relation to the local ministry with acceptability and usefulness. Sept. 28, 1788, he was married to Miss Mary Lees, a worthy member of the same church. Removing to Philadelphia about the year 1795, he continued to exercise his gifts, both as class leader and local preacher. In the year 1802, having been recommended to and received by the Philadelphia Conference, he entered upon life in the itinerancy. At this time a preacher with a family had to endure many privations and make large sacrifices, as the provision, in a pecuniary point of view, was scanty in the extreme. The circuits were of great extent, and rides long and wearing, which for many years Mr. Walker performed on horse-back, often preaching every day in the week, and three times on the Sabbath, besides meeting the classes. At the Conference held in Soudersburg, Pa., May, 1804, he was ordained a deacon by Bishop Asbury, and an elder, by the same Bishop, at the Conference of 1806, held in Philadelphia. His parchments which certify to these ordinations, have been carefully preserved as precious relics of the past.

Although Mr. Walker did not fully enter upon his great life-work till in his thirty-eighth year, yet he continued to go through the toils, privations and hardships of an effective traveling preacher, for thirty-three consecutive years. He served the following charges: 1802, Trenton, N. J.; 1803, Flanders; 1804 and 1805, Salem; 1806, Chester, Pa.; 1807, Bristol; 1808, Philadelphia; 1809, Chester; 1810 and 1811, Lancaster; 1812, Bristol and Northampton; 1813, Smyrna, Del.; 1814, Dauphin, Pa.; 1815, Trenton, N. J.; 1816, Gloucester; 1817 and 1818, Salem; 1819 and 1820, Burlington; 1821 and 1822, New Mills; 1823 and 1824, Freehold; 1825 and 1826, Trenton; 1827 and 1828, Salem; 1829 and 1830, Bargaintown; 1831 and 1832, Camden; 1833 and 1834, Swedesboro. About this time his health became very much enfeebled, not only from increasing age, he having passed beyond the Psalmist's limit of three-score yers and ten, but also owing to severe suffering, endured for many years, from a painful disease; and in the spring of 1835, he reluctantly consented to have his relation changed from effective to supernumerary, in which he continued to the end of life.

He never asked for or refused an appointment, but always cheerfully went, wherever the authorities saw proper to send him, only praying in the name of the Lord, for success in winning souls to Christ. His whole soul was in the work of his Master, and he never failed to secure the love and confidence both of the people and his brethren in the ministry. He loved the preachers; indeed his large and benevolent heart embraced all mankind. But to the preachers, and especially those of the New Jersey Conference, he was ardently attached. He never forgot them in his prayers, frequently mentioning name after name, in his supplications at the blood-sprinkled throne of grace.

January 15, 1833, he was called to endure a severe trial,—the death of his beloved wife. She had been the companion of his joys and sorrows upwards of forty-four years. Converted to God in her sixteenth year, she had attached herself to the M. E. Church in Mount Holly, then in its infancy. Always walking worthy of the profession she made,

> "None knew her but to love her,
> None named her but to praise."

Dying of consumption, she suffered long and much, but her mind was calm, clear, full of confidence in and submission to God, and the closing scene of her life was one of glorious triumph.

At this time he and his daughter Mary Ann, took up their residence in an humble little cottage-home at Clarksboro, Gloucester County, N. J. This resting place for the weary, he called "The Pilgrim's Retreat." Here he kept a little chamber, a bed, a table, a stool and a candlestick, for his friends, who, from time to time, would call and spend a night or two with him. He always welcomed them with the warmth of a truly benevolent heart, and with a sincere friendship, shared with them the best he had.

In this pleasant retreat he spent the balance of his days, but not in inglorious ease. His zeal for God and his cause continuing unabated, he preached and held meetings, even beyond his strength. He took his regular appointments on the plan of the circuit with the local preachers, often meeting two engagements on the Sabbath, besides preaching frequently at funerals. When urged by his presiding elder to desist from so much labor, he said, and his eye sparkled with divine love while he said it, "Brother Neal, God gave me a commission to preach the gospel, many years ago, and he has not taken it from me. He blesses me and the people whenever I attempt it. While he gives me strength of body and blesses my soul in the work, I believe it to be my duty to labor, and I dare not refrain. Through his grace sustaining me I expect to continue till he calls me home."

He preached his last sermon in Clarksboro, Sept. 10, 1848, from the words, "But if we walk in the light, as he is in the light, we have fellowship one with another, and the blood of Jesus Christ his Son cleanseth us from all sin." He loved holiness, and preached it by his life as well as in the pulpit.

A few days after preaching the above-mentioned sermon, he fell and injured his hip so seriously, that he never walked afterward. He now suffered extremely, and for nearly seven months languished on a bed of severe affliction and pain. Yet when he could no longer *do* the will of God, he calmly submitted to *suffer* that will, with a truly Christian patience and meekness. Still, the trial was very great, and he had frequently to pray for sustaining grace. Often he would say, "It takes more grace to *suffer* than to *do*, but blessed be the Lord, I can say, 'Thy will be done,' it is all right, he knows just what to do with me, my confidence is strong in the Lord, his promises are all yea and amen in Christ Jesus. I trust in nothing I have done, but clinging to my precious Saviour, I rest on the atonement he has made. I am a sinner saved by grace. Glory to God, for victory over the fear of death, hell and the grave."

Through all his affliction, he was never known to murmur, but with holy joy, would look forward to the time of his release. He was ready winged for his upward flight. Yet with Job, he would say, "All the days of my appointed time will I wait till my change come." Sometimes for hours together, he would appear absorbed in deep meditations and lost to all below. On one of these occasions, his devoted daughter, laying her hand on his head, said, "Papa, what is thee thinking about?" Opening his eyes, while his countenance beamed with delight, he said with great emphasis, "I am thinking about heaven and the blood-washed company before the throne." Conversing, one day, with one of his friends and admirers, he was drawn out to speak of some of the hardships and privations he had endured on the first circuits he traveled. But suddenly stopping and looking his friend full in the face, he said, "My dear Brother Shaw, I put no dependence in anything I have ever done or suffered, in the cause of my Lord and Master.

'In my hand no price I bring
Simply to the Cross I cling.'

Jesus is my great high priest. He has made an all-sufficient atonement, and it is the consolation derived from the precious gospel, I have so long tried to preach to a perishing world, that sustains me now. Oh, I would like to have the privilege of proclaiming that glad news once more!" and added, with energy, "I would like to give the devil's kingdom one more stroke." After a pause he further said, "But my work is done, and I must die;" and, with rapture kindling in his eye, he added, "I am not afraid to die. Glory to God, the Judge is my friend, yes, *my* judge, *my* friend. Glory, glory, glory!"

A few days before his death, Rev. Mulford Day, preacher in charge on the Circuit, and his faithful friend, called upon him, and after some profitable conversation, said, "Father Walker, what shall I tell the preachers at Conference?" With much animation, he said, "Tell them I am going to heaven; there is no doubt of that; no, not a doubt. I am going to heaven." He also said to Brother Day, "My sufferings are great, but they will soon be over. Oh, how gladly would I exchange time for eternity!"

His sun set without a cloud. To him death was a kind angel, that opened the gates of bliss. He calmly laid his head on Jesus' breast, and without a struggle, a groan, or even a sigh, sweetly breathed his life out there, about one o'clock, on Thursday morning, April 5th, 1849. His funeral took place on the following Sabbath afternoon, when an immense concourse of friends and acquaintances, from ten to fifteen miles around the country, convened together. A very appropriate sermon was preached by his long-loved and kind friend, Rev. John K. Shaw, the Presiding Elder of the district, from the words, "To die is gain."

He left five children and twenty-two grandchildren to mourn their loss. He was buried in the grave-yard attached to the

Methodist Episcopal Church in Clarkesboro. On the top of the humble stone which marks the place of his interred remains, is carved the figure of a flying angel blowing a trumpet, and underneath this the inscription, "Not dead, but sleepeth." Rev. John Walker departed this life, April 5th, 1849, in the eighty-fifth year of his age. He was sixty-three years a member, and fourty-seven years an itinerant minister, in the M. E. Church. Ardent in zeal, abundant in labors, and emniently successful in winning souls to Christ.

"Servant of God, well done!
Thy glorious warfare's past;
The battle's fought, the race is won,
And thou art crowned at last."

On his grave the Summer rose sheds its fragrance, the evergreen myrtle creeps silently, entwining itself among the graves, and the weeping-willow at the head, bends its graceful branches to the breeze, all planted by the hand of bereaved affection.

"'Tis a happy thought that our loved and lost,
Forever are hovering nigh;
That they kindly would all our footsteps lead,
To the home of the blest on high."

An extract from the Conference Obituary, showing the estimation in which he was held by his brethren at the time of his death, must close this memoir. "Since our last Conference one of the fathers has fallen asleep. The aged, the venerable, the beloved Father Walker is no more. A volume might be written concerning the excellencies of our dear departed friend. As a man, he was universally beloved. He loved everybody, and everybody loved him. As a Christian, his piety was deep and genuine. He possessed much of the spirit of the beloved John, whose name he bore. As a preacher, he was plain, simple, and unadorned. 'Jesus and the resurrection' was his constant theme. As a minister of the New Testament, he was successful in winning souls. He was in labors more abundant, not only while in health and strength, but in old age and infirmities. He did not think that because he was a supernumerary, his work was done, but even during his last year on earth continued to fill his appointments till he was disabled. The past, the present, and the future all smiled upon him; and when his work was done, like Paul the aged, he looked back upon his life with pleasure, and forward with joy; exclaiming, 'I am now ready to be offered and the time of my departure is at hand. I have fought a good fight, I have finished my course, I have kept the faith; henceforth there is laid up for me a crown of righteousness.' His reward will be great, his crown bright; for 'they that be wise shall shine as the brightness of the firmament, and they that have turned many to righteousness, as the stars forever and ever.'"

REV. RICHARD LANNING.

"How beauteous are their feet
Who stand on Zion's hill,—
Who bring salvation on their tongues,
And words of peace reveal!"

RICHARD LANNING was born in the beautifully-undulating county of Sussex, N. J., on the 13th day of June, 1809. Remote from church privileges, and the blessed advantages of the Sabbath-school, he enjoyed in the very beginning that which is of unspeakable value to every child, the prayers and councils of pious parents. These produced impressions so deep and holy, that at the age of eighteen he gave his heart fully to God. His religious experience was at once clear, and his renewed life so consistent, that when twenty-one years of age, he was licensed to exhort. How often his native hills echoed with his voice, as in school-house and cabin he urged sinners to flee from the wrath to come, we may not know; but we are well assured he was faithful in this work, for in 1833 the Church enlarged the sphere of his usefulness, and gave him authority to preach the gospel.

In those days Rev. M. Force was Presiding Elder on Asbury District, and finding Brother Lanning, whose young wife had just been torn from his side by death, cast down, yet intelligent and zealous, employed him, in 1835, as a supply on Hamburg Circuit.

In 1836, he was received on trial by the Philadelphia Conference, and appointed with Abraham Gearhart to Asbury, a circuit numbering about five hundred members, and of considerable influence and financial strength. The word of God, as uttered by these devout men in that region of country, was quick and powerful, and accomplished that whereunto it was sent.

The New Jersey Conference became a separate organization in 1837, and Rev. Sedgwick Rusling and Richard Lanning were appointed within its bounds to Newton, another large and important circuit, in Sussex County. Here Brother Lanning labored one year, and was then placed in charge of Milford station, on the west bank of Delaware River, in Pennsylvania.

In this field his labors were more circumscribed, and he had larger opportunities for those intellectual pursuits in which his mind so greatly delighted, and for which he had such an intense thirst. These opportunities were so perseveringly improved, that when he left Milford, not only was his own mind greatly enlarged and strengthened, but the church also was much benefited by his diligent course of study. His class-mates and committees of examination acknowledged his intellectual power, and readily pronounced him first in the class with which he graduated.

In 1839 he was stationed at Bloomfield, a beautiful village a few miles west of Newark.

Milford and Bloomfield were both small stations, too weak financially to support men with families, yet they were of such importance as to require the best talent amongst the young men of the conference, and the appointment of Brother Lanning to these fields is proof of the high estimate placed upon his ministerial abilities.

While stationed at Bloomfield, he was married the second time, and Miss Harriet Pitts, of Orange Co., N. Y., became his wife, who was a devoted, affectionate, and sympathizing companion.

Leaving Bloomfield, he was appointed in 1840–41 to Nyack, N. Y. Nothing could have been more congenial to a cultivated mind than the beautiful scenery of this romantic place. The towering hills on the north, between Nyack and Haverstraw—the noble Hudson, spread like a vast sheet of molten silver beneath the sun—villages and princely mansions, sleeeping in the hazy distance on the farther shore—the scores of steam and sailing vessels dashing proudly on their way, to or from the distant city—were all calculated to inspire exalted sentiments, while the quiet of the village itself gave ample opportunity for cherishing those sentiments, which, incorporated with the blessed teachings of the Bible, would make him a wiser man and a better minister.

The Church felt the influence of such exalted thoughts, and his well-prepared discourses advanced it in knowledge and Christian holiness.

In 1842 he was sent to Rome and Wantage, and in 1843, to Belvidere, where his health so far failed that he became a supernumerary, and his disease, a bronchial affection, continuing to increase, he remained in such relation to the close of life.

In the spring of 1846 he removed his family to Trenton, where he was known as a man of sweet spirit, modest pretensions, and unimpeachable integrity. His whole life inspired confidence in the genuineness of his piety. His religion was more than form, —it was the "love of God shed abroad in the heart, by the Holy Ghost given unto us." The means of grace were a special joy to his heart. The songs of Zion—the voice of prayer—the class-meeting—the love-feast, the word of God, read or expounded,—the sacrament of the Lord's Supper—Christian fellowship—every form of religious service gave him great delight. Often while engaged in the house and worship of God, his lips would exclaim,

> "My willing soul would stay
> In such a frame as this,
> And sit and sing herself away,
> To everlasting bliss."

Residing, the latter part of his life, in the extreme suburbs of the city, remote from the church, he was often deprived of its holy privileges. This was much regretted, as the privation, in connection with his physical debility, sometimes produced mental depression. But a visit from a Christian friend, religious conversation, singing, and prayer, would soon revive his desponding spirit, and his heart again was glad.

He was much afflicted, but afflictions are not in vain; even trials and sorrows have their mission, and if properly received, will not only wean us from this world to which we are so often unduly attached, but will bring our hearts to such a condition, as under the Spirit's influences promotes purity, even as the fire purifies the silver. Then, let us hail afflictions, when divinely sent, not as stern expressions of a Father's anger, but as handmaids of the Lord, effectually working together for our good. Such was their influence with him. As time rolled on, his rapid approach to the grave became more and more evident.

On Saturday morning, January 5th, 1850, he was not able to rise from his bed, and complained of great weakness. Two or three times through the day he found it very difficult to breathe. The night was one of severe physical suffering, but his mind was unclouded. About midnight it was thought he was dying, and his children were called up to receive his parting blessing. He kissed them, bade them farewell, and, laying his cold hands upon their heads, commended them to their heavenly Father for protection. His companion then asked him if his way was clear. In a whisper, he replied, "All is right; God is my rock, I trust in the atonement." Looking up to his physician, he said, "If I am to die to-night it will be a solemn hour, but I die in peace with God, and all mankind." At a later period, looking at his sorrowing companion, he said, "O, my dear, weep not for me! I shall soon be at home, I am almost over the stormy banks, we shall be parted but a little while, we will soon meet in our Father's kingdom to separate no more." Just before he took his flight from earth, she asked him if Jesus was precious. He immediately replied, "Oh, yes! Jesus is precious, precious, precious." And thus, at five o'clock, on Sabbath morning, January 6th, 1850, he fell asleep in the arms of that Jesus whom to the very last he found so precious to his soul, leaving, in this valley of tears, a widow and three children to mourn his loss.

Brother Lanning was a man of great natural diffidence, and of retiring habits. He was, therefore, easily embarrassed, either publicly or privately, in the presence of strangers, and yet, of such strength of mind, that when he had carefully examined a subject, was fearless, even to boldness, in its presentation. He was capable of great mental efforts, and in Sussex County, during the second year of his ministry, waxed so mighty in controversy, that strong men of opposing theological views, feared to enter the arena with him, though publicly invited so to do. But a frail body prevented much mental toil, and when the immediate occasion, which called forth his energies, had passed away, he would shrink from view almost with the timidity of a child.

He was an excellent preacher. His sermons abounded in rich thought, manly argument, and appropriate illustration. He instructed and profited his hearers. His, too, was a blessed experience—he lived well, and died well.

> "Oh! may we all like him believe,
> And keep the faith and win the prize;
> Father prepare and then receive
> Our hallowed spirits to the skies,
> To chant with all our friends above,
> Thy glorious, everlasting love."

REV. WILLIAM R. ROGERS.

"How sweetly flowed the gospel sound,
From lips of gentleness and grace,
While quiet listeners gathered round.
And joy and reverence filled the plaee."

WILLIAM READING ROGERS, was born at Pemberton, Burlington County, N. J., on the 20th of September, 1817. His parents, James and Mary Rogers, were members of the M. E. Church, and brought up their son in the fear of the Lord, who at the early age of twelve years, gave his heart to God, and became an experimental Christian.

From the commencement of his religious life, his piety was deep and ardent, which, together with the natural amiability of his disposition, arrested the attention of the Church, and drew forth predictions that he would be called to the work of a gospel minister. Soon, it was found his mind was laboring with convictions of duty in that direction, and these predictions were fullfilled. But never, perhaps, was a young man more timid, or distrustful of his own abilities, called to that important work; and, but for the stern conviction, "Woe is me if I preach not the gospel," it is very certain he never would have attempted to lift up his voice in public: and when he did consent to do so, it was with the utmost fearfulness and trembling.

In 1834, his father resided at Medford, and Rev. Abraham Owen had charge of the circuit. William, who was now about seventeen years old, was at school in Philadelphia, but, spending his vacations at home, would frequently, during these times accompany the preacher in charge to his appointments around the circuit; but it was only after much solicitation that he could be induced to take even the smallest part in the public exercises. Finally, however, Brother Owen succeeded in getting him to deliver his first exhortation.

Three years after this, in 1837, Rev. T. Neal, Presiding Elder of Camden District, called him to fill a vacancy on Salem Circuit, with Rev. Charles T. Ford, preacher in charge. While on this circuit, his natural timidity, and strong tendency to doubt and discouragement, so nearly overcame him, that he was on the point of giving up the work, to which God had evidently called him. He and his colleague were holding an extra meeting. Brother Rogers had preached, and urged upon the impenitent the importance of a speedy return to God. But after the united efforts of Brother Ford and himself, there being no signs of contrition anywhere in the congregation, he concluded probably it was owing to him—that he stood in the way, or was not an acceptable ambassador for Christ; and he then and there decided to quit the field. With such decision in his mind, he was walking gloomily to his lodgings. It had been raining, and was a dismally dark night, so dark that objects could not be distinguished. Suddenly he came up close to two persons who were talking about the meeting, and overheard one of them say, "Well, no one ever before made me feel as I did to-night when that young preacher was talking. Had he continued much longer, it would have overcome me. I shall attend the meeting to-morrow night, and have decided to give up my wicked ways and lead a new life." His companion agreed to unite with him. This conversation, uttered providentially, it would seem, in the hearing of Brother Rogers, gave a new impulse to his drooping energies, and, on the wings of faith and hope, he rose high above all his discouragements. The next evening, true to their word, these men presented themselves at the altar upon the first invitation, and in due time were hopefully converted. They had been leaders in sin, and their changed lives influenced many others. But for this timely encouragement, Brother Rogers often said, he knew not what would have been his future course.

Becoming more established in his views and feelings, he consented to continue his work as a gospel minister, and in 1838, was received on trial by the New Jersey Conference, and appointed to New Germantown Circuit, with Rev. G. F. Brown.

He was then appointed successively to Elizabethtown and Elizabethport, Crosswicks Circuit, Lambertville Mission, and Key Port Circuit. At the conclusion of his labors on the last named charge, he was married to Miss Sarah McGalliard.

He was then appointed to Cape May Circuit, and he and his young wife went to their work with joyful hearts. But a few months passed, however, before sorrow darkened his peaceful home, and the wife of his bosom was borne away by death. Soon after this, he and the writer, who had a little while before passed through a similar bereavement, enjoyed frequent and intimate communion with each other. I shall never forget the pious and joyful feelings with which he looked forward to the recognition and reunion of loved ones who had left us for the spirit world. In the silence of the midnight, he would often say, "O Brother, I hear their voices now; I see them by an eye of faith, they bid us come;" and all seemed to his faith so real, that he enjoyed it, as if it had already taken place.

In 1844, he was appointed to Cumberland Circuit, with Rev. D. Duffel, and in 1845, with Rev. S. Townsend to Salem Circuit. Towards the close of the last named year, he was married to Miss Margaret Bullic, and his sensitive heart found comfort in the sympathy of another fond companion.

The following two years he was on Moorestown Circuit. Rev. T. G. Stewart and J. I. Morrow were his colleagues the first year, and Rev. Z. Gaskill, the second.

His last appointment in 1848–49, was New Egypt, where he ceased to work and live. The Sabbath before he died, he preached with great power, for *one hour and a quarter*, at Goshen church, from the text, "As Moses lifted up the serpent in the wilderness, even so must the Son of man be lifted up, that whosoever believeth in him should not perish, but have eternal life." John iii. 14, 15.

The discourse was remarkable, and so unlike anything the people had heard from him before, that many thought, and some said, it would be his last sermon. And so it proved.

For months, his system had been much enfeebled by a complication of diseases. He had been quite ill for some days previous to preaching the sermon just referred to, but nevertheless, he concluded on the following Monday morning, to ride over to his father's, at Mount Holly, hoping the change might benefit him. He was so weak that he had to be assisted to and from his carriage, and immediately on his arrival, went to his chamber, which he never left alive. The next Saturday morning, with the assistance of his wife, he walked from his bed to the window, and sat for a short time listening to music on the street. While sitting there he remarked, "The music of this world is nothing compared to that of heaven, which I hope soon to hear." He sank rapidly, and the next day, seemed to have a presentiment of his approaching dissolution, notwithstanding the encouragements given by his family. and physician. His father entering his room, said to him, "I will get some one to fill your appointments to-day." He answered, "Yes, and hereafter my place must be supplied, I shall preach no more. my work is done; how thankful I am that I did not defer a preparation for death, to a dying hour. A sick-bed is a poor place to get ready to die." His father, trying to encourage him, remarked, "The doctor thinks you are only suffering from debility now, and will soon be better." "Oh no," he replied emphatically, "*My work is done.* But I would like to preach one more sermon." His father asked him, "What subject he would select." He said, "The inconsistency of professing Christians. Oh, how the thought of it presses upon me now."

About two o'clock, on the following morning, Sept. 10th, 1849. he was taken with a heavy chill, and soon became insensible. A few hours after, without a struggle or a groan, his meek and quiet spirit passed to its eternal rest.

"So fades a summer cloud away:
So sinks the gale when storms are o'er;
So gently shuts the eye of day;
So dies a wave along the shore."

"If Christian character receives its perfection in becoming 'like unto a little child,' Brother Rogers possessed it; for added to all his other excellencies, he was *amiably simple.* His love was unabating, and his ministry, if not like a Boanerges, certainly resembled that of an Apollos."

He had delicate and refined sensibilities, and all his tastes were elevated.

With a constitution naturally frail, he possessed a lovely mind, from which were darting forth occasionally, such beams of light and brilliancy, as only come from off the throne of God. These gave to his preaching an attractiveness which all acknowledged. His soul too, had deep and earnest breathings for a closer walk with God, and as he found the bliss, urged others to its enjoyment.

The following sentence, uttered with great fervency and pathos, while addressing believers at a camp-meeting, shows his views of the extent and blessedness of our privileges in Christ. "There are many green spots in the fields of Christian experience, upon which the eye of our faith hath not yet rested." On these delightful spots he desired his own faith and vision to rest. And it is a pleasing thought to the Christian, that however extensive may be the range of his spiritual vision, and however lovely the objects his faith unfolds to view, there are ranges more extensive and objects still more lovely which his spiritual perception may comprehend and enjoy. In such exercises his soul greatly delighted. But in the temple where he now worships, these views, blessed and ennobling as they were, are exchanged for those more elevated and sublime. The vision is no longer clouded. Glory has thrown off its last veil, and the soul is changed into the same image, from glory to glory. The eye now rests on greener spots than those for which he longed on earth,

> "Where hope in full fruition dies,
> And faith is lost in sight."

There have been few more artless, innocent or sweeter-spirited men. He was loved by all. In Lambertville, where the writer labored a few years after him, was an aged, and highly-esteemed Presbyterian minister, who often spoke of his excellencies in the strongest terms. We seldom met, that he did not ask, "Where and how is Brother Rogers?" To him, to all, we may now say, "He is well, for he lives with God, and his home is in heaven.

> "Sin for ever left behind him,
> Earthly visions cease to blind him,
> Fleshly fetters cease to bind him;
> Heaven, sweet heaven at last."

REV. CHARLES T. FORD.

"Beautiful being, thou art come in love,
With gentle gales from the world above,
Breathing of pureness, breathing of bliss,
Bearing our spirits away from this
To the better thoughts, to the brighter skies,
Where heaven's eternal sunshine lies;
Winning our hearts with a blessed guile,
With thy holy look and thy saintly smile."

THERE is much of beauty even in a fallen world. The sun as he throws his gorgeous beams upon the morning sky, or paints the smallest flower with mellow hues—the queenly moon, pouring her silver floods upon the sleeping earth—and all the sparkling stars, are beautiful. The rose, too, has its brilliant dyes, and the lily a stainless purity. Even the blade of grass is beautiful in perfection. The lowly vale unfolds itself in dreamy quietude, while the mountains rise in wild sublimity towards the skies. The ocean in calm or storm is beautifully grand. But the loveliest thing beneath the sun is a blood-washed human spirit, redeemed through Christ, and walking with God in white. This is the concentration of moral glory, the beauty of holiness, the counterpart of God.

"Goodness is beauty in its best estate."

Such goodness and such beauty it is our privilege to portray in the meek and holy life of Rev. Charles T. Ford of blessed memory.

He was the second son of Charles T. and Mary Ford, and born at North East, Cecil Co., Md., June 23, 1811. Both father and mother were devout members of the Methodist Episcopal Church.

One year after his father's death, Charles wrote as follows: "One year has been added to the ages past since my beloved and most excellent father departed this life. He died in his sixtieth year. His piety was deep and uniform, and secured the confidence of all who knew him. For many years he filled the responsible offices of Trustee, Steward, and class-leader, and continued to do so up to the period of his death. He was an affectionate husband, a tender parent, and a good master. He brought up his children in the fear of the Lord, and had the unspeakable happiness of seeing them all embrace a Saviour's love. Like his divine Master, he was made perfect through suffering, and was then received into the joy of his Lord. In his death I feel that one of the strongest ties to earth has been severed. I can hardly survive his loss. Still I can sing,

> 'A while in flesh disjoined,
> Our friends that went before
> We soon in Paradise shall find,
> And meet to part no more.
> In yon thrice happy seat
> Waiting for us they are,
> And thou shalt there a husband meet,
> And I a parent there.'"

Charles, though naturally amiable, was early impressed with the fact that he was a sinner, and needed the entire renewal of his nature. In accordance with these convictions, on the 16th of August, when only a little past fifteen years of age, he bowed at the foot of the cross, and found salvation through the blood of the Lamb.

He immediately united with the church, an example which all who find the Lord should follow, if they would retain the evidence of their acceptance with God, or increase in the knowledge of his ways.

The light upon his pathway shone brighter and brighter, until his soul was all glowing with glory.

The eye of the Church was on him. The meekness of his spirit, the gentleness of his manners, the humility of his daily walk, the purity of his life, and his untiring zeal in his Master's cause, were matters not only of general observation, but of universal commendation. In a little over a year from his conversion, a paper, yet in excellent preservation, of which the following is a copy, was handed him:

> "This is to certify that Charles Ford is authorized to exhort in our Society at North East, Strasburg Circuit, being satisfied with his grace, gifts, and usefulness. HENRY BOEHM.
>
> *Done in the Society, this* 23*d day of December,* 1827."

From this time his zeal became, if possible, still more ardent, burning like a steady flame, but so intense that many of his friends predicted that a few years would utterly destroy his physical energies, and he be brought to a premature grave.

Still he went on; and though a stripling of only seventeen years old, would often walk, after the labors of the day, from three to eight miles, holding meetings, and endeavoring as God gave him the ability to lead sinners to the cross.

He was licensed to preach in 1829. Soon after he was sent to fill a vacancy on the Harford Circuit, Baltimore Conference, as an assistant to Rev. J. Poisal, for whom he afterwards retained the warmest feelings of friendship. He remained on this field until the session of the Philadelphia Annual Conference, in the spring of 1830, when he joined that body. His first appointment was to Dauphin Circuit, Pa. His subsequent fields of labor were in New Jersey, viz., Burlington and Pemberton Circuits, Somerset Mission, Pemberton and Mt. Holly Stations, Salem Circuit, Sharpstown and Woodstown Station, and finally in 1841—44, Presiding Elder on Camden District.

He was ordained a deacon at Wilmington, Del., on the 15th day of April, 1832. by Bishop Hedding, and an elder at Philadelphia, on the 13th day of April, 1834, by Bishop Andrew.

In all his fields of labor he was a useful and greatly-beloved minister of the Lord Jesus.

While engaged in the faithful performance of his duties as a Presiding Elder on the Camden District, his health failed, so that after much prayer and consultation with friends whose judgment he esteemed, he concluded in the spring of 1845 to ask for a supernumerary relation. The Conference readily, but sorrowfully, granted his request.

He immediately removed his family to North East, where he lived in the midst of relatives and friends, useful and honored, until October 20th, 1849, when he sweetly fell asleep in Jesus.

Such is a brief outline of the life of a precious saint of God. But in all this life there is so much of the morally beautiful that we may linger and look, admire and be profited. To the Christian eye and heart there was much to admire and imitate in his EXPERIENCE.

He was a devout and holy man. From the beginning the constant and intense aspirations of his heart were for the closest possible walk with God. Nothing satisfied his ardent soul but divine communion and fellowship. He fixed his eye upon the high places of privilege, and rested not until his feet stood on the very summit of the mount of vision, and then, as he beheld the unbounded glory, longed to launch into the divine immensity.

A friend says in a letter, "I was present at the camp-meeting at which he was converted: the change was one of great power. I was also present a few months after when he received the blessing of entire sanctification. I have seen many as they professed to secure this great blessing, but have never witnessed any case so remarkable as his. Heaven beamed from his countenance, and his soul was full. At that moment he received his call to preach. Looking at his sister, he exclaimed with great sweetness and solemnity, "Oh, I shall have to leave you and go forth to preach the gospel of my blessed Lord!" His constant theme everywhere was perfect holiness, through the cross of Christ.

In a letter to his beloved wife, he says, "I thank the Lord for all his benefits towards me, particularly for the comforts of his love. True, I have made but little proficiency in the divine life, and my infirmities are great, yet the Lord allows me to approach him. But oh, I sigh to be implunged and inwrapt in the bottomless abyss of love. At times I am privileged to stand upon the mount, and by faith behold the glories of the heavenly world, and while contemplating the nature of its felicity, so perfect and eternal, I am filled with rapture, and exclaim, 'I am entering into life, eternal life.' Oh, my dear C. let us hasten to the coming of the Lord, by following him fully, and by passing through holiness to glory!"

His thoughts were continually upon heavenly things. The last letter he ever wrote to his wife was while she was on a brief visit at Burlington, N. J. A part of it is as follows:—

"NORTH EAST, *May* 25, 1849.

"MY DEAR CATHARINE:—The season has advanced very rapidly since you left. The fields and grass are now clad in their vernal beauty, and the flowers begin to exhale their grateful fragrance, so that we are frequently reminded of that bright and happier world,

'Where all things are pleasant,
And the fields growing green,
And the parting of Christians
Shall never be seen.'

"May we aspire with new vigor and perseverance to those plains of light where God shall wipe away all tears, and there shall be no more death, neither sorrow nor crying, neither shall there be any more pain. Farewell in Him who is the resurrection and the life, and in whom I trust our lives are mutually hid. Yours affectionately,

C. T. F."

His spiritual solicitudes so deep and constant were the means of bringing his soul, as far as is the privilege of mortals, into all the fullness of the blessing of the gospel of Christ. His pathway shone brighter and brighter, until his whole life was like a luminous sun amidst the surrounding gloom and darkness of sin. But beautifully bright as was his whole example, and majestically as he moved amongst the children of men, he seemed to be entirely unconscious of all, and was as humble as a little child. Possessing such a spirit, and enjoying such an experience, as might be expected, he was wonderfully powerful in

PRAYER.

In this holy exercise his talents were of an extraordinary character. There was in his language such clearness, comprehension, and appropriateness, as is rarely equaled, perhaps never excelled. Overmastering faith and power, and pathos accompanied all his petitions, and all felt that his prayers took hold of the right arm of Jehovah's power. Answers to these prayers generally came in copious showers, sometimes in overwhelming floods. The church was baptized under their influence, and from the abounding consolations, the people wept and praised the Lord.

On a certain occasion he was engaged in family devotion at the house of a relative in Burlington, N. J. His soul was unusually exercised. He was drawn out of self and into God. Salvation descended. God was present; glory filled the house. For a long while the whole family seemed transfixed to the floor, helpless and speechless:—

"A solemn awe that dared not move,
And all the silent heaven of love."

When appointed Presiding Elder, in 1841, he did not reach home, after the adjournment of Conference, until ten o'clock, P. M.

He met his wife with a full heart, and, after saluting her with an affectionate kiss, she asked where they were appointed, but he was so overcome with a sense of his entire unfitness for the work, that, unable to answer, he fell upon his knees by the bedside, and remained in that position, supplicating grace and strength, until one o'clock in the morning. Arising, he said, "The work is too great, I cannot perform it." But these three hours of prayer were not in vain. Strength and grace were given, and, though he was young for such an office, yet he was a successful and most saintly Presiding Elder.

At one of his quarterly visitations on Saturday afternoon, he became greatly interested. The congregation was not large, but he felt their spiritual wants were many. He applied to God, the inexhaustible and eternal fountain. Soon the cloud arose from the boundless sea—it spread over the sky—then descended, first in drops, then in showers, then in inundating floods, until the whole house became so filled with the glory of God, that, for half an hour, the congregation remained moveless upon their knees. His prayers will never be forgotten.

He was also a godly MINISTER.

He commenced in great earnestness. When only an exhorter he attended a camp-meeting in a strange neighborhood. His unremitting labors and powerful prayers arrested attention. But he seemed to be alone. There was no tent or company where he had a home. One day there was a little respite from public exercises, and the people were at dinner.

Young Ford was sitting alone on one of the rude seats in the circle of tents, engaged in meditation and silent prayer. A couple of brethren sitting at their noon-day meal, observed him, and spoke of his untiring zeal for God. Instantly it flashed upon their minds, perhaps he had nothing to eat. They immediately approached, and asked if he had dined.

"No," he meekly answered, "Nor have I had any breakfast."

"No breakfast!" they responded with surprise; "how is it you do not eat?"

"I do when I am invited," was his calm reply, "but when I am not, I work on for God the best I can."

In his regular ministry, all who saw and heard him, felt that he was God's ambassador. Clear, chaste, plain, and practical in his expositions, his whole manner and appearance was commanding and dignified, but at the same time sweetly and intensely solemn. Even the most careless felt they were in the presence of a man of God, while his tender and touching appeals awed them to silence or melted them to tears.

To the Church he was a son of consolation. The blessed promises of the gospel were clothed with new beauty as they fell from his lips, and were often effectual in awakening fresh courage in the minds of the timid, or inspiring hope in the hearts of the desponding.

His zeal was unmeasured, for the love of Christ constrained him. This was evident from the first, and the ruling passion of his heart was,—

"To tell to sinners round,
What a dear Saviour he had found."

The Sabbath he regarded as belonging in a very peculiar sense to God alone. After family-prayers on that day, he seldom spoke to any one; so impressed was he with the greatness of the work he had to do, that he took no notice of things around him. From the house to the church, and returning, he walked in silence. His wife remarks, "I became so accustomed to this, that at such times I never asked a question or made an observation."

It was no uncommon thing for him to remain upon his knees, in deep devotion, till long after the midnight hour, and the place would sometimes become so solemn, and the awe so great, that words could not describe it.

On one occasion, he had prepared his subject for the Sabbath, as usual. But at ten o'clock, on Saturday night, it was all taken from him. From that hour, until twelve, he was in an agony of prayer. He retired to rest with his mind in darkness. In the morning a new subject was presented to him. He preached with uncommon liberty, and a great and glorious revival of religion followed.

His zeal knew no abatement as his years increased, but, like a consuming fire, continued to burn within him.

When, through failing health, he was compelled to desist from the active work of the ministry, his spirit was almost crushed. He felt that not to work for God was not to live. He seemed to be unconscious of the fact that his whole life, though a silent, was, nevertheless, a sermon of marked and marvelous power.

A member of the society of Friends, who lived next door to him in Salem, N. J., said, "Charles Ford preaches all the time, even when he feeds his horse or puts him to the carriage."

It was so. His daily example was like a perpetual declaration from the mouth of God, "Be ye holy."

Even after he gave up his work in connection with the Conference, he visited the sick, prayed and preached as often, and, in the judgment of his best friends, sometimes much oftener, than his health would justify.

One of the most powerful sermons of his whole ministry was preached at Beacon Hill Camp-meeting, Md., while he was a supernumerary at North East, only a few months before his death.

His theme was the richness and fullness of the gospel feast. The word was accompanied with wonderful power, and while his own soul, and the souls of the people, were feasting upon the rich banquet, his expansive vision took in the myriads who were starving for the bread of life, and then referring to the instrumentalities employed for their relief, his impassioned soul cried out, "Oh, that the Church, and all the ministers were alive to their duty, and would put forth a more vigorous and powerful effort, that the whole world might become partakers of the blessings of salvation!"

His last sermon was preached at the Brick Meeting House, a few miles from North East, about one month before he closed his earthly pilgrimage, from, "Behold, I lay in Zion for a foundation, a stone, a tried stone, a precious corner-stone, a sure foundation; he that believeth shall not make haste." Isaiah xxviii. 16.

God was pleased to own this last effort of his servant in a most blessed manner. He had extraordinary clearness of perception, together with great power of utterance, and the result was glorious beyond description.

In his last sickness he often referred to this subject, and delighted to rest on Christ as his sure foundation.

As a man and minister he was justly held in high esteem, and yet the applause of earth only brought out more conspicuously his HUMILITY AND GENTLENESS.

The humility of his life was as marked as his gentleness was sweet and attractive. Towards his superiors he was reverential; to his equals kind and affectionate; over the failings of men he threw the broad mantle of his fervent charity, and while he dealt with his opponents faithfully and fearlessly, it was, at the same time, in tenderness and love. The force of these last remarks may be seen by a few introductory sentiments affixed to a sermon which circumstances required him to preach on the subject of Christian baptism.

His text was 1 Corinthians, x. 2, "And were all baptized unto Moses in the cloud and in the sea." He then says,

"Before entering upon the merits of the subject, I wish to premise a little. *First*, It has ever been my desire to live in peace and love with all Christian people; and in accordance with this desire, I have uniformly invited all who love our Lord Jesus Christ to the Sacrament of the Lord's Supper, the true sign of Christian communion. I have also, in my preaching, purposely avoided all controversy on doctrinal points, excepting when the nature of the subject and the wants of the congregation required it, and then I have endeavored to do it in the spirit of love and meekness, for the defence of the truth, and not for victory. But while I have been endeavoring to follow peace with all men, the tocsin of war has been sounded, and we have been challenged to the conflict.

Secondly. The great noise and bold assertions which have of late been made on the subject of baptism, and the undue importance which has been attached to the mode of its administration, are calculated to unsettle and perplex the mind of the young and inexperienced, and give rise to unprofitable reasonings, and unstable conduct, which may result in the return of some to sin and folly, or, in the bereavement of our church, by proselyting, of some of her lawful children.

These things have led me to interpose, lest any should be spoiled "after the tradition of men, and not after Christ."

"Having thus premised, we proceed to the discussion of the subject."

How lovely were these traits of character! And while they shone out so conspicuously in all his public walks, it is pleasant to know that their lustre was equally bright and holy in all private ways and relationships.

As a husband, his affection was of that fervent and fixed character, which arises from all that is noble in man, tender in nature, and sanctified in grace.

The tenderness of his paternal feelings may be gathered from an incidental allusion in a letter to his wife, written at the Cumberland camp-meeting, Aug. 12th, 1843.

"We have had a very excellent camp-meeting thus far. There are but few preachers with us, but they are in the spirit of their holy calling, and have preached with great power. Professors have been quickened, the careless have been aroused, a number have already been converted, and the good work appears to be extending greatly. Last night was a time of great power. I have enjoyed the meetings from the beginning, but the recollections of the past awaken the sorrows of a wounded heart, and in spirit I cry out, '*O my son, my son.*'* This state of feeling is only relieved by the hope of the resurrection. The day hasteneth when death shall be swallowed up in victory; and those who sleep in Jesus shall God bring with him. Then we shall meet in the air, and sorrow and sighing shall flee away. Then we shall see again our beloved Charles, and together praise our great deliverer.

"*Affectionately, your Husband.*"

Though a man of the most tender affections, he was a man of few words. This was true, even in his family, and with his best friends. Sometimes his wife would urge him to talk, especially when they had a good deal of company. His usual reply was, "It is constantly impressed upon my mind, that for every idle word I must give an account. I cannot talk, even for the entertainment of company; you must do it; I will talk when it is necessary."

At the polls, on a certain election day, his vote was challenged by some hostile politician, on the ground, that he had not paid his tax. He left the place, went to his house, procured his receipt, returned to the polls, deposited his vote, passing through the whole transaction, without uttering a single word.

But this silent and solemn deportment gave to him at home and abroad, in the church and in the world, an influence almost unbounded. His dignified and measured walk was a silent, yet irresistible rebuke to sin, and at the same time an inspiration to the child of God.

Christians of his own, and other denominations, looked upon him as a model man.

The writer has traveled over much of the ground where he labored for years. Brother Ford was often a subject of conversation. But before, and after his death, there was everywhere, with young and old, within and without the church, but one sentiment.

* Referring to his eldest son, who died in 1842.

"None knew him but to love him,
Or named him but in praise."

It is sometimes a matter of grief that such a man should ever die, and yet, it is often the case, that they are amongst the earliest called. Beautiful therefore as was the light of his holy example, we must now contemplate his CLOSING SCENES.

The good man dies well. "Thanks be unto God, who giveth us the victory through our Lord Jesus Christ."

His last sickness was bilious dysentery, superinduced as his friends believed, by over exertion in attending the funeral of a person who died of that disease.

It immediately assumed an unparalleled violence, and his sufferings were intense. His recovery was soon considered doubtful. With marked composure he at once commenced the arrangement of his temporal affairs.

"I feel," said he, "that my work is ended, and the Lord no longer needs my poor services in his church below." From the very commencement, his chamber became a privileged place—the house of God—the very gate of heaven. Many flocked to the house to behold and enjoy the abounding glory. Physicians forbid their entrance, but the anxiety was so great, that it was often difficult to prevent it.

To his mother, he said, "Dear mother, you will have to bury another of your family before you go home, but your loss will be my infinite and eternal gain. My hope is founded on Jesus, the rock of my salvation. If I go before you, I shall welcome you with shoutings and songs of salvation as you enter the skies."

In his communications with his beloved companion, there were many tender utterances, such as a heart overflowing with love alone can give. Looking upon her with unutterable affection, he said, "*You*, my beloved wife I know are sincere. Be faithful. God will watch over you. You have leaned upon me, a poor worm of the dust. I am taken away, that you may lean more implicitly upon the Saviour. Look to him. He will more than fill the void my absence will create. Endeavor to train up the children in the nurture and admonition of the Lord. Attend to family prayers; and the Lord will sustain you."

Just before the final hour he said to her, "Do you think I am dying?" With a choked utterance, she answered in the affirmative. "Oh," said he, "how kind and faithful you have been to the very last!" "May the Lord reward you." Then clasping her to his bosom, imparted the last fond farewell kiss upon her brow, saying, "We part for a little while, but we shall be united again in heaven forever."

His daughter Eliza had been absent; on her return, he said, "Farewell, dear Eliza, I had not expected to have seen you again. But I am still on these mortal shores. This day I expect will introduce me to the company above. How it rejoices you father, that you have given your heart to the Saviour in the days of your youth. Be faithful. Though your father may die, it is but the narrow stream of death that separates us; *soon, very soon*, you will join your Pa, in that happy country where farewell words are never uttered.*

Speaking to his son Budd, he said, "My dear son, your father is about to be taken from you. Strive to attend to the great work of salvation. Do not hesitate to attach yourself immediately to the church: and if you are good and faithful, you may be called to fill the station your Pa has vacated."

Counseling his youngest son Stephen, he said, "Be a good boy, obey your mother, serve the Lord, and, like Stephen of old, may you be filled with the Holy Ghost."

Addressing his brothers Stephen and John he gave the tenderest counsels concerning his wife and aged mother. When they had promised to do what they could, he said, "I know you will." Then placing his dying hands upon their heads, he said, "May Benjamin's portion be yours. May you be blessed in your basket and in your store. May prosperity attend you in this world, and in the world to come eternal life." The scene resembled that of the dying Jacob pronouncing a blessing upon his several sons. True, it was not a father's blessing, but that which was scarcely less sacred, the benedictions of a sainted brother.

* In just one month, Eliza passed away from earth, and no doubt joined her father in the skies.

To an unconverted person who approached his bed and inquired how he was, he answered, "Nearing the haven of eternal repose, with the city just in view. I stand upon the heights, beholding the glory, and feel that my *entrance is sure.* The religion I have recommended to others, is now sustaining me." Sometimes, after he had spoken in these hallowed strains, reflections of the glory he was so fondly anticipating would light up his attenuated features, until all radiant with bliss, his lips would break forth in loftiest songs of praises.

Recovering partially from one of his frequent sinking turns, he said, "I thought I was nearly through the dark valley,—but I feared no evil, Jesus was with me;—up—up—my soul mounts higher and higher, and soon will clap her glad wings and soar to the dwelling-place of angels and of God."

About this time, in addition to his previous difficulties, typhoid fever seized him, and reduced him still lower than before. But his spirit triumphed in God. After a restless night, as the light of the morning sun broke in, he said, "Glory to God, there shall be no wearisome nights there,—the day that dawns upon us shall know no close. Oh, it fills my soul with rapture to think of the glories I am about to enter!"

Two days before his death, such visions of glory burst upon his view, that he exclaimed, "Oh, can't you sing of Jesus and heaven?" Rev. A. Simpers and his brother John sang

"And let this feeble body fail."

As they reached the words—

"My soul shall quit this mournful vale,
And soar to worlds on high."

his countenance glowed like the face of an angel, and though too much exhausted to speak, the triumphant waving of his feeble arms expressed that which language was too poor to do. When the words—

"O what hath Jesus bought for me,"

were uttered, it seemed as if he had already entered the city, and was wearing the crown and bearing the palm of victory. But when the last verse was finished,—

> "Let me find them all again
> In that eternal day,"

supernatural strength was given, and he broke out in the most rapturous strains, exclaiming, "Glory be unto God! I will praise him; I have had many sore conflicts in my sickness, but thanks be unto his precious name, through his redeeming blood, He has given me the victory over my last foe. Oh, unite with me to praise Him; call upon all the ends of the earth to praise Him! Oh what a salvation is this; it flows from the very centre of the throne of God! How deep and wide the stream! enough to wash away the sins of all the world." His strength was gone. Pausing a little, he again resumed. "I shall soon have strength to shout the praises of God in heaven; in the resurrection morning this shattered frame shall rise, clad in immortal vigor. Oh, I shall have strength *then.*" After a little, he waved his hand, and looking as if gazing upon the innumerable company, he exclaimed, "These are they who have come up through great tribulation, and have washed their robes and made them white in the blood of the Lamb."

The day before he died, he said, "I feel *happier* and *happier* as I near the haven; do *you* not feel happy?" he inquired.

The reply was, "We cannot feel happy when we think of being separated from you."

"Not feel happy," said he, "to give me up to Jesus? O my friends, weep not for me, all is well, all is well."

A change was observed to come over him, and according to his request, he was informed that he was probably dying. Said he, "If this be death, it is sweet to die.

> 'Jesus can make a dying-bed
> Feel soft as downy pillows are.'

"I am in the floods of death, but the Saviour is around, above, and beneath me; I fear no evil." Awaking from a brief slumber, he said, "How sweet to die! death is a welcome messenger." Again he dozed. Awaking, he said, "*Pray, pray mightily;* just as I was entering the promised rest, the enemy was permitted to drive me back."

In the last conflict Satan thrust sorely at him, but at half past seven o'clock, on the morning of the 20th October, he waved his hand in token of final victory, and his pure spirit entered into rest.

> "Life's labor done, as sinks the clay,—
> Light from its load the spirit flies.
> While heaven and earth combine to say,
> How blest the righteous when he dies!"

REV. DAVID BARTINE.

THIS great and good man cannot easily be assigned to his true position in Methodistic history. The remoteness of the period in which he lived—the fact that he left but few private papers, and kept no journal—the absorbed and uncommunicative nature of the man, the disappearance in death of his cotemporaries both in the ministry and society, make it impossible to collect the *facts* which alone, could do justice to the man. Yet, living at a period when the name of *Methodist* was a synonym for all that was romantic, perilous, and self-sacrificing in religion, and being of a stern, determined, and energetic character, it is certain that his life *was* full of incidents, noble sacrifices, and glorious successes, and his status is rightly given as among the giants of those days.

He was born of reputable parentage in New Rochelle, Westchester County, New York, on January 26, 1767.

His boyhood is without record except that, under the ministry of Freeborn Garretson, he passed through the experience of the despised Methodists, and connected himself with their society in that place, where he remained an earnest and devoted member until God and the church called him to the work of the ministry, which he commenced by preaching with great acceptability and power, from John xiv. 31: "Arise, let us go hence." This, in application to those times of itinerancy, which made its every votary a homeless wanderer, was peculiarly appropriate, and illustrated fairly the sentiment acted upon by all who entered then upon the work of a traveling preacher, among the Methodists.

This was before the days of Presiding Elders. There was no intervening medium between the bishops and the preachers, by which the inclinations and the wants of societies and preachers could be jointly consulted. When the episcopacy wanted a man it appealed at once to *him* to leave all and preach the gospel. There were few *places* prepared to which they could be sent, fewer still houses of worship, and scarcely any parsonages either rented or owned by the societies in which their families could be accommodated. Indeed, in many appointments there were no houses where they could be sure of a welcome for a single night, and many communities deemed it infamous to harbor them at all. There were no pledges of specified salary, four or five dollars on some occasions being the cash receipts of a year,—they were allowed to remain but an average of three months upon a circuit embracing a hundred miles, and on which they preached once a month to the same congregation.

It was at this rough period of our history that Bishop Asbury, attracted by the wonderful argumentative power of the youthful Bartine, selected him for one of his assistants in the work of spreading scriptural holiness over the land. In those days of single-heartedness, if a man felt called of God to preach the gospel, the appeal of the bishop was imperative, and, "conferring not with flesh and blood," such a man left all and followed him, and young Bartine, though distrustful of his ability, and inexperience in the work, was no exception to the noble rule.

His first appointment was with Benjamin Abbot, the Methodistic Boanerges, on Salem Circuit, in New Jersey. He arrived at the place while Abbot was holding one of his peculiar meetings, in which spiritual thunderings and lightnings were thrilling all the people and prostrating them by scores. At first he was simply *startled* by these exercises—then he began to fear that the preacher must be some escaped maniac, and at last, fairly frightened, he nearly concluded to run away. Abbot alludes to the case in his book, although he does not give the name of the preacher. Yet, this same young man afterwards entered with both zeal and zest into this class of exercises, although his singularly calm and self-possessed temperament never would have originated them. He saw that they were *from* God and led *to* God, and that fact was sufficient to sweep away all prejudices regarding them.

His earlier labors were intensely severe. In Dr. Peck's "History of Methodism in northern New York," reference is made to his traveling and preaching there, years before the populous towns which now dot its surface had anything beyond a name. His first circuit here, which was the first appointment following his reception into the Conference, was "Herkimer," and embraced all that part of the State of New York, west of Albany, and was bounded northward only by Canada. His work here was to preach, form circuits, and prepare the ground for permanent occupancy. The report made to the Conference at the close of the year's labor gave proof that although an extremely young man, yet the bishop had exercised wise judgment in the selection of his agent for the important and responsible enterprise, and it is no doubt largely owing to his wise and comprehensive arrangements, that the Methodism of that region has evinced so solid and aggressive a character in its steady and thorough advancement. In 1794 he was appointed to Albany, taking charge also of a large portion of contiguous territory, which was then the custom when a minister was appointed to a city. In 1795 he traveled Delaware. 1796 he labored in Trenton Circuit, and contributed largely by the use of his splendid argumentative power, in compelling the enemies of Methodism to respect her.

During all the period of his ministry in New Jersey, the Churches of the most ultra Calvinistic stamp were dominant in its middle and northern parts, while the coldest Quakerism held the lower portion. However they might differ in other matters they agreed in paying but scanty respect to the invaders of what they deemed their peculiar domain. Among communities so constituted, his style of address was a tower of strength. His wit was caustic and unsparing, his judgment clear and penetrating, his powers of perception comprehensive and discriminating, and his memory astonishingly retentive. Few persons could resist the power of his cold steel-like arguments. Never discomposed, never angry, never careless, watching for the slightest mistake on the part of his adversary, and pressing with terrible power all its consequences upon him, never allowing him to escape, but pitilessly pursuing his arguments to their remotest possibilities; his name became a terror to them over all the country. Bible in hand, he would enter a store, and by his caustic remarks would soon force a controversy upon a Hicksite Quaker. It would be maintained by him with skill and power. Passages from the word would be hurled like shot and shell at his opponents, the arguments of the Hicksite would be held up in the shortest, clearest, and most ridiculous forms; his own views would be presented with the most majestic solemnity, and he, himself, quiet and unexcited, exhibiting neither smiles nor passion, would talk on until he cleared the ground of his adversary, and left his hearers, often, convinced of the truth of his views, and impressed with their power, and they would frequently afterwards be found among the attendants upon his ministry. Such a man *enforced* respect toward the denomination he represented, and successfully made the fear of an attack, the basis upon which he founded his demands for consideration to his Church, and in the region of Trenton his ministry was eminently successful in this regard.

In 1797 he traveled Milford Circuit, where the same characteristics were made a blessing to the feeble and despised societies. In 1798 he labored in the same section on Flanders, with the same results. In 1799 he was removed to Elizabethtown, a strong centre of Calvinistic influence, where he taught the Methodist people the strong arguments which would enable them to give a reason for the faith that was within them, and give that reason in such shapes that discomfiture would be impossible.

* * * * *

While stationed here, he made an occasional visit to the city of Newark, and had the honor of forming the first class in that influential place, a city which now contains twelve Methodist Churches, some of them magnificent and costly, and nearly three thousand members. This fact was distinctly remembered by old Father Baldwin and Mother Bonsel, names both venerated and loved by Newark Methodism; and Pierson's Directory of the City of Newark, a valuable and accurate statistical work, ascribes to him that honor. If further proof were needed, the writer of this sketch heard him publicly declare it in a sermon preached in the Halsey Street—the mother-church—during a session of the Conference in that city.

In 1800, he went to Freehold, the county-town of Monmouth, teaching as prayerfully as ever the tenets of his faith. In 1801 Trenton was added to Freehold, and he successfully repeated his previous efforts in confirming the churches. In 1802 he ministered in Burlington, bringing the powerful armament of his mind to bear against the Hicksite influence of the Friends, which he attacked unsparingly. In 1803 he returned to Freehold. In 1804 he crossed into Pennsylvania, and traveled Bristol. In 1805–6 he again labored with his unvarying success in Elizabethtown. * * * * In 1807 he went to the lower part of the state, in Cumberland, and in 1808 he was stationed in Philadelphia, which was, at that time, perhaps, the most influential centre possessed by Methodism. Here his peculiar talents were largely appreciated. Our congregations compared favorably, for intelligence and position, with other denominations, and, while our mission was specially to the poor, a fair proportion of the wise and noble were numbered among our members and attendants upon our worship. By these, especially, his ministry was received with delight, as it combined the keenest, sharpest intellectuality with the richest experience of personal and spiritual religion, while the poorer and less educated persons found in his comprehensive simplicity of thought, a full satisfaction in receiving through him their portion of the bread of life in its due season.

In 1809 he was re-appointed to Bristol, which, as in the case of every other circuit which he traveled, was glad to welcome him again, and learn from him afresh the defences of the religion they possessed. In 1810 he preached in Northumberland. In 1811–12 he returned to New Jersey, and traveled Asbury, apparently as willing to minister in that rough mountain district as he had been in the more comfortable stations of the city. In 1813 he extended his labors to Hamburg. In 1814 he returned once more to Bristol, which seems to have been a favorite field of usefulness. In 1815 he went back to his old ground of Freehold, and in 1816 he took charge of the societies among the mountains of Sussex, where his ministry was both popular and effective.

In 1817–18 he labored on New Mills. In 1819–20 among the

sands of Gloucester. In 1821–22 he crossed the Delaware again to Chester, and in 1823 recrossed and went back to his old friends in Asbury. In 1824 again to Sussex. In 1825 he remained in the same region at Warren. In 1826 he opposed Methodism to the extreme Calvinism of the Dutch Reformed Churches in Bergen. In 1827 he worked on the line of the Hudson at Haverstraw. In 1828–9 he traveled Essex Circuit, which was inhabited by a population more than ordinarily intelligent, and peculiarly susceptible, from their Presbyterian education, to his public ministrations, among whom he is still remembered as a king in the Methodistic Israel. In 1830 he continued his ministry in the same region, at Bloomfield, and with the same success. The writer, when a boy, heard him at a camp-meeting in North Belleville, on the Bloomfield Circuit. There was no appearance of passion about his address: he did not excite the emotions like the exhortation preachers, but stood calmly asserting a superior cause, which he was strong enough to prove. To the writer's childish mind he decidedly failed in accomplishing the expected results of a sermon at camp-meeting. But the *people* estimated differently. Abstruse points had been cleared up to the mind's vision, painful doubts had been set at rest, impregnable arguments furnished and simplified, "against the foreordination of whatsoever came to pass," the sinner clearly shown the results of his path of transgression, the Christian shown where stood the rock upon which his feet securely rested, and it was universally conceded to be the greatest and best sermon preached at the encampment. In 1831 he traveled a mission circuit in Somerset. In 1832 he once more passed over the old ground at Freehold, and in 1834 he closed his traveling ministry upon a circuit which he had occupied three times before—his favorite Bristol—and in 1835 he took, for the first time in his life, a supernumerary relation to the Conference.

That ministry had extended over a period of forty-one years without a single one of interruption. No discouragements from hardships or inadequate compensation which draw so many into locations, had induced him to lay down his ecclesiastical weapons for a single month. None of these things had moved him from his integrity. His constitution was iron, and his health firm, and both were used to their full capacity: but God mercifully preserved them, and they were continually dedicated to his work, and his descendants can point to his record and say, "Here was a man who, in times that tried men's souls, never faltered in his work for forty-one years, and who only laid it down when age and infirmities made its continuance impossible."

He traveled a number of years after entering the Conference, as a single man. Probably the meagre support which was accorded to the preachers influenced him to this, for home was the paradise of life to him, though it was but seldom he could enjoy its blessings. He was then united to Miss Louisa Knowles, a relative of Rev. Enoch Knowles, of Pennington, N. J. She was a lady eminently qualified to aid him in bearing the burdens of his ministry, and nobly filled the position of a helpmate to him. Among the children of the marriage may be named the late Hon. Judge Stephen North Bartine, of Bucks County, Pa., and Rev. D. W. Bartine, D. D., the efficient and popular Presiding Elder of the North Philadelphia District.

After her decease he married Miss Elizabeth Hunt of Princeton, N. J., near which he afterward settled his family, while he traveled his extensive and laborious circuits. This lady managed successfully his domestic interests in his long absences, and it was largely owing to her energy and ability that he was enabled for so long a time to leave all domestic cares, and give his entire attention to the one work to which he had consecrated his life. She is still living, and resides in the City of Trenton. Dr. O. H. Bartine, a son by this union, is a popular practitioner of medicine in Princeton, near the old homestead of the family.

In that *homestead* this veteran of the cross spent the declining years of life, after taking his supernumerary relation in 1835, until on the 26th day of April, 1850, in the eighty-second year of his age, and the fifty-eighth of his ministry, the angel of death bore him to his homestead in the new earth, which the master he served had prepared for him beyond the silent river.

Brother Bartine was altogether a *self-made* man. He tasked his powers to the utmost, until he attained to a respectable proficiency in the languages. He was a good critic in the Greek, and read its Testament accurately. Such attainments in days when text books were not only scarce, but so arranged as to confuse any but an instructor, argued more than mediocrity of mind and energy. His *memory* was rightly denominated *prodigious.* He relied upon it exclusively for his sermons, with all their multitudinous divisions and subdivisions, as well as illustrations and delicate statements of abstract ideas. He also trusted it entirely for all the studies which he was regularly prosecuting. His private affairs were all carried on from the simple power of recollection. His mind acted as a piece of machinery which printed indelibly its own results upon the memory, to be read by him in all after time, whenever he chose.

This habit of studying from memory gave him a gravity of demeanor, which interfered somewhat with the sweet amenities of life. His children reverenced and loved, but never became *intimate* with him. That same reticence of disposition exists in all his writings, which say but little of himself, so that a *complete* analysis of the character and life of one of the noblest names of our church cannot now be given. In person he was tall and spare, and his frame dignifiedly erect. In preaching, his motions were angular, but in perfect harmony with the mathematically demonstrative lines of his discourse. He frequently preached with great unction, and large revivals were not uncommon during his ministry. He never allowed himself except in severest sickness to miss an appointment. In his preaching his aim was to make out whatever he took in hand. His disposition was kindly, and found happiness in efforts for the happiness of those around him.

During the last years of life, the most of his time was spent in reading the Bible and prayer, giving to Rev. D. W. Bartine, as a reason for such constant perusal of the word, that he found so much in it that was new. For the last year of his life infirmities confined him to the house, and in the few weeks that preceded death, it pleased the Lord to try him with fiercer forms of affliction. But his faith did not fail him, and he stayed himself on GOD. When a brother referred to his abundant labors in the ministry, he replied, "I can see nothing in it all upon which I would dare to rest the hope of salvation; my trust is *altogether* in the atonement made for me by my gracious Redeemer." As he neared his end, his affectionate wife asked, "If he felt the Saviour with him." With evident peacefulness and satisfaction, he answered, "*He* is *with* me. I fear no evil." Expressions of entire confidence in God, and of a clear knowledge of his safety, frequently fell from his lips, until just as life's lamp was darkening, he looked around lovingly upon all present, mantled his lips with a heavenly smile, and breathed them a farewell. And then with the same calmness which had distinguished all his life, he folded his hands upon his breast, closed his eyes, and uttered, "Now Lord, lettest thou thy servant depart in peace, for mine eyes have seen thy salvation," and sweetly fell asleep in Jesus, to waken in a land where his long services and patient endurance would be graciously rewarded, with the stars and crowns which mark the kings and priests in the kingdom of the Father.

REV. PETER VANNEST.

HE was born in Bethlehem Township, Hunterdon Co., N. J., on the 5th of August. 1759. In 1771 he removed to Philadelphia. During his residence in this city, he was often terribly alarmed at his awful condition as a sinner. So intense was the anguish of his spirit that the very pavements, as he walked over them, seemed to bend beneath his feet, and he actually feared the earth would open and swallow him up. His religious solicitude seems to have subsided, for a time, without having led him to the fountain of cleansing. About this time our Revolutionary struggle commenced, and he was induced to offer his services to his country, and in 1776 he entered upon a privateering expedition, and, after a year's absence, returned in his vessel to Philadelphia.

The next year he repeated the experiment, but was taken prisoner by the British, and carried to New York. After his release, in order to avoid the British press gangs which infested the city, he took ship for Halifax, and sailed thence for the Island of St. John. Here he remained until near the close of the war, then returned to Halifax, and embarked for England. On the passage the ship was found to be unsafe, and they put into Bear Haven, the first port on the western coast of Ireland. He made his way across the country to the City of Cork, where he remained until February, 1784, when he set out for Bristol, England, from which place he intended to embark for the United States. The execution of his purpose, however, he found impracticable at the time, and finding employment at anchor making, spent the next four years at this business in the City of Bristol. During this time he boarded at a tavern; a young man in the same house being ill of pulmonary consumption, requested Mr. Vannest to go for him to a Mr. Bundy, a

Methodist class-leader, who resided in the neighborhood, and procure him his services as a religious counsellor. Mr. Bundy made several visits to the sick man, and in this connection became acquainted with Mr. Vannest, in whose religious welfare also, he took a very deep interest.

At first he found it difficult to understand why the class-leader should come with the subject of religion, since he was not sick, nor likely soon to die! He thought religion very well for dying people, but what interest could it have for those who had before them the prospects of life? "Such," says he, "was my ignorance." The good man invited the stranger to his house, and, with his consent, read to him out of the Bible, and kneeled with him in prayer. This was immediately followed with an invitation to go to the Guinea Street Chapel and hear the Rev. Thomas Warwick preach. At this time Mr. Vannest had never been at a Methodist meeting, and complied very reluctantly, as he felt he would somehow compromise his good name by going to such a place. "The man," he says, "was so kind, I could not refuse his request. So I went, and crept away under the gallery stairs to prevent any one seeing me, thinking it would be a reproach to have it said that I went to a Methodist meeting. As he listened to the discourse, he found that every part of it so exactly applied to himself, that he supposed the preacher must have had him in his mind, and that nothing but delicacy kept him from calling out his name. He went from the chapel with feelings which could not be described, and spent much of the night in prayer to God for his pardoning mercy; and here fully resolved that religion, from this time, should be the great business of his life.

He immediately commenced to exhort his fellow-workmen to flee the wrath to come, reproved them for swearing, and, finally, prevailed on them to go with him to the house of prayer, and with him they all at last embraced religion. Within a few days after his awakening he joined the Methodist society, and attended the class, as a penitent sinner inquiring the way of life, in which condition he remained for nearly two months, when he was happily converted in a class-meeting held in Richard Bundy's house. In narrating his conversion, he says, "When the leader on that occasion spoke to me I could not arise, but fell, like Dagon before the ark of God. I lay about an hour helpless, had no use of my limbs, but thought I was as active as ever. It appeared as if I passed by the very gate of hell; but, glory be to God, my blessed Jesus met me there and proclaimed pardon for all my sins. My strength returned, and, oh, the unspeakable joy I then felt; if there had been ten thousand people there, and I had possessed ten thousand tongues, I would, with them all, have praised the Lord in the presence of all the people!"

Having been the instrument of leading his fellow-workmen to Christ, even before he had himself emerged from the sorrows of penitential grief; the light and love which now stimulated his zeal for the salvation of souls greatly increased his efficiency, and others were awakened and brought to God through his agency.

The change in the men with whom he worked was so remarkable as to become the subject of general observation. Their employer, an irreligious man, worldly and vain, and who dressed very elaborately, generally appearing among them with powdered hair and ruffles on his wrists, was deeply impressed with the altered character of the men, instead of drunkenness and profanity, there was now the utmost decorum; and, interested to learn the secret of this marvelous change, he determined to go to the meetings and see for himself. He went to inquire, but remained to pray, was happily converted, and became a most zealous member of the Methodist Church. He had been accustomed to have great and fashionable entertainments at his house; now he put them all away, and his house was made a house of prayer. His wife was indignant at what she deemed his fanaticism, and, not being able to dissuade him from his course, she finally left him. He, however, continued steadfast, visiting and praying with the sick, relieving their wants, and, by a life of earnest devotion, became himself a striking illustration of the power of this religion.

In the beginning of 1790, two years after his conversion, he joined an association, whose object it was to relieve indigent strangers, who had no parish, nor friends to help them, to visit jails and hospitals, and to look after the sick who needed aid in all parts of the city. Finding difficulty in selecting an appropriate name, and in drafting suitable rules for its government, the society appointed a meeting, and invited Mr. Wesley, who was in Bristol at the time, to meet with them and aid in its organization. When he came, he made some inquiries as to its object, then sat down and in a few minutes wrote half a sheet full, containing fifteen or sixteen rules for its government, and naming it the "Strangers' Friend Society." The society distributed between two and three hundred guineas (more than one thousand dollars) annually.

Mr. Wesley usually visited Bristol in the fall and spring of each year, so that during the seven years of Mr. Vannest's connection with the society in that place, he had frequent opportunities of seeing him, and also of hearing him preach. He led all the classes during each of these visits, and has led as many as *seventy of these classes in three days.* It was his habit when he found three absent-marks connected with any name, to announce publicly the expulsion of the person, and to state that it was for the neglect of class. One evening in the pulpit, he observed that the night before a very extraordinary thing had happened him; he did not recollect anything like it happening to him for many years. The house was full, and all ears opened to hear what it was. After a pause, he proceeded :—"Last night when I went to bed I believe I laid awake above five minutes"—an illustration of one of the secrets of Mr. Wesley's wonderful achievements: he never wasted time. Dr. Samuel Johnson said of him: "Mr. Wesley's conversation is good: he can talk well on any subject; but he is never at leisure. He is always obliged to go at a certain hour. This is very disagreeable to a man who loves to fold his legs and have out his talk, as I do."

In the year 1791 Mr. Vannest was appointed leader of a class which met about a mile out of the city. He assumed the duty with great reluctance, trembling under a sense of its heavy responsibility; but God was with him, and it prospered greatly, so that in a short time it became necessary to divide it. In attending to the duties of his class, he was obliged to pass through the village of Bedminster, whose inhabitants were both very poor and extremely wieked. They would eall derisively after him as he passed them, and bespatter him with the vilest and coarsest epithets, and their children, under the influence of these vieious examples, were likely to surpass even the parents in wiekeducss. He became interested in these people, and with his wonted energy undertook their rescue from the demon viee. While a quiet passer through their streets, they were fieree as eurs, but when he turned upon them, with his earnest and affeetionate exhortations, they beeame alarmed, and rather avoided than sought his attention. One of the worst of these was a Richard Wakefield, who as Mr. Vannest passed along called after him; but as he was used to this, he kept on without notieing the man "until he got to the top of his voice; then," writes Mr. Vannest, "I looked baek and the man beckoned me, and I went to him, and he began with the worst language I ever heard, part of which was personal abuse of me. When he paused I thought it my turn to say something for my Master. When I had spoken a few moments, he shook as if he had the ague, and invited me to come into his house and see him. A time was arranged, but when I came he was not at home. I went several times, but eould not find him; his wife seemed to be a respectable woman, and was mueh affected on account of his wiekedness. She engaged to keep him in on a eertain Sabbath until one o'cloek if possible if I would come. I went at the time and found him at home; he was so agitated when I went in that he shook from head to foot, so that at dinner it was diffieult for him to earve. I entertained him with talking, reading, singing, and praying until five o'clock, and then invited him to go with me to a meeting at Guinea street Chapel; turning to his wife, he said: 'Get the children ready—let us all go to meeting.' This family on their way to meeting was so novel a sight that the people all through the village stared at them as if they had been wild beasts; but the man was sineere, and himself and wife became deeply penitent, and immediately joined the society. In about two weeks they were happily eonverted; he felt such unspeakable joy that he started immediately to bring the joyful news to me, a distance of two miles; and as he went through the village, he told all he met what the Lord had done for his soul.

About a year after this his wife died in great triumph, shouting and praising God to the last."

He also became interested for the children of this wicked community, for whese souls "no man seemed to care." He opened a Sabbath-school, and went from house to house, and invited the children to attend, and succeeded in collecting about seventy of them into a room which he had rented for the purpose, and which he supplied with the necessary furniture and fuel at his own expense. After the school on each Sabbath he took them to the Episcopal Church, where he had two large pews provided for them. The children made great improvement, and his success led him to devise still more liberal things for them. He opened a subscription, which he headed with a considerable contribution, for the purpose of furnishing them with a week-day school, and soon had some forty of them in regular attendance. Other liberal-minded people were drawn into the enterprise by its wonderful success, which continued to increase while under his efficient management.

While thus engaged, the Rev. Henry Moore sent him "a plan of six months' work as a local preacher," bearing date, January 1794, he was unwilling to accept the responsibilities of so sacred and important a work, notwithstanding his "determination to do good to the bodies and souls of his fellow-men to the utmost of his ability," and went to Mr. Moore to return him the plan and to say the work was too great, that he could not undertake it; the minister, however, had no authority to release him from the obligations of a work, to which God had evidently called him and left with him, the whole responsibility of refusing to obey the call. Unwilling to take such a responsibility, he went, though not without considerable reluctance to the work; but soon found abundant encouragement in the gracious fruits with which God crowned his earnest, faithful labors.

He continued to serve the church in this office for about two years when a gentleman in Bristol, who had control of certain shipping interests, learning of his desire to return to America, offered him a passage in his vessel to Philadelphia; and in the beginning of the year 1796, he bade adieu to England, and returned to his native land.

He found "the captain and his crew all very wicked, swearing, brawling, quarreling, fighting and doing many acts bordering on desperation." With his wonted fearlessness he "commenced reproving them;" his remonstrances kindled their rage, and they threatened to throw him overboard, but as they did not do it he continued his reproofs; the contest for a time was severe, but in "about two weeks," he writes, "I got swearing out of the ship, and there was a great calm. All was now peace and good order where fighting and disorder had reigned; and, when after this, by accident, I fell overboard, they gladly came to my help, and got me on board again; and when we landed at Philadelphia our parting was truly affecting, even to tears."

He continues; "I brought a certificate from Rev. James Cole, which I gave to Mr. Bostwick, who took it to the Philadelphia Conference, upon which they received me, and appointed me to Salem Circuit, N. J., with Robert McCoy, but I did not go. I suffered more affliction that year than I had for many years before. I did not know but that it was for disobedience, so I promised the Lord that I would go the next year, if he would go with me. I went to Conference the next Spring, 1797, which was held at Duck Creek, (Smyrna, Del.), and Bishop Asbury said to me, 'I am going to send you to England, will you go?' I said, 'Yes, sir, if you say so.' He said, 'I mean *New* England, and they are a wise people there: it will be a good school for you. Last year I gave you an appointment, and you refused to go; now I will send you a great way from home, and you will not run away.' So I went to Middletown, Conn."

At South Britain, which was a part of his charge, he found a society of four members, one of whom, a boy, it became necessary to expel: but he left there at the end of the year, about forty members, and four local preachers. On another part of the circuit lived a man who had recently been reclaimed from a backslidden state, who came to Mr. Vannest, and requested him to hold a meeting at his house: he appointed a day, and went to the place, a distance of fourteen miles, through extremely bad traveling, "there being nearly two feet of hail upon the ground with a hard crust upon it." Having had two other appointments at different places the same day, it required considerable effort to meet this engagement; he was the first preacher of his denomination to visit the place, and the people stared at him as if he had been a monster.

He found the woman of the house to be a perfect termagant, who "swore if he ever came there again, she would have him rode on a rail." Her conduct was indeed so violent in general, toward ministers, that the Presiding Elder, who saw her after this, said, he never saw a woman possessed with so many devils; yet even this woman was converted, ere the year closed, "and became a remarkably humble and pious follower of our Lord Jesus Christ, and was a blessing to her family and the neighborhood." The Lord raised up during the year in that place, also, a good society.

In 1798, he was appointed to Croton Circuit, from which, after three months, he was returned to Middletown.

From the New York Conference in 1799 Bishop Asbury sent him to Wittingham, Vermont, to form a new Circuit, after he had arranged a round of appointments occupying two weeks, his circuit was merged by the Presiding Elder in that of Pittsfield.

Among the converts this year was a young woman named Deborah Butler, the daughter of a Baptist minister. This person was subject to singular paroxysms; she would fall suddenly and lay like one dead for a few moments, and then begin to talk and continue her discourse nearly as long as the state lasted: previously to her conversation her utterances were coarse and vulgar, afterward they were purely religious. Mr. Vannest says, "I have heard her when in one of these fits, compose a hymn and tune and sing them; then pray, take a text and preach a good sermon, compose another hymn and sing it, pray and dismiss the congregation with the benediction, and then in a few minutes come to herself, but without any recollection of anything she had said. She had a wonderful gift in prayer, and sometimes would exhort individuals in a masterly manner. I have heard her in conversation with her father tear his Calvinistic system to pieces; she seemed to have the whole Bible at command. When I last heard of her she was married, and living a very pious life."

While on his way to preach at a place called Petersburgh, on this circuit, he was sorely tempted to abandon the work of the ministry; and the impulse so far mastered him, as that he actually turned his horse to go home, but recollecting several difficulties in the way of so sudden an abandonment of his charge, he concluded to fill that appointment and then leave: that night, however, a good work of religion commenced, which resulted in an ingathering of nearly a hundred souls in that place.

At a place called Dalton, they met with much opposition. "But God carried on his own work," writes Mr. Vannest, "and a number were converted: among whom was a young woman of respectable family, an only daughter. When under conviction the Presbyterian minister waited on her, and wished her to join his church, saying that it was more honorable to be a Presbyterian than a Methodist. She said she did not want honor—she would rather go on her hands and knees to heaven than to ride to hell in a coach. When she went home after joining society, her father bade her leave his house. She found shelter in the house of a poor man named Durgy, where she was entertained in the best they had; and the Lord blest her visit to the conversion of both this man and his wife. After this she taught school at a place called Adams, about twenty miles distant, but whether she ever returned home or not, I cannot tell."

In the village of Clorane were two Presbyterian churches: one of them was without a preacher. The late incumbent, having violated the law in marrying a couple, and finding there was a reward offered for his arrest, hurriedly took his departure. The people worshiping there had paid their pastor four dollars per week. After he left they wrote the preacher in charge on the Pittsfield Circuit, requesting him to fill the pulpit, with the offer of the four dollars per week. The preacher complied, but refused the money, asking only the privilege of a quarterly collection. A revival soon commenced, and the first convert was the son of the Presbyterian minister settled over the other church, a Mr. Tagert. Under the stimulus of so grave a provocation as the perversion of his son, this minister immediately set himself to write a book against this new sect, which, Mr. Vannest says, "was to be the great magazine to destroy Methodism, but, Rev.

Wm. Thatcher of the N. Y. Conference wrote a reply with such weighty arguments and strong, scriptural truths, that it completely damped all the combustibles of the magazine so that they did not explode, to do Methodism any harm."

In 1800, he was sent to the Essex Circuit; and in 1801, to New London. There he met with the eccentric Lorenzo Dow, and gives several anecdotes characteristic of the man: one of which is in substance, as follows: Dow prevailed on many to pledge themselves to pray three times a day, and would engage himself to pray as often for them, and he always called upon God to witness the agreement; his manner of doing this was peculiarly solemn, and often caused those thus pledged to tremble. One man engaged to pray the required number of times per day, after exacting a promise that he would not call *God* to witness: but Dow immediately on the man pledging himself called on the devil, and all the damned ghosts to witness! The man declared that language could not describe the sense of horror which this awful invocation produced: it was however the means of his conversion, and he thanked God for it.

The yellow fever was fearfully prevalent during the summer within the bounds of this Circuit. "At Norwichtown the bell would toll at daylight each morning, and men go from house to house to call for help to bury the dead. "As I was going to meeting on a Sabbath morning," he says, "I saw a horse standing at a door, the grave dug, and the man not dead. I returned in about two hours, and the man was buried. I could hear the groans of the afflicted at my lodgings. The custom was as soon as one was dead, to wrap the corpse in a tarred sheet, and bury as soon as posible.

"The fever continued about three months. We attended our appointments regularly. I was taken with the symptoms, which were a pain in the back and head, very violent. It was a very warm day, and I had an appointment in a dwelling-house which was full. I was in much pain, but commenced the meeting and got into a great perspiration, and at the close felt well in soul and body."

The following incident given in one of his letters illustrates some of the prevalent peculiarities of the doctrinal and practical religion of those days in New England.

"On my way to Bozrah a man came up to me in great haste, and inquired if I was a Methodist preacher. I told him I was. 'Well,' said he, 'I have been looking and watching and waiting for several years to catch one.' Well, sir, what do you want with him? 'To make him ashamed of his erroneous principles.' What are they? 'You hold to falling from grace.' Not so; we hold to getting grace and keeping it. 'But you say that we *can* fall from grace?' That is another thing. There is a possibility and a danger: angels fell, Adam fell; and Paul said, 'I keep under my body and bring it into subjection, lest when I have preached to others I myself should be a castaway.' The man said, 'I do not believe it possible to fall from grace.' Sir, will you give me liberty to ask you a few questions? Have you ever had grace? He said, 'Yes, sir.' Have you any grace now? 'To be sure I have: I could not lose it.' Now, be honest. Do you not get mad sometimes? Do you not swear sometimes? Do you not get drunk sometimes? He answered, 'Yes, I do.' Sir, if you do these things, you have no more religion than the devil. He said he believed in falling *foully*, but not *finally*. I said I believed in two degrees of falling: 'the first is to fall from grace, as you have, if you ever had any: and if you do not repent, and do your first works, and find forgiveness, your next fall will be into hell, and you will be lost forever.' The man's countenance changed, he put whip to his horse and hastened away. I thought he would not be in haste to catch another Methodist preacher, as he had such poor success with the first."

At the New York Conference, of which he was then a member, there was in 1802 a call for preachers to go to Canada. As the church authorities did not make appointments to the British Provinces, the request was for volunteers. Mr. Vannest went upon this call to Oswegatchie Circuit. Here he had long and dangerous rides over frozen rivers and through deep snows, often with nothing to direct his course but marks upon the trees, and had at times to travel where for twenty miles he did not see a single human habitation.

His next charge, Bay of Quinte, was through even a more desolate region. On one part of this circuit the appointments were separated by a distance of *thirty-four miles* without a stopping-place. In the summer his horse would find grass in a place where the Indians in other years had made their fires, and in the winter he carried oats in his saddle-bags, and made a trough of the snow, out of which to feed his horse.

The year 1803 was spent on the Niagara Circuit with Samuel How as his colleague. This year they had no Presiding Elder, and he attended to the duties of this office for his own and the adjoining circuit. They found the work here even more difficult than in the other parts of the Province: for in addition to long rides, dangerous exposures and hard fare, they suffered persecution from wicked men, who were so stupid as to charge the unselfish evangelists with a desire for money and ease, in their ill-paid toils and voluntary hardships.

He was, however, more than compensated for these trials, by the successes which crowned his faithful ministry. On one occasion a man of genteel appearance came to request him to preach at his place: he had a large ball-room, (for he kept a public house,) the use of which he offered him for the service. After some searching inquiries which led the man to believe that the preacher could see into his heart, he arranged to go: it became one of his regular appointments, and as a result the man and his six brothers with their wives. in all fourteen, were happily converted. He gave up his tavern, extinguished the fires of his distillery, and gave his ball-room to the Lord for a place of worship, until the society could provide a better.

In 1804 he returned to the States, and was appointed to Burlington, N. J.; in 1805, to Elizabethtown Circuit; in 1806, to Somerset, Md.; in 1807, to Holland Purchase Mission, N. Y. During the years 1808 and 1809 he was Presiding Elder on the Cayuga District. In 1810 he was preacher in charge on the Gloucester Circuit, N. J. From 1811 to 1814 he traveled the East Jersey District. His subsequent appointments as an effective man were a year on each of the following circuits: Salem, Freehold, Bergen, and Gloucester, all in New Jersey.

At the conference of 1819 he was made supernumerary, and appointed to Pemberton, and in 1821 became superannuated. From the time he ceased to be effective till his death—a period of about thirty-one years—he had his home at Pemberton, N. J., where he was highly respected and eminently useful. He watched over the church in that place with exemplary fidelity, and felt a lively interest in whatever related to the purity and prosperity of the general Church to the last. When in his ninety-second year, he was often seen with staff in hand going from house to house, inquiring with great interest in respect to both the temporal and spiritual welfare of the inmates.

During his last years he wrote several articles for the *Christian Advocate and Journal*, giving personal reminiscences mostly of his earlier life and ministry. They were characterized by great simplicity, and often by deep feeling; and they excited so much interest that persons in various parts of the country wrote him, expressing a wish for a continuance of these contributions.

On Tuesday, Oct. 8th, 1850, he was attacked with paralysis, which totally disabled one side, and so affected his speech, that it was with difficulty he could be understood. On the following Friday his speech returned, and he conversed fluently with his numerous Christian friends. He was fully aware that death was approaching, but instead of viewing it with terror he hailed it with rapture as the introduction to a glorious and an eternal rest. The exultations of his triumphant spirit made the place of his departure a truly privileged one: it seemed radiant with the light of heaven. An inquiry concerning his prospects elicited the response: "Glory, glory, glory! Hallelujah to the Lamb for ever and ever." Indeed the language of praise and thanksgiving was continually upon his lips until death sealed them in silence on the 17th of October, 1850, in the ninety-second year of his age.

Mr. Vannest was of middle height, of stout build, and in his old age slightly corpulent; he possessed great simplicity and cordiality of manners, and in natural temperament was ardent and sympathetic. He was a man of strong, positive character, whose convictions were very decided, and always maintained with great tenacity. These qualifications, connected as they were with excellent judgment and a rare prudence, gave him great power with the people, and, despite his defective education, made him eminently successful as a minister of Jesus Christ.

His piety was of a high order; like Stephen, he was a man full of faith and the Holy Ghost, and lived in unbroken fellowship with God. His whole life was in a remarkable degree controlled by religious considerations and influences. He regarded Methodism in her doctrines and polity as nearly as possible a *perfect* embodiment of the teachings of the New Testament, and consequently always deprecated what are called improvements in our economy when they seemed to involve a departure from the established usages of the Church.

Like Asbury, McKendree, Whatcoat, Cooper, and other leading men of the heroic age of our Methodism, Mr. Vannest remained a bachelor.

His preaching was plain, practical, thoroughly evangelical, and more than ordinarily effective. He attracted very considerable attention in his day, and well deserves an enduring memorial.

REV. THOMAS CHRISTOPHER.

THE subject of this sketch affords some useful lessons, illustrative of the ways of God to man. He was one of the many humble and unpretending men, from obscure walks in life, and without superior talents or special advantages, whose self-denying and devoted labors in the vineyard of the Lord are crowned with large success. God thus shows us that he selects his own ambassadors, and that, with him, a single eye and a zealous enlistment in the great work, are more acceptable than many talents or varied learning. Not that either of the latter is to be lightly esteemed. One is the direct gift of God, and both are signally owned when rightly used; but neither separately, nor both combined, will make up for the lack of single-hearted devotion to the work of cultivating the Lord's vineyard. When large native talent is developed by extensive culture and research, and, especially, when it employs a splendid oratory, it may attract attention and secure applause. It may also go far to disarm prejudice, instruct ignorance, convey important truths to the popular mind, and in many ways accomplish good. But all this, apart from a distinct consecration of the whole man, a living sacrifice to God, will avail but little in bringing sinners to Christ, while medium ability and ordinary acquirements, fully devoted to God, are often rendered strangely efficient in this highest department of usefulness. How invaluable is this lesson to the many who are called to this difficult and responsible work, and yet painfully feel deficient in both native and acquired ability.

Thomas was the son of Joseph C. Christopher, and was born in Cambridge, Dorchester Co., Md., June 12th, 1805. His mother died when he was a child, but his father, who was a farmer and local preacher, was twice subsequently married. He died when forty years of age. Thomas was converted and joined the Church when only twelve years old, and ever after maintained a Christian profession with unusual steadiness. How lovely is such a sight! How few rise superior to native evils, avoid the snares, and resist the enticements that beset the paths of childhood, and thence to life's end exhibit a consistent Christian demeanor! And if the reformation of a debauched sinner shows a wonderful efficacy in the atonement, a case like this does more. It proclaims Christ a Saviour from sin in the highest sense, *i. e.*, from the commission of it, and that the lost image of God may be restored, before guilt has been contracted or native depravity increased. It also shows that the whole of life may be employed in the service of God.

Thomas had a frail body, for which reason his school advantages were increased, and his early conversion and after faithfulness render it probable that he had a good religious training. He loved books, thirsted for knowledge, acquired a fair English education, and adopted teaching as a profession, which he followed till he became an itinerant.

For a long time he was exercised on the subject of preaching. Feeling incompetent to the task, and that the idea of his being called to such a work was preposterous and must be a mistake, he earnestly resisted his impressions. But, though repressed for a time, they would return with redoubled power. At times his distress was so great as to interfere with his duties. He would often resort to the grove to commune with his own heart, with nature, and with God. The feathered songster, gleefully hymning its Maker's praise, and even the roaming beast, so free from responsibility and care, added to his sadness by force of contrast. And when we call to mind how early he was converted, how late he entered the ministry, and that his attention was called to the subject soon after he embraced religion, a long interim is left for this painful conflict. But, as relief only came in the measure of his ascent to the truth of his impressions and his willingness to follow in any path that Providence and the Church pointed out, he was finally led out of the mazes of doubt and perplexity, into the clear light of a call to the ministry.

In 1833 he was employed under the direction of the Presiding Elder. The next spring he was admitted to the Philadelphia Conference, and in due course of time, elected to deacon's and elder's orders. In 1835 he came into New Jersey, in which state he spent the balance of his life. The following were his fields of labor: 1834, Kent, Md.; 1835, Salem, N. J.; 1836, Gloucester; 1837–8, Cumberland; 1839, Bargaintown; 1840–41, Cape May; 1842, Gloucester; 1843–4, Bargaintown; 1845, Medford; 1846, Cumberland; 1847, Lower Penn's Neck: 1848–9, Atlantic.

About the middle of the second year at Atlantic his health failed. Under medical advice, he gave up the charge and sought rest and invigoration, expecting soon to return to his loved employment. He opened a store in order to secure a support for his family and healthful exercise for himself. For a few weeks he seemed to improve, but then took a severe cold which resulted in bilious pleurisy. He took to his bed the day after Christmas, but soon partially recovered. Meanwhile, a heart disease, which had at times troubled him, developed quite alarming symptoms. This was on the 16th of January. His friends yet cherished hopes, but he had a presentiment that he would not recover. His prostration and distress were very great. "Yet he talked much of dying without fear or dread." He took comfort from the assurance given by Paul, that "our light affliction, which is but for a moment, worketh for us a far more exceeding and eternal weight of glory." 1 Cor. iv. 17. The day before he died, his friends painfully felt that his end was near. When asked if he had any fears, "Oh, no, all is well!" he replied, and added, "my work is done, I shall soon go."

He commended his children to God, and urged his wife, son, and other friends, to meet him in heaven. The next day he said, "This world is not worth a thought, I am almost gone, all is right." He also sent this message to his brethren of the Conference: "Tell them I love them all. For sixteen years I have not failed to preach Christ and him crucified. Tell them I have finished my course with great joy." As the closing hour drew near, his mind assumed a triumphant frame, and he awaited his release in tranquil peace and holy ecstacy. He again took leave of his family and friends, desired them to pray that he might be taken away from his sufferings, frequently exclaimed, "Glory to God!" and uttered, as his last words, "I am almost home." After this he was only able to raise his hands in token of victory. "He sweetly fell asleep in Jesus, without a sigh or a groan," at seven o'clock, P. M., January 31st, 1850, aged nearly forty-five years. Thus lived and died another champion of the cross, another trophy of the Redeemer. And thus, too, was illustrated the power of the religion of Christ, fully to sustain the believer through the toils and trials of life, and in the stern reality of death.

As a preacher, Thomas Christopher was earnest, pointed, and practical. He belonged to the old school as to the structure of his sermons, the warmth of his manner, and the extent to which he dealt with the affairs of every day life. He gave no quarter to the follies of fashion, the frivolities of the giddy and trifling, or the bold inconsistencies of those who put the claims of business before the duties of religion, or allow trivial things to come between them and their religious obligations. In all these respects he trimmed closely. Of his earnest manner one colleague says, "As a preacher he was very ardent; he could not preach unless he felt." Another says, "A prominence of his ministry was ardency." This arose from an intense and absorbing anxiety to secure success. To this everything else was secondary, and was made subservient. His deep reverence for God, high appreciation of the sacred office and strong desire to win souls, combined to exclude all attempts at mere display, and even seem to have led to a neglect of style. He wrote but little, and depended mainly, in preparing for the pulpit, upon thinking out his subjects, and fixing the substance of them in his memory. But he was chiefly anxious to enlist his feelings in them, and secure an attending divine unction. He believed that people are benefited in about the measure that their feelings are impressed, and that deep feeling must be had before it can be communicated. Acceding the correctness of this position, it does not follow that deep feeling or divine imbuement is incompatible with thorough mental preparation. Our subject possessed a fine imagination, and, at times, when aided by a special inspiration, there were passages in his discourses of unusual pathos and power. But if he gave too little attention to style and thus failed to develope his full power as a preacher, it arose from the purest motives. Blessed is he who adopts the happy mean between too great neglect and over-attention to the arts of oratory.

Concerning his success, and the manner of securing it, his widow bears this remarkable testimony: "He was always successful. He was never satisfied without success. He never served a circuit or station but what he had a revival. When he commenced an extra meeting, he began extra prayer for the descent of the Holy Spirit. I have awaked at the midnight hour and heard him praying, and when I asked him what was the matter, he would reply, 'Oh, the weight of souls, and the responsibility I feel.' Often when finding him awake, I have asked if he had not been asleep. He would say, 'I have preached two or three sermons since I came to bed.' He was a man of strong faith, and would hear no prophesying of failure, but went to work, relying on God, with the assured expectation of success. He was seldom disappointed. The greatest revival of his ministry was on old Gloucester Circuit, as the colleague of Rev. A. K. Street, when they received five hundred on trial."

His mode of studying his sermons so developed the power of abstraction, that he could even be oblivious to the confusion of crying or rollicking children. The habit of close, consecutive thought was also thereby fostered and some measure of mental discipline secured. This much, at least, was gained as an offset to the loss arising from the neglect of a more thorough and vigorous use of the pen. But without this it is not possible for any one to develope his full power in the use of his mother tongue.

He was blessed with a large stock of kindness, which overflowed in all directions. He was a good husband, a considerate father, a fast friend, and a genial, pleasant companion. Combined with an ever-present desire to do good, it gave him access to the people, disarmed prejudice, put the timid at ease in his presence, made all feel that in him they had a friend, and thus aided him in his pastoral work.

He spent sixteen consecutive years in the ministry, and his strong desire to cease at once to work and live was quite fully accorded. Most of the time he traveled large circuits, and received but a light support. He bore a full share of the hardships of the itinerancy, nor did the ardor of his zeal tend to lighten its burdens. He went through all kinds of weather and roads, promptly meeting all his engagements. And what we regard as a special virtue, he was scrupulous about being punctual as to time. Nor did he fail where fidelity is put to its strongest test, *he spent much time from home.* His whole career was marked by uncomplaining cheerfulness, for he was warmly attached to the church, and counted no personal sacrifice too great to aid in a full development of her economy. If reminded that he might thereby hasten his end, he would reply, "I shall die in a good cause; better to wear out than to rust out."

His piety was deep and uniform, and his course steady. And though not free from severe spiritual conflicts, yet his tenacity knew no yielding till he gained the mastery. And then the religion that he enjoyed and commended to others did not fail him in the dying hour.

His mortal remains were first buried at Tuckahoe, but afterward removed to Glassboro, where, four years later, those of his only son, a promising youth of nineteen, were laid by his side. His widow, a daughter of Joseph Albertson of Glassboro, and mother of Rev. G. C. Stanger, of the New Jersey Conference, and two daughters, still survive him.

REV. MULFORD DAY.

MULFORD, eldest son of Rev. Stephen Day, was born at New Providence, New Jersey, on April 8th, 1800.

His father was one of the oldest, most devoted and useful Methodists in all that country. When he was born, the Methodist Episcopal Church had no existence, and the infant colonies were battling for national life. Twelve years only had elapsed since Philip Embury preached his first sermon in New York, and *all* the societies numbered but about six thousand members and less than thirty preachers. In the year that he united with the church (1803,) there were but little over one hundred thousand members in all North America. He was always found on the side of the progressive Christianity of the day, hating drunkenness, hating slavery, and hating rebellion. In early life he was married to Miss Sarah Mulford, who remained with him but for a year, when she died, leaving an infant son, only nine days old, the subject of the present sketch.

He was immediately adopted by his maternal grandfather, Cornelius Mulford, Esq., in whose family he spent most of the years of infancy, boyhood and youth. They were loving and kind, but no kindness can supply the lack of a mother's gentle ministrations. No class of circumstances *can* compensate for *this* loss. The tender sympathy which attracts the boy to his *home* and thus preserves him from vicious associations, the watchful solicitude which guards the early errors of the mind, the intense regard which embraces *all* opportunities for temporal or spiritual welfare, could be given by no one *but* a mother, and in *his* case the loss was most severely felt. His grandfather's family made no profession of religion, and consequently he was left without those moral restraints, or religious instructions, so essential to the rightful direction of the youthful mind. As was natural, he did *not* choose the better part. While he did not yield to gross immoralities, he still chose a life of sin, in preference to one of godliness. His moral nature was too strong to bear this, without strong reproofs from an accusing conscience, and, at the early age of sixteen, he openly adopted the principles of infidelity, as a refuge from its power. Referring to this in his diary, he says, "Oh how fearful is such a course! My depraved heart, almost, if not quite, (under Satan's influence,) embraced the horrid doctrines of Atheism." But though the convictions of his soul were thus deadened, and his principles were so averse to the reception of religious truth, God did not leave him to reprobacy of mind. The light of the gospel of Christ found its way to the darkened moral sensibilities of his nature, and when about nineteen years of age, while attending a camp-meeting near Rahway, and listening to a sermon delivered by Rev. Lawrence McCombs, a strange feeling came upon him, and he felt impelled to seek the Lord. The convictions were not pungent—there was no deep distress—but a "drawing from above" both seized and kept possession of his soul. Under its influence, he openly avowed his need of the religion of Jesus, and expressed his determination to seek it until it was obtained; although, without the impulsion of that deep anguish which so generally accompanies conviction of sin. With characteristic energy and perseverance he devoted himself to this one work. No opportunity was neglected, no meeting of the church allowed to pass unimproved, until, a few weeks after his first convictions, while struggling for salvation at the altar of the church at New Providence, all his sense of guilt disappeared, and he involuntarily arose to his feet and sang with the rest of the people, the praises of his Divine Redeemer. He continued, however, to pray, and soon the evidence of his acceptance became so clear and full as to free him from every doubt, and enable him to rejoice in God with joy unspeakable and full of glory.

This great change through which he passed he dates on the thirteenth day of October, 1819, a day of precious memory in his history. He had already, while a penitent seeker of religion, united with the church on probation, thus giving evidence of that calm determination of purpose which was a marked characteristic of all his future life. Soon after his conversion he was appointed a class leader, in the exercise of which office, he gave promise of future usefulness, while his consistency of life and conversation impressed the church with unbounded confidence in the purity of his principles and the reality of his conversion. Soon after this he was licensed to exhort. A new field of labor opened before him, for while his work as a class leader had heretofore only brought him into contact with those who held like precious faith, he was now to face the ungodly in his public efforts for the cause of Christ. But, accepting the labor, he toiled with all the calm energy of his soul in impressing sinners with their danger, and urging them to flee the wrath to come. He labored in this sphere until 1824, at which time he was united in marriage to a worthy and pious lady, and almost immediately afterward received impressions of his duty to preach the gospel. These impressions were shared fully by his wife. But such was the modesty of the man, and so high his estimate of the sacred office, that it was not until June of 1831, that they were allowed to overcome his hesitancy and compel their public avowal. From that hour, he states, "he never had a doubt of his Divine call to the work of the ministry." In the August following he received verbal license to preach, and delivered his first sermon at Union Valley. This was deemed by his brethren a satisfactory evidence of his call to the work, and at the Quarterly Conference of the November ensuing he was regularly licensed to preach and recommended to the Philadelphia Annual Conference. At this session of the Conference, however, no married men were received, and he continued to exercise and improve his gifts, by preaching in the appointments adjacent to his residence until the Spring of 1833, when he was admitted on trial and appointed to Freehold Circuit.

The position he now occupied, though felt to be a duty, was emphatically a cross. His nature was diffident and retiring, his estimate of himself unusually low, and he was conscious that his preaching lacked that intense and fiery energy which gave so great a popularity to many of his brethren in the ministry. But, the Holy Spirit pressed him on, and he dared not disobey, working faithfully and usefully throughout the year. The succeeding year he traveled Crosswicks, where the same results followed. At the Conference of 1835, he was admitted into full connection and ordained a deacon by Bishop Emory, who appointed him to Cumberland Circuit, but to accommodate some want of the work, he was subsequently changed to Freehold, where his calm and loving manner had impressed the people with a sense of his worth, and remained there as preacher in charge for two years, to the general satisfaction of the people. In 1837 he was ordained an elder by Bishop Waugh, and appointed to Staten Island, where he also served the church for two years, winning the love of the people among whom he labored, and realizing a fair amount of spiritual success in his endeavors to do good. In 1839 and 1840, he traveled Haverstraw Circuit, magnifying the office of the ministry, and by the purest possible walk and chastest conversation, impressing the people with the reality of the religion he professed. Indeed a large part of his pulpit power lay in this consistency of life. No man who knew him, had any doubts, when he came to the house of God to hear the minister, of his entire holiness. From the general habit of his life, the people were sure that he was what he professed to be, and his influence over them was correspondent with their confidence. Oh, what holy power over men exists in a pure and godly life! The weakest talents illuminated with *this* light of God, are made his power unto salvation, and when their talents are of a superior cast, the dignity of a solemn and devoted life adds double power to their impression upon the minds of men.

In 1841 and 1842, he was favored with an appointment among his native hills at New Providence, the place both of his natural and spiritual birth. It is no small tribute to the worth of the man, that the usual rule of itinerancy was reversed in his case, and he was sent to labor among the very people who had known him from his childhood, up through all the stages of his career to manhood, and had also been familiar with his feebler earlier efforts in public speaking, and where impressions of its power must necessarily be below the real standard of the man. Here, too, he gave the most faithful attention to his work, and saw his reward in the general prosperity of the church under his care. In 1843 and 1844, he was preacher in charge at Woodbridge, where he left also a large circle of appreciative friends. In 1845 and 1846, he labored in Sharpstown and Woodstown. Here the people esteemed him highly. The members of the church still speak of his dignity, of his gentleness, of his tenderness, and of his deep and self-abasing humility, while some who came into the church under his ministry, revere him as a father, and all regard him as a friend. Brother Abraham Richmond, a prominent official man in the charge, says of him, "The most marked characteristic about him was his *humility*. His views of himself, his talents and ability were so low that they would sometimes call forth the gentle remonstrances of the official men. They feared that the people might be induced to take the same low views of him that *he* took of himself, and which *they* knew to be unfounded so far as their views compared him with his fellow-laborers in the ministry. But their fears were groundless, for the people who knew the *worth* of the man were brought to yet more serious reflection, by the contemplation of his humility." The same authority says, "He was always burdened with a sense of his responsibility for the congregation to which he ministered. It was the theme of his conversation and his prayers. In the classes, his advice was tinctured with it, his public exhortations were full of it, and even his pastoral prayers among the people were filled with the same feeling, while in his public ministrations his flowing tears told with powerful effect of the same absorbing thought." Here his ministry was blessed, and the Church feels its good effects even still.

In 1847 and 1848 he traveled Swedesboro Circuit, a large and important field of labor, where incessant effort and work were essential to the successful prosecution of his ministry, and which incessant effort was freely made. In 1849 and 1850 he was returned to Staten Island and stationed at Bethel, renewing the associations of earlier days, and zealously endeavoring to fulfil the high duties of his calling. In 1851 he was sent to Hackettstown, which proved to be his last charge. He entered upon his work with earnest zeal and hope, and planned largely for the extension of the Redeemer's kingdom. But "man proposes and God disposes,'' and on the sixteenth of June in that year, he was attacked with pneumonia, and ere the twenty-sixth of the same month surrendered his life to him who gave it. In these trying times the power of the gospel, which he had spent the strength of his life in proclaiming, was found sufficient to sustain him. When the death river chilled and the pains of death gat hold of him, he exclaimed, "How long it takes me to get over this Jordan of death." His ardent soul was longing for the other shore whose prospect, the darkness which overhung the veil had no power to dim, and he uttered, "I am almost home, I mean my heavenly home." And with glory in his view, his happy spirit took its flight to the heaven his soul had gazed upon while dying.

Mulford Day was a man of marked character. His powerful moral and religious nature, arising both from constitutional make and deep acquantance with God, compelled a *distinctness* from other men in this regard. His countenance was singularly solemn, verging on sadness, and his religious feelings left their impress unmistakably upon it. He was *never* morose, but *always* solemn. In gay and frivolous company though he uttered no reproof, his presence always brought the sense of condemnation. No *words* betrayed his belief in the sinfulness of trifling sports, but it seemed impossible to trifle in the presence of a man, who evidently had but recently come from God's presence in his closet. More than once, when the exuberant spirits of young preachers, at camp-meetings and other places, had passed the bounds of strict propriety, and the reproofs of their elders had been unheeded, the solemn gravity of his presence has hushed them into silence, and stimulated them to the substitution of devotion in its place.

His voice shared the solemnity of his countenance. Said a sturdy weather-beaten pilot on one of the Hudson River steamers while his vision was dimmed by tears, "I was converted under the preaching of Brother Day. When he left Haverstraw he came up into the pilot-house, and putting his hand upon my head said, 'Brother, be faithful.' The *solemnity* of his *tones* will never be forgotten. Tempted as I have frequently been, the recollection of his words has kept me from sin and apostacy." It also gave a powerful weight to his public ministrations. No adult candidate for baptism ever heard him pronounce the formula, "I baptize thee in the name of the Father, and of the Son, and of the Holy Ghost," without feeling that the rite was something more than mere ceremony. In the repetition of the marriage service, the most careless and inconsiderate were compelled by his very *tones* to feel that they were entering their union at least in the *fear* of the Lord. Seldom indeed could the bride refrain from tears or the bridegroom feel otherwise than grave, when they left the presence of God's servant, by whom they had been joined in the life-long ties of holy matrimony.

At the sacramental table it was the same. Unworthy persons were deterred from approaching by a voice which seemed to come from the realities of a spirit world, while those who received the sacred elements in sincerity, found their power of appreciation deepened from the same influence, and few ever received it from him who had not reason to call him blessed.

This intense seriousness of expression was also a strong element of his pulpit power. When the first words of the exposition of some great truth contained in his text, fell upon the ears of the congregation, they produced a more than common effect. The listener who had formed his taste from hearing the greatest preachers forgot his models—the captious critic laid aside his rules—the learned attendant upon a learned ministry buried his contempt of ignorant Methodism—fortified sceptics came out of their intrenchments—hardened sinners abandoned their hostility to the word, and apostates their defiant attitudes when he spoke, for they were made to feel that the "Lord was in his holy temple," and that the "earth must keep silence before him."

In speaking of his deportment, one who loved him says, "Such solemnity as his, approaching gloom, and which sometimes rendered its possessor unhappy, would have been unlovely had it not fortunately been free from even a tinge of misanthropy. It was as pure as that of Elijah. His moments of exhilarating joy and hope were rare, but when they came, they threw over his soul's features such lights as the setting sun pours upon the retreating clouds. There is no transition of feeling so touching as that of deep reverence when it banishes its fear and melts into liquid love. Many who have stood beside him in the altar while laboring for souls recollect with pleasure, these rare moments when his faith triumphed over every fear, and his soul was filled with celestial rapture."

"He was a man singularly free from the lower motives which usually actuate our humanity. The ambition which often leads to prominence and greater influence found no place in him. During the eighteen sessions that he occupied his place in the Conference he never made a speech or took any prominent part in its discussions. He shrank modestly from the Presiding Elder's office or a station in a city. Impressed with a nice appreciation of the merit and worth of his brother preachers, yet none could sooner detect their weaknesses than he, while he conscientiously forbore from making those weaknesses a subject of discussion. To his younger colleagues he was frank and open, privately pointing out to them their faults of life or manner, but pursued the same unvarying rule of never speaking to others of these faults, which were only named to their possessors in hope of their removal.

His religious experience was of a most solid character. Of its power there can exist no doubt. His own utterances in this matter are too emphatic to be misunderstood. Holiness of heart and the fellowship of the Spirit were asserted by him to be facts of constant reality in his spiritual life.

As a husband and father, he modeled his practice upon the precepts of the gospel.

His early educational privileges were only those of the common schools, and he did not acquire an accurate knowledge of the rules and principles of the English language till he was thirty years of age. As soon as he began to preach he made himself thoroughly conversant with the outlines of history and theology, studying and remembering such books as Rollin, and Josephus. His library contained the works of the standard Methodist authors, and their contents were carefully read and digested. His acquaintance with the Bible was as great as a retentive memory added to a philosophic power of generalization could give him. His mind was stored with great doctrines and moral facts, while light literature he never allowed himself to read.

Brother Day was a successful man. In no appointment did he labor where his ministry was not a blessing. "Methodism in New Jersey is probably as much indebted to him for its solidity and purity as to any other of its deceased ministers. He did not study so much to mould mind as character. He swayed the moral nature rather than the intellectual, and disseminated principles rather than opinions. Just as his own great conscientiousness moulded him, so he stood to mould others and make every man a preacher of righteousness unto himself. It has been said in reference to him, "The results of a great man's life are what he *does*. The results of a *good* man's life spring from what he *is*," and this latter character applied especially to him. The successful power of his ministry can perhaps be illustrated by its results in New Providence, his native place. Night after night scores of penitents crowded the altars, and many witnesses, living still, refer to him as the instrument through whom they were awakened and brought to God. No man's ministry was ever blessed in that appointment to a greater extent than his, and probably no minister ever labored among them who was more highly esteemed. His value to the church may be estimated from the fact that during his eighteen years of service he received into her communion over a thousand souls.

As a preacher he was calm, but not unimpassioned. One who was converted through his instrumentality, says of him: "His face preached—his voice in its ordinary tones preached—the tears that came from his heart when he was silent preached—and all preached to the heart." There was a power of tenderness about his ministrations which forced its way into the soul. Men attended his ministry to go away better than they came. Without any use of the machinery of the professed revivalist, his ministry was yet productive of sweeping revivals, and his churches always assumed a purer and more devoted caste. He did not seek to charm or entrance. Poetic flights, impassioned appeals, and irresistible argument were with him exchanged for the one single faculty that aroused men's consciences and led them to faith in Christ, and while it blessed the believer, melted the sinner into penitence. It was logical, clear, and simple; the meaning of his message could not be mistaken, nor the ardent earnestness with which he pressed it be misunderstood. He told the story of the cross both with simplicity and pathos, and the longer a congregation remained beneath his ministry the more deeply they felt its power.

He now rests from his labors, leaving behind him the record of a stainless life and a successful ministry as a precious heritage to his bereaved family, who remain behind him following in his steps. Of that family the Rev. George B. Day, a popular and talented minister, occupies the place made vacant by his father's death.

REV. ZERUBBABEL GASKILL.

THE subject of this brief memoir was a native of Newport Neck, Cumberland County, N. J., and was born June 10, 1805. He took the Christian name of his father, who died when he was an infant. Of the father no account can be given, but God rendered this bereavement an inestimable blessing to the stricken widow. By it she was led to a sense of her condition as a sinner, to seek a saving interest in Christ and a home in the M. E. Church. She remained a consistent Christian to the end of life, and then at the advanced age of eighty-two or eighty-three, was transferred to her home in heaven. Nor was this long life in vain. God so answered her prayers and blessed her pious care to the Christian nurture of her son, that he sought religion at the early age of eleven. He did not, however, join the church till in his seventeenth year. Yet he did not backslide, but maintained a consistent demeanor amid the alluring snares that everywhere beset the slippery paths of childhood and youth.

His early educational advantages were very limited. It is said that he was sent only "a little while at a time to a small country school. Yet he made rapid progress in learning." Taking both parts of this statement as true, they furnish a clear presage of his after career; for the child that could make rapid progress in learning, by no other helps than a small country school afforded forty or fifty years ago, and that attended only a little while at a time, displayed both studious habits and vigor of intellect. At the age of eighteen he began to teach school, which he continued at intervals for several years. During part of the time he farmed in the summer and taught in the winter.

He did not enter the itinerant ranks till in his twenty-eighth year. Prior to this he had labored to some extent as an exhorter, but had not been a local preacher. He seems to have been much afflicted and retarded by diffidence. Perhaps this is the explanation of his delay in joining the church. It certainly delayed his entering upon the great work to which God undoubtedly called him. After much hesitation he began his ministry in 1833 on Salem Circuit, under the direction of the Presiding Elder. The next spring he was received on trial in the Philadelphia Conference, and was elected to full membership and to deacon's orders in 1836. When the New Jersey Conference was constituted, he was left in the old Conference, but at the end of one year was transferred to the new one, and in 1838 ordained an elder. He occupied the following fields: 1834, Moorestown, New Jersey; 1835, Smyrna, Delaware; 1836, Caroline, Maryland; 1837 and 1838, Bargaintown, New Jersey; 1839, Crosswicks; 1840, Crosswicks and Bethel Mission; 1841 and 1842, Middletown Point; 1843 and 1844, Quakertown; 1845 and 1846, Haddonfield; 1847 and 1848. Blackwoodtown; 1849 and 1850, Tuckerton; 1851 and 1852, Clarksboro.

Nothing from his pen has come into our possession. But few of his relatives are yet living, while those of them who could be found were able to furnish but little information. Still, though our facts are meager, we have learned enough to show that his whole career was marked by a steady aim, a devout and dignified bearing and genuine sincerity and faithfulness. Rev. Dr. Quigly, with whom he traveled Caroline Circuit, says, "My personal recollections are clear and strong concerning him, as a humble follower of Christ, a faithful minister of the gospel and a pleasant colleague. His personal appearance did not at first sight, make a favorable impression, but when heard and known, he made a *good* impression, where he labored. His character and standing as a man, a Christian and a minister, were unimpeached and unimpeachable. I considered him a very good preacher. He labored very acceptably in this region."

Though genuinely modest, and diffident even to a fault, yet in clear cases of duty, he was fearless and unflinching. In this respect he imitated the great apostle, when he said, "None of these things move me, neither count I my life dear unto myself, so that I might finish my course with joy, and the ministry which I have received of the Lord Jesus to testify the gospel of the grace of God." In one instance, at least, he displayed the martyr spirit, with an unobtrusive fidelity and courage, which challenges our admiration.

He found the Quakertown Circuit in a condition so deplorable, that there were scarcely enough living to bury the dead. Bacchus, that fell demon of discord, "said in his heart, I will ascend into heaven, I will exalt my throne above the stars of God: I will sit also, upon the mount of the congregation, in the sides of the North: I will ascend above the heights of the clouds; I will be like the Most High." Isa. xiv. 13. And he did get the upper hand of many of the stars of the congregation, *i. e.*, the leading men, and also in the place of the Most High; for these men discarded minister and church and God, all at the bidding of Bacchus. Mr. Gaskill prudently but fearlessly opened the batteries of truth against this citadel of Satan. Men are always extremely sensitive when conscience is silenced at the demands of interest or self-indulgence. This was the case now, and their combinations and show of fight looked formidable. They first tried by raising a storm of popular indignation, to silence the stupid, one-ideaed fanatic, who was capable of the senseless temerity of insisting that Christians ought not to make, sell, or drink rum! And they did succeed in awaking the elements. "The rain descended, the floods came, and the winds blew." But, like the sturdy oak, he only bent to the blast, till its fierceness was spent, and then stood up as firm and defiant as before. Failing in this they changed their tack and raised the cry of "persecution." And if their version had been reliable, it would have been true, that they were the most thoroughly abused men in the land! This also failing, and finding that neither words nor tufts of grass would do, they tried the virtue of stones.

Two trustees of the church at Everetstown demanded the key of the sexton and closed the house against him. For the sake of their descendants their names are omitted from this page. But Amos Opedyke, a trustee, backed by others, and aided by Wm. Johnson, a Presbyterian, who made a key, opened it for him to preach on the subject in question. Being foiled again, a mob took the matter in hand, and tried the persuasive power of rotten eggs and other missiles, together with street fires, and yelling and whooping like a pack of savages. Fortunately for the minister and the cause, the ladies of some of the malcontents attended the service, and received in part the application of the egg argument. Meanwhile the appeal of the speaker was so calm, logical, and convincing as to enlist the favor of the better part of the people, and thus to secure a triumph. The turbulent party then threatened to waylay and lynch him, if he attempted to fill an appointment at another place. But he did meet the engagement, and that, too, without being maltreated. These expedients failing, they next resorted to the desperate alternative of an attempt to starve him out. When told of this design, he replied, "They might as well try to starve a bear." Nor was this a vain boast. The sum he received cannot be named, but he was driven to perplexing straits. Friends aided him, he exchanged wheat flour for Indian meal because it would go farther, sold part of their scanty furniture, and thus procured the needed pittance for his family. At the same time he stood up to his convictions with manly and unflinching firmness to the end of his term. I cannot say whether or not members of the church participated in the mob or threats of violence. They did the other things charged, and were the occasion of these being done. And when it was found that he could neither be moved from his position nor driven from the field, several withdrew from the church. And as it seemed necessary to show their faith by their works, one went to keeping tavern, became and died a drunkard, while others became more bold and shameless in their tippling habits than before. Some lived to lament their folly, and one, at least, has since died sustained by hope, but others still tread crooked paths.

But these were not the only or heaviest trials that fell to his lot. Life's closing year was covered by dark clouds, which cast over him gloomy and lowering shadows. They came from unusual domestic afflictions, which pressed upon him with a weight to which his strength was not equal. And though his faith did not fail nor his hope grow dim, yet his shattered frame could not long sustain the throbbings of a broken heart. He had met the rum demon with heroic boldness, had faced and defied the taunts and missiles of the mob and their threats of violence, had sacrificed his salary, stripped his house of needed furniture, scanted the table and wardrobe of his family, and had come out of the conflict with a good conscience and robust health. But this poignant shaft, coming from an unexpected quarter, found him unprepared and unequal to the hard necessities of the trying hour.

A short time before his death, he left the charge, entirely broken down, and repaired to the house of his brother Charles, in Philadelphia. Here, as the Conference Obituary shows, he closed life's checkered scenes in full prospect of an inheritance with the saints in light.

"The text selected for his funeral discourse, Acts xi. 24, 'For he was a good man, full of the Holy Ghost and of faith,' is a very fit illustration of his character as a minister. His life exemplified the text. Consistency and fervor were marked characteristics in him. We do not know that he possessed what some have called the divine art, yet he loved sacred song. One Sabbath, when near his end, while contemplating the holy temples of the Lord, and the gathering together of the people, he repeated these expressive lines:

"Thousands, O Lord of hosts, this day
Around thine altars meet,
And tens of thousands throng to pay
Their homage at thy feet."

"Deprived am I," but continued:

"I may not to thy courts repair,
Yet here thou surely art;
Lord, consecrate a home of prayer
In my surrendered heart."

Contemplating death, he exclaimed,

"How shall I meet this foe,
Whose frown my soul alarms?
Dark horror sits upon his brow,
And vict'ry waits his arms."

He answered,

"But with an eye of faith,
Piercing beyond the grave,
I see that friend who conquered death,
Whose arm alone can save."

In conversation with a brother in the ministry, a little before his departure, he was very happy and praised the Lord; and when raised up a little, he said, "Let me go! Hallelujah! Praise the Lord!" and calmly folding his hands upon his bosom, he ceased to breathe. In this ecstatic frame of mind he passed from trial and suffering to his home in heaven, Nov. 13, 1852, in the forty-eighth year of his age and twentieth of his ministry.

As a preacher Zerubbabel Gaskill occupied a very creditable position. The qualities of his mind were substantial, and his reasoning faculties of a superior grade. Had imagination given wings to his thoughts, so as to render his powers of description and graces of style equal to the cogency of his logic, his pulpit abilities would have been decidedly superior. He was generally acceptable, frequently popular, and always useful in his fields of labor. Many were brought to Christ through his instrumentality. But his efficiency did not consist alone in this nor in his pulpit performances. He was affable and genial in social life, and at the same time maintained a dignity, gravity, and thoughtfulness befitting the man, the Christian, and the minister. He thus wielded an undivided influence in aid of his ministerial duties. Nor did that religion, which by precept and example he commended to others, fail him in life's severest trials, nor in the dying hour, but lighted his pathway in the dark valley and bore his soul in triumph to the home of the saved.

REV. J. F. CROUCH.

THIS devoted man of God, was born May 27th, 1804, at a place called, Head of North-east river, Cecil Co., Maryland.

His paternal grandfather was of German extraction, and possessed a valuable estate on the Elk river in the same county. He was an ardent patriot, and, during the Revolutionary war, sacrificed his entire fortune to his country, but, like many other noble-hearted men, gave it cheerfully, rejoicing that he had it in his power to aid in securing the blessings of liberty and equality to his descendants.

His maternal ancestry were English, and among the first settlers in the colony, occupying a large tract of land on the same river, known by the name of Johnson's Addition, by which appellation it is still distinguished.

Both his parents were members of the Protestant Episcopal church, and illustrated their membership in a life of consistent and devoted piety. Under their faithful instructions, and godly example, he became firmly impressed both with the reality of religion, and the beauty of a religious life. These two facts, under the power of the Holy Spirit acted constantly upon his nature, and led him to write in regard to his early experience, "I know nothing of that ignorance of sin for which some plead. Since I could tell my right hand from my left, I have been conscious of inward reproof for every sin of my life. From earliest recollection I have been the subject of deep conviction and alarm in my conscience combined with an awful dread of the judgment day. These convictions followed me and spoiled all earthly pleasures." He attempted to stifle them by resorting, on Sabbath days, to the companionship and sports of the young people of the neighborhood, but seldom succeeded in so doing. On one of these occasions the conversation between him and one of his associates assumed, unintentionally, a religious character, and they found themselves discussing the judgment day, when the great hail storm of the "Revelation" should fall upon them.

Just at that moment a terrific storm of thunder and lightning, rain and hail burst upon them, impressing with its awful grandeur the fact they had just been contemplating, and they made earnest promises to God of amended life, which, alas! only waited the advent of sunshine to be broken, but the impression was never forgotten.

At the session of the Conference of 1819, William Forbert and John Woolson were appointed to Cecil Circuit, and came to their work in the demonstration of the Spirit and of power. In August of that year they held a camp-meeting near Elkton, at which such powerful ministers as Ezekiel Cooper and Joseph Rusling preached. Many persons were awakened, a large number converted, and the whole church revived. He says, "My own convictions were pungent, but the enemy raged fearfully within. To rid myself of tormenting reflections, I joined the ranks of the persecutors, and employed myself outside the circle in hurling missiles at the colored people as they passed along the highway. On Sabbath I returned home to allow my elder brother to come. When alone, my misery became almost insupportable. When I returned to the camp, they were marching around it preparatory to closing, and among the ranks of the saints I saw my brother, sister and an intimate associate. It made me tremble to see this, but I still resisted.

"After this there was no peace for me at home. The warm and ardent worship of the family was misery to me, and I usually fled to the barn for retirement. Among my companions I spoke sneeringly of the *Methodist* church, for which one of them, ungodly as he was, so strongly reproved me, that I ceased, and began to be thoughtful. This was on Sabbath, and on the following Wednesday evening I attended a prayer-meeting, where my heart was greatly softened. For the first time I *cherished* these feelings, and resolved to give my heart to God. I drank deeply of the wormwood and the gall, but it was soon accompanied with a lively faith in the Friend of sinners. God accepted the faith, and it was accounted to me for righteousness. Everything seemed to have undergone a change, and I was filled with rejoicing, and,

> 'Could not believe
> That I ever should grieve,
> That I ever should suffer again!'

I soon however found severe temptations, but found also that 'the Lord knew how to deliver the godly out of temptation.'

I was ouly about fifteen, but felt deeply concerned for the spiritual welfare of sinners around me. All leisure moments were spent in reading, attendance upon religious worship, prayer and meditation. At the decline of the excitement attendant upon the revival, the love of many waxed cold, but though astonished at this, my faith was in no degree shaken, and I toiled more earnestly than ever to maintain my integrity, and on the 19th of September, 1819, united with the Methodist Episcopal church."

He now felt deeply, and toiled faithfully for souls. His warm, ardent, and nervous nature employed itself unceasingly in warning sinners to flee the wrath to come. The judgment was ever before him, and their exposure to its penalties compelled him, day and night, to warn them faithfully and with tears. In private conversations, in public meetings, everywhere, he urged upon them their danger, and besought them to return penitently to God. He came fresh to his work from communion with the Lord, and many could not resist the wisdom and power with which he spake. This continued for five years, when the church publicly recognized his ability and devotion, by licensing him to exhort. This official recognition stimulated his zeal yet more, and emboldened him to expand his thoughts in giving to the people a *reason* for the *hope* that was within him, and he soon developed capacities which induced the church to add to his power for usefulness by assigning to him, in 1831, the position of a local preacher. From this hour the necessity of an entire devotion to the work of the ministry was a feeling interwoven with his life. It was a work of toil and sacrifice. Large circuits were to be traveled with but slender pecuniary recompense.

The work of incessant preaching was exhausting to a slender constitution, the sweet associations of domestic felicity must be largely abandoned, the world's fair prospects must be ignored, but "none of these things moved him," and he united with the Philadelphia Annual Conference, on probation, and was appointed to Dover Circuit, Delaware, on which, though with much trembling, he preached with acceptability and usefulness.

In 1834 and 1835 he traveled Gloucester Circuit, N. J. His ministry here was eminently successful, and his personal popularity was perhaps unsurpassed by any of the numerous ministers who had preached the gospel on that classic ground of Methodism. Many years have elapsed since that time, but the remembrance of his ministry is still as ointment poured forth, among the older members of the church in that locality. In 1836 he labored in Cohansey Mission, and gave to the feeble interests of the Church a substantial support. In December of that year he married Miss Margaret Synnott, a lady who accompanied him the rest of his pilgrimage, and was his valued companion and counselor.

In 1837 he exercised his ministry over a region of country now filled with numerous circuits and stations, but then known simply as Cape May Circuit. The Bishop had assigned him as junior preacher upon the circuit, a young man who fell into evil habits, and was afterwards expelled. He took a deep interest in the reclamation of this young preacher, and, after preaching, stood out in the cold, chilly night air, hour after hour pleading with the misguided young man to forsake his ways, and assume a better course of life. When he left the place, his intense mental anxiety, added to the chill of the suddenly arrested perspiration, sowed within his frame the seeds of the consumption which steadily germinated and brought forth their deadly fruit, until, a few years later, they sent his body to its grave, and his soul to its heaven. In one aspect, it is sad to contemplate a noble and useful man stricken down because of the errors of another, but in a different one it is pleasing to record that his life went down as the result of an effort to reclaim a wanderer from God and restore him to the fold.

The fatal effects of his imprudence were not immediately apparent, and in 1839–40 he was appointed to Cumberland Circuit, where a ministry of power left its impression indelibly upon the people. In 1841 he was sent to Medford, in which place he labored with some success for a year, when his health, previously broken, gave way entirely, and he was returned the next year as supernumerary. While he resided there, holding that relation to the Conference and cut off from all active means of support, Brother William Alston, now of Bordentown, relates, that on one cold Christmas night, after all the money received from Conference except one quarter of a dollar and a one cent piece, was gone, his wife informed him that they were out of flour, and gave him a vessel in which to procure a supply. As he started for the store, a man met him at the gate, who stated to him that his wife and children had eaten nothing all day, and were then entirely without food, and asked him if he could not put him in the way to obtain some.

As Brother Crouch saw the tears coursing down the man's hunger-stricken features, his heart, ever responsive to suffering, was moved, and he thrust his hand into his pocket, determining to give him the piece of money which his fingers should first grasp. He drew out his hand, and found that he had drawn with it the quarter, and at once gave it to the man. It was no use now to go to the store, and he silently returned into the house. His wife asked him for the flour, and he replied by saying that he had given his last twenty-five cent piece to a poor man, and had but one penny left. The poor woman burst into tears, but he sat quiet and composed, perfectly happy in his mind, expecting to see the salvation of God. So calm were his feelings that he took a book and commenced to read. At about nine o'clock a sleigh drove up to the door containing a couple who wished to be married. The ceremony was soon performed, and the happy couple left, the gentleman presenting him, as they did so, with a five dollar gold piece, which relieved his immediate wants, and filled his soul with rejoicing and gratitude.

During the next summer, three persons, one of whom was the narrator of this incident, were conversing together about Methodist ministers, when one of them remarked, "I esteem Mr.

Crouch very highly. I *ought* to do so, for he married me." "When, and where?" said Mr. Alston. "On last Christmas night, at Medford," was the reply. The peculiar circumstances connected with the *Christmas* marriage had been narrated to him previously by Brother Crouch, and he felt interested to know *why* the gentleman went to him at Medford to get married, when it was so great a distance from his home. As the story proceeded, he learned that the first arrangement was, to go to Rev. Mr. Dandy, at Mount Holly: that when nearly there, the lady said, suddenly, "I feel as if I ought to have Mr. Crouch to marry us." "Why," said he, in surprise, "are you acquainted with him?" "No," said she, "not particularly: but I have heard him preach several times, and think he is a very good man." "But," said the gentleman, "the night is very cold, and it is six miles further to ride." "I know it," said she, "but I feel as if I *must* go to *him*." Of course, under *such* circumstances the lady could not be denied, and they came to Mr. Crouch and were married, as before stated, and presented him with the five dollars which came so opportunely in his time of need.

Upon further inquiry it was ascertained that the hour when the lady felt impelled to change her mind as to the officiating minister, corresponded exactly with the time when Brother Crouch gave his last quarter, to relieve the family of the starving man.

Incidents like these were spread over his history, and contributed largely to imbue him with that unfaltering trust in the Lord, both as a God of providence and grace, which never deserted him in the darkest and most trying hours of his history, and which kept him serene and hopeful, when all was apparent storm and wreck around him.

While residing here, another incident of a still more remarkable character, and proving itself to be of God, occurred to him.

The venerable James Moore, of precious memory, whose services in the cause of early Methodism cannot easily be overestimated, and whose purity of heart and life secured the respect of all who knew him, was visiting there. His health had long been declining, and he was an object of special solicitude to Brother Crouch. The latter was one day walking in his garden, when suddenly, sweet and seraphic music filled all the air above him, the green leaves of the trees seemed alive with it, and the golden light trembled under its power, everything appeared as spell-bound, and his heart was entranced with its celestial sweetness. In looking upward to see whence these ravishing sounds proceeded, it seemed as if a body of angels were passing over, who in some inexplicable manner impressed him that they were conveying old Brother Moore to his eternal home, leaving the impressions of their glory ineffaceably upon his mind and heart forever. Subsequent inquiries ascertained that at precisely that moment, the spirit of James Moore passed from earth to heaven, and there can be no doubt that God took him Elijah-like, in celestial chariots with angel bands to the place of the blessed, and that he allowed the vision for the purpose of confirming and rewarding the faith of the godly minister who witnessed it. "Heaven waits not the last moment, but owns its friends on THIS side death," and makes their death a blessing. His supernumerary relationship continued for 1842, 1843 and 1844, when his health being much improved he resumed the active work, and in 1845 and 1846, served the church at Winslow, where his devoted spirit impelled him to the performance of more labor than was consistent with his state of health, and at the close of his term there, he again regretfully retired to the supernumerary ranks, where he remained till the Conference of 1849, when he once more attempted the work of the ministry in Sharpstown and Woodstown, where his efficient services are still gratefully remembered by the people. In 1851 his broken constitution sank again, and he sorrowfully abandoned the work, never more to resume it upon earth. After this he resided at Glassboro, until the 23d of September, 1852, when his life of labor and suffering closed in peaceful triumph. In the early part of that year he observed to a friend, "If I am not to *preach* any more, my *work* is done, for I feel myself to be a man of but *one* work, which is, to preach Jesus and him crucified." His sufferings were excruciating, but a holy patience and resignation crowned them all with victory. In the beginning of this last illness he said, "I have not a doubt of my acceptance with God, nor have I had, at any time through my afflictions. My sky is clear. Sweet Jesus, sweet Jesus." Rev. J. Loudenslager, who witnessed his dying hours, speaks of them as exhibitions of glorious triumph. With both worlds apparent to his view, his attention would turn first to one and then to the other, as one who possessed both. The same communion with the other world which had been vouchsafed to him before, was given to him again. His departed children met his dying vision, and as they appeared before him, he kept turning to his weeping wife and exclaiming with ineffable rapture, "Little lambs, little lambs." They asked him if he was happy, and as calmly as if speaking on an ordinary topic he replied, "Yes, I *am* happy," and in this sweet frame of mind he fell asleep.

In the Conference obituary he is delineated as a holy and devoted minister with a talent above mediocrity. His power lay principally in *enlightening*, rather than *dazzling* his hearers. He *penetrated* the truths of the gospel, and presented them in an easy and familiar style, so that the feeblest and most uncultivated of his hearers could grasp their meaning. In doctrine he was purely Wesleyan. His manner was consoling and encouraging to the penitent, but intensely alarming to all classes of sinners. With boldness and earnestness he exposed the errors and backslidings of the church, and the danger of ungodly men.

His sermons were carefully prepared, full of *points* calculated to alarm the conscience, and delivered in a style so perfectly simple and natural, that it was impossible not to be interested in them. One of his hearers said, "He always preached as though he was full of matter, and never humdrummed on a text to try and squeeze a sermon out of it." His important propositions were fixed upon the mind either by the use of *unusual* terms or illustrations. He *felt* deeply himself, and the feeling usually communicated itself to those who formed his auditory, and, taken altogether, he was a noble type of a successful Methodist preacher.

His *social* qualities were of a very high order. He conversed with ease and fluency upon almost every subject. He never wearied by tediousness or degenerated by levity. His life had been rich in incident, and his habits those of close observation, and from these, his philosophic mind had gathered valuable results which it was his delight to impart, and which made his society an object eagerly sought after by all classes of men.

As a *friend* he was warm and faithful. He was very tender of the *reputation* of his brethren in the ministry, and exceedingly careful to make no unfavorable impression regarding their talents or usefulness. At one time he had spoken unfavorably of the abilities of a brother, but subsequently hearing him preach, became convinced that he had done him injustice, and wrote at once to the brother to whom the remark had been made, acknowledging its injustice and expressing his sorrow for ever having given it utterance. The *character* of a brother was safe in his hands, and his friendships embraced the minutest opportunities of benefiting their object.

As a Christian he had more than an ordinary experience. The spiritual world was sometimes revealed to him, as is not common to man. Such special revelations as have been alluded to, were bestowed upon him, while in the more *important* one of the "witness of the Spirit," his soul had full knowledge of God. For a long time he *enjoyed* entire sanctification, though he did not so fully profess it as his later convictions taught him to believe he should have done. His communion with God lifted him above earthly cares and sorrows, and enabled him to live with his conversation in heaven. From that experience he lived, from that experience he preached, and *with* that experience his soul was finally lifted to heaven.

May his mantle fall upon his brethren who still remain below, and stimulate them to a successful emulation of such a minister as John F. Crouch.

NOTE.—The writer desires to acknowledge his indebtedness to Rev. J. S. Hiesler, for a large portion of the material from which the above sketch was prepared.

REV. WILLIAM SMITH.

AFTER careful research we are left without sufficient materials, from which to prepare a proper memoir of this venerable man. Neither the place nor date of his birth—the name, occupation, nor circumstances of his parents—any of the surroundings of his early life—the place, date, nor manner of his conversion, or call to the ministry, nor, indeed anything respecting his early history can be given. He was a tailor by trade, but it is not known where or with whom he served his apprenticeship. He was favored with some school advantages, or else was a careful student privately, for he acquired some mental discipline, a fair knowledge of his mother tongue, and a considerable range of theological and general literature. At different times and places, after he ceased to be "effective," he taught Greenleaf's English Grammar, of which he was an amateur, and became an expert master. His appearance, together with the date of his entering the Conference, indicate an early conversion and call to the ministry. But the record of his name in the minutes for 1802, is the first definite item in his history that we are able to furnish. His fields of labor were the following:—

1802. Annamessex, David James, William Smith.

1803. Caroline, Ephraim Chambers, William Smith.

1804. Northampton, Richard Lyon, William Smith.

1805. Ontario, William Smith, Lawrence Riley.

1806. Seneca, William Hill, William Smith.

1807. Salem, William Mills, William Smith.

1808. Cumberland, William Smith, Charles Reed.

1809. Elizabethtown, William Smith, Thomas Stratton, John Sharpley.

1810. Freehold, William Smith, John Woolson.

1811. Salem, William Smith, Daniel Ireland.

1812. Cumberland, William Smith, Joseph Bennett.
1813. Gloucester, Daniel Ireland, William Smith.
1814. Freehold, Joseph Totton, William Smith.
1815. Asbury, Manning Force, William Smith.
1816. Sussex, David Bartine, William Smith.
1817. Gloucester, Solomon Sharp, William Smith.
1818. Bergen, Joseph Lybrand, William Smith.

In 1819 he located on account of feeble health, but in 1825 his name re-appears as supernumerary at Queen Ann's and Centreville. Then at Caroline, and then Greensboro alone. In 1828 it is not assigned to any place, but in 1829 to Lewistown; 1830, Accomac; 1831, Freehold. In 1832 he became superannuated, and so remained during life.

No literary remains have come into our hands, and it is now so long since the close of his effective ministry that but few items respecting it can be gathered. A number of elderly people have been found who remember the man and his ministry, and can give their impressions respecting both, but no facts. During his first term on Salem Circuit a revival occurred, which for many years was spoken of as "the great revival." This was one of those gracious, all-pervading outpourings of the Holy Spirit that but rarely occurs. "There were two conversions in particular that occasioned considerable remark. They were brothers, both large men, who had been great sinners, but became characterized as large stones in the building."

Mr. Smith was twice married, first to the daughter of a Mr. John Smith, of Salem Co. She lived but a few years, and left one child, who became the wife of Mr. Henry Barber, but also died early. Mr. Smith remained a widower for many years, but in the fall of 1830 he was married to the widow of Rev. James Quail, late of the Philadelphia Conference. He then settled at Long Branch, Monmouth Co., N. J. Mrs. Smith, who is highly spoken of, died Sept. 26, 1834. She left three children, only one of whom is yet living, and is married and settled in one of the north-western States. While at the Branch, his occupation was farming, but after the death of his wife he broke up housekeeping and spent the balance of his life chiefly in Philadelphia and New York.

We have not the means of forming a definite estimate of his character and abilities. We infer that he was accorded a medium rank as a preacher. His manner was not in a high degree impassioned, but grave, earnest, and impressive. His style was lucid, argumentative and convincing. His discourses were instructive, entertaining, and profitable. He studied to show himself "approved unto God, a workman that needed not to be ashamed, rightly dividing the word of truth." He felt a decided aversion to jumping, shouting, and all such modes of manifesting religious joy, deeming them disorderly extravagances. This interfered with his acceptability in some places. But without being specially popular, he was generally acceptable and useful.

He is said to have been a strict disciplinarian. This fact deserves to be mentioned to his credit. The Church is now deeply suffering the evil consequences of a loose exercise of discipline. But the responsibility for this discreditable state of things must be traced to a later period than that of the ministry of Mr. Smith and his cotemporaries.

In some respects our subject seems to have been poorly fitted for the trials and hardships of an itinerant at that period. His social and domestic feelings were strong and controlling, so that a companion and a home were almost as essential to his comfort as food and raiment. Yet in the inscrutable providence of God he was doomed to spend most of a long life without either. This bore hard upon his spirits, and was a constant source of annoyance and disquiet. His first wife was soon taken from him. Then, for some cause, now inexplicable, he reluctantly remained a homeless wanderer for many years. From these causes, and perhaps partly from natural temperament, his spirits were often depressed, and his head bowed down, so that he had many desponding and gloomy seasons. Nor was he favored with robust health. This, doubtless, added to the depression of his feelings, while this very depression made his health seem poorer to himself than it did to others. Yet it is conceded on all hands, so far as we have been able to learn, that while he was effective, he labored earnestly with some good measure of success. The list of his appointments shows that he occupied a fair share of important and responsible positions. It is also evident that from first to last he maintained the life of a humble, consistent follower of Christ. Rev. Eliphalet Reed, who became acquainted with him in 1819, and knew him well afterward, says, "He was a sincere Christian." The closing scenes of his life give assurance that this opinion was well founded. The following account is taken from the Conference Obituary:

"Rev. Wm. Smith departed this life at Long Branch, Monmouth Co., N. J., on Saturday, April 8, 1854.

"In July, 1853, he visited Long Branch for the benefit of his health, intending to remain there only during the warm season, but it pleased the Lord to direct otherwise; his health, instead of improving, continued to decline, until death released him from his sufferings. On the Tuesday previous to his departure, when interrogated as to his prospects for heaven, he responded with strong emphasis, 'My hope is full of immortality; my way is clear; I have peace with God through our Lord Jesus Christ.'"

Evidently aware of his approaching dissolution, he was anxious for the hour to arrive when he should depart and be with Christ. His sufferings at times were great, but he endured them with Christian fortitude and resignation. He expressed a warm affection for his brethren in the ministry, especially of the New Jersey Conference, remarking, "I shall meet with them no more on earth, but I rejoice in the prospect of meeting them in heaven."

From this time until Saturday he failed rapidly, when without a struggle he fell "asleep in Jesus."

REV. CHARLES PITMAN, D. D.

"Who that has sat beneath that silvery voice,
So like the chimings from a purer sphere,
Can e'er forget the compass of its power?
How rose and fell its thrillings on the ear,
Melting to tears the soul which earth had steeled,
As erst the flinty rock its lucent tide could yield."

Charles Pitman, son of Daniel and Hannah Pitman, was born at Cookstown, Burlington Co., N. J., on the 9th day of January, 1796. At the tender age of six years, his father died, and he was left to the care of his widowed mother. Through her pious teachings, his mind was early impressed with the evil of sin, and the importance of a religious life.

His mother's health was frail, and as she possessed but little of this world's goods, Charles was compelled, at a very early period, to bear a part in obtaining a support. For a considerable time he worked upon the farm of Daniel Smith, an old Quaker gentleman, whose only fault with the lad, seems to have been, that he loved his books, and occupied too much of his time in reading. After leaving the farm, he was engaged in the snuff mill of William Foulks, at New Egypt.

When quite a youth, and while his mother's teachings were yet fresh upon his mind, he went to Philadelphia, on a visit. He was soon invited by some of his young friends who were fond of theatrical exhibitions, to accompany them to their favorite place of resort. He yielded to their solicitations, but as soon as he reached the scene of these forbidden pleasures, conscience commenced its workings, he saw his mother's tears, he heard her spirit groanings and her prayers, a sudden trembling seized him, and unable to support himself, he clasped one of the pillars of the building, against which he leaned, until more composed, when he fled from the place of temptation as from the pit of destruction.

When in his sixteenth year, the prayers and godly example of his mother, together with the influences of the Divine Spirit, had so impressed his heart, that he became deeply interested for his soul. Soon, a meeting was held in the old M. E. Church at Wrightstown, only a few miles from the place of his birth, where he sought and found the pardon of his sins. His conversion was powerful, and attended with considerable physical excitement. He fell to the floor, where after remaining for a time in prayer and praise, he rose, not only freely justified by the grace of God, but so full of zeal for the salvation of his young companions, that he felt assured if he should only touch them, they would yield to the Spirit's influences and be saved. Thus impressed, he started for the door. Some fled before him, while all the others whom he could reach, surrendered themselves as willing captives to the Lord, and immediately sought his favor.

Shortly after this, on a Sabbath morning, his heart still burning with Divine love, and yearning with intense desire for the salvation of others, he visited five or six of his irreligious friends. His object was to exhort them to repentance and faith in Jesus. When he arrived, his heart was so full of sympathetic sorrow, that his utterance was choked, and bursting into tears, he turned away and left them. He was greatly mortified at his weakness, and yet these tears, silent though they were, had an influence which words and arguments often fail to produce, and in a few weeks all but one of those thus visited, were partakers of the great salvation, attributing their awakening to those floods of tears, of which at the time he was so heartily ashamed.

About this time, he received a letter from Rev. Joseph Bennett, a local preacher, and relative, a few passages from which are here appended.

"O my cousin, seek pure and undefiled religion. I have not been without the hope of seeing you in your Lord's vineyard, tilling Immanuel's ground. But knowing as I do, by experience, the many snares of the devil, the lusts of the flesh, and the allurements of the world, I sometimes fear my hope will be baffled. O, my dear Charles, cast away every Babylonish garment: like Joseph, tear away from every smiling mistress, and with Samuel say, 'Speak Lord, for thy servant heareth.'

"Wait the Lord's command, and the openings of Providence. Watch and pray. Take up your daily cross, read and meditate; keep out of company as much as possible, and I shall have hope of yet seeing a relation in the vineyard. May the God of all grace bless you with all spiritual blessings.

"I am, dear cousin, yours in love."

A new era in his life had now commenced. The latent fires of intellect were stirred, and he was athirst for knowledge. But there were difficulties in his way. Books were few, and opportunities for study were not only limited, but even these had their embarrassments. The day was occupied with labor, and at night he had only shavings, or a few pine knots, by the light of which to read the occasional volume that came within his reach. But the determined mind does not easily despond. He persevered and, by the time he had attained his seventeenth year, had so far qualified himself, as to take the charge of a small county school. At one time he taught in Pemberton, and the little brick building which he occupied, is still standing, in the rear of Benajah Antrem's store.

Advancing rapidly in piety and knowledge, he was licensed to exhort at New Mills, in September, 1815; so that with studying, teaching, and warning sinners to flee from the wrath to come, his time was wholly and profitably occupied.

In the winter of 1816, Rev. E. Page, then a local preacher, and young Pitman, yet an exhorter, held a meeting at Three Tuns, now Hedding, near Columbus, which was visited in a most wonderful manner with the out-pourings of the Holy Spirit. There was great excitement. One young woman was so powerfully wrought upon, that in the hope of escaping the influences which she felt, fled from the place, but, unable to flee from the Spirit of God, yielded her heart to the claims of the gospel and was saved.

Beholding such fruits of his labor the conviction that it was his duty to preach the gospel, grew clearer and stronger from day to day. He felt it was his duty not only to preach, but to devote all his time to preaching. But, notwithstanding this, he continued his work as a teacher, and as he well knew the hesitancy with which the Conference at that time received men with families, and hoping to get clear of the obligations which he felt to become an itinerant, entered into the marriage relation, and Miss Mary Newbold became his wife.

But this course did not silence his convictions. There was a voice, by day and by night, perpetually whispering or thundering, in his ear and heart,

> "Go sound the gospel jubilee,
> And tell poor sinners Jesus died.
> Say to a bondaged world, Be free,
> For mercy's arms are open wide."

Finally, in March, 1817, he so far yielded to his convictions, as to consent to receive license to preach. Here he thought his anxieties on the subject would cease, for as he was now married, he supposed the barrier in his way to the Conference was insurmountable. But, God's ways are not as our ways. After one short year of wedded life, Brother Pitman was bereft of his companion, and an infant son was left to his paternal care. How true are the words of inspiration, "Son of man, behold I take away from thee the desire of thine eyes with a stroke." This stroke, falling so suddenly and unexpectedly, he always regarded as a punishment for refusing to yield to what he knew was duty. He now felt that longer resistance would expose him to still further visitations. Like an obedient son therefore, he laid himself upon the Divine altar, and in the spirit of an entire consecration said, "*Here am I, send me.*"

Some time during the year 1817, the health of Rev. Daniel Moore so far failed, as to require him to give up his work on Trenton Circuit, and Charles Pitman was appointed to supply his place. It is worthy of remark, that his first sermon as an itinerant, was preached in the old church, corner of Green and Academy streets, in that city, the scene of so many of his subsequent efforts, and within thirty yards of the spot where after thirty-seven years of almost unparalleled toils and triumphs, he yielded up his soul to God.

In the spring of 1818, he was received on trial by the Philadelphia Annual Conference, and returned to Trenton Circuit. His itinerant career was now fully inaugurated, and though he shrank at first from the high and sacred responsibility, yet, having now given himself to the work, it absorbed his physical and mental energies to an extent rarely equaled.

In 1819, he was appointed with John Potts to Bergen Circuit. A little memorandum book, still in excellent preservation, shows the several preaching-places, the texts from which he preached at each place, and the number of members in every class connected with this charge. As these things may be matters of future interest, I append the names of the appointments on the circuit, with the number in society at each place. Belleville, thirty-two members; Spring Garden, twenty-five; Bloomfield, thirty; Caldwell, twenty; Paramus, two classes, sixty white, and seven colored members; Sherwood's, ten members; Widow Guiness's, thirty-two; Drummond's, sixteen; Johnson's, seven; Babcock's, twenty-five; Thiell's thirty-eight; Haverstraw, fifty-nine white, and four colored; Nyack, twenty-seven white, and four colored; Pond, twenty-six; Taylor's, eleven; Williams's, five; Fort Lee, twenty-seven, and four colored; Bull's Ferry, one; Ringwood, twenty-two white, and five colored; Paterson, three classes, fifty-six members; making twenty preaching-places, with four hundred and eighty-two white members, and eighteen colored.

Most of these places are now flourishing charges of themselves, and what was then comparatively a moral waste, now blooms and blossoms like the rose. Pitman was returned to Bergen in 1820, in company with Rev. G. Banghart. The revival flame spread in every direction. Young Pitman was exceedingly popular, and multitudes flocked to hear him. Among those converted was Charles Dougherty, who up to this time had been a Roman Catholic. Through much opposition he now became a decided Methodist. Soon after his conversion, he was elected to fill the office of a trustee. Not being acquainted with the duties of such an office, he inquired of some of his brethren what he was to do; and, among other things, was told he must assist in taking the collection on the Sabbath. Willing to serve the church in any way, he commenced his duties at once. Accordingly on the following Sabbath, he took the purse, which in those days was suspended at the end of a staff, some five or six feet long, and passed it among the audience to receive their contributions. A large number, however, gave him as he passed, only *a very respectful bow.* This, in his simplicity, he supposed meant, they were willing to contribute, but not having the means at hand to do so then, wished him to do it for them and charge to their account. Anxious to do the best he could, and as far as possible accommodate all, he went to the house of God on the following Sabbath, *with his pockets filled with change.* As he passed along from seat to seat, the people began to bow again, and every time they bowed, *he dropped a penny in the purse to their account.* They looked amazed. What does the new trustee mean? The third Sabbath, however, all were prepared, and instead of *bows*, they gave their *money.* Brother Dougherty had *cured them.*

About the middle of this conference year, Rev. Jacob Moore, who had been laboring at New Brunswick. failed in health, and it became necessary to supply his place. Charles Pitman was selected for this important work, and on the eighth of October, 1820, he left his friends on Bergen Circuit, by whom he was greatly beloved, and entered upon the duties of his new and responsible charge in the city. He found but twenty members of the church there, and the very name of Methodist, was a term so full of reproach, that few were willing to bear the scorn associated with it. and the cause had been languishing for years. The arrival of Pitman gave a new impulse to the drooping energies of our Zion, and crowds soon gathered to hear the eloquent words which fell in such harmonious accents from his lips. The fame of the preacher spread far and wide, so that at the expiration of his term of service, the church had not only increased from twenty to one hundred members, but the public sentiment in favor of Methodism had advanced an hundred fold. The memory of his labors is still cherished in New Brunswick. and a vigorous church. in an enterprising part of the city, called by his name, stands as a living and lasting monument of his fame.

Leaving New Brunswick, he was appointed in 1823–4, as the first pastor of the Bridgeton Station. He commenced his ministry in that place on the eighth of June, 1823, with a sermon from the text, "Finally brethren, pray for us, that the word of the Lord may have free course and be glorified." Pitman was a stranger in that community, and the number of his hearers was small. At six o'clock in the evening, he preached from the text, "He that goeth forth and weepeth bearing precious seed, shall doubtless come again rejoicing, bringing his sheaves with him." In this sermon there were overwhelming tides of gospel eloquence, and the copious showers of tears shed on that occasion are remembered to this day.

It was soon noised abroad that a man of marked ability was in their midst, and the church henceforth, was always filled with earnest listeners. Rev. James Ayres, Presiding Elder of Newark District, Newark Conference, says, "The first time I ever heard him speak was on the following occasion. Passing through the street in Bridgeton, N. J., one evening in warm weather, I heard at a distance a voice which sounded so sweetly that I was instinctively drawn in the direction of it. As I advanced, I saw the door of a house ajar, and soon learned that a minister was leading class in a private room. I listened, and such was the mellowness of his voice, and the unction with which he spoke, that I was perfectly entranced, and impressions were made, never to be effaced. From that hour, I became interested in the man. As the class-meeting was held weekly, on a subsequent evening, although an impenitent youth, I formed one of the number present. After Mr. Pitman had spoken to the other persons in the room, he addressed some kind inquiries to me. Finding I had not experienced converting grace, he led me in a short series of questions and answers, to promise that I would pray to God for a new heart. He then laid his hands upon my head, and, in a most solemn and melting prayer, called upon God and angels to witness my pledge, and entreated the Lord to accept me as his own dear child. Such was the commencement of my own religious career, and surely, I have cause to remember with reverence and gratitude, him, who under God, led me to such a course."

On the 21st of October, 1823, Mr. Pitman was married to Miss Lucy Ann Gillespie, of Philadelphia, who up to the close of life shared in his toils and triumphs, and still survives him.

The church in Bridgeton more than doubled under his ministry, so that when he left, after deducting for removals, expulsions, deaths, and other losses, there was a membership of two hundred and eleven.

In 1825 he was placed in charge of St. George's, Philadelphia, embracing several churches, and a membership of over two thousand souls. Revs. William Barnes and Joseph Holdich were his assistants. This year was one of great labor, wide-spread popularity, and much success, several hundred being added to the church. But large and important as was this city charge, there were other and still more important posts to occupy, and he remained at St. George's only one year.

In 1826, when just thirty years of age, and only eight in the ministry, he was appointed Presiding Elder of West Jersey District. The condition of the Church in all that region was low. Methodism, indeed, in many parts of the district scarcely had a name. Calvinistic churches were scattered here and there throughout the territory, and, even where there was no regular church organization, the people held largely to Calvinistic sentiments. Here, then, was a vast and magnificent field for the exercise of his popular talents, and the dissemination of the doctrines of Methodism—doctrines which were embalmed in his soul by a blessed experience, and cherished by his intellect as giving the only true exposition of the word of God. Never, perhaps, did a man go forth better qualified by natural endowments and gracious influences for the work to which he had been called. During the eight years of his previous ministry his mind had been enlarged by careful discipline and study: his elocution was at times, and especially on great occasions, over-mastering and resistless, his piety sincere and deep, all of which, when added to his official position, gave him an influence almost unbounded. He went to his district, not only like a son of thunder, striking terror to the souls of ecclesiastical opponents, but like the silver-mouthed Apollos, soothing the sorrows of the penitent, and gladdening the hearts of Christians, until tears of holy joy fell in showers like summer rain.

During the camp-meeting season, when it was known that he would preach, the whole country for many miles would be on the move. Not unfrequently he would have five, six, or even seven thousand persons to hear him on such occasions. His audiences were often chained to the spot for two hours and a half at a time, forgetful of everything but the great theme of the redemption of a lost world, upon which he dwelt. Towards the latter part of his sermon unconsciously and instinctively the people would rise, one after another, until the whole were on their feet, and when he finished it was difficult to distinguish between the rejoicing of Christians, and the weeping of awakened sinners. It would seem as if heaven had been drawn down to earth, or earth had been elevated to heaven. At one of these great gatherings in the pines of lower Jersey, he preached three times with such remarkable power, that three hundred and sixty professed conversion.

At a similar meeting in Salem County, he had taken strong and unanswerable positions in antagonism to Unitarianism, and likewise crossing the views entertained by the followers of Elias Hicks, the distinguished Quaker. These positions were sustained as usual with great eloquence and unction. His opponents, unable to present a single argument in refutation, feeling all he said was true, but mortified beyond endurance by defeat, gave vent to the pent up fires of passion by declaring aloud that the preacher was vile and ought to have his throat cut. On the following day, Pitman, who had heard of the utterances of these men, was giving directions concerning a collection. When he was through, the collectors, hat in hand, were starting to wait upon the people, but the preacher cried out to them, "Stop." Halting, and looking towards him, he said, "Brethren, I understand there are some persons here who declare that any man who could utter such sentiments as I did yesterday, ought to have his throat cut; now I don't want you to take a cent from such persons; just pass them by, and let them enjoy themselves with their hands in their pockets." No one was willing to be reckoned among those who had made these rough remarks, and the result was, everybody contributed, and a very large collection was obtained.

He held a meeting at Cape May Court House, before there was any society in that neighborhood, and so powerfully were the people wrought upon, that he dismissed them three times before they would leave the place.

His quarterly meetings were seasons of so much interest, that persons often traveled all night in order to be present, and his congregations were composed of all classes of community. The rich and the poor met together, and learned and illiterate were alike moved to penitence and prayer.

He continued on the district four years, and the present prosperous condition of the churches in West Jersey is in a large measure attributable to him. Through all that region he was peerless in his power, and his name to this day is a synonym for all that is grand and glorious in our Methodistic Zion.

His next field of labor was the East Jersey District, comprising all that part of the State lying north of Trenton, including Staten Island; and several appointments north of the lines separating New York from New Jersey. This was another vast territory in which Methodism, though in some localities comparatively strong, had in many places only a feeble and sickly existence, being overshadowed by its old, well organized, wealthy and influential competitors,—the various Calvinistic churches.

Here, in this field, too, like causes produced like results with those which had been realized on the West Jersey District. His quarterly visitations and camp-meeting occasions were still seasons of great interest and spiritual power. At all of these meetings marked displays of the Divine presence were expected and experienced. God came up with his people, and the eloquence and tears of Pitman, like a swelling flood, swept down all opposition, and left him, an intellectual and spiritual giant, sole master of the field.

A camp-meeting was held near Newton, Sussex County. Pitman was a stranger in that mountainous region, but his popularity had preceded him, and the expectations were great. The congregation gathered was immense. Lawyers, physicians, judges, men of wealth and influence from all parts of the country came to hear the gospel of the Son of God. The preacher seemed to have special qualifications for the work before him, and torrents of baptized eloquence fell from his lips with such over-mastering power, that strong men were bowed to the earth like the tempest-swept forest, and multitudes yielded to be saved.

Many persons of wealth in the community, supposing money could secure all they might desire, made large offers if he would remain and preach for them again. But he had his work, and no offers, which man might make, could induce him to turn aside from his God-appointed path.

"During the Summer of 1831, a camp-meeting was held near New Brunswick. Charles Pitman preached on the first day of August. At the close of his discourse the people were so overwhelmed, that a deathly silence prevailed all over the ground. Tears, copious and glistening, gushed up from every heart. The heaven-inspired minister himself, removed almost beyond the power of utterance, motioned to one who sat near him to pray. The congregation knelt, and for five minutes not a voice was heard. Eventually, a prayer-meeting was commenced, and 'then came a sound from heaven, as of a rushing, mighty wind.' Believers were sanctified, and sinners were brought to the foot of the cross. Two preachers, Brothers Petherbridge and Bull, fell prostrate to the ground, and lay in a state of apparent unconsciousness for several hours." An old man, who had not heard a sermon for many years, led hither by curiosity, fell beneath the power of conviction, yielded to be saved on the terms of the gospel, was blessed, and returned home, rejoicing in hope of future glory. And "so mightily grew the word of God and prevailed."

The appointment of Pitman to these two districts, which, at that time, occupied the entire state, seemed providential. Our young and growing, but in many places weak and feeble Church, seemed, just then, to require the presence of a great master-spirit, who could arrest the attention of the masses, and then move and mould, control and direct them for the glory of God. Pitman was that master-spirit, and for seven consecutive years.

as Presiding Elder on these two districts, he moved and moulded the entire state of New Jersey Methodistically, as no man ever did, and probably as no one man ever will again. During these years thousands were added to the Church, and public sentiment, concerning Methodism, everywhere was changed. Calvinism received checks from which it will not soon recover, and the doctrines of free grace and an unlimited atonement were disseminated from Cape May to the hills of Upper Sussex, and from the Delaware River to the sea. The fires of his eloquence consumed the rubbish of doctrinal error, his evangelic arguments ploughed the deep field of the human heart, the gospel of free grace was living seed cast deep into the soft soil of the soul, and his prayers and tears, the sunshine and the shower, fostering the seed thus sown; and if it is yet true, "They that be wise shall shine as the brightness of the firmament, and they that turn many to righteousness as the stars forever and ever," how bright and glorious must the eternal future of Charles Pitman be!

Called to leave the district at the close of his third year, he was appointed, in 1833, to Union Church, Philadelphia, where he remained two years.

Rev. S. Y. Monroe, who experienced religion and joined the Church towards the close of his first year in that charge, says:

"At the period of Mr. Pitman's appointment to the Union Church, the present noble edifice on the west side of Fourth street, below Arch street, was in course of erection. Divine services, for the time, were held in what was known as Keyser's Church, in Crown street, below Callowhill. This was a building of moderate size, which had been kindly loaned for Sabbath afternoon and evening service.

"Pitman's reputation for pulpit eloquence, strengthened by the remembrance of his labors at St. George's in 1825, and occasional opportunities of hearing him during the years of his eldership, had awakened expectations of no ordinary character, and he found, on his arrival, crowding throngs eager to listen to his words.

"The accommodations at Keyser's were far from being sufficient to provide even comfortable standing room for the numbers who came, and those who wished to secure a place, found it necessary to be present a long while before the hour of service. Often were the side-walks, as far as the adjoining streets, filled with a multitude patiently waiting until the opening of the doors should give them an early ingress.

"On the completion of the new building in Fourth street, the society removed to its commodious audience room, and morning services were added to those previously held. Here the sittings were, perhaps, three-fold the number of those in the place temporarily occupied, but, considerable as the enlargement was, not only was every part needed, but, in a little time, the pressure was as great as it had formerly been. From all parts of the city the people poured into the new sanctuary, until the society might have said again, 'The place is too straight for me, give place to me that I may dwell.'*

"The spacious auditorium, when the congregation had assembled, presented, often, a thrilling and inspiring scene. Seats, aisles, vestibule, and, not unfrequently, gallery and pulpit stairs were crowded to their utmost with an interested throng, where every ear was open, and every eye was fixed upon him who occupied the sacred desk. The preacher was worthy of such an audience."

A man of commanding physical appearance, six feet high, somewhat inclined to corpulency, a fine, large head, covered with a luxuriant growth of dark and slightly curling hair, a moderately high forehead, slightly sunken eyes, rather short upper lip, dark complexion, and, with all, a voice of great compass and power, whose every note was melody. His countenance, too, was an index to the various emotions of his soul, while his manner was grave, dignified, full of earnestness and feeling, and, so far as the exterior was concerned, every element which constitutes the orator seemed to be possessed.

Then came the thoughts, just, appropriate, forcible, so warm with sympathy, so powerful with unction, and so eloquently ex-

* Words from which Dr. Holdich had preached the last time they worshiped in the "old Academy," previously to its being torn down to give place to the present beautiful church.

pressed, that those vast congregations, which at the commencement of the services, were like a sea of upturned faces, melted in tears, and bowed at last, like willows by the water courses.

It was on a Sabbath afternoon, during this popular career, at Union Church, about the first of March, 1834, the writer of this memorial first beheld him. The venerable Dr. Gough, a local minister in connexion with the church had preached, and the services were closing, when I, a youth, from motives of curiosity, ascending the northern stairway, stood upon the upper step, in full view of his majestic form. Pitman, who was then in his thirty-eighth year, and in the very zenith of his manhood, and ministerial glory, was reading the hymn, commencing,

> "O, that my load of sin were gone;"

the first words that reached my ear, were,

> "The cross all stained with hallowed blood,
> The labor of his dying love."

All the deep sympathies of his nature were poured into these two lines. The voice seemed almost divine, and the blessed sentiments, fell into the soul, softly and smoothly as drops of liquid silver, never to be forgotten. This was the commencement of my own religious history, and now, at the expiration of thirty years, that majestic form and mellow voice, are fresh and beautiful in memory, as things of yesterday.

Revival scenes were witnessed during most of the months of his ministry at the Union, the fruits of which remain unto this day. Large numbers of young men were brought into the church, many of whom are now preaching the gospel, living epistles read and known of all men.

At the expiration of his term of service there, in 1835, he was appointed in connexion with Rev. E. S. Janes, agent for Dickinson College.

It is questionable whether this kind of work was congenial to him, but, whatever his personal preferences were, he yielded to the call of the church, which in all such matters, he obeyed as the voice of God.

Thrown out of the regular pastorate, in which all the sympathies of his nature were enlisted, where his mind, too, was engaged in regular and systematic study, he was now largely occupied with the financial interests of the cause of education, and yet, the fires of his ministerial zeal were not extinguished.

Traveling in the duties of his agency, he came one day in the vicinity of a camp-meeting, and, like the war horse snuffing the battle from afar, hastened towards it. His arrival was near the middle of the day. He said to the Presiding Elder, "I have come to your meeting, and must leave this afternoon, but God has given me a message to this people, will you let me preach?" The elder replied, "There is a brother engaged to preach this afternoon, if he will yield the appointment, I shall be glad to have you." The arrangements were made, and Pitman was to preach. At three o'clock, however, the sky was overcast with dense black clouds, fierce lightnings glared, and the thunders roared terribly. All the indications were that a fearful tempest would immediately burst upon them. But notwithstanding these angry premonitions, the preacher took the stand, and falling upon his knees, cried, in an agony of spirit, "O! Lord God Almighty, if thou hast sent me to preach to this people, hold back these threatening clouds for one hour." This prayer was thrice repeated; each time with increasing faith and fervor. It was a bold request, yet it was heard, and the rain was staid. He preached for an hour and ten minutes, like one newly commissioned from the skies, and, as if when through, he must immediately return to report the manner in which he had performed his work. Men stood aghast, or, feeling that the day of doom had come, fell prostrate to the earth, under the power of the convicting Spirit. Thousands were present at the service, and as soon as he had finished, the clouds no longer restrained, poured out their contents in such ceaseless floods, that the multitudes fled to the tents for refuge. The whole congregation convinced by the power of truth, and now held captives by the storm, were kept within the reach of religious effort. Prayer-meetings were opened simultaneously all over the encampment, and such were the gracious displays of Divine power, amid the tempest, that five hundred souls were reported among the saved on that memorable afternoon and evening.

Closing his labors in the agency at the expiration of one year, he was stationed in 1836 and 1837, at old St. George's in Philadelphia, to engage once more, in the great business to which he had devoted his life, and for which he was so pre-eminently qualified, preaching the gospel in connexion with the regular pastorate. It was just ten years since he left this charge, and he now returns to it, with an enlarged experience, greater popularity and pulpit power, and in just so much, better prepared for more extended usefulness.

Much of the year 1836 was taken up with extensive improvements to the church edifice, which interfered somewhat with those direct efforts which he was accustomed to make for the salvation of souls.

Wm. P. Corbit, then a worldly-minded young man, assisted as one of the workmen, in these repairs. Pitman used often to say to him, "Friend Corbit, when we get our church done, you must get religion, and come and join us."

In the fall and winter of 1837, some time after the church had been re-opened, it became evident that the streams of salvation were rising to such an extent, that all former banks between which the gracious tides had flowed, would be overrun, and a general inundation would take place. God's saints cried out, "Let it come, Lord, let it come," and the newly garnished walls of old St. George's, echoed back the earnest cry, "Aye, Lord, let it come, and come quickly."

While they were thus looking and waiting for the coming flood, Pitman appeared in the pulpit one Sabbath evening, and announced as his text, "He that goeth forth and weepeth, bearing precious seed, shall doubtless come again with rejoicing, bringing his sheaves with him." As he advanced in his subject, the people were wrapt in silent astonishment at his utterances, and like a volcano, heaving with emotion, were endeavoring to smother the fires within. Strange as it may appear, at the very moment when the multitudes thought they were listening to little less than an angelic ministry, clouds and darkness so surrounded the speaker, that, incapable of proceeding further, he suddenly stopped, and, turning round in the pulpit, fell upon his knees, and wrestled with God for deliverance. In an instant, such a

Divine influence swept over the congregation, as had never been witnessed in that time-honored church. Scores immediately rushed to the altar for prayer, crying, "God be merciful to us sinners." From that evening, the work of the Lord swept on with increasing grandeur and glory for many weeks.

It was no ordinary revival, it was a flood, an inundation, going far beyond all that the strongest faith had dared to hope for.

Five prayer-meetings were sometimes held at once. Three in the gallery, one on either side, and one in the front, while below there was one at the altar, and another by the front door. All hearts seemed surcharged with divine power. A man took his seat in the gallery one night with knife and stick in hand to keep tally of the number who went to the altar. When the prayer-meetings commenced, the whole congregation seemed ready to go forward. He looked in amazement: "My Lord," said he, "they are all going," and dropping knife and stick, exclaimed, "I will go too!" He was soon converted, and, returning to the gallery, gathered up his things, feeling glad, not merely because this and that man were born there, but that he too was included in that happy number.

The interest became so general through the city that sometimes rows of carriages, bearing the rich and gay, extended all along Fourth street, from Race to Vine, and often their converted owners, re-entering their carriages, were driven to their homes, shouting the praises of God along the streets. Men and women laid for hours, like those who had been slain in battle, and when they returned to consciousness, "Glory—glory!" were the first utterances that fell from their lips.

There was a southern lady of great beauty and wealth who was devoted to fashion in all its wildest and extremest forms. The theatre and ball-room were her favorite places of resort. She heard of the meeting, and came with her jewelry and splendor to see what was going on. Arrested by the power of grace, she too bowed at the altar of mercy, repented of her folly, wept, and prayed, and asked to be forgiven. God sent the baptismal floods upon her, and she shouted aloud the praises of her King. Tearing off her gewgaws and jewelry, she cast them at the feet of God's servants in the altar, who, gathering them up, sold them, and gave the proceeds to the cause of missions, while she became not only a devout Christian, but gave her time, talents, wealth, and influence to extend the knowledge of her redeeming Lord.

The meeting swept on with such unwonted power that, in the period of twelve or thirteen weeks, seven hundred and fifty souls professed conversion, among whom were William P. and Israel S. Corbit, both of whom became influential members of the New Jersey Conference; and, it is estimated, that nearly fifty others entered the ministry from that revival alone.

Some time before his labors closed at St. George's the membership was far too large for one pastoral charge, and quite a number from this church and others entered into a separate organization, purchased the building on Eighth street, above Noble, which had been used by a Dutch Reformed congregation, and in 1838 Charles Pitman became their pastor. It was a new field of labor, and in some respects calculated to try the preacher's faith; but, however sorely he may have been tempted, he rose above the shafts of the enemy, and in that neighborhood, then so largely occupied by butchers, poured forth, as was his wont, the precious gospel of the Son of God. Soon large numbers of these earnest and honest men became, not only his warm admirers, but the lovers and followers of his Lord.

His labors in this new church were attended with large success.

In the year 1839, when it became known that in the opinion of Bishop Waugh, there were legal barriers in the way of his return the second year, a petition containing the names of a great proportion of the citizens of Spring Garden, was carried to the Bishop in the hope of changing his mind upon the subject. But the Bishop seeing, as he thought, the constitutional difficulty, said he could not return him, no matter who, or how many, might ask it to be done. This, however, was not the exercise of an arbitrary power on the Bishop's part, but, as he believed, a just adherence to law, which he must observe in Pitman's case as well as in reference to the humblest minister in the Church.

When, therefore, the Philadelphia Conference of 1839 adjourned, he was transferred to the New Jersey Conference, and, when that body met, was stationed at the large new church in Green street, Trenton, which had just been completed under the administration of Rev. A. Atwood.

His congregations were large, and here, as elsewhere, souls were added to the Lord.

For a number of years his peculiar adaptation for special services, such as corner-stone laying and the dedication of churches, had been manifest to the Methodistic public, and his calls on such occasions were numerous.

The years of his sojourn in Trenton were far from being exceptions to this kind of labor. About this period, a vast number of those plain old God-honored churches, erected and occupied with so much religious faith and fervor by our fathers, had served their generation, and were passing away, while a new era in church architecture had come. Buildings, more commodious, costly, and better adapted to the growing interests of our Zion, were rising on every hand. At that time, few of those within a circle of several hundred miles were opened, where he did not take some part in the dedicatory services. Rev. Wm. P. Corbit, who spent one year in study with Mr. Pitman, while at Trenton, thinks his calls for such labor while there, averaged three per month, and, during some of the later periods of his ministry, he often attended three in a single week. There were few churches erected in New Jersey between the years 1825 and 1850 whose walls did not first echo with the gospel from the lips of Charles Pitman.

Towards the close of his term of service in Trenton a vacancy occurred in the secretaryship of the Missionary Society of the Methodist Episcopal Church. Letters from several leading ministers were soon received by him, soliciting his views concerning the acceptance of the office. While Mr. Pitman was not insensible of the honor such a position would confer, he knew its responsibilities were vast, and, feeling that his great mission was more directly to preach the gospel for the immediate conversion of sinners and the general upbuilding of the Church of God, declined entertaining the proposition, and when the Conference of 1841 adjourned, he was appointed Presiding Elder of Trenton District.

He immediately entered upon the duties assigned him, and passed partly around his district, when, in June following, on the assembling of the New York Conference, with which, at that time, was vested the power of filling vacancies in the General Conference offices, in the interval of its sessions, notwithstanding his expressed reluctance, he was elected Corresponding Secretary of the Missionary Society of the Methodist Episcopal Church. Subsequently, he was elected to the same office, by the General Conferences of 1844 and 1848.

It was a position of great importance, involving interests wide-spread and vast as eternity, and yet, whatever his own views and preferences in the matter were, now that he was called by the voice of the church, the obligations were felt too strongly to allow him to refuse.

He therefore accepted the position, removed his family to New York, and commenced his new and onerous duties.

His thoughts and labors were now to a large extent in channels new and strange. The general oversight and direction, under the advice of the Board of Managers, of all the missions in connection with our church, together with the promotion of the financial interests connected therewith, devolved, to a great extent on him.

In the prosecution of this work, he traveled far and wide, and a new impulse was given to this divine cause, which under the administration of wise and judicious successors has continued to increase to the present day.

But, though his mind was so largely engrossed in these matters, he found time for the more direct work of a gospel minister. The next year after his appointment to the Secretaryship, he dedicated twelve churches in widely different localities—preached every Sabbath unless prevented by sickness, and oftentimes through the week; sometimes in Boston in the east, and then at Petersburgh at the South—everywhere calling sinners to repentance, and building up the church in its most holy faith. At Petersburgh, he says, "Had a good time, and twenty were at the altar." At Green Street, New York, "Felt at home, and between twenty and thirty were at the altar." At John Street, New York, "an interesting time, and thirteen were at the altar."

These things, however, were in the intervals of his official business, the large proportion of his time being taken up with missionary sermons, addresses, collections, reports, correspondence, plannings, &c.

But numerous and pressing as were oftentimes the duties of his office, he could not forget or desert his old summer resorts—the camp-meetings. In 1842, one of these meetings was in progress near Bellville, New Jersey. Thither he repaired. At an appointed time he was to preach, but when the hour arrived, there was every indication of an immediate and heavy rain; indeed, a few drops had already fallen, and the people were hurrying to their tents for shelter, when Pitman, mighty in faith, called aloud for them to stop, assuring them that in as much as he was the Lord's ambassador, the rain would not fall till his message was delivered. Rev. A. E. Ballard, then a young man, and present at the meeting, says. "At this announcement, I looked incredulously at the blackened heavens. but remembering to have heard that once before, on a similar occasion, he had made a similar declaration, I determined to wait and see, although trembling for God's honor in the result. He then knelt, and prayed fervently that God, for the glory of his cause, would hold back the rain until the sermon was delivered, and in his prayer, felt more strongly that it would be so. He arose, told the people again there would be no rain until he was through with preaching. All this while, however, the clouds were hanging over the assembly like a funeral pall, and to human vision, a moment could not elapse, before the storm would burst upon us. But the people waited, and he preached for nearly two hours, with great power and unction. At the close of the sermon, he shouted, 'To your tents, O Israel, for the Lord's message having been delivered. the rain will now descend.' We fled for refuge, but had scarcely time to shelter ourselves, before the floods poured upon us in greatest fury."

Sometimes on these great occasions his sympathies were stirred to their very depths, and he could only find relief in tears. At one of these meetings in the woods, a solemn and impressive discourse had been delivered, without producing much visible effect. During its presentation, Pitman had been in his imagination, placing all that vast congregation before the judgment, where they were to receive their final award. He thought the matter over and over, until it seemed to be a reality. With these views and feelings, he arose to exhort. But the awful danger to which the people were exposed, so overwhelmed his burdened heart, that utterance was choked, and he could not speak a single word. He stood for two or three minutes, and then covered with confusion at his awkward position, waved his hand towards the altar, and burst into a flood of tears. The people who had sat unmoved, though solemnly impressed under the sermon, quite unprepared for this outburst of sympathy on their behalf, yielded to the truth, and came—ten, twenty, fifty, a hundred, two, three hundred, crowded around the rude altar in the forest, all seeking the forgiveness of their sins, and renewal in righteousness. Glorious power had attended Pitman's *words* a thousand times, but in this instance, an equal, if not greater power, attended *Pitman's tears!*

But we must turn away from these soul-stirring scenes, and follow him to his office work in the dry and dusty city. It is not intended, however, to examine the details of his missionary labor, during the nine years of his secretaryship. That which he did one year, he did the next, with this difference, that, like the waves, when the pebble has been dropped into the smooth waters, circling wider and wider till they reach the shore, so he enlarged and increased the circle of his toils, until reaching the shore of human weakness he could toil no more.

If then, we take the year 1843, the third of his new position, as one of the early or inner circles of his missionary labors, when he traveled six thousand miles, delivered forty-one sermons, thirty missionary addresses, dedicated six churches, and collected ten thousand dollars, and that too, at a time when missionary funds were contributed with a hand vastly less liberal than now; then enlarge these labors each year, in proportion as the missionary cause enlarged and took a stronger hold upon the judgment and sympathies of the church, remembering too, that his calls to corner-stone layings, dedications, camp-meetings, and protracted efforts, were augmenting, rather than diminishing.

and we shall have some idea of his work during the six years succeeding 1843.

But the labors just enumerated, are such only as appear upon the surface, and could readily be seen by the church. They do not include the drudgery of the office, the wide-spread correspondence, the editorial supervision of the Missionary Advocate, the preparation of reports, the devising of large and liberal schemes of benevolence, and the urging of these upon the attention of annual conferences, hundreds of miles apart, arranging for missionary meetings, in which to give a practical application and developement of all these schemes in the churches throughout our wide-spread territory, the entertainment of missionaries, assisting them in the out-fit for their voyages and travels, supervising their embarkation and departure; these, and a thousand nameless things, which even good men could neither understand or appreciate, added to his labors in the pulpit and on the platform, made up a weight of toil and care too great to be long endured.

In the year 1844, he received the following communication, which explains itself:

"TO REV. CHARLES PITMAN.

"METHODIST MISSION ROOMS, NEW YORK.

"REV. AND VERY DEAR SIR:—It gives me pleasure to communicate to you officially, that the *Academic Senate* of the *University* of *North Carolina*, conferred upon you the honorary degree of *Doctor of Divinity*, on the 6th inst., in Gerard Hall, at the celebration of the annual commencement of the institution.

Allow me to embrace this occasion to tender an expression of the high regard for you sincerely cherished, by

"Yours, affectionately, and obediently,

"CHARLES M. F. DEEMS."

UNIVERSITY OF N. C. *June* 10, 1844.

In regard to the honor thus bestowed, it may be added, that although he never manifested any fondness for such things, yet, as it came unsought, he received it in silence as an expression of kind regard, and wore it without resistance to the end; but, if a deep practical, and to some extent critical knowledge of the word of God, if power to preach that word so that sinners in vast multitudes were converted and the Church built up, if a thorough knowledge of theology and Church usages in his own and other communions, and a burning love for Jesus, constitute claims for such distinction, Charles Pitman possessed them all, and was, in the highest and truest sense, a Doctor of Divinity, entitled to all the honors which such a degree could confer upon him.

In the closing part of the year 1847, after an extended and protracted official tour westward, accompanied by Mrs. Pitman and Bishop Waugh, Dr. Pitman, in the most fraternal spirit, addressed a missionary letter to the ministers of the Liberia Annual Conference, which was so highly esteemed by that body, that by resolution copies were ordered published at their missionary printing office for the use of the members and other friends. The first and closing paragraphs are here appended.

"Dear Brethren, for some time past I have felt a strong and increasing desire to address you on the subject of the great work in which you are engaged, and, if possible, to encourage your hearts and strengthen your hands for the more successful prosecution of the duties which devolve upon you as missionaries of the cross. But, as yet, neither time nor circumstances have allowed me an opportunity of gratifying this desire. Nor am I now able to communicate with you individually. I have, therefore, determined to address you collectively, and in your Conference capacity."

He then treats of the magnitude and importance of the work, the qualifications with which a missionary should be endowed, the difficulties and dangers connected with missionary enterprise, and closes in the following words:

"In conclusion, permit me to remark that, although the magnitude of your work, the difficulties and dangers which surround you, in connection with the weakness and infirmities which attach to human nature in its best state, are sufficient to cause the stoutest hearts to quail, yet the prospect before you is not without its encouragements. The cause itself is the Lord's. You are but agents employed in this great work, yet, we trust you are agents selected by God himself. And who can tell what he will accomplish by instruments of his own choosing? Your hopes of success are based upon the word of everlasting truth. Prophecy and promise unite to sustain the long cherished hopes of the Church, in regard to the salvation of the heathen. 'Ask of me,' says God, 'and I will give thee the heathen for thine inheritance, and the uttermost parts of the earth for thy possession.' For these, the Redeemer suffered and died. And 'he shall see of the travail of his soul and be satisfied.' Individually, you may indeed be nothing; but you are connected with an agency which is Divine, and which cannot fail to give efficiency to your efforts. What is the pebble in the brook, or the sling? or what the slender arm of the youthful shepherd? Yet, that pebble in the sling, and that sling in the hand of David, and his arm connected with the name of the God of the armies of Israel, and the vaunting Goliath lies prostrate at his feet.

"How simple, and even foolish, in the ear of worldly wisdom, is the story of the cross! how feeble and inefficient the instrumentality of man! and yet this simple weapon drawn from the brook of truth, though directed by the most insignificant instrument, becomes 'mighty through God;' and by it the giant forms of pagan idolatry, and superstition, which for centuries have reared their brazen fronts and proudly defied the God of heaven, shall, in the midst of their vauntings, be tumbled into ruins.

"With these animating prospects before you, dear brethren, let nothing deter you from the faithful prosecution of your holy work. Ever remember that you are not at liberty to entangle yourselves with secular concerns, and that you are expected to consecrate yourselves and your families entirely to the missionary work, though it may be at the sacrifice of ease, of the refinements and socialities of polished society, of health, and even of life itself. Go forward, then, in the name of the Lord, and push the conquests of Messiah's kingdom farther, and still farther, until the vast interior of Africa shall become vocal with the songs of Christian triumph. And remember for your consolation, that the Church under whose direction and patronage you labor, is identified with you in all that legitimately belongs to your mission. She will hold herself responsible for your necessary supplies. She will sympathize with you in all your trials; she will weep with you in all your sorrows; and she will rejoice with you in all your successes. And should any of you, in the providence of God, be destined to find a premature grave in the land of your voluntary exile, she will most devoutly pray that, like others of your noble predecessors and coadjutors, you may fall at your post, sword in hand, with your clustering honors thick upon you; and that with Cox, and Wright, and Barton, and Stocker, and Williams, and others who have been associated with you in this interesting field, you may wear a faithful missionary's crown, and 'shine as stars in the kingdom of heaven forever and ever.'

"And now, dearly beloved, '*I commend you to God, and to the word of his grace, which is able to build you up, and to give you an inheritance among all them which are sanctified.*'

"Yours in Missionary bonds."

As years passed, it was more and more manifest that the varied and protracted labors connected with his office were prostrating his physical energies, and in the early part of 1850 he had so far declined, that it became necessary for him to resign his position as missionary secretary, and withdraw from all public labors. Immediately his thoughts were engaged in making suitable arrangements for his family, and he addressed the following affecting letter to his old friend, C. C. Yard, Esq., at Trenton, dated New York, March, 1850.

"My health is so feeble and my nervous system so much prostrated that the labor and difficulties, connected with moving, seem to me almost insurmountable.

"My infirmities, if not my age, make the weight of a grasshopper to be a burden. I have arrived at that crisis in a Methodist preacher's history which calls for a large share of sustaining grace. I had intended to rent my house and get a smaller one for a moderate sum; but I cannot hear of one anywhere to suit me, and I am, therefore, driven to the necessity of occupying my own. It is true, it is not a better house than

I need for my comfort, but I do not know how I am to live without the rent. My whole income, without the house, will be less than one hundred dollars per annum. And you know the amount we receive from Conference is very small and very precarious. But stern necessity compels, and I must submit and endeavor to trust in God. It is impossible for me to describe my feelings for some weeks past, but I think I do not murmur."

During the years of Dr. Pitman's secretaryship, he had frequent prostrating attacks of sickness; sometimes at home amid the affectionate solicitude of his family, and sometimes far away prosecuting the duties of his office. From these, however, with careful and kind attentions he generally soon recovered, but for some months previous to his resignation there seemed to be a permanent decline, and after his settlement at Trenton a steady increase of debility and suffering marked his course.

For years he had cherished a high appreciation of poetry, and sometimes courted the muse himself. Some of his articles are touchingly pathetic, while others are full of playful humor or biting sarcasm. Each year after his retirement to private life, on the 9th of January, his birth-day, he wrote an article, entitled "*Birth-Day Reflections.*" The following verses are parts of a poem written on that day, in 1851, the next year after his removal to Trenton:

"Two score and fifteen years have gone,
Since life with me commenced its dawn.
How like a race that's swiftly run
Life's tale is told, soon as begun.

* * * * *

"I've labored long and labored hard,
Nor have I toiled without reward.
Thousands of souls in mercy given
Shall own my ministry in heaven.

"In retrospecting by-gone years,
How short our fleeting time appears!
How evanescent all below,
How dark these grounds where sorrows grow!

"Friendship is often but a name,
Prompted by selfish love of fame;
It fawns and flatters for a day,
And then it cools and dies away.

"So I have found my summer friends,
Friends only while it served their ends,
And when I could no longer serve,
Their love was changed to cold reserve.

"But, yet, there are a worthy few,
Who still remain both kind and true,
Whose tender sympathies I share
Who for my comfort kindly care.

"May these unwavering friends be blest,
With present peace and future rest,
And I with them sweet notes employ,
Where all is health, and life, and joy."

The views here taken of the friendships of life are somewhat gloomy, but it must be borne in mind that at the time of this writing his nervous system was entirely prostrated, and, physically. he was a wreck.

In the year 1852 the New Jersey Conferenee held its annual session in the city of Trenton. Although the ehurch was but three or four minutes' walk from Dr. Pitman's house, and dearly as he loved to mingle in these gatherings of his brethren, his health was such as to allow him but a single visit. That visit will never be forgotten by those who were present. It was about ten o'clock in the morning, several days after the Conference had convened. Bishop Janes was in the ehair, and the business was progressing with quietness and dispatch. Suddenly a wail of unutterable sorrow burst upon the assembly. Startled by the unexpeeted sound, and ignorant of its source, every eye was instantly turned in the direction from whence it came. What a seene was then presented! There was the form of the onee majestic Pitman bowed and broken; his noble, and in times past often divinely-illuminated face bathed in a flood of tears; the lower jaw was relaxed and so fallen as to give him a most unnatural appearance; and, as he passed up the northern aisle, supported by a friend on either side, the sight of his ministerial brethren in health--brethren whom he had so often met under more favorable circumstances, and with whom he had so long and so sweetly labored, still strong to battle for the Lord, while he, with all his early and earnest sympathies for poor humanity, was but a wreck unable to do anything, so overwhelmed him, that a wail expressive of the deepest anguish burst from his almost breaking heart. On reaching the platform, Bishop Janes descended and kindly assisted him to a chair beside him, where he sat till the close of the session bathed in tears. The scene was so deeply affecting, that for some time no business was transacted, and when resumed, it was in tones subdued by sympathy and sadness.

Having followed the narrative of Dr. Pitman's life thus far, and witnessed some of the gracious results of his labors, it seems appropriate to refer now a little more particularly to his style of preaching and the sources of his power.

"When I first knew him," says Rev. Jas. Ayres, "I thought, and, after the experience and observations of thirty-six years, I still think, he was, taking him altogether, one of the greatest preachers of his time.

"His oratory was not of the scholastic or fictitious type. Like Patrick Henry's, it was the true oratory of nature. His voice was mellow and full, its intonations were pleasant, and the modulation entirely under his control. The expression of his countenance, when preaching, was glowing and sympathetic, evincing the deep interest he felt in the spiritual welfare of his congregation.

"He equally despised witticism and bombast, and used plain words to express sound and sober sense. He respected his hearers, and they respected and reverenced him. He recognized the true relation between judgment and feeling, and when, by solid argument, he had convinced the understanding, he knew no law of philosophy or religion which forbade his appealing to the emotions, and enlisting them in the fear and service of God. 'The unction of the Holy One,' was a favorite expression with him, and rarely in any man's ministry has it been more gloriously exemplified than it often was in his.

"In the commencement of his sermons he was usually argumentative, but, having stated his doctrinal points and defended them, he would pass to the Christian duties based upon those doctrines, and after sufficiently enforcing them, would again pass to the Christian privileges connected with them. As he advanced in his sermons, his emotions would rise, and, carrying his congregation with him, he often became overwhelmed with his subject, and the responsibility of his position as an ambassador of Christ, and at such times would give utterance to his feelings in the language of the weeping prophet, 'Oh! that my head was water, and mine eyes a fountain of tears, that I might weep day and night for the slain of the daughter of my people.' Upon such occasions, his congregation would sympathize with him to such an extent that scarcely a heart could be found unaffected, or cheek not bathed in tears." Often, too, the exhibitions of feeling were those of unbounded joy.

An illustration of this occurred at a camp-meeting, near Plainfield, while he was on the East Jersey District. His text was, Romans viii. 17: "And if children, then heirs; heirs of God, and joint heirs with Christ; if so be that we suffer with him, we shall also reign with him." Having treated the subject doctrinally, practically, and experimentally, rising by degrees all through his discourse, when he came to speak of the blessedness of the heirship, he was wholly absorbed with the grandeur and glory of his theme, until reaching a sublime climax of emotion and oratory, he asked triumphantly, "Heirs of *what?* a hundred acres of land? *No!* A few thousand dollars in gold? *No!* A kingdom or a throne on this earth? *No!*" Then, ascending to the loftiest possible summit of overmastering eloquence, his voice full, melodious, and clear as the tones of a silver bell, yet towering to its sublimest pitch, the echoes were heard through the forest a mile or more, as he asked again, "*Heirs of what?*" Then with a soul overflowing with divine emotions, answered, "*Heirs of* GOD *and joint heirs with* JESUS CHRIST, to an inheritance incorruptible, undefiled, and that fadeth not away, reserved in heaven for YOU."

The effect was overpowering, and the saints of the Most High in an ecstacy of joy felt they were scarcely any longer heirs, but had already entered upon their bright and eternal inheritance.

Here, then, in his commanding style, his well-arranged discourses, his sound theology, his earnestness of spirit, his sympathetic nature, and his baptized soul, we have the key to his great popularity and power.

His love of books became a passion, and, during a large portion of his life he spent a considerable part of his limited receipts in the purchase of volumes that he prized, so that, notwithstanding the inconvenience of frequent removals in the itinerancy, he accumulated and continued to keep near him an extensive library.

"Although uniformly an extemporaneous speaker, he was accustomed to make laborious and careful preparation for the pulpit by means of the pen. He wrote many sermons in full, not for the purpose of either reading or memorizing them, but for the sake of disciplining his mind to thought and language, and also for the purpose of putting his best thoughts on important subjects into convenient form for reference, when he might have occasion to treat those subjects again.

"When in the full exercise of his noble powers, he once said to a friend, 'I should perhaps write no sermons, were I sure I should always have the same activity of mind that I now possess; but, as I cannot reasonably expect this, I deem it but prudent to make preparation when I can, for coming days of mental decline or physical feebleness.' To his friends who were cognizant of the state of his mind and body during the last few years of his life, these words will seem as prophetic as they were discreet and full of wisdom for the guidance of others.

"His natural temperament was highly nervous. At times he was subject to a great flow of spirits, which made him exceedingly companionable—at other times to great mental depression, which very much abridged his personal enjoyment. He was a fast and firm friend. He was ambitious, but his ambition was of an exalted kind. It was his pleasure to place others on a proper level, and then endeavor to rise above them—not so much, however, in position, as in usefulness.

"In the Missionary Secretaryship, he excelled in the eloquent presentation of the glorious provisions of the gospel, as adapted to every descendant of fallen Adam, and most powerfully would he urge the motives for its dissemination. The management of finances, however, was not congenial to his mind or habits; a large correspondence was a burden to him; and he always delighted less in platform speeches than in the more substantial, and, as he regarded it, more *religious*, mode of pulpit address."

But with all his talents as a man, his faith and zeal as a Christian, his power as a minister, called and anointed from on high, there were better things in reserve for him, and so, on Saturday, the 14th of January, 1854, in the triumphs of the glorious gospel, God took him to himself, aged fifty-eight years and five days.

The funeral services were conducted at the Green Street Methodist Episcopal Church, Trenton, on the following Tuesday afternoon, by Bishop Janes, in the presence of a large congregation, in which were between thirty and forty ministers. The remains were then interred in the Mercer Cemetery, over which, at a subsequent period, the New Jersey Conference erected an appropriate monument to his memory.

The Rev. Edward C. Jones says, "When a boy, I frequently attended the ministrations of the lamented Pitman. I was attached to him as an awakening preacher of righteousness; and now, though a member and minister of another branch of the Israel of God, I desire to express my feelings at the sad event of his departure from the earth."

These feelings he embodied in a beautiful little poem, published in the Christian Advocate and Journal, entitled, "*The Unbroken Rest*," a verse of which stands at the commencement of this memorial, and with two other verses of the same, we close our account of the loved—the lamented—and the now sainted Pitman.

"In slow decay thou passedst to thy rest;
  But faith had pinions mighty in their sweep!
And hope and trust were thine while sinking thus,
  So wrecked in body, to thy dreamless sleep.
The crown bedecked with gems revealed its light
And pain forgot its power, and death disowned its night.

"In that blest realm where all the hosts of God,
  Though differing here in name shall meet at last,
The travel-dust of time, the strife with sin,
  The fierce temptation, all forgot and past,
How sweet the hope! how rapturous the trust!
That there shall meet, *as one*, the glorified—the just."

REV. JOHN P. M'CORMICK.

"At church, with meek and unaffected grace,
His looks adorned the venerable place;
Truth from his lips prevailed with double sway,
And fools, who came to scoff, remained to pray."

AMID the quiet and rural scenes of Phillipston, New York, on the 13th of May, 1822, John P. M'Cormick had his birth.

Reared under the influence of pious example, his parents being members of the Methodist Episcopal Church, he beeame a conscientious, and to some extent, even a devout child. His mother declared she never knew him to tell a falsehood.

When about eight years old, being in company with some rude boys, who were in the habit of using profane language, they dared him to follow their example; he finally yielded, and uttered an oath. In a moment he felt as if a dagger had pierced his heart. His peace of mind was gone, and he found no relief, until with tearful eyes he confessed his sin unto the Lord, and then in the middle of the night, his eyes still streaming with tears, arose, and went to his father's bedside and asked him to arise and pray for his forgiveness.

Through all his childhood, he was a subject of the Spirit's influences, but the first religious impressions which he could distinctly remember, were made upon his mind when about thirteen years of age, through the instrumentality of Methodist ministers, laboring in his neighborhood. These impressions and convictions remained with him, with greater or less force, up to the time of his conversion. Under the influence of these convictions, he often made resolutions to become a Christian, but, like many others, failed to fulfill them. Often when returning from the place of worship, where he had listened to a heart-searching sermon, he would kneel by the road-side and pray to God for the pardon of his sins. But notwithstanding these strong convictions and earnest way-side prayers, there was not a full yielding of the heart to God, and the work of salvation was deferred. One obstacle in the way of his immediate conversion, he says himself, was an intense love for what is called *light reading*. Every novel or romance that fell in his way, no matter what its character, was read, indeed fairly devoured by him, until a taste had been formed which was only overcome at last, by the powerful help of the Holy Spirit.

At the age of sixteen he went to Orange County, N. Y., to learn a trade. The situation he occupied was not favorable to religion. Fortunately, however, he was in the immediate neighborhood of an elder brother, who in his regular visits to the house of God, some three or four miles distant, invariably invited John to accompany him. Under the heart-searching appeals of such men as S. Landon and T. Newman, who labored on the circuit at that time, the young apprentice often wept like a child, and was soon influenced so far as to engage in the duty of secret prayer every night and morning. But the great deep of his heart was not yet reached. Pride and sin were not subdued. Still he continued to visit the sanctuary. On one of these occasions, Rev. T. Newman preached. God was with his servant, an inspiration from the Holy One came upon him, and his word was with power. Many hearts were deeply affected, and amongst these was young M'Cormick. It was the Sabbath day. There was no extra meeting, yet seeing the influence that was abroad amongst the people, an invitation was given to such as felt like giving their hearts to God to come forward to the altar. A number embraced the opportunity, sought and found the Saviour. But John, timid and fearful, felt the cross was heavy, and although bathed in tears, and greatly desiring that some one would ask him to go forward, yet as no one spoke to him on the subject, he could not go alone. After the services closed, a friend seeing his condition, said to him, "You desire salvation, come to-night, and go to the altar." He went home with a sad heart, but when evening came, though the church was three miles off, he was again in the congregation, and at the proper time bowed at the altar, a heart-broken penitential seeker of pardoning mercy from the hand of God.

On the following Sabbath evening, before the hour of Divine service, while singing

"Religion! 'tis a glorious treasure,"

in a social company, at a friend's house, his soul was set at liberty, and he felt he could sing with the spirit and with the understanding also.

Soon after this, on the 9th day of December, 1839, then in his seventeenth year, he united with the M. E. Church on probation.

He immediately adopted rules of holy living, which greatly promoted his religious growth and strength. Amongst these rules was one requiring him to observe stated times for private prayer three times a day. In these devout spiritual exercises, he was greatly built up and blessed, and he thought, in after-life, that, but for the adoption of such a course, he might have backslidden, and finally become a cast-away.

From the commencement of his union with the Church, he was convinced of the necessity of holiness of heart. He said, "I heard it preached, saw it to be my privilege, and earnestly desired to possess it." But in the attainment of it, he had agonizing and protracted heart-strugglings with unbelief and sin. In these struggles his physical strength was sometimes exhausted, and he felt cast down, and almost destroyed, still he persevered until, in the simplicity of a child-like faith, he cast himself unreservedly upon the all-cleansing blood. Then the divine baptism came, and he exclaimed with a heaven-inspired rapture, "*My joy is full!*"

During these spiritual efforts to obtain the higher forms of Christian experience and knowledge, his mind was greatly exercised concerning the gospel ministry. But, as he was young and of a retiring disposition, it was only through much prayer and the advice of reliable Christian friends, that he was able to reach a right conclusion on the subject. God had often blessed him in exhortation, and some degree of success had crowned his labors, still, his mind was not as clear as he desired until his removal to New Jersey and his way was opened for him to attend the Pennington Seminary, where he spent a year, using every means in his power to qualify himself for the great work to which he now felt and believed he was divinely called. Here his piety and meek spirit soon secured the confidence of the Church, and he was licensed to preach.

In 1845 he was admitted into the New Jersey Conference on trial, and appointed to Middleville charge, where his labors were blest in the conversion of a score of immortal souls. His subsequent appointments were, in 1846, Rockaway; in 1847–8, Vernon; in 1849–50, Chapel, a part of Hope Circuit; in 1851–2, Clinton Circuit, when his labors closed.

In all these fields of labor he was greatly beloved and useful. True, he had his conflicts and trials in connection with his work as a Methodist minister, particularly on the Chapel Circuit, where there was much dissatisfaction growing out of a division of the charge at the previous Conference. This, Brother M'Cormick felt most keenly, but, he said, "I believe it is the duty of a Methodist preacher to go to work, even though formidable obstacles present themselves before him." He did go to work, and, although for a time the difficulties seemed unyielding, yet God was with him, and, notwithstanding all, he said, "My soul is full of peace—calm, settled peace."

> "That lays the rough paths of peevish nature even,
> And opens in the breast a constant heaven."

He had success, too. Concerning a woods-meeting held on the charge, during his first year, in August, he wrote, "Our contemplated woods-meeting is past. The Lord was present to bless his people, and it was a good time." They then concluded to continue the meeting in a school-house near by during another week. He said, "The object of this meeting is the glory of God and the salvation of immortal souls," and then subjoins the prayer, "Oh, if my heavenly Father would sanction my efforts, and pour out the spirit of revival upon the Church, I would try to cleave closer and closer to his blessed side."

He had married a Miss E. Crosby, of New York City, a lady of deep piety, who greatly aided him in his work. In a note appended by her, some time after his death, she says, "This prayer was answered. A work broke out which resulted in the awakening and conversion of scores of precious souls, and the valley echoed and re-echoed with the praises of God."

At this meeting a circumstance occurred, illustrating the power and prevalence of persevering prayer. There were three young men, all sons of a devout old Christian.

For these young men Brother M'Cormick felt a deep solicitude. He wept, and prayed, and labored for their salvation. But their minds seemed wholly absorbed in worldly matters, and the work of their salvation was delayed. Still, the minister was unfaltering, and prayed and labored on.

Finally, feeling that these young men were not only neglecting salvation themselves, but that they were standing in the way of others, he asked the Lord to give him a message particularly adapted to them, and then so direct the word that it would reach their hearts. This prayer was likewise answered. That night, after having preached with power, on "Quench not the Spirit," and while inviting persons to the altar, to which none had yet come through all the week, one of these young men arose, and said aloud, "I am going to the altar—*pray for me.* I came here this evening, striving to quench the Spirit, resolved to defer seeking my soul's salvation to some other time, but I fear I may never have another opportunity. *Pray for me.*" Immediately his wife arose and followed him. Then the two other brothers fell at the mercy-seat, and, side by side, they sought the Saviour, and, side by side, rejoiced in his love. Believing prayer prevailed, and the gospel triumphed. To these gracious displays of saving power Brother M'Cormick referred with profoundest satisfaction in the closing hours of life.

On Clinton Circuit, his last charge, he was greatly honored of God, and beloved by the people. He moved amongst them in the discharge of his various duties, like his divine Master, meekly, devoutly, and cheerfully, preaching with system, pathos, and power. Every sermon seemed to be attended with that divine unction, which clothes the pulpit with a halo of glory. As the people looked up, they saw not the man, but the blessed Master; heard not a human voice so much as a divine message. Rev. Wm. Stout, then a lad, but now a member of the Maine Conference of the M. E. Church, was amongst those converted while he was on this charge.

He loved every department of his work. He was an excellent pastor, a friend of the Sabbath-school, temperance reform, educational interest, missionary enterprise, everything connected with the cause of God had his prayers, and his hearty co-operation, yet all was done without ostentation, quietly, and almost unseen, but felt. For one so young, he was a model minister.

In his intercourse with men, he was of a modest and retiring disposition, seeming to develope the teachings of the Apostle Paul, "ever esteeming others better than himself." "While his scruples, of which he never lost sight, were of the most commanding and influential character, yet he was sweet-spirited, and one of the most desirable companions; still, he threw off restraint less, and carried out his habitual gravity more, than any man I ever knew."

He was deeply pious. With him religion was not a theory only, but a divine and heartfelt reality; a reality which gladdened his heart in its deepest sorrow, and brightened all the future with hope and joy. He professed and enjoyed holiness of heart, a glorious attainment, one which adorns the Christian life with whatsoever things are pure and lovely and of good report. It was this that gave him that genuine meekness of spirit, and true humility of soul, which rendered his heart so blessed, and his life so influential. Religion with him became a habit, Christianity a settled principle. His reliance upon the atonement was thorough, his experience mature, and his fitness for heaven seemed to be complete. He said, "I am the Lord's, and I am determined to be his."

The last Sabbath of the Conference year, April, 1853, came. He had preached his farewell sermon to the Clinton congregation, in the morning, previously to going to the Conference on the following day, as he supposed, a well man. In the afternoon, he went to another appointment, to give his valedictory there, but he was attacked with hemorrhage of the lungs before entering the church. He called on a brother to officiate in his place, he had preached his last sermon.

At the ensuing Conference, he was returned to Clinton Circuit, a supernumerary.

His decline was rapid; but such is the power of dispensing

blessings which God has attached to the truly good, that they cannot even die without benefit to their fellow-creatures; for death consecrates their example, and the influence which may have been by some slighted through life, becomes efficacious in death and mighty at the tomb. It was so with John P. M'Cormick. His death chamber seemed to all, like the vestibule of glory. He awaited the arrival of the pale messenger, like a Christian hero, trusting in his God. While passing down the declivity which leads to the river, he said, "I am not afraid to die; the everlasting arms are around me. Oh there is glory up yonder. I suppose if the veil were drawn aside, we should see it all about us now. Glory to Jesus! Glory to Jesus! *Why it is all glory.* I am a worm of the dust, a child of mortality, but the Lord is my all, and in all, forever."

The last Sabbath but one, that he spent on earth, he asked those around him to sing,

"And let this feeble body fail."

When they reached the third verse,

"O what hath Jesus bought for me,
Before my ravished eyes,
Rivers of life divine I see,
And trees of paradise,"

his heart was full to overflowing, and he triumphantly exclaimed, "Hallelujah! my adorable Jesus has purchased this for *me.* shall soon be at home with him, and the innumerable company who are washed and made white in the blood of the Lamb."

Calling his wife to his bedside, he said, "When I am gone, say to my brethren in the ministry, preach holiness of heart; in that I have been deficient. I now see and feel its importance. Only the pure in heart shall see God."

He gave up his family with great confidence, saying, "The Lord has promised to provide." Hearing his wife say to a friend, "O what shall I do when he is gone?" He immediately responded, "Jesus will be left, in him you will find, Husband, Brother, Friend."

The morning before his departure, recovering a little from his great prostration, his wife and some of his neighbors being in the room, and his countenance all radiant with glory, he said, I seem to catch a view of the outer sanctuary, not of the inner, but of the outer sanctuary; I see an innumerable company of redeemed ones; and they say to me, "Brother come, Brother come," and then, referring to a little child whom they had buried four months before, he said, "I see my own dear Sarah with them. Glory to God, I shall soon be there."

On the 31st of July, 1853, he whispered softly, "*Jesus, precious Jesus*," and then passed up to be forever with the Lord. So he lived, and so he died. His life a beautiful example of purity; and his death a bright ascension to the joys of heaven. His remains lie among the people he last served, and whom he loved so much, at Clinton, Hunterdon Co., N. J. He has gone before us,

"Just gone within the veil, where we shall follow,
Not far before us, hardly out of sight,
We down beneath him in this cloudy hollow,
And he far up on yonder sunny height.

"Forever freed from this, his lonesome prison,
How shall we greet him in that day of days,
When He who died, yea rather who is risen,
Shall these frail frames from dust and darkness raise."

REV. ABRAHAM GEARHART.

THE grandfather of our subject was a German, who emigrated to this country and settled in Hunterdon Co., N. J., when Abraham's father was a youth. He was a Christian of the Calvinistic school, and was a member of the "German Reformed Church," to which he was warmly attached, and in the faith and usages of which, he strictly trained his children. After coming into New Jersey, the family became associated with the "Reformed Protestant Dutch Church," that of their former fellowship not being accessible. Of this Abraham's father was long a member and an officer, being, at the time of his death, a Ruling Elder. The children, of whom there were sixteen, were reared in accordance with the usages of this church, and to observe a strict morality.

Abraham was the thirteenth child, and was born, July 15, 1788. In addition to his moral and religious training, he was afforded a fair common school education. Being of sedate and thoughtful temperament, he turned his opportunities to good account. When of suitable age his father allowed him to choose between a collegiate education with a view to the ministry, and a continuance on the farm. He preferred the latter. This decision, so strange in itself, would probably have been different, had there been no condition appended to the offer. But not being a Christian, he could not have felt a special interest in such a work as the ministry, and must naturally have thought it improper to commit himself to it, in the absence of any assurance that God would approve the undertaking. Nor is it unlikely that Providence influenced his choice, as a means of reserving him for a work for which the proposed course would have failed to fit him and from which it might have kept him.

He remained at home till May 23, 1811, when he was united

in marriage to Miss Elizabeth Jolly. She was an excellent Christian lady, and a member of the M. E. Church, to the doctrines and usages of which she was warmly attached. Her prudent course and Christian influence led to his conversion, and to a change in the current of his whole life. In 1813, Rev. Manning Force was invited to preach at their house and baptize their eldest child. After this they frequently had preaching at their residence, and as he had not been strongly biased by his former training, he generally attended the meetings preferred by his wife. In 1817 they moved to New Providence, where there was a Methodist church, which, from this time, he regularly attended. In 1819 he was converted and joined the church, under the ministry of Revs. Asa. Smith and Bartholomew Weed. Though he had always led a moral life, yet when the Holy Spirit discovered to him his real condition, his load of guilt and sense of deep depravity were so great that for about a week he passed through an earnest penitential struggle. But his conversion was very clear, and occurred while he was alone in the barn. He at once felt that he must begin to pray with his family, but on reaching the house his courage failed him. He returned to the barn and wrestled in prayer till he felt strong enough to obey his sense of duty. This course was repeated three or four times before he conquered. But never after to the end of life, did he fail to keep the fires of incense burning on the family altar. His next embarrassment arose from the decided opposition of his parents to his joining what was now the church of his choice. To cross their wishes, so earnestly expressed, was a great trial, but both his convictions and religious interests summoned him to cast his lot with those who had been instrumental in his salvation, and he obeyed the summons.

From about the time of his conversion he felt that God designed that he should preach the gospel. In 1820 he was licensed to exhort by Rev. M. Force, and to preach not long afterward. In this capacity he traveled extensively, and labored with great zeal and success. He and other local preachers established an appointment at Mount Horeb, formed a society, and were instrumental in promoting an extensive work of grace. He often preached several times through the week, besides filling his regular Sunday appointments on the "local plan." On one occasion, while preaching at a watch-night service, in Union Village, near New Providence, he was so overwhelmed by divine power that he remained insensible for several hours. The surrounding scene was grand and glorious beyond description. The slain of the Lord were many. The altar was crowded by weeping penitents, while songs and prayers, cries of distress and shouts of triumph mingled in great confusion, and yet in sweet harmony. The whole night was thus spent, during which many were converted, among whom were two young men who came to scoff, but remained to pray, and who afterward joined the itinerant ranks.

While thus actively and usefully employed, he felt a growing impression that his devotion to the great work ought to be uninterrupted and entire. Still he felt an unaccountable shrinking from the itinerancy, and earnestly strove to so labor in a local sphere as to satisfy his convictions. About the year 1825, this impression became more clear and distinct, and as he still resisted it, he thought he saw God's displeasure in pecuniary reverses and trials, yet he hoped this was not so, and continued to hold out. Finally, he was prostrated by severe illness. Friends and physicians gave up all hope of his recovery. But to his mind it was made clear that if he would consent to follow the calls of duty, his life would be prolonged. He acquiesced in the will of God, and was restored to health.

A printed copy of his last license is preserved. It was conferred by the Quarterly Conference of Essex Circuit, held at New Providence, March 22, 1828, and signed by "L. M'Combs, Presiding Elder, and Philemon Dickinson, Secretary." Rev. D. Bartine and A. Atwood traveled the circuit the following year. After a few months Brother Atwood was sent to Morristown to superintend the wonderful revival that then prevailed there, and Brother Gearhart took his place, and remained about three months, till Brother Atwood returned.

In 1829 he was received on trial by the Philadelphia Conference, then in his forty-first year. He passed in due course to membership in the Conference and to deacon's and elder's orders, both ordinations being conducted by Bishop Hedding. His fields of labor were the following: 1829, Warren; 1830, Asbury; 1831. Hamburg; 1832–33. Warren; 1834. Caldwell; 1835. Kingwood; 1836, Asbury; 1837, New Germantown and Somerset Mission; 1838–39, Tuckerton; 1840, Bargaintown; 1841–42, Cape May; 1843, Cumberland; 1844–45, Atlantic; 1846–47, Cedarville; 1848–49, Salem; 1850–51, Gloucester; 1852–53, Pittsgrove; 1854, Tuekerton. Thus it will be seen that, though he began so late in life, yet he filled out twenty-six eonsecutive years as a traveling preaeher, by which time he had reached his sixty-seventh year. The territory he traversed was almost entirely within the boundaries of New Jersey. A large portion of it lay in the more mountainous and rough northern seetion of the State, while other portions required long and wearisome rides in the southern sandy region. His eircuits were mostly large and laborious, subjeeting him to great exposures and severe trials and hardships.

Of the last year of his ministry the Conference Obituary says, "Half of the year he was left without a eolleague, yet not discouraged, he commenced a series of extra meetings, and with the aid of the local preachers, kept them up with little intermission through the entire winter." It thus appears that he was alone during the time of his extra meetings, and it is not unlikely that the excessive labors thus bestowed, overtaxed his strength and hastened his end. The same authority says, "He was taken suddenly sick on his way to an appointment at Pleasant Mills, on Saturday, and halted at the house of William Sooy, at Greenbank. The disease increased with great virulenee. On Monday he was removed to his home in Tuckerton, where he lingered till the following Wednesday, when he fell asleep in Jesus. When he reached home, he was too much redueed to hold conversation in regard to his future prospeets. But he had said to Brother Sooy, before his removal, 'I have no fear for myself. So far as I am eoneerned all is well; my only anxiety is about my family.' His last words were, 'My work is done.' He died of typhoid fever, March 28, 1855, aged sixty-six years, eight months, and thirteen days." One son has joined his father in the spirit-world, while the aged widow, one son, and three daughters are still (1864) living.

As a preacher, Abraham Gearhart was plain, practical, stirring, and sometimes eloquent and powerful. A diligent student of the Bible, and blessed with a memory of wonderful tenacity, he stored away its treasures in large abundance. To this both his public ministrations and private conversations bore ample testimony. His sermons were richly imbued with Bible truth, and the positions taken in them, strongly fortified by well selected and forcibly applied Scripture proofs. His all-absorbing aim was success, in seeking which he fully taxed his powers of both body and mind. He selected his subjects, prepared for the pulpit, and delivered his sermons with unswerving reference to practical efficiency. Nor were his labors confined to preaching, but diligently extended to the social means of grace, to pastoral oversight, and especially to the wearing toils of protracted meetings.

As might be expected from such a course, his ministry was richly fruitful. From the time he commenced to preach in a local capacity, he was eminently a revivalist. He expected immediate fruits, and God, who giveth the increase, honored his faith and crowned his labors with large success. This was the general fact with reference to his whole ministry, and yet we are unable to give an extended record of particulars. At Tuckerton, in 1839, thirty or forty were at the altar of a night, and the flame of revival spread all over the circuit. Nor was his last term there scarcely less prosperous. In the evening of the day he died, nineteen were added to the church, as the fruit of an extra meeting he had just closed. Such men are always popular, and his frequent return to the same charge shows how well he sustained himself and how eager the people were to enjoy his ministry.

"He was a man of great simplicity of character, very fervid in his religious exercises, and decidedly spiritual as a Christian." More than thirty-five years intervened between his conversion and death. During this period his outward life was correct and uniform, his fidelity true and unfaltering, and his devotion to God heart-searching and ingenuous. Thus he attained an enlarged and mature Christian experience. Hence if he had been permitted to give a distinct dying testimony, it would have been clear and full, and while it would have been a comfort to his friends, would also have added another to the innumerable list of triumphant deaths. But this was not necessary. His faith, piety, and zeal, nobly witnessed for him, and furnished a ground of assurance of a safe exit from earth, of infinitely more value than mere words, for the grace that furnishes to such a life, never fails in the end to save to the uttermost.

A brief editorial in the *Jersey Blue* newspaper, issued at Camden, April 7, 1855, will appropriately close this sketch. In the comparison instituted the language may be too strong, and may have resulted from an insufficient knowledge of all the circumstances. Yet it can never harm ministers to listen to the views laymen take of their doings.

"By the death of this excellent man, the Methodist Church has lost one of its most sincere and devoted ministers, society an unassuming kind-hearted member, and his family an excellent and exemplary husband and father.

"Few men in the ministry have endured greater toils and privations and received less earthly emolument in the service of God, and the attempted imitation of Him who 'went about doing good,' than Mr. Gearhart, and none were ever more cheerful or more active in the 'good work.' Circuits embracing a wide extent of territory, composed of sea-coast and sand, and a wilderness of woods, were often assigned as his part of the vineyard, while younger ministers, more able in body and less able in mind, less 'learned in the law' of God were placed in 'Stations,' where the pay was more abundant and the labor, in a physical sense, nothing. Yet, he murmured not, but traversed the wilderness in sunshine and in storm, by night and by day, with a light heart and a cheerful temper, content to wait for God's good time to rest. That time has come and he has found rest. Let those ministers who would pray at his grave, pray not for him, but that they may be like him!"

REV. JAMES H. PRIMROSE.

He was born in New Castle County, in the State of Delaware, October 5, 1827. Being deprived of both parents at the age of six years, he was left to the care of a pious aunt, with whom he remained until about his seventeenth year, when he went to reside with a married sister in Wilmington, Delaware. Here during a revival in the old Asbury Church he sought and obtained the Divine favor. After a residence of two years in Wilmington, he removed to Philadelphia and connected himself with St. George's Church, where he entered the Sunday-school as a teacher, and took an active part in prayer-meetings, class-meetings, &c.

In the fall of 1849 he removed to Beverly, New Jersey. The Methodist Episcopal Church at this time had no organization in this village. He found, however, a few members there, and they arranged a meeting through the week for prayer and exhortation, which increased in interest until in the spring of 1850, Rev. Edward Page, then preacher in charge on Moorestown Circuit, formed them into a class and made Beverly a regular preaching-place. From this time Mr. Primrose was very zealous in promoting the interests of the church both spiritual and material in that place. During that year a very gracious revival occurred under the ministry of Revs. Messrs. Page and Hanly, and more than one hundred persons were added to the little society. In all these revival meetings our friend was abundant in labors, and contributed largely to their success. While engaged in these services he exhibited such decided qualifications for the work of the ministry as led his brethren in the beginning of 1837 to confirm his undoubted call to this work. While these meetings were going forward, the society were engaged in the erection of a church edifice, and to this enterprize he devoted much of his time and energy, and had the satisfaction of seeing it dedicated to the service of God in the following May.

This spring Beverly became a part of Burlington charge, and in the latter part of May Mr. Primrose was called to supply the place of junior preacher on Moorestown Circuit.

In 1852 he was admitted on trial in the New Jersey Annual Conference, and appointed to New Egypt Circuit; in 1853 to Rhodestown Station. In 1854 he was admitted into full connection and appointed to Atlantic Circuit. On the fourteenth of June following this last appointment, he was married to Miss Hannah Jones of Beverly. He now entered upon what he deemed his life-work with great diligence; having felt deeply his want of suitable qualifications for so responsible a position, he did not until after many struggles and some considerable experience fully settle the question of duty. The line of duty was now clear, and he seemed to "scorn delights," and devote himself to laborious days: he studied closely, was much in prayer and attended with great fidelity to all departments of his work.

In the spring of 1855 he was returned to the same charge, and met with no interruption to his labors until the following November, when he had an attack of illness from which he never recovered. His last sermon was preached on the Sabbath before Christmas, though, through all his sickness, which continued about four months, he continued to look forward to his recovery, and fondly cherished the belief that he should again resume the work in which he had found so much pleasure. God, however, had ordered otherwise.

On Sunday evening, March sixteenth, he inquired of his wife if the light in the room was not very dim, saying he could scarcely see. It then became apparent that he was approaching the dark valley, and that its shadows were already obscuring the light of life. He inquired of some friends who were present if they thought he was dying, and on receiving an affirmative reply he said, "Amen! I am ready. My work is done! Hallelujah!" He then took an affectionate farewell of all present. Calling his wife to his side he said, "I leave a good-night for all my friends." Taking her hand he said to her tenderly, "Trust in God, it will not be long till we meet again: I shall look for you in every ship that arrives." About midnight he opened his eyes, and gazing upward exclaimed with seeming surprise, "The clouds are clearing away. The sky is bright." His pure spirit had doubtless caught some glimpses of those bright and cloudless skies which canopy the redeemed: these were his last words. In a few moments his soul, calmly trusting in the Saviour of sinners, took its departure to the paradise of angels and God.

Our dear departed brother possessed a remarkable combination of energy and amiability. He was eminently unselfish, ever ready to sacrifice interest to duty, esteeming the rewards of well doing in the cause of his Redeemer far above any merely earthly gains. His generous nature adorned with the graces of religion made him a very agreeable companion ; hopeful and cheerful, he presented a beautiful embodiment of the spirit of our blessed Christianity.

As a preacher, he was earnest, practical and faithful, and was, accordingly, a successful minister of Christ. He had many seals to his ministry, and many in the day of eternity will rise up and call him blessed.

"Servant of God, well done!
Thy glorious warfare's past;
The battle's fought, the race is won,
And thou art crowned at last."

REV. CURTIS TALLEY.

CURTIS TALLEY, was born Nov. 19, 1807, near Wilmington, Del., and died at Pennington, N. J., Dec. 5, 1855, aged forty-eight years.

His parents were respectable people, and his mother was a member of the Methodist Episcopal Church, connected with one of the societies of old Chester Circuit, Philadelphia Conference.

Brother Talley spent his youth at home, dividing his time between labor and books, except a winter or two, passed at an academy in a neighboring town. His father's house being not far from one of the regular preaching-places on the circuit, he was, from his earliest years, an attendant on the worship, and familiar with the doctrines and usages of the Methodists.

In the 23d year of his age, he was converted, and united with the church, and the next year, was appointed class-leader, and licensed as an exhorter. He was zealous, laborious and acceptable in conducting religious service at little neighborhood gatherings, and saw much good done. Two years later, (in 1833,) at a quarterly meeting held by Lawrence McCombs, at the Grove Church, he was licensed as a local preacher, and three months afterward, was recommended to the Philadelphia Annual Conference, as a candidate for the itinerant ministry.

Brother Talley often referred to his labors as an exhorter and local preacher on Chester Circuit. Among his neighbors and friends, many souls were converted, during the last year of these his early ministrations; and he seemed to regard this period as the happiest, and he sometimes said, the most useful part of his life. One incident which he used to relate, is worthy of record as an example of the "diversities of operations" wrought by "the same God which worketh all in all." Brother Talley had been conducting a series of meetings at a school-house, and a revival was in progress. One evening, the little room was filled with people, and the meeting waxed warmer and warmer. Seven persons were kneeling at a bench, seeking the pardon of their sins. While all were engaged in fervent, importunate prayer, there came an overwhelming influence, as sudden as the rushing mighty wind and the tongues of fire on the day of Pentecost. Every believer at the same moment felt its power, and either bowed beneath it in speechless rapture, or shouted aloud in an ecstasy of holy joy. And at the self-same instant, the seven persons seeking peace with God, "passed from death unto life," and began to weep happy tears, or praise the Lord aloud for his pardoning grace.

Brother Talley was received on trial by the Philadelphia Conference, in April, 1834. His subsequent appointments were as follows:—

1834–5.	Asbury Circuit.	1844–5.	Crosswicks.
1836.	Caldwell Circuit.	1846–7.	Nyack.
1837.	Belleville.	1848–9.	Springfield.
1838.	Madison.	1850–1.	Pennington.
1839–40.	Somerville.	1852.	Rahway.
1841–2.	Woodbridge.	1853.	Quakertown Circuit.
1843.	Perth Amboy.		

In Nov. 1836, he was united in marriage with Miss Agnes C. Crane, who, with their only child, a daughter, survives the husband and the father.

Twenty years, as shown above, filled the measure of Brother Talley's life in the effective ministry. For some years previous to his death, there were indications of a tendency to pulmonary disease, and his health was gradually declining. He struggled on, however, hoping against hope," until at last, his disease became so aggravated, that he could no longer hide from his own eyes the fact that he must seek at least a temporary respite from labor; and at the New Brunswick session of the New Jersey Conference, in 1854, he was constrained to ask for a supernumerary relation. The love of life was strong within him, and love for the work of the ministry was even stronger. As the weary months passed on, and his flesh wasted, and strength declined, and while the cough of the consumptive grew more and more hollow and painful, he clung to the idea that he should yet return to the work with new energies of body and soul. While the process of inexorable decay was apparent to every other eye, he talked continually of recovering; and his almost invariable reply to inquiries after his health was, that he hoped he was gaining somewhat. In the last stages of his disease, he was confined to the house only nine days, and to his bed only three. And even when prostrated to rise no more, he manifested a strange tenacity of the idea of living, remarking on one occasion that "No one could tell what the Lord might do for him even yet." But in all this delusive hopefulness, this eager grasping at longer life, there was no murmuring, no dread of death, no desire to live, save for good purposes, and in accordance with the Divine will. A few days before his departure, he said, "Oh, if I could only preach the blessed gospel once more to my fellow men, how would my heart rejoiee." When he felt that the end was at hand, he was perfectly resigned to the Divine will, saying, to a brother in the ministry, "I feel that my work is done; if my good Lord would cut the cord that now binds me to earth, how delightfully would I pass away and be at rest. I wish you, my brother, to give my love to the Conference. Say to the preachers that I still love them; and that the same doctrines preached by me while in health, afford me the greatest comfort now, when I am about to die." He then exclaimed:—

> "Jordan's streams shall not o'erflow me
> While my Saviour's by my side;
> Canaan, Canaan, lies before me,
> Rise and cross the swelling tide."

This ealm faith and hope sustained him to the last. His mind never wandered for an instant. Reason and memory were clear and strong to life's utmost verge; and thus his dying testimony is unclouded even by the flitting shadow of a momentary delirium. He died a little past midnight, on the morning of Wednesday, Dec. 5, 1855, so gently that they who watched the scene, knew not when the freed spirit passed away.

As a Christian, Brother Talley was devout, earnest, and consistent, publicly and privately, in word and deed. The gospel of peace was his chief joy, and he clung to its blessed truths with a confidence that never wavered. The leading features of his piety were reverence and conscientiousness.

As a preacher, he did not excel in those qualities which attract the superficial hearer. His sermons were eminently scriptural, abounding in the very "words which the Holy Ghost teacheth," and deriving their illustrations principally from the Scripture narratives. His knowledge of the Bible, indeed, was uncommonly full and accurate. In preaching, his range of subjects was not extensive. Christ the Redeemer, the Holy Ghost the Purifier and the Comforter, were his favorite themes. He loved to exhort to repentance, faith, hope, and holiness, nor did he care to travel in speculation beyond what God has revealed. The general effect of his ministrations was to "edify the Church" rather than to impress the careless. The matter and the method of his sermons were far better than the manner of delivery. His utterance was not loud nor violent, and yet it was somewhat constrained, and to himself laborious, not exactly in accordance with the *mechanics* of natural modes of speech. Had his style been more easy and conversational, his ministrations would have been more attractive to general audiences, and very possibly might not have terminated so soon.

As a pastor and general manager of church business, Brother Talley excelled. A friendly nature and conciliatory manners won the love and respect of the church and the community wherever his lot was cast. He paid unusual attention to the records of his various charges, and looked closely after all that pertained to the church debts and church improvements. Through his instrumentality, parsonages were erected at Somerville, Woodbridge, and Springfield, and the church at each of those places, as well as that at Perth Amboy, was repaired and put in good order.

Comparing his annual reports with those of his predecessors, we find that during his pastorates there was, in the aggregate, an increase in the membership, though this increase is not great, and it is probably safe to say that he left all his charges stronger, religiously and financially, than he found them. In the number of conversions reported, his first year at Pennington was the most successful one, the Minutes of 1851 recording sixty-five probationers in that place.

As a Methodist, Brother Talley was loyal and enthusiastic. He was clear and decided in his views of doctrine, and strongly conservative in regard to polity and usage. He hoped for nothing better than the "old paths," and denounced, in unsparing terms, all departure therefrom as needless changes and false reforms.

In intellect, he was a strong and patient thinker, looking at things in a matter-of-fact way, with but little play of the imagination. He had a remarkably tenacious memory, especially stored with Scripture facts and language. In heart he was friendly, "easy to be entreated," and without much of what men call a knowledge of the world. He was accordingly scrupulous in paying his debts, but aside from this, set little value on money. In fact, he was too generous toward others to be just to himself. On one occasion, at least, the anniversaries and other appeals for money at the session of the Conference completely emptied his scanty purse, and he was compelled to borrow a few dollars to enable him to reach his new field of labor.

REV. ISRAEL SAUNDERS CORBIT.

It is always a sadly-pleasing task to sketch the lines which are to delineate the life and character of a deceased *friend*. Love will hallow the labor, tears will bedew it, and memory be tenderly careful of the facts which make up his record, and, although a review of his past history will tinge the heart with mournfulness, yet the hand will perform gladly the labor which rescues that history from the waters of forgetfulness.

With feelings of this nature, the writer has approached the work assigned him by the Conference in the preparation of a sketch embracing the brief but brilliant career of Israel Saunders Corbit.

He was born in the city of Philadelphia, February 16, 1817. His parents were members of the Methodist Episcopal Church, and strove to imbue him deeply in the days of his childhood with the truth and excellence both of the principles of religion and their practice in the life. In this laudable effort they were more than ordinarily successful, and the character of the boy assumed a seriousness and solemnity which even at that early age led him to prefer serious reading and meditation to the usual sports of boyhood, and probably gave the color to all his future life.

At the age of twelve he was taken from school, and placed in the store of Mr. Jacob Carrigan, of Philadelphia, whose kindly watchfulness over all those dangerous years when boyhood passes into manhood, secured from its recipient a grateful friendship which only ended with his life.

His brother, Rev. Wm. P. Corbit, says of him, "To the best of my knowledge, in all these years he was never known to be guilty of falsehood, profane swearing, or Sabbath-breaking. His evenings were generally spent at home with the family in the study of useful works, especially those which treated of the doctrines and usages of the Church, to which he afterwards consecrated his labors and his life. Even in those days the impression would sometimes come upon him that this would be his duty. He shrank from this idea, and trembled at the possibility of its fulfillment, but amid all his fears and doubts, it would often force itself upon him, and cause unspeakable misery to his tender mind, as he realized his own incompetency for so great a task. He was still unconverted, but no inducements could win his consent to enter a ball-room or a theatre. His tastes led him on the contrary to wander alone amidst the scenery which surrounded his native city: and while his companions were spending their hours in the excitements of those places, he was reveling in the glory of God's splendid handiwork, and tinging his nature with that love for everything beautiful which afterward lent so chaste and delicate an eloquence to his public ministrations.

His Sabbaths were uniformly spent in attendance upon Divine worship, and in the labors of the Sabbath-school. At an early age he was made a teacher, which office was filled with unswerving fidelity. After his own class had been taught he would walk over into the more destitute parts of the city, and, gathering the neglected little ones of that locality into a class, would endeavor to teach them the subline truths of a religion which he reverenced and loved, but as yet had never experienced. Years after he was dead, the writer attended the Quarterly Conference of a colored church, where its pastor declared in language of grateful enthusiasm, that he had acquired a deep love for the Sabbath-school interests from experiencing the beneficial effects of one which was carried on among these people by Brother Corbit. A nature like this *could* not be left unnoticed of God. Powerful religious emotions began to agitate him, the great deeps of his soul were broken up under the power of the Divine Spirit, his nature *felt* the need of a renewal in righteousness, and in the winter of 1837 in St. George's Church, under the ministry of the Rev. Mr. Pitman, he made a public acknowledgment of his need of Christ, and sought him for a Saviour.

He afterwards said it *seemed* to him as if the happiness of his whole eternity hung upon the plea that he presented on *that* night. Hour after hour he struggled on with a passionate energy and fervor that would not be denied. So intense was the struggle that he was lost to all surrounding circumstances. The perspiration started from every pore—his physical energies were exerted to their utmost capacity, his mind seized the sins of his life and forced them toward the atonement, and his spirit struggled to compel their union. So prostrated was his frame by these exercises that it was weeks before his system regained its usual tone. But the conflict was not in vain, for late on that night the Divine Saviour came to his assistance—the hard-fought battle was over, and his soul rejoiced in God his Saviour.

He now devoted himself with freshened zeal to the moral and religious duties which had previously engaged his attention, and soon began to feel the revival of his boyish impressions regarding the preaching of the gospel.

Day and night, at home and abroad, an inward voice was continually saying to him,

> Go sound the gospel jubilee,
> And tell poor sinners Christ has died,
> Say to a bondaged world, Be Free,
> For mercy's door is opened wide.

A period of deep distress now commenced its reign within his soul. The call of God was clear and unmistakable—his own sense of unfitness was positive—he was naturally extremely diffident, and his soul heaved and surged in the conflict, till he was almost driven to despair. Over and over would he exclaim in the anguish of his spirit, O Lord, send by whom thou wilt, but oh, send not me! I cannot, oh, I cannot, do this thing that thou requirest. The cross is heavier than I can bear. But the pressure of God's Spirit upon his own, became so powerful that he dared not longer resist, and sorrowfully exclaiming, "Thy will be done," he devoted his whole attention to the work of preparation for his solemn calling.

In the autumn of 1843 he was invited by Rev. James Ayers, who was then stationed at Long Branch, to assist him in filling some small appointments contiguous to the charge. The invitation was accepted, and he labored with both energy and success in Eatontown, Rumsum, Red Bank and other places near Long Branch.

He was there but a few months, and his labors were extended over a considerable territory, yet, many persons still remember, with fond affection, his graceful eloquence and gentle qualities, and "weep his memory still."

In the spring of 1844 he was unanimously recommended by the Quarterly Conference of Long Branch Station, to the New Jersey Annual Conference as a suitable person to enter the traveling connection, and was received on trial at its session in Trenton, and appointed to Madison Circuit, as a colleague of Rev. L. R. Dunn. The circuit was small, embracing but four or five appointments, only two of which had churches, and these small and incommodious. At Madison, which was the head-quarters of the circuit, they preached in an umbrella factory, and at Washington Square, another important part of the charge, in a school-house. Both these brethren were of fastidious tastes, taken from cities where church accommodations were constructed with a view to refinement and comfort, and in *ordinary* matters the transition would have been a most repulsive one. Besides this, the support was meager, and the members few; but, they were laboring for souls, and no appointment of his work was ever more cheerfully taken or faithfully executed than this one. This was largely a year of spiritual conflict. His brethren accorded him the possession of superior natural powers, and his close attention to study made those powers still more efficient. But his own estimate of himself differed from that of his brethren, every sermon seemed to him a failure, every comparison between himself and other ministers to his vision sank him lower, and he was often tempted to abandon the work in despair, and return to his former occupation. But the *Divine impression* was too strong, and he fought the battle successfully, and at the close of the year consecrated himself afresh and for life, to the work of the ministry.

His next charge was Somerville, an important county town, in the centre of the state. Here his pulpit manner, as well as the dignity and propriety of his life, gave him large congregations, and produced a favorable impression upon the community for the cause he represented. Members of other denominations charmed by the elevated style of his preaching, and allured by the eloquence of its delivery, were frequently found among his hearers, while his own people received from his devoted attention to all their interests, strong encouragement in maintaining their Methodistic position in the community.

Perhaps by no portion of the people was he held in more grateful remembrance than by the colored portion of the church. Nearly one-third of the membership was composed of these people, and their class in which they generally had a 'good time' met immediately after morning preaching. It was his practice to remain with them and listen to their rude and uncultivated expressions of experience, join with them in the excited spirituality of their worship, and advise them as to the best mode of resisting the peculiar temptations of their lives. They loved him with a fervor correspondent to his efforts for their welfare, and while the refined and cultivated sorrowed over his removal from their midst, these humble servants of Christ probably mourned his loss more deeply than any others, while he himself always remembered his labors among them with peculiar spiritual gratification.

In the spring succeeding, he was sent to Orange, a beautiful village, situated on the margin of the City of Newark, where he remained two years. During this time he devoted himself unremittingly to the improvement of his powers in order to more extended influence in the work to which he had been called, and made rapid advancement both in mental culture and physical oratory. He had been in the habit of constantly violating one of those sanitary rules of our Discipline which require a man not to speak *too loud*. Earnest to a fault, he had acquired a style of delivery which verged upon the boisterous, and which both lessened its effect and deteriorated the powers of his physical system.

His esteemed friend, Samuel Hurlbut, Esq., called his attention repeatedly to this fact, and finally succeeded in making him sensible of it for himself. "To show you how important I esteem it," said Brother Hurlbut, "I will engage to present you with a complete set of Clarke's Commentaries as soon as in your own opinion you have succeeded in overcoming it." He aroused his attention to the matter, and soon succeeded in relieving his efforts from the overloading of a style, which had already seriously injured his lungs and impeded the success of his preaching, and it may be proper to add that a short time afterward Mr. Hurlbut sent him the Commentaries as fairly earned, and which were used by him in pulpit studies till the end of life.

At the close of his labors here he was enabled to report a fair addition to the membership of the church and a considerable improvement to its property, while his Conference examinations won him high encomiums from the committees to whom they had been referred.

The appointment which succeeded this was Camden, where he was sent as colleague to Rev. D. W. Bartine.

The membership of the Third Street church in that city had for a considerable period of time been watching with interest the growth of the southern portion of their municipality, and waiting for a proper moment to locate a new church enterprise in its midst. In their judgment that time had arrived, and they solicited the authorities to organize it. Their judgment concurred with that of the brethren, and Brother Corbit was appointed to them in view of the successful forwarding of their enterprise. During all the early part of the year his weakened lungs forbade active exertion, and he became seriously alarmed for his health. But rest, and proximity to his native air restored him, and the fall and winter were given to vigorous exertion. A school-house was procured, in which to hold Divine service. A Sabbath-school was organized, Bible classes were formed, the people pastorally visited, Trustees elected, subscriptions solicited, contracts made, and the church pushed rapidly forward and completed. A series of meetings were held which resulted in the conversion of many precious souls, a number of whom still stand among the most efficient members of the society, and revere his memory with the fondest and tenderest love.

At the close of his labors here he was united in marriage to Miss Mary, daughter of the late General Reed of Mount Holly, and appointed to Princeton Circuit. For a long time the Conference had been desirous of establishing a Methodist society in that classic and beautiful town, but until a short period previous to this, had been entirely unsuccessful. The mass of the people had not regarded the project with favor, and a suitable location at a reasonable price had been found an impossibility. A lot was finally purchased by a private individual, resold to the society, which had been previously organized by Rev. T. T. Campfield. Rev. Joseph Ashbrook succeeded him, and commenced the building, and the whole conference interested itself in taking collections for the furtherance of the object. It was at this period that Brother Corbit received his appointment and commenced his work. He interested himself immediately in the Sabbath-school, ever a favorite field of labor. He begged money in adjacent places, often receiving only a quarter of a dollar as the result of a personal application. He made the acquaintance of the prominent citizens, many of whom contributed liberally to the cause. The students of its noble seminary, charmed with his brilliant oratory, largely attended his preaching. Many of the people, impressed with the intense earnestness of his manner, were found among the attendants upon his ministry, and a fair congregation soon rewarded his exertions. All this time the church was being pushed forward to completion, and was dedicated in the fall by that "Master in Israel," Rev. Charles Pitman. A revival of religion speedily followed, through the instrumentality of which, over eighty persons connected themselves with the infant society, giving it at once, a standing and a power in the community. So rapidly had the interests of the church advanced under his care that at the close of his first year, it was deemed advisable to separate it from the circuit, and erect it into an independent charge, which was accordingly done, and Brother Corbit reappointed to Princeton alone. This year also he labored with unswerving fidelity in *all* the departments of his work, confirming and strengthening all the interests committed to his care, and superadding many an irksome hour to the care of its finances.

In 1852 he received an appointment to Trinity Church, Jersey City, one of the most important stations in the Conference.

Here as elsewhere his pulpit popularity gave him large congregations, and frequently commanded the attention of the press. A powerful revival of religion blessed his ministry, and quickened the church. Its property was materially improved, and he closed his labors there with a reputation for effectiveness in his work which was scarcely surpassed by any of the "strong men in Zion" who had preceded him in the appointment.

His last appointment was Bordentown, a beautiful location on the Delaware.

His health was now good and his mind expanded, and he felt himself at liberty to make large additions to his previous plans of systematic study, the result of which was soon apparent in the increased efficiency of pulpit service. A mile below the town lay the village of White Hill, occupied principally by the employees of the Camden and Amboy Rail Road Company. There was no place of worship in the village, but few of the inhabitants felt sufficiently interested in religion to walk to Bordentown to church, and he determined in addition to his other labors to supply, if possible, their lack of accommodation. The Rail Road Company co-operated with him, some prominent members of the church at Bordentown assisted, the people of the village did what they could, and a house of worship soon crowned the efforts which they made, in which the community still gather for their worship. But his ardent spirit could not rest even with this additional. labor. The boatmen of the Delaware and Raritan Canal, which terminates at Bordentown, as well as the raftsmen and boatmen of the river, generally spent their Sabbaths in utter disregard of all the claims of religion. While engaged in their occupations, their opportunities were rare, and when lying at the town, their inclinations did not lead them to the house of God. His soul became deeply exercised in their behalf. Could not he do something for them? became a question to be spread before the Lord. After mature consideration he decided to establish afternoon preaching in the open air, at the confluence of the river and canal. Here, upon one inclement day, when worn down with labor, and still wet with perspiration from the exercises of the morning, he waited half an hour, chilled and shivering, for the gathering of the congregation. He returned home with a violent cold, which immediately settled upon his lungs. An intense inflammation succeeded, and he was prostrated at once. All possible efforts under the direction of the best medical skill were made to arrest its progress, but in vain, and it soon became apparent to his friends, though not to himself, that consumption was fast settling upon his vitals. He was now to enter upon a new phase of Christian experience, and one which tried his spirit to the uttermost. The valley of affliction was before him, and God was calling him to travel it. Hitherto his life had been all active labor, and in that activity for God his soul had found its elements of happiness. In the strong excitements of the ministry, in the prayer and class-meetings of the church, in pastoral visiting, in church enterprises, and, above all, in the preaching of the gospel, the morbid melancholy of his temperament had been counteracted, and his inward spirituality increased. But now all this was to be changed. The knee was to be bent no more amidst the families of his people, the mind no longer gratify its energies in the preparation of his sermons, and the voice never again utter the "cross story" in the pulpit. He knew not how to meet this. In his own opinion his capacity for usefulness was just beginning, and it was impossible to suppose its close. He was not afraid to die, for both his heart and imagination had long since clothed the second Eden in forms of beauty, but to him the work of the vineyard, while the power of manhood endured, was preferable even to heaven. He could not believe that his work was done, and his nervous system fretted at an inactivity which seemed an ignoring of the great objects to which he had consecrated his existence. The dew of early manhood was yet upon his brow, his intellect was just reaching its maturity, his luxurious imagination had been chastened and subdued, his language had acquired a plain and beautiful polish, his sweet and solemn voice was never more sympathetic, and all his powers were capable of a more intelligent and successful labor than ever before. His contemplations of heaven had been of the victor's crown, whose splendor was proportioned to the amount of toil and battle, and for death to seize him *now*, appeared like destroying his power to contest the prize. He had not yet understood that the passive graces of the Spirit were as costly jewels in that crown as those of active warfare. He had not seen the road to heaven as lying through much tribulation, or that the loftiest sanctification was attained through suffering. But he was to understand it *now*. His physical strength was prostrated, the fever was eating out his life, his nerves sank into hopeless depression, and his mental power weakened till he wept over its imbecility. His spirit shared the general prostration, and a mist of darkness stood between him and his Maker. God's face was dark to him, and Christ he could not see at all. But soon all this darkness disappeared, and the light of God shone clearly to the last. The imaginative power of his soul was resurrected from its stupor, and lined the further shore with beauty, while his heart exerted its faith afresh, and rejoiced in tribulation, and his whole nature resigned itself for direction to the providence of God.

His love for the church of his choice was absorbing. A short time before he died he said to the writer who was standing by his bed, to receive his last message to his brethren in the ministry, while the dying hand clasped the living one, "Tell the preachers that I love them, that I am happy in God, and that I want them to pray for me. I *had* hoped to meet them at the Conference, but I cannot do so now." He was silent for a little time, and then bursting into tears exclaimed, "Tell them I die with the love of the Methodist itinerancy as strong in my heart as ever." To Rev. Charles E. Hill, on the last morning of his life he said, "When! oh when! will the fetters break that bind me to this clay? When shall my triumphant spirit go to grasp the God I seek?

> "In rapturous awe on him to gaze,
> Who bought the sight for me,
> And shout and wonder at his grace,
> To all eternity."

He paused a little and then resumed, "When! oh when! on *spirit* wing shall I rise *above* this clay, and look down upon the stars as burning dust beneath my feet? I am very, very, *very* unworthy, but I lean upon the atonement. 'Tis not by works of righteousness which I have done, but by his mercy he saves me." Then turning his head he faintly, but distinctly uttered, I am happy, happy, happy—farewell.

On that same morning he exhorted a friend to seek the Lord. I am now, said he, about to pass through the valley of the shadow of death, but I fear no evil; *He* is with me. His rod and *His* staff they comfort me. There was then a profound silence which was broken by his little boy, who said, "Nobody talks." Once more that solemn voice broke the stillness of the death chamber as he replied, "Yes, my son, *God* talks." His brother, Rev. W. P. Corbit, asked him "if he had any fears?" "*No*" was the immediate reply. "Are your prospects bright?" he asked again. "Yes," was answered as quickly. Then simply saying to his brother, "Be good," eighteen months after the commencement of his illness he sank into the arms alike of death and Jesus.

He died during the session of the Conference. Resolutions were passed by them, appreciative of his character, and tendering sympathy to bereaved friends. A committee was also appointed to attend his funeral at Mount Holly, a member of which, Rev. J. K. Shaw, had been previously selected by him to preach his funeral sermon. After its delivery his body was deposited in the beautiful cemetery of that town, there to await the general resurrection at the last day.

In a sketch kindly contributed to this memoir, by Rev. L. R. Dunn, his character is sketched with a fidelity so discriminating that no other could, with propriety, take its place. "Refined in his tastes and feelings, noble and high-minded, he scorned any action that bore the slightest impress of littleness. In appearance he was commanding, in apparel neat to an extreme, and in intercourse with the people both prudent and careful, while there was no appearance of stiffness or chilling reserve. He observed great regularity in his habits, rising in the morning, between four and five, and pursuing his studies until twelve. After dinner his time was principally spent in pastoral duties. His preaching at that time was of a high order for one so young in the ministry, his sermons being both clear and carefully studied. His descriptive powers were superior, and some portions of his sermons were adorned with the most beautiful and eloquent language. His manner was very earnest, employing a large amount of physical energy in delivery without degenerating into boisterousness. The most refined taste could not be offended either with the sermons or their delivery, while their impression upon the community was that of a workman that needed not to be ashamed. Had he been spared, he would, no doubt, have become one of the ablest ministers in the Connection."

In association with others he was especially careful lest some inconsiderate remark might wound their feelings.

If in conversation, a level below that of ministerial dignity was reached, he would gently rebuke it, and in the pulpit he *never* descended from that dignity. In friendship he was capable of the strongest attachments, and few sacrifices were too great for those he loved. In his family his constant endeavor was to develop the character of the *Christian* husband and father. His devotion to the church of his choice was unbounded. All her peculiarities were dear to him, and he had small sympathy with those who were continually speaking of her infirmities. The sentiment sent from his dying bed to his brethren in the ministry may be taken as the abiding one of his life.

But he has gone from her altars to those of a higher worship.

"Gone in life's golden prime,
Its sunlight in his eye,
He might not find till gray old age,
A nobler time to die."

REV. WILLIAM V. DARROW.

"Go preach my gospel saith the Lord,
Bid the whole world my grace receive,
He shall be saved who trusts my word,
And be condemned who won't believe."

WILLIAM V. DARROW, the subject of this brief sketch, was born in Camden County, New Jersey, on the 20th day of March, 1819. At a very early period of life he felt he was a sinner, and needed a change of heart to make him happy. Still, though convinced of duty, he did not consent to its performance until his twenty-third year. Unable longer to resist the Spirit's influences without great violence to his moral nature, he then yielded to gospel claims, and was clearly and happily converted to God.

His situation in life was not the most favorable for intellectual or spiritual growth, and yet his advance in both was commendable. The best evidence of his talents, zeal, and piety, is in the fact that he secured the approbation of the church, and in 1849 was licensed to exhort. In this department of the church's labor, he went forth industriously, and was so far successful, that the next year he was licensed to preach. Here, too, he was diligent.

An important period of his history soon arrived. Recommended to the Annual Conference, he went up with fear and trembling, to the session held at Jersey City in 1851, where he was received on trial, and sent to Allowaystown and Hancock's Bridge.

There are few scenes on earth more intensely interesting, than a young man going forth to dedicate his life to the work of saving souls. The wide world is before him. Hearts steeped in sin are hard and will resist the appeals of truth. Discouragements multiplied in number, and various in form, oppress his spirits. He may be led sometimes to distrust the divinity of his call, and yielding to Satanic influence, be almost ready to relinquish effort, and return to his home. But retiring to his closet his case is once more laid before the Lord. Relieved of a degree of sadness he resolves to persevere. With an encouraged faith, he repairs to the pulpit and preaches the simple gospel of the grace of God, relying on him whose word he utters. Hearts are touched, and eyes overflow with tears. He labors on, and gathers a rich harvest of immortal souls. So, if the man be earnest, and his heart sincere, success in some degree will always crown his efforts, and whatever men may say, God will approve at last.

Every position in life has its trials, and the gospel ministry its full share, but the inspiring consideration, "He that converteth a sinner from the error of his ways, *saves a soul from death*," has caused many a noble youth to exclaim with the Apostle Paul, "None of these things move me, neither count I my life dear unto myself, so that I might finish my course with joy, and the ministry which I have received of the Lord Jesus, to testify the gospel of the grace of God."

It was so with William V. Darrow. He went forth to his life-work, though fearing, yet unmoved by fear, trusting in Him who said, "Lo I am with you always, even unto the end of the world."

He was not without success. At his first appointment he remained one year, and some souls were added to the Lord. In 1852 he was placed in charge of Atlantic Circuit, a position of considerable importance for so young a minister, and so well did he sustain himself in that important field, that after being ordained a deacon in 1853, he was returned to it again. His labors while there, were blest in the conversion of more than a hundred souls, all of whom we earnestly hope, will rise up in the day of eternity and call him blessed.

In 1854 he was stationed at Winslow. In this interesting little manufacturing town, there were also seals to his ministry, and more than a score were added to the church.

At the session of the Conference held in the Central Methodist

Episcopal Church, Newark, in the spring of 1855, he was ordained an elder, and appointed to Bargaintown Circuit. He entered upon the duties of his new charge with much spirit and promise of usefulness. His labors in the early part of the season resulted in the conversion of over half a hundred souls, and the church was greatly encouraged. But the days of his activity were numbered. He was laid upon a bed of sickness where his sufferings were extreme. Here he was patient, and his reliance upon Christ unbroken.

During an interview with his Presiding Elder, Rev. I. N. Felch, he referred to the probability of meeting no more on earth, then exclaimed exultingly, "We shall meet in heaven, hallelujah, glory to God." On another occasion he expressed his deep regret that he had not lived more holy, and that his ministry had not been more successful in bringing sinners to Christ, but his trust was in the blood of atonement which would cover all his imperfections. Four days before his death he referred to the approaching Quarterly Meeting, and said, "I shall meet my brethren no more in the church below, but while they worship God here, I shall be enjoying his presence before the throne above."

Near the closing hour he expressed anxiety for his family, but he quieted himself with the Divine assurance, "The Lord will provide." "As for me, it is better to depart and be with Christ, where I shall be free from all pain and suffering." These were his last words, then calmly and quietly on the 24th of January, 1856, he fell asleep in Jesus.

"Father, to us vouchsafe the grace,
Which brought our friend victorious through;
Let us his shining footsteps trace;
Let us his steadfast faith pursue;
Follow this follower of the Lamb,
And conquer all through Jesus' name."

REV. ICHABOD B. CARMICHAEL.

"Happy, if with my latest breath,
I may but gasp his name;
Preach him to all, and cry in death,
Behold, behold the Lamb!"

ICHABOD B. CARMICHAEL was born in the year 1823. In early life he was brought under religious influences, and when only eleven years old, gave his heart to God.

From the very beginning he had a high ambition. Having himself experienced the blessing of God's free grace, he was not satisfied to enjoy it alone, but wanted society generally to reap these saving benefits, and in all things secure the glory of Him, whose mercy and power he had so gloriously realized. Is it not always so? Can a soul be brought from darkness to light, and from the power of sin and Satan unto God, and not have strong desires for all to enjoy the same knowledge and salvation?

One of the surest evidences of the genuineness of the work of God in our own souls, is a burning desire to communicate the same blessings unto others.

Brother Carmichael's heart glowed with Divine love, and that love found its legitimate out-growth in earnest efforts to do good. In all these efforts he was so eminently successful, that he exerted a commanding influence in the Barryville charge, of which he was an honored member.

As years, knowledge, and experience increased, his exemplary deportment, conciliating manners, industrious habits, liberal spirit, his earnest prayers and exhortations, rendered him greatly serviceable to the cause of Christ wherever he was known.

Regarded by all as a young man of marked piety and promise, he was early appointed class leader, and soon after regularly licensed to exhort.

Blest himself, and benefiting others in these labors, the impression became general that it was his duty to preach the gospel. In this impression his own heart shared largely. But, as he considered the subject, the work in all its far-reaching influences and proportions rose up before him, and yielding to timidity and fear, declined assuming its responsibilities.

The gospel ministry is indeed a great work, and its responsibilities vast, but he who is called to its performance, and declines compliance, assumes responsibilities even greater, than he who with all its magnitude accepts it, trusting in the help of God.

In 1847 he was married to Miss Rebecca G. Vansickle, with whom he enjoyed connubial happiness for five years, when she died, in hope of eternal life. Her last words to her husband, were, "I am going home, now do your duty, go and preach Jesus Christ, and him crucified." These words, together with his previous convictions, and the urgent solicitations of his brethren, settled his purposes for the future, and although he had two interesting little boys left to his care and council, he immediately arranged his business, and gave himself up to a more thorough preparation for the gospel ministry.

In 1853 he was employed by the Presiding Elder on Harmony Circuit, Newton District. At the session of the Conference held at New Brunswick, in 1854, he was received on trial, and returned to Harmony. In 1855 he was appointed to Sparta Circuit. While on this charge, he was married to Miss Sarah P. Vansickle, younger sister of his former wife. In 1856 he was ordained deacon, and returned to Sparta. At the Conference held at Trenton, in 1857, he was assigned by Bishop Scott to Vernon Circuit, which proved to be his last appointment. Here, his life and labors closed.

He was not well while at Sparta. Chills and fever prostrated him. But his last illness was caused by over exertion in the pulpit, after which he took cold. Disease followed disease in quick succession for three months, when it became evident to all that he must die.

But he was not afraid. "Tell my brethren in the ministry," said he, "I trust in the atonement; my sky is clear; I shall meet them in heaven." When his deeply afflicted companion said to him, "I can go with you no further, you must pass through the dark valley alone;" he looked up with a triumphant smile, and said, "Oh no, not alone, Jesus is going with me through the valley and shadow of death, his arm supports me." After a while he said softly, but emphatically, "*Jesus is with me.*" These were his last words, and soon after, on the eleventh day of January, 1858, aged thirty-five years,

> "The weary wheels of life stood still,"

and the worn servant of Jesus was no more on earth.

Brother Carmichael was an earnest minister, too earnest possibly, for his feeble strength. But the love of Christ constrained him, and he felt, even though he died in the effort, he must publish the glad tidings of salvation to all, and urge them to come to that Jesus who had done so much for him.

These earnest efforts were, from time to time, signally owned of God, and many were brought from the darkness of nature, into the light of truth. He held an extra meeting of great interest which continued a long time, and closed just one week before he was taken sick. On the last night of the meeting, he told the people he felt impressed, "That one of their number was soon to be taken from time to eternity," then added, though he was then in usual health, "possibly it will be your speaker." Such proved to be the case, and the words he was then uttering, were his last to that people.

His wife says, "I never saw him so anxious for the salvation of souls, as at that time." "Sometimes," she continues, "I would plead with him not to labor so hard, but his uniform reply was, 'I have a great work to do, and but a short time to do it.' He never murmured during his sickness, but when asked if he would love to get well, would always answer, '*Yes, to preach Jesus.*'"

He had a conscientious regard for the Sabbath. A few weeks before his last illness, he arose very early on Sabbath morning, that he might have more time for reflection and prayer. Just at day-break, in going to the door, he saw a person in high official position, hauling in a load of hay. During the day, he went to the Sabbath-school, told the children what he had seen, and pointed out the sin of Sabbath-breaking, without mentioning the name of the person involved.

The children told what they had heard at school. This coming to the offender's ears, who, knowing he was the guilty man, had his anger aroused, but in future desisted from Sabbath violations.

His experience was of a high order, and yet the continual cry of his spirit was,

> "The seed of sin's disease,
>   Spirit of health, remove,
> Spirit of finished holiness,
>   Spirit of perfect love,"

until the New Year's eve before he died, when he experienced that perfect love which casts out fear, and rejoiced in all the fullness of the blessing of the gospel of Christ. In this blood-washed and purified condition he remained, until he exchanged earth for glory, and was eternally saved.

> "Saved by the merit of his Lord,
>   Glory and praise to Christ he gives;
> Yet still his merciful reward,
>   According to his works receives;
> And with the seed he sow'd below,
> His blisss eternally shall grow."

REV. JOHN KNOX SHAW.

THE annals of New Jersey Methodism present few, if any, nobler names than that of the self-sacrificing man at the head of this memorial. All over the State it is known as symbolizing one of the most devoted of all the men who have graced and strengthened the advancing Church, while in those parts where he more immediately labored, it is still regarded as a household word.

John Knox Shaw was born of respectable protestant parentage, in Ireland, April 10, 1800. This was in the days when the Church of Rome exercised her domination over that beautiful but hapless country with a fierceness of intolerant cruelty which expatriated many of the most valuable citizens, and compelled them to seek a home upon the distant shores of other and freer lands. Impelled by persecution, his parents decided to relinquish the attachments of a life-time—the comfortable property which they enjoyed and the country they loved—in order to obtain repose for themselves and secure for their growing family, among whom John was then an infant, immunity from the pernicious example and teachings of that ignorant and fallen Church. Their property was sold for a trifle, their household goods gathered, and with their children they embarked for the United States, and settled in Washington, Cambridge County, New York.

Here the earlier years of his life were spent. Blessed with the best of parental influences, trained in the knowledge of religious principles, and encouraged in a fondness for books which early developed itself in his character, he soon manifested a strength of moral purpose which not only held him aloof from the vices common to youth, but also induced a spirit of reliant independence, which, added to a disposition naturally adventurous, impelled him at the early age of sixteen to leave his loved parental home, determined, as he said, "To seek his fortune." Youthful as he was he obtained the position of a school-teacher. It must have been a strange sight—that slender stripling, with very many of his scholars rude, uncultivated, impatient of restraint, and older by years than himself, yet, submitting quietly to the rigid government he maintained, a sight which must have compelled the belief even then, that the boy teacher would develope into no ordinary man. He maintained his government by mingled firmness and gentleness, by a thorough comprehension himself of what he attempted to teach them, and by an identification of his ardent and sympathetic nature with their well-being and advancement. The roughest and the rudest scholars, who obeyed no one else, would obey him, because they both felt his competency to instruct them, and his deep interest in their welfare. After more than twenty-five years had passed away, the writer heard the people of a neighborhood in which he had exercised his profession speaking of his superiority, and asserting that no teacher who succeeded him had ever filled his place.

After an absence of three years he returned to visit his home, and while there was attacked with bilious remitting fever, the same disease which finally terminated his life. He sank so rapidly beneath its power that his physicians gave him over as past all aid, and announced to the family that nothing could save him, and he must die. His pious mother, however, could not so give up her son. In deep anguish she exclaimed "I *cannot* give up my poor boy, for he is not *prepared* to die." Speaking of this in his journal he says, "My mother bowed before her God in prayer. It was the wrestling, effectual prayer of faith. God heard that mother's prayer and prolonged the life of her boy. I was awakened to a sense of my danger. I saw myself to be poor and miserable, helpless and wretched. The future to me was most appalling. No ray of light from Bethlehem's Star shone upon my pathway. All was gloom, all was misery. Cheerfully would I have given the world had it been in my possession for one single hour: so invaluable is time and so trivial is earth when eternity appears in view to an unprepared soul. In that state of mind I resolved to make an effort, and if I perished, to perish in the act of seeking for redeeming mercy. Sincerely, earnestly, and importunately did I cry, "God be merciful to me a sinner." After many days of deep distress deliverance came. I was enabled to rest my burdened soul on Jesus, who kindly spoke to me, saying, "Said I not unto thee that if thou wouldst believe thou shouldst see the glory of God." I had not left my sick-room, but so transforming and renovating was the blessing which I then received, that both mind and body participated in the restoring influence. I immediately arose to my feet, clapped my hands in an ecstacy of joy, and with a loud voice praised the God of my salvation, for, from a realizing sense could I say, "O Lord, I will praise thee, though thou wast angry with me, thine anger is turned away, and thou comfortest me." So delighted was I with what I had obtained that I sent for my friends and neighbors, testifying to them that all my sins were forgiven, that I had been brought from the power of darkness and translated into the kingdom of God's dear Son. Some heard me, and like Nicodemus were ready to say, "How can these things be?" Others concluded that my mind, through severe and dangerous illness had become deranged, and that when the physical strength should be regained, these things would pass away. But, though many years have passed since the day of my spiritual birth, yet I have abundant reason to be unfeignedly thankful to God, that the blessing then received still remains, and I fondly anticipate that to the end of my earthly pilgrimage I may be enabled to testify from personal experience that Christ Jesus came into the world to save sinners, and to be ready always to give, in answer to every man that asketh me, a reason of the hope that is in me, with meekness and fear, and then throughout the annals of a blissful eternity, may it be my happy privilege to unite with the ransomed, and joyfully sing, "Unto him that hath loved us and washed us from our sins in his own blood, and hast made us kings and priests unto God and the Lamb, to him be glory and dominion forever and ever. Amen."

Almost immediately following his conversion, he became impressed with the conviction that it was his duty to call sinners to repentance, and spent large portions of time in studying the

Scriptures in order to learn the will of God concerning him. He does not appear to have had at this time any clearly defined views about preaching, or any settled theological belief. His parents were Presbyterians, but while his heart inclined toward the religion of his ancestry, he found himself utterly unable to accept the Calvinistic doctrines upon which their church was based. He knew nothing about the Methodists, and so for a time remained unattached to any branch of the Church of Christ, simply endeavoring to improve himself in a knowledge of the Scriptures, and to deepen his experience of God, while at the same time he earnestly warned sinners to flee from the wrath to come. Soon, however, a situation was obtained in a community in which the Methodists were largely represented, and he began to attend their preaching. The doctrines were such as coincided with his plain, strong intellect, the experience they preached corresponded exactly with his own, while their earnest manner found an echo in the ardent feelings which burned within his own bosom, and he soon, without a doubt upon his mind, attached himself to their communion. He writes, "On the day in which I joined the Methodist Church, the leader of the class examined me as to my Christian experience, and after hearing my testimony, he placed his hand upon my head, and said in a most affectionate and paternal manner, 'My son, I have somewhat to tell thee. Be thou faithful unto death, and thy Lord will give thee a crown of life.' Often in after years did I think of the advice thus given in my first introduction among the Methodists, and often have I resolved to live conformably to it, fully believing that, if true to my Master and faithful to his cause, I should, through grace, ultimately shine in the glories of the heavenly world. My first leader has, doubtless, long since finished his course, for he was then a venerable man, and will be pleased to meet him whom he thus advised, on the farther blissful shores of immortality, to receive from the Judge the diadem of life."

During the leisure hours allowed by his profession, he gave special attention to the study of the sacred Scriptures. In order to facilitate his meditations upon them, he committed the whole New Testament, and a considerable portion of the Old, to memory. Besides this, he read and wrote largely upon religious subjects, bringing the whole power of his young and vigorous mind to bear upon this one class of facts. He noted daily all the occurrences which transpired in reference to his soul, whether of inward experience or outward providence. Every moment of time and every fact of life was pressed into the spiritual education through which his soul was passing, and which God was using as a preparation for the higher work that he intended soon to place in his hands. The value of these exercises to his after ministry cannot be over-estimated. The abundant fund of Scripture language which gave so solid a strength to his preaching, the thorough expositions of the mind of the Spirit accompanying the quotations which satisfied the hearts of so many believers, and the clearness of an experience which drove away difficulties from the minds of others, were all, probably, referable to the entire devotion of his powers in this morning of his spiritual life, in the manner which has just been indicated.

The attention of the Church soon became attracted to the singleness of purpose with which he endeavored to make religion the one business of his life, and they increased his usefulness by conferring upon him authority to exhort. A deeper sense of responsibility rested upon him now, and the privilege was used diligently and usefully. His gifts rapidly improved, his earnest manner deepened, his knowledge expanded, and in the spring of 1825 the Church again recognized his usefulness by licensing him to preach the gospel, and at the same time evinced their confidence by recommending him to the Philadelphia Annual Conference as a suitable person to travel in the bounds of their connection. That body received him by a unanimous vote. and appointed as his first field of labor Hamburg Circuit, where on Sabbath morning, May 8th, 1825, he began his itinerant career, with the now venerable father, George Banghart, for his senior. Now he passed through that experience which in more or less of power comes to all whom God sends out into the vineyard. Satan tempted him fearfully with his unfitness, with his want of experience, and with the sore discomforts of the work. His circuit was three hundred miles around; there were thirty appointments; there was but one church, and that unfinished, and the rest of the preaching was performed in school-houses, court-houses, the mean log houses. or the open air, as Providence might afford. The rides were long, the fare coarse, the remuneration slender, and the labors abundant. But the spirit which had thrust him forth into the ministry, sustained him in all conflicts; and of it in his journal he writes:

"It was fraught with much profit though I passed through many trials and discouragements. The word sown in weakness was raised in power. I felt that my labors, though severe, were not in vain, and that my strength had not been spent for naught."

The Conference of 1826 gave him their mark of highest appreciation by returning him to the Circuit for another year. This was extremely unusual in those days, and nothing but a full conviction that young Shaw had acquired more than ordinary influence in that circuit, and also that he possessed preaching ability of more than average culture for his years, would have induced them to do this for so young a minister. This time Rev. Benjamin Collins was his colleague, a name famous in Methodistic history, and in whom Brother Shaw found a father as well as a preacher in charge, and whose memory he ever cherished with profound regard. Modern facilities for study were then unknown to the young itinerant, books were scarce and difficult to carry, and by daily preaching and traveling the time was fully occupied, and unless the junior preacher found a friend both capable and kind in his superior, any material progress in study was impossible. But such a friend was found in Benjamin Collins.

Possessing a massive intellect whose power had been refined by acquaintance with the best of the poets, and a strong nervous and physical system, his nature was just of the kind needed by Brother Shaw for companionship and improvement, while the kindly interest taken in his advancement in the power of usefulness and cultivation of mind, gave him all the advantages which the circumstances could possibly allow.

The preaching of Collins was often with extraordinary power. A Divine afflatus seemed to overflow him, and his full sonorous voice, sweet as strong, would pour forth sentences burning with spiritual fire and elevated as the sublimest conceptions of the poets of our Israel. Such a man could not fail deeply to impress and benefit the young preacher, and ever after he was spoken of by him in terms of the strongest appreciation and affection, and his untimely end, which occurred soon after, deeply intensified these feelings. Of him he writes, "A friendship was formed which was not transient, but destined to continue through life and then to be perpetuated through a blissful eternity." In the early part of this year, he was invited to preach in the town of Milford, Pa. There was no Christian church in the place, and but little Christian influence. He preached in the Court House, and succeeded in winning the approbation of the people. He was well calculated for work of this kind, from his almost intuitive knowledge of those avenues of human nature most accessible to the gospel, from his strong vein of common-sense thought, from his almost perfect knowledge of the Scriptures, and the ease with which he made their application, from his power of adapting himself to all classes of men, using their own familiar modes of illustration, and most of all from the deep well of sympathy within him, which was forever overflowing the language of his preaching. The people crowded round and urged him to come again, which he consented to do, and added it to the already abundant list of his appointments. During the year he had the pleasure of receiving here over fifty converts, of organizing a church, and of commencing a house of worship, which was completed during the following year. Among the converts were many prominent persons, including two members of the bar and others who gave promise of much usefulness. "Thus the word of the Lord grew and multiplied."

During this year he planted Methodism also a few miles below Milford. He had no Sabbath to give them, as every one was employed to its fullest extent, but so anxious were they to hear the gospel from him that they dismissed the school upon a week day, in order that he might preach to them, and upon these terms it was taken in and made a part of the circuit. Here too he was successful, and it is now an appointment in the Conference.

In these first two years of itinerant life, he preached over five hundred sermons, besides delivering numerous exhortations and leading a large number of prayer-meetings. When to this is added the facts, that he almost invariably led class after preaching, that he raised funds for the erection of churches, five being built, two of which were dedicated during his term of service, that he supervised their construction, that he visited from house to house, warning the people to flee the wrath to come, and that all this time he was regularly pursuing theological studies—when all this is considered, we may have some idea of the Herculean labors with which this devoted man of God commenced what was in truth to him the *work* of the ministry.

At the close of his labors here, amid the profound regrets of the people, he was removed to Asbury Circuit, where he also remained two years. This circuit then embraced considerable parts of Warren, Hunterdon, and Morris counties. There were twenty appointments, only six of which were in churches, and the rest were filled in school and private houses. But the people heard the word of the Lord gladly, and gave him sufficient work "to keep him well employed." Indeed, the rule which always governed his conduct was, "Be diligent, never be unemployed, never be triflingly employed, never trifle away time." In his colleague, Rev. John Finley, he found, as with Benjamin Collins, an able counselor and faithful friend. There were many revivals during these two years on different parts of the charge, the largest of which was at Flanders, where God's Spirit was poured out in a wonderful manner, and the whole community shaken by its power. Among the converts were two young men who afterwards entered the ministry, and became useful laborers in the vineyard of the Lord. He writes in his journal at this time, "I have set out to be more faithful, and am resolved, whatever may oppose, to discharge my duty. When I take into consideration my calling, I think of a remark made by a Jewish Rabbi in reference to the sacerdotal office. The work is great, and the reward is great. The day is short, and the Master of the house is urgent. When I retrospect the past, I see that much of my time has been poorly spent; and shall I be prodigal of the present? The Lord forbid. Oh that in me there might manifestly appear the work of faith, the labor of love, and the patience of hope. From my heart, I can say, I desire to be useful in the kingdom of my Lord and Saviour Jesus Christ; and my prayer is, O Lord, enable thy poor dust to proclaim the glad tidings of salvation to my perishing fellow-creatures with success. Open their dark understandings, warm their cold affections; make me strong in faith, unabated in zeal, patient in tribulation, and indefatigable in labors to promote the prosperity of Zion, and extend the peaceful kingdom of the Prince of Peace." Such was the lowly estimate placed by himself upon his usefulness and devotion while performing an amount of labor which to us at this day seems almost an impossibility.

It was while traveling this circuit that he formed the acquaintance and enjoyed the friendship of Rev. William Loder, a local preacher of deep piety, extensive learning, and wide experience. who had introduced Methodism in the neighborhood, had formed and led the classes, and preached regularly and successfully the word of the Lord in the godless regions round about; and the two men, though widely apart in years, soon discovered a unity of spirit in each other which cemented them together in the bonds of a Christian friendship, and his house became a favorite home for the young gospel preacher. Among the members of his family was an only daughter, whose modest worth soon made an ineffaceable impression upon his heart. Her deep and unaffected piety, her grace of mind and person, her gentle womanly ways, combined to deepen that impression until they won from him the offer of all he had to give,—his hand and heart,—pledging with them the tenderest care and fondest affection which it was possible for his ardent nature to bestow, a pledge which his life amply redeemed. No burden that he could bear was permitted to fall on her, no calamity which he could suffer visited her, and no happiness which he could procure was wanting to her. He never hesitated to acknowledge the depth of his affection, but in a befitting and manly way openly avowed the intensity of his appreciation of the qualities of mind and heart which at first had drawn him to her side, and which in his estimation made her value 'far above rubies.' He found in her a companion suited alike to his nature and his work. Her disposition was as generous as his own, though controlled more largely by prudence, a quality needed in the government of his household, for he was generous to a fault. Her heart was as deeply interested in the salvation of sinners as his own, and her mind delighted in the cultivation of all that was pure and good and beautiful in life. He esteemed her counsels of inestimable value to him in the prosecution of his work, and the home that her presence filled with sunshine to him was the sweetest spot in life. She bore cheerfully with him all the sacrifices and hardships that the itinerant life compelled, and, relieving him largely from the care of a numerous family, left him free to pursue with an almost entire consecration of his time the work to which he had given his life. Her praise is in all the churches which they served, and many whom her gentle persuasions led to God rise up and call her blessed. She is still living, residing in the city of Newark, waiting for the summons which shall permit her to rejoin her husband at their home in the city of God, where he has passed before her.

His next appointment was Paterson, one of the four stations which then existed in New Jersey. There he passed through many difficulties, but still met with a considerable degree of success. His journal written at the close of that year says,

"Though the beginning was not auspicious yet, upon the whole, the year has been in some degree successful. About fifty have been added to the church, whom I hope to meet in that better country where there are no misrepresentations, no tribulations, but where peace, love and harmony shall forever prevail."

The year succeeding this he labored upon Essex Circuit, with his beloved friend, Benjamin Collins, again for a colleague.

During this year they added Plainfield to the circuit, of which he says, "Here I preached in a wheelwright shop the unsearchable riches of Christ to all who were disposed to hear. At first the number was small, but as our efforts were continued it increased, and in a short time a class was formed. From such humble beginnings arose what is now an important appointment in the Newark Conference. About the middle of this year his beloved colleague was removed for the purpose of establishing a mission in Somerville, the county town of Somerset County, leaving the charge of the extensive circuit entirely in the hands of his junior, a work, however, which he performed faithfully and usefully till the close of the year.

His next charge was Staten Island, one which always lived in his memory as among the pleasantest of his long and useful itinerancy. Healthily located, an affectionate and appreciative people, and abundant success in the work of the Lord, all contributed to leave this spot among the greenest and most beautiful of the recollections of his ministry. He writes, "During my labors on the island the Lord was pleased to make the preaching of the gospel his power unto salvation to many souls." More than a hundred were added to the church, the whole membership were greatly quickened and blessed with a deeper and fuller power of religion, and he collected the funds with which to build a parsonage. His place in their affections was of a far more than ordinary depth; and so firmly were they entwined around him, that his numerous friends, both in and out of the church, offered to purchase him a house and surround it with a number of acres of land if he would consent to locate and remain among them. But, he says, "I had consecrated myself to the work of the ministry, and believing that I must preach the gospel in other places also, for therefore was I sent, I declined the generous and affectionate offer." His own heart was deeply affected at leaving this people, but his unswerving devotion to the itinerancy left him no choice, and willingly, though sadly, he repaired to New Providence, his next field of labor, where he toiled with the same untiring energy in the service of his Master. Of this year his journal says, "I had the pleasure of seeing my congregations increase, and of adding some to the church of God." His next appointment was Long Branch, where for two years he fully proclaimed the gospel of Christ and surrounded himself with friends whose affections followed all his life. He says, "I spent two very agreeable years in this appointment, during which I tried to perform the various duties obligatory upon me, and had the pleasure of seeing the cause of my Master to some degree prosper. I also made some progress in my studies, paying particular attention to Greek, which I find of great benefit to me." He next went to Pennington, which was then called a station, although there were three appointments to which his enterprising spirit soon added a fourth. His parish was fifteen miles in one direction, and five in another, which, as he says, "kept him constantly employed." A part of the time he was engaged in two extra meetings at once with four miles of distance between them, (dividing his labor as the most pressing necessities seemed to demand,) and in each of which there was a a good measure of success. At all the appointments on the charge, the work of the Lord was revived, and while a number of the converts connected themselves with the Presbyterians, where they had always attended, yet the Methodist church received an addition of over one hundred and fifty as the result of his labors here. It was during his pastorate there that the Pennington Seminary was projected. Into this movement he entered with all the ardor of his nature. The educational necessities of the church had long been a subject of deep consideration with him, and to this project, which promised to contribute so largely to their successful solution, he gave all the labor and interest which was within his power. Interesting prominent men of the connection in its favor, soliciting subscriptions from those who had means, and supervising largely the details of both its plans and their execution, it is not too much to say that to his labors the seminary is largely indebted for the useful position it has occupied in the developement of New Jersey Methodism. From this he was removed to Swedesboro, where there were two more years of abundant labor. A school-house was the only place in the town where the society were permitted to meet, and this they might not occupy on the Sabbath, lest it should interfere with the attendance at "The church." Under his effective administration a noble Methodist man, named Wolfe, purchased a lot in a central location, and donated it to the society, and Brother Shaw succeeded in collecting sufficient funds to erect a house of worship, which was both built and dedicated during his ministry. Two other churches on the circuit were repaired, two parsonages were bought, and many added to the societies, so that he was enabled to say, "His labor was not in vain in the Lord."

While here he was called to suffer the loss of one of his dear children, which deeply affected him, but did not stop the current of his labor. With a heart sad and burdened he toiled on indulging his grief only in the privacy of his sympathizing family and remitting no labor because of his saddened spirit. So deep was this feeling that twenty years ago when in company with the writer he visited the grave in the beautiful cemetery of that ancient town, his feelings overcame him, and he could scarcely resist the impulse to have the dust that remained disinterred, and laid in the resting-place where he expected to repose himself when his earthly career should be terminated.

From there he was appointed to Camden Station. There was then but one church of the denomination in the town, and the work was laborious and incessant. But his spirit pressed him beyond the regular duties demanded at his hands, and he instituted preaching at five o'clock on Sabbath mornings in addition to the regular duties of the day. Besides this, he preached in the public gardens to the pleasure-loving Sabbath-breakers, and in every possible way endeavored to promote the work of calling the attention of men to the demands of the gospel upon them. His labors were blessed with a good degree of success, and he left the charge feeling that his appointment there had not been without the Master's approval.

He was now sent to Mount Holly, in which place he witnessed the largest revival which ever occurred in the place. The power of God seemed to attend every service of his ministry, and the whole town was moved. Several of its most prominent men and women were converted—the altar was crowded with mourners—people were kneeling, weeping, and praying, in all parts of the church at once, and over three hundred were added to the society, of whom a number still remain to call him blessed.

The appointment following this was Burlington, where he labored in 1844. At this session the Conference avowed its sense of his ability by electing him a delegate to the General Conference. His duties were discharged in a manner satisfactory to those who sent him, and opened the way for higher influence and usefulness in the future. He labored one year in Burlington with great acceptability, when he was removed from there and made Presiding Elder of Camden District, which office he filled to the general satisfaction of both preachers and people for four years. Of these years he writes, "I traveled in my carriage ten thousand miles, preached one thousand sermons, was present at many quarterly meetings and love-feasts, gave an oversight to the building of and dedication of churches, &c.," spending his whole time in work as one who expected the Master when he came to find him toiling in the vineyard. In 1848 the Conference again honored him with an election to the General Conference, and the bishops continued him in the eldership, appointing him to Trenton District, where he committed himself to his labors with the same untiring devotion. He says, "During my term of service there I traveled between eight and ten thousand miles in my carriage, preached about five sermons a week, and attended to the various duties which the office imposed upon me. I had the pleasure of seeing the work of the Lord prosper to a greater or less degree in all parts of my field of labor, and a goodly number were added to the church of God. The Lord was very merciful to me in giving me health to perform all my journeys and fill all my appointments. Upon a review of the past I may gratefully exclaim, 'What shall I render unto the Lord for all his benefits toward me? I will take the cup of salvation, and call upon the name of the Lord.'"

In 1853 he was stationed in Franklin Street, Newark. In this appointment far more than ordinary effort was needed to keep up the status of the society. A hundred and fifty members had left that spring for the purpose of organizing the new and splendid Broad Street Church, and many of these were among their most prominent men. But undismayed by the discouraging aspect of affairs, he vigorously commenced his labors, devoting a large proportion of his time to visiting the sick and among the members, working in the classes and managing all the church interests. There was a long standing debt on the church of $2000, which he succeeded in liquidating, and at the close of his term of service it was found that two hundred had been received into the society.

He next served the church in Morristown. Here also was a church debt of $1400, which he removed, thus greatly relieving the society. A revival accompanied his labors, from whose fruits the church received one hundred and fifty members, and the interests of the church generally prospered in his hands. He writes of Morristown, "Frequently as I saw the altar crowded with those who desired admittance on probation, I thought, will all these prove faithful? will they endure hardness as good soldiers of Jesus, and finally hear the Master say, 'Come ye blessed of my Father, inherit the kingdom prepared for you from the foundation of the world; enter in to the joy of thy Lord?'" At the close of his two years there he again writes, "I found some kind warm friends in Morristown, friends who evinced their love not in word only but in deed and in truth. One of them, Hon. G. F. Cobb, gave me a beautiful lot in the cemetery here, so that when my labors shall have terminated, my body will find a resting-place in this sequestered and beautiful spot, but only for a season. When Christ shall awake the slumbering dead, I also shall hear his voice and obey his bidding. I shall rise in the likeness of my Lord, and live to die no more."

The last appointment filled by him on earth was Warren street, in the city of Newark. The officiary of that church, impressed by the success of his labors in Franklin street, and anxious to secure the spiritual privileges of his ministry, made a unanimous and earnest request to the appointing power for the services of Brother Shaw, which request was granted, and accordingly in the spring of 1857 he entered upon his ministry in that charge. Here again the necessity for excessive labor was apparent. The society was small, the church was only completed in the basement story, with the upper part enclosed, and the finances of the people had been nearly exhausted in their previous gifts toward the enterprise. But nothing daunted he immediately inaugurated a series of movements which looked to the speedy completion of the building. He was encouraged in this by witnessing a very considerable increase in the congregation, a revival of religion, and the fresh zeal with which his own indomitable spirit inspired the membership.

In this matter, all the financial care and labor came upon him. The smallest details were to be adjusted, the most trivial accounts kept in shape, the contracts to be made and settled, the material to be examined, and the money needed for carrying on the work raised, principally by appeals personally made to the prominent Methodists of the city, whose patience and liberality had already been severely taxed by repeated applications for the same purpose. All this came upon him in addition to the regular duties of the pastorate, which were faithfully discharged. Day by day in the prosecution of his cross-bearing labor, he plodded wearily on foot through the streets of the city, endeavoring to fully carry out to a successful issue the labor he had undertaken. It cannot be surprising to any that these labors were too much for his toil-worn frame.

His friends observed his failing health and urged him to desist, but his feelings were so strongly enlisted that he could not get the consent of his mind to do so. He toiled on, striving against the lassitude induced by increasing weakness until the church was almost ready for dedication, when a bilious remitting fever supervened upon his already broken powers, and confined him to his bed, from which alas! he never rose again. The fever was so violent as to occasion delirium during the most of his sickness, but occasionally his mind was clear, and he would speak of possessing the "peace that passed all understanding." His friend and Presiding Elder, Rev. J. S. Porter, D. D., visited and conversed with him frequently, and the following transcript of one of the conversations will illustrate perfectly the spirit of mind with which he met the approach of the last evening. Said Dr. Porter, "The eye and the heart of the great Father are upon you, and in this way he magnifies you, for we are all called upon to *endure* when we pass through the furnace of affliction." Brother Shaw replied, "Yes, and it is always our privilege to know that 'He doeth all things well.'" Dr. Porter again said, "I hope Brother Shaw that it will please the Lord to counteract the present visitation, so as to bring you up to renew your labors in the vineyard, in the extension of the cause of his kingdom among men." "Yes," said Brother Shaw, "I hope so, for I would love so much to be spared a while longer to preach the gospel of my blessed Saviour. Ah! *how much more diligently would I labor in the vineyard.*" Dr. Porter then said to him, "You have done what you could, you could do no more, this is the belief of your fellow-workers, and of all that have known the extent of your labors." At once Brother Shaw responded, "I would not rely upon that. I have a better, a surer foundation. For he that spared not his own Son, but freely delivered him up for us all, will he not with him freely give me all things? The *unspeakable* gift. Through him that loved me, and gave himself for me, I expect to be saved." "Yes," said Dr. Porter, "but it is pleasant to know that the ministry, the church, and all with whom you have been associated, give expression to the faithfulness of your labors." "*Oh yes*," said he, "*but I think I would do better.*"

A few days before he passed away, Dr. I. M. Ward, one of the attending physicians, a devoted and pious Christian, said to him, "Mr. Shaw, do you want to live?" "Yes," he replied. "If it be the Lord's will." "But," said the Dr., "if not his will?" "All is well," was the reply, "all is peace within." On the morning of his death which took place Oct. 5th, 1858, several of his brethren in the ministry gathered round his bed and sang "Homeward Bound." The sentiment apparently lingered in his mind, and the last words he utttered, about half an hour previous to his death, were, "Most home! Most home!" He was unable to speak without painful effort, but always responded audibly his hearty Amen! whenever prayer was made in his room, until he gave up what remained of mortal life into the care of the Christ he loved and served. He was buried from the church which his labors had completed, and which his bereaved flock had draped in mourning. His beloved friend, Dr. Porter, officiated at the funeral, taking for his text, "He was a good man, full of the Holy Ghost and faith," words which in themselves were descriptive of the character of the departed.

Afterward amid the tears of his family, his people, and his brethren in the ministry, they conveyed him to the beautiful resting-place in the cemetery at Morristown, where two years before he had written that he wished to lie, and where the worn-out frame reposes until Christ shall call him from the dead.

Brother Shaw was possessed of a vigorous physical system. In all the long years of his ministry no sickness had so prostrated him as to interfere seriously with his work, and this was perhaps one reason why he was so unwilling to believe that repose was necessary to him when he was literally giving his life for the Church. It sustained him in a class and variety of labors which would have broken down the most of men, and contributed largely to the cheerfulness of spirits which made his society a charm. His mental powers were naturally strong, and had been cultivated with a view to their increase in that direction. While he loved and appreciated the beautiful both in literature and oratory, his own peculiar power lay in strong simplicity and logic. He knew his power, and increased it in the manner which could be rendered most available in the great work of his life. He gave a very considerable attention to his mental cultivation, studying the languages, reading and digesting the best authors, and writing freely upon all subjects which came within the purview of his labors. He had partially prepared an autobiography of his life, reaching six hundred pages, containing many things of general Methodistic interest, besides being a faithful transcript of his life, and which, had he lived, would have been published and found to contain many valuable materials for a history of the Church in our State. The word which will probably best describe his preaching is "powerful." Not that kind of power which consists chiefly in the arousing of excited passionate emotion, though that entered to some considerable extent into the results of his labors, but that kind of power which left an impression capable of being developed into an immediate invitation of sinners to seek God, while the Church would at the same time be built up in its most holy faith. His sermons were always the result of careful preparation, and thoroughly studied, the time for which he found by an habitual system of rising at four o'clock in the morning during all the years of ministerial life. At home or abroad it was all the same, and unless some insuperable obstacle prevented, no matter what hour he retired, that hour in the morning found him awake and attending to his duties. He preached with deep feeling, baptizing his sermons with his tears, and the occasions were rare indeed in which the tears of the congregation did not accompany his own. In the minor details of the work he had few superiors. In the successful conduct of prayer-meetings, in the leading of classes, in visiting the sick, in pastoral visiting, in personal efforts to induce men to seek Christ, and in the instruction of penitents, he was a workman that needed not to be ashamed. His sermons always attracted good congregations, and while specially adapted to the masses, yet in their strong, true logic found appreciative hearers among the cultivated and refined members of community. He possessed in a remarkable degree the power of adaptation. The writer remembers hearing him preach a sermon to a congregation on the Sabbath, composed largely of intelligent people, where the strength of thought and lucidity of argument illustrating the truths of the gospel was the theme of universal commendation, and on the following day preach a sermon to a congregation of unlettered people in the mountains, and which was the theme of commendation equally strong. When he went to the church on this occasion, there were but ten persons present, and as there was considerable official business requiring attention, he at first thought he would not preach, but on hearing that one lady had walked seven miles to hear a sermon, and carried her babe all the way, he at once decided differently, and for over an hour held the congregation of ten spell-bound, while he delivered in the simplest yet most eloquent manner, with illustrations drawn from surrounding circumstances, a sermon on "One thing is needful."

As a preacher in charge his large charity and general insight into the motives which governed men, made him uniformly successful. If he erred anywhere it was in excessive leniency to offenders, which sometimes worked against the best interests of the Church, yet on the whole we have had but few men who managed the difficult and delicate duties of a preacher in charge with greater efficiency than John K. Shaw. His business talents were superior, and fully consecrated to the Church. The number of parsonages and churches erected under his ministry, the debts removed from others, the refitting of many of our houses of worship, all attest both a capacity to plan and an ability to execute which fully entitles him to the character which we have given; and the remark made in the cabinet of Bishop Waugh in reference to him, that "Brother Shaw would be useful anywhere," is borne out by his success in all these various departments of labor.

As a Presiding Elder he was generally esteemed. In the official discharge of his duties as an adviser of the Bishop, it sometimes became necessary to recommend a brother for an appointment which appeared oppressive, but his genial sympathy with the circumstances and his willingness to share the burden soon disarmed any opposition of feeling which might exist. His administration of discipline was mild, and not so closely bound by technical rules, as to prevent the accomplishment of greater good by sometimes giving larger latitude.

The welfare of the preachers rested heavily upon his mind, and many are living still who can bear ample testimony to his persistent exertions to secure them a comfortable support. Sometimes he would beg money from door to door to supply the wants of such of them as were sick and destitute. If any cases of misconduct occurred among them, while he did all that appeared requisite for the honor and welfare of the Church, yet he studied how the blow might fall upon the offender in such a way as to redeem instead of entirely crushing him, and in the general, the people regarded him as a friend, and the preachers as an elder and beloved brother.

In the construction of his moral nature, conscientiousness was probably the most powerful element. His sympathies were wide and deep. His generosity was profuse, and frequently led him beyond the bounds of propriety, and, but for the prudence of his wife, would often have occasioned embarrassment. No one was turned empty away. The writer has known him to give away his last dollar to an object of questionable worthiness, but which appealed warmly to his sympathies, and it was a principle with him to give something to every applicant whose imposture was not clearly proved. As a husband and father he was devoted, the spiritual or temporal welfare of his family occupying a large portion both of his thoughts and prayers, and any possible sacrifice was cheerfully made for their advancement.

In his friendships he was firm and confiding. Those who enjoyed that friendship feared no betrayal, counting it among the pleasant blessings of their lives, and feeling assured that it could be successfully appealed to, whenever the friend in need was requisite.

His religion was an experimental realization of a God of love. The witness of the Spirit was not only a doctrine preached but an experience realized. His theological views were as broad as his sympathies. Atonement for all men in the fullest Scriptural sense was the foundation upon which he based his public efforts. He loved his race with sympathies that spanned all time, and took in their wide circle the sweep of immortality.

But, he rests from his labors. His work is done, and well done. His memory is precious to the churches, and precious still to those he honored with his friendship. His record is on high, and his works do follow him.

REV. ROBERT LUTTON.

"Like snow that falls where waters glide,
Earth's pleasures fade away,
They melt in time's destroying tide
However bright their stay;
But joys that from religion flow,
Like stars that gild the night,
Amid the darkest gloom of woe,
Smile forth with sweetest light."

THE life of Rev. Robert Lutton was full of romance and variety. He was born in Ireland, in the year 1791. His father was a man of considerable wealth, liberal education, and fine social position. At an early period Robert became fond of society and dress, and the position of his family gave him ample opportunity for indulgence in these propensities.

This fondness soon grew into a passion which broke over all restraints, and convivial fellowship and sports were the legitimate results.

He not only neglected religion, but the church and her ministers were objects of frequent ridicule and scorn. His parents, who were deeply pious, mourned over the waywardness of their son, but their praiseworthy efforts to restrain him, gave offence, and he left home clandestinely, joined the British service, found his way to the West Indies, took the yellow fever in its severest form, and while lying in the hospital, attended by an old colored woman, with the bullets of the enemy flying around him in all directions, he resolved, if he ever reached home, which he did after many adventures, he would receive advice with more attention.

Some time after his return to his friends, he was prevailed on to attend church. Very soon he became thoughtful, and even penitent. He desired to know the way of salvation. In this state of mind, a work on predestination was put into his hands. He read it with care. The teachings of the book were, that God had from all eternity ordained a certain portion of the human family to eternal life, and the remaining portion to eternal death; and that these numbers were so fixed and definite that they could neither be increased or diminished. The influence of such reasoning upon young Lutton's mind was unfavorable. He at once became despondent, and concluded, that in consequence of his great crimes, he was numbered amongst the reprobates, and that the longer he lived the greater the accumulation of his guilt would be, and so, the heavier his punishment to all eternity.

These thoughts were so overwhelming, that he came to the terrible conclusion to destroy his own life, and announced this intention to his friends. Shocked at such a purpose, his parents were vigilant in their efforts to prevent it. But the gloom upon his mind continued to increase, until it could be endured no longer, and he resolved to rush unbidden into the presence of his God.

On a bright moonlight night he went down to the River Bann, took off his coat, and in the act of plunging into the water, it was suggested, "Look into your Bible once more before you die." He drew from his pocket a little well-worn book, opened it at random, and the first passage that met his eye, was, "But we see Jesus, who was made a little lower than the angels, for the suffering of death, crowned with glory and honor; *that he, by the grace of God, should taste death for every man.*" It was a voice from heaven, and the rash deed was prevented.

He hastened home, went to his chamber, fell upon his knees, and prostrate in the lowest depths of humility and penitence, yet encouraged with gleamings of hope, pleaded with God until three o'clock in the morning, that for Christ's sake his multiplied and aggravated sins might all be pardoned. He did not plead in vain. Mercy came, first in drops, then in showers, then in overwhelming floods. He was inundated with the surging glory, filled with the unfathomable love of God. This change so wonderfully glorious, was accompanied with loud and long utterances of praise. The family was awakened by the unusual cry, and his mother who had been driven almost to frenzy, expecting every day he would put his terrible threat of suicide into execution, rushed into the room, supposing she would find her son weltering in his blood. Falling upon him as he lay upon the floor, she exclaimed frantically, "*O he has done the deed at last.*"

Thus interrupted, the happy young man cried out, "O mother! mother, your son is saved, saved through the blood of the Lamb. God for Christ's sake has pardoned all my sins; now I am his child, filled with his Spirit, unspeakably happy in his love. O mother, happy—so happy."

The poor mother brought up thus suddenly from the lowest depths of mental agony, to the highest emotions of blessed relief, exclaimed in an ecstacy of surprise, "Now Lord, lettest thou thy servant depart in peace, for mine eyes have seen thy salvation," when her nervous system, too severely taxed, gave way, and she swooned with unutterable joy.

This conversion, so marked and powerful, had its influence upon others. His sister Anna, a lady of superior talents and education, was at that time, a rigid formalist, but seeing the wonderful change wrought in her brother, felt deeply convinced that there was a power in experimental piety, to which she was an utter stranger. She therefore sought, and soon found, the pearl of great price, and became henceforth a decided, happy, and useful Christian. For many years she led *six classes every week*, and frequently held meetings in private houses, when she expounded the Scriptures, and set forth as the high privilege of all believers, "The fullness of the blessing of the gospel of Christ." She was an authoress too, and her published poetry is not only imbued with the spirit of her Divine Master, but is marked with equal literary taste.

Soon after his conversion, young Lutton found that he had a proud heart to contend with, and at once set about its mortification.

His love of dress was extreme. He felt it must be conquered, or it would conquer him. What should he do? After a little reflection, he concluded to array himself in the most homely attire, then tying a rope of straw around his loins, started down the road.

He soon met a man on horseback, who supposing him crazy, asked, what was the matter?

"O," said Brother Lutton, in a pitiful tone, "I am afflicted with a very loathsome disease, the most terrible to which human nature is heir." The man alarmed, asked excitedly, if it was contagious. "Yes," replied the young Christian; "It is the most contagious of all diseases in the world; I believe everybody takes it." The man was about putting spurs to his horse to fly from the presence of so much contamination, when Brother Lutton quietly exclaimed, "Do not be alarmed, I refer to the inward corruptions of the human heart, and I am taking this method to mortify my pride."

He prayed earnestly for purity, and immediately after the commencement of his religious pilgrimage, sought with great earnestness the higher forms of Christian life and experience.

He burned with a Divine zeal, and longed to be useful to his fellow-men. Everywhere, publicly and privately, he exhorted to repentance.

He soon secured the confidence of the church, and was licensed to preach. After this, he did not wait for invitations to labor, but sought appointments, and then filled them with power.

While thus engaged, he was frequently associated with that distinguished man of God, Rev. Gideon Ouseley, for whom he cherished the fondest recollections, and of whom he always spoke, as the *sainted Ouseley*.

Pursuing his Master's work, Brother Lutton found in a part of the country noted for its wickedness, an organization, styled the "*Hell Fire Club.*" It was composed of infidels of the lowest grade. They held an annual festival, at which they built an altar, and with horrid oaths and obscene rites, burned upon it the sacred Scriptures. Lutton heard of it, and fired with holy indignation, resolved, if possible, to put a stop to such blasphemous sport. His friends tried to dissuade him, but asking God for help, he ventured to go forth. The leader of the club was an Irish giant about seven feet high, and desperately wicked, called Big Tom. He swore if the preacher came there he would kill him. Entering the building, the young minister found a large concourse of people, to whom he preached Jesus and the resurrection. As he was about passing out of the house after the discourse, Big Tom stood at the door with a huge club, but while in the act of striking the minister to the ground, fell prostrate himself, paralyzed in every limb.

It was not long before he began to cry most piteously for mercy. Young Lutton fell upon his knees beside him, and, after a protracted struggle, the lion became a lamb, and horrid oaths were turned to songs of praise. It was a great victory, and henceforth Big Tom became the preacher's fast friend, and while he remained in the missionary work in that region, went with him as a kind of body-guard, and, thus protected, no one dared molest him. A number of the members of the club, seeing so great a change in their leader, sought salvation, and the "*Hell Fire Club*" was effectually destroyed.

Soon after this, the circumstances of the family changed. His father, by injudicious endorsements, lost his fortune, and was entirely dependent upon a small annuity settled upon him for life by those whom he had befriended.

This was quite insufficient to meet all demands, and Robert felt the importance and necessity of doing for himself. His mind was strongly turned towards America. But he had no means of going, and no friends when he should arrive there. The former, however, was unexpectedly supplied by a generous relative, and, thus assisted, he resolved to leave the latter in the hands of God.

Filled with an inexpressible sorrow, he bid farewell to friends and dear old Ireland on the 4th day of May, 1823, and embarked on board the good ship Woodbine, bound for Philadelphia. Coming on deck after a poor night's rest, just as they were leaving his native shore, he says, "I was wonderfully struck with the prospect presented to my view. The ship was in full sail, the weather fine, favorable breezes filled our canvass, and we moved along with a majesty indescribable, while the sun in his glory, vying with every other part of creation, added lustre and beauty to the scene. A number of ships were in view, which, together with the landscapes everywhere greeting the wondering eye, presented a lovely picture. The white chalk cliffs of County Antrim on the one side, and the romantic mountains and valleys of County Down on the other; the fields clothed with verdure, the flocks feeding and sporting on the plains, altogether formed a prospect which caused my astonished heart to exclaim, "O Lord, how manifold are thy works, in wisdom hast thou made them all; the earth is full of thy glory, so is the great and wide sea."

On ship-board he labored successfully for the spiritual welfare of the passengers and crew until prostrated with sea-sickness, when he gave up with great reluctance.

During the passage, which lasted about six weeks, they were visited with a terrific gale, which carried away the vessel's rigging, and threatened to engulf them all.

As they approached Philadelphia on the 16th of June, and saw vast multitudes standing upon the wharf, awaiting their arrival, he says, "A strange mixture of sensations exercised my mind. In this crowd were persons with eager expectation inquiring for their friends. Some were looking for a wife, some for husbands, some for a father, and others for a mother, &c. But there was no friend to take me by the hand. I was a stranger in a strange land, with but little money, and little knowledge of the world, afraid to trust any one, and knew not where to go. I lifted my heart to heaven for direction, and was soon encouraged to hope in the Lord." He went to a respectable hotel, staid all night, and found the people kind.

On the third day after his arrival, he sought out a Mr. Kelly, an influential and wealthy member of the M. E. Church, for whom he bore a letter from a brother in Ireland.

Mr. Kelly and family received him most cordially, and bid him make their house his home until he should get settled. This unexpected kindness filled the young stranger's heart with gratitude, and he praised the Lord with unfeigned lips.

Mr. Lutton had brought with him from men of the highest position in the church numerous testimonials of his deep piety, unabated attachment to the cause of Methodism, and his great usefulness as a local preacher. In a few days he presented these to Rev. William Thatcher, then Pastor of Old St. George's, in

Philadelphia, and was at once received into the communion of that church.

His zeal and talents becoming known, his services were soon required to fill a vacancy on the Burlington Circuit, in New Jersey. In the following November, the district conference for West Jersey was held at New Mills, now Pemberton. To this conference he applied for a recommendation to the Philadelphia Annual Conference as a suitable person to become a traveling preacher. As the applications were numerous, and some little prejudice existed against him, on account of being a stranger and foreigner, his request was at first denied. He felt afflicted, but, as he had often done before, committed his case to his covenant-keeping God. After the transaction of some additional business, the brethren thought perhaps they had acted hastily in reference to the application, and finally, in order to be more fully satisfied, invited him to preach before them that night. He modestly consented. God baptized him in a wonderful manner, all hearts were melted, the opposition gave way, and the next morning Brother Lutton was unanimously recommended.

In the spring of 1824 he was received by the Philadelphia Annual Conference, and appointed to Elizabethtown, N. J., then to Salem, N. J., and afterwards to St. George's, and Bristol, Pa. About the time of the last appointment he was married. Mr. Kelley, who had so kindly received him into his family on his arrival in this country, having reached an advanced age, died, leaving a young widow, and several children. Mr. Lutton's intimacy with the family continued, and at a proper time, after Mr. Kelley's death, had so ripened into a mutual attachment, that he and Mrs. Anna Margaret Kelly were united in holy wedlock. She was a lady of amiable qualities, high social position, of considerable wealth, and as the attachment was mutually strong, few unions in a fallen world proved more congenial. With this marriage, the whole current of his life was changed. He soon ceased from the regular work of the ministry, and settled with his family in a princely mansion in Burlington, N. J. Here interesting and beautiful children were born unto them, their home was the abode of Christian refinement, their grounds spacious and attractive, and for a time the cup of their happiness seemed full.

One fine afternoon in the lovely month of June, Mr. Lutton and his wife were sitting in the back piazza, the children were playing amongst the flowers, birds were singing in the branches above, while the soft winds of summer, loaded with delicious fragrance, so filled the air, that existence became bliss, and the whole scene was such as mortals rarely enjoy.

But a cloud of sadness soon passed over Mrs. Lutton's mind, and a presentiment of coming evils seemed to possess her. "O, Robert," she exclaimed, "this is too perfect to continue."

In a few weeks, that terrible scourge of children, scarlet fever, appeared in their family. One and another were taken, then *three* of their little ones lay in death at the same time. Neighbors fled as from a contagion, so that when the time for interment came, there being no one else to do it, the broken-hearted father performed the solemn burial service over his own children. *Five were thus taken in six weeks*, and in the short space of *nine months*, *seven* of their children slept in death, by this terrible disease. It was a dark day, but,

> "Let us be patient! these severe afflictions
> Not from the ground arise,
> But oftentimes celestial benedictions
> Assume this dark disguise."

Then Mrs. Lutton herself was taken ill. It became a time of heart-searching before the Lord. Why are these afflictions upon us? She concluded they were not living in the line of duty, and felt, unless her husband speedily re-entered the active work of the ministry, she too would be removed. She told him her feelings.

He thought so, too. In a short time word came to him from the Presiding Elder of Camden District, that death had made a vacancy on the Swedesboro Circuit, and asking him if he would fill it. His wife urged him to do so at once. Brother Lutton consented, went to the charge, procured a dwelling, a small two story, unpainted house, with but a single rough coating of plaster on the walls, in strange contrast with their Burlington mansion, not only without attractions, but without comforts.

In a few weeks they moved, entered upon their work, Mrs.

Lutton got well, and declared she was far happier in their humble Swedesboro home doing their duty, than in their Burlington mansion, neglecting it.

His subsequent appointments were, Bargaintown, Medford, Whippany, Belleville, and Elizabethtown, N. J., Quarantine and Port Richmond, N. Y., and Perth Amboy, N. J.

Then in 1846, they settled at Camden, N. J., where he became connected with the Third St. M. E. church in the capacity of a local preacher, and labored in the city and surrounding country as opportunity offered.

Here, as years increased, his Christian character ripened toward a beautiful perfection, so that in 1858, he was unanimously re-admitted to the New Jersey Conference, and in connection with the writer, as preacher in charge, received his appointment to the Third St. Church, Camden, as supernumerary.

Our connection there was of the most pleasant and profitable character; while his labors were abundant and successful.

As a friend, Brother Lutton was ardent. To the gushing sympathies of his warm Irish nature were added the holier impulses of Christ's religion; both together, made him a generous and noble friend. The writer will never forget, how, when worn with protracted toil, and needing rest, Brother Lutton came to him one day, with a heart so full of sympathy, that it showed itself in trembling lips and tears, and placing a considerable sum of money in his hands said, "Brother, a few of your friends desire me to give you this, (and I wish," said he, "it was twice as much,) with a request that you will give up the cares of your charge for a few weeks, and seek rest, anywhere that your inclination may lead you." The money and relief were both valuable to a weary minister, but doubly so, because of the genuine sympathy with which they were bestowed.

His ministry was popular. In all his stations he was acceptable, in some eminently successful. His preaching was almost invariably accompanied with that holy unction from above, which cannot fail to find its way to the hearts of men. He felt *himself*, and others felt. In his pulpit efforts his own soul often became very happy, and God's people sat under his ministrations with great delight. He did much good, and many, some of whom are now in the ministry, will rise up in the day of judgment and call him blessed.

He had an elevated and joyful experience. This was true of many periods of his life, but especially so during the later years of his history. His path and his example grew brighter and brighter, even to the perfect day. The last year of his life was a perpetual triumph. He seemed to live, not only for heaven, but in heaven. Often while listening to the word of the Lord in the sanctuary, as he lifted up his voice in the high praises of God, every faculty he possessed seemed to say,

> "My willing soul would stay,
> In such a frame as this,
> And sit and sing herself away,
> To everlasting bliss."

He seemed for many months, to stand like Moses, on the top of the mount, while Jordan smiled in his view, and the promised land was but a short way off.

In this state of mind, the final summons came. He was attacked with hemorrhage of the lungs; the struggle was brief, and on Sabbath evening, Dec. 5th, 1858, in the 67th year of his age, he passed over, to be with Moses and the Lamb forever. Thus closed a varied and useful life. His end was so sudden and yet so peacefully triumphant, that we have felt like saying,

> "There is no death! What seems so is transition,
> This life of mortal breath
> Is but a suburb of the life elysian
> Whose portal we call death."

REV. GEORGE LANE.

THE subject of our sketch, who, for a number of years occupied one of the most prominent and important positions in the M. E. Church of this country, was born in Kingston, Ulster Co., N. Y., on the 13th of April, 1784. His early years were spent amid the toils and hardships incident to a residence in a new country.

Almost entirely destitute of the privileges of the sanctuary, at a period anterior to the era of Sabbath-schools and of Sabbath-school literature, the people there, in those days, enjoyed but few religious advantages. The heroic itinerant following closely the pioneer of civilization, would occasionally awaken the echoes of the wilderness with his messages of mercy to dying men. But our frontier was so extended, and the little groups of population so scattered, that their visits were necessarily quite infrequent. George, however, was more fortunate than most of the youth in his community, for he had a most excellent mother—a Puritan of the old type, who exerted a controlling influence over her son. Through the pious efforts of this earnest woman he was often the subject of deep religious convictions, which led him to go alone before God and pour out his soul in fervent prayer.

In his twentieth year, under the preaching of Rev. James Herron, he was more powerfully awakened than ever before. This season of penitential sorrow, however, was brief, for he soon emerged into the light of a clear, blessed religious experience, and united immediately with the Methodist Episcopal Church. Though he had no early advantages for mental improvement he soon became conspicuous, not only as a man of eminent Christian virtues but also of superior mental power.

Indeed, such was the estimate in which he was held by the Church that the year following his conversion, in 1804, he was employed by the Presiding Elder of the Genesee District as an assistant preacher on the Tioga Circuit. In 1805 this new recruit to the itinerant ranks was received on trial in the Philadelphia Conference, and appointed to Scipio Circuit, New York, which was six hundred miles in circumference. In 1806, he traveled Pompey Circuit, New York. He was sent in 1807 to Accomac Circuit, on the eastern shore of Virginia. In 1808 he was appointed missionary to the Holland Purchase, New York. This mission included all the state west of Canandaigua, and was a field involving hardships and privations of no ordinary character. His incessant exposures on this charge greatly impaired his health, insomuch that after a year spent on the Wyoming Circuit, Pennsylvania, at the Conference of 1810 he found it necessary to ask a location. He was suffering when he went to Wyoming with an affection of the lungs which his zeal, stimulated by his success on that circuit, had so increased as to make his retirement from the work a necessity. Ministers in these days cannot realize the extent of his privations and sacrifices during his year on the Holland Purchase mission. He found it no easy matter to procure even the barest necessaries of life. He was reduced to the necessity of making his own garments, and, though without the slightest knowledge previously of tailoring, or the use of the needle, he actually fitted himself with a coat in which, such was the skill with which he executed the task, he made a very creditable appearance at the Philadelphia Conference the following spring. Thus, amid discouragements which must have driven one not Divinely inspired from the field, he continued, esteeming it a privilege to suffer for such a Master and in such a cause. Here we have the sublime spectacle of a man with business capacities which would have placed him among the merchant princes of the world, living laborious days in the midst of poverty and reproach, until his failing health absolutely forbade his longer continuance therein, impelled solely, as we believe, by the power of Christ's constraining love.

In a letter to the author, the Rev. Dr. George Peck says of him:—

"For the pioneer work he was admirably fitted. He had the heart, the nerve, and the muscle for the hard work, the scanty fare, and the persecution which were the lot of the early preachers of this country. Neither mud, snow banks, swollen streams, nor starvation could turn him aside from duty. Saving souls, with him, was the noblest work in which a mortal could engage, and no labor or sacrifice should be regarded as real difficulties in the way of its accomplishment. Though he commenced his itinerant career in 1805 evidence still exists of the zeal, courage, and success with which he battled with the difficulties of that rugged period of Methodistic history."

He entered into business in Wilkesbarre, Pa., immediately on withdrawing from the Conference, but continued to preach quite as often as was consistent with his condition of health. Being diligent in business and fervent in spirit, he not only succeeded in the former, but was respected and loved wherever known, as a devout Christian and an excellent minister of Jesus Christ.

Rev. Dr. Elias Bowen, who knew him well at this period, says:—

"When I first became acquainted with Rev. George Lane he was engaged in mercantile business in old Wilkesbarre. This place was situated near the centre of the old Wyoming two weeks' Circuit, on which it was my happiness to travel during the years 1817 and 1818, and, being a single man, I made my home at the house of Brother Lane, where I had been cordially invited. It was here I found in him a man to whom I could always go amid the various trials and perplexities of a young itinerant for sympathy and council, and I have always felt that my success on the circuit (and I had a continual revival of religion during my second year especially) was very much owing to the countenance of such a man, the savor of whose name 'was as ointment poured forth' in all that region of country.

"In private life embracing his every-day intercourse with friends and neighbors and the management of his domestic affairs, he was a pattern of piety; and I have yet to become acquainted with the man who excels him in the observance of the principles and duties of family religion. His countenance ever beaming with benignity and affection as he mingled with the loved ones at home; and his family devotions exhibiting, like the matins of the feathered songster, the same unfaltering animation from day to day, could but spread a cheerful solemnity over the entire scene of family associations.

"With regard to secular affairs he was a model business man. It was not enough for him that he went not beyond the letter of the law or the maxims of the business world, the law of the Golden Rule. Nay, he 'was a law unto himself,' 'doing as he would be done by' from the spontaneous impulsions of his heaven-born nature. In all his business transactions it might be truly said of him that he was not only honest, but honorable; commanding the respect of all with whom he had any dealings; and being referred to as the ultimate authority—the universally acknowledged standard among business men, who felt themselves covered in any transaction for which they could allege his example. It was enough to be able to say of their acts and deeds, 'Mr. Lane does so and so,' or 'Mr. Lane sells at such and such prices.'

"Mr. Lane was a man of large benevolence, bestowing of his earthly substance with a bountiful hand as well for the carrying forward and sustaining our benevolent institutions, as for the relief of the poor within his reach, who everywhere recognized him as one of Heaven's divinely-appointed almoners."

After a period of nine years spent in mercantile pursuits his health was so far restored that in 1819 he re-entered the traveling connection, and was appointed Presiding Elder of the Susquehanna District, where he labored during the disciplinary term with great acceptance and success. In 1823 he was returned to the Wyoming Circuit, where he saw abundant fruit of his labor. In 1824 he was again appointed to the Eldership, and placed in charge of the Ontario District, within the bounds of which during the year more than a thousand souls were added to the Church.

The health of his wife, and his family circumstances, were such at the close of this year as to make it necessary for him to ask a location for the second time; and he entered into business again, this time, however, in Berwick, Pa. During the next eight years he was found sedulously ministering to the necessities of an invalid wife and a large and dependent family, and filling with great usefulness and success a large circle of appointments extending some twenty miles around Berwick. "He never allowed a Sabbath to pass," writes an eminent cotemporary who knew him intimately, "without an appointment or an opportunity to help in a revival to be unimproved. While located he was always ready to assist the traveling preachers in their work, and so fully did he retain the confidence of the Church during these periods of retirement from the regular ministry, that at the termination of them he was appointed Presiding Elder with the hearty approbation of the preachers and people." "For the work of a Presiding Elder," continues this gentleman, "Mr. Lane was well adapted. The gravity of his manners and the earnestness of his spirit made a deep impression upon all, and were an example to be imitated by the younger preachers. He held tenaciously to the Discipline and usages of the M. E. Church, and labored to 'keep' the rules. and not to 'mend them.' When he traveled districts, he was a powerful preacher, and was the means of the conversion of many souls. His pungent appeals fastened upon the conscience and left life-long impressions. Under his terrible denunciations of the wrath of God at his quarterly meetings, or from the stand at camp-meetings, hardened sinners would often tremble and sue for mercy. Many precious souls from his old districts in the day of the Lord will rise up and call him blessed. He dealt in the staple truths of the gospel, he was not fond of novelties, and he studied more to do good to the souls of the people than to excite their wonder or tickle their fancy. There was a simplicity, a fervor of spirit, and a power in his language, both in his sermons and his prayers, which told of deep communion with God and a thorough sense of the worth of souls."

In 1832 his beloved wife was called from suffering to reward, and he then began to carry into effect a long-cherished purpose of entering again the regular work of the ministry. He was re-admitted in 1834 into the Oneida Conference, and appointed Presiding Elder of the Susquehanna District, where he remained until he was appointed assistant book agent at New York by the General Conference of 1836.

After his removal to New York he formed the acquaintance of Miss Lydia Bunting, of that city, to whom he was married the following year. In the spring of 1840 he was re-elected assistant agent. The office of principal agent becoming vacant in the following September, he was appointed by the book-committee to fill that place, and so efficiently did he serve the Church in this important position, that the General Conference elected him to its high responsibility in 1844 and again in 1848.

Rev. Dr. Peck, whose relation to the publishing interests of the Church gave him ample facilities for forming an accurate judgment of Mr. Lane's qualifications for, and success in, the office of book-agent, says, "His attention to business was unremitting. He was a perfect fixture in his office. He lost no time. He took no recreation. During business hours he was at his table, and idle gossip was lost upon him. He was always polite and accommodating to those who called upon him at his office, but always made the impression that he had no time to waste in idle conversation. His business matters were conducted with method and despatch; they were never entangled or confused. George Lane was a man of strict integrity. The vast interests committed to his trust were managed carefully and to the best of his ability. As strong evidence of the wisdom of his measures as can be furnished is to be found in the steady advancement in power and usefulness of those great institutions of the Church, the Book-concern and the Missionary Society, while he was Agent of the one and Treasurer of the other. Mr. Lane was an unselfish man. He was a strict economist, never practiced nor tolerated any waste, but was possessed of a noble and generous heart. He patronized every noble charity, and his house was always open to his friends, and his table always spread to supply them comforts. While he begged incessantly for the missionary cause he gave liberally as well."

After having managed successfully the interests of this great publishing house for a period of sixteen years, and having served the Church in the important office of missionary treasurer most of this time, at the General Conference of 1852 he found his retirement from public labors and responsibilities demanded by his increasing years and infirmities. Having cast about him for a congenial locality, in which to spend the evening of his days, he determined upon Mount Holly as his future residence, to which place he removed in 1852, and became a member of the New Jersey Annual Conference. He found his home and associations here highly satisfactory, and did not hesitate to express his conviction that a special Providence had led him to this place. He stated, on one occasion in a meeting for religious experience, that after his retirement from business he "could find no rest for the sole of his foot until he came to Mount Holly, that here he had felt a union of soul and a blessed sympathy with the people of God, and he hoped to live and die with them." He was wont to say, he feared he loved his home almost too well, and was too happy in it.

For several years after his removal to New Jersey he preached regularly in Mount Holly and surrounding villages, and found congenial employment in visiting and praying with the sick. The poor and destitute of his town, during these years, found in him not only a sympathizing friend, but one always ready to supply their necessities with a liberal hand. Indeed, he carried his charities so far as often to diminish his own comforts, preferring to give to the needy what he might himself otherwise enjoy. He had himself been called to suffer, and had learned in his own sad bereavements and bitter experiences to sympathize with others' woes. Two gifted sons, thoroughly educated and eminently qualified for usefulness as ministers in the Church of his choice, had been early called away from earth. He had borne to their graves also two lovely daughters who had grown to womanhood under his affectionate care. But that which he felt, perhaps, more keenly than any other of his bereavements, was the loss of his only remaining daughter, a bright and promising child of ten years. From this, it is thought, he never fully recovered. His affections clung to this little girl with intense fondness. He would often exclaim with flowing tears, "Was she not a precious little one? might she not have been spared?" Even in these sad moments, however, he was wont to say, "The Lord gave and the Lord hath taken away, blessed be the name of the Lord."

Mr. Lane's declining days were marked by all the grace and

gentleness of virtuous age. His life's busy day, as was fitting, had its calm and tranquil evening—an evening, around which clustered the pleasant memories of a well-spent life. He spent hours every day upon his knees in communion with God. He had a room set apart for this sacred audience with Deity, and lived and walked in unbroken fellowship with his Divine Saviour. He was solemn but not austere, grave but not dull; he exhibited a tender concern for the well-being and comfort of all about him, and his countenance uniformly beamed with heavenly light. He enjoyed greatly his correspondence with friends. During the sixteen years of his connection with the book-room he found, amid its numerous cares, but little leisure for reading. After his removal to Mount Holly he turned with great interest to his books, and found them a source of great pleasure and profit.

The last year of his life was spent at Wilkesbarre, Pa., where he was surrounded by the friends and scenes of his earlier days. It was, however, a year of great suffering, for very soon after his arrival there he had a severe attack of paralysis, which greatly prostrated him, not only physically, but, for a time, his mind was also much affected. Though nearly helpless he was not only uncomplaining but prayerful, devout, and happy. So tender and grateful was he that even the slightest attentions from his numerous and anxious friends always received the most affectionate recognition. He often praised God aloud, and almost to the last would repeat and sing those sweet familiar hymns of our Church. The one in which he specially delighted and which truly and beautifully expressed the exultation of his triumphant spirit was that of Charles Wesley:

> "And let this feeble body fail,
> And let it faint and die."

In the lips of such a man, under such circumstances, how fitting was that charming hymn! Though his memory had been much impaired, yet it was never at fault in calling up his favorite hymns. These he would repeat entire without missing a word.

On the evening of the fifth of May, 1859, after commending himself and friends to God in prayer, he entered into conversation with a young member of his own family on the importance of the study of the Holy Scriptures. He said to this person, "Read the Scriptures, love them, treasure them in your heart, and let them be your guide, and you will never be left desolate." These were his last words. He retired to rest, as usual, but was soon seized with convulsions, and at two o'clock in the morning the weary wheels of life stood still, and George Lane, having faithfully accomplished life's great mission, entered into rest.

The subject of our sketch is not to be ranked among the brilliant intellects of the age, but is entitled to a very high place among practical and useful men. As a preacher, he was neither noisy nor ostentatious, but in his best days was unusually effective. Though simple, and unpretending, he was intensely earnest, too much in earnest indeed to be either demonstrative or showy. His success was not due to extraordinary endowments so much as to the concentration of all his powers of mind and heart, upon the one great business of his life: he was never unemployed, nor was he ever uselessly employed, but brought all his energies with intense and persistent devotion to bear upon the great aim and end of probation. His piety was a steady blaze, and his whole life bore most unfaltering and consistent testimony to the power of Christ's redeeming blood, to cleanse "from all sin."

I cannot, perhaps, more appropriately close this brief memoir than by a resume of his character as a Christian and a minister, furnished by his life-long friend, the Rev. Dr. Bowen, of Oneida Conference, who says: "In his character as an eminent Christian minister, taking him for all in all, he had few equals. There have been many, doubtless, who possessed a higher school education, many whom the cold critic would pronounce more eloquent than he; but if there have been many among us who were capable of preaching with more zeal, pathos, and tender Christian affection, many who could appear before their audiences, with a more effective pulpit oratory, I have not known them.

Few public speakers have been favored with a more commanding voice. Few have been wont to employ a more chaste and impressive style of language. This last mentioned qualification arose, not so much from his scholastic attainments, as from his fine natural taste, and the habitual reading of the best authors. I need not say to those who knew him, that 'he was mighty in prayer,' or that in exhortation, that most desirable and useful gift, he had scarcely an equal.

"It was the spirit of his Master, however, connected with his purity of life and exemplary deportment, which clothed him with that tremendous power of utterance under which the most obdurate were often melted into tears. No man, in all the Wyoming Valley where he lived when I first knew him, exerted the same wide-spread and controling moral influence, with George Lane. He was social without dogmatism; cheerful without levity or trifling; having no fellowship with the unfruitful works of darkness, but rather 'reproving them.' A single example of his fidelity and kindness in giving reproof must here suffice. A man coming into his store one day, when I happened to be present, asked, 'Have you playing cards here?' 'No, sir,' was the reply, 'We have Bibles.' The disappointed customer, in a mortified and subdued tone, as he turned to go out, said, 'I suppose you good folks don't keep such things.'

"But I must close my remarks upon one whom I venerated more than any other man I ever saw, by saying of him, as Mr. Wesley said of the immortal Fletcher, that, 'After an acquaintance of more than thirty years, I never saw him do an improper act, or heard him speak an improper word.'"

REV. THOMAS NEAL.

THOMAS NEAL was born in the state of Maryland, April 9th, 1778. His parents were members of the Methodist Episcopal Church, and occupied a respectable position in society. Thomas, notwithstanding his religious training, and the fact that he was reared on a farm, apart from the more corrupting associations of town or city life, was disposed to seek worldly pleasure and sinful amusement, especially in the ball room, and kindred places of merriment and frivolity. This course was a great grief to his parents, and his mother earnestly strove to persuade him to leave his ungodly companions who were leading him to ruin. And, as her concern increased, she made his case a subject of special prayer, beseeching God, for hours together, to arrest him in his evil course, and bring him into the fold of Christ. Nor did she pray in vain, for God, who answers prayer, turned her sorrow into joy, by leading the object of her solicitude to a thorough and happy change of life.

The date of his conversion is not known, but on returning home from a gay party one evening, with his mind filled with the mirthful scenes through which he had passed, he retired to rest as careless as usual. That night, however, the Lord spoke to him in a dream. Eternity was opened to his view, the abode of the lost was uncovered, and he was assured that such would be his portion, if he continued in the ways of sin. So deeply was he affected, that he resolved to lead a new life, and at once set about making his peace with God, nor did he rest till he had secured a saving interest in the blood of Christ. His conversion was clear, the change in his after life so marked as to be evident to all, and his zeal in the cause of religion as great as it had been in seeking worldly pleasure.

When about the age of twenty-four or twenty-five, he was

married and went "West." But his expectations in regard to the country, were not realized, and learning that his mother was dangerously sick, he returned to his native place, and resumed the occupation of farming.

For some time the Spirit of God had been whispering to his heart, that he was called to the work of the ministry. But, like many others, feeling unworthy to occupy such an important post, he endeavored to stifle his convictions, and persuade himself that he was not competent for so responsible an undertaking. Yet the voice still said, "Go and preach my gospel." In the midst of this conflict, God, by his providence, solemnly spoke to him. He was suddenly bereft of his beloved companion, and left with two little ones to care for. He felt that the great affliction which was thus permitted to overtake him, was the voice of God calling him to duty. "Now," said he, "I must go, lest a worse thing come upon me. Woe is me if I preach not the gospel." About this time a Presiding Elder visited him, and after a long conversation on the subject, persuaded him to go at once into the regular work. He reached a decision, left the corn field, still needing his labor, made provision for his motherless children, gave up his farm, and abandoning all worldly prospects, went forth, trusting in God, to the holy, but arduous and responsible work of the ministry.

He was received on trial by the Philadelphia Conference April 26th, 1808, and, after the usual time, passed to full membership and to deacons' and elders' orders. The following long list gives his appointments; 1808, Annamessix; 1809, Smyrna; 1810, Trenton; 1811, Essex; 1812-13, Sussex; 1814, Asbury; 1815, Trenton; 1816, Freehold; 1817–18, Cumberland; 1819–20, Salem; 1821–2, Essex and Staten Island; 1823–4, New Mills; 1825–6, Lancaster; 1827–8, Dauphin; 1829–30, Bristol; 1831, Freehold; 1832–3, Crosswicks; 1834–5, Western Church, Philadelphia; 1836, Camden. When the New Jersey Conference was formed he remained within its bounds and filled the office of Presiding Elder eight consecutive years, four on the Camden and four on the Burlington District. He was a delegate to the General Conferences of 1824, 1828, 1832, and 1844. He settled in Burlington, N. J., as a supernumerary, in 1845, in which place and relation he continued till September 9th, 1859, when, in the seventy-eighth year of his age, and the fifty-first of his ministry, he was transferred to heaven.

The space here allowed is quite insufficient to give a full account in detail of what was accomplished for God and humanity by the abundant labors of this faithful minister of Christ. The success which attended his efforts in nearly all his appointments afforded conclusive evidence that he had not mistaken his calling, but was a chosen vessel for the Master's use. Some of the most powerful and sweeping revivals in connection with Methodism in New Jersey, commenced under his ministry. At what is now Pemberton a great work prevailed, of the fruits of which there are yet living and grateful witnesses. It began in a prayer-meeting in his own house, and one says, "It broke out like fire in the woods, and spread from heart to heart, and from house to house, until the whole community was in a blaze of salvation." Eminent servants of God, who have long stood on the "walls of Zion," and been the means of bringing thousands to Christ; and many esteemed members of the Church, who still adorn the doctrine of God their Saviour, were converted in that revival. This was only one of many places that shared largely in the fruits of his evangelical and faithful labors. Trenton, Salem, Cumberland, Harrisburg, on Dauphin Circuit, Lancaster, and Bristol; and, indeed, nearly every place he served was favored with a gracious revival.

Sometimes he was sent to places where religion was low, and matters, in other respects, most discouraging. Perhaps no house for the new preacher, and no one who seemed to care whether any were provided or other comforts procured. Yet this man of God, who had faith in the reformatory power of the gospel, and believed that he was in the order of Providence while engaged in the work assigned him by the Church, entered upon it, expecting the attending blessing of Heaven. Sustained by this faith, he was happy in God, happy in his work, and seldom failed to reap thirty, sixty, or an hundred fold, and to see the wilderness and solitary places made glad, and the desert rejoice and blossom as the rose.

In 1810 Miss Jemina Rulon, of Trenton, became his second

wife, a most estimable lady, who became a faithful, affectionate companion and a helpmate indeed. The truths he proclaimed she manifested and confirmed by her saintly walk and pious conversation. She was wise in council, strong in faith, earnest in prayer, consistent in life, and thus wielded an undivided influence in aiding to promote his great work.

As a preacher, Thomas Neal occupied a creditable position. He did not lay claim to learning or eloquence. "His preaching was not with enticing words of man's wisdom, but often in demonstration of the Spirit and of power." He had clear views of the theology of his own Church, dwelt mainly upon the cardinal doctrines of the gospel, employed plain, familiar language, brought to his task a warm, honest heart and the accompanying unction of the Holy Ghost, and with these weapons earnestly sought immediate practical results. The writer once heard him say, that, as he went to preach at a certain place where religion was very low, he felt a great desire to see a revival. His subject was a free and full salvation, and while delivering it, his soul was filled with glory; Divine power came upon the people. Some trembled, others were prostrated upon the floor, others cried for mercy, while many shouted for joy. The presence of God filled the earthly temple, and a revival continued with increasing interest for weeks, and resulted in the conversion and sanctification of many souls.

In manner, he was warm, earnest, and impressive. The fire usually kindled in his own soul, as he advanced with his subject, and enabled him to throw much spiritual life, tender feeling, and stirring energy into his efforts. He was an advocate for short exercises, whether in preaching, praying, or singing, and he seldom transgressed his own rules in this respect. The people were wont to say, "He knew when to stop." But on one occasion, at least, he found it necessary to stop sooner than he desired. He was preaching in one of our large churches, and became so embarrassed that, at the end of fifteen minutes, he was compelled to take his seat. He closed by saying, "Brethren, I am out at sea and cannot get back again; pray for me." But they could not help him back, yet, in that sea, many another, before and since, has sunken, as well as he.

Thomas Neal was a man of the people. His plain and unpretending manners, frank and open generosity, fervent and earnest exercises, pleasant social habits, and prompt and sympathetic attention to the afflicted, together with the fact that he was never tedious, rendered him popular everywhere, and made his visits to be hailed with pleasure and his services to be highly appreciated. Whatever impression his ministry made in other respects, it never failed to carry the conviction that he was a good man, and hence his influence in the sick-room and among the bereaved and those passing through life's heavier trials, was most salutary. While on Staten Island an awful storm arose one Easter Sunday morning. The rain poured in torrents, and many of the people thought a second deluge was coming. They flocked around their pastor, asking him to pray for them, and seemed to feel safe in his presence.

His heart was in his work, and he endeavored to perform every part of it with conscientious fidelity. He met all his appointments with great punctuality, in all kinds of weather and under all circumstances, except when providentially prevented. He visited from house to house, seeking to do the work of a faithful pastor, and took a deep interest in the children and in promoting the cause of Sunday-schools. In a number of places, where there was occasion for it and where it seemed feasible, he organized new schools, and thus set many to work in the vineyard of the Lord. He also took an active part in seeking to improve our Church property. The Western Church, Philadelphia, was built while under his pastoral care. Much of the money had to be raised in small sums, and it is said that he never failed to secure through the week the means of paying the workmen on Saturday evening.

The multiplicity of his duties and cares, were not allowed to interfere with his domestic obligations. He was a considerate husband and a kind father, but at the same time, carefully trained his children, and was strict with them in religious matters and especially in regard to the observance of the Sabbath. Yet a somewhat amusing incident is related in respect to his home duties. While absent on one of his circuits, he was detained beyond the expected time. Before he returned, the prepared fuel became exhausted, and Mrs. Neal went to a neighbor's and asked the woman if her son might saw some wood. She became angry and declared her son should not saw wood for such a man as Mr. Neal, who was running round the country and neglecting his own family. Said she, "Do you know what the good book says?" 'If any provide not for his own, and especially for those of his own house, he hath denied the faith, and is worse than an infidel.'" Mrs. Neal keenly felt the rough repulse, but as her custom was, she went in private and told the Lord all about it. Before she ceased praying she heard a knock at the door, and to her astonishment, there was the boy with his saw, and the woman with some good things for Mrs. Neal. "Oh," said she, as she passed the basket over, "how sorry I am that I talked so about your husband. I believe now he is a good man, and is about his Master's work. Forgive me, and accept this, and I shall always be your friend;" and she kept her word.

An incident or two will illustrate the singular care of Providence in connection with the slender income and varied trials of his times. On one occasion he was detained from home several days longer than was expected, by a severe snow storm. The provisions became exhausted, and with a trembling hand Mrs. Neal gave the last piece of bread to her hungry children, and retired supperless, herself, feeling confident, however, that he who sent the ravens to Elijah, would not forget her. That night a brother in the church had a strange dream about the preacher's family, which so disturbed him that he could not rest, until he ascertained if anything was the matter. Thinking it would be safe to take some provisions along, he arrived at the house about daylight. He soon learned the condition of affairs, and felt assured that God had sent him to relieve the family of his servant. At another time Mrs. Neal was taken sick in the absence of her husband. The woman who came to take care of her, wanted money to procure some needed articles. Mrs. Neal who thought there was none in the house, and was afraid to let it be known, lest the nurse should leave, asked for the Bible, intending to seek comfort from its holy counsels, when at the first place she opened it, to her surprise and delight, she found a five dollar bill. How it got there she did not know, but thanked God for help in a time of so great need.

When father Neal settled in Burlington, and ceased to do the work of an effective minister, he still continued to labor as he was able. For years he took his place on the local preachers' plan, and often filled the pulpits of his brethren. When the Second M. E. Church in that city was projected, he identified himself with, and took a lively interest in the enterprise. After the society was organized he took charge of it till a regular pastor was appointed. By its members he was much beloved in life, and lamented in death.

He was also held in high esteem by the people of this city generally, of which they gave many substantial tokens. When it came to be known that some three hundred dollars were all that he had laid aside for old age, though his arduous ministry had covered near half a century, it was proposed to purchase and present to him the property on which he lived. This noble enterprise was started among some friends at the house of the late Col. Hays, who by purse and active efforts evinced a lively interest in the matter. And when the project became known abroad, donations came pouring in from all quarters, and especially from his brethren in the ministry, until more than enough was realized to accomplish the object,

Nor was the generosity of his friends exhausted in this one valuable gift. Again and again was their affection and esteem substantially verified. Having no income but his small annual quota from the Conference, he would have suffered had it not been for the liberality of his friends, but these the Master did not fail to raise up. The people of Burlington constantly testified their appreciation of his character and services in this way. Nor were his friends confined to that city, as a few facts will in part show. One year his money was gone by about camp-meeting time. The question arose, how shall we get our winter stores? But the conclusion was, the Lord will provide. He attended one of those modern feasts of tabernacles, and while there, two unconverted young men introduced themselves, and after some conversation, to his great surprise, each gave him twenty-five dollars. At another time, he received a telegram, directing him to go to the freight depot, at Burlington, and he would learn something to his advantage. He went, but found nothing, and as it was the 1st of April, he concluded some one was playing off a joke upon him. About noon, however, the freight wagon delivered a barrel of flour and two bags, one of sugar and the other of coffee. But whence they came he never learned. Evidence is also furnished of the very high esteem in which he was held by the citizens of Burlington, in an obituary notice, written by a gentleman of the place at the time of his death.

Father Neal lived the life of the rightcous, as those who knew him intimately, fully learned. That his end should be peace was therefore confidently to be expected. The sickness that conducted him down to the chambers of death. came upon him some six weeks before his departure. He attended the camp-meeting at Penns Grove, N. J., where he preached his last sermon, in the delivery of which he was greatly baptized with the Holy Spirit. He returned home as he said, "with his soul full of glory, happy, happy in God." The next week he was much prostrated with a chronic disease; yet his friends did not anticipate a fatal termination. His sufferings were great, but he was fully sustained through them all. "His peace flowed like a river," and sometimes he had such views of heaven as filled his soul with ecstacy. He was often heard to say, as the tears of joy coursed down his cheeks, "I have had precious views of heaven to-day, and it is so delightful. O glory, glory. glory!" During his illness. his nerves were much affected, and sometimes he could get no bodily rest day or night. A friend who was attending by his bed while he was suffering much pain, repeated the words of Paul, "For our light affliction, which is but for a moment, worketh for us a far more exceeding and eternal weight of glory." "Oh, yes," he replied, "the glory, the glory is coming." At another time a friend inquired if he was fully accepted of God. "Yes," he said, "I am the Lord's, and he is mine." A few days before his death, he had an attack of quinsy which very much increased his sufferings. During his last hours, however, he seemed to be relieved from all pain, so that he was permitted to quit the mortal strife in a condition of perfect tranquility. The summons to cease from labor and suffering, and enter into rest, was evidently most welcome; for though his speech was gone, his beaming countenance and speaking eye, expressed more of peace and joy within than any words could convey. Thus lived and died this veteran of the cross. Well might those exclaim who witnessed his departure, "The chamber where the good man meets his fate, is privileged above the common walks of virtuous life, it is the gate of heaven."

His venerable companion went home to glory about eighteen months before her husband. Death was not permitted long to divide them. They lived and labored together for nearly fifty years, in the cause of their blessed Master, and are now reaping abundantly their reward in heaven. May their children with the writer and reader hail them in their happy home!

REV. EDWARD STOUT.

"But on he moves to meet his latter end,
Angels around, befriending virtue's friend;
Sinks to the grave with unperceived decay,
While resignation gently slopes the way,
And all his prospects, brightening to the last,
His heaven commences ere the world be past."

REV. EDWARD STOUT, the son of Joseph and Sarah Stout, was born in Burlington Co., N. J., near the city of that name, on the 26th of July, 1786. When but a child, his father removed to Salem Co., where the whole family resided for many years.

During the early part of his life, young Edward followed the water, and became inured to the trials and hardships incident to such a calling.

At that day, and especially situated as he was, opportunities for spiritual and mental culture were few. Sabbath-schools did not exist, and while there were a few inferior day-schools, he could only attend a short time in the winter season.

Still his mind and heart were under the influence and teachings of the Holy Ghost. He saw and felt that he was a sinner, and needed salvation.

In 1806, a gracious revival of religion broke out in Perkintown, N. J., and a number of his young companions sought and found the Saviour. These things, however, while they deepened his religious convictions, did not lead him to give his heart immediately to God.

Shortly after the revival ceased, one of these new converts died in the triumphs of faith. He attended the funeral; and while listening to the sermon, preached on this occasion by a local minister, familiarly known as "Uncle John Vaneniman," he wept freely, and determined that he too would be a Christian.

In May, 1807, true to his resolution, he joined the M. E. Church as a seeker of salvation. In the following month, at the first camp-meeting ever held in West Jersey, at Pilesgrove, Salem Co., he was happily converted to God. The change was marked and influential, and, from the first, he became a decided Christian.

In 1809 he was married to Miss Clarissa Mulford. Shortly after this he was appointed to the charge of a class. In this department he was laborious and successful, and so secured the approval of the Church, that Rev. Daniel Ireland gave him license to exhort. Here he was zealous and efficient, holding meetings whenever he found an open door, and his labors were blessed in the pulling down of the strongholds of sin, and the edification of the people of God.

A few days after New Year's, 1814, Rev. Michael Coates, Presiding Elder of West Jersey District, called him to fill a vacancy on the New Mills Circuit, with Rev. John Woolston, preacher in charge.

The January snows were deep, and the journey, at that time and season of the year, from Salem to New Mills tedious. Still, with a strong faith and heart full of love to God, the young itinerant took his saddle-bags, mounted his horse, and, facing the north-east blast, set out for his new and important life-work.

He remained there until the session of the Philadelphia Conference, in the following April, the last which Bishop Asbury ever attended in that city, at which he was received on trial, and appointed to Gloucester Circuit, having at that time some twenty-five or more preaching places, with Rev. J. Woolston for his colleague again.

His itinerant career, now fully inaugurated, continued for a long series of years, exhibiting a degree of mental determination to be faithful in all departments of his work, accompanied with corresponding physical energies, rarely equaled, perhaps never excelled.

In 1815 he was appointed to Centreville Circuit, Queen Ann's

County, Md., with Rev. William Leonard. Up to this time his family had been stationary. He now moved them to his field of labor. The Parsonage was a low, one-story, oak weather-boarded house, without even the cheap adornment of white-wash to give it a cheerful appearance. It was equally divided into two apartments—kitchen and parlor. The loft, which was reached by a ladder from one corner of the kitchen, served as a bed-room. It was a poor affair, and the itinerants felt it so, but under the persuasion that it was even better than the Master had, tried to be contented.

His salary, with a family consisting of five persons, was $174, all of which he did not receive. But the flame of revival spread with such irresistible power and glory, that the preachers sometimes had scarcely opportunity to eat, or to enjoy the luxury of a fine parsonage, for they were on the go, from point to point, and from house to house, both day and night, and the slain of the Lord were many.

In 1816 he was elected to deacon's orders, but owing to the death of Asbury, they were without a Bishop at that conference, and he was not ordained. From that Conference he was appointed to Cecil Circuit, with Rev. John Sharply, who, he says, was a good man, a good minister, and a good colleague.

In 1817 he was ordained deacon by Bishop George, and with Rev. Thos. Miller appointed to Smyrna Circuit, to which, in 1818, he was returned with Rev. J. Moore.

His labors in Maryland and Delaware closed with these years. These labors had been arduous, but pleasant, and to his latest hours he often referred to them and his numerous friends there with sentiments of the warmest affection

His subsequent charges, with one exception, were in New Jersey, where he continued to labor without interruption on Cumberland, Gloucester, and Salem Circuits until 1825. While engaged on one of the above fields, he wrote a letter to his Presiding Elder, Rev. Lawrence McCombs, in reference to the interests of the charge, and other matters. As the Presiding Elder's answer is of some historical interest, we insert the larger part of it for the reader's benefit.

TRENTON, *June 5th*, 1820.

DEAR BROTHER:—I received your kind letter of May 22d. I am glad to hear of your health and the prospect which appears on your circuit favorable to religion. But I perceive that it is with you as it is in most other cases in this life, that with the sweet there is some collection of bitter. I am not able to tell what to do, nor how to do, with some cases which I meet in this world. The case you mention is one of the unaccountables. That dear brother is an old preacher, but nobody wants him. I do not know any place where I could put him that would answer any better than where he is. I think preachers who cannot, or will not, serve the people as they ought, should locate. I have made my observations, and find that those preachers who labor hard, even if they have not very brilliant talents, will generally be received by the people. But he is too old to be taught much on such subjects. I hope our brethren will do the best they can under their peculiar embarrassments.

You want to know something about our General Conference. I wish it was in my power to give you a favorable account of all our doings.

We had a great time, and a disagreeable one, in discussing the subject of electing Presiding Elders. The answer to the question in the Discipline, "Who shall choose the Presiding Elders? which is, "*The Bishops*," we wanted changed to "*The Annual Conference.*" After the subject had been under discussion for about two days, there was a proposition presented for accommodation, which was, "*The Bishops shall nominate three, and the Conference elect one from the three nominated.*" This was carried 61 to 25.

In this state the matter rested for five days in peace and harmony. In the meantime J. Soule was elected Bishop, and he wrote a letter to the other Bishops that he could not, and would not, administer the Discipline under this arrangement. Mr. McKendree came into the Conference with Soule's letter and his own talk, and entered a protest against the dictation of the General Conference. It was then moved to reconsider the vote, and we stood twice 43 and 43. So there was no reconsideration. After this S. G. Rossell got a proposition written to suspend the rule for four years. He got forty-five signers to it out of doors, and came into the Conference determined to carry it without argument, and, of course, succeeded. * * * * *

"I must give a view of what was done about local preachers. There is to be annually in each Presiding Elder's district, a district Conference, of which all the local preachers in the district who have been licensed two years, are to be members. The Presiding Elder to be president. This is similar to our annual Conferences, and is to have power to license, and to renew licenses, to recommend persons in the local connection for ordination, and also persons to be admitted into the traveling connection, to expel, suspend, or censure, as the case may be. This is a new thing under the sun, amongst us. There were many things done besides, and some of them out of our line of things, of which, at some convenient season, I will give you as much knowledge as I can. * * * *

"Accept of the affections of myself and family,

"L. McCombs."

The closing months of Brother Stout's labors on Salem Circuit, in 1824–5, were times of great prosperity and power. The young and earnest Anthony Atwood was his colleague. They were true yoke-fellows, each intent on doing the largest possible amount of good. Late in the summer of the year named, the wife of Brother Stout, being sick, dreamed that her husband sat by her bed-side, looking pale, haggard, and worn. She was alarmed, and expressed her fears that he was about to die. He made no answer, but, with a sweet smile, pointed to another part of the room, and asked her if she saw that beautiful star, which seemed to be waving back and forth, with unusual brilliancy.

"Yes!" she exclaimed, "I see it;" and the star still burned with increasing brightness. Some time afterwards she chanced to mention her dream to a pious female friend. That friend immediately replied, "I think I can interpret your dream. Brother Stout," said she, "is going to have a great revival on his circuit, in the labors of which he will become greatly prostrated in body, but do not be discouraged, his reward is sure, and stars will be added to his crown of rejoicing." The interpretation was full-filled. A great revival broke out in the fall, which continued up to the next Conference, in which hundreds upon hundreds were converted and added to the Church. The preachers were much worn, Brother Stout, in particular, to the last extreme, so that, haggard and faint, he went to Conference, and was appointed to Bristol, another large circuit in Pennsylvania, where, with much physical embarrassment he labored for the next two years.

At the expiration of this time, in 1827, utterly exhausted, he was compelled to ask for a supernumerary relation. He then removed his family from Germantown, where he had resided while on Bristol Circuit, to Camden, N. J.

But, though a supernumerary, a man of his active habits could not be idle. Camden was part of a large circuit. The regular ministers could only preach there once in two weeks, on Sabbath afternoons. Brother Stout soon saw that with such an arrangement, while it was the best the circuit preachers could do, was, at the same time, doing but little for the Church there. Camden, so contiguous to Philadelphia, was continually drained of its denominational strength, by its larger and more wealthy neighbor.

Something must be done to consolidate the Church and keep the people at home. As one means of accomplishing this, he proposed to the Society to establish a Sabbath morning appointment, and, as far as he was able, preach himself, and when he could not, secure the services of some one else. The proposition was accepted, and from that day the cause has advanced in Camden, until we now number four flourishing churches, and a prosperous mission with several appointments occupying the outposts of Zion.

Leaving Camden, in 1828, he removed to Sharpstown, afterwards to Woodstown, and finally to Allowaystown, in each of which places he kept a country store, a course rendered necessary, from the fact that the little means he possessed when he commenced to travel had been exhausted in the support of his family, the limited amount of salary received from the Church failing to accomplish that result.

In 1831, his health so far recovered that he re-entered the regular work, and was appointed to Bargaintown Circuit, where he remained two years.

From 1833 to 1845 he labored on Gloucester, Cumberland, Salem, Moorestown, Medford, Swedesboro', Gloucester, Tuckerton, Haddonfield, and Columbus Circuits.

On the last named charge, his physical energies, so long strained and overworked, gave way, and he was compelled, reluctantly, to give up the cherished work, to which he had devoted so many years of his life. These fields were, many of them, large and laborious, yet, though much of the time infirm and broken, he persevered to such an extent that few young men could equal, and with whom, on that account, many felt reluctant to be associated.

On all these charges there were additions to the Church, on some of them large and wonderful revivals of religion, in which the foundations for churches and parsonages were laid, which have since sprung up, and now flourish through all these regions.

His style of preaching was plain, pointed, and practical, adapted to the wants of the people, accompanied with the unction of the Holy Ghost, and sometimes with wonderful exhibitions of Divine power.

His themes were the great fundamental principles of our holy religion. He had no time or taste for speculation. Human depravity he knew was a mournful fact, and Christian holiness he had experienced as a glorious privilege. In all his pulpit efforts, therefore, his great and only object was to bring the world from the gloomy depths of the one, and then to the exalted enjoyment of the other. Christ was his sovereign remedy for sin, the Alpha and Omega, the beginning and the end of all gospel preaching.

On the great practical duties of Christianity, he dwelt with frequency and fervor. His observance of the Sabbath was rigid, and he continually enforced the same duty, both publicly and privately, upon all.

In all things he was strict with himself. He fasted regularly, and from principle. He was an early riser, and spent much of his time in secret prayer. His walk was close with God. Even in the smallest matters he was conscientious to the last extreme. He was a thorough disciplinarian. "He did not mend the rules but kept them; not for wrath but for conscience sake." He wanted others to do the same,—first, because they were the rules of the Church with which they had voluntarily united; and, secondly, because the observance of these rules promoted order in the societies, and holiness in the souls of men, while a violation of these disciplinary requirements, founded, as they are, upon the word of God, resulted in spiritual declension, if not in everlasting ruin. As a faithful shepherd, he constantly enforced the rules.

In so doing, he sometimes made enemies. This, he regretted, but still he discharged his duty fearlessly, not in malice, but in love.

His library was small, but well selected, and wholly Methodist. No work of doubtful tendency, was admitted to his shelves, or recommended to others. Clark, Wesley and Fletcher, were oracles, which he regarded, next to inspiration.

His reading was almost, if not wholly confined to the Scriptures and Wesleyan theology, in which he became proficient, and therefore a sound and successful minister.

He was conscientiously plain, in manners, dress, and equipage. On one occasion, he had ordered a new carriage. When it came home, there were some ornamental parts of it, plated with silver. Although there was nothing really objectionable, yet, fearing the influence of such an example, he carefully wound black tape all around the plated parts, that every appearance of show might be concealed.

In 1840, he located his family in Haddonfield, Camden Co., where they still reside. Here, when unable to engage longer in the active service of his Lord, he retired, to await the arrival of that messenger who should summon him to the spirit world. He waited solemnly, patiently, and prayerfully for fourteen years. But he was not idle. During these years, he often walked several miles and preached, and felt it a blessed privilege so to do. His influence was always good, and the light of his holy example shone with increasing brightness to the last. But the close of his pilgrimage came on. It was a calm autumnal day, November 3d, 1859. The sun shone brightly, and the atmosphere was bland. He walked some two miles that morning, as he generally did when the weather would permit. Returning about eleven o'clock, he rested upon the lounge. At twelve o'clock, he arose, and sat down with the family to dinner. With a low trembling voice he offered thanks to God for every mercy. and solemnly implored a blessing upon their meal. Each member of the family had been served, and they were about to eat, but.

> "A voice that moment came,
> He started up to hear,
> A mortal arrow pierced his frame,
> He fell, but felt no fear."

His son, a physician, who, providentially was at home, sprang to catch his falling father. It was too late to be of service, the tongue and throat were paralyzed; in a few moments he ceased to breathe, and the toils and sorrows of *seventy-four* years were ended. What a scene was here presented.

> "There was weeping on earth for the lost!
> There was bowing in grief to the ground
> But rejoicing and praise, 'mid the sanctified host,
> For a spirit in Paradise found!
> Though brightness had passed from the earth,
> Yet a star was new born in the sky,
> And a soul had gone home to the land of its birth,
> Where are pleasures and fullness of joy!
> And a new harp was strung, and a new song was given,
> To the breezes that float o'er the gardens of heaven."

On the following Monday, a funeral discourse was preached by the Presiding Elder, Rev. George F. Brown, D. D., and his remains were deposited in the burial ground of the Haddonfield M. E. Church, to await the resurrection of the just,

> "When death shall yield his ancient reign,
> And, vanquished, quit the field."

The following letter, written by a venerated and venerable minister, now in heaven, may properly close this article.

PENNINGTON, *Dec.* 30*th*, 1859.

DEAR SISTER STOUT, AND FAMILY:—I have for some time desired to send you a few lines of sympathy and condolence, upon your late painful bereavement, but I have been hindered through a succession of difficulties.

It had always been my purpose, should I outlive my dear brother, if possible to attend his funeral obsequies, for I always esteemed him one of my dear brethren in the Lord. Yes, I loved him most affectionately. Our mutual toils and sufferings endeared us to each other. And now that he is taken from us, his memory will be cherished with the most kindly thoughts and feelings. I do hope that his saintly life may have a holy influence upon us, as long as we may be permitted to stay in this valley of tears. His example is your legacy; yes, and it is mine; for I knew his life. "He being dead, yet speaketh." I shall ever think of him as a man who lived and walked as in the presence of God; and God has taken his blood-washed spirit to Himself. It is his gain to have died, yes, entire, and eternal gain. This blessed fact should soothe the sorrows of our hearts, while we feel painfully our loss. May the God of all grace support your hearts, as he did his, in his many and long sufferings. You may feel some regrets that his exit was so sudden, but was it not a great mercy to *him;* for when the time came that he should be removed, quick almost as lightning flash, without those convulsive struggles which make death-bed scenes doubly afflictive, he was released, and taken up to rest with his God.

Three of our oldest ministers have been taken in regular succession from amongst us, and I stand the next upon the list. Oh that my loins may be girded about, and my light be brightly burning, when the Master comes and calls for me. Should I be so happy as to find my future home where my dear Brother Stout has found his, we shall have many mutually pleasing reflections upon the way which the Lord led us in our pilgrimage on earth.

Let me say to you, trust confidingly in the sure mercies of your covenant-keeping God. He has promised to be a husband to the widow, and a father to the fatherless.

My dear wife sends her love, and unites her sympathies with mine.

Your brother in Christ, most affectionately,

RICHARD W. PETHERBRIDGE.

REV. EDWARD SANDERS.

Of the early days of the subject of the present memoir but little is known, save that he grew up to youthful manhood in the practice of the severest morality, but with no clear teachings of experimental religion. The first religious fact that it seems possible to recover, connects with an evening which the neighborhood had devoted to pleasure. There were jest and dance and song—sparkling wit and gushing music; while the obligations of life and the solemnities of death were forgotten. Among this group was Edward Sanders. Tall and spare, with thoughtful brow and eye, strong in physique, mind, and spirit, he stood prominent among the revelers. In the midst of all this, like the flash of the summer's lightning, the Spirit of God awakened his conscience. Where were his steps tending? What was to be the end of his path? Would not its sunlight go down in cloud and storm? Was he not a sinner, and would not God require an account of transgression? Might not eternal woe lie at the end of any moment of his life? Impressed with these questions his anguish soon became intolerable. The contrast between the scenes around him and the facts of his condition was too strong to be resisted, and he rushed from the house into the fields and woods, where the darkness of the night corresponded with the blackness in his mind. The hours drifted past him, but brought him no relief. The morning found him weeping and sorrowing, and, like the pilgrim in the world's allegory, with but *one* concern—the salvation of his soul; and of *that*, alas! those around him could tell him nothing. He repaired to his father's house, but the sight of pleasant faces brought no comfort to his spirit. He secluded himself entirely in his room, praying and reading the Bible, and endeavoring by a sorrowful repentance to merit some favor at the hand of God. Weeks passed thus, and still gross darkness covered his mind. His bread was eaten in bitterness and his water mingled with tears as he felt the arrows of the Almighty in his wounded spirit. His health began to fail, and friends trembled for his reason. They endeavored to divert his mind, but God alone could satisfy it, and to Him he knew not the way, and he began to fear that he was lost forever.

At a little distance from his father's house there resided a devout and humble Methodist, who was generally regarded by the pleasure-loving community as a fanatic. It occurred to him that possibly *he* might help him, and he was sent for at once. The good man spent some time instructing him more perfectly in the way of salvation, illustrating the gospel theory by a matured and clear experience, till faint glimmerings of the light began to appear. A camp-meeting was held near him, and there he took his weary spirit, hoping for freshening life. Nor did he hope in vain. Under the preaching of the word he *believed*, and all sorrow passed away. Radiant with hope and joy he returned, an astonishment to the friends, who, unable to understand his previous depression, now looked wonderingly on to see if this were indeed the "great power of God." His experience of salvation inspired him with ardent desires for the welfare of others, and he began with strong crying and tears to warn sinners to flee from the wrath to come. Impressed by his earnestness the people heeded the claims of religion, and a revival, subjecting all classes to its power, was the immediate result. Night and day he labored among them, bringing all the stalwart strength of his character to bear upon his work. In private houses, in school-houses, in the rude churches of the country, his powerful voice was heard constantly warning sinners and instructing penitents, until the evidence was clear to all that God had called him to preach the gospel; and at the session of the Philadelphia Conference held in 1834 he was regularly commissioned for the work. For a short time he remained in that section which is now termed the "border country," but when the Conference to which he belonged divided into that of Philadelphia and New Jersey, he chose the latter, and in 1835 was appointed to New Providence Circuit, which at that time covered the territory which is now divided into several circuits and stations. At the close of his term in this charge he was assigned to Plainfield, where, as usual, he labored abundantly. During the term of his appointment here he was united in marriage with Miss Rachel Egbert, of Morristown, a lady every way qualified to assist him in the great work he had undertaken, and who cheerfully made all the sacrifices which were then so fully required in the itinerancy. Her cheerful faith upheld the heart of her husband, and her attention to domestic duties relieved him from their care.

He relied largely upon her judgment; and when passing into eternity, summed up his estimate of her character by saying to the writer, "She has been a *good wife* to me—a *good wife* to me. I do not know what I could have done without her." Even with the lips of death her husband spoke forth her praise.

A fair amount of spiritual success attended his labors in this place, when he was removed to Flanders Circuit, at that time comprehending a large part of Warren County. Here he labored faithfully and zealously, and the Lord's work prospered in his hands. His next removal was to Kingwood, where in labors abundant he still pursued his unflagging course, and won souls to God. Afterward we find his name connected with Newton, the county town of Sussex County, where he preached acceptably the gospel of the kingdom. Next he was stationed at Hope, where the usual success attended his labors, which appointment was succeeded by Flemington, and that again by Asbury, where it pleased God to grant him the largest revival of religion which occurred during all his ministry. The power of God was with him, and large numbers of strong men and thoughtful women gave their hearts to God, producing almost an entire revolution in the Methodistic status of the whole community. At the close of his labors here he was appointed to New Germantown, where he spent the usual term of ministerial labor, after which he was sent to Parsippany, where for two years more he preached the word. Here his health began to fail. Long, earnest preaching—cold, damp rides home in the winter nights after protracted meetings, began to tell even upon his iron constitution, and at the close of his labors there he was assigned to the "River Church," in the hope that a lighter appointment might recuperate his impaired health. But the disease had gone too far to be arrested, and at the next Conference a supernumerary position was deemed indispensable. Now came the trying hour of his life. He was broken down with labor in the prime of manhood, with a numerous family who, from their tender years, were yet incapable of battling with the world, and the probability of a long future in which he would be unable to add anything to his resources. But his trust was in God, and he bore the trial bravely. He selected Pennington as a place of permanent residence, where year after year he lived and suffered, becoming feebler as time kept passing, till the fall of 1859, when it became evident that his days were numbered, and that the emaciated form which had appeared so regularly in the streets of the village would soon be at rest forever. He was now confined to his room. The long years of wasting disease had done their work upon the highly irritable nervous system of a powerfully organized frame, and his physical sufferings were consequently intense. His worldly circumstances were in an unfavorable condition. His eldest son, a young man of brilliant promise, was rapidly sinking into a consumptive's grave, and several young and helpless children were to be left when most they needed a father's care. All these dark shadows kept closing round him as he went down into the valley of death. But his faith never wavered, and his heart never failed. He calmly contemplated and discussed these prospects, and, in view of them all, exclaimed, "My feet are on the rock. I cannot be moved. I can trust *everything* to God." At one time, after passing a sleepless night, he said to the writer, "I have had a blessed time—my soul has been full of the praises of the Lord all the night long;" and again, just before his departure, "I am quite cut loose and am perfectly free from everything on earth; wife and children are given up to God, and I am fully ready to depart." Some time before, he had expressed his inability to understand the plan of Providence in leaving him so long upon the earth without the power to labor. "But," said he, "I can see it all now, and understand how God has left me so long to suffering and uselessness. My character needed *perfecting through suffering*, so that I could be capable of something better in the world to come." When the last struggle came, and his pastor was kneeling by his side in prayer, he held him by the hand while he prayed, and kept assuring those around him that all was peace in his soul, till on the last day of 1859, he gently passed away. He was buried from the church where he so long worshiped; and though the day was one of intense cold, yet the mass of the people were there to testify their respect and love. He had selected Revs. J. Winner and R. W. Petherbridge to preach at his funeral, but the one was absent, and the other ill, and the sermon was preached by the writer, after which his remains were deposited in the old grave-yard of the Methodist church at Pennington. The subjoined sketch of his character is from the pen of his friend and colleague, Rev. G. R. Snyder, and will appropriately close this memoir.

"He was a man of magisterial bearing, though possessing unusually humble views of himself. His delicacy, nice sense of honor, strict scrupulousness, enlarged benevolence, together with his high-toned moral feelings, led him to set the standard of moral and religious conduct so high as to give a lofty appearance to all his movements. And this standard, in his view was the true one for all, while the simplicity and unsuspiciousness of his character. together with the lack of a ready insight into human nature disqualified him to make those allowances which the marked differences between men demand. If to this is added his instinctive contempt for everything mean and vulgar it will not be surprising that his strictures were often sarcastic and severe, and were perhaps the cause of whatever ripples marred the peace of his ministerial career. As a preacher, he was of more than medium ability. The current of his thoughts naturally flowed in speculative channels, and even in conversation he delighted to discuss theories, and trace them to their logical conclusions. Had he bent his mind to purely intellectual exercises, and from early life accustomed himself to penning down his thoughts, he would have made one of the giants of our theological literature. But he was so diffident of his power to write, that he could only be induced to make the most meager preparations for the pulpit, from which alone he generally excluded those speculative processes in which his mind so much delighted. While there his aim seemed to be to reprove sin, correct irregularities, stimulate to Christian faithfulness, and help men to heaven. He was cheerful and pleasant in social intercourse, and in his private friendships, formed attachments that could only be alienated by the clearest acts of perfidy. But once alienated, his aversions were strong and decided, and he lacked all patience with those who had proved themselves unworthy of his confidence.

His religious exercises were often very severe. At times he was inclined to despondency, and the question, Am I to blame? often perplexed him, and he would carry it into his closet with earnest pleadings for light. He would sometimes almost be driven to locate, and abandon his ministry. But the conscious integrity of his motives sustained him, and the answers of God to his soul would send him on his way rejoicing. He could do anything for the good of the cause of God, but neither men nor devils could drive him from what he saw to be his duty. He did not allow enough for the possibilities of mistake, yet it was impossible not to honor his unflinching devotion to his belief. His communion with God was so clear, that more than ordinary religious enjoyments sometimes fell to his lot, and those who knew him best, knew best both his moral worth and the power of his religion, and had the fullest confidence in the motives which actuated his life.

REV. THOMAS M'CARROLL.

THOMAS M'CARROLL was born of Scotch parentage, August 12th, 1800, near West Chester, Chester Co., Pa.

The only son in a family of nine children, his parents aged and infirm, and mainly dependent upon his care and exertions for their comfort, he was early in life obliged to assume responsibilities requiring much self-reliance, as well as self-denial. To this exigency much, doubtless, was due toward developing that thoughtfulness and gravity which pertained to his manners, and which, in his maturer years, rendered him a wise counselor and prudent minister of Christ. It was during these years of labor and anxiety he laid the foundation of his education. Business hours being over, he would turn his attention to his studies, prolonging them far into the night, with but little assistance from friend or teacher. His thirst for learning was always a controlling passion of his life. No difficulties were so great as to discourage him; no disheartening circumstances repressed his ardor in the pursuit of knowledge. In his determination to acquire a critical acquaintance with the best authors of his own language, he very early in life learned to deny himself of many comforts, in order to purchase such books as were not obtainable from friends or acquaintances.

When about sixteen years of age, he was thrown into the society of men of skeptical principles, and through their influence and the perusal of infidel works, imbibed some of their pernicious opinions. The bright example and pious teachings of Christian parents, however, exerted a moral power too strong to enable him to accept without grave doubts, their fallacious arguments. Still, the influence of his infidel associates, and the specious arguments against the truths of revealed religion thus presented to his mind, yet susceptible to new and peculiar views.

produced, to a considerable extent, their legitimate fruit. In after years he trembled, when reviewing the dangerous ground upon which he had well nigh been ruined. Referring to this period of his life, he would say, "There was a something in my father's life speaking so strongly in favor of the truths of Christianity, that I could not rest entirely satisfied with my opposing views."

In the year 1819, while in this state of mind, he with several of his young companions, concluded to attend a Methodist meeting, at the Washington school-house, Chester Circuit, at which Rev. Mr. Price, M. D., was expected to preach. They had arranged, in a spirit of mischief, to disturb, and if possible, to break up the meeting. Accordingly, it was planned that young M'Carroll should stand directly in front of the preacher, and without removing his hat, stare him in the face, until some confusion should thereby occur in the congregation, when the rest of the party were to rush forward, seize the preacher, and carry him out of the house. On the night of the meeting a deep snow had fallen, which prevented the attendance of Dr. Price, and the services were conducted by Rev. Alban Hooke.

The young men were present, and still fully determined to carry their anticipated sport into execution, and the subject of this memoir stationed himself immediately in front of the preacher's stand.

Rising to preach, Mr. Hooke announced his text, "Thou fool, this night thy soul shall be required of thee." With the power and unction of Divine truth the preacher portrayed the perilous condition of the sinner; the awful character of the "fool, who saith in his heart there is no God," and his fearful end. Soon, a strange feeling came over the thoughtless boy's heart. His hat was seen hanging by his side. The solemn truths as they fell from the lips of the man of God roused him to a sense of his lost condition as one awakened from a sleep, and he began to feel that God was dealing with him as a child of wrath. His emotion was not easily controlled. With bowed head and alarm rising in his soul, he felt as never before that he was a sinner in the sight of God, exposed to danger and eternal death. The sermon ended, and without waiting for his companions, he hastened home, fell upon his knees in prayer for mercy and forgiveness. For some months he continued in great distress of mind. Certain Calvinistic views with reference to election troubled him, and for a long while he was unable to resist the impression that he was not included in the covenant of grace. Earnestly he struggled for deliverance, and nights were passed in prayer, but still he could obtain no sense of pardoned sin. The heavens seemed as brass, and he felt as if God had left him. He now gave way to discouragement, and for a time discontinued his efforts to seek the Lord. He went one Sabbath to an acquaintance, and told him the state of his mind. "Well," said his friend, "Brother Hooke will preach to-day at Washington school-house, let us go and hear him." "No," he replied, "I feel that I am not of the chosen ones. I believe, now, the doctrine of Calvin is true, that God saves his own elect, and the rest must be lost," and quoted these words, "Many are called but few chosen." After much entreaty he consented to attend the meeting.

To his astonishment, Brother Hooke who had been greatly troubled about a text and subject for the occasion, selected the words quoted by him that morning, in support of the doctrine of a limited atonement: "Many are called, but few chosen."

In its discussion, the preacher was led to make frequent use of the fifth chapter of Romans, and dwelt particularly upon the nineteenth verse, viz., "For as by one man's disobedience many were made sinners, so by the obedience of one shall many be made righteous."

Light and hope broke in upon his mind, and he at once resumed his efforts to obtain religion.

Shortly after, he attended a camp-meeting near Chester, Delaware Co., Pa., and there, amid the out-pouring of the Spirit of God, after wrestling like Jacob of old, through the darkness of the night, the day dawned, the shadows fled: by faith he was enabled to see Him who was pierced, and with tears of joy coursing down his face exclaimed,

"I know thee, Saviour, who thou art,
Jesus, the feeble sinner's friend;
Nor wilt thou with the night depart,
But stay and love me to the end."

His conversion was clear, and the work of grace abiding, as his after life gave evidence. It was said by one of his quaker neighbors, "That he could perceive a change in young M'Carroll as far as he could see him."

Two weeks after his conversion, in 1819, he was received into the church, by Rev. Alban Hooke. The love he entertained for Brother Hooke, his spiritual father, cannot be expressed, and after forty years of life's toils and experiences, his heart beat as warmly at the mention of his name as when in youth they rejoiced together in the service of their Lord.

Soon after his connection with the Church he was placed in charge of a class at Laurel Church, which stood near the Western branch of the Brandywine river. In 1823 the Rev. Thomas Miller gave him license to exhort. In 1825 he was united in marriage to Miss Mary Ann Bruce of Guthrieville, Pa., a lady, whose piety and pleasing manners, associated with more than ordinary strength of mind, not only rendered his domestic life one of peculiar happiness, but conduced greatly to his usefulness as a minister. At the Quarterly Conference of 1825 he received license to preach, the saintly Joseph Lybrand being in the chair, and the Rev. Henry Boehm, now of the Newark Conference, preacher in charge of Chester Circuit. At the Quarterly Conference held in the spring of 1829 he was recommended to the Philadelphia Conference, and by that body received into the traveling connection, from which time he continued to labor as an effective itinerant preacher, uninterruptedly, for thirty-one years.

The following are the charges occupied by him during this period:—

Stroudsburg Circuit, one year; Chester Circuit, one year; Port Deposit, Md., two years; St. George's, Philadelphia, two years. The New Jersey Conference being formed in the spring of 1837, he was then transferred, and labored successively at Commerce street, Bridgeton, Franklin street, Newark, South Street, Salem, Pemberton, Morristown, Franklin street, Newark, again, and Elizabeth, in each of which appointments he continued two years. His next charge was Plainfield; from thence, at the end of one year, he was removed to fill the office of Presiding Elder on the Newark District. After four years he was transferred to the Paterson District, and there continued until April, 1860, when he received his appointment to East Newark, where, almost literally, "he ceased to work and live." Besides these positions of honor and trust, he was elected a delegate to the General Conference in the spring of 1852, and performed his duties faithfully as a member of that body. Brother M'Carroll was a diligent student, and this remark applies to the later as well as the earlier years of his ministry. He thus became thoroughly versed in the theology of our Church, and acquired a very considerable knowledge of the languages in which the Holy Scriptures were originally written. To the close of life it afforded him the highest pleasure to read and study the word of God in these languages. He was an excellent preacher. But this statement can be appreciated fully only by those who sat statedly under his ministry. His diffidence almost always prevented the full exhibition of his pulpit power on special occasions; but in the stated ministrations of the pastorate he not unfrequently proved himself to be "an eloquent man and mighty in the Scriptures." He possessed a nature of great kindness. In fact, he was sometimes gentle and forbearing to a fault. He loved his brethren of the ministry as he loved no other class of men on earth, and to all of them, old and young, he was uniformly kind. This sanctified and sanctifying element of his character, wherever he went, was as precious "ointment poured forth."

His devotion to the Church of his choice was intense. From his admission as a probationer to the last hours of his life, his prayers were offered in her behalf, his labors and sacrifices were for her prosperity and welfare. As an instance of his conscientious sense of duty in this respect, it may be stated that when preparing for the ministry, in the early period of his life, urgent and repeated offers of a free collegiate education were extended him by a sister denomination upon the condition of his uniting with them in Church fellowship. His love for learning, and the knowledge that such an opportunity for acquiring a systematic mental training would probably never again occur, rendered his rejection of this proffered kindness a sacrifice of no little importance.

Few preachers ever experienced deeper anxiety for the welfare of the Church in all her relations. He was a man of great sensitiveness, and this led him to feel acutely whatever in the discharge of his ministerial duty was necessarily afflictive. As Presiding Elder, he was greatly distressed when he knew a brother was grieved with his appointment, or felt that his claims had failed to receive the attention they deserved. With men of sterner mould, much that was a source of deep anxiety and mental solicitude to him, would have been regarded as matters comparatively trivial and productive of no disquietude.

In the performance of his regular pastoral labors he was influenced by a solemn conviction of duty and accountability to God. Whether in his ministerial efforts in the pulpit, or when pointing the penitent "to the Lamb that was slain," or whether encouraging the faltering or chiding the erring, he never forgot the serious responsibilities of his position as a minister of the word.

An instance of his moral heroism is related in reference to this feature of his character that may appropriately be mentioned.

While pastor of a church in one of the large towns in New Jersey much alarm was created in the minds of the people by the prevalence of the small-pox, which began to assume the character of an epidemic. One night a messenger called at his house, informing him that a poor woman in the neighborhood was dying with the fatal disease, and was earnestly desirous to see a minister. She had neglected the interests of her soul, and now on the threshold of eternity was unprepared to meet her Maker. The messenger observed, that he had called upon two or three other clergymen, but they could not feel, under the circumstances, that duty required them to go.

After a moment's reflection, he replied, "I will go," and at once started on his errand of mercy. Two hours he remained by the bedside of the dying woman, telling her of Jesus who suffered and died for the world's guilt.

When remonstrated with by his family, who were exceedingly fearful of the consequences, he exclaimed, "I felt it my duty; had I shrunk from it I fear I could not die calmly; let us trust in God."

During the first years of his itinerancy his style of preaching was florid, but in after life he possessed those more sterling qualifications which gave him a high position in the ministry of his Church. In the regular labors of the pulpit he was always clear, forcible, and interesting, bringing to his subject the products of a mind well stored with biblical knowledge, acquired by constant study of the Scriptures in their original languages. Wherever in the providence of God he was called to labor he was successful in winning souls to Christ, and in building up the believer in the truths of the gospel. In very many instances his Master owned and blessed his efforts to a remarkable degree. Many who are at the present day in the ministry of the Methodist Episcopal Church—noble servants in the cause of the Redeemer—were brought into the fold through his instrumentality.

The last sermon he ever preached was from the text, "In the last day, that great day of the feast, Jesus stood and cried, saying, If any man thirst, let him come unto me and drink." It was more than usually impressive, and will long be remembered by those who were privileged to hear it.

A natural diffidence often prevented the display of his gifts as an extemporaneous speaker. Seldom could he overcome this constitutional peculiarity so far as to enable him to manifest his full powers with perfect freedom.

There were times, however, when his feelings more than usually controlled by the interest or importance of the occasion, or when discussing a subject in which the powers of his mind were fully engrossed, he would rise superior to every influence, and exhibit a latent power of eloquence which, if more frequently exercised, would have placed him in the first rank of platform speakers.

In his intercourse with the world he was always the courteous Christian gentleman. Possessing the gentleness of a woman, with the dignity inseparably connected with the character of a Christian minister, he gained the respect and confidence of all with whom he associated. The only brother of eight sisters, brought up to manhood subject to the kind and softening impressions of woman's influence, it is not strange that his whole life and character were to an unusual degree moulded in conformity with his earliest associations.

As husband and father he was an example of what the sanctifying influences of grace operating upon a nature abounding in kindness can effect. He was the idol of his children, and though governing by affection, he did not the less succeed in securing their obedience to his will. Living, he exemplified to them the doctrines he had preached so many years: dying, he gave them a glorious evidence of his title to a home in heaven.

The disease of which Brother M'Carroll died—congestion of the lungs—attacked him suddenly and with great violence. But he suffered patiently, and even joyfully. On the Sabbath of his illness he said to one of the lay brethren whom he had long known, "I want you to say to my ministerial brethren and the church, that I die in the faith of the atonement, and in full belief of the doctrines of the M. E. Church as taught by Wesley, and which I have tried to preach, for over thirty years." Soon after, calling his youngest son to him, he said, "Be a good boy, and take the counsel of your mother and Christian friends, and the Lord will take care of you. It is a great mercy to me that the Lord has called you into the kingdom of his grace before I die." Then addressing his only daughter, he said, "I have consecrated you to the Lord from your childhood." She said, "I cannot give you up;" when he replied, "Religion requires it." The next day it was said to him, "You are very sick, but I trust you feel all is well." He replied, "I feel that all will be well. Many years ago God awakened me, and when I sought him by faith in Christ Jesus, he forgave me all my sins, removed my guilt, received me into his gracious favor, and gave me his Divine and Holy Spirit to witness my adoption into his family. And I am fully assured that the blood of Jesus is able to cleanse from all the remains of sin. For several years I have been seeking this great blessing, at times with a good degree of success." On Tuesday afternoon he said, "I am not ashamed nor afraid to trust in Jesus. I have said this for many years, and I say it still."

The same day, he inquired of his physician whether he thought there was any probability of his recovery. The doctor replied, "Mr. M'Carroll, you have in the discharge of your duty, always been frank with me, and I feel I should now be equally so, with you; there is no hope." "Well," responded the dying man, "I am entirely resigned to the will of God." As night drew near—the last he spent on earth—he remarked, "If it is God's will that I should die, I would rather die to-night;" and then added, "For a number of years I have not had the slightest doubt as to the firmness of the foundation, on which I stand. My faith has long been settled, confirmed, and fixed." A short time after one of the preachers present quoted the passage: "And they shall come from the east and from the west," etc. After a pause he said, "I am fully persuaded that Christianity in its essential principles is able to take the soul to heaven."

A few hours before he breathed his last, his son stood by his bedside weeping. Seeing his distress, the father said, "Don't weep, Thomas, it is all right, all right, I shall soon be with the Saviour, don't forget me, but try to meet me in heaven."

To his wife he said, "Don't weep, Mary, it won't be long before we shall meet again."

Bidding farewell to all his children, he said, "Be good, be kind to your mother, I shall always be near you."

These and kindred expressions, many of them noted as they dropped from his lips, evinced the power of grace to sustain him in his sickness and death even more abundantly than it had done during his long and varied life. His faith, always steady, became bold and heroic in the final conflict. Thus lived and thus died on the 9th of May, 1860, in the sixtieth year of his age, a great and good man in our spiritual Israel, leaving to his wife, to his children, and to the church the rich legacy of a holy example, a useful life, and a victorious death.

REV. THOMAS W. PEARSON.*

THOMAS W. PEARSON, was born in Hull, England, Dec. 8th, 1804. He came to this country when eleven years of age, but at what precise period he gave his heart to God, his family or the church have no means of knowing.

He was licensed as an exhorter at seventeen, and traveled under the Presiding Elder in the Baltimore Conference. In the secession of 1825, when Francis Waters and others left the M. E. Church, Brother Pearson was among the number.

He occupied a prominent position in the Methodist Protestant Conference, for several years, and was once its President. He was stationed successively in some of their most prominent appointments, among which were Philadelphia, Newark, New York, and Albany. From this last charge he rejoined the M. E. Church, was admitted into the Troy Conference, and received successively, the following appointments; Gloversville, two years; Esperance and Fonda, each one year; Burlington, Vt., Middlebury, Vt., North Adams, Mass., and West Troy, each two years; and Castleton, Vt., one year.

While at Castleton, his youngest son sickened, and his physician prescribing sea air and bathing, Brother Pearson was transferred to the New Jersey Conference, and stationed at Asbury, Staten Island. Here his son died and was buried. With him lies also the Rev. T. B. Pearson, the eldest son, and now likewise the father. It is a retired and charming spot, and side by side they shall sleep sweetly until the morning of the resurrection. His appointments in the New Jersey and Newark Conferences were, Asbury and Trinity, Staten Island, each two years; Asbury again, two years, and New Providence, which was his last.

* Originally published in the Newark Conference Minutes.

Brother Pearson was a good scholar, a clear thinker, an excellent pastor, a superior preacher, a firm friend, a devoted father, and loving husband.

At his first appointment, Gloversville, Troy Conference, he enjoyed a most gracious outpouring of the Spirit. Hundreds were converted, and among the rest, Rev. George W. Carpenter, for some years a prominent minister in the Providenee Conference.

Rev. Stephen H. Parks, of the Troy Conference, was also converted under his ministry.

When appointed to the Fonda Mission, he found but one member of the church, and that one a female. He left the mission at the end of one year, with one hundred members. At North Adams, three hundred were converted during his two years' stay among them.

The Christian experience of Brother Pearson was singularly uniform. He was constitutionally inclined to look on the dark side of things. The clouds, however, were never so dark, but they contained the silver lining which Christ's presence reflected; and however fatigued or way-worn, however distracted with care and anxiety, when Christ's name was mentioned, or his worship approached, it was always with a reverential delight. He entered upon the duties of his last charge with unusual interest and efficiency. Indeed all his exercises at New Providence were attended with a peculiar unction, and seemed like the works of one rapidly ripening for the skies.

Among the last texts from which he preached, was, "Blessed are they that do his commandments, that they may have right to the tree of life, and may enter in through the gates, into the city." Rev. xxii. 14. Especially did he dwell upon the city of God, the abiding place of them that do his commandments, with peculiar unction and fervor, until the people wept and praised God with joyful hearts.

He had always desired, if it might please the Master, that he might cease at once to work and live. And this desire was fully gratified. The Sabbath but one previous to his death he preached three times. The next Tuesday he was confined to his bed. On the following Monday, his physician had just expressed hopes of his recovery, but he said, "No, I shall not recover;" then turning suddenly to his wife, who stood at his bed-side, he grasped her hand, exclaiming, "It is all over, my dear;" and thus, on the 28th of May, 1860, expired this holy man of God.

He died as he lived, at his post. And if to toil well is to rest well, he rests well from his labors, and his works do follow him. His wife and daughter remain to the care of the church he served so well.

The funeral services were held at the church on the following Wednesday, attended by a crowded assembly of weeping friends, with a number of the members of the Conference to which he belonged. On Thursday the remains were taken to Staten Island, where another weeping assembly awaited the sad rites of burial.

"Thus star by star declines,
Till all are passed away,
As morning high and higher shines,
To pure, and perfect day;
Nor sink those stars in empty night,
They hide themselves in heaven's own light."

REV. DAYTON F. REED

"I saw this man, armed simply with God's word,
Enter the souls of many fellow-men,
And pierce them sharply as a two-edged sword,
While conscience echoed back his words again;
Till, even as showers of fertilizing rain
Sink through the bosom of the valley clod,
So their hearts opened to the wholesome pain,
And hundreds knelt upon the flowery sod,
One good man's earnest prayer, the link 'twixt them and God."

THE annals of Methodism contain few worthier names than Dayton F. Reed. He was born in the town of Simsbury, Connecticut, on the 16th day of March, 1817.

When about four years of age, his parents removed to Herrick, Bradford County, Pa., where he remained until twelve years old, after which he lived in Brooklyn, N. Y., until the year 1837.

He then returned to Pennsylvania, and on the evening of his twentieth birth-day, attended a prayer-meeting under the care of Brother E. Owen, now a member of the Wyoming Conference. Young Reed went to the meeting wild and thoughtless, and, as he afterwards confessed, for amusement alone. But while listening to the exhortation, he was so powerfully awakened, that at its close he arose, confessed his need of Christ, and. with characteristic frankness, said. "Pray for me, but do not be too sanguine in your hopes, for I may never be converted. I am very proud, and apt to think I know more than others. I came here with such feelings, and I feel pride in my heart while I am speaking. Pray for me, and I will try to pray for myself." After seeking Christ for many days, and being brought to the borders of despair, his soul obtained deliverance.

He straightway commenced laboring with zeal and earnestness for the salvation of others. He felt he had a work to do, and engaged in it as one who had no time to lose. This work henceforth became the chief business, the all-absorbing passion of his life. In school-houses, in barns, in workshops, by the wayside, and at the corners of the streets, in any place where sinners could be found, the voice of the young disciple was heard calling them to repentance. After laboring thus for a while, he received license to exhort, and shortly after, in April, 1839, was licensed to preach.

Having now the sanction of the Church, he went forth with an intenser zeal, upon wings almost like the wind, in his high and holy work. A few weeks after receiving his authority to preach, we find him out in the State of New York, laboring like one who felt that an immortal soul was of more value than ten thousand worlds.

The following life-like and touching sketch of his manner, and the power which he exercised in such a remarkable degree, when only twenty-two years of age, and but two months in the ministry, is from the eloquent pen of the Rev. Joseph Cross, of Tennessee.

"In 1839 I was stationed in Ithaca, N. Y. One Wednesday morning in June, a young man in coarse shoes, threadbare coat, and superannuated straw hat, called at my study, and said: 'My name is Dayton F. Reed; I am a local preacher; here is my license; will you let me preach to-night?' His very youthful appearance, together with the abruptness of the introduction, made me hesitate. Desiring him to be seated, I questioned him as to his whence, his whither, and his wherefore. The child-like simplicity of his conversation, and the great humility of his spirit, soon won my heart: and if he had asked me for my eyes, I could scarcely have denied him. But how to publish an appointment, how to get the congregation—that was the question. 'Leave that to me,' said he; 'I'll certainly have the church full if you'll allow me to take my own course; don't be displeased if it's a little uncommon.' 'Very well,' said I. And away he sprang as if impressed with the conviction that his Master's business required haste. Half an hour elapsed, when the sound of a horn drew me to the window. There, to my great mortification, was my new acquaintance on horse-back, riding slowly along the crowded street, alternately blowing a tin trumpet, and pausing to harangue the wondering multitude. Arriving at the corner, he delivered an exhortation of about ten minutes, which he finished with the announcement that he would preach at seven o'clock in the Methodist Church; then galloped to another street, where he repeated the performance; and so went throughout the town, tooting, exhorting, and publishing his appointment for the evening.

"Dinner over, he spent about half an hour upon his knees in my study, and then went again into the street. Walking out soon after, I found him upon a box at the corner preaching to about two hundred people. The discourse abounded with brilliant wit, pungent satire, quaint remarks, beautiful sentences, and pathetic appeals. It was over in less than twenty minutes. Then he exhibited his old saddle to his hearers, and told them he wanted to buy a new one; it would cost ten dollars, three of which he had in his pocket. 'Take your hat and go round,' cried a voice in the crowd. He picked up his straw roof, upon the torn rim of which he had been standing to keep it from being blown away by the wind, and passed to and fro among the people. 'Now throw in, boys,' cried one. 'Yes, throw in, all of you,' shouted another, 'and buy the man a saddle; you don't hear such preaching as that three Sundays in a year.' Very freely went the change into the old straw hat. Not half had contributed, when the preacher, shaking it up, perceived that he had more than seven dollars, and returned to his box, refusing to take another cent, though several urged him. He knelt down, offered a short but fervent prayer, repeated his appointment for the evening, and rode rapidly away. In a few minutes he was preaching to another company in another part of the town. And so he went on till sunset, delivering not less than seven or eight short discourses during the afternoon; and true, indeed it was, that the people did 'not hear such preaching as that three Sundays in a year.'

"Seven o'clock came, and the church was thronged, and many failed to effect an entrance. All classes were there, young and old, rich and poor, flaunting belles and rustic laborers. My young friend knelt full fifteen minutes in silent prayer, during which his soul seemed to be in an agony. He arose and read his hymn in a tone of unaffected modesty, and with such a tremor in his boyish voice, that I could not help feeling a deep concern for his success. The singing over, he knelt, buried his face in his hands upon the pulpit cushion, and almost sobbed out one of the most touching prayers I had ever heard. He began by asking for Divine aid to preach to "such a crowd of gay and fashionable people." He was like a timid child, earnestly imploring his father to stand by him in an hour of danger. Before he finished, I believe he had the sympathy of every heart in the audience, and many were dissolved in tears. He announced his text: 'It is appointed unto men once to die, but after that the judgment.' Every eye was fixed, and every ear was open. Seldom had they listened to so solemn and earnest a warning. And never, perhaps, save three times in my life, have I witnessed a more profound impression under the preaching of the word.

"The next day he preached ten or twelve short sermons in the streets, and at night again occupied the pulpit. The crowd was greater than before, and the discourse was of a very different character. It was addressed especially to the young, and the manner in which he described the follies of fashionable life, and exposed the common sophistries of sinners, the delusions of the devil, and the perils of procrastination was equally inimitable and irresistible. His rapid sketches of character, and brilliant sallies of wit, mingled with histrionic passages of uncommon power, and occasional touches of the pathetic, made everybody laugh and weep by turns. The morning following he went on his way, I know not whither; but the impression left upon my own mind, and I believe upon all, was, that 'a holy man of God' had been among us.

"In July, 1840, he spent some days with me at Binghampton, and attended our camp-meeting. It was not far from town, and multitudes of young people went out with no other motive than that of hearing him preach. His first sermon was from the text: 'What went ye out into the wilderness to see? a reed shaken by the wind?' Toward the close of the discourse he described the sinner as dying, and 'spinning down into hell;' at the same time leaning over the pulpit, pointing downward with the index finger, with a rapid horizontal revolution of the hand; and so vivid was the picture, that many rose up and bent forward to see the accursed soul, as

'Quick and more quick he spins in giddy gyres'

into the everlasting night! I was forcibly reminded of this in the first sermon I heard from Mr. Spurgeon; when he drew the procrastinator to the verge of life, trembling, and clinging to his failing hopes, cried, 'Hands off!' then pointed after him as he fell!"

Perhaps the annals of the pulpit nowhere present evidence of equal power attained at so early a period of ministerial life. Nor were these successes confined to Ithaca and Binghampton. Immediately on leaving the camp-ground and rural districts, we find him in the great city of New York, where he labored incessantly until December, 1840. It was now about fifteen months since he was first authorized to preach, and yet so simple and artless was his manner, so increasingly quaint and original his style, so convincing and irresistible his appeals, now causing the people to smile at their folly, and then producing overwhelming consternation, as they saw themselves whirled by that folly to the crumbling verge of ruin, that, melted in penitential sorrow, they fled to the cross in teeming multitudes. Hundreds in a single church oftentimes professed conversion chiefly through his instrumentality.

The houses were always crowded when he preached. He would have the people. Bar-rooms, beer saloons, oyster cellars, work-shops, every locality where a sinner could be found, was visited, and after a word or two about their souls, he would inform them who he was, that he was laboring at such a church, and then kindly say to his amazed auditors, "*Come and hear me preach to-night.*"

The whole transaction was so natural to him, so evidently sincere, and withal, so uncommon, that crowds always flocked to hear him, and many,

"Who came to scoff, remained to pray."

His zeal knew no bounds, and his powers of invention, always fruitful, were taxed to the utmost, to bring all within the sound of the gospel. Not satisfied with his personal visits to those found in shops, cellars, taverns and stores, he sometimes placarded himself in large capitals, thus,

PROVIDENCE PERMITTING,
DAYTON F. REED
will preach to-night in the Methodist church.
COME AND HEAR.

Then with this huge card fastened to a staff five or six feet long, swung across his shoulder, he would pass for hours, in meditative mood, up and down the crowded streets of a great town or city, studying the very sermon that would startle and convince the people, who were in this novel way invited to hear him preach. Some thought him crazy, but however strongly this idea impressed them when they saw him in the street with his placard on his shoulder, they changed their minds, when at night they heard from his lips, truths the most solemn that had ever fallen upon their ears, accompanied with an imagination as brilliant as light flashing from polished diamonds, while it soared to the loftiest summits of the mountains of God, and dilated on the bliss of eternal saintship, then, to show the sinner his awful and imminent peril, plunged to the indescribable depths of unending blackness and darkness, where the worm dieth not, and the fire is not quenched.

Sometimes his satire was so keen and pungent, that men would get angry, and under the influence of excitement, make harsh threats of what they would do to the preacher, and vow they would never hear such a man again. But the threats were seldom executed, and when the time arrived, they were generally found in the house of God, listening once more to the man, whom conscience told them, uttered only truth, and whose sincerity and zeal they could not do otherwise than approve.

His labors in Philadelphia were sometimes followed with remarkable results. He was connected with Nazareth church as a Local Preacher, and often occupied the pulpit. There was a protracted meeting in progress. On a certain night the house was crowded in all its parts, and he was to preach. The close of his sermon was overwhelmingly convincing and terrifying, death, judgment, and eternal perdition, with all their awful scenes stood out before the congregation, as visible realities; they almost heard the groans of dying men, and the clang of the judgment trump, while the countless millions of earth stood with breathless silence, waiting to hear their doom; heaven too, with its harps, and palms, and crowns, and thrones, its endless light, and love, and bliss, depended upon the activities of that passing moment.

The scene which followed was indescribable. Men and women shrieked for mercy. All over the house they knelt and wept and prayed, while a hundred and fifty crowded around the altar, where the pleas for pardon, and the songs of the newly saved mingled together, like the sound of many waters. That night will never be forgotten. Many who yielded then will bask in eternal sunlight, while those who resisted such power, run the fearful hazards of endless ruin.

But no one place could keep him long. Like his Divine Lord, he felt called to "*go about doing good.*" He traveled extensively in Pennsylvania, and through his native Connecticut. The interior of the state of New York too, was a frequent field of his labor. We find him at one time at Rochester. As he saw the multitudes passing to and fro in the streets, they presented to his mind, not merely so many persons engaged in the pursuit of business or pleasure, but a vast procession hurrying on to death and judgment. His soul sympathized with them, and he felt he must warn them to flee from the wrath to come.

Mounting a box, or barrel, or any thing that would elevate him a few feet above the pavement, like John the Baptist, he cried aloud to the passing multitudes, "Repent ye, for the kingdom of heaven is at hand." Crowds stopped to listen. The sidewalks were blockaded, and some, seeing the quiet routine of every-day business life disturbed, and unwilling to devote a few moments to the higher interests of the immortal soul, conducted him to the magistrate who committed him to prison.

But even there, his heart still burned with an unextinguishable love, and climbing to the window, preached through grates and iron bars, the unsearchable riches of Christ. The crowd around the prison window was soon greater than it had been while preaching in the streets, and the authorities, finding, that while moved with an unconquerable zeal, he was inoffensive and kind, concluded to release him and let him go.

In all these things his sanity has been sometimes questioned. I shall not attempt to decide the matter, but feel safe in saying, if he was at any time in the least degree insane, it was of such a saintly character that it left the world better for its existence.

After ten years of his life had been spent as an evangelist, years which were abundant in labors, and rich in the ingathered harvest of immortal souls, he was employed in 1849, by Rev. T. Sovereign, Presiding Elder of Newark District, as a supply for Harsimus, in the vicinity of Jersey City. The next year he was received on trial by the New Jersey Conference, and sent to Salem Circuit. His subsequent appointments were, in 1851, Gloucester Circuit; 1852 and 1853, Financial agent of Pennington Seminary; 1854, Stanhope; 1855, Bloomfield; 1856, Ladies' City Mission, Newark; 1857, Stapleton Mission, Staten Island. Here his health failed, and in 1858, he became a supernumerary, remaining in that relation to the close of life. In all these fields he had success in leading souls to Christ, and the church was strengthened through him, and yet it is doubted whether his regular ministry in connexion with the conference, equaled in power, that which he exerted when as an evangelist he went from place to place, stirring the masses by his able arguments and startling appeals. To that work he seemed especially called, and for that work he was especially qualified.

Something has been said of his style of preaching, and yet there has been no special reference to his powers of illustration. In this, he had few equals, perhaps no superiors. He was a word-painter. His audience saw his pictures, not pale, cold, lifeless scenes; but living, moving, breathing—full of intense heat. They were not merely a panorama to admire, they were a power to be felt. Preaching at one time on, "Behold I stand at the door and knock;" and referring to the hostility of the human heart, and its unwillingness to yield to the claims of Jesus, he exclaimed, "See that lordly mansion—how perfect and beautiful its architectural proportions—how attractive its situation;—it is night, and all its rooms are brilliantly illuminated; rich music sounds from every window—a gay company fills its halls and chambers—it is a festive scene and hour. But the owner is without. Approaching, he looks with intense surprise at what is going on. He tries the door, but it is bolted against him. He knocks, but the sound of music and dance drown his efforts. He knocks again,—there is a momentary lull of revelry,—and the sound is heard. Looking from an upper window, they ask, 'Who's there?' 'The lord of the mansion—let me in.' 'Not now,' they exclaim, 'wait till the dance and mirth are over.' Then the music sounds high, and the dance goes on. Again he knocks louder and louder still. Once more they answer from within, 'Wait, not now, after a little while.' The music still sounds out more merrily than ever, and still the knocking continues louder than before, 'Let me in, let me in; the night is dark, and I am weary; haste, oh, let me in to my own house.' But the answer now is fiercer and more stubborn, 'Not now—go away—the house is ours. We will not let you in,' and deadly missiles are hurled upon the exiled owner's head." Then, when every eye was fixed, and every ear was ready for the application, he exclaimed with overwhelming power, "O, sinner, thou art the man. Your heart is barred against the Saviour; you will not let him in." His sermons were set with gems and precious stones, all sparkling with living light.

He was a writer too. In addition to his frequent contributions to the periodical literature of the church, he published a volume on enlarged and systematic beneficence, &c., entitled, "*Duties, Tests, and Comforts.*" Dr. McClintock, who wrote the introduction, says of it, "The book is animated throughout, by a burning love to God and for the souls of men; everywhere it is clear that 'it is the love of Christ that constraineth' the pen of the writer. It is terribly in earnest, and I commend it to the Christian public, as eminently practical and truthful. It cannot fail to do good to all that read it attentively; and there is in it a power of Christian sympathy and earnestness that will *command* the reader, unless his heart is utterly out of harmony with the great laws of God's kingdom."

The following just and eloquent estimate of his character is from the pen of Rev. Charles E. Hill, of the New Jersey Conference:

"In him dwelt no guile. He was one of the most transparently pure souls that ever blessed the world; and he adapted himself to all parties, not by the accommodation of his principles, but by his amiable and loving manners. What he *seemed* to be, he *was*. Among the many that I love, and whose memory I cherish, none have ever entered more thoroughly into my heart's best affections than Dayton F. Reed. All that I could say of him in brief, would be comprehended in the points I shall mention.

"*He was severely plain in appearance and in language.* This peculiarity was not the result of eccentricity, as many supposed. He had to be plain in his habits to *live*. His was a frail and delcate organism, and he knew from experience what was best adapted to sustain it. His preaching was plain, for he preached to win souls to Christ. Yet at times he would so far transcend his ordinary style, both in language and figures, as to startle his hearers.

"*He was free from all worldly ambition and vanity.* It seemed to me, when listening to him, that he *knew* Christ stood beside him, and would demand a strict account for every word he uttered. Hence he reproved sin when some of the most refined of his hearers practiced it,—he inculcated the forgiveness of injuries when they ridiculed the idea,—he taught great moral truths which the world was unwilling to believe. He literally lived without books, (Webster's Dictionary, the Bible, and Baxter's Saint's Rest composed his library) and without instructors; poor, unpopular, persecuted; and continued such to the end. Look at him when we will, he evidences the most consistent humility which no applause could inflate and no reflections dissatisfy. In him no attempt was seen to display his humility. Through all his ministry not a word was said to bring it before us as a mark of his piety. He exposed the faults of his friends; he reproved the malice of his enemies; he spoke under all circumstances as a man of God, and yet he was humble. After preaching he retired to pray, and never remained to listen to his own praise. Nothing in him could be construed into a motive of personal aggrandizement or desire for worldly show.

"*He was unusually endowed with intellectual strength.* They were in error who thought him a fool or a madman. His ministry throughout, was what we might expect from a *great* man, embarked in a great undertaking. Firm without obstinacy, strict without superstition, and cautious without concealment or disguise. His ordinary social conversations and his public ministrations never failed to convey an irresistible impression of the greatness and originality of his intellect. Each word was so full of meaning, and every action so full of example, that even if we could question his *heart*, we are compelled to admit the strength and comprehensiveness of his mind.

"*He was a truly good and benevolent man.* If the warmth and ardor of devotion—if long-continued seasons of prayer—if hourly meditation and reading the Scriptures—if fasting and watching—if charity and kindness, make up the elements of a good man, then surely he was one. I have known him to spend hours upon his knees with the word of God open before him. I have seen him bathed in tears whilst uttering the prayer, 'Make me understand the way of thy precepts: so shall I talk of thy wondrous work.' Frequently at midnight would he arise and pour out his soul to God. He lived, moved, and had his being in the atmosphere of prayer. Like his Master, he 'went about doing good.' In all places, and at all seasons, he sought and found opportunity to proclaim the 'unsearchable riches of Christ Jesus.' He lived only for others. Self did not enter into his calculations or plans. All he received, he gave; and the record of eternity will show that but few more disinterested men ever adorned the ministry or blessed humanity. He was considerate, and never occasioned trouble *in his behalf.*

"As a speaker, he had some faults, but many *excellencies.* Had he devoted himself to the stage or the bar, he would have attracted more than ordinary attention. Such were the number and variety of his qualifications for efficient oratory, that had he indulged his genius in these particulars, the common consent of his hearers would have awarded him no small degree of applause. But chastened and subdued, he wielded his gifts to win men to

Jesus. His manner arrested attention instantly, and almost riveted his hearers to their seats. He delineated every subject upon which he discoursed. He was punctual to his engagements, and faithful *to his promises.*

"*He believed in being led by the Spirit.* This fact will account for the manner and matter of his sermons. I have heard him say after preaching, that God gave him the sermon, and in a few days he would forget all about it."

His last illness was a brief but violent attack of congestion of the brain, which terminated in death on the 9th of October, 1860. Such was the nature of the disease, that he was unable to give any expressions of hope or triumph in his final moments. But, he has left to his family and church a testimony more precious than dying words—the testimony of a *good life.*

I close this account of the eccentric, but devout and excellent Dayton F. Reed, in the language of Rev. Joseph Cross, whose pen furnished the beautiful sketch of his early ministry at Ithaca, in the first part of this paper. He says:

"Twenty years have passed since then. I have wandered far from Ithaca and Auburn. A thousand new scenes and associations have arisen around me. But in the ever-shifting kaleidoscope of life, I have never lost the image of Dayton F. Reed; for, with all his eccentricities, I loved him as a brother, and honored him as a saint. Often, within those years, had I thought of him; and wished to know where he was, if living; or how he died, if dead. But I had never heard of him, nor seen his name in print, till, on opening the METHODIST of November 10th, 1860, my eye fell upon his obituary. How beautiful! What a life, what a character is portrayed in those four brief paragraphs! A hundred pages of panegyric could add nothing to the testimony. Faith, humility, purity of heart, perfect conscientiousness, habitual self-denial, and the most absorbing devotion—what more could any one desire? And my heart tells me it is just. It accords with my recollections of the man. No wonder the lamp of life burned out so soon, for his was truly a seraphic fervor. With all his fidelity of admonition, and occasional severity of rebuke, he was no raven among the birds of paradise, no melancholy croaker over evils which others failed to see. He was as loving as a John, and an angel of God could scarcely be freer from envy. None of his good qualities were more remarkable than his humility. He was never obtrusive and dictatorial; but loved to be subordinate to his brethren; and often, with the sweetest modesty, sought their advice. Such was the Dayton F. Reed of my personal acquaintance, and such seems to have been the Dayton F. Reed of the obituary.

"Farewell, my dear brother! Thou hast entered into rest, and 'thy name is as ointment poured forth.' May the God of the widow and the orphan bless the beloved ones thou hast left behind thee! And may thy poor brother, who rejoices to bear this testimony to thy worth, share something of thy joy 'in the presence of our Lord Jesus Christ at his coming.'"

"O safe in port, where the rough billow breaks not,
Where the wild sea-moan saddens thee no more;
Where the remorseless stroke of tempest shakes not,
When, when shall I too gain that blissful shore?

"O bright, amid the brightness all eternal,
When shall I breathe with thee the purest air?
Air of a land whose clime is ever vernal,
A land without a serpent or a snare."

REV. JOSEPH J. HANLY.

THIS young and excellent minister was a native of Philadelphia, a son of John and Margaret Hanly, the eldest of eight children, and was born May 3d, 1830. His parents are devoted and active members of the M. E. Church, to which his father has long held an official relation. They have observed with tender solicitude, the command, "Bring up your children in the nurture and admonition of the Lord." Providence, also, seems to have thrown a special shield over Joseph's childhood. When scarlet fever, that fatal enemy of children, invaded the family circle, and removed an infant brother, he revived, though for a long time there seemed no hope of his recovery. At another time his mother gave him poison by mistake, and to her consternation, he lay for hours in what seemed a dying state. But God spared her the extreme anguish of being even the unwilling instrument of his death. Then again, when about three years old, he was one day playing at the front door. His guardian angel, probably, made his mother uneasy. Her glances through the window were frequent. Presently he was gone. She hastened out, looked in every direction, and was startled by the thought, *he is stolen.* She cried an alarm, and rushed to the street corner, where she caught a glimpse of what proved to be his scarlet colored dress. She soon overtook a burly negro, apparently a sailor, and snatched from him her precious boy. She was so excited and overjoyed that she failed to have the monster arrested.

His great life work was foreshadowed when he was a mere child. The Sunday-school and other means of grace with which he was early made familiar, so arrested his attention, that he would often collect other small children and hold meetings. To them this was only play, but he was serious, and would sing and pray and preach, with solemn earnestness. His natural disposition was meek and amiable, and his surroundings religious, genial and tender. Both nature and friends did much for him. Nor were these influences lost, for he was remarkably thoughtful, obedient and affectionate.

Being the only living son, and of a studious turn, his father intended to give him a liberal education, and then have him succeed to his own business. For a short time he attended the New London Academy, and then, at the age of fifteen, entered the Pennington Seminary. Notwithstanding his home training, and that he had prayed daily, and thought and felt much on religious subjects. yet he did not enjoy religion. The parting scene, as he left for Pennington, made a deep impression on his mind. And as he now entered distinctly upon his educational career, he felt that new responsibilities were crowding upon him, and yet that earthly props were taken away. Never had he so deeply felt the need of taking hold of the Divine hand as his stay and guide. He earnestly prayed that "The Spirit itself might bear witness with his spirit that he was a child of God." Nearly six months thus passed, and the holiday vacation brought fond home greetings. "A watch-night" was held at Ebenezer Church, and God was in the sanctuary. It was a time of close heart-searching. Many approached the altar, seeking either purity or pardon, and among them, Joseph, for the first time, publicly consecrated himself to the service of God. Thus he closed the old year, and began the new. But the joyful, "Happy new year," found no answering response in his burdened heart. In this state of mind he returned to Pennington. "His agony became intense: he could not study; he could scarcely eat or sleep." This night was long and dreary, but was followed by a bright, beautiful morning. He was converted, Jan. 18, 1846, in the midst of one of the gracious outpourings of the Holy Spirit with which that institution has been favored. At this time the interest was so great that, "For days their regular studies were suspended, and the cry for mercy might have been heard from almost every room." Joseph, having been powerfully blessed, was constrained by the love of Christ, to strive to lead his fellow students to the same Saviour. After the revival subsided, all went prosperously for a season. Then he was severely assaulted by the tempter. His mind became so clouded and confused, that he doubted the truth of religion, and even the existence of God, and was driven to the extreme length of taking steps toward ending his own life. But an unseen hand held him, and after he learned some of the devices of Satan the cloud was removed.

In October, 1846, he was compelled by failing health to leave the Seminary, and also to abandon the cherished purpose of pursuing a college course. When his strength permitted, he entered his father's store, attending chiefly to such calls as gave him out-door exercise. The father's purpose now, was to work the business, at first gradually, and then fully, into the son's hands. But God ordered otherwise. The son's heart was being strangely moved in another direction. He found the store an extremely irksome place, but was deeply interested in his religious duties. He was much grieved with hints that his fellow-clerks thought him indolent, and especially to find that his father was disappointed. He explained by referring to his impressions, but his age and health were pointed to, in order to reconcile him to the store.

Meanwhile he kept quite an extended diary, which fully reveals the tenor of his thoughts and feelings. How devout was his spirit! How closely he searched himself! How carefully his self-denial extended to little things! How earnestly he sought the path of duty! Gladly would we show all this and more in his own words, if space permitted.

In the summer of 1847 he enlisted some young men to aid him in holding meetings in neglected neighborhoods, and anxiously strove to do good in every practicable way. At length he fully felt, "Woe is me if I preach not the gospel!" Yet his father, reluctant to give up his long-cherished hopes, did not seem to sympathize with his views of duty. Nor did the Church at first appear to second the call of God. This gave him great anxiety lest his way should be hedged up, and he became a little impatient at the delay. This seeming discrepancy between the call of God and of the Church is readily explained. His entanglement in business was forestalled by an early divine call, and then the attention of the Church was directed to him as soon as his age and health warranted. And when his father saw that this call was from God, he too acquiesced, and sent him away with his blessing. And now that the son felt that he was loose from the world, and that his way was open, he seemed like an unfettered bird, as free and as buoyant, but he rejoiced with trembling.

He was first employed by Rev. R. W. Petherbridge, Presiding Elder of Trenton District, New Jersey Conference, on Freehold Circuit, as the colleague of Rev. J. S. Beegle. He took an affecting leave of friends, and started for the scene of his labors May 19, 1848, a few days after he had reached eighteen years. His great concern had been to find the path of duty, and to obtain permission to walk in it. Now he saw that he had reached the position of a preacher without having provided anything to preach. But prayer and study helped him out of the dilemma in a way that confirmed him and impressed others that he was truly called of God. This gave hope that his health would yet become firm, while his meek spirit, amiable temper, and trembling timidity, together with ready gifts and burning zeal, gave large promise of usefulness. He was soon endeared to the people, and received everywhere with much favor. A brief extract will give an idea of his labors. "I preached to the people of Squan on Monday night, held prayer-meeting in the Church on Tuesday night, in a private house on Wednesday night. Thursday night I preached at Newman's school-house, and on Friday night at Point Pleasant." This was in midsummer, and in addition to the work of the Sabbath. About twenty were converted in July; and as the evenings lengthened, a campaign of extra meetings was entered upon, which lasted through the winter. Revival succeeded revival till one hundred and twenty-five were added to the Church. At the close of the year he was received on trial in the Conference, and returned to the same field with the same colleague.

In 1850 he traveled Moorestown Circuit, with Rev. E. Page. This was also a year of incessant toil and great success. There were large accessions to the Church at different points. Of Beverly he writes, "We commenced last May or June with a class of about seven, and we now number, under the blessing of

God, about one hundred and sixty. It has been the most powerful work I have witnessed since I have been in the ministry. They have a new church, and at the coming Conference will ask for a stationed preacher."

In 1851 he was admitted to membership in the Conference, ordained a deacon by Bishop Janes, and appointed to Columbus. A few days later he was married to Miss Joanna P. Reynolds, of the vicinity of Tom's River, Ocean Co., N. J., in whom he found an affectionate companion and a good helpmate. Now he had a home, and a strong centralizing attraction; still his ardor in the great work was not thereby lessened. For some months but little visible fruits appeared. He became uneasy, and, indeed, somewhat desponding. On the 2d of November he returned home after preaching twice, and retired to his study in an agony of prayer. He then went to the pulpit, attended by an unusual divine unction. The audience was greatly moved, Christians rejoiced, sinners were awakened, and seekers crowded the altar. A revival was thus begun which prevailed till four appointments were reached and large numbers converted. He returned to this charge the next year, and aided in building a church at Georgetown, where a good revival followed. God gave him much favor with the people and success in his work. But his incessant and wearing toils quite reduced his strength.

In 1853, he was ordained an elder by Bishop Morris, and sent to Tuckerton. With the lighter work and sea bathing of the summer, his health somewhat recruited. But with the return of extra meetings and spreading revivals, he again overtaxed his powers, so that he was forced to a sick-bed about the first of February. In one sense, this was "the beginning of sorrows." He only preached a few times till March 25, 1854, when he delivered a farewell sermon and retired from the field. The thought that his work was done, and the loss of a loved pastor, combined with his emaciated appearance and tender, earnest manner, to render this a deeply affecting occasion.

He repaired to Chestnut Hill, and as soon as able, entered a branch store of his father's. Here he slowly recruited. Then, after much deliberation and consultation, and in order to provide against the contingency of being unable to resume the ministry, he began the study of medicine, August 14, 1855, under Dr.

Keichline. A few months later, he was admitted to the Lectures of the University of Pennsylvania. The next summer he was partially employed as agent of Dickinson College, but spent much time on the sea-shore in quest of health. In August, 1856, he took the place of Rev. J. H. Knowles, whose health had failed, as pastor of Broadway Church, Camden. While here, he continued his studies, and was honorably graduated as an M. D. in the spring of 1858.

His term at Camden was eventful. At the same time that he kept up with his class in college, he attended promptly to his pulpit duties, and gave considerable time to pastoral oversight, and also passed through varying experiences. He had long been exercised on the subject of holiness. It had entered largely into his prayers, private conversations, and public ministrations. Yet his experience had been somewhat fluctuating. Now he took an open, distinct stand. February 10, 1857, he writes:—"This day, I believe, will prove in eternity the best day I have seen. This afternoon I was led to hear Rev. James Caughey preach from, 'Blessed are the pure in heart, for they shall see God;' and upon reading his text, he suddenly and boldly exclaimed, '*And nobody else!*' These words fixed my attention and led me to search my heart. * * * Oh, why have I been hobbling along at such a poor, dying rate, when I might have flown upon wings? Here, Lord, bear witness to my record: henceforth and forever I dedicate all that I have and am, and may be, and give up everything contrary to thy will. I have no other desire but to lay myself, a living sacrifice, upon the altar. O my heavenly Father, be thou my gracious and saving helper." Thus was God leading him under a safe covert from the coming storm, the first blast of which was in domestic affliction. Their precious Katie, not quite three years old, after weeks of painful solicitude, was taken from their fond embrace, on the 4th of April. After this, the summer and autumn passed away without the usual success of his former ministry. Whispers were also circulated, that if part of the time given to his medical studies were spent among the people, things might go better. As these hints reached his ears, they went like daggers to his heart. But as he had tried to consult duty at the outset, and had felt no qualms of conscience thus far, and as these complaints did not reach him till near the close of his course, he did not feel it his duty to halt then. He hoped that God would send them a revival, and thus heal all wounds. Oh, how he agonized with the Lord; and as his extra meetings approached, became so anxious that he could sleep or rest but little. He secured able help, and prosecuted a vigorous campaign for five weeks. Yet but little fruit of all this labor could be seen, while the failure under the circumstances, and the thought that he was blamed for it, almost crushed and overwhelmed him. His soul writhed in the deepest anguish, and vented its bitter cries to the Lord, while he still felt, "Though he slay me, yet will I trust in him."

In 1859, he was stationed in Woodstown, and from the first it seemed like entering a new world, so free were his feelings and so heartily did the people rally around him. Nor was this merely spasmodic, but as time rolled on, and his face grew more pale, and his frame more feeble, and especially as his soul ripened for heaven, the unction on his ministry and the interest of the people in it, steadily increased. Many were converted, and the whole church edified and prospered. Thus matters moved on till June 14, 1859, when he preached from, "He that goeth forth and weepeth, bearing precious seed, shall doubtless come again with rejoicing, bringing his sheaves with him." God touched his lips and filled the house with his glory. The scene was in a high degree affecting and profitable. But his rapt soul led him beyond his bodily strength. He did not preach again till July 3d, nor ever after, except in great feebleness. His situation excited much anxiety. Brother Elias Mattson kindly took him on a health-seeking tour, which, however, availed but little. August 14, he preached from, "My heart and my flesh faileth, but God is the strength of my heart and my portion forever." How appropriate for his last sermon! After this he took but little part in any religious exercises, though he did considerable pastoral visiting. As his nerves became weak, his spirits were often depressed, but Christian conversation seldom failed to revive him. A slight hemorrhage added to the alarming symptoms. Thus the winter passed till the last Sunday in February, when, at the close of the sermon, he entered the church and took an affectionate and deeply affecting leave of the congregation, and the next day repaired to his father's. After this his health fluctuated, and his time was spent among his friends at different points. But in October, he finally returned to his father's at Chestnut Hill.

He never expected to live long, and frequently spoke of dying early. He once said, "When I entered the ministry, its solemn weight seemed to be crushing out my very life: I looked to God in earnest prayer, and asked him to spare my life and give me *ten years* to preach the gospel to poor, perishing sinners;" and he did preach ten years. Death to him did not wear a gloomy aspect. He would talk about dying with great composure, and once said, "A Christian has no death,—only a dying unto sin." When he finally reached home, he said, "Mother, I have come home once more, to remain with you now until I either get better or am taken to my better home." When nearer his end, he was asked if his pain was relieved; he replied, "Not much; but the everlasting arms are underneath me. It is that, oh, yes! it is that which supports me." When asked how he felt, he exclaimed, "I have very little to do with feeling: if I had trusted to that alone, I might have sunk into deep mental depression; for my sufferings have been so great, and my nervous system so shocked, that at times I have had but little feeling. But God has promised that he would never forsake me. I believe him, yes, I do believe him. This is all that I can do." Again he said, "Nature can't stand this much longer," and then prayed, "Good Master, deliver me." He gave his dying blessing to his children; and, after drinking some water, exclaimed, "Oh, that is good, but I will have it from the rock." He was too weak to say much after this, but his whole manner indicated a triumphant frame of mind. Sabbath morning, October 28, 1860, in a quiet, peaceful way, he sweetly resigned his spirit into the hands of Jesus, aged thirty years and nearly five months. His mortal remains were conveyed to Woodstown, and after appropriate services, deposited in front of the church, where his friends have erected a monument to his memory.

A widow and two children survive him. She has also reared to his memory an enduring monument, in the form of an interesting memorial volume, from which the materials for this sketch are derived.

REV. RICHARD W. PETHERBRIDGE.

"He stood the messenger of truth; he stood
The legate of the skies; his theme divine,
His office sacred, his credentials clear.
By him the violated law spoke out
Its thunders; and by him in tones as sweet
As angels use, the gospel whispered peace."

It is a pleasing task to review the lives of virtuous men. Purity has a charm, and holiness commands the esteem not only of human hearts, but all heaven resounds with highest commendations. Even after the earthly career is run, and such persons go down to the tomb, the mind reverts with sacred interest to their loving words of friendship, or, to their still more valuable admonitions, administered with the tenderest concern for our eternal welfare. Heaven designs such men shall never be forgotten. "The righteous shall be in everlasting remembrance."

There are few persons to whom memory recurs with profounder pleasure than Richard Whatcoat Petherbridge. Not that he was perfect; who is? But even his failings had in them so much honesty of purpose and frankness of spirit, that they ceased almost to be failings, and the beholder involuntarily covered them with the mantle of charity.

He was born of devout Methodistic parents, in the city of Philadelphia, on the 6th of October, 1792. Of his childhood and youth we know but little, save that he was early impressed with the importance of a virtuous life. When quite small, his mother said to him, "Richard, you are now young; be careful of your character, for if you receive a stain upon it now, it will remain with you through life." Referring to this advice a short time before his death, he said, "I am now an old man, and, while my life has been subject to the ordinary infirmities incident to humanity, yet by the grace of God I have maintained an unspotted character until now."

His first religious impressions were received under the preaching of Rev. Manly Smallwood, a local minister, whose name was precious to him till the close of life. He became a decided Christian under the labors of that eminent minister of Christ, Rev. Joshua Wells. Soon after his conversion he was convinced that it was his duty to preach the gospel; but the call was resisted, and it was not until he was prostrated by a severe attack of sickness that he consented to yield, and consecrate himself entirely to the service of God.

In the early part of 1815, having consented to have his name brought before the brethren for recommendation to the Annual Conference as a traveling preacher, he attended Quarterly Conference for the first time. It was a great trial to him. He was to be examined on doctrine and discipline, but the Rev. Henry Boehm, who was Presiding Elder, conducted the exercises with so much consideration, that he was almost wholly disarmed of his fears, and as it was a very stormy night in the month of January, he was allowed to retire to a distant part of the church, while they discussed his case. While there, he was busy with his own thoughts, not hearing or caring to hear what was said, until he was startled from his reverie, by some one coming in and saying in a loud voice, "I oppose the sending of that young man on the circuit, it is too soon, he has not had experience enough, I should like to see him, where is he?" He was immediately called up, and stood in the presence of the learned Dr. Sargent. The doctor soon began proposing questions, and the young candidate, who was but twenty-one years of age, trembled like an aspen. "Young man," said the doctor, sternly, "you ought to stay at home at least two years before you go out to preach." Young Petherbridge, whose mind had yielded to convictions of duty with extreme reluctance, had nothing to say, but while afflicted at the doctor's sternness, felt strongly inclined to his view of the subject. Still, as the church had taken the matter in hand, he was disposed to submit to its decision.

After some further discussion, the doctor's objections were

overcome. Petherbridge was recommended, and in the following April was received by the Philadelphia Conference.

His first appointment was to Talbot Circuit, on Chesapeake District, Md., and his first Presiding Elder, who became his life-long friend, the reverend, and now venerable and venerated Henry Boehm, who had so gently passed him through his first examination.

From Talbot Circuit, he was removed in 1816, to New Mills, where he became acquainted with the family of Mr. Budd, which henceforth shared the unmeasured affections of his heart, and into which he subsequently married, three successive times.

In 1817 he was appointed to Asbury Circuit, with Rev. George Banghart, and there was considerable religious interest.

During these years, his own experience was maturing rapidly. Convinced that holiness of heart was a high and glorious privilege, he sought and obtained it. While passing round the circuit with his heart filled with Divine love, he wrote to a dear friend as follows:—

"I adore our gracious God for the riches of his grace bestowed upon you. Improve that grace, and he will give you more abundantly. Your thirst for sanctification is one of the strongest evidences that it is the will of God concerning *you;* for believe it, this is the necessary disposition in order to obtain it, and may I not add, the *only necessary* disposition.

> 'All the fitness he requires,
> Is to feel your need of him.'

"Should the suggestion be made, 'You have not improved the talent given;' I would ask in reply,

> 'Will you tarry till you're better?'

if so,

> 'You will never come at all.'

"'To whom shall we go but unto the Lord, for he has the words of eternal life.' You have been bold enough to ask for this great blessing, continue your importunities; God loves the soul most, that asks the most: put no limits to the riches of his grace, for the Saviour has come that you might have life, and have it more abundantly. Have you been so presumptuous to expect so great a blessing? It was by *such* presumption, that you first obtained *forgiving love*, and by the same presumption you shall obtain that perfect love that casteth out all slavish fear. But does the thought arise, 'let me receive it, and then I will believe it?' Remember, as we received Christ Jesus the Lord, so we must walk in him. We first believed, and then received, now believe, and thou shalt receive,

'All the depth of humble love.'"

Such an experience possessed and urged upon others, gave him great religious strength, and as a result, in all the embarrassments of life, he had a perfect trust in God. On leaving Asbury, he was appointed in 1818, with Rev. Geo. Wooley, to Essex and Staten Island Circuits.

From representations made to him previous to entering upon this charge, he had high anticipations, but these were not realized. Methodists were few, and vital piety was low. He felt sometimes greatly discouraged, but tried to labor on, looking to God for aid.

In 1819, he went to Hamburgh Circuit in the extreme northern part of the state. Here he remained one year, and the next two he was on Gloucester Circuit, the first year with Rev. D. Bartine and the last with Rev. E. Stout. In those days parsonages were few, and the preachers had to get along the best they could.

Brother Petherbridge had married while on Gloucester Circuit, and his family, and the family of Brother Stout resided in one house. These things, while they had some disadvantages, had likewise their compensations; in this case, a friendship was formed between the two ministers residing beneath the same roof, which was as lasting as life. Their wives too, were bound together in love, but this attachment was short, for in a few months death came to the quiet home of the country preachers, and Sister Petherbridge was borne to the silent tomb.

His next appointment, in 1822, was Hamburgh again. He had been absent, but two years, and how it came he returned so soon, we are not informed, but so the minutes state.

He was married this year to Miss Theodosia Budd. They kept house in one room, in Deckertown. He said to his mother-in-law, Perhaps you ask, how we get along without goods? "Our kind friends have furnished us with a few articles, and as necessity is the mother of invention, we are now learning by experience what wise men have said, that the real wants of mortals are but few." He received that year but *forty-two dollars in money*, and yet he says, "We never lived so well. We are more than comfortable, for happiness has its seat in the mind. We are happy in each other and in our God."

In 1823 he and his friend Stout were again together, this year, on Salem Circuit. The following year he was on New Mills Circuit, the home of his wife, with T. Neal for his colleague.

From New Mills he was sent in 1825 to Trenton Circuit with John Walker. The next two years his name stands in connection with Allentown as Supernumerary.

In 1828 he was appointed to the charge of Freehold Circuit, with William Granville.

While engaged on one of these large circuits, there came a terribly stormy day. His appointment was distant some ten or twelve miles. His family endeavored to dissuade him from going, on the ground that no one would be present. But he felt he must be there, if no one else was. He went. On reaching the place of meeting, he found twelve persons awaiting his arrival. He preached, led class, and gave an opportunity to any who wished to unite with the church. Seven of the number joined on probation, among whom was a man and his wife, four of whose sons subsequently became ministers of the Gospel.

Having now labored largely through New Jersey, he was sent in 1829 and 1830, to Kensington station, in Philadelphia.

From that charge he was returned in 1831 and 1832 to Trenton Circuit, the first year effective, and the second as supernumerary.

During these years, he was not only afflicted in his own person, but the hand of God was frequently laid upon him in domestic bereavements. His companions were not long-lived, and his heart was frequently bowed and rent with unutterable sorrow.

In 1833 he was appointed Presiding Elder of the West Jersey District; where he remained until 1837.

His work wholly absorbed his mind. On one occasion, he started from home in such haste that he forgot to change his coat, and preached in his old seedy garment, without noticing his appearance. Not so with his hearers. They took compassion on him, and desired him to call at a tailoring establishment before he left town. He did so. The merchant requested him to look at some pieces of cloth and make his selection. One piece he particularly admired, and said, "That suits my taste, but this," referring to another piece, "would be good enough for me."

He was then requested to stand and be measured. "Oh," he remarked, "that is not worth while, as I am not prepared to get a suit now." "No matter," replied the merchant, "I have orders to get your measure, please satisfy me." Greatly wondering what all this could mean, he finally complied. Shortly after, greatly to his astonishment, he received a whole new suit. It was a great surprise, being the *first*, and as it proved, the last present of the kind he ever received; and this grew out of the fact that he had unintentionally worn his old coat to church. In referring to the matter, afterward, he humorously remarked, he had learned for the first time, how to get a present.

As he passed round his district, his quarterly meetings were seasons of great interest, for his preaching was sound, spiritual and practical, while his prayers had such an unction, that one person remarked, if they could only hear him pray, it was as good as a sermon from almost any other minister.

When the New Jersey Conference was formed in 1837, he was appointed to Trenton District, when he remained four years.

Firmly attached to the church of his choice, he ably vindicated her doctrines and discipline, and was one of the safest leaders in our general and annual conferences.

In the administration of discipline he was mild, but decided, and his conclusions were generally satisfactory to all.

He had now a considerable family claiming his attention, and he said, "My children shall have an education, no matter how hard I have to work. I shall give them that, if I never give them anything else, that can never be taken from them, and will make them independent in any situation."

When the Pennington Seminary opened, he entered his son John as its first boarding student, and he remained the firm friend of the institution through life. While his son was there the father's solicitudes for him were very great, and he wrote to him as follows, "I wish you to write by Mr. Winner, and inform me how you like the place, how you succeed in your studies, and if you are trying to be good. For be assured my dear boy, learning, riches, or anything else, will be of little service unless you are good. But learning and goodness will make you everything your affectionate father desires you to be, a respectable man, and a happy Christian. Do not neglect to read that precious book, the Holy Bible. It will be as a lamp to your feet, and a light to your path through life, and will conduct you to heaven, the home of the good. Neglect not to pray every morning and night in your chamber, that your heavenly Father will keep you from evil. Forget not my advice when with you, to keep out of the company of wicked boys. The wise man says, 'My son, if sinners entice thee, consent thou not.'"

At the close of his term on the district, in 1841, he removed to Pennington as supernumerary, and became steward and financial agent of the Seminary, in which position he remained four years.

He then opened a small store in the town, and did considerable business, but his benevolence was too great to make it very profitable. A poor man came in one day, and bought a pair of shoes. "Please charge them," said the man, and left. A person standing by, said, "Mr. Petherbridge, why did you trust such a man?" "I could not refuse," said Mr. Petherbridge; "did you not see how much he needed them? The Lord will never let *me* want, for helping *him*."

His ideas of fair dealing often made him in the world's view of it, at least, the loser. If he had a horse to sell, he would invariably ask less than he gave, even though it had improved on his hands, because he would argue, "I have had several years' service out of it."

Honest to the last extreme himself, he thought others were

the same, and acted towards them as such. He often loaned money, with a simple promise to pay, many of which loans were never cancelled. After four years' experience of this kind, he closed his store, and resumed his work in the itinerancy.

In 1849, he was appointed to Burlington District, where he remained three years. In 1852, he was stationed at Third St., Camden, and in 1853, returning to Pennington, he took the charge of the River Church in that vicinity, and with that church, ended the years of his active ministry. About this time, his son-in-law, Dr. Cory, in view of his retirement from the regular work of the ministry, dedicated to him the following lines, and their insertion here seems appropriate.

THE MINISTER'S FAREWELL!

"My three-score years and ten,
Are almost numbered now;
The lines of furrowed age are plain
Upon my cheek and brow,
And soon the last adieu
I shall be called to take
The pitcher at the fount of life,
I feel must shortly break.

"These locks as dark as night,
When I was in my prime,
Now fully frosted o'er, bespeak
The lightning march of time.
And like the tender plant
I must submissive bend,
Beneath the ruthless, certain stroke;
Time knows no favorite friend.

"But how can I depart
From earth's endearing scenes?
From the beloved, happy ones,
Saved by my humble means?
From those at home so dear,
That love so well, but then,
There is a pure eternal home
Where we shall meet again?

"I'm ready; long I've fought,
The votaries of sin,
And well I know there's life for me,
At death will life begin.
No name I ask but this,
When friends my tomb-stone scan,
Let them in simple accents read,
'He was a holy man.'"

Pennington now became his settled home, where he was greatly loved and honored by all. Here he lived in the enjoyment of his family and friends.

He was a man of stern appearance. and on that account often misunderstood by those who did not know him; but though these things were so, his heart was full of the holiest and tenderest sympathies, and among his friends he was *intensely loving.* He often said, "My happiest moments are with my family bowed around the altar of prayer;" and his surviving loved ones will never forget those sacred hours and scenes.

He greatly delighted to have his children round him. He frequently said, "As long as I have a roof, my children shall have a home."

His youngest daughter felt it her duty to go South to teach. An older sister went down to the house to bid her good-bye, but found she had left. The almost broken-hearted father met her at the door with open arms, and after giving her the most affectionate embrace, exclaimed, "Oh how glad I am to see one of my children again!" He could say no more, his heart was too full for words, and he wept like a child.

When his eldest daughter died, his grief was so great that he prayed, "O God, spare me from seeing another one of my children die."

He taught his children the great duty of Christian charity. "You must *forgive* and *forget* too," was his constant exhortation. "Many persons," said he, "will do one, but not the other; if you will be Christ's disciples you must do both." He likewise taught them the important principle of trust in God. "Seek ye first the kingdom of God and his righteousness, and all these things shall be added unto you." "Trust in the Lord, and do good, and verily thou shalt be fed," were subjects to which he called their attention with great frequency and earnestness.

He had humbling views of his own efforts, and rarely said much about the success of his ministry. Sitting in the porch one pleasant afternoon in conversation, Dr. Cory said to him, "Father, it must be a pleasing reflection when you think of the good you have done during the many years you have been in the service of the Lord." He responded with a sigh, "I do not know that I have ever done *any* good." Several listeners begged him never to think so again, for he had done them good, and they were sure many would rise up in the last day and call him blessed.

Brother Petherbridge possessed a clear, strong, and comprehensive mind. He took his positions deliberately and carefully, and then was a bold and unflinching advocate for the right. Sometimes in this advocacy he seemed to be stern, almost to anger, and often, aware of the impression his appearance and manner might produce, would stop, and say, "Brethren, I am not angry, I am in earnest."

He took a great deal of interest in questions involving the welfare of the State and country, especially in the TEMPERANCE REFORM, and urged the passage of a law similar to that of Maine with all his energies of voice, vote, and pen. He said, "Such a law would relieve the industrious tax-payer of at least *three-fourths* of all the taxes raised to support paupers, and the prosecution and maintenance of criminals." Not having the statistics of his own State at hand, he refers to those of New York, as follows:—"The Board of Supervisors of Livingston County paid for the support of paupers and the prosecution of criminals in 1852, *eighteen thousand, four hundred and forty-three dollars*, and of this sum, *fourteen thousand and seven dollars* were for cases resulting directly from rum. In Saratoga County there were similar facts. If we were to stop, then, in matters of dollars and cents, who can be so blind as not to see that a law of prohibition would be of incalculable benefit to the community? Let it be remembered, too, that the greater part of legislative acts refer directly or indirectly to monetary interests. Why, then, inflict this enormous imposition upon the public, or why authorize such oppressions?

"Repeal the present license system. Prohibit the sale of liquor as a beverage, and you save in this item of taxation three out of every four dollars thus assessed. Let any legislature impose a tax upon the people of three out of four dollars for any purpose of even doubtful expediency, and the last hope of their return would depart with their footsteps. But let any legislature impose a *direct* tax of this ratio for an object that everybody admits does more harm than good, and if there was no other way of dispensing with their services, the people in the majesty of their strength would do as Oliver Cromwell did to the long parliament, with fixed bayonets show them the way to the outer door. Now, though we may admit the license system is not a direct tax, yet it does as certainly affect the pecuniary interests of the people in this ratio as if it were direct. The expense is incurred as the result of the license system, and the tax must be paid. It is then plain that the legislature can save the people three out of four dollars in this item of taxation alone; and do they do their duty when they neglect to protect the people from such enormous impositions? We hear much of retrenchments, and they are made the hobby of politicians. Here, then, is a matter in public expense that may be retrenched without injury to any one, but of incalculable good to all, and the amount is enormous—one dollar tax instead of four. Three dollars saved out of every four in the items of paupers' and criminals' expense. We repeat, the monetary interests of the community demand prohibition."

So deeply interested in this noble cause, his friends were anxious to secure him a seat in the State legislature, and in order to bring about such a result, placed his name on an independent ticket. The election came, and he was defeated. Returning to his family, he said, "I am not disappointed; they don't want such men as I am in the Legislature."

He was a true patriot. At the Presidential election in 1860 he was not in sympathy with the ascendant party. Pennington, however, was illuminated, and he placed the words, "OUR COUNTRY," in bright lights in his window. Upon being called to an account for it by some of his political friends, he replied, "*For my country I will ever illuminate, no matter what party triumphs; that is always appropriate and right.*"

He was the subject of much personal affliction. A severe neuralgic affection of the head and eyes was not only a frequent, but sometimes for days and weeks a constant source of suffering.

He likewise passed through many and severe domestic bereavements. It was his sad lot to follow four loved companions to the grave, while the last remains a stricken widow, who, with his children, mourn his loss.

Through all these trials he conducted himself with becoming resignation, exclaiming, "The Lord gave, and the Lord hath taken away, blessed be the name of the Lord." In all his sorrows he found comfort in the glorious doctrine of a future sinless and painless life. Heaven loomed up before him, especially towards the close of his pilgrimage, with all its divine realities. About a month before his death, visiting his old friends at Hightstown, he was going from the house of Brother Winner to Brother Morrison's. On the way he had a sudden and severe attack of his old complaint, neuralgia of the heart, and came very near dying on the street. Speaking of it afterwards, he said, "Oh, my daughter, I had no fear, I saw heaven opened; and though I seldom shout, my hands went together, and I felt like crying, Glory. I felt as if I was *almost home*, and I had no desire to stay but for my family's sake."

His sight, from the pain he so constantly suffered in his head and eyes, was rapidly failing, and the prospect of its entire loss sometimes made him sad. Visiting at the house of the writer one day, while sitting at the dinner-table, finding it difficult to discern the objects before him, he said, "I am afraid I have not grace enough to be blind." I said to him, "Father Petherbridge, God may never require you to be blind." "Oh yes," he quickly responded, "I shall be totally blind in less than three months." "Well," I replied, "in less than three months you may be in glory." Immediately his whole countenance became radiant with joy, and his heart seemed greatly relieved with the possibility that it might be so. And so it was.

Fifteen days after this conversation, on the 15th of March,

1861, seemingly as well as he had been for some time, with his wife and a few friends he paid a social visit to the house of his pastor, Rev. A. E. Ballard. This he enjoyed very much, indeed. All the afternoon his countenance was peculiarly serene and heavenly, and his prayer at the close of that Christian interview was so full of tenderness and love, that those who were privileged to be present will never forget it. He prayed for all, but especially for the beloved pastor whose term of service was just expiring—that God would go with him to his new field of labor, and that the blessed Master would control in the choice of his successor; that he, too, might come in the fullness of the blessing of the gospel of Christ.

It was his last prayer, and worthy of being the last. It was now dark, and a friend assisted him in returning to his house, which was just across the way. He sat down, spoke a few words upon some ordinary subject, was seized with neuralgia of the heart, then looking towards his wife, exclaimed, "O my dear, my dear," fell side-ways in his chair, and so, without being blind, and without realizing the agonies of death, which for years he had so much dreaded, gently and peacefully he fell asleep, and awoke in the bright land of glory, where the eyes grow not dim, and sufferings are no more.

"Christ himself the living splendor,
Christ the sunlight mild and tender,
Praises to the Lamb we render,
Heaven, sweet heaven at last."

The day of his burial was stormy, yet there was a large assembly, and the occasion was improved by Rev. Isaac Winner, for many years his co-laborer in the ministry, in a very impressive sermon, from the words of the Apostle Paul, "For we know that if the earthly house of this tabernacle were dissolved, we have a building of God, a house not made with hands, eternal in the heavens."

His remains were then conveyed to the family burial-ground, connected with the M. E. Church, Pemberton, where they now repose, awaiting the resurrection of the just.

REV. MANNING FORCE.

FEW names, during the last half century, have been as familiar in the Methodist families of New Jersey, as that of Manning Force. His ministerial career began and ended in this state, although some portions of it were passed in Philadelphia, Baltimore and the state of Delaware. During all the lengthened period referred to, he went in and out before the "many thousands" of our Israel, as preacher, pastor and Presiding Elder, sustaining an unblemished reputation, "preaching Jesus and the resurrection," and gathering multitudes into the fold of Christ. The life of such a man is an inestimable treasure to the church of God and to humanity. In an obituary notice which appeared in the minutes of the Newark Conference, the writers well say, "A life so eminently given to the church of God, should receive more than a passing notice; it should have a fitting memorial." Such a memorial we would gladly furnish, were it within our power. But the scantiness of the materials which have come to hand, and the brief space allotted in this volume, will forbid more than a notice of the prominent events of his life.

He was of French descent, his grand-parents, on his father's side, having emigrated from France at an early period of our country's history. He was born in the city of New York, in the year 1789, only five years after the adoption of the Constitution of the United States.

His mother was a pious and devoted Christian woman, and endeavored to bring up her children "in the nurture and admonition of the Lord." With her husband and family she attended service in what was called the "Brick Church." Under the training of this Christian mother, and the instructions of the men of God occupying the pulpit of that once honored church, young

Force, doubtless, received those instructions which early ripened into the consecration of all his powers to the service of Christ. His early education was as good as ordinarily obtained in the schools at that period. When about sixteen years of age, anxious to do something for himself, he was at his own request, apprenticed to a Mr. Banks, in the village of Denville, N. J., to learn the hatting business. Only a few months after he had entered upon his new employment, his mind became profoundly impressed with his need of a Saviour. Whether this was through the direct instrumentality of the Methodist ministry, then traveling in that region, or the fruitage of seeds carefully sown in his heart by his mother, is not known. But having, as the result of his impressions, made up his mind to become a Christian, although as yet destitute of the knowledge of sins forgiven, he joined the little band of Methodists in his neighborhood, as one "desirous of fleeing from the wrath to come, and of being saved from his sins." For three long and dreary months he went bowed down under "the spirit of bondage." No ray of light penetrated his dungeon; no voice of mercy spoke peace to his troubled and often anguished heart. At length, however, the time of his deliverance came. His night of sorrow, apparently so long protracted, was to be succeeded by the day-dawn; and that day-dawn by the increasing brightness of "the path of the just."

It was in the house of Benjamin Munn, Parsippany, N. J., at a general society meeting, that the burden rolled from his heart, and Jesus was revealed to him as his personal, precions Saviour. His heart was now all aflame with the love of Christ, and with his tongue he endeavored to express that which can never be expressed, the joy and the peace of the new-born soul. Such, indeed, was his zeal for the glory of God and the salvation of souls, that he attracted the attention of Revs. David Bartine and William McClennahan, who were then traveling on Elizabeth Circuit. They at once urged him to hold religious meetings, for prayer and exhortation, wherever the opportunity might be presented.

To their solicitations, although opposed to his natural diffidence, he yielded, and began a work which was to "make his heart rejoice," and in which he was to spend "the remnant of his days." Although but a youth, yet his tall and commanding appearance, his natural dignity and grace, the mellowness and sweetness of his voice in singing, prayer and exhortation, attracted the people and won many to Christ. He was now urged to accept license to preach, which was given to him at a quarterly meeting held in Turkey, (now New Providence, N. J.) on the 14th of Oct., 1809. This license bears the signature of Joseph Totten, Presiding Elder of the New Jersey District. Soon after this he was pressed to enter the traveling connection. But here a difficulty occurred with his employer. He, Laban-like, seeing the services of the young man were profitable to him, refused to give him up. But, after much persuasion, and by the payment of a sum of money, he released him from the last year of his apprenticeship. That year he devoted to preparing for the work before him, working at his trade to obtain the means to pay his employer, and procure for himself the humble, yet necessary outfit of a Methodist itinerant. When in his twenty-second year, he was received on trial in the Philadelphia Conference, and appointed to Asbury Circuit as the colleague of Rev. David Bartine. His first preaching place on the circuit, was Flanders, where in the house of Judge Monroe, he found an hospitable home whenever he was on that part of the circuit. Here too, he became acquainted with Miss Nancy Monroe, whom he married, on the 24th of Nov., 1814, and with whom, for more than two-score years, he lived in peace and harmony. Mrs. Force still resides in Flanders, cherishing the profoundest affection for the memory of her departed husband, and longing to rejoin him on the glorified shore.

He had now fully entered upon his great lifework. Cut loose from all worldly entanglements he was henceforth to "know nothing among men, but Jesus Christ and him crucified." Inflamed with zeal in his Master's service, he labored by night and by day, in public and in private, to fulfill his mission. Nor were his labors and those of his colleague without success. Many souls were saved, and his convictions of his call to the ministry were confirmed and strengthened by the manifest approval which God gave him. His next circuit was Dover, in the state of Delaware, to which he was appointed with Asa Smith. In 1813 and 1814, we find him on the Philadelphia Circuit, as junior preacher, laboring the first year with those blessed men of God, Robt. R. Roberts, Thomas Boring and John Emory; and the second, with Robt. R. Roberts, John Emory and David Best; two of whom, Robt. R. Roberts and John Emory, subseqently became Bishops of the M. E. Church. In 1815 he was re-appointed to Asbury Circuit, this time as preacher in charge, with William Smith for his colleague. He continued on the Circuit during the year 1816, and had George Banghart, now an honored superannuated member of the Newark Conference as his co-laborer. It was a rare thing to return a young man so soon to a circuit in those days. What were the particular reasons influencing this appointment we know not,

Having traveled extensively over the eastern and northern parts of N. J. at the Conference of 1817 he was appointed to Trenton Circuit with Daniel Moore as the junior preacher. From there, in 1818 and 1819, he was transferred to the Baltimore Conference, and stationed in Baltimore City, with Thomas Burch and John Bear. In 1820 and 1821, he was returned to the Philadelphia Conference, and placed on Bristol Circuit, with Phinehas Price as his colleague. In 1822 he was appointed to Bergen Circuit, with Benj. Collins, a name dear to many of the Methodists of N. J. And now, after he had preached and labored from the Blue Mountains and the Delaware to the Atlantic, after he had traveled through a large part of Delaware and been stationed in the cities of Philadelphia and Baltimore, he was appointed in the spring of 1823 to the East New Jersey District, on which he continued for four years, from 1823 to 1827. In 1824 he was elected for the first time a member of the General Conference, an honor, which was likewise conferred upon him in the years 1828, 1832, 1836, 1840, and 1848. His labors over on the district, he was stationed in the Union church, Philadelphia, in the years 1827 and 1828, with Rev. T. F. Sargeant as junior preacher. In 1829 and 1830, he was appointed to St. George's, having as his colleagues the first year, B. Weed and Anthony Atwood; and the second year Levi Storks and Levi Scott, the last named now one of the bishops of our church. These four years in the city were years of incessant toil, but also years of great peace and prosperity in the church. Many souls were converted to God, and the borders of Zion were greatly enlarged. The years 1831 and 1832 find him on the Philadelphia District.

This district was then divided, and he was brought back to New Jersey amid the scenes and associations of his early ministry. He was appointed to the Asbury District, where he remained from 1833 to 1837. At the close of his labors on the Asbury District, the Philadelphia Conference was divided, and he was then appointed to the Newark District, in the New Jersey Conference, where he labored with great success from 1837 to 1840. Here, in 1838, his health began to give way under the pressure of long-continued labors and exposures in the service of the Church, and he began to think that it would be necessary for him to retire for a season and seek rest. It was under these circumstances that he was led to accept the nomination of the Democratic party for congressman of the district within whose bounds he resided. This called forth the very severe, and, in some instances, bitter animadversions of some of his brethren, both of the ministry and the laity. These things greatly pained his heart. Yet, conscious of the purity of his motives, he made no complaint, he uttered no murmur. He was persuaded that he had acted conscientiously, and was willing to leave the whole matter with God. With such an array of influence, however, as was brought to bear against him, it was but natural that he should have been defeated. And, perhaps, it was well for him and the Church that it was so. Defeated in the election, he went forward quietly and faithfully in the discharge of his duties as Presiding Elder, laboring, as aforetime, for the upbuilding of the Redeemer's kingdom. From the Newark he went to the Paterson District, where he remained from 1841 to 1844. This closed his labors on the districts for several years. In the meantime he traveled Clinton Circuit in 1845–6, was stationed in Morristown 1846–7, on Warren Circuit, 1847–8, Stillwater, 1848–49, and in 1850–1 at Stanhope. And now once more, and for the last time, he is appointed Presiding Elder. This was on the Newtown District, where he remained from 1852 to 1855. But, although verging on towards seventy years, he traveled through the entire district—the hardest within the Conference bounds—

with energy and success. His labors on the district ended, and still unwilling to desist from the active duties of his calling, he was appointed to Cokesbury Circuit. This was his last field of labor. At the Conference of 1857, with many regrets, both in his own heart and among his brethren in the ministry, he took a supernumerary relation, in which he continued until 1861, when he became, by the law of the Church, superannuated.

But while sustaining this relation to the Church, he was unwilling to be idle. He felt great solicitude for the welfare of the Church in Flanders. There he had commenced his itinerant ministry—there he had found the companion of his youth and of his riper years—there his leisure days had been chiefly spent during the periods of his Presiding Eldership, and while traveling those circuits contiguous to it. He saw the society there worshiping in an old, dilapidated building, and desired to see before his departure a new and commodious church. Having pledged himself to the trustees to see the work accomplished, he gave from his own private funds $1000, besides devoting his time for the purpose of collecting funds for the enterprise. The church, a neat and beautiful building, and an ornament to the village, was erected, also a comfortable parsonage—and both were free from debt. This gave him great satisfaction during the short period in which he was permitted to enjoy these fruits of his liberality and toil. And even on his dying-bed he said, "Well, there is a good church and parsonage in Flanders, and, I believe, out of debt; I don't know that there is anything more for me to live for."

Thus he labored on until the summons came to call him to his reward and rest. And what a record do the labors of such a life furnish! Forty-five years of active ministerial and pastoral work, scarcely ever intermitted by sickness, persevered in amid discouragements and difficulties almost innumerable;—and then six years, which, although nominally supernumerary and superannuated, he spent in visiting the scenes of his former labors, and seeking still the advancement of the cause of Christ. Fifty-one years of the seventy-three of his life were thus spent—*a little more than half a century consecrated to Christ.*

A life so devoted, we might justly conclude, would have a fitting and glorious termination. And in this we are not disappointed. Blessed be God! our ministers and people "die well." He was taken ill while absent from home, and with difficulty reached the house of an old and valued friend, John V. Vansyckle, Esq., in Sussex Co., N. J. He had been attacked with a general inflammation of the kidneys and bowels, and, in addition to this, the quinsy—a disease which frequently assailed him—came upon him, which rendered his breathing and articulation very difficult. A few days before his death he was visited by two of the members of the Conference, Brothers Hilliard and Nelson. "His mind was clear, and his soul was full of rapture." He said to them, "Of myself I can say nothing good. I am less than nothing. The atonement of Christ is my trust, and it is all-sufficient." Then, as his emotions became overpowering, he exclaimed, "Oh the goodness of God to me! Praise the Lord! Glory to God! I have had toil and suffering in my ministry, but had I my life to live over again, I should choose to be an humble Methodist minister." To his wife, who had been hastily summoned to his bedside, he said, the day before his death, "Child, pray that my faith and confidence may hold out to the end." Frequently she heard him whispering, "Precious Jesus! Oh the atonement of Christ, my Lord!" With such holy confidence and rapturous joy did this man of God, at the close of his pilgrimage, come to his eternal rest in the heavens. Calmly and peacefully as the child sinks to rest upon his mother's bosom, did he repose upon his Saviour's breast. There were no clouds upon his sky, casting their gloomy shadows over the cold waters of Jordan; for the Sun of Righteousness had chased them all away, and flooded the whole horizon with his heavenly radiance.

Thus lived, and labored, and died the Rev. Manning Force. And now, in attempting a brief resume of his ministry, we would say, *His life exhibits the spirit of deep, untiring devotion to the cause of God.* As we have seen, he consecrated himself to this service in his youth. And, having "put his hand to the plough, he never looked back." When *he* entered the itinerant ministry, it involved no small amount of hardships and privations. But no one ever heard him murmur or complain of sacrifices, scanty fare, meagre support and incessant toil. He loved his work with all its embarrassments and discouragements. His whole time and attention were given to it. And whether he was on the circuit, or station, or district, he was day and night employed for the extension of the Redeemer's kingdom. Perhaps few men have ever mingled more with the people than he. As a pastor, he was remarkably faithful—visiting from house to house—and in a most winning, earnest manner entreating all to come to Christ—comforting the sick, the sorrowful and the dying, and gathering in this way many sheaves for the garner of his Lord. While stationed in the city of Philadelphia, he generally commenced his pastoral work before breakfast, in order that, at an early period in the day, he might see all the sick. And this fidelity to his Master and his cause he exhibited up to his last hours. No better evidence of this could be furnished than is found in a letter addressed to his "beloved wife" only a short time before the close of his effective ministry. This letter bears date of January 18th, 1856, and is written from Port Jervis, in the State of New York. He says: "No worldly emoluments could induce me to be wandering about through rain, and snow, and cold as I do. But, as it is not worldly honor or wealth I am seeking, but the salvation of souls immortal, for whom the adorable Redeemer suffered, and bled, and died, I can do it all cheerfully, without murmur or complaint. If I had not satisfactory evidences that my unworthy labors were made a blessing to the church and the people of the world, I should become disheartened and leave the itinerant field. But while I have the unmistakable evidences that God crowns my efforts with his special blessings, I feel like spending my strength in his holy cause." He was on his last round, on his last district, when he wrote this. He had suffered greatly from cold and exposure in reaching his appointments; "but none of these things moved him." He says: "I suffered more with the cold last week, than I have done since last winter. I had to face the cold up the Delaware River, on the tow-path of the Delaware and Hudson Canal, with the snow knee-deep to my horse, and the road not broken for about forty miles, with the thermometer from twenty to thirty degrees below zero." So intense was the cold, that one man traveling the same route became insensible, and was carried home just alive—losing, however, it is said, his hands and feet. But the "Lord blessed him with good health, and he escaped with only a frosted face." This language and these exposures need no comment. They speak for themselves.

His early ministry was eminently successful, and his entire ministry was a blessing to the church. Thousands of souls from New Jersey, Philadelphia, Baltimore and Delaware will doubtless "rise up in the last day and call him blessed," and acknowledge him as God's instrument in their salvation. As we have seen, for many years he was a Presiding Elder, and it is difficult for one in this position, or in the general superintendency of the church, to trace clearly the results of his labors. There can be no doubt, however, that under his sermons, always preached to crowds at his quarterly meetings, not only was the church greatly edified, but multitudes were saved. He thus sums up the results of his four years on the Newton district:—"The cause of God through the instrumentality of Methodism has been constantly, and in some places, rapidly advancing ever since my return to the district. When I came on the district, it called for seventy-two quarterly meetings in the year; it now calls for 100, and next year it will call for 104, and perhaps 108 or 112. Thus, if I live to finish the Conference year, I shall leave the church in a peaceful and prosperous condition. We have now several glorious revivals in progress, several new churches under contract; and others have been remodelled and handsomely improved. At the same time we have paid off all the old debts on our meeting-houses, besides building and repairing the parsonages."

This is certainly a cheering record for this veteran of the cross. But statistics give only a faint and feeble idea of such a man's labors; and never, until the records of the last day are unrolled, will we *begin* to know them—while eternity only will fully develop them. Brother Force did the Church great service, also, in selecting and calling out young men into the work of the ministry. His long service as Presiding Elder gave him a fine opportunity for doing this, and no man ever better, or perhaps more extensively, improved it.

Like Barnabas, Manning Force was eminently a son of conso-

lation." He was not one of the "legio tonans." He seldom dwelt upon the terrors of the law. But he delighted chiefly to expatiate upon the consolatory truths of the gospel. The great atonement of Christ he often dwelt upon with interest and power. This, in fact, was the anchorage ground of his own hope, and the source to which he pointed many thousands for life and salvation. It may also be said of him as of Barnabas, that "he was a good man; full of the Holy Ghost and of faith; and much people was added unto the Lord." Brother Force also carefully obeyed the apostolic injunction, "Be courteous." He was, indeed, a fine specimen of the Christian gentleman. This gave him great favor in the eyes of the people, and was, doubtless, one of the reasons of his being called upon so frequently, while a pastor in Philadelphia, to perform the marriage ceremony. In his intercourse with his brethren, the law of kindness was ever on his lips. We very much doubt whether any one ever heard him speak evil of his brethren in the ministry or laity. And if the conduct of others was animadverted upon in his presence, he would always have something apologetic or explanatory to say which would serve to shield the absent one, and to rebuke the fault-finder or the slanderer. Hence, while he had some enemies, he had many friends.

He was a man of wisdom and firmness in settling difficulties in the Church.

The following illustration is furnished by Rev. J. P. Dailey: "While he was traveling on Clinton Circuit, a difficulty which had long existed between two of the members, was settled by him as follows:—Each of the parties claimed that a certain amount of money was due him; and neither would be satisfied unless it was paid. He finally obtained their consent to settle the matter in his own way, and their joint promise to consider the difficulty amicably and permanently settled when the claims were met. These points gained, he took the money from his own pocket, and paid to each one what he demanded. This they promptly refused at first. 'They would not take it from Brother Force: they could not think of such a thing.' But seeing his advantage of them, he said, 'Brethren, you have called on me to settle a difficulty which you could not settle yourselves.

You have promised to be at peace when your claims were met. You have agreed that I should settle this matter in my own way,—*this is my way.* You must take the money, the matter is settled on your own conditions.' They took the money, but afterwards called on Brother Force, and made it all right."

He had a deep and blessed experience. While on Dover Circuit he had high spiritual enjoyments. Here, too, he writes, "The Lord sanctified my soul."

He was a "good minister of Jesus Christ," and he has left to his family, to the church, and the world, a bright example of devotion to Christ—of ardent piety—of Christian purity—of unaffected humility—and of "unflinching religious integrity." Then, too, when we think of the multitudes who were strengthened, comforted and encouraged by him—of the multitude saved from their sins through his instrumentality—of the moral and religious influence he exerted in the family, the community and the church—we cannot fail to see the rich inheritance to which we have fallen heir. And who can look upon his peaceful and triumphant death-bed-scene, without being convinced of the reality and glory of the religion of Christ? When we see him, an old man, at the close of a long and weary pilgrimage—dying away from home—with only a few friends hurriedly gathered around his bed-side; and then listen to his exclamations of unshaken trust and confidence in the atonement of Christ, of his assured acceptance with God, and hear his shouts of praise as he plumes his wings for his upward flight—we must say that *Manning Force neither lived nor died in vain.*

"The pains of death are past,
Labor and sorrow cease;
And life's long warfare closed at last,
His soul is found in peace.

"Soldier of Christ! well done!
Praise be thy new employ;
And while eternal ages run,
Rest in thy Saviour's joy."

REV. JOHN L. LENHART.

JOHN L. LENHART was born in Lock Haven, Pennsylvania, October 29, 1805. Of Methodistic parentage, his early days were favored with religious instruction, which, under the blessing of the Holy Spirit, led him to the practice of a life of piety before he had passed the age of childhood. While yet young, he connected himself with the church of his fathers; and, by consistency of life, together with earnest efforts for the good of others, soon attracted the attention of the society. His natural capabilities for usefulness were good; and, at an unusually early age, he was licensed to preach the Gospel. For several years he exercised his gifts in the regions round about his home, increasing steadily in efficiency, and also in the favorable regard of his brethren, until in the spring of 1830, he was recommended to the Philadelphia Annual Conference as a suitable person for the regular work. By this body he was received on trial, and appointed to labor in "Neck Mission," situated in the lower part of the City of Philadelphia. This appointment for so young a man was one of severe trial. He was fresh from the country, where the people were quiet and orderly, and here they were mostly uncultivated and somewhat turbulent. At home, he had been surrounded by loving and devoted Christians, while here the people were generally irreligious and careless. But, the zealous fervency of both his character and labors impressed them favorably; and before he had been long among them, a considerable number of people, who had heretofore cared for none of these things, were found among his congregations as serious and attentive listeners to the word of God. In 1831–2 he traveled Caroline Circuit in Maryland. Here his warm and ardent nature found congenial spirits, and the time passed in this charge, as well as in that of Cambridge, which he traveled for the two succeeding years, were remembered by him as among the pleasantest of his life.

In 1835, he labored, in connection with Rev. J. O. Rogers, on Flemington Circuit, New Jersey, where his labors were eminently successful in strengthening and enlarging the society. In 1836–7, he served the church at Long Branch, where he was perhaps one of the most popular preachers that that time-honored society had ever received from the Conference. In 1838–9 he was stationed at Mount Holly. In this town his pulpit abilities attracted considerable attention from all classes of the population; and here, also, his ministry was successful in its grand object of winning souls. In 1840–1 he preached in Bridgeton, in which important county town he was greatly esteemed. In 1842 he served the society in Camden with no diminution of ministerial prestige or power. In 1843–4 he took charge of Franklin Street Church in the City of Newark. Here he zealously identified himself with all its various departments, and filled up his two years of labor with the most active exertions for its success. Unusual embarrassments arising from the prevalence of Millerism and other causes, sometimes attended the administration of discipline while stationed here, but his fertile invention always succeeded in extricating the church from such embarrassments without serious loss.

During this time a pleasurable circumstance occurred which afforded him more than ordinary gratification, one of a kind not often given to a Methodist itinerant. His father, a talented local preacher, visited and preached for him. His exercises impressed favorably the energetic ladies who had charge of the Home Missionary organization of our church, in that city, and they tendered him an appointment in that work. Their offer was accepted, and, as he was a widower, he established his residence with his son. Father and son lived together in the same house, preached the gospel in the *same* city at the *same* time, in the *same* denomination, and were both esteemed as able workmen in the vineyard of the Lord.

In 1845–6 he was stationed in Cross street, Paterson. In this place his labors were attended with great difficulties. His health under a severe affection of the throat had long been declining, and he was now never without pain. The general *tone* of his system was gradually sinking, and a nervous irritability which it seemed almost impossible to control fastened itself upon him. Words, unintentionally abrupt, would be spoken by him, whose remembrance would occasion him the keenest sorrow, and almost drive him to the determination of abandoning the ministry altogether. After the utterance of such words he would often spend the whole night in sleepless anguish, pacing the floor for all its weary hours, weeping and praying, and allow himself no rest until he had sought the forgiveness of the person to whom they had been spoken.

It soon became evident to him that it would be impossible to sustain longer the position of an *effective* minister, and he submitted to his prospective lot with sorrow and tears. Poverty and sickness stood before him in all their hideousness, and for a time he could not embrace them as welcome ministers of God. The severance of the tie that bound the Conference laborers together was something he could not contemplate except with deepest misery. But at last he accepted these sorrows as part of God's great plan for his salvation, and in humble dependence upon Providence began to make his preparations for retiring from the work, and, as he termed it, "to be laid upon the shelf." God, however, did not intend to try him so far, for just at that time a position was offered him as chaplain in the United States Navy. He accepted it with gratitude, and retained it with honor until the time of his sad but noble death. He was appointed to the *Brandywine*, and immediately commenced the preparations necessary for his absence. His heart, however, still clung to his old work, and he employed the evenings of the intervening time between his appointment and reporting for duty in holding a series of extra meetings in his charge, closing the last hours of itinerant opportunity with energetic itinerant labor. The ship was soon ordered off for a three years' cruise in connection with the Brazilian squadron, and Brother Lenhart bade farewell to his native country and entered upon his untried but promising field of labor with those "who go down unto the sea in ships"—the sailors of our navy. In this position he was far from idle. He had entered it with an earnest desire to benefit the "sons of the ocean," and opportunities to do so were abundant. He possessed in an eminent degree that dignity of manner so highly prized by the officers of our navy, and in consequence they gave him their unqualified support in the performance of his duties, a support which, if withheld, renders a chaplain's labors almost nugatory. Whenever it was possible they attended his preaching on the Sabbath, and thus contributed their influence over the "tars" to his efforts. His familiar and cheerful address made fast friends of the man-of-war men, while his evident interest in both their secular and eternal welfare gave him ready access to their hearts. He sought out those who were religiously inclined, and put them into classes. He established public prayer-meetings, and in every way possible on board a ship, endeavored to interest the men in the subject of religion. He found the greatest opportunities for good, however, in personal conversation. He had been successful in gaining their confidence, and the confidence of a sailor, once gained, is boundless. Often, seated beside them on their watch, he would lead the conversation to eternal things, and amid the solemn silence of the night make impressions upon their minds which, he firmly believed, the Holy Spirit blessed to their spiritual good.

During all this time, the cultivation of his mind was not neglected. His health improved rapidly, and with renewed health came corresponding activity of the mental powers. From the nature of ship duties, a large amount of time could not be occupied with active labor, and a great part of this time he devoted to the reading of solid literature, and writing upon such themes as would best develope the intellectual power. Nor did he neglect his spiritual nature. Much of the time was employed in prayer. He says, "Before I devoted such large measures of time to it upon the boundless ocean, I never knew how much happiness it could be made to give." In a letter to the writer he says, "I am happy to assure you, my dear brother, I have not lost anything, either in religious principle or enjoyment. Indeed, sometimes I am led to think I am making some little advancement in the Divine life, for, Bless the Lord, O my soul! in my little seven by nine room, I have often sweet access to a throne of grace, and am enabled to rejoice in the Lord." He was also a close observer of the manners and customs of the people where the vessel was stationed. At one time he had the oportunity of a presentation to Royalty, which he thus graphically describes: "Having dressed myself in proper uniform, cocked hat and all, I accompanied a number of our officers to the Imperial Palace. According to previous arrangement, we here met Mr. Tod, our minister to this court. In one of its rooms, called the Diplomatic Saloon, we found the foreign ministers, charges de affaires, consul-generals, foreign army and navy officers, with others who had been invited to attend this levee, all awaiting the pleasure of the emperor to receive them. After some little delay, the announcement was made by the chief lord chamberlain that his Imperial Majesty was upon the throne, and ready to receive us. General Giddo, the Buenos Ayres minister, led the way, and Mr. Tod as next oldest followed, and, consequently, we were among the first who were presented. The audience chamber is, perhaps, fifty feet long, and at the extreme end of it stood the throne, upon the upper steps of which the Emperor and Empress stood. On the right of the Emperor stood a body of guards, and on the left of the Empress a long row of *wall flowers* called maids of honor.

"The room was richly furnished with drapery, chandeliers, and lustres, while the whole court was gorgeously decorated with diamonds. Upon entering this chamber I made my first bow to royalty, in the person of Don Pedro II., Emperor of the Brazils. At about midway of the room, I made my second bow. We then approached within ten or fifteen feet of the throne, and waited while General Giddo made a short speech. After this we each in turn approached; first bowing to the Emperor and then to the Empress, which bow they returned. And now came the worst part of the business, which was the 'backing out.' This I assure you was no small matter. But, I got out safely, and upon the whole was pleased with my first visit to royalty."

Writing of the cemetery of Gamboa, he describes it as covered with flowers in mid-winter. This place possessed for him a peculiar interest in being the last earthly resting-place of the deceased wife of the Rev. D. P. Kidder, formerly a missionary at that post, but at that time a member of his own Conference and the accomplished editor of the *Sunday School Advocate.* Many hours, he states, were spent meditating among the tombs, which he hoped were not without profit to him. In the society of Brother Lore, our missionary to that city, he also found great pleasure, and in preaching for him was much blessed. What he saw of the slave-trade in that port seems to have aroused his righteous indignation. He says: "Several slavers have been fitting out here for the coast of Africa, intending to sail under the stars and stripes, and commanded by American captains. Two have been captured recently and sent home; the others are not disposed to venture out at present. Our commodore is determined to put a stop to it so far as American vessels and American captains are concerned. And to it I say *amen* with all my heart. It is a singular fact, that the captains generally engaged in this nefarious business are *down easters*, none farther south than New York. Unless some more active measures are adopted to suppress the trade, I should not wonder if this country becomes a second Hayti, for it really seems to me that there are more blacks than whites here now, thousands of whom remain in the most abject bondage. Surely another *Moses* will be raised up when the cries of the afflicted shall have fully entered into the ears of the Almighty." While absent at sea his regard for his conference-associates did not diminish. "If possible," he writes, "I love them better than before. During the session of the Conference, I assure you that I felt no ordinary degree of solicitude. It was the first Conference from which I had been absent for nineteen consecutive years, and the remembrance of the fact that I no longer had an active connection with a body of men whom I love so dearly, afflicted me sorely. But the recollection of the facts, that my severance from them originated in a desire not to burden them—that in this way I could secure a support for myself and family, while at the same time I continued to labor in the vineyard of the Lord—assisted me to bear up under this, and even to rejoice in the kind providence which had placed me here." After three years of active service at sea, he was relieved and appointed to the receiving ship off Staten Island. For a couple of years he resided in Newark. but afterwards purchased a residence on Staten Island, which he made his home for several years, taking great delight in beautifying and adorning it. Here he would often gather his friends around him; and, in the exercise of a generous hospitality, add largely to the happiness of his life. He was often permitted to visit and preach for his ministerial brethren, in which he received rich spiritual blessings. But there is no *earthly* state without its darkening shadow, and that shadow now began to brood over his otherwise pleasant hours. The health of his wife, whom he loved with a most devoted affection, began to manifest symptoms of decline. All that skill and science could do for her was tried without avail. Day by day he saw her wasting away, and slowly but surely approaching the tomb. He would contemplate her altered appearance with deep sadness, and say: "What are all these blessings of Providence to me while I see my wife dying before my eyes. Yet," he would continue, "I thank my heavenly Father, that for so long a time he spared me so good a wife." His worst anticipations were realized, and although it was a number of years after he took up his residence upon the Island that she left him—she passed away before him to a better land.

After an unusually long period of duty on shore, he was ordered again to sea, and appointed to the United States ship Cumberland. His letters now speak of deeper piety and broader patriotism, and evince the most complete abhorrence of the "Slaveholders' rebellion." They speak also of a willingness to lay down his life sooner than allow their Satanic purposes to be accomplished—a willingness which he soon after illustrated in the gift of that life for his country's defence. In one of these letters written to a friend (Rev. J. M. Tuttle) he says: "It is just as near to my heavenly home from the old Cumberland as from any other place." In another to Rev. J. S. Porter, he says: "I indulge the hope that I may be able to meet you at the Conference. Should I not be permitted to do so, tell the preachers that I love them and love the work. Should I *not* meet them again upon the earth, tell them I *hope* to meet them in the morning. Death to the Christian is a sleep—they that sleep sleep in the night, and the glorious resurrection will bring us together—soul and body—once again."

In another letter he says, "I hope, my dear Brother Tuttle, that I have an interest in your prayers. I wish very much to be a devoted Christian and a useful, happy minister of the Gospel of Christ. Some of our officers are praying men. Would that all of us lived nearer to God and enjoyed more of the divine power of godliness. I spent new year's eve in my little room, reading and praying. The new year found me upon my knees pledging myself to live nearer to God, and to press with greater ardor toward the mark for the prize of my high calling."

The letters also evince a strong interest in the prosperity of the Conference. Of the decease of Rev. Manning Force he writes mournfully and lovingly. Of the success of Brother Kelley on Staten Island, he says: "Who would have thought that Bethel Church would be enlarged and beautified, and that St. Paul's would so soon have a new building. God bless them, and give the church of our choice a wide place. The older I get the more I love her and the more I love to love her." And again: "I am very glad to see from the *Christian Advocate and Journal* that in some places in God's heritage showers of mercy are falling. Would that a glorious revival of religion would break out in all the churches in Newark."

His health had now become much enfeebled, and in view of its condition the naval authorities tendered him the privilege of returning home. Under more favorable circumstances he would gladly have accepted it, but *now* he preferred to share with his comrades the perils of their situation, and see the last of the eventful cruise of the Cumberland. He wrote to his friends in Newark that he felt a presentiment of speedy dissolution if he remained, but that his honor and duty commanded him to stay, and he must obey their voice. The Cumberland, with the other vessels of the United States fleet, was at this time lying in Hampton Roads. The rebel steamer Virginia (formerly the Merrimac) had been encased in iron plating and supplied with a projecting ram which was capable of piercing and sinking any wooden vessel that floated the waters.

For days the United States fleet had been in momentary expectation of her appearance, and the whole country felt a nameless dread of the evil she might inflict. It was under these circumstances that the Christian patriot and minister refused to leave his post of danger, choosing rather to suffer affliction in serving his country and God, than to enjoy the pleasures of home for a season. The government had made every possible effort to finish the "Monitor," the only vessel at all likely to successfully oppose the Virginia, but up to the day on which the monster made its appearance in "Hampton Roads," she had not arrived at her destination. Wooden vessels only, such as the Congress, the Monongahela, and the Cumberland were at the command of the government, and they were almost powerless in such a conflict. The shoaling banks and narrow channel which destroyed all opportunities of successful manœuvering, added to the perilous chances against them. Still, when on that bright morning the Virginia steamed down upon them, the battle was not declined. The fleet rained shot and shell upon her, but they rolled off harmlessly from her invulnerable plating. She steamed on steadily toward the Congress—paused a moment to receive her defiant refusal to surrender, and then plunged the iron prow through her sides, leaving her in a sinking condition. The Monongahela ran aground where the monster could not follow. She then stood for the Cumberland, pausing as before to demand her surrender. The Cumberland replied with a broadside, when the iron ram of the rebel vessel was thrust through her timbers. A few moments more and it crashed through again, and she began rapidly to sink. Still there was no thought of surrender, but she went down beneath the crimsoned waters with her guns firing, her broad pennant flying in the breeze, with the stars and stripes still asserting their supremacy even in the midst of rebel triumph. Such of the crew as were enabled to escape did so in any manner which was most available. Some few in boats, some upon loose planks, but the most by throwing themselves into the sea and swimming amid the shot and shell of the enemy, until they were picked up by the boats or made the shore. A large number, however, went down with the vessel, among whom was the first ministerial martyr of the war, chaplain John L. Lenhart.

According to the statement of Lieut. Morris, when it was announced that the ship was sinking, and the crew were directed to escape in the best manner possible. Brother Lenhart went below to his state-room, probably to secure some papers. It was supposed that there was ample time for this before the vessel would go under. But the orifices made in her side by the ram were very large, and she sank rapidly. The water was already above the level of the state-room floor, and rising fast; and probably her careening as she went down rolled an immense volume of water against the door and prevented its opening. There—prisoned by the waters in his state-room, with the roar of battle still around him, with the groans and cries of wounded and dying men whom he had *not* deserted in their hour of need still sounding in his ears, amid the sound of the guns of the Cumberland hurling their defiance as the vessel gasped in the death-clutches of the sea—there he met his last enemy—alone with *it* and *God!* For a death under *such* circumstances the country inscribes his name upon its monument of *heroes*, and his *God* upon the list of those eminent and martyred saints who shall have part in the first resurrection.

God's honor needed that the Church should not be silent upon the grave questions involved in the slaveholders' rebellion, and also that she should give the lives of her sons in whose blood her record might be written for the reading of after ages. And so she gave her members by thousands, and her ministers by scores, that the name of Jesus might be identified with the cause of her country's morals, and that the world might see that in such a cause they loved not their lives in comparison with their principles; and John L. Lenhart was *honored* of God, in being selected to lead the van of the numerous ministers who have since sealed their devotion with their blood.

Exhibitions of God's presence and power to save in the hour of death are not possible in a case like this, and we must look for our evidences in the record of the life. Peaceful death-beds, surrounded with loving Christians, whose holy sympathies and prayers compose a spiritual atmosphere, afford facilities for such testimonies, but a death like his forbids all revelations. Yet we are not left to conjecture to gather his own estimate of his future condition. His long life of Christian experience, in which there was a constant avowal of fellowship with God,—the letters written just before the battle, in which he expressed a presentiment of approaching death,—are filled with expressions of undoubting confidence in his spiritual prospects, and there can exist no reasonable doubt that the God who was his companion in life was present, cheering and comforting him in his lonely death. The wreck of the old Cumberland still lies off Newport News, with its bow toward the shore, and probably in one of its state-rooms still remains whatever is left of the mortal frame of the brave and noble-minded minister who went down with her, while the spirit which animated that frame is at home in that land where there is neither slave nor war, and where he rests from his labors forever.

The patriotism of Brother Lenhart was absorbing. With him it was a development of religion. He was a Democrat of the old Jeffersonian school; but in the hearty support of his country all political distinctions were ignored. His later letters show this fully. In one of these he says: "Oh, when will this dreadful and unnatural war have an end? May the God of battles—our heavenly Father—speed the time when rebellion shall cease, and our beloved constitution and government be triumphantly maintained; which I doubt not sooner or later will be the case." Again he says: "I believe our government has the right and must eventually triumph, and the Union will be preserved; but it will be at an immense cost of money and sacrifice of life."

He writes thus of the croakers: "How apt people are, when one has done well, to ask, why has he not done better? Our fleet did well, they say, in taking Forts Hatteras and Clark, but they ought to have gone on and taken Beaufort—altogether forgetting that we had no troops to retain it if we *had* taken it."

He was also a prominent member of the Masonic fraternity, and held with credit several of its prominent offices. He was held in high estimation by that body of men both from his ability in their craft, and the high-toned sense of honor and generosity by which he squared his life.

His domestic attachments were strong. Toward his wife he exhibited a devotion both intense and constant. She was a widowed lady at the period of her marriage to him, somewhat his senior in years, but adorned with noble and womanly qualities which fully justified that devotion. Her gentle dignity could disarm his most impetuous moments, and lead him to the rectification of any error. She moved among the people in an atmosphere of meekness and love, and thus added largely to his power for usefulness. He was never happy if she was absent from his house, and her long affliction clouded sorrowfully the last years of his life. At one time when the physicians had given her up to die, and told him that a few hours would close her life—he went to God in her behalf. He afterward said to the writer: "When I found how little hope there was from the physicians, I went directly to the Lord. I paid no attention to *them.* I went to *God*, and pleaded with *him* to spare her. I told him that he *knew* I could not get along without her, and that if he kept *me* here he *must* spare her to me. I said it humbly but fervently, and kept the plea before him until he *did* spare her; and from that hour she improved until she regained her usual state of health." Any sacrifice on his part, which might tend to alleviate the terrible pains of her disease, or bring even momentary relief to her suffering frame, was not deemed too great to make; and previously to the breaking out of the war, he several times proposed to resign his commission in the navy in order that he might devote himself entirely to her while she remained on the earth.

His grief over her loss was deep and lasting. Every letter written afterwards, to his friends, is full of the most touching allusions to her. In one letter to Rev. J. M. Tuttle, he says: "At times when I think of my once happy but now desolate home, and that I am now bereft of my dear Nancy, I am greatly depressed in spirits. However, God has thus far sustained me, so that, whilst I sigh because of my great loss, I do not murmur." Again: "Often is my pillow wet with tears because she who was the light and life of my once happy home, has gone to return no more."

His warm-heartedness developed itself strongly also in his love for *children.* God gave him but one child, who died in infancy, but he cherished its memory with a fondness that only such warm natures can understand. His ideas of heaven were always associated with his child, and the fact of its being there was felt as a strong incentive to him in struggling for the prize. A child of Mrs. Lenhart by her previous marriage, was always treated as if it were his own. In addition to this, he received other orphans to his home, and the generous feelings of his soul found a peculiar pleasure in endeavoring to compensate them for the bereavement they had suffered. He said: "God had taken *his* child away, and evidently meant by so doing, that he should supply a father's place to others." From these he always required unquestioning obedience, while at the same time he entered into their childish sports with all the zest of a fresh and genial nature; and he is wept by them still with tears as earnest as would have been called forth had he been their natural protector.

In form Brother Lenhart was magisterial and imposing. His movements were dignified and gentlemanly. His features were dark and swarthy, and when lighted up with the enthusiasm of his soul, harmonized grandly with the bearing of his frame. His eyes were black and penetrating, and when on fire with his subject, seemed to pierce the sinner through. His voice was sweet and powerful and, especially when reading the Scriptures, possessed a mellifluous tone which seemed to float their spirit into the very heart of the listener. His manners were courteous and agreeable. His physical strength was great, and his courage equaled his strength, as lawless and disobedient men sometimes discovered to their cost. While preaching at Long Branch on one warm summer evening, he was seriously annoyed by the conduct of a number of persons who had attended for the express purpose of disturbing the meeting. He was not of a disposition quietly to bear this, but he politely and gently requested their attention. They disregarded the request, and increased the disorder. He next desired the officiary to enforce the order of the meeting. But the disturbers were numerous and composed of the best fighting material on the shore, and the idea of a close engagement with the desperadoes was not inviting. So they sat still, with their eyes fixed upon the minister—never by any chance looking the other way. This emboldened the men, and the disturbance grew worse. Then he announced that if the brethren did not enforce the rules of the meeting and preserve order, *he* would do it himself. The prospect of a melee in which the preacher should be engaged delighted the band, and they redoubled their efforts to produce the desired battle. He continued to preach until, when the back of the leader, who was standing in the aisle, was towards him, he suddenly descended from the pulpit, twisted his fingers in the neck-band of the ruffian's shirt, tightening it till he choked him, then ran him down the aisle, through the door, out upon the platform, and, administering a farewell kick, re-entered the church, just as the man's astonished companions were hurrying out to ascertain the fate of their comrade. Nowise discomposed by the occurrence, he ascended the pulpit again and finished his sermon. But this was not the finale of the matter. The rioters, indignant at being so shamefully beaten,—more indignant still at the kicking of their leader from the church by its minister,—and having a wholesome dread of both the disgrace and danger of a personal assault, entered a complaint against him for assault and battery, before a justice of the peace upon whom they could depend. Brother Lenhart appeared before the Justice's court to answer the charge. The memory of their defeat and the sight of their captured foe was more than they could bear, and their rage was almost boundless. Dire threats of vengeance were uttered, clenched fists were flourished in his face, and it was with difficulty the magistrate could restrain them from active violence. Brother Lenhart demanded the interposition of the magistrate for his protection, but to no purpose. "Well," said Lenhart, "since *you* cannot protect me, I will protect myself. When you think you *are* able to protect me, send for me and I will come." Then grasping his heavy cane in the middle of his length, he brought it on a level with the eyes and noses of his assailants as they stood on either side of him, when whirling it rapidly, it became a matter of necessity if they would preserve those useful appurtenances that they should "fall back," which they promptly did, while their again victorious enemy walked quietly away, never again to be troubled with their opposition.

At a camp-meeting near Belleville a number of men were engaged in inciting a disturbance. The Presiding Elder quietly remonstrated with them, but to no purpose. They were informed by him that if they persisted, the law would be enforced against them. This enraged them, and one of their number, a stalwart and powerful man, doubled his fist and aimed a blow at the Elder. Lenhart was standing near, and quick as thought the cane was leveled and sent with the precision of a rifle shot, striking and felling the man senseless to the ground before his blow had time to reach the person of Brother Porter. The man recovered in about half an hour, humbly begged forgiveness for what he had done, promised all kinds of future amendment, and was soon permitted to go on his way with his head bound up, sadder and wiser, and largely enlightened upon the different varieties of *power* attendant upon a Methodist camp-meeting, and the widely-extended *gifts* of the Methodist ministry.

Brother Lenhart justified the act upon the ground that the person of his friend was in danger, and that it was his duty to defend his friend, and no logic could convince him that the action was not acceptable to God.

He was gifted with a large share of wit and humor, which was often made available in the affairs of the church. Sometimes when the trustees were passing the collection baskets, he would insist that each person who had been sleeping during the services should contribute at least ten cents, instead of the customary penny, as the church could not be expected to furnish lodgings and preaching both for the same price she did preaching alone. In matters of church discipline also it would often manifest itself in an unexpected manner. Among other incidents of his life he one day related to the writer the following. In one of the earlier charges of his ministry, the members of the church almost universally neglected the class meeting service. He preached about it in public, he prayed about it in private, he urged it upon them in personal exhortation but all to no purpose. They heard him respectfully, always promised amendment, and then neglected precisely as before. At last almost in despair, he penned a note to each of the absentees, marked it private and confidential, and sent it to them. The note simply stated that there were certain reports affecting their characters, about which he desired to see them at his house at two o'clock on a specified day. When the hour arrived *every one was there* in one room together. Each regarded the other with suspicion as somehow implicated in his difficulties, and as a consequence conversation was at a discount. He allowed them to sit for about half an hour in gloomy silence before he entered the apartment. Gravely and solemnly he asked them if a note had been received from him requesting their presence. All responded in the affirmative, wondering what would come next. He then, turning the key in the lock of the door, and putting it in his pocket, told them, that he thought it proper to explain, that the reports alluded to in his notes, were not directed against their moral, but religious character. The leader had reported to him that they habitually neglected their classes, and it was now his duty to ascertain the truth or falsity of such reports. Each one, in turn, admitted their truth.

He next stated that the Discipline made it the duty of the leader under such circumstances to call their attention to the neglect, and asked if it had been done. This was also admitted. He then told them that the Discipline made it obligatory upon the preachers to urge the duty upon them. They confessed that this had been attended to. He then informed them that there was but one thing more left to do, which was to proceed to try them for their contumacy, and inflict upon them the penalties of the church, which he was now about to do.

He selected five of the most derelict, and informed them that they were a committee to try the rest. One peremptorily declined, upon the ground that he was not competent, as he had not been to class in five years. Another remarked that the committee were the most guilty of all. Brother Lenhart reminded them of the adage, "Set a rogue to catch a rogue," and insisted that they were the proper persons.

By this time the lurking smile around his mouth betrayed him, and they all saw that in this humorous manner they were receiving a most unmerciful castigation for their evasion of a rule they had solemnly promised to observe. Then after a tender, pleading prayer, he dismissed them, most of them with tears pledging themselves to a performance of their duties, and a goodly number kept the pledges which they there made.

When the writer was associated with him at Paterson and Red Mills, many persons were reported by their leaders as willfully and repeatedly neglecting their class. "Well," said Brother Lenhart, "turn them over to me and I will form a new class of them, and lead it myself." This was accordingly done, and he opened a book with their names upon it, and himself as leader. Perhaps he would meet one of its members in the street, surrounded by ungodly associates, and begin at once to question him about his experience. An effort would be made to evade it and talk about something else, but he would cling to the question until he had extracted what little he had to say about his spiritual condition. After which he would give such advice as he deemed suitable. Then he would state to him that he had been transferred to his class, and he would be glad to receive the amount of his class subscription. Surprise would be expressed at the change of classes, especially as it had never been requested. The reply would be, that it was supposable there must be some objection either to the leader or class-mates as his attendance with them had ceased; and, as it was not likely there was any objection to him, he had been placed upon his class. Vehement protestations of regard for the old class would follow without however producing any effect. Finally they would ask where his class met, when he would be informed that it was called the *street* class, and met generally in the street, or if not there, then anywhere where he happened to find a member, unless indeed the member preferred a regular attendance upon the old class, in which case he would transfer him back again. The prospect of being questioned in every company about an experience of which very little was possessed, was more than could be borne; and in every case solemn promises to faithfully perform the duties were given, and many of them were as faithfully kept.

In personal character he was impulsive, but his impulses were founded upon correct principles of religion; and when they ran beyond legitimate bounds, it was generally upon the generous side. Once convinced that they had led him wrongly, he was as quick in atonement as in error. Any kindness done to him was sure to be repaid with interest. He experienced almost a childish delight in making others happy, and many a dollar sorely needed by himself was spent in relieving the wants of others. His general deportment was cheerful—some thought too cheerful. But those who knew him best knew the depth of the controlling spiritual influences which gave him fellowship with the Father and with his Son Jesus Christ. Probably with his temperament, had he possessed less of cheerfulness, he would have been less effective as a minister.

In his habits he was orderly and methodical, always having stated times for stated things. In appearance he was never otherwise than neat. Soiled apparel or unblacked boots were in his eyes a crime. Never over dressed but always well dressed, he was in this respect a model for his younger brethren in the ministry.

In his friendship he was both ardent and constant. Once a friend always a friend. He always placed himself at the service of a friend, ready to illustrate his professions of attachment in his deeds.

As a preacher, he was above mediocrity. His natural advantages of appearance and voice were only supplementary to solid logical thought. The arrangement of his sermons was simple—generally textual, and always embodied some central, powerful principle. His voice was frequently overflowing with emotion, and an almost inexpressible tenderness would then bathe his audience in tears. Often the baptism of the Holy Spirit would be poured upon his soul in preaching, until men felt that he spake as he was moved of the Holy Ghost. The writer heard him preach at a camp-meeting, where, during the delivery of the sermon, the Divine power was realized in an extraordinary manner, and where he was so overcome by the afflatus, that at the close of the sermon he was unable either to stand or sit, but lay in the preacher's tent, shouting, weeping, and rejoicing, exclaiming, "Who would have believed that the Lord could have blessed so unworthy a minister as me in so wonderful a manner?"

His sermons always aimed at immediate effects. No matter how abstruse the general subject of his discourse, he compelled it to strike heavy blows at the sinfulness of men or the inconsistencies of Christians, while at the same time it urged the necessity of immediate repentance, and the privilege of immediate holiness. His election by his brethren to represent them in the

General Conference, and the occupany of several prominent appointments in the Conference are fair proofs of their estimation of his mental ability and pulpit talents.

Take him all in all, he was a man to be loved and a workman who needed not to be ashamed. The Church feels that in his death she has lost a valuable servant, and his friends mourn his loss with a deep and abiding sorrow. But they look for the time when the sea will give up her dead and both Church and friends will honor and love the patriot martyr who sleeps now beneath the blended flags of his country and the cross, but who will then arise to everlasting life with them at the right hand of the Father.

REV. SYLVESTER ARMSTRONG.

THE native place of this talented Christian minister was Greenfield, Saratoga Co., N. Y., and the date of his birth, July 7, 1825. His history previous to his conversion cannot be given. Nor can the precise time be named, when he entered upon the experiences and services of the Christian life. But that he did heartily embrace the Saviour and become largely imbued with the love of God and the spirit of the gospel, his character and course as herein portrayed, fully attest. He once said that at the time he sought religion, the Spirit clearly witnessed to his acceptance with God, but he still felt a strong desire for some confirmatory token of the reality of the change. His daily labor was so exhausting that the rest of the night did not relieve him from a sense of weariness. He therefore prayed that if what he experienced was a true conversion, he might be thus relieved on the ensuing morning. The time arrived, and the usual sense of enervation was gone. He believed that the desired token was vouchsafed, and never after had any doubt of his acceptance with God.

In 1852 he entered the Troy Conference as a probationer, but after a ministry of two years, concerning which we have no account, he again retired to secular life. In 1855 he took charge of the church at Passaic, N. J., under the direction of the Presiding Elder. At the close of the year he was received by the N. J. Conference, and returned to the same place. The next year he was stationed at Flemington, and when the Newark Conference was formed in 1857 his field of labor placed him in connection with that body. He regularly passed to membership in the Conference and to deacon's and elder's orders. His subsequent appointments were; 1858 and 1859, Mendham; 1860, West Bloomfield; 1861, Franklin St., Newark; 1862, Plainfield.

Here his earthly life and labors were finished, and though the account of them is very brief and meager, yet all that we have to add can best be given in connection with an estimate of his character and abilities.

Sylvester Armstrong was a man of marked characteristics, and had he been favored with a liberal education and a vigorous constitution, he would undoubtly have taken high rank among the intellectual celebrities of his day. His powers of perception, classification and deduction, together with his strong moral sense, led him to take clear and controlling views of moral evil where-ever he found it. To it he felt a mortal repugnance that impelled to the attack at every opportunity, and that allowed him to show it no quarter in any of its forms, or in connection with whomsoever it might stand associated. This led him into many collisions, some of which were not a little sanguinary and unpleasant. The natural result common in such cases, followed as a matter of course; he made warm friends and bitter enemies. Those who held like sentiments greatly admired the ability with which he advocated them, and cordially ranged themselves with him, and even many who did not approve his whole course, could but admire his skill, fearlessness and unswerving fidelity; while such as felt that their moral delinquencies and bad affinities were depicted and exhibited by his keen criticisms and scathing sarcasms, responded in bitter resentments. He was not distinguished in the pulpit by emotional manifestations. But his clear, ringing voice which was well cultivated and controlled, gave unusual power to his comprehensive expositions and forcible arguments. He took a wide range in his themes of discourse. He mainly dwelt upon the fundamental doctrines of the gospel, in the portrayal of which he employed a careful analysis of the word of God, interpreted in the light of a personal Christian experience. He also dealt with topics, which, by many, are thought to be out of place in the pulpit, such as the citizen's relations to civil affairs, the obligations of patriotism, the ethics of politics and of slavery. On a Saturday evening while stationed in Newark, he announced in a city journal that on the next evening he would preach on, "Christ, not cotton, the Nation's King." This may be taken as a specimen of the special theme he was wont to discuss. He evinced considerable familiarity with American civil history. He also took a deep interest in public affairs, not from the motives and impulses of the partizan, but from an abiding conviction that both the interests of religion and humanity are closely connected with the conduct of civil matters. He eminently displayed qualities, which, under other circumstances, would have made him a popular political orator.

His earnestness knew no bounds but the measure of his strength. His convictions were of the most positive character, and on whatever subject his opinions were formed, they were strongly held. His feelings became intensely enlisted on the side of right, and against wrong, whenever he came in contact with either. He had a vivid sense of the sacred character of his calling and the grandeur of his work, believing that preaching the gospel is the great instrumentality by which a lapsed world is to be restored. And then the frail body that he was doomed to carry, helped him to see that the time is short, and that what his hands found to do must be done with his might. Hence preaching with him was no mere pastime. And as he saw sin stalking abroad with brazen face and impudent mien, intrenched behind law, fostered by those in the high places of trust and influence, sustained by wicked combinations, holding the masses in its iron grasp and hastening them to perdition, his soul yearned with longing desire to snatch them as brands from the burning, and to break the fetters by which they are enslaved. In order to this he dealt with the wrongs that most concerned his hearers, and tried to convince and lead them to better views and practices. And he so saw the great issues at stake and felt the responsibilities of his mission, that he could but be intensely earnest, and was usually impelled to an extent of exertion that resulted in much exhaustion. And as his great aim was practical efficiency, he sought in each discourse, and by each word, and look, and gesture, to accomplish some distinct object. If the theme was repentance, faith, the Christian life, the sin of drunkard making, of slavery, or whatever else, he employed his whole power in his effort to make out the case in hand, and as he had a ready command of language he used but few pointless words. His talents both as a thinker and a speaker were far above the average, and he was especially effective in argument and as a debater. When free enough from pain and in his best frame of mind, his eloquent periods had a thrilling effect, and will long be remembered by those who heard him. When in such a mood his clear, pointed, original thought, flowed in a stream of well-chosen words that seemed to know neither obstruction nor exhaustion. Whatever discussion engaged his powers, was treated with the ability of a master, and whether his hearers agreed with him or not, all were ready to acknowledge that the subject was ably handled.

Fearlessness and fidelity were conspicuous traits of his character. He did not confer with flesh and blood in any exigency that involved the welfare of the church, the honor of the gospel or the good of mankind. He did not shrink from a bold utterance of the truth, from a regard to consequences personal to himself. He believed in humanity, and that the gospel is hostile to all unrighteousness. He also believed in progress, and that God's truth is the invincible foe of every wrong and selfish prejudice and practice, and the grand revolutionizer of men's hearts, of society and of the world. And thus believing, he spoke, and while for thus speaking, storms raged around him, and the evils assaulted, resisted to the death, he never on that account, swerved from a manly, steady and fearless exposure of whatever could not bear the light of truth. Some of the officers and members of the churches he served, thought he brought improper things into the pulpit. But impelled by a sense of duty, bring them there he would at all hazards, and denounce them too, and in a way that would make his opponents wince. In a certain charge he was threatened with removal at the end of the first year, parties absented themselves from his ministry, earnest protests were urged that neither their congregations nor finances could be kept up under such a bold and unusual style of preaching. But neither threats nor importunities turned him aside, nor yet the fact, that heavy trials thus fell to his lot. Not that he was indifferent, either to popular favor or the interests of the church, but personal considerations were held in abeyance, while he believed the proper work and ultimate good of the church were thus promoted. In the spirit of a true reformer, and a noble hero did he make all things bend to the will of God, as he understood it, and bravely fought life's great battle, till, in the meridian of his noble powers, he fell at his post, with the scars of battle fresh upon him, an unflinching and triumphant warrior for the right.

Such was the malignity he encountered that he was indicted, a short time before his death, by the grand jury of Union Co., because of certain relations he bore to a public meeting at New Providence. Two conclaves, representing different political opinions, were assembled near together, and each addressed by speakers of its own choice. A collision occurred during the evening, between the two parties, and though Mr. Armstrong rendered important service in restraining the violence of the excited throng, he, with several other supporters of the measures of the Government, was held to answer the charge of violating the public peace. The case excited much solicitude, but closed with a verdict of acquittal by the jury. On the evening of his return home from the court-house, his Plainfield friends, from the several denominations of the place, gathered at the parsonage to express their approval of his course, and sympathy with him in his persecutions and afflictions, in a testimonial of cheering words and a sum of money. Worn and feeble, he rose from his bed to receive them, and then and there declared that he would fearlessly utter the truth as long as he should be able to speak.

His manner would sometimes lead a stranger to infer that he was austere and exacting, but this impression was dispelled by acquaintance. While he claimed the largest liberty for himself, he freely accorded the same to all others, and never allowed his friendships to be disturbed by differing opinions. A stern appearance covered a generous nature, a kind and genial heart. He was ever ready to aid in relieving the needy and in helping every deserving cause, his benevolent promptings often leading him beyond his means. He loved society. His hospitalities were cordially extended, and many are the recollections of pleasant hours spent with him at his house and his board by his brethren and friends. At such times he would unbosom himself to them in the unreserved fullness and frankness of a genuine confidence and affection. He was certainly one of the most kind, open and generous of men. The impress of his noble, Christian character remains vividly upon the hearts of those who enjoyed his friendship. To many, the name of Sylvester Armstrong will ever be suggestive of some of the most kindly and loveable traits that adorn sanctified human nature, and long will his memory live redolent with the fragrance of undying virtue.

But a few days elapsed between the close of the exciting litigation above referred to, and the end of his earthly career. He encountered the final foe with sublime confidence and composure. He watched life's failing currents as they slowly ebbed away, and kept feeling his pulse to ascertain the progress with which death invaded the citadel of life. He said he had faithfully preached the truth, and all he had to regret concerning his ministry, was that he had not labored more as a pastor. He declared, "all is well," repeated the sweet verse beginning, "Jesus the name that charms our fears," and as a victorious conqueror, passed from the toils and struggles of his militant life to the endless triumphs of the church of the first-born in heaven. He died on the morning of January 7th, 1863, in the thirty-eighth year of his age, and tenth of his itinerant ministry.

But he being dead yet speaketh, for the echoes of his voice still ring eloquently in many ears, and the impression of his peculiarly earnest, uncompromising and able ministry, yet lingers in many hearts. Had he lived till now he would have greatly rejoiced to witness the widening sway and brightening triumphs of truths, for which he battled with the intrepidity of a hero to the end. But though he is gone, the truth lives and shall live forever.

N. B. The above memoir was enlarged from one kindly furnished by Rev. John Atkinson, of Newark Conference, whose services are hereby gratefully acknowledged.

REV. JAMES LONG.

It is painful to sketch the life of a useful and aged minister, when the material of which that sketch should be composed is almost inaccessible. The heroes of the battle-field receive memorials from their country, and the soldiers of the cross deserve no less remembrance. But in the paper here presented, such a recognition of the power and usefulness of James Long as would be worthy of the man, is an impossibility. His cotemporaries have nearly all passed away. The few who remain can remember but few of the incidents of his career. His diary, upon which his friends relied with confidence for the facts from which to illustrate his life, and to which he always referred them when questioned as to his history, was lost or destroyed. And his life, undoubtedly rich in early Methodistic incidents, occurring at a period which is now the classic age of our church, must be given, if given at all, in so meager a shape as to fail in fairly representing his status in the ministry.

James Long was born in the town of Enniskillen, Fermanagh County, Ireland, September 27, 1789. At the early age of nine years he experienced the saving power of the Gospel, and connected himself with the Methodist society. While yet a youth, he became a local preacher, and exercised his gifts in his native county with acceptability and usefulness. At the age of twenty-six, he immigrated to this country, and sought immediately to connect himself with the church, rightly esteeming her safeguards to be the surest protection of a stranger in a strange land. At St. George's, Philadelphia, he found kindred spirits, and realized from their communion all that spiritual aid and comfort for which his soul constantly thirsted. Of the four years succeeding his arrival in this country little is known, except that by consistency of life and depth of experience he grew in favor with his brethren; while at the same time, the exercise of his gifts impressed them with the belief that the Lord designed him for more extensive labors in the grand field of gospel effort; and in 1820 he was recommended by them to the Philadelphia Conference, by whom he was received and sent to Essex and Staten Island Circuit in New Jersey. These early days were full of toils and sacrifices to the itinerant Methodist preacher, and none bore them more uncomplainingly or cheerfully than the now sainted Father Long. The communities among which he preached had accepted quite generally the more repulsive doctrines of "High Calvinism," and against those doctrines he directed his attacks in a mode so novel and yet so simple that they were entirely swept away from the minds of many of his hearers. He would announce the doctrine, and then proceed to tell what the *Scripture* had to say about it. Line after line, verse after verse, paragraph after paragraph, occupying sometimes almost the entire sermon, was poured out before them until their creed was made to appear in perfect antagonism to such masses of Scripture truth as to render confutation impossible, and the labor of its attempt more than they were willing to assume. After a year of active effort here, he was appointed to New Mills Circuit, where he labored, though among a different community, as zealously as before. In 1822 he was received into the Conference, ordained a deacon, and in connection with the Rev. Edward Page, appointed to Trenton Circuit. He had been married the winter previous to Miss Ann McLaughlin of Mount Holly—a worthy and estimable lady—and now with his colleague and family occupied a house in Crosswicks. Parsonages were not very numerous in that day, nor were the means of furnishing them very largely at the command of the preachers. The best that could be done was to secure one small house for both the preachers. Brother Page and family occupying the lower, while Brother Long and wife dwelt in the upper story of the building—room enough, probably, for the furniture they possessed. But the pleasant family associations more than compensated the inconveniences—and a year long remembered with pleasure in their history was passed by both these families.

He next traveled Caroline Circuit, in Maryland. Here his

life was saddened by the loss of his young wife, who was seized with a malignant fever, and after an illness of a few days died, leaving to his care an infant daughter. This child is still living, and resides at Allentown, New Jersey. His next appointment was Cecil Circuit; following that, Milford and Smyrna, in Delaware, then Hamburgh and Warren, in New Jersey; afterward Milford and Bristol, in Pennsylvania; then Asbury, Freehold, Crosswicks and Gloucester, in New Jersey. At the General Conference of 1836, the State of New Jersey, together with some slight portions of New York and Pennsylvania, were set off from the Philadelphia and erected into the New Jersey Annual Conference. In this last-named division of the work Father Long was stationed at the time, and remained during the rest of his life. The first session of this Conference was held in Newark, from which he was appointed to Haddonfield Circuit, where he did good service for the cause. Following in regular succession, were Middletown, New Egypt, Tom's River, Tuckerton, Swedesboro', Woodbury, Gloucester, and lastly Salem circuits, in all of which he labored with indefatigable zeal, and with success.

In 1851, after an effective ministry of over thirty years, he was—sorely against the wish of his heart—made supernumerary. But age and excessive labor had weakened the powers of his frame, and, while the desire to work for God burned with as intense a heat as ever before, his infirmities left him no choice, and he reluctantly gave place to younger officers in the Methodistic army, and continued on the list of either supernumerary or superannuated ministers until the time of his decease.

He died at the house of his son-in-law, Mahlon Poinsett, Esq., near Imlaystown, N. J., on January 13th, 1863. His life had been extended to nearly seventy-four years, and all but the first nine passed in active connection with the Church of God, and those nine years were probably filled with such religious activities and experiences as were consonant to his age and opportunities, so that it might be said with truth, he had spent his life in the service of his God. Such a life might be expected to close in calm and peaceful hope. And those expectations were fully realized. Brother Edwards writes of his last hours, "It was my privilege to occasionally visit him, and invariably I found him resting on that atonement which for so many years had been the theme of his ministry. The immediate cause of his death was a fall, in which he had fractured a limb, besides receiving serious internal injuries. Strange to say, however, he suffered but little, and sank steadily and calmly into the arms of death. Just before he departed he said to his daughter, 'From the hour of my conversion until now I have never doubted my acceptance with God,' and then passed away to the regions of the blest."

He was a man whose life was especially devoted to *work*. He traveled in every county of New Jersey except two, besides extensive labors in other States.

In the meekness and simplicity of his manners Father Long was a pattern to the Church. The sweet and childlike addresses made by him in the Conference when his aged lips uttered his sentiments upon some subject which was before them, or else detailed his experience of the power of God to save from sin, are still remembered lovingly by his brethren in the ministry. Guileless as an infant himself, he suspected no guile in others, and was perhaps as perfect an illustration of the charity that thinketh no evil as could easily be found. His religion reflected a pure life among his fellow-men, and those of them who knew him best bear testimony to the eminent Christian holiness of his character. In pastoral intercourse with the people the same simplicity and godliness were manifest. His conversation was tinctured with religion, his spirit sweet and agreeable, and his prayers fervent, breathing out the fullest desire for the well-being of the household. He was especially fond of children. Their bright, glad faces were always welcome, and it was his delight to converse with and instruct them in those gospel truths which he desired should influence their future lives. Many men and women still remember his godly admonitions, and account them among the influences which afterward led them to God.

As a preacher he was plain and unpretending. His principal study was the word of God, and in the pulpit it was almost his only weapon. Chapter and verse were always at command and given to his auditors in profusion. So thoroughly was his memory stored with its language, that at Haddonfield his hearers styled him a "walking concordance." He attacked an opponent with Scripture, his own positions were defended by Scripture, he solved all doubts by Scripture, he consoled Christians with Scripture, and unbelief was demolished with the same powerful weapon. An illustration of his manner is given by Rev. E. H. Stokes, upon whom the venerable brother called one morning, and after lamenting the low state of religion in a particular church, and stating various erroneous habits into which the people had fallen, proceeded to say, "that they sat up when they prayed." "And Brother," said he, "I can prove by *forty-two* distinct passages of Scripture that is not the position to occupy in prayer." But he has gone, leaving the record of a blameless life and peaceful death as a precious heritage to his family and Church.

REV. GEORGE W. BATCHELDER, A. M.

"Oh! he was fair, on earth a while
He dwelt; but transient as a smile
That turns into a tear,
His beauteous image passed us by;
He came, like lightning, from the sky,
He seemed as dazzling to the eye,
As prompt to disappear."

INSPIRATION has lifted up its voice, exclaiming with solemn emphasis, "The flower fadeth." How we feel this truth! The flowers all fade. Not one of the vast bright family, whether it smiles in the valley, or blooms on the mountain, whether it rejoices by the river, or expands in the forest, whether nurtured by the hand of poverty, or gracing the grandeur of palace halls, but is short-lived, frail and perishing.

Sad that things so beautiful should be so brief, and yet, perhaps, because so brief, they are so beautiful. Flowers have their mission, to inspire exalted sentiments, to call forth admiration for the beautiful, to awaken love. How much like the flowers, are many lives, brief, but beautiful! We are about to record the narrative of such a life; a life which, like the flowers, had its high and holy mission; filling the social atmosphere with the rich fragrance of piety, inspiring exalted sentiments, calling forth admiration for the true and beautiful in nature and grace; awakening love for God and man; then, like the flower, falling from the stem, leaving the chill and gloom of life's sorrowful autumn on the soul, and yet, even in death, producing immortal longings for that land, where the leaf shall not wither, and the flower never fades.

George Washington Batchelder, son of George W. and Eliza Batchelder, was born in the season of flowers, which through all his life he so much loved, June 15th, 1836.

Philadelphia was his birth-place, but the years of his early childhood were spent at Moorestown, Cross Roads, and Medford, Burlington Co., N. J.

At the latter place, when he was eight years old, the writer became acquainted with him. He was then of full height for his years, but pale and slender, with a finely developed head, covered with long, light and gracefully curling hair. Neither shy nor bold, his countenance and manners were frank, while his soft blue eyes always beamed with love. He was a child of intense affection, loving his parents and an aunt, residing with them, almost to idolatry.

But parental precept and example, aided no doubt, by the Divine Spirit, had already taught him, there was a Being above all earthly friends who claimed his heart, and so, when only seven years old desired his name recorded upon a class-book where, week after week, in company with his parents or aunt, he expressed his childish longings to be good.

Talent soon began to develope. One of his early teachers says, "Foremost among those of my charge who enlisted my sympathies, was George W. Batchelder, a fair-haired modest boy, who with a younger brother, occupied a seat near me on my right, always neat, smiling and attentive. Seldom was there a day passed without something being added to the storehouse of knowledge which he had thus early commenced accumulating for future usefulness.

"He often preferred remaining by my side, asking questions and receiving explanations, while others were enjoying the recess in noisy play. When an exhibition of the Sabbath-school, to which we were both attached, was about to take place, it devolved on me to hear him rehearse his pieces.

"Never shall I forget the anxiety he manifested to catch the tone and manner, and the lightening up of countenance when these efforts met with approbation."

Early in 1847, when George was between ten and eleven years old, the writer, then stationed at Gloucester City, sent for father and son to visit him at that place. The occasion was a Sabbath-school missionary meeting. George was to speak. His voice, soft, clear, and somewhat plaintive, terminating in a slight lisp, had, on that account, a ten-fold interest. He arose before the crowded audience with graceful modesty, holding in his hand a small copy of the word of God, and delivered a poem, entitled, "*My Mother's Bible.*" So touching were the sentiments, and so tender the tones of his voice, as he clasped the volume to his bosom, exclaiming,

"She dying gave it me,"

that many wept. When the youthful orator beheld the effect which his speaking had produced, the fountains of his own heart were touched, and speaker and people both were bathed in tears.

In the spring of 1847, his parents removed to Burlington, N. J., where his opportunities for mental and spiritual culture were enlarged, and he diligently improved them.

Here, when only twelve years old, during the pastorate of Rev. C. H. Whitecar, he bowed an humble penitent at the foot of the cross, seeking salvation, and united as a probationer with the church of Christ.

It was not until the eleventh of February, 1850, however, under the ministry of Rev. D. W. Bartine, that he obtained a clear evidence of pardoned sin, and an adoption into the family of God.

Two months after his conversion, when not yet fourteen years old, he wrote, and entered into the following solemn covenant.

"I, George W. Batchelder, this Sunday evening, April 27th, now make a covenant with God, that I will try, through his assisting grace, to devote myself wholly to His cause, to set an example to those around me, and never give up trying to serve him while this paper lasts. Hereafter I consecrate myself to Him, asking God's divine blessing upon me for ever; and, O God, fit me for any part of Thy service which Thou seest I am capable of filling. Amen. I here promise never to leave my God while this paper lasts. Sealed with God's divine blessing, and, I trust, my everlasting consecration to Him.

"Amen. Amen. Amen. God help!

GEORGE W. BATCHELDER.

"Burlington, N. J., *April 27th*, 1850."

This paper is still in good preservation, and how he kept his promise this narrative will reveal, and those acquainted with him know.

He developed rapidly. Not that he possessed the gravity or the wisdom of advanced life. He was a youth, with the feelings of others of his age ; but his whole life was so controlled by Christian grace and principle, that his mental and spiritual growth was rapid.

Dr. Joseph Parrish, who knew him well, and loved him as a younger brother, says, "When he was a boy, at work in his father's shop, there shone from his quiet life a gentle spirit, the memory of which still lingers about me like the sweet fragrance of a morning in spring. He often came to me for counsel, but there was a beautiful consistency in his own example which always counseled me."

On his fifteenth birth-day he commenced a journal, which he kept with few interruptions to the time of entering the ministry. At that important period, it is much to be regretted, his journal ceased. This youthful production, while we may not be able to make many extracts from it, is interesting, from the fact that it shows his interior life with such wonderful transparency that we see to the very depths of his soul. All he thought, and all he did, seems to be recorded. To surviving friends it is a subject of profound gratitude, that in looking through this glass to his inner nature, we discern a guileless spirit, refined and elevated by intense longings after God.

Whatever the occupation of the day,—whether at work with his father, or engaged in the amusements usual to his years, in company or alone—whether flushed with the bright hopes of youth, or depressed by the frequent embarrassing circumstances of life, and the pains inflicted by a frail constitution—how much he worked and how much he played—how much he walked for pleasure, and how much he went to meeting to pray,—all were set down with beautiful simplicity; and he closes up every day with regrets for any failures or omissions of duty, devoutly asking God to make him wiser and better for the morrow. These are not the occasional, but the continual aspirations of his heart. To whatever page we turn, or wherever the eye may rest upon that page, the day is closed with God.

Early in his journal he adopted the motto, "*Integrity, Industry, Economy,*" and his life was an exemplification of these traits of character.

At an early day he exhibited a rare love of books. Histories, biographies, and scientific works, such as came within the grasp of his intellect, were read with an eagerness which showed his intense thirst for knowledge.

The life of that distinguished servant of God, John Summerfield, made a deep impression on his mind. Occupied with thoughts of his saintly life and successful ministry, he closed his record for December 4th, 1851, with this brief prayer, "*Oh for the eloquence of Summerfield!*" a prayer which, as we shall see in the course of this narrative, was, in the estimation of competent judges, answered in a large degree.

Believing the position he occupied at home was not his proper sphere, in his sixteenth year, with the approval of his parents, he entered the drug store of Mr. Roberts, in Salem, N. J. How he felt as he started for his new situation, is recorded in his journal thus:—"The Lord has guided me, and He will protect me. I am about leaving the paternal roof to seek a living in the wide friendless world. I have no friend, O God, but Thee. Oh guide me; keep me from stepping into the ways of sin and Satan. Farewell, friends, home and kindred." He refers to the same subject in one of his sermons,—"When you cross the mystic bridge that starts from the threshold of home, followed by tearful eyes and the echo of low farewells, you enter a wilderness *alone.*" With this feeling of heart desolation, and his habitual piety, it is not surprising that in this trying hour he should make this renewed and unreserved committal of himself to God.

While at Salem, he heard Rev. Mr. Vandewater present the claims of Dickinson College. Listening to his statements, the ever-present desire for knowledge was so strengthened that he wrote, "*I am determined to have learning, school or no school.*"

After a trial of seven months in the drug store, where he was highly esteemed for his many virtues, it was the mutual conclusion of father, employer, and himself, that his love of books was so strong as likely to interfere with successful business life, and the engagement was dissolved.

Returning to Burlington, he longed for school, but as his father was unable to do all that was desirable in that direction, George agreed to work during the interval of school hours, and so bear his own expenses.

With this arrangement his heart was full of joy, and the morning he took his books under his arm and started for school, he heads his journal with this brief, but triumphant exclamation; "LIGHT BREAKS IN."

But in addition to his work at home, and his studies at school, he was an active and earnest member of a debating society, where his talents as a speaker were developed, and his knowledge increased. When the question was to be discussed, "Are fictitious writings beneficial?" He says, "I am on the negative, the side of conscience, for there is scarcely a greater evil comes in our midst. The pen is a powerful weapon; when it is used wrongfully, its influence is pernicious."

When the new church on Union St., Burlington, was formed in March, 1853, he, by invitation of his friend, Dr. Parrish, united therewith, and at once, as from earliest childhood, identified himself with the interests of the Sabbath-school.

His privileges and efforts in this new church were brief, however, for in the following May, when nearly seventeen years old, having by adherence to his early motto, "Integrity, Industry, and Economy," secured enough to pay his way, he left his Burlington school, and went to Pennington Seminary. A few days after his arrival there, he prayed in public for the first time. In the following July, in company with Rev. J. G. Crate, likewise a student at Pennington, he went to Cedar Grove, where, after Brother Crate had preached, he closed the services, and then led class for the first time. It was a great cross, but the Lord blessed him in the effort.

Leaving Pennington in the following October, he took charge of a school at Long Branch, where he remained one year. This was a new sphere of action, and he entered upon it with many fears. He commenced with seven scholars, but such was his success, that the number soon increased to nearly seventy. His labors as a teacher, were not allowed to interfere with his religious duties, and the church soon felt, that he was called to preach the gospel. It was mentioned to him, and he was urged to receive license to exhort. But his health was such, that his own judgment, as well as that of his father, was, that for the present it had better be deferred.

In November, 1854, he left Long Branch, and went to Cassville, Pa., in the double capacity of student and teacher, where he studied Greek and Latin, with a recitation in Theology once a week. He remained at Cassville one year.

Returning to New Jersey in the autumn of 1855, he opened a classical school at New Egypt. This school prospered beyond his most sanguine expectations. While residing there, the church saw he was a young man of talents, and feeling the power of his consistent life, gave him license to exhort.

During the following December, in company with Rev. B. D. Palmer, going to the village of Goshen, four or five miles through the pines, Brother Palmer insisted that he should preach, and gave him a text. When they arrived at the church, with much fear and trembling, yet impelled by a sense of duty, he opened his mission and preached his first sermon from the words of Paul, "Cast not away your confidence, which hath great recompense of reward," the text which Brother Palmer gave him.

With this verbal license from Brother Palmer, he preached a few times, to the great delight and profit of his hearers.

On the 15th of June, 1856, he wrote in his journal as follows: "To-day ushers in the first day of my twentieth year. To-day I peculiarly feel my eternal obligations to Him who has preserved me so long, given me so much that I needed, and preserved me from so much that would harm. I have been trying within a few weeks, to walk with God, but too much like Peter, I have walked afar off. Whose heart is so prone to sin as mine? Thy power, *thy* power, O Lord of heaven and earth, alone can keep me. My feelings to-day are peculiar. The Lord has opened a way for me here; my salary is sufficient for all my wants, after assisting my parents some; pleasant school and well advanced; but is this my proper sphere? God only knows! During my stay here, I have tried to speak for my Saviour and his cause, and have been blessed. The other Sabbath Brother Palmer made me try to preach at Pemberton, and there I was not forsaken. Oh! that

I knew how to act. A calm spirit of resignation is what I need, but how hard to maintain it? Brother Palmer finally drew from me the promise, that if the way should again be opened, I would not hesitate. Considering my health, and general want of preparation, it seeems like a rash promise, but father thought it best, and why should I not be in the hands of the Lord? My determination, Christ strengthening me, is at all events to live for Him, and to live in Him, that I may finally dwell with Him.

"On this my birth-day, I wish to covenant with my heavenly Father to live in all humility of heart the life of a Christian. *I am persuaded I shall not count another twenty years on earth.* My life will be short, but Oh, if useful, how cheering will be its close. Lord, guide me, and whether thou givest me life or not, oh, give me thy Holy Spirit. May this year of my life be the happiest, the most productive of good to thy church and the world, and whatever its unseen future may reveal, prepare, Oh prepare me for it. Amen."

About the last of July of the same year, while in company with his father on a visit to a fellow-apprentice, Rev. S. H. Smith, of New York East Conference, then stationed at Bethel, Connecticut, he received a letter from Rev. Wm. A. Wilmer, Presiding Elder of Trenton District, informing him that the illness of Rev. B. O. Parvin left the church at Millstone, eight miles from New Brunswick, without a pastor, and asking him to take charge of it. He was only an exhorter, and but twenty years and two months old. What should he do? His father said to him kindly, "Go, my son." The work of the ministry had long occupied his mind—the scales of inclination and duty were poised on even beam: but these few words from a parent's lips turned the balance, and his life work was decided.

He at once procured a teacher for the New Egypt school, made arrangements for his higher calling, and started for Millstone; but as he bore a letter of introduction from Rev. C. E. Hill, of Burlington, to Rev. S. L. Johnson, a local minister of New Brunswick, he stopped at that place for its delivery. The acquaintance thus commenced between these two Christian men, ripened into an intense and sanctified friendship, which continued until dissolved by death. By special invitation brother

Johnson's house became his frequent and pleasant home. Reaching Millstone, the place of his destination, he says: "I arrived here on Thursday, August 20th, 1856. And is it possible I am here to take charge of a church? Is it not presumption? It is not my work; I throw the responsibility on my friends. Lord, if it be thy will that I work in thy vineyard, in this department, Oh bless and encourage me! In thee I trust. On thee I rest. Thy blessing—thy blessing I crave—I *must have*, or I fail. Oh the responsibility—the account I must give in the day of judgment for the immortal interests of this church and this community. It overwhelms me; it would crush me; but I know who is leading me, who is sustaining me; and he will bring success—God help."

The people looked at their new minister, and though he was but a youth, yet impressed by his boyish appearance that he was much younger than he really was, shook their heads in fear, that in a community like that, so long accustomed to the ministrations of staid and able men, he could do nothing.

The Sabbath came. He preached in the morning from the text, "Brethren, pray for us;" and in the evening, "Seek ye first the kingdom of God," &c. Not only were all fears dispelled, but an angel from heaven would have produced little more surprise. They expected little or nothing, but when his fervid thoughts and glowing eloquence fell upon their cars, they scarcely knew how to express their feelings. His reputation as a speaker was at once established, and his power increased from week to week.

The quarterly meetings for Liberty Street, New Brunswick, and Millstone were at that time held together. At the first of these, after Brother Batchelder's appointment, he was regularly licensed to preach.

While stationed at Millstone, he preached for the writer several times at New Brunswick. A newspaper of that city spoke of him as follows:—"For a young man, Mr. Batchelder is the most promising public speaker it has been our good fortune to listen to for years, and if health is continued, he will soon rank among the ablest for eloquence and oratory. He is only a little over twenty years of age, of liberal education, has a retiring yet pleasing manner, and sweet and pathetic voice, over which he has excellent control; language chaste, pertinent and forcible, while his thoughts, if not always original, are original in their presentation."

Of a missionary address delivered there, the same paper says: "Rev. G. W. Batchelder's earnest and soul-stirring remarks upon the subject of missions, given in his own happy and eloquent style, will long be remembered by those privileged to hear. They reached the heart and opened the fountain of tears. Many wept who are not to weeping given."

His brief ministry at Millstone, which closed on the 5th of April, 1857, will never be forgotten by those who had the opportunity of sitting under it.

The week following, the New Jersey Conference commenced at Trenton, where he was received on trial. On the succeeding Sabbath, while the Conference was yet in session, he was sent to fill the pulpit at Princeton, where he preached twice to the admiration of all. Great was the delight of that people, therefore, when on the adjournment of Conference, they learned that the eloquent preacher of the previous Sabbath was to be their pastor.

Of this appointment he wrote: "Conference has thus disposed of me. O my God, sustain me! Let this be a year of usefulness in my history, and to the church a year of power."

He commenced his work in that far-famed and time-honored seat of learning on the 19th of April, 1857. The elevated character of his ministrations soon arrested attention, and while the citizens generally were interested, the Professors and students of Old Nassau Hall were his frequent, and some of them his constant hearers.

In speaking of Brother Batchelder, S. L. Johnson, of New Brunswick. says:—"The question as to the best method of pulpit preparation was one frequently discussed by us. On one occasion I showed him my plan: which was to select two or three themes, write them down, and then in the course of reading, hearing, thinking, or conversation, if anything offered illustrative or applicable to either, place it at once under its appropriate head. Some six months after this, and while he was stationed at Princeton, I was paying him a visit, when he said to me in his familiar way, 'Johnson, your plan of preparing discourses is excellent, but, under the blessing of God, I think I have improved upon it.' He then produced his plan, and said, 'I first go to God in prayer, and ask Him for a text or subject; and I seldom take anything that does not come in this way. Then I write them down as you do, and in my reading, conversation, study, or hearing sermons, anything that bears upon my subject I place where it belongs; thus I have always material for thought and reflection; and my very best illustrations have been gathered in this way.' "

His sojourn in Princeton was pleasant. He often spoke of its refined society, and its beautiful flowers. He loved both. But while he enjoyed these, there was that which gave him sadness —his want of larger success in winning souls to Christ. True, there was a religious interest, and some were converted while he was there, but not such numbers as satisfied his zeal. He wanted to see scores and hundreds brought to Jesus. But the ministry of such a man cannot be estimated by immediate results. The truth in reference to him is contained in a newspaper notice:— "The young preacher is a remarkable man, and take him for all in all, I never listened to his equal. A dignity, the natural result of great purity of character, a sweetness of utterance that no affectation could attain, united with a command and adaptation of language that seems like inspiration, renders George W. Batchelder one of the most effective and useful ministers. Such a man sows the seeds of virtuous life deep in the souls of strong men, silently to germinate, the fruits whereof the sower may not know until preacher and hearer are summoned to appear before the eternal throne." Sometimes, however, fruits of this gracious sowing appear in this life to gladden the heart of the tearful sower. A gentleman in Princeton, who subsequently joined the church, said, "I received my first religious convictions under the preaching of Mr. Batchelder." And here and there, through succeeding years, though the form of the preacher may lie in the silent earth, persons will continue to arise with similar declarations, and the light of eternity will, no doubt, reveal many more.

In the main, however, he was one of those deep but silent workers, so beautifully described in one of his own brilliant lectures:—"But the world's work is not waiting for conspicuous workers, neither is the most of it done by those whom history will recognize. Nature teaches us by the might of noiseless laborers. 'There is no rushing sound when the golden gates of dawn swing round, and the broad tides of sunlight break in on a darkened world, flooding it with glory as one bright wave after another falls from the fountain millions of miles away. There is no creaking of heavy axles or groaning of cumbrous machinery as the solid earth wheels on its way, and every planet and system performs its revolutions. The great trees clothe themselves with boughs, the plants cover themselves with buds, and buds burst into flowers, but the whole transaction is unheeded. The change from snow and winter winds to the blossoms and fruits and sunshine of summer is seen in the slow development, but there is scarcely a sound to tell of the might of the transformation. The river rolling voiceless, forever and forever, is eloquent of strength. The beat of the heart is muffled, and the lapse of time that sweeps the living world far out to sea, is silent. The past is dumb, the future still, and the present makes but a slight ripple, like the traveling of a steamer on a quiet sea.' If then Providence, the mightiest worker in the universe, is the least noisy and obtrusive, the unseen influence exerted by the unheard name may be most significant."

Still we long for the immediate and visible results, and in the absence of these, no applause, however merited and wide-spread, can satisfy the earnest soul of a faithful minister.

His career at Princeton secured the esteem of the first intellects of that literary town, and closed on the 20th of March, 1859, with universal approbation.

Meanwhile a new church had been organized in Trenton, having in view the erection of a beautiful and costly edifice for the worship of God. The minds of its official members were at once directed to the youthful Princeton preacher as every way adapted to their wants. The proper authorities coincided with these views, and George W. Batchelder became the first pastor of the State Street Methodist Episcopal Church. It was a responsible position for one so young, and yet he proved himself eminently qualified for the important work. This new society worshiped until the completion of their own edifice in Temperance Hall, corner of Green and Front streets. Batchelder commenced his labors there on the 3d of April, preaching in the morning from the text, "Christ sent me not to baptize, but to preach;" and in the evening, "Without faith it is impossible to please God,"

His graceful elocution and oratory, connected with his fervent piety, arrested immediate attention, and made a profound impression. The large room was regularly filled with intelligent hearers, from all classes, and representing all denominations.

The church was greatly encouraged by the auspicious commencement of their enterprise, and workmen were immediately engaged in laying the foundation of the new building corner of State and Stockton Streets. While matters were thus pleasantly progressing, his friends experienced an agreeable surprise in the fact announced by a morning paper, that at the annual commencement of Princeton College on the 27th of June, the honorary degree of Master of Arts was conferred upon the eloquent pastor of the State Street Church. This was the more interesting and impressive from the fact that it was the second distinction of the kind ever conferred upon a Methodist minister by that ancient and honorable institution, the first being upon the saintly Summerfield.

The corner-stone of the new edifice was laid with appropriate ceremonies on the 21st of July, 1859, by Bishop Scott. The building advanced with great rapidity, and was dedicated on the 14th of the following June. Bishop Janes preached in the morning, and performed the dedicatory services; Dr. Kenneday preached in the afternoon, and Dr. Bartine in the evening.

The popularity of the pastor was sufficient to fill the fine large audience room, and the prospects of the society were of the most flattering character.

A correspondent of a city paper said, "Being in Trenton on Sabbath, I went to the new M. E. church on State Street. I found the interior finished in exceedingly good taste, combining simplicity and beauty. The preacher is a young man of almost boyish appearance, and yet there is a quiet unaffected religious dignity in the expression of his features, and in his whole bearing that cannot fail to secure respect even from the most lightly disposed. I never saw a face more thoroughly stamped with the expression of sanctity. I never listened to a more interesting sermon. I have heard the most eminent clergymen of this country, but I know of none superior to this young man in all those rare gifts that combine to give power and influence to the pulpit. I have heard men more eloquent, more argumentative, and more logical, but in the happy blending of all these, I have never listened to the superior of George W. Batchelder. His eloquence never oppresses, his arguments never weary, his logic never confuses. A gentleman and a Christian, with a zeal governed by rare intellectual discrimination, he is the very man demanded by the emergency which called this new church into existence."

Though he was the subject of frequent newspaper remarks, and universally applauded by his congregations and the community generally, he never seemed elated, but moved on with the artlessness and simplicity of a child.

There was that which gave him greater joy than all human commendations; the penitent's cry for mercy, and the song of new-born souls. These he longed to hear, and felt, unless he heard them, he could scarcely live. To accomplish this, he preached and prayed and toiled, and lived.

He did not toil in vain. A gracious revival of religion closed up the year 1860, and sweetly extended its influences into the year 1861, in which between forty and fifty professed conversion. In this revival his joy was unbounded. He often referred to it as the most blessed period of his life.

These things improved his religious experience; he grew as a Christian, and consequently rose higher as a minister. In one of his sermons, after this, he speaks of personal experience.

"There is a spiritual stature we are to arrive at; there is a spiritual form we are to be moulded into. It is not of Pharisaic figure; it is not of philosophic size and cast. Do we say with little more meaning than a child's answer would contain, 'It is Christ's? Yes, it is Christ's. Thankfully, joyfully, triumphantly, we cry, as the work goes on within us, It is Christ's, his image his likeness.' He is our ideal, and the mind that was in him, must be in us."

While stationed at Trenton, he was called to pass through the greatest grief of his life, the loss of his mother. In the last sermon he ever prepared, he refers to the subject in such instructive and tender words, that we are sure the reader will be pleased with their insertion. "'Come home immediately, your mother is dying,' read a telegram handed to a young man, who had even to manhood clung to the endearments of mother and home. As the sorrow fell into his heart, he crushed the paper in his hand, and with an agitation that shook his frame, offered the prayer, 'Spare her, O merciful Father, yet a little while, spare her.' It is no new thing for a mother to die. Every day orphanage weeps and the world takes no heed. But to every one who has stood within the veil, and known the sacredness of a mother's love, and then by the coffined form, and known the unfathomed grief of a mother's death, it is *new once.* And what child or man, if he retain anything of the innocence of childhood, will not feel the strange, terrible novelty in his history, of a 'home without a mother?' She passed away to the family in heaven. Now see the struggle, and victory. Though a Christian in his habits of thought and aims of life, his religious vitality was numbed. There was a bitterness in the cup that tinctured the spirit. There was an intensity of agony in the wound that paralyzed the frame. Religious exercise, friendly counsels, the conclusions of reason, availed nothing. One day when journals and letters relating to the bereavement had revived the emotional strength of grief, and the heart was turning away from earth for comfort, God sent into its meditations this much of his word: 'If any man love father or mother more than me, he is not worthy of me.' It struck the Horeb of his heart, and tears of repentance flowed freely. In the rebuke was hidden consolation. Day after day the comparative claims of Christ and the parent were weighed; the appropriate work of Christ in affliction beheld, and the place he would occupy in the stricken spirit revealed, till every barrier to peace was broken down, and the contrite soul of the mourning one sobbed out the ejaculation: 'No! no, blessed Jesus, not *more* than thee, thou

31

art the first and the last, thou knowest that I love thee more than these,

> 'Give what thou wilt, without thee, I am poor;
> And with thee rich, take what thou wilt away.'

The victory was final."

His ministry in Trenton approached its close. It was brilliant, and in many respects satisfactory to himself—the crowning glory of his life.

A distinguished jurist, the late Judge Dayton, Minister to the Court of France, who knew him well in Trenton, said, "He was more like Summerfield than any man he had ever known."

A gentleman, who made no profession of religion, deeply impressed with the excellency of his ministry, said: "When I meet him in the street, though a stranger, I can hardly refrain from grasping him by the hand in token of my profound admiration."

But Batchelder was frail. He had been so from a child. His popularity, though it seemed not to affect him, was nevertheless exciting. To meet its demands he toiled many a weary hour when his admirers were asleep.

Not only did his own church require his energies, but he was in demand for all kinds of labor at home and abroad. Sabbath-school and missionary addresses were very numerous. He addressed Young Men's Christian Associations in various places. Pic-nic and Harvest Home speeches were frequent, sometimes two or three a week. He delivered addresses at school commencements at home and abroad. He likewise delivered a Fourth of July address before the Washington Monumental Association of Trenton, and an address before the Normal School.

He frequently lectured for the relief of churches in different localities. At the Annual Sessions of the Conference he was invariably called upon for an address at some of the anniversaries. He spoke at corner-stone layings, and preached at the dedication and reopening of churches. Such were his labors outside of his regular pastorate.

He was worked hard, and his frail constitution could not otherwise than feel it. He longed for repose, and looked forward to the annual Conference as a time when he might retire to some little country charge to rest. But this was not his privilege. When his term expired in Trenton, April, 1861, he was appointed to Bayard Street, New Brunswick.

He entered upon his work there with all the energy his failing strength would allow. He officiated one Sabbath, and on the next was called to preach at the dedication of the new church on Market Street, Paterson, New Jersey.

Flattering notices of his sermon appeared in the papers of that city, and were copied abroad. When a friend called his attention to these notices, he replied: "My dear brother, I am convinced that my time in this world is short, and such is my agony of soul for the salvation of sinners, that I would much rather hear the cry, 'What must I do to be saved?' produced by my efforts, than to have the eulogies of all the world. O, my Master, give me souls; I feel I cannot live, unless souls are converted under my ministry."

The time of Mr. Batchelder's appointment to New Brunswick was one of great excitement in our country. Sumpter had just been fired on, and the great national heart was stirred to its depths. It was not only Sumpter that had been assailed, but the Northern mind, loyal and liberty-loving was insulted, and stood aghast with profound astonishment. When the first stunning shock was over, the cry to arms rang through the land in tones of thunder. To sustain the government and encourage enlistments, large and enthusiastic meetings were held in almost every locality. New Brunswick was astir, and on the 22d of April, just two weeks after Mr. Batchelder's appointment, the greatest popular demonstration ever known in that city took place in the First Reformed Dutch Church. The galleries were thronged with ladies, and the lower floor of that vast church was packed with men. All classes were there, from the College President and Theological Professor to the humblest mechanic and laborer. Judge Van Dyke presided; and the meeting was addressed by Rev. Dr. Campbell, president of Rutgers' College; Rev. Dr. Crosby, Hon. G. B. Adrain, Rev. G. W. Batchelder, Rev. Dr. Woodbridge, G. A. Vroom, Esq., Rev. D. Cole, Rev. Dr. Proudfit, J. Van Rensalear, Esq., Rev. Dr. How, Rev. Mr. Riddell,

Rev. Mr. Harlow, Rev. Mr. Jeffreys, Rev. Dr. Wilson, Rev. Dr. Webb, Rev. Wm. J. Thompson, Dr. Morrogh and R. Adrain, Esq.

Amid this vast array of age, experience, and talent, Batchelder stood *youngest of all*, and yet, in energy of thought and gracefulness of style, *a peer!* He said, "I cannot conceive why I am called to speak, unless it be to represent the young men of New Brunswick. The question has often been asked, What will the young men do? I answer, The young men will speak for the Union, vote for the Union, give for the Union, and fight for the Union. I am not of an excitable nature, but my blood has been heated by the events of the past few months, and I am surprised at the course the South has taken. We look back to 1776 and find causes sufficient for the revolution which then took place. We look over to Italy, and do not wonder that Garibaldi springs upon his enemies. Has the South been taxed heavily, or any of their rights infringed upon? I can find nothing of this kind on record. But I do see that the Government has suffered, petted, and coaxed them, until like rebellious children they become outlaws. The South asked for Louisiana, and we bought and gave it her; she wanted Florida, and we bought and gave it her; she wanted a Missouri Compromise—we gave it her; she wanted Texas—we fought and bled and conquered, and gave it her; she wanted New Mexico—we bought it and gave it her; she wanted a Fugitive Slave Law—we gave it her; she wanted the repeal of the Missouri Compromise—we repealed it; and yet she complains that she is wronged! Why I myself am outraged by all this, and I will now speak for the Union, vote for the Union, give for the Union, and fight for the Union.

"Now what has been done? Our Flag that no foreign nation dared to insult has been trodden under foot—our vessels taken on the seas, our forts and arsenals and mints seized, and the young blood fired until it is ready to speak, vote, give, fight, and die for the Union. When I see laws violated, property stolen, harvests destroyed, men outraged, and the liberties of the people in danger, I can no longer cry 'Peace, Peace,' but must declare in trumpet tones, 'Thus far and no further.' For this purpose I appeal not only to New Brunswick, but ask, Will

New Jersey be true to her past history? I say, Yes. Her sacrifices and privations were second to none in the Revolutionary struggle; and her sons have been as brave as the bravest. She has given a Morgan, a Lawrence, a Bainbridge, a Pike, and a host of others who never flinched in the cause of their country. New Jersey to-day lives and breathes the same big breath of patriotism, and will not be trampled upon.

"I have looked at this contest in various lights—in the light of a Jerseyman—as a Christian man,—and I believe it to be as much my duty to fight for my country now as it is to preach the gospel, and I will do it. The Government has been very lenient, but the first gun that fell upon Fort Sumpter decided that we must be lenient no longer, and must be ready for war. We must sustain the Government, and if needed I stand ready to go to-day. Let every one who can go do so at once. The cross may be great, but go, and if you should fall, a grateful country will honor and remember, and the God of the fatherless protect those dependent upon you..

"But I close my remarks to give place to others. The cry is, To arms. Let us rush to the battle, with the spirit of the poet in our hearts,—

'What God in his infinite wisdom designed,
And armed with his weapons of thunder,
Not all the earth's despots and factions combined
Have the power to conquer or sunder!
The union of lakes—the union of lands,
The union of States none can sever—
The union of hearts—the union of hands,
And the flag of our Union forever.'"

These efforts and excitements had their influence upon one so frail as he, and were noiselessly, but surely, undermining the foundations of life, and hastening him to an early grave.

His summer at New Brunswick was passed, however, with comparative comfort, but as the season advanced, and autumn with its fading glories came, his infirmities increased.

On the 15th of September he preached in Newark, at Central Church, in the morning, and Broad Street at night. Concerning this visit he wrote to a friend, "I spent rather a pleasant day in

Newark, though I have not preached so poorly for a long time. Hear the voice of the rod, says the Good Book; and I hope this slight chastisement will tend to produce a state of healthful humility. It seems to me it would be pleasant, though, if ministers could be whipped like other people at home. Do not blame the clergy for publicly chastising their congregations when the former suffer so much more largely—for theirs is a narrower surface, and the corrections much more frequent."

But poorly as he preached in his own estimation, more than a year after a lady of piety and intelligence said, "I have the pleasantest recollections of Mr. Batchelder, owing to the great benefit derived from his sermons on the above occasions."

The following Sabbath he preached at home, after which, being attacked with hemorrhages, he was laid aside from pulpit labors for three months.

Sometimes during this period he was tolerably comfortable, and his friends with himself entertained the hope that care and rest might possibly restore him.

On the 21st of October he was married to Miss Helen, daughter of Rev. D. W. Bartine, D. D., of the Philadelphia Conference, a young lady eminently fitted to become his companion, who by her gentle ministries not only soothed the hours of his affliction, but, no doubt, prolonged his life for months.

A few weeks after his marriage, he wrote from Philadelphia to his friend, Rev. Wm. H. Jefferys, at New Brunswick thus, "I scarcely know what to say of my health. It had been improving, until a slight cold received last week, brought into prominence again the old features of my disease. Confidentially, my dear brother, I fear my time of work on earth is not very long, at most only a few years. Oh! how I wish I had done more, worked harder, with a more single eye, and won more souls to Christ. If my allotted time should close this winter, I will have preached five years. But how have I preached? Where are the souls? Where my abundant labors through the week in pastoral work? Oh! there is no hope in such a review, and I have only one feeling in surveying it, besides deep regret; and that is thankfulness, 'that we are not saved by works.' Where O my soul would be thy salvation? But now, thank

God, I can by the exercise of a present faith, cling to a living Redeemer, whose work on the cross wrought a salvation independent of my poor life history, and while it lifts me up, 'nearer my God to thee,' rolls through my soul its gentle waves of consolation. No text has impressed my mind during my sickness like the sixth chapter of Hebrews, from the seventeenth verse, to the end. Oh! the weight of comfort there is in it."

He returned to New Brunswick with his wife, in December, making their home in the family of Brother Jeffery's, pastor of Liberty St. church, whose parsonage was next door to the chapel which Brother Batchelder served. They were pleasantly situated, and hoped for days of health and usefulness.

On the 23d of December, he preached from the words, "If any man will do my will, he shall know the doctrine." He commenced his remarks as follows:—

"It pleased God recently to lay his chastening hand upon me, and for months to seal my lips. Many hours of restiveness I spent, mourning that I could not, when the Sabbath came, preach Jesus and the resurrection. But why? It was not the desire of standing as the speaker, or the teacher of hundreds; from that responsibility I shrink with trembling. It was not love of fame, for even if desirable in health, it dwindles when earth loosens its bond, and eternity draws nigh. It was not love of excitement connected with the preparation and delivery of sermons, that had already shattered me. It was the desire I had to take up once more the blessed old gospel cry, 'Whosoever will let him come and take of the water of life freely;' that I might stand where John stood, and point to where John pointed, and re-echo, though with a feeble voice his shout, 'Behold the Lamb of God.' Oh! there is pleasure in placing gold in a poor man's hands; joy in saying to those who ask, 'Where shall I go;' there is a rock higher than I. It is sweet to give bread to the hungry, and to lead those who are athirst, to fountains springing up unto everlasting life. Therefore I resolved, that if restored, whatever my past remissness, hereafter,

'Only Jesus would I know,
And Jesus crucified.'

And here I stand, for myself, crying, God forbid that I should glory save in the cross of our Lord Jesus Christ,' and for you, 'Behold the Lamb of God.'"

On the first Sabbath of January, 1862, he preached from the words of Paul, "I beseech you therefore brethren, by the mercies of God, that ye present your bodies a living sacrifice, holy, acceptable unto God, which is your reasonable service."

This was his last sermon, and henceforth, the pulpit was eloquent with his voice no more.

It was yet three months till conference. During this time the professors and students of Rutgers College, and the Theological Seminary, supplied the pulpit in the morning, and Rev. Dr. Howard Crosby, pastor of the First Presbyterian church of New Brunswick, magnanimously volunteered his valuable services, and preached for Mr. Batchelder every Sabbath evening with great acceptability and profit, for a period of three months; an act of Christian kindness, for which he will long be held in grateful remembranee. This distinguished divine, in speaking of Mr. Batchelder, says, "I first knew him as pastor of the Bayard St. Chapel, and loved him at once. As I met him on various public occasions, I learned more and more to esteem his gentle spirit, and his warm zeal. It was only a few months after I first knew him that he was taken ill; and his rapidly increasing weakness incapacitated him for pulpit duties. He had continued them too long, when I was permitted to take his place in the evening service of every Sabbath. During the three months of this intercourse with his flock, I had abundant opportunity to witness their affection for, and their pride in him.

"From time to time, I visited his sick room, and found him always the same patient sufferer. He was a Christian of a broad Catholic spirit, of winning manners, cultivated mind, and beautiful life. He reminded me of the Scotch M'Cheyne, having that remarkable mingling of the mild and energetic in his character, which so distinguished that eminent servant of Christ. The Lord has given him an early crown. Happy morning, when we shall meet him there."

During the months of Mr. Batchelder's sickness, his friends in various parts, were deeply solicitous for his welfare, and numerous substantial tokens of their regard were given. To one of these friends, Wm. Hutchinson, Esq., of Trenton, he wrote, "Permit me before I close, to thank you again, for your unceasing kindness. God only can reward you for the interest you have shown in my welfare, and may his best blessings ever rest upon you and yours. Next to my wife I thank God for my friends; no man ever had better or truer."

When Conference came, his health still declining, he took a superannuated relation to the church, cherishing the hope, however, that still further rest might, to some extent, restore him.

Having followed Mr. Batchelder thus far, it seems appropriate, at this point, where the activities of his ministry close, to introduce the following estimate of his abilities as a preacher, prepared expressly for this volume, by Rev. Isaac W. Wiley, D. D., the accomplished editor of the Ladies' Repository.

"There was something in Mr. Batchelder's preaching that attracted among all classes of people, not only of his own church, but of the community generally. What that something was is an interesting and important inquiry. If we can discover it, and it is something that is generally attainable by young men, then his success, though short-lived, may yet be made a great blessing to the world. We are quite willing to present his character, his style, and his success to the young men of New Jersey, as in the highest degree exemplary.

"Let us inquire, then, as well as we can, into the secret of this popularity and success.

"1. We claim that the popularity of Mr. Batchelder was genuine, and of that kind which every true minister desires to have, for the sake of giving him acceptability with the people, that he may have power and influence over them. It was not ephemeral, such a false popularity as would have soon worn out; but on the contrary was of that substantial and well-merited character that would have grown with his increasing years and strength, and if he had lived would doubtless have carried him to a high place among the preachers of the country. It was gained by no false arts, and was fostered by no special efforts on his part. It came to him; he sought not after it. In fact, the writer has good reason to know, that he was but little conscious of his own popularity, and but little thought that he deserved any great amount of reputation. His aim was for success, ministerial success, but I do not think he ever would have accepted mere popularity as an accomplishment of his aim.

"2. While listening to Brother Batchelder in the pulpit, judging from the easy flow of his words, the regular order of thought, the smoothness and appropriateness of the language, I concluded that his sermons were fully written out and were delivered memoriter; and when he passed away, remembering the excellent contents of many of his sermons, I felt satisfied that the young preacher had left behind him some written sermons that by their beauty and value would compensate somewhat for his own absence. When his papers fell into my hands, I was surprised to find but one fully written sermon among the entire number, and that too, in the hand-writing of another, doubtless written out by that other under dictation from him, to be preserved as a memento of a dying loved one. Mr. Batchelder, then, was not a memorizer; his sermons were not written out, and that easy fluent utterance, that purity of diction, that accuracy of grammar, those sentences composed with elegance and accuracy that would have answered at once for the press, and that perfect self-possession were but the evidences of the mastery the young orator had already attained in the art of extemporaneous preaching. For some of the sermons that I had heard with great interest, and which I had seen produce most excellent effects, I at once looked among his papers. Some of them I found in the form of skeletons, some more fully elaborated, but none written out.* His sermon on 'JESUS THE SINNER'S FRIEND,' which many have heard, and have felt its beauty and power, and which on one occasion I saw followed by the coming forward of seventeen young ladies and gentlemen to give themselves to Christ, was only a fully prepared skeleton. The filling up, the beautiful language, the rounded sentences, the pathetic appeals, and of course the sweet and loving spirit, were the spontaneous work of the pulpit.

"3. Mr. Batchelder, then, was an extemporaneous preacher. But I do not mean by this that he was a preacher who entered

* And yet it must be stated, that his sketches are very numerous, and for *sketches only*, very full.—E. H. S.

into the pulpit unprepared for his work, and depending on the inspiration of the occasion, and as a consequence dealing out to his people uninteresting common place, and empty repetitions. He was a hard student, for his delicate constitution, too laborious a student. His early opportunities had been limited, his education was only academic, but he had already built on this foundation a good superstructure of learning. His learned admirers of Princeton did themselves no dishonor in conferring on him the degree of Master of Arts; but the fact that the young self-taught preacher won for himself this distinction from one of the oldest colleges of the land, and one, too, very careful in the distribution of her honors, is a proof of his studious industry and his commendable attainments. His sermons though not written out were fully prepared. You can readily see by his skeletons that his own mind had gone carefully over the whole ground; that he had thought out every part of it, and that when he went into the pulpit he knew what he was going to say; *how* he would say it was the skill of the orator. And this is what we mean by extemporaneous preaching.

"4. Mr. Batchelder was an original preacher. And here again we do not mean that he preached thoughts that no body else had preached, or that he depended simply on the resources of his own mind for the subject-matter of his sermons, or that he was disposed to discard old truths and methods, and to be perpetually seeking after novelties. An originality of this kind is rather a dangerous feature in a minister of the gospel. But his sermons were his own; his style, his language, his methods, his choice of subjects, were his own. He was natural, perfectly so. Mr. Batchelder in the pulpit was exactly the Mr. Batchelder you knew out of the pulpit. He imitated no one; he copied from no one. Yet he drew from every possible source within his reach, materials for his sermons, and inspiration for his thoughts. He was a great reader, and a judicious reader. His library drew into it the most recent and valuable works. He kept up to the literature and learning of his own day. His books were well marked with notes referring important passages to their appropriate places for use; his skeletons refer you to his books; his common-place book abounds in references to places where good thoughts, good illustrations, good examples and incidents were to be found. And on these sources he drew for suggestive thoughts, for illustrations and examples, and they abundantly enriched his sermons. Yet I think I can safely say he never merely copied anything, but imbibed the thoughts he read, digested them, used them to expand his own mind and develop his own powers of thought. His books furnished him excellent food; his own intellect digested it, and he furnished it in his own style and methods to the people. The result was that he always appeared in the pulpit with a freshness and newness of thought; always had new facts, new illustrations, new modes of presenting truths; that is, was not constantly repeating his old illustrations and old methods. The people went always expecting to find a preacher prepared to address them, and to give them old truths to be sure, but with the freshness and brightness of a new coinage. The truths, of course, were the same, the changeless truths of the gospel; for he always preached the gospel; yet they were presented in new and varied modes of thought, with new illustrations, and even in new language. His reading up to the times kept his thinking up to the times; and the people listened to a preacher who was talking to them in their own current order of thought, about matters moral and religious, of present interest and concernment, and who was bringing the religion of Christ to bear on the needs and questions of the present hour. He preached the gospel of Christ, both as a regenerator of society and as a salvation for the soul. He seemed to understand his congregation, and to aim at preaching Christianity to his own people in such a manner as would interest and impress them, and as a consequence was never in want of a large and attentive congregation to hear him.

"5. A great part of the attraction and power of Mr. Batchelder lay in the man himself, and in his manners in the pulpit. Personally he was one of the loveliest of men. Of course there was a charm in his youth, a charm in his personal beauty, a charm in the pale cheek, the brilliant eye, the fragile frame, all which were assuring you that you were listening to a youth whose life lay close along the borders of death. But all of these would have failed without the gentle, loving spirit that gave real beauty and charm to them all. I am almost afraid to write all I know and think of this remarkable young man—the simple truth may seem like over-wrought praise. And yet it is simply true that with all his talents and success, he was humble, meek, diffident, modest, gentle in spirit and in manners, loving and lovable; a true friend, an earnest patriot, a devoted brother and son, the tenderest of husbands, and the most genial of companions. Everybody loved him—it would have been impossible not to love him. And best of all, he stood the fiery ordeal of early popularity and wide-spread praise without producing a scar on this pure and lovely character. These personal attractions and these traits of character he carried with him into the pulpit. There, as I have said, he was perfectly natural, perfectly himself. He did nothing for show, nothing for effect. The same elements that made up his constant character marked also the delivery of his sermons—meekness, modesty, gentleness.

"We conclude, then, that the attractiveness of Mr. Batchelder's preaching lay in his pure character, loving spirit, gentle and amiable manners; in his youth, becoming diffidence and modesty, and the touching delicacy of his health; in the excellent subject-matter, careful preparation, and special adaptedness of his sermons; and in the naturalness, ease, chasteness and sincerity of his delivery. We have spoken of all these things as if they were personal accomplishments and acquirements of Mr. Batchelder, and yet we wish to be understood as implying all along, that many of them were the direct fruits of the Holy Spirit, and all of them interfused and sanctified by Divine grace."

All who knew Brother Batchelder will appreciate the justice of Dr. Wiley's tribute.

It will be our privilege to follow this amiable young man only a little further. His earthly career is near its close.

After becoming superannuated, a change of climate was recommended; and accompanied by his wife, he started on the 11th of June, 1862, for Minnesota. Reaching the Mississippi, he wrote to a friend: "We embarked on board the steamer 'Northern Light,' for a ride of four hundred miles up the river. If I could see you, I could infuse into your imagination some idea of my enthusiastic enjoyment of this trip on the 'Father of Waters!' But my pen and my lungs both give out in writing. Bluffs six hundred feet high, beautifully wooded, with here and there rocks that look like the fallen masonry of old castles, border the river on both sides nearly its entire course.

"For miles there is not a habitation to be seen. Our boat hauls up occasionally at some log-house, where we take a load of wood, then for miles again, the grandeur of solitary nature, till a western town is announced by the ringing of our bell. The river is dotted all along with beautiful islands, covered with tall slender trees, whose branches interlace and form arches and trellises, while the richest and deepest green carpet the ground. At night, when from the pilot-house or upper deck, you look out upon these spots as the moon silvers them with her rays, it seems like fairy land. You think, too, of eastern tales, travels, and beauty, until sleep is driven away, and you revel in enjoyment that seems too fairy-like to be real.

"We were two days thus enjoying the grandest travel one can take this side of the Rhine, if not this side of heaven."

They were pleasantly situated at St. Paul's, and as health was the grand object of pursuit, their time was spent in such ways as were best calculated to secure that end. While there, they were in constant correspondence with their friends, and many a joyous greeting from New Jersey cheered their hearts. His letters, too, were flushed with hope, as long as hope could be entertained; finally, however, that last sweet refuge and support of poor mortality failed, and he wrote to his friend Hutchinson: "I must give up all expectation of recovery. My lungs are too much diseased, and my constitutional vigor too little to hope for anything but a few months' more battling with the destroyer. It is foolish to attempt concealment from myself or friends. I believe I do better here than I could in any other climate, but climates can do but little. Though discouraged in the things my friends and myself hope for, I am not unhappy. My heavenly Father is most gracious, and my Saviour is ever with me."

While in Minnesota, too weak much of the time to sit up, or hold a pen, he dictated, while his wife wrote the sermon on "Heavenly-mindedness," from which several quotations are made in this narrative, the last of his numerous productions, and, as was fitting, the *sweetest of them all.*

On the 5th of November he wrote to Brother Jefferys, "I am just able to write you a line. Have been confined to my room for nearly four weeks with hemorrhages. It seemed more than once that I was going home, but I am now recovering. I was taken at a hotel where I called. Helen was sick, and we were separated more than a week: she at our boarding-house, and I at the hotel. It taxed our fortitude, but we were sustained. She came to me as soon as possible, and we are now at the Merchant's Hotel. Many, many thanks to you, my dear friend, for the evidences of your regard and care. May God bless you as you deserve. But I am trespassing on my strength. Providence willing, we shall leave for home within two weeks. Oh how I want to see you!"

Again he wrote to his friend Hutchinson, "I am just able to sit up. Have had a hard time of it, but 'still live.' All thanks of my *swelling heart* for your kindness. May God bless you as you deserve."

He had gone to Minnesota in search of health, but now, in compliance with the earnest solicitations of deeply-interested friends, he turns his face homeward, with the last hope of prolonged life obliterated, and, as he believed, to die. It was, therefore, a sad yet joyful hour, when on the eleventh of November this young minister and his wife, together with their little son, who had been given them during their stay in Minnesota, started for Philadelphia, which place, weak as he was, a kind Providence enabled them to reach, on the eighteenth of the same month, 1862.

After spending some time with their relatives in Philadelphia and friends in Trenton, they finally fixed their residence at Princeton. Although every effort was put forth that human skill and kindness could devise, no remedy was found for the fatal disease, and it became more and more evident his end was near.

On one occasion interested friends from Trenton came to see him. They found him a little despondent. After a few remarks, one of them said, encouragingly, "You must look on the bright side." A brief pause followed, in which he thought of his interesting family, the Church, his many friends, and of that beautiful heaven to which, he believed, he was so rapidly hastening; then with a sweet smile, which indicated the serenity of his soul, he answered, "*Both sides are bright.*"

His chamber of sickness and death was rendered pleasant by gentle ministries, sweet flowers, and the smile of God. How much he loved all these. Sometimes during his illness he would kiss his friends in the fullness of his affection. Flowers he almost worshiped; but God was over all, blessed forever.

It was now the dreary month of March, and he was very low. Rev. Mrs. Jefferys, who, while the invalid was at her house in New Brunswick, had rendered many comforting services, now received a present of a valuable bouquet of natural flowers, which had been made to bloom in winter by means of artificial heat. Passionately fond of these beautiful gifts of God, she esteemed the bouquet highly. But she thought of the sick and dying minister, and knowing how much he would prize it, cheerfully sent it to him. These flowers reached his bedside a short time before his departure to a better world. As they were held up before him, he opened his languid eyes, and gazing on them, exclaimed, "*Oh they look like heaven!*" Yes, they *looked* like heaven, but that was all, for they were perishable. *Here* flowers all fade; *there* they will bloom forever.

On the 18th of March, 1863, the New Jersey Conference convened at Burlington. On Saturday the 21st, information of his critical condition was received, and Rev. William H. Jefferys was immediately delegated to bear to their dying fellow member, assurances of sympathy and fervent prayer in his behalf.

Brother Jefferys found the patient sufferer at the door of death, calmly waiting for the final summons. The light of divine grace shone in his eye as he said: "Last night I thought I was dying, but all was bright and clear before me." "Oh, I have such peace, I ought to be willing to suffer in body, for God so greatly blesses me in mind." He then repeated the words of our Lord Jesus, "My peace I leave with you. My peace I give unto you." He received the message of sympathy and condolence from the Conference, and remarked: "No language can express how much I love the members of the New Jersey Conference." Said he, "The appointments will soon be made. Brother Hanlon will go to Lambertville, Brother Stokes to Bordentown, Brother King will come here, you will go to Trenton, and *I will go home to heaven.*" Then with a sweet smile upon his wasted cheek, he said, "*Do you not think I have the best appointment?*" The interview was protracted, and remarks of a similar character continued to fall from his lips.

On Friday night, the 27th, his sufferings were severe. He remarked to Rev. T. Hanlon, who was with him at the time, "Patience, patience. He is teaching me to say, *Thy will be done.*" The next morning he had a season of peculiar brilliancy of mind. "What a calm and beautiful morning this is," was his oft-repeated expression, and his soul seemed as calm and peaceful as did nature around him. In the midst of his pious rapture, his beloved wife inquired, "Are you asleep, my dear?" "Yes, asleep in Jesus," was his calm reply. His uncle said, "Is Jesus precious?" "Yes, precious Jesus, he is precious," was his answer. To the friends who now gathered around his dying bed, he remarked: "I did not expect to die so calmly, I expected to suffer in death; but I die so quietly, and so triumphantly!"

He said to Mrs. Bartine: "Mother, do you think this is death?" She replied, "Yes, George, I think it is." "Then it is sweet to die," was his response. She said: "George, we have gone with you as far as we can, you must leave us. What do you see before you?" "Pleasures for evermore," he triumphantly exclaimed. He sent a message to his brother and brother-in-law, who were both in the army of the Union. "Tell them to meet me in heaven, and tell them I send this message with heaven in my view." He then said: "Jesus is a friend that sticketh closer than a brother; my brother is far away, but Jesus is here with me." "Tell my dear father that the Father of fathers is with me." Of Dr. Bartine he said: "I have loved him, O, how I have loved him!" To his uncle he said: "I love you, uncle, and I am glad I came to your house to die." To his wife he said, "I love you next to Jesus." He sent messages of love like these to his various friends and relatives, not forgetting his brethren in the ministry, for whom his affection in death was very strong. Finally he became exhausted, and sank into a quiet, calm repose, in which condition he remained during all the following day, which was the Sabbath. Its sacred hours were spent by him in deep and silent communion with God. The only utterances that are remembered as falling from his lips on that day, are, "Jesus shed his precious blood for me, to him be power and dominion, amen, amen, amen," and he concluded with the Angel Anthem, "Glory to God in the highest, peace on earth, good will to men."

On Monday morning, the 30th, just a few moments before his death, as if he saw the Saviour coming, he exclaimed: "Jesus, my hope! my all! take me! take me now!" He then added: "Glory, glory to—" and with these words dying upon his lips, his pure spirit passed away from the earth, leaving a heavenly smile upon the face of the lifeless clay, which was all that remained of the once eloquent, lovely, and beloved George Washington Batchelder.

The funeral services, on the following Thursday, were held in the Methodist Episcopal Church, in Princeton, under the superintendence of Rev. S. Y. Monroe. The Rev. Dr. Maclean, President of Princeton College; Rev. Dr. McDonald, pastor of First Presbyterian Church; and Rev. I. D. King, pastor of M. E. Church, all participated. The eulogies upon the character of the deceased, which were pronounced by the two distinguished Presbyterian divines, afforded proof of the fact that denominational walls do not hide from the eyes of great and good men intellectual and moral excellence.

From Princeton, his remains were taken to the State Street Methodist Episcopal Church, Trenton, where a vast concourse of people had assembled to participate in the solemnities of the occasion. Nearly all the evangelical churches of the city were represented in the persons of their pastors. A delegation of ministers appointed by the Newark Conference was present, as also, a large number of the members of the New Jersey Conference. Rev. I. W. Wiley, D. D., pronounced a beautifully appropriate funeral oration over the sainted dead, and his remains were deposited in the Mercer Cemetery, where his numerous friends have since erected to his memory a beautiful Italian marble monument some fourteen feet high, on which is inscribed—

ASLEEP IN JESUS.

REV. GEORGE W. BATCHELDER, A. M.,

OF THE NEW JERSEY CONFERENCE.

FIRST PASTOR

OF STATE ST. METHODIST EPISCOPAL CHURCH IN THIS CITY.

BORN JUNE 15, 1836,

DIED MARCH 30, 1863.

A CHILD OF GENIUS, CULTURE AND GRACE.

BRILLIANT AND LOVELY IN LIFE, PEACEFUL AND TRIUMPHANT IN DEATH.

CROWNED WITH IMMORTALITY, HIS MEMORY LINGERS A BEAUTIFUL VISION, PRECIOUS FOREVER.

REV. WILLIAM M. BURROUGHS.

THE subject of this sketch was a son of Benjamin and Sarah Burroughs, and was born in Hopewell Township, then Hunterdon, but now Mercer Co., N. J. His parents occupied a respectable position in society, and sustained a reputable character, but did not profess religion. He received a careful moral training, and being reared in the country on a farm, he was not brought in contact with the corrupting presence of large numbers of boys. Still there was no family altar or domestic religion in his home, or Sunday-school in his reach, so that but slight religious influences were thrown around his childhood and early youth. He was trained to industry and economy, and by nature was sedate and thoughtful, and remarkably kind and affectionate, always acting the part of a peace-maker among his schoolmates and companions. His literary advantages were only ordinary, but by diligent application he was enabled to acquire a fair common school education.

At the age of sixteen he was apprenticed to Joseph Burn, of Pennington, to learn the cabinet making business. In this new position he was industrious and attentive, and gave good satisfaction. Here he was brought in reach of the M. E. Church, and at once became a regular attendant upon its services. In 1832, Pennington for the first time is named upon the minutes as a separate appointment, and assigned to Rev. Wm. H. Bull. Through his instrumentality Mills was brought to a saving knowledge of the truth, and was baptized and received on probation Oct. 13th of this year. His conversion was very clear, and he took a prompt and decided stand with the church, evincing a deep interest in whatever pertained to its welfare and success.

He began his religious life by strictly attending the means of grace and taking part actively and acceptably in social worship.

His parents resided six miles from Pennington, which distance he usually traveled every other Saturday, in order to spend the Sabbath at home. On his first visit after he was converted he felt that he ought to pray with the family. But the cross was so heavy and his nature so shrinking and timid that he could not muster the courage to say anything about it. Reflecting upon the matter as he returned to his work, the Holy Spirit helped him to see in contrast what the Saviour had done for him, and what he was doing in return, and he felt much ashamed for his unfaithfulness. Feeling depressed and condemned, he asked the Lord for forgiveness, and promised to do better next time. As the fortnight rolled away the subject was much in his thoughts and prayers, and as the time approached he felt deeply anxious. But to his great relief and joy, his mother, who had been recently converted on a sick bed, invited him to conduct family worship. He gladly complied, and ever after continued the practice when at home. From the time he was converted, he thought deeply on the experimental and practical phases of religion, prayed much and watched closely, was solemn and earnest in manner, devout in spirit, and was largely influenced by the promptings that actuated the Saviour in his great work. The class-meeting attracted his special attention, and was richly blessed to his profit. Of this part of our economy he became and remained a warm advocate, striving especially to lead all young converts to form the habit of conforming to it.

In the fall of 1836 he changed his residence to Flemington, but continued at his trade. In the mean time he was much exercised on the subject of preaching, but he did not entertain it cordially. The idea of his ever occupying the position of a minister of the gospel, seemed extremely foolish. His religious advantages had been quite inferior, his education was very limited for such a work, he was timid, retiring and slow of speech, and so far as he could see, had not a single qualification for so great an undertaking. Surely the thought must come from the adversary, and the design be to lead him into trouble and effect his ruin. Thus he reasoned, and earnestly strove to dismiss the subject. But in this he failed, and the impression so far from leaving him, continued to deepen, till it became a source of great perplexity and even distress. This struggle was of four years' continuance, till finally he became fully satisfied that the salvation of his soul depended on his consenting to warn sinners to flee the wrath to come.

His first license to exhort bears date, Pennington, May 27, 1836, and is signed by "J. K. Shaw, preacher of the gospel." It was renewed Feb. 26, 1837, and signed by "Thomas J. Thompson, P. E." While acting under this authority, he was sent, in the fall of this year, by Rev. Manning Force, to assist Revs. J. Chattle and C. S. Vancleve on Asbury Circuit. His first attempt to preach was at a woods meeting after he reached the circuit. A brother who was present says, "He began in great fear and with much trembling, yet those who then heard him, felt that God had called him to preach, and that he would be a useful minister of the gospel." After filling out the balance of the year, he was transferred by the same elder, to Newton Circuit, where he spent the next year with Rev. J. S. Swaim. When he first started on his itinerant mission, his father gave him a horse and equipments, saying, "Go, Mills, and do all the good you can, for I have never done any."

In 1839 he was received on trial by the New Jersey Conference, and afterward regularly passed to full membership and to deacon's and elder's orders. His fields of labor were the following: 1839, Warren; 1840, Vernon: 1841, Hudson; 1842, Port Jervis; 1843, Milford; 1844-5, Ramapo; 1846-7, Dover and Millbrook; 1848, Bergen; 1849-50, Rome and Wantage; 1851-2, Stillwater; 1853-4, Hope; 1855-6, Newton and Tranquility; 1857-8, Frenchtown and Milford; 1859-60, Kingwood; 1861, Wesley Chapel; 1862, Piermont and Tappan; 1863-4, New Prospect.

In 1841 he received intelligence that his father, then in his sixty-fifth year, and five or six other members of the family, had embraced religion. This was joyful news indeed, and deeply affected him. It conveyed a new and grateful confirmation of the fact that "the effectual fervent prayer of a righteous man availeth much." It took from his mind a heavy load of anxious concern. And, most of all, he could now feel that those he loved so tenderly enjoyed a good hope of heaven.

April 11, 1849, he was united in marriage to Miss Sarah A. Thrall, of Milford, Pike Co., Pa., an estimable lady and excellent companion, well fitted to share the toils, responsibilities, and burdens of his ministerial life. One fact in connection with this union is worthy of record as helping to delineate the simplicity of his character. During his term there in 1843, the young lady who afterwards became his wife, and for whom his affections became warmly enlisted, then resided in the place. And though he had been preaching six years, and had graduated to elder's orders, yet so humble were the views that he entertained of himself, and so fearful was he of burdening the Church, that he felt it his duty to defer marriage. At the same time his great prudence led him to withhold from the lady all expression of his regard, lest she might become unduly entangled at too early a date. His purity and freedom from suspiciousness are also shown by what was to many an amusing incident. On the evening before their plighted vows were consummated, he consented to preach to the congregation at Milford, and with great solemnity announced for his text, "Set your affection on things above, *not on things on the earth.*"

Mills Burroughs, as he was familiarly called, was of medium height, rather stout build, somewhat inclined to corpulency, robust constitution, and vigorous health. He seldom had to halt in his work on account of any physical disability. All his engagements were met with prompt and uniform faithfulness.

As a preacher he occupied a fair position, which he attained notwithstanding serious obstacles. His voice was heavy and unmusical, and owing to the lack of early helps, was never properly cultivated. And then he failed to overcome his great natural diffidence, which rendered him so timid and fearful as to often seriously embarrass him, and lead those who heard him to form too low an estimate of his abilities. And perhaps he erred by yielding somewhat to the notion that attention to style belongs rather to those who are more highly endowed by natural gifts. Yet he was a diligent student, acquired a fair knowledge of theology and general literature, carefully prepared his sermons and delivered them with great solemnity and earnestness. All were impressed that they were listening to a man who felt that he had a message from God, and whose great aim was to so deliver it as to conceal himself, magnify the cross, and to the fullest possible extent accomplish the objects of his embassy. And if his ministry was not specially attractive, it was highly instructive, and well adapted to warn sinners and to edify and comfort believers. "Plain in manners and retiring in disposition, he passed for far less than he was worth, as such men are wont to do, yet he never failed during a ministry of more than twenty-five years, to leave behind him in every charge abiding fruit of his unpretending but useful labors. His record is on high, and that record will one day show that through his godly example and steady, persevering efforts many were turned to righteousness, and from the power of Satan unto God." There is other testimony to his uniform success and varying usefulness. Many were saved from their sins through his instrumentality, but his chief strength lay in his capability of inciting Christians to a deeper spirituality and increasing faithfulness, and thus building up the Church in faith and holiness. Could we but give the items in these respects, they would furnish an interesting and noble record.

The above quotation, and that which follows, are taken from an obituary notice by Rev. N. Vansant: "Few men have sustained a more irreproachable character. In all his relations he was a true man." As a son, a husband, a father, a Christian and a minister, he adorned the doctrine of Christ, and beautifully exemplified the Christian religion. His unflinching integrity, the modesty of his views in regard to his own claims to consideration, and the tender solicitude with which he deferred to the rights and feelings of others, rendered him a true Christian gentleman. From the time of his conversion, his motto was holiness. And as is true, more or less fully, of all really spiritual Christians, his inner life was marked by conflicts and struggles, but his steady faith and unfaltering devotion, enabled him to maintain outward uniformity, and, at the same time, a constantly increasing spirituality.

In the midst of a laborious career of usefulness, he was suddenly and unexpectedly stricken down by congestion of the brain. The attack was of such a nature and so violent that he was not able to converse on any subject, and of course could not communicate anything respecting his future prospects. But this, though it would have been a satisfaction to his friends, was not necessary. His life testified for him with great distinctness, in behalf of the efficacy of the blood of Jesus to save from sin and to sustain under the severest trials. There is hence no room to doubt that the same saving efficacy was abundant and availing in the dying hour. He was attacked on Friday evening, and died the next Sunday morning, April 19, 1864, in the fiftieth year of his age and twenty-sixth of his ministry. A widow, and three daughters, whose ages range from fourteen to six, are left to the sympathy and care of the church. May they follow him as he followed Christ.

REV. WESLEY ROBERTSON.

"Friends of my mortal years,
The trusted and the true;
You are walking still thro' the valley of tears,
And I wait to welcome you."

WESLEY ROBERTSON, the subject of this sketch, was born at New Providence, New Jersey, on the 14th day of May, 1807. At a very early period, bereft of both parents, and left in a world of change and sorrow, he experienced with many an orphan before him, the truthfulness of inspiration, "When my father and mother forsake me, then the Lord will take me up."

When about fifteen years of age, he left the scenes of his boyhood, and went to Newark to learn a trade. While there, he did not despise the sanctuary or the Sabbath, but soon found his way to the Old Halsey St. Church, the birth-place of so many immortal souls, where he heard the gospel from the lips of Rev. John Creamer, the first Methodist sermon to which he ever listened.

Remaining in Newark a short time, he changed his mind in reference to his employment, and finding a situation in Rahway, removed to that place.

In the winter of 1828, during the early ministry of Rev. Thomas B. Sargent, he came out from the world, experienced religion, and immediately united with the church. He soon felt it his duty to labor for souls, and do all in his power to promote the interests of the Redeemer's kingdom.

It was not long before he was promoted to the leadership of a class, then to exhort, and finally, in February, 1834, he received license to preach. In all these positions of responsibility, he labored with intense zeal, and was honored of God.

On the 10th of March, 1829, he was united in marriage, with Miss Margaret T. Worth, of Rahway, between whom there always existed the fondest and purest affection.

In the spring of 1835, Rev. E. Page, who had been appointed to Freehold Circuit, needed a colleague. Rev. J. J. Matthias, Presiding Elder, of East Jersey District, found Brother Robertson at Rahway, and immediately sent him to fill the place.

Here, he was both popular and useful, and the next year being received on trial by the Philadelphia Conference, was returned to the same circuit.

In 1837 and 1838, he was appointed in charge of Caldwell Circuit. Here, he was blest in his efforts to do good, and succeeded in establishing a society and building a church at Little Falls. Woodbridge was his next field of labor, where he remained until 1841. He then removed to Westfield, Staten Island, which appointment covered all the ground now occupied by Woodrow, Bethel, and St. Paul's charges. The present church edifices at Woodrow and Bethel, were built under his supervision, and during the two years of his stay there, about *four hundred* were added to the church.

In 1843, he was appointed to Clinton Circuit, where over *three hundred* professed conversion. The next year the circuit was divided, and he was sent to that part comprising New Germantown and Parkersville. The flame of revival spread this year also, and their borders were so far enlarged, that a society was formed, and a church commenced at Mechanicsville.

Leaving New Germantown in 1845, he was appointed to Middletown Point. He remained until 1847, and was then sent to Flemington. He removed from Flemington in 1849, and was stationed at Bordentown. His residence at this place was most agreeable, and his labors successful, the fruits of which remain, a permanent blessing to the church. In 1851, he was sent to Woodrow, Staten Island, but the health of his family suffered so much, that he removed the next spring to Nyack, being the first instance in his history, where he did not remain the full term allowed by the church, and this one year removal was caused, as stated, by the health of his family.

At Nyack he remained two years. His next appointment in 1854 was Quarry St., Newark, where his ministry was blest in the salvation of many souls. In 1856, he was stationed at Belleville. Here his health failed, but though feeble, he labored on, and saw some fruit.

The following spring, having been twenty-two years in the ministry, sensible of rapidly failing energies, he was compelled, reluctantly, to ask a supernumerary relation to the conference, and removed his family to Newark.

During his years of itinerant life, he received nearly *two thousand* persons in the church, an average of nearly *one* hundred per year. Among these were several now in the ministry of the church he loved and served so well.

What was the secret of Brother Robertson's success? He was a good preacher; but there was something back of this, that gave him access to the hearts of men, whereby he won them to the service of his Lord.

He was a good man. None doubted his piety. He was in daily and hourly communion with God. He believed in, and enjoyed holiness of heart. He did not make such a parade of his profession, however, as said to those around him, "Stand back, for I am holier than thou," but sweetly exemplifying the grace of humility and heavenly charity he drew all persons to him, and then, by the purity of his life and example, made them better by the association. A minister said, "I was never so impressed with the truthfulness of the doctrine of Christian holiness, as when I saw it exhibited in his consistent life." Another, who knew him equally well, said, "I never knew a man so intimately, of whom I wish to remember so much." This purity and perfection of Christian character was one great element of his power.

He had strong and unceasing faith. It never wavered. He had strong faith in the atonement, on which, in sunshine and in storm, he rested the interests of his own soul. Christ was his personal refuge and rest. This refuge he felt was so secure, and this rest so blessed, that with a heart overflowing with love, he invited all to the same enjoyment. He had faith too in God's providences. Dark clouds could not make him despondent, nor could fierce tempests shake him. Rooted and grounded in the faith, he stood like a rock in the sea. He had faith for others, faith for the church, and faith for his bleeding country. This faith in God gave him a heart to labor, and, as a consequence, he seldom knew defeat.

In all his pulpit ministrations, he was aided by the blessed influences of the Holy Ghost. The Spirit of the Lord God was on him. He was thereby a man of power. Thus anointed, Wesley Robertson went everywhere preaching the word. A minister asked him, one day, "Brother Robertson, what is the highest number of sermons ever preached by you in one day?" He replied, "It is difficult for me to tell; *twenty, thirty, and sometimes more.* As I go along the street, I try to preach a little sermon wherever I find an open ear."

Another element of his usefulness was his uniform cheerfulness. He was never trifling, but always cheerful. He knew nothing of what the world calls gloomy godliness. His soul was always full of the sunshine of religious joy, and that joy beamed out through every pore of his benignant countenance, until, like the face of Moses, it was all glowing with the light of God. He carried no clouds with him, but left the influence of his happy spirit, and the light of his cheerful example wherever he went. This cheerfulness was not the result of worldly prosperity, or exemptions from the trials of life. He had been called to stand where Habakkuk stood, and while there, could say, as triumphantly as he, "Although the fig tree shall not blossom, *yet will I rejoice in the Lord; I will joy in the God of my salvation.*" While a supernumerary in Newark, he entered into business, and though not successful, yet he was happy; not because of disappointment, but in defiance of it.

Residing in Newark from 1857 to 1864, he was deeply interested in all that involved the welfare of immortal souls and the prosperity of Zion. During this time he worshiped mainly in the Halsey street church, where several members of his family belonged. On one occasion, Brother Bryan, who was pastor at the time, found it necessary to be absent a few days, and left the week evening prayer-meeting in his charge. When the pastor returned, he found, to his great surprise and joy, that the *worn-out preacher* had, under the blessing of God, started a revival, and several had already been converted.

We now reach an interesting, but, to us, sad period of his history, the summer and autumn of 1864. The rebellion, with all its terrible consequences, still raged. The colored man, freed from the rigors of slavery by the victorious march of our armies, was within our lines without spiritual care, and the soldiers of the Union were languishing by thousands in Southern hospitals. Rev. John S. Swaim, of Newark Conference, and brother-in-law to Brother Robertson, had been sent by the Mission Board at New York to Jacksonville, Florida, to look after the interests of the church there, and to do what lay in his power for the freedmen also. To that very place, a few months after, Providence seemed to open the way for Brother Robertson as an agent for the United States Christian Commission. In the fond hope of doing good to these noble but suffering men, and possibly of benefiting his own health, he accepted the appointment, and, though it involved a separation from his family, which he tenderly loved, yet he looked forward to an entrance upon his duties with the same strong faith and cheerfulness of spirit which had characterized him in all the pursuits of life.

On the 18th of August he took an affectionate leave of his family and friends, and on board the transport Fulton, left New York for Jacksonville. The first evening he was out, in a letter to his family, he says, "After tea, I went to my room (alone), and had *family prayers*, or did my part towards it. I remembered you all, and thought I was uniting with you." Two or three days after, having had but a few hours' sea-sickness, he wrote, "I have enjoyed myself much. My state-room has been a Bethel to my soul, morning, noon, and night." When near the end of their voyage, the wind blew a perfect gale. He wrote to his wife, "Just think of your husband kneeling on a chair, (which was likely stationary) engaged in prayer for those around, while the vessel rolled backward and forward to such a degree, that I had to hold on to the chair to keep from falling over, and yet feeling as calm and as much composed as when worshiping in the Halsey street church. He arrived at Jacksonville on the 24th of August. He felt there was a work for him to do there, and entered upon it with spirit. On the 5th of September he wrote, "I have just returned from distributing the papers for the various offices, gun boats, wagon masters, and regiments, which are away from here, up at Magnolia Springs, and other places. * * Yesterday was another precious Sabbath to me. At eight o'clock I prayed with the Fourth Massachusetts Cavalry; at nine went to Sabbath-school, and taught a class of colored persons—ages from *ten* to *thirty-five*—some in reading, some in spelling, and one, the oldest of the class, in her A B C's; oh, what an interest she manifested! She said, 'I can say them *forward*, but I don't know them *backwards*.'" Soon after writing this letter, he had a severe attack of typhoid fever, which continued several weeks. Recovering somewhat, he wrote to his wife on the 10th of October, saying, "The Lord has done it. He sent Dr. Marcy, and he sent Sister Swaim, and with her, your own *dear self*, in those tokens of love, from your own hand, grapes and apples, and pears from Sue. I told Sister Swaim it *brought home right here in my sick room:* Brother Swaim has watched over me with the kindness of a brother. Then too I have seemed to be *at home* with you; I could see you all around me, and Minnie, (a grand-daughter, whose mother was dead,) the dear little girl, how she has looked up in my face while sitting on your lap, and called my name. *The Lord has given me these home scenes to keep me up.* And then I have been so happy all through. Thank you all for these tokens of love. Thank Sue, and Will, and Carrie, and Mary, and Wesley, and kiss Minnie *ten times for me.* I expect to see you again in this world. Lean on the Arm Divine, that will support you."

Soon after this cheerful and hopeful letter, he grew worse again, and on the 28th of October, Brother Swaim wrote a long letter to Sister Robertson, the first sentence in which is significant and alarming. "Since Wesley wrote to you concerning his rapid improvement, he is not so well again. Getting well a little too fast, he has *suffered a relapse.*" The letter assures her that medical stores and attendance were ample, every delicacy that could be named was at hand, while friends were lavishing in kindnesses, and nothing would be left undone in his behalf. In a note appended to this letter, dated Nov. 1st, Brother Swaim continues, "All our efforts to arrest the progress of disease have not availed, and he is now *lying very low.*" On the 2nd of November, 1864, he writes again, "Dear Sister Margaret, with feelings of sorrow I cannot describe, I have now to say to you, that our worst fears, as expressed in my note of yesterday, have been realized. To-day, at *twenty-three minutes before one o'clock*, your dear husband *quietly breathed his last.* But for the pain which he experienced, for some days previously, it would hardly have seemed like death; so calmly, so quietly, so peacefully, did he sink away into rest, his very features assuming a sweet and holy smile." Chaplain

Hobbs, who sat up with him the last night of his life, said, "He was very happy, and seemed to hear music and singing. Ten minutes before he died, he rose up, as if he wanted to say something, but unable to speak, he pointed upwards with the index finger, then lying down, folded his arms across his breast, and quietly fell asleep in Jesus." Brother Swaim continues, "I must now confine myself to an account of the disposition we make of his body. We put him to-night in a zink case, air-tight, inclose it in a firm box, and on Friday shall bury him in our *own yard*, a few paces only, from the door, to be taken up when the very first trading schooner returns to New York. It so happened however, that he did not return by a trading schooner, but was brought on, by the Transport Fulton, the same vessel, on which a few months before, he had gone forth with such fond hopes of doing good. His remains arrived safely in Newark, and on the 8th of Feb. 1865, a solemn funeral service was held in the Halsey St. Church, where *forty-three* years before, he heard his first sermon from the lips of a Methodist minister. Rev. James Ayres, preached an excellent sermon from Acts xi. 24, and all that remained of Wesley Robertson was borne by his brethren in the ministry to Mount Pleasant Cemetery, to await the resurrection of the just.

Farewell, dear brother, the loved ones thou hast left behind thee, are cheered in their sorrow, by the sweet assurance that thou hast gained thy rest, while by the ear of faith they hear thee say,

> "I shine in the light of God;
> His likeness stamps my brow;
> Through the shadows of death my feet have trod,
> And I reign in glory now."

THE END.

CPSIA information can be obtained
at www.ICGtesting.com
Printed in the USA
LVHW100509130422
716029LV00002B/43

9 783752 590418